A Wrinkle in Time

MADELEINE L'ENGLE'S

A Wrinkle in Time

THE GRAPHIC NOVEL

ADAPTED AND ILLUSTRATED BY
HOPE LARSON

Margaret Ferguson Books
FARRAR STRAUS GIROUX · NEW YORK

For Charles Wadsworth Cano and Wallace Collin Franklin
—M.L.

To Mom and Dad
—H.L.

Text copyright © 1962 by Crosswicks, Ltd.
Pictures copyright © 2012 by Hope Larson
All rights reserved
Distributed in Canada by D&M Publishers, Inc.
Printed in the United States of America by R.R. Donnelley & Sons Company,
Harrisonburg, Virginia
Designed by Hope Larson and Andrew Arnold
Colored by Jenn Manley Lee
First edition, 2012
7 9 10 8 6

mackids.com

Library of Congress Cataloging-in-Publication Data
Larson, Hope.
   A wrinkle in time / Madeleine L'Engle ; adapted and illustrated by Hope
Larson. — 1st ed.
      p.   cm.
   Summary: A graphic novel adaptation of the classic tale in which Meg
Murry and her friends become involved with unearthly strangers and a search
for Meg's father, who has disappeared while engaged in secret work for the
government.
   ISBN 978-0-374-38615-3
   1. Graphic novels.   [1. Graphic novels.   2. Science fiction.   3. L'Engle,
Madeleine. Wrinkle in time—Adaptations.]   I. L'Engle, Madeleine. Wrinkle
in time.   II. Title.

PZ7.7.L37Wr 2012
741.5'973—dc22

                                                        2010044120

Table of Contents

A Wrinkle in Time

1

1
Mrs Whatsit

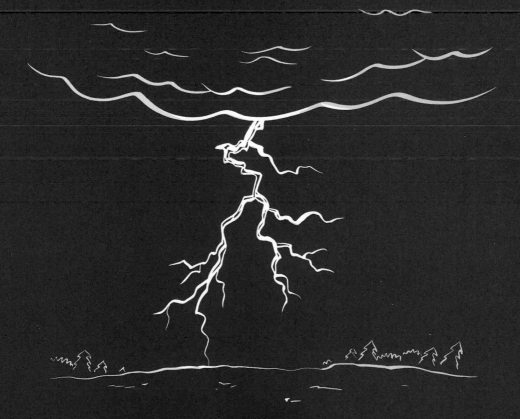

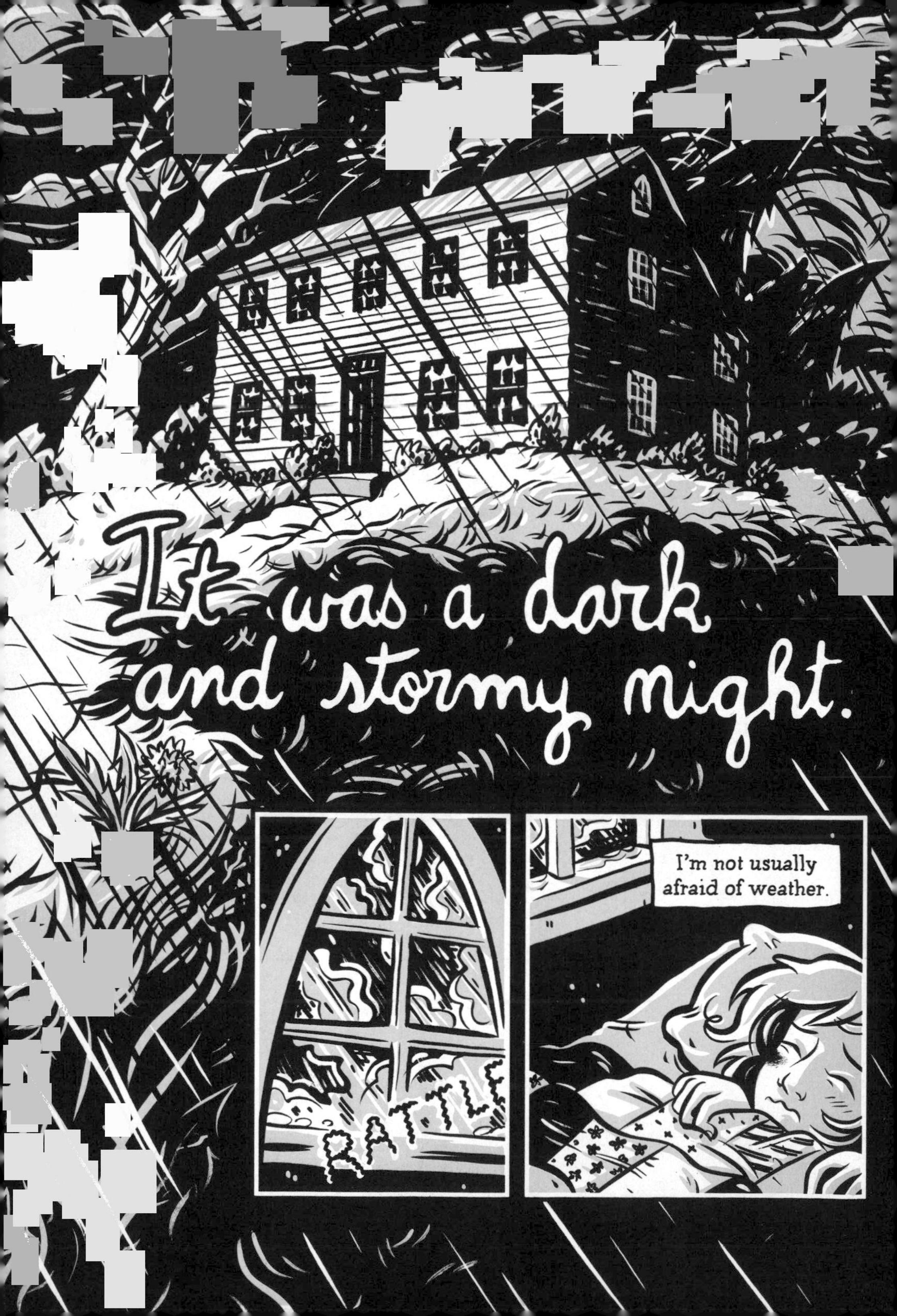
It was a dark and stormy night.
RATTLE
I'm not usually afraid of weather.

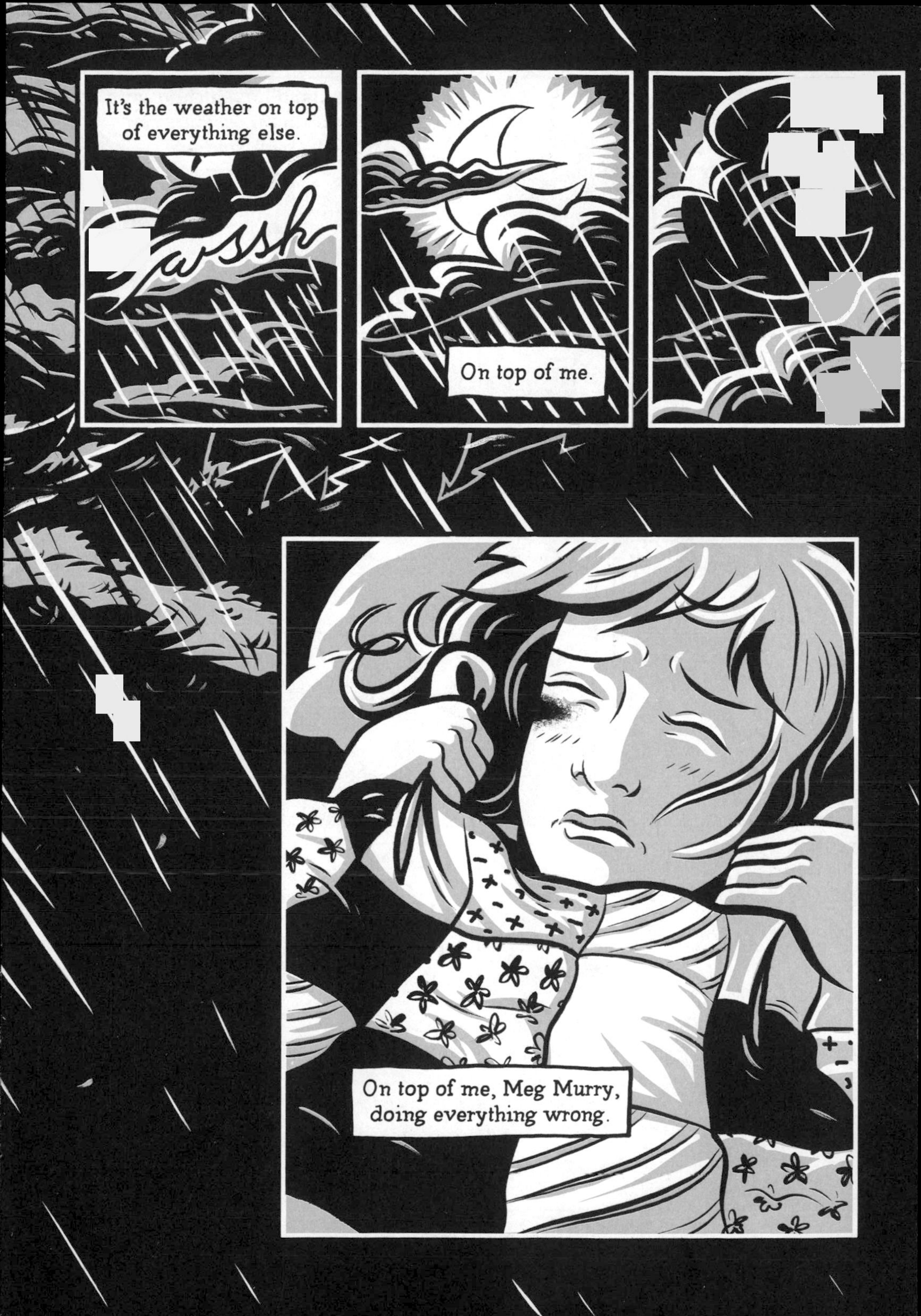
It's the weather on top of everything else.
wssh
On top of me.
On top of me, Meg Murry, doing everything wrong.

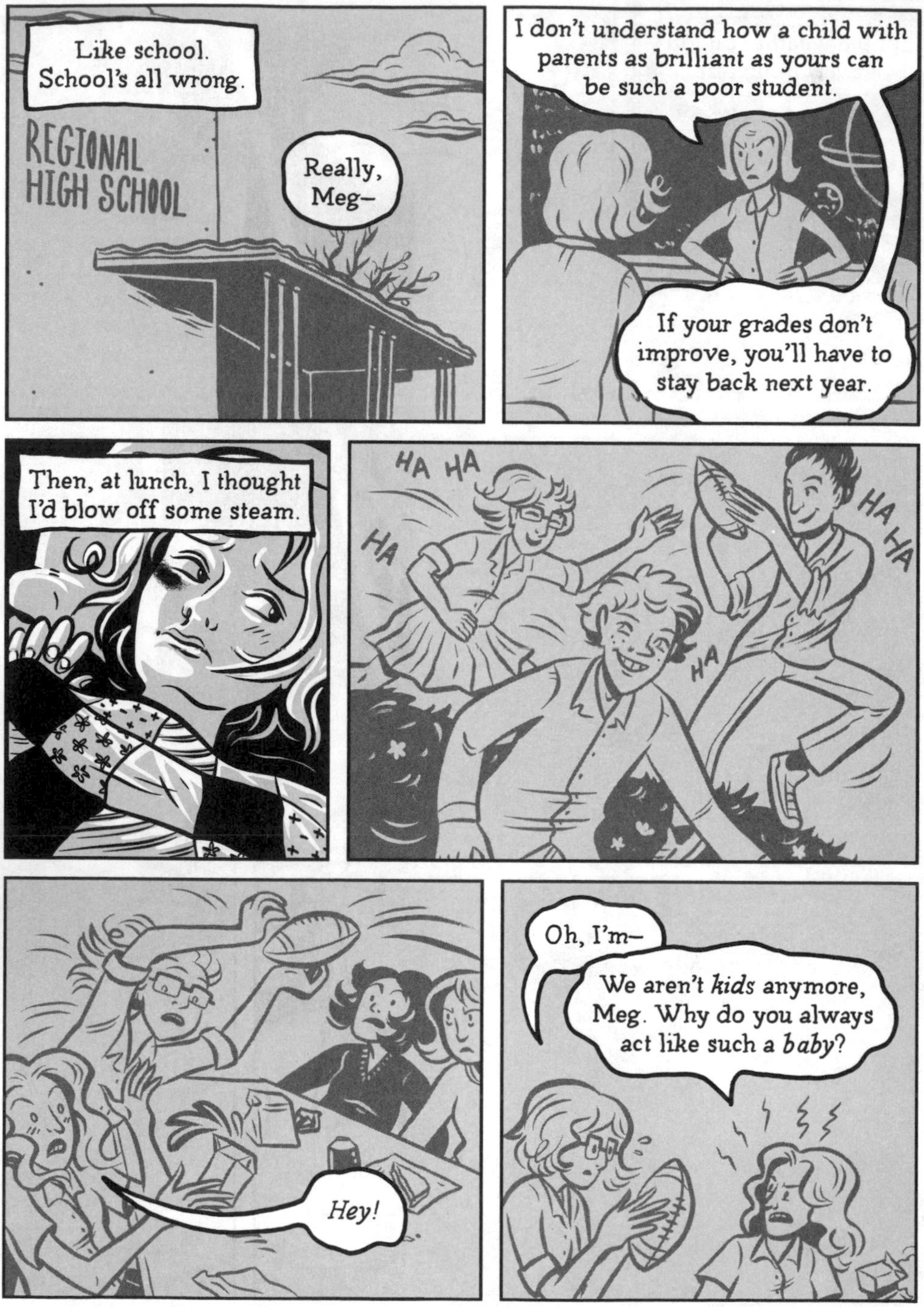

Like school. School's all wrong.
REGIONAL HIGH SCHOOL
Really, Meg—
I don't understand how a child with parents as brilliant as yours can be such a poor student.
If your grades don't improve, you'll have to stay back next year.
Then, at lunch, I thought I'd blow off some steam.
HA HA
HA
HA HA
HA
Hey!
Oh, I'm—
We aren't *kids* anymore, Meg. Why do you always act like such a *baby*?

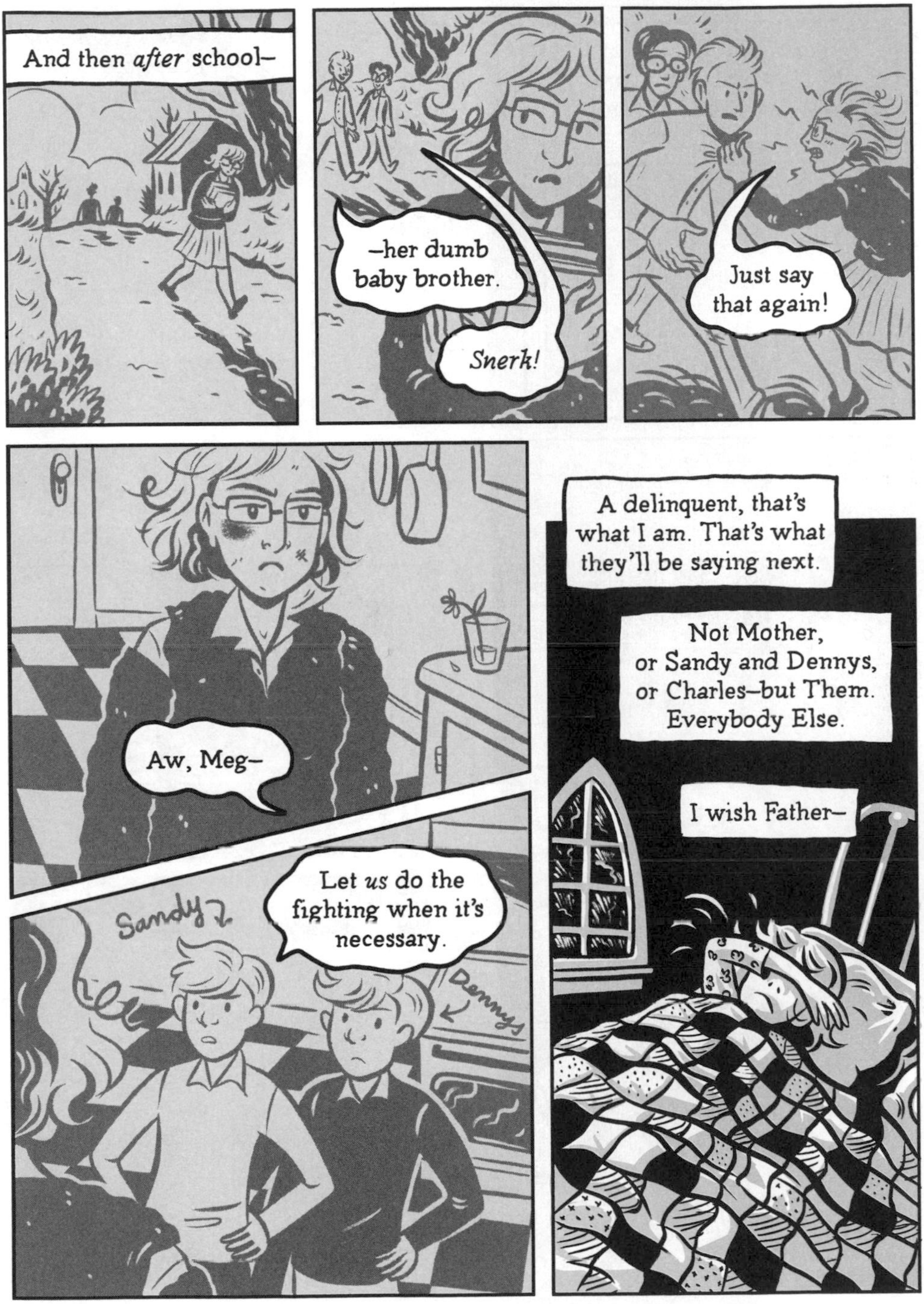
And then *after* school–
–her dumb baby brother.
Snerk!
Just say that again!
Aw, Meg–
Let *us* do the fighting when it's necessary.
Sandy
Dennys
A delinquent, that's what I am. That's what they'll be saying next.
Not Mother, or Sandy and Dennys, or Charles–but Them. Everybody Else.
I wish Father–

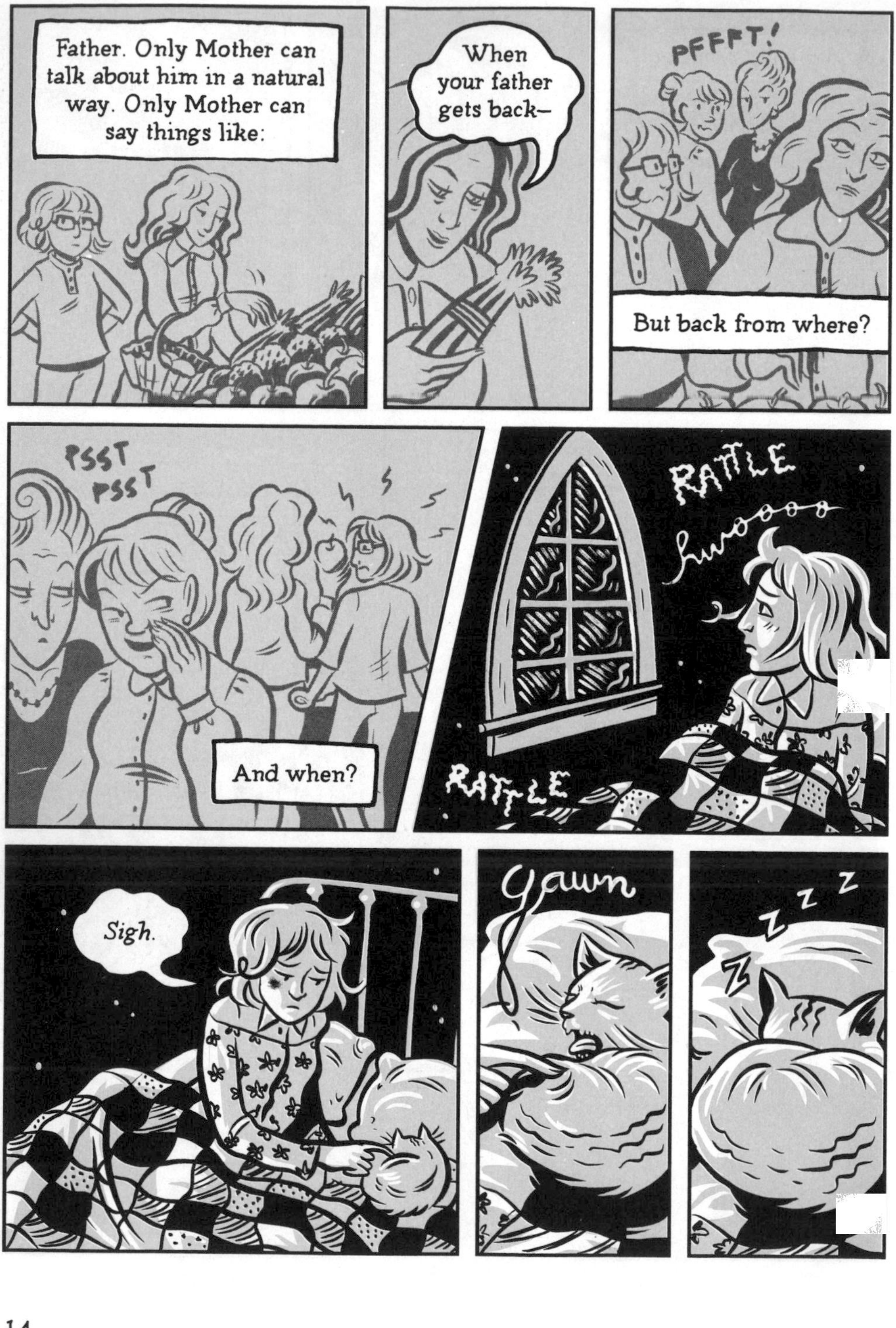
Father. Only Mother can talk about him in a natural way. Only Mother can say things like:
When your father gets back–
PFFFT!
But back from where?
PSST PSST
And when?
RATTLE
hwoooo
RATTLE
Sigh.
yawn
Z Z Z Z

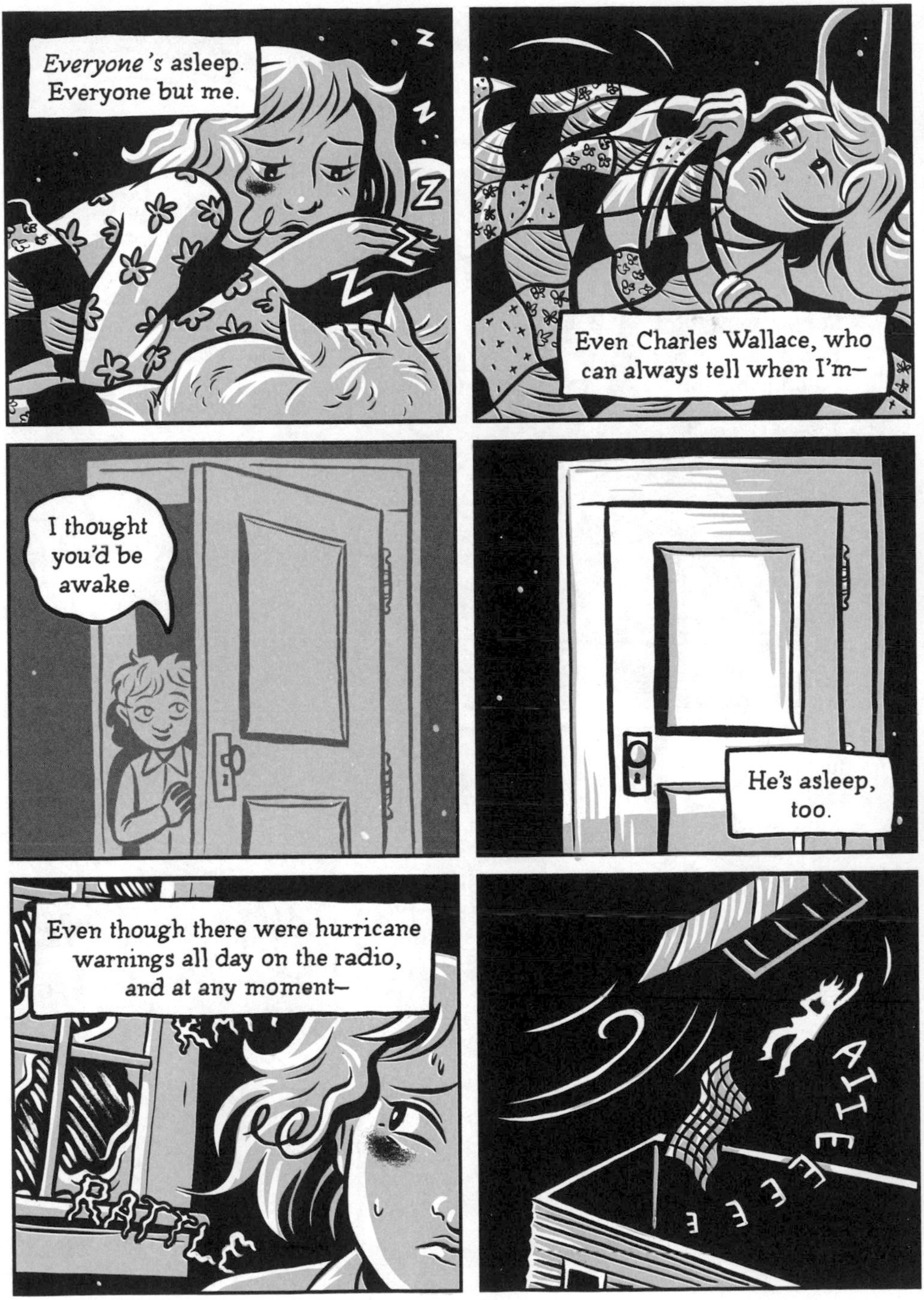

Everyone's asleep. Everyone but me.
Z Z Z Z Z
Even Charles Wallace, who can always tell when I'm—
I thought you'd be awake.
He's asleep, too.
Even though there were hurricane warnings all day on the radio, and at any moment—
RATTLE
AIIEEEEE

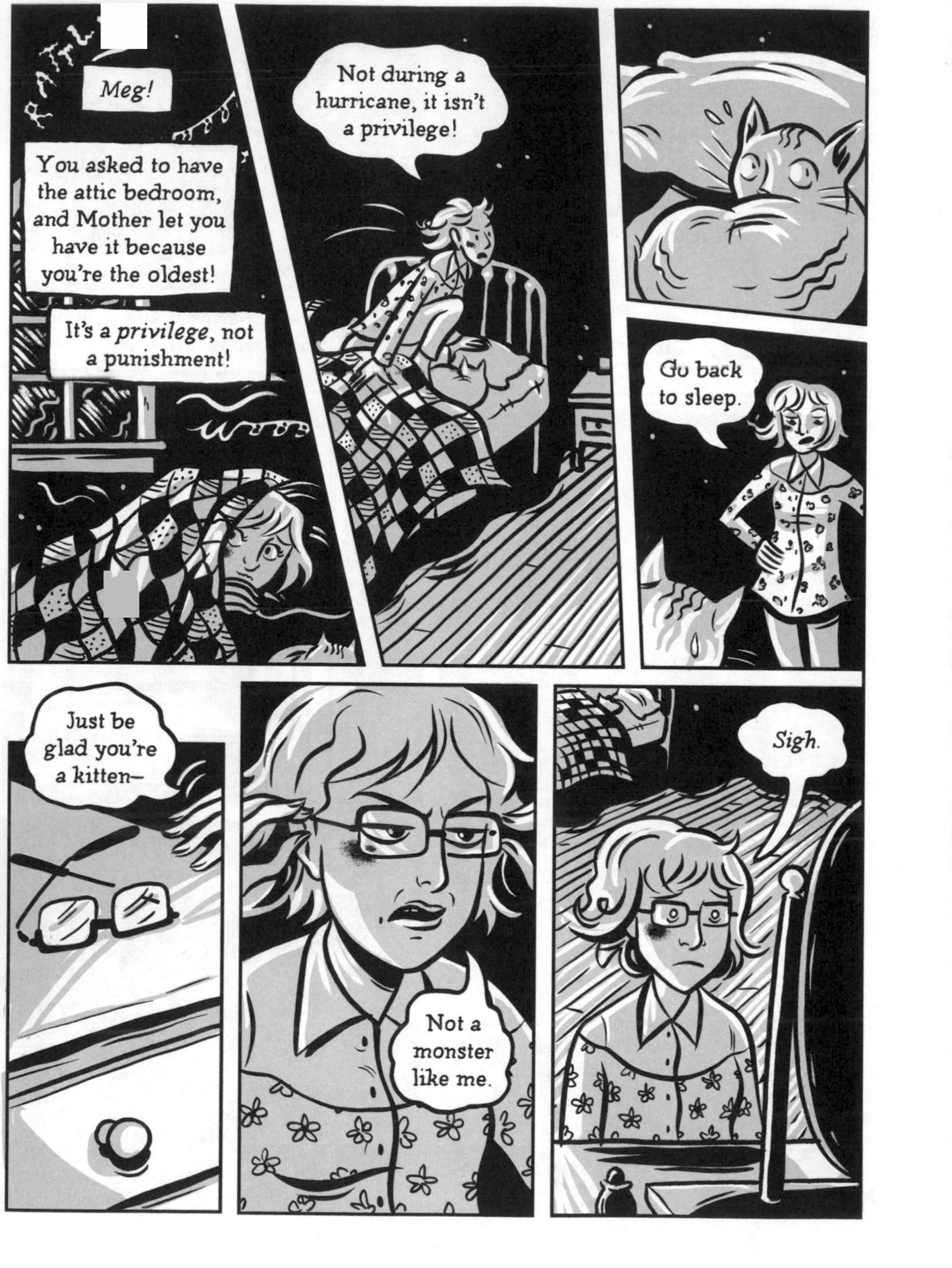
Meg!
You asked to have the attic bedroom, and Mother let you have it because you're the oldest!
It's a *privilege*, not a punishment!
Not during a hurricane, it isn't a privilege!
Go back to sleep.
Just be glad you're a kitten–
Not a monster like me.
Sigh.

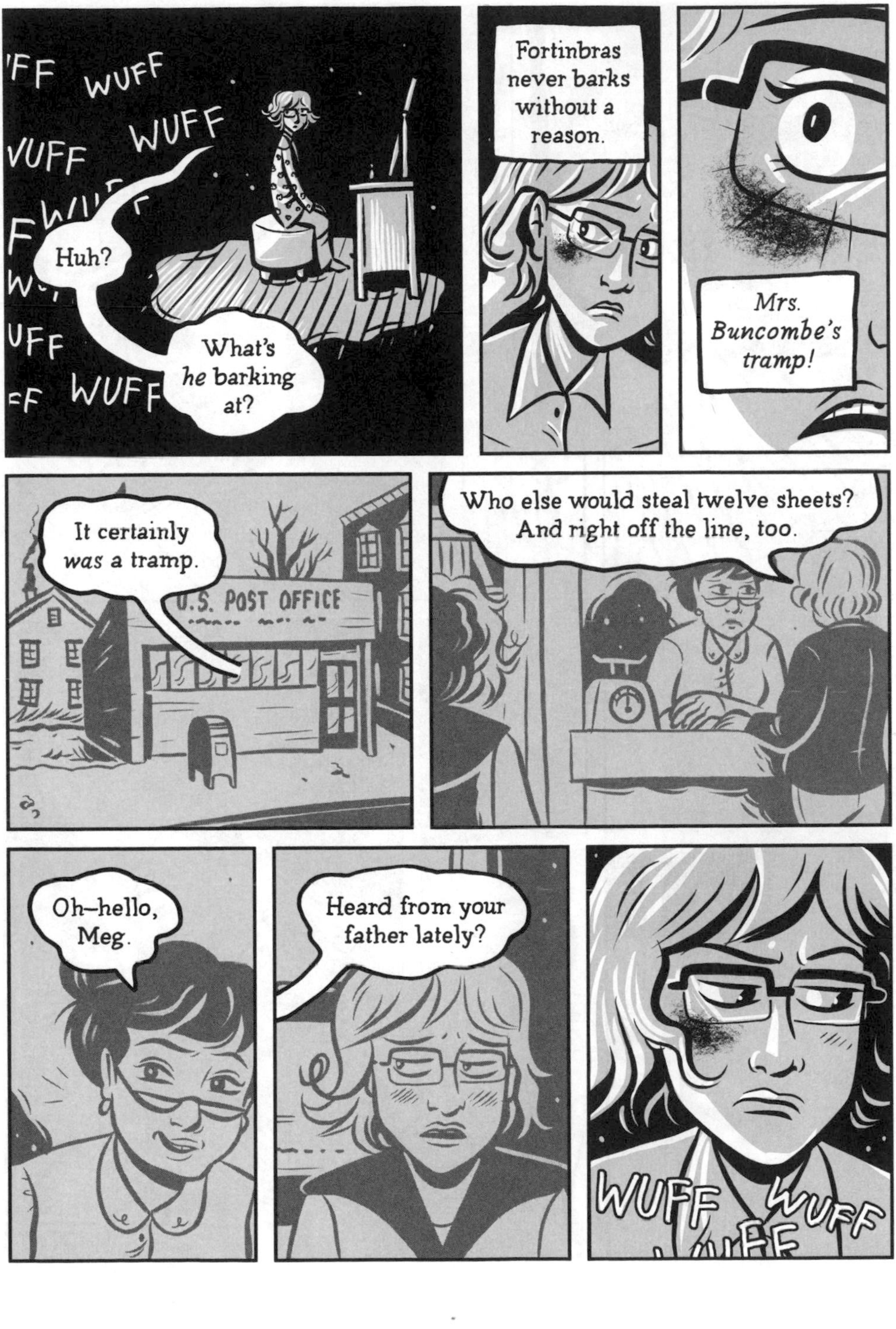
WUFF WUFF WUFF WUFF WUFF
Huh?
What's *he* barking at?
Fortinbras never barks without a reason.
Mrs. Buncombe's tramp!
U.S. POST OFFICE
It certainly *was* a tramp.
Who else would steal twelve sheets? And right off the line, too.
Oh—hello, Meg.
Heard from your father lately?
WUFF WUFF

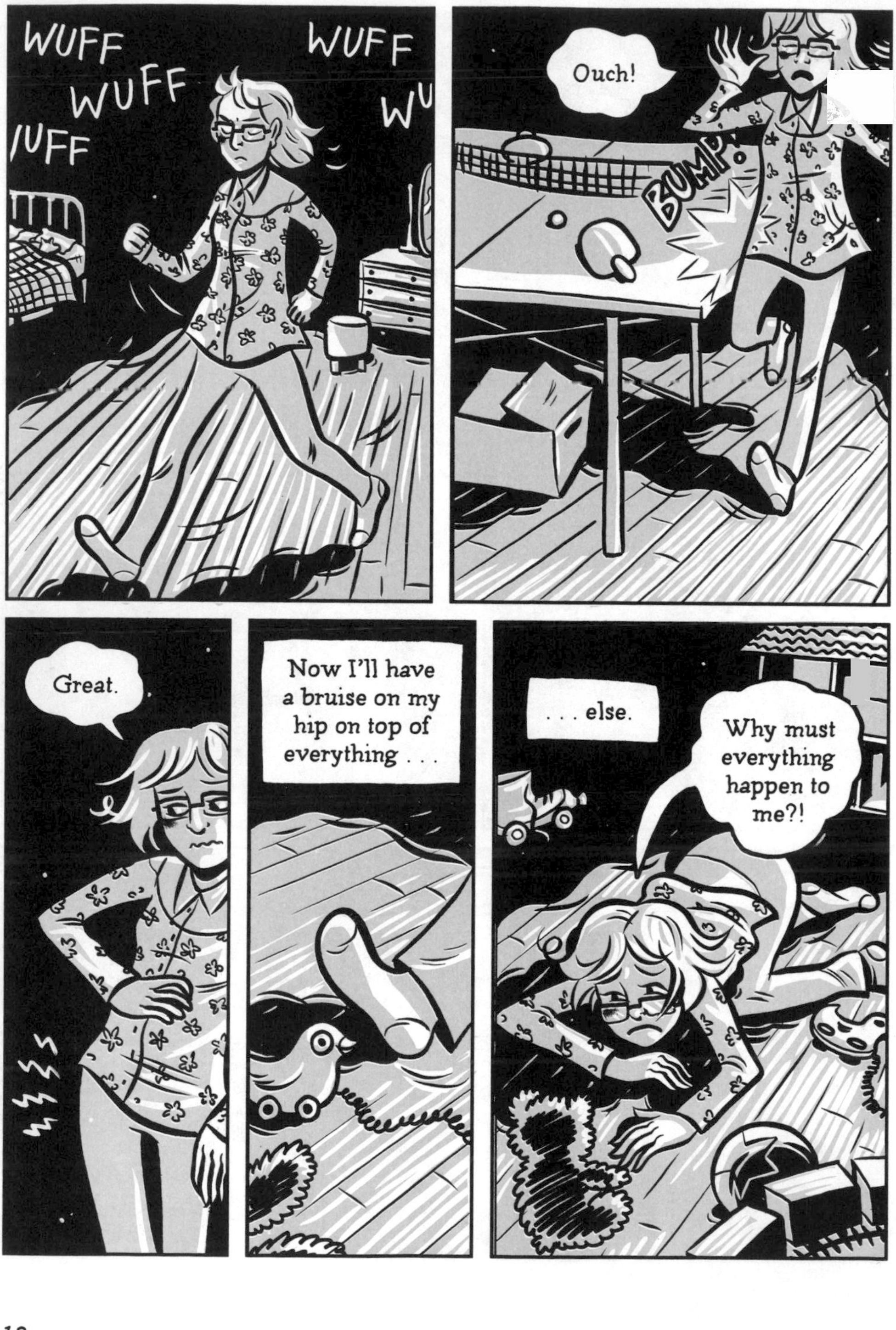
WUFF
WUFF
WUFF
WUFF
Ouch!
BUMP!
Great.
Now I'll have a bruise on my hip on top of everything . . .
. . . else.
Why must everything happen to me?!

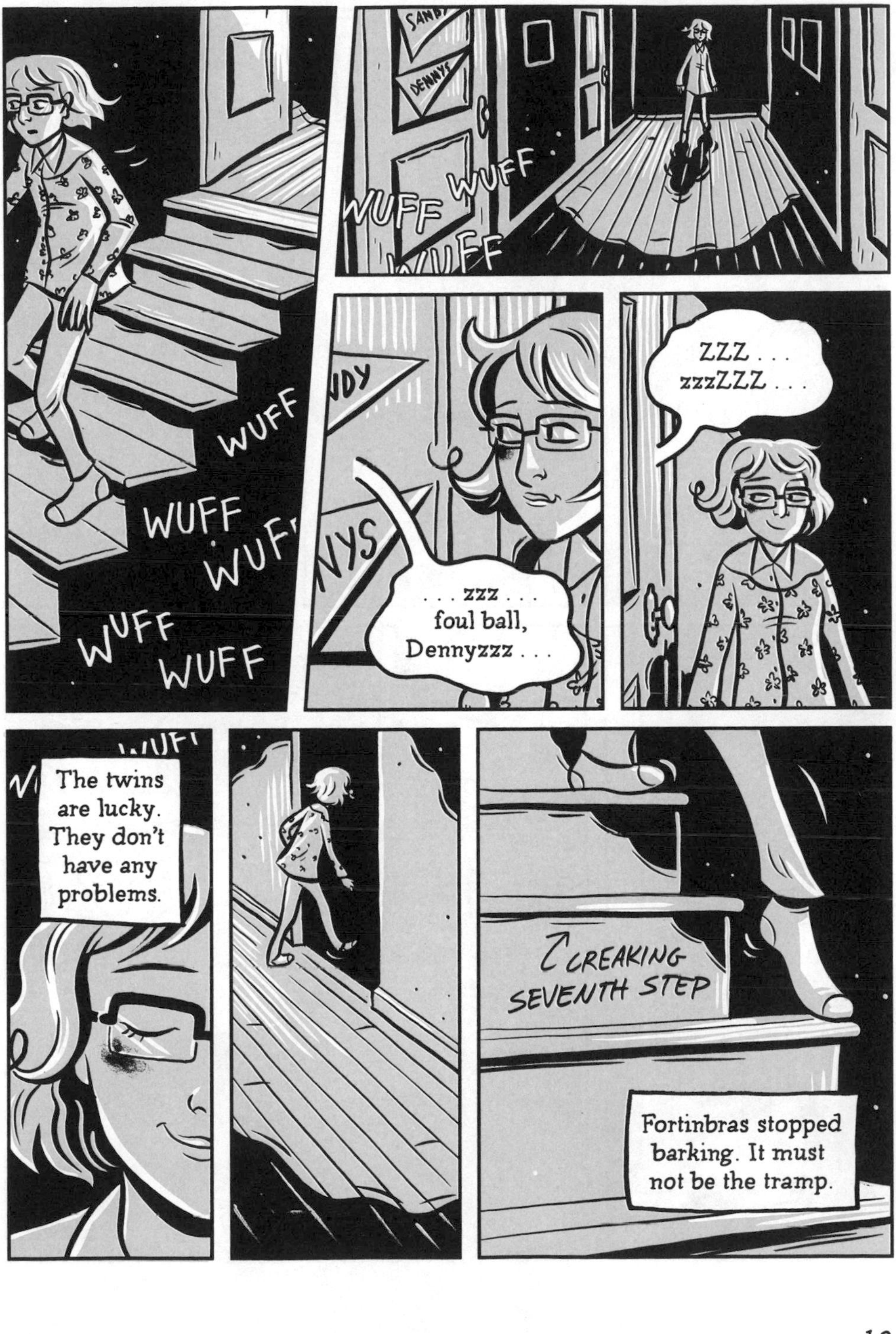
WUFF
WUFF
WUFF
WUFF
WUFF
WUFF
WUFF
WUFF
. . . zzz . . .
foul ball,
Dennyzzz . . .
ZZZ . . .
zzzZZZ . . .
The twins
are lucky.
They don't
have any
problems.
CREAKING
SEVENTH STEP
Fortinbras stopped
barking. It must
not be the tramp.

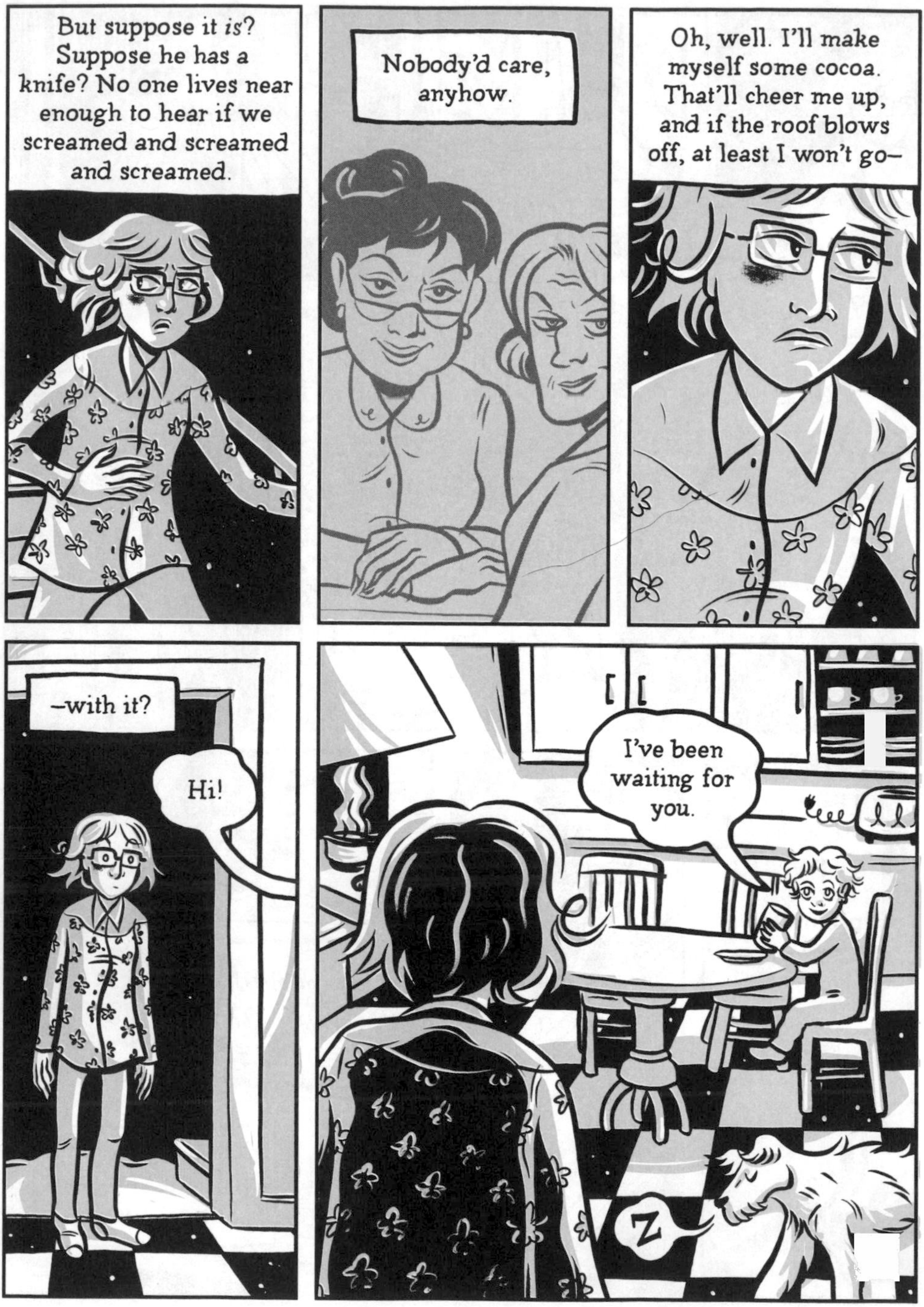
But suppose it *is*? Suppose he has a knife? No one lives near enough to hear if we screamed and screamed and screamed.
Nobody'd care, anyhow.
Oh, well. I'll make myself some cocoa. That'll cheer me up, and if the roof blows off, at least I won't go–
–with it?
Hi!
I've been waiting for you.
Z

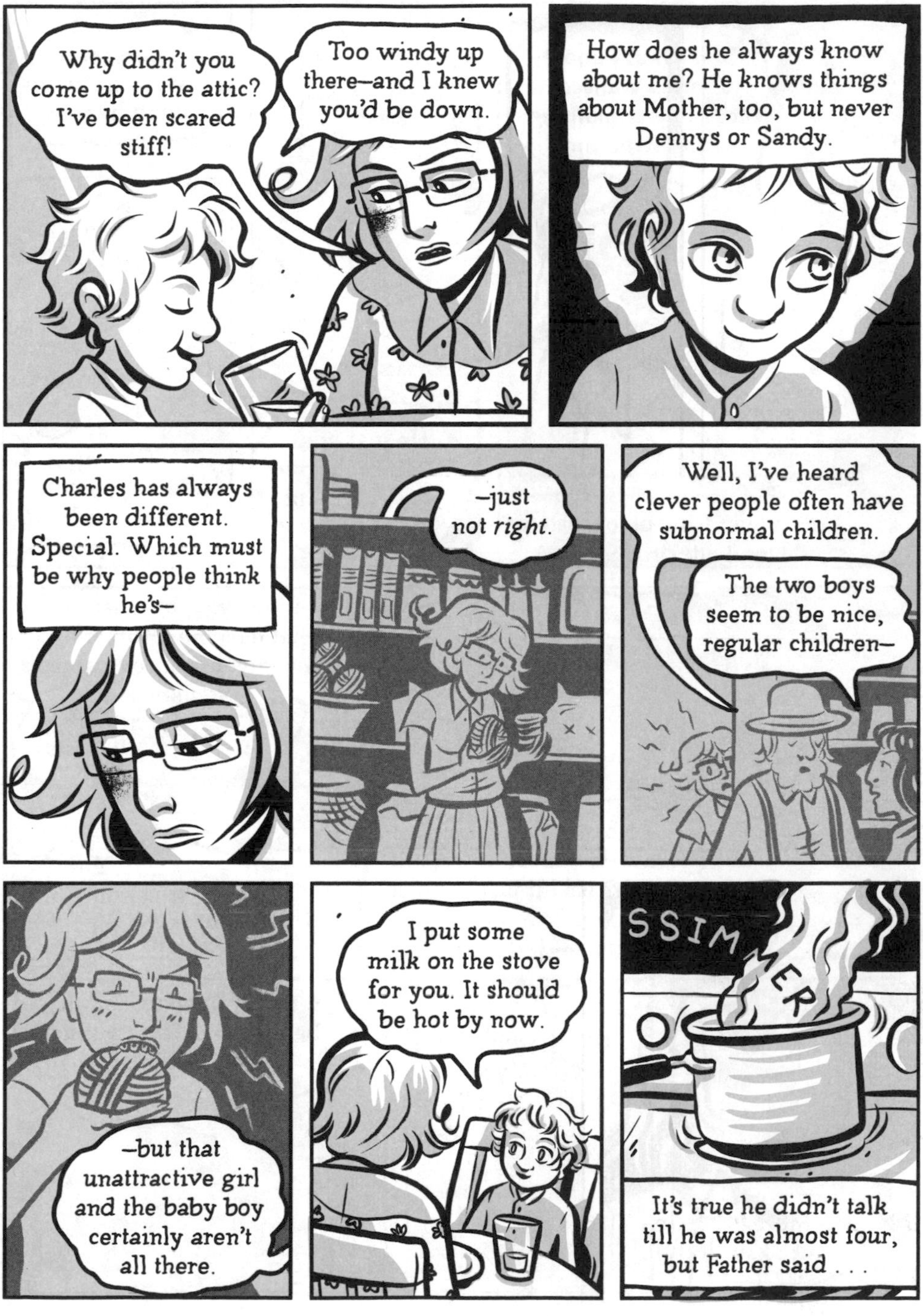
Why didn't you come up to the attic? I've been scared stiff!
Too windy up there—and I knew you'd be down.
How does he always know about me? He knows things about Mother, too, but never Dennys or Sandy.
Charles has always been different. Special. Which must be why people think he's—
—just not *right*.
Well, I've heard clever people often have subnormal children.
The two boys seem to be nice, regular children—
—but that unattractive girl and the baby boy certainly aren't all there.
I put some milk on the stove for you. It should be hot by now.
SSIMMER
It's true he didn't talk till he was almost four, but Father said . . .

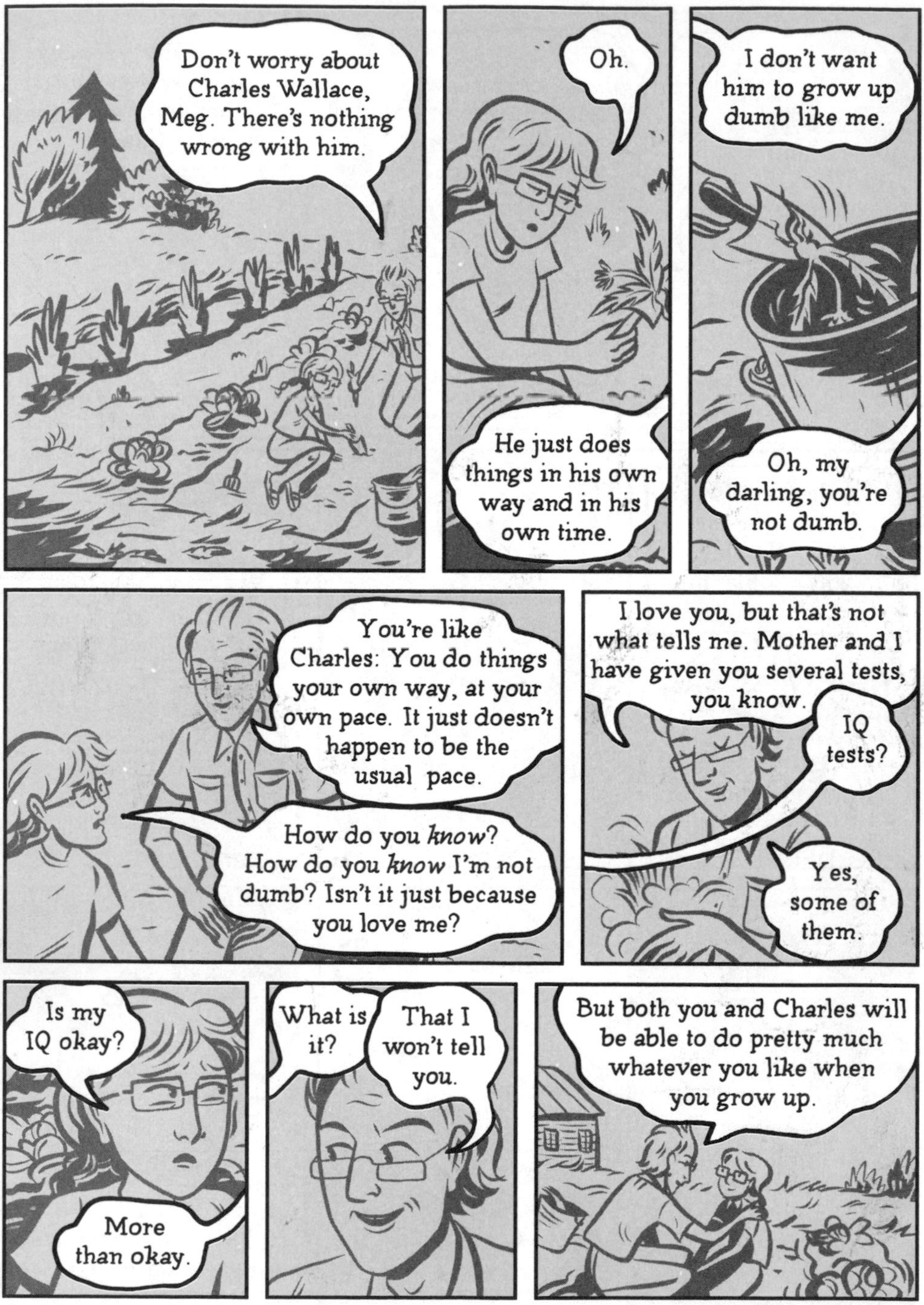
Don't worry about Charles Wallace, Meg. There's nothing wrong with him.
Oh.
He just does things in his own way and in his own time.
I don't want him to grow up dumb like me.
Oh, my darling, you're not dumb.
You're like Charles: You do things your own way, at your own pace. It just doesn't happen to be the usual pace.
How do you *know*? How do you *know* I'm not dumb? Isn't it just because you love me?
I love you, but that's not what tells me. Mother and I have given you several tests, you know.
IQ tests?
Yes, some of them.
Is my IQ okay?
More than okay.
What is it?
That I won't tell you.
But both you and Charles will be able to do pretty much whatever you like when you grow up.

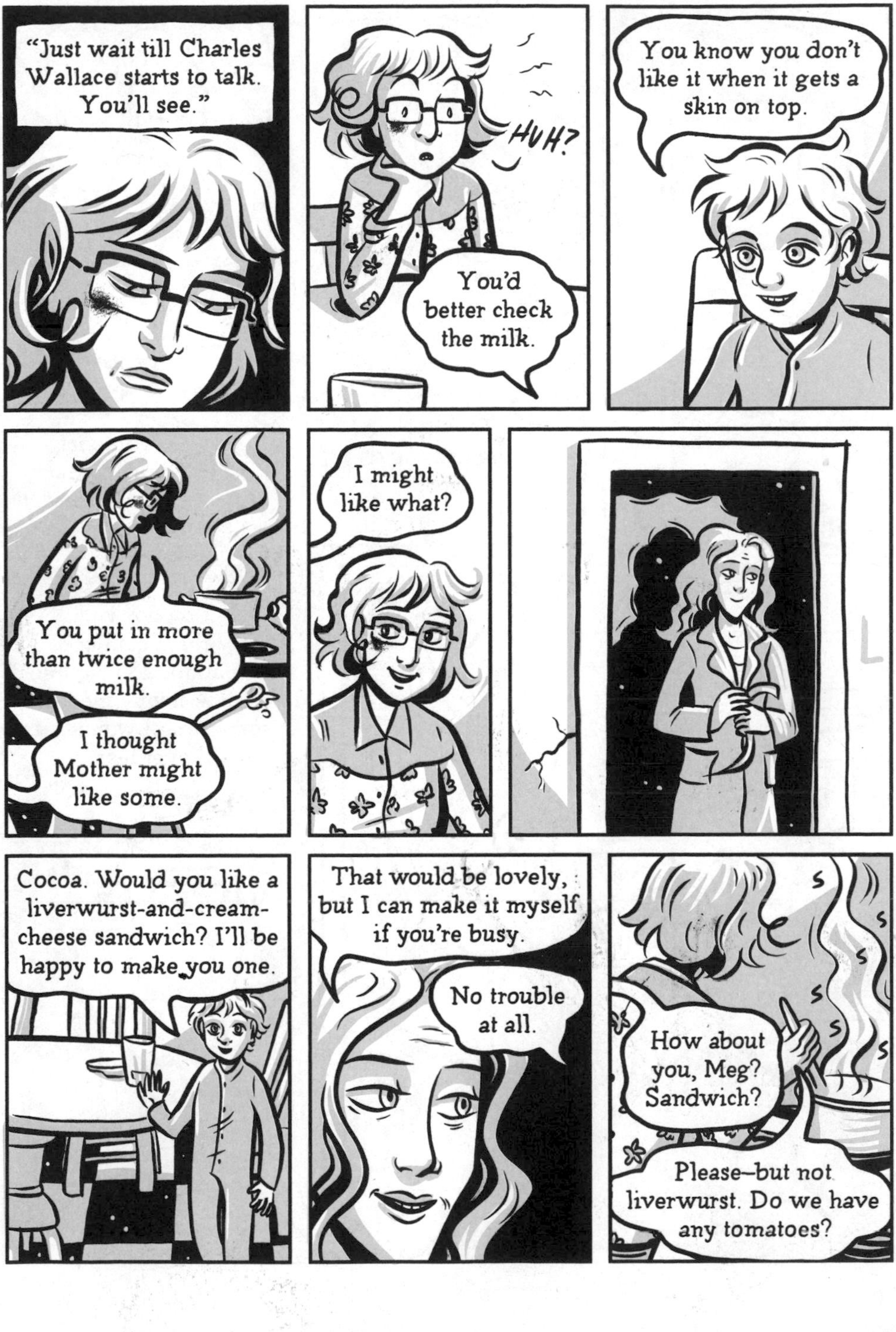
"Just wait till Charles Wallace starts to talk. You'll see."
HUH?
You'd better check the milk.
You know you don't like it when it gets a skin on top.
You put in more than twice enough milk.
I thought Mother might like some.
I might like what?
Cocoa. Would you like a liverwurst-and-cream-cheese sandwich? I'll be happy to make you one.
That would be lovely, but I can make it myself if you're busy.
No trouble at all.
How about you, Meg? Sandwich?
Please—but not liverwurst. Do we have any tomatoes?

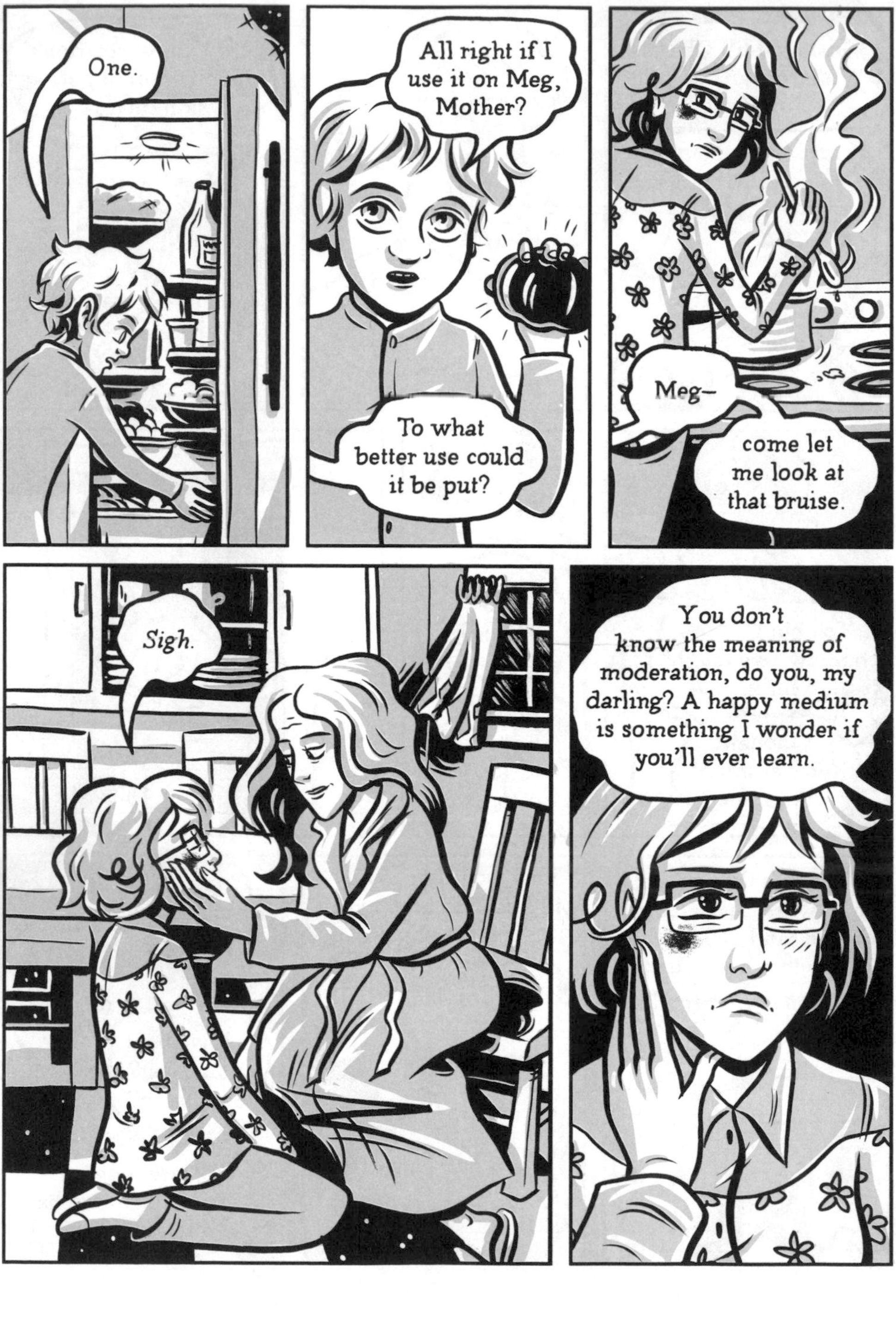
One.
All right if I use it on Meg, Mother?
To what better use could it be put?
Meg–
come let me look at that bruise.
Sigh.
You don't know the meaning of moderation, do you, my darling? A happy medium is something I wonder if you'll ever learn.

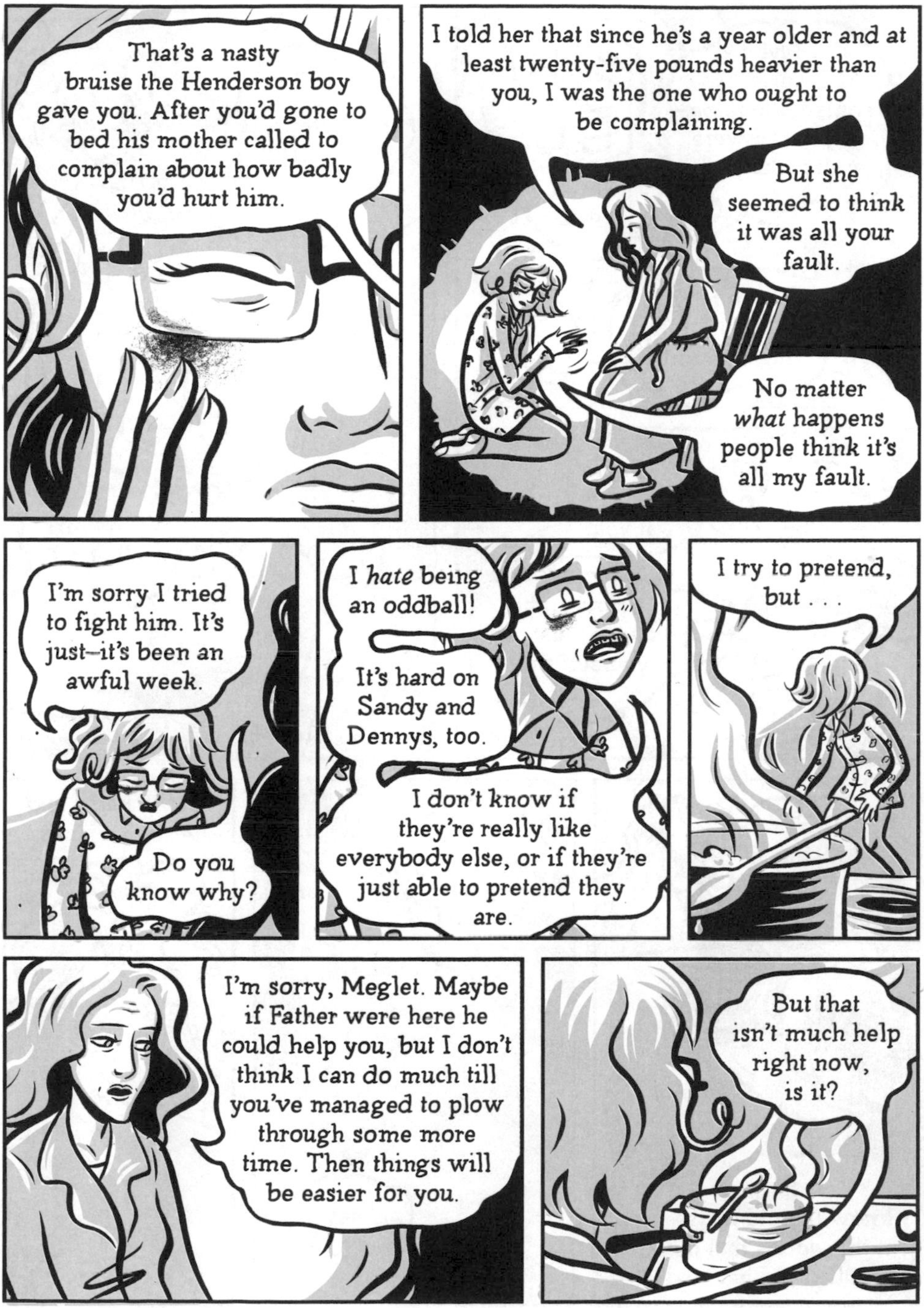
That's a nasty bruise the Henderson boy gave you. After you'd gone to bed his mother called to complain about how badly you'd hurt him.
I told her that since he's a year older and at least twenty-five pounds heavier than you, I was the one who ought to be complaining.
But she seemed to think it was all your fault.
No matter *what* happens people think it's all my fault.
I'm sorry I tried to fight him. It's just–it's been an awful week.
Do you know why?
I *hate* being an oddball!
It's hard on Sandy and Dennys, too.
I don't know if they're really like everybody else, or if they're just able to pretend they are.
I try to pretend, but . . .
I'm sorry, Meglet. Maybe if Father were here he could help you, but I don't think I can do much till you've managed to plow through some more time. Then things will be easier for you.
But that isn't much help right now, is it?

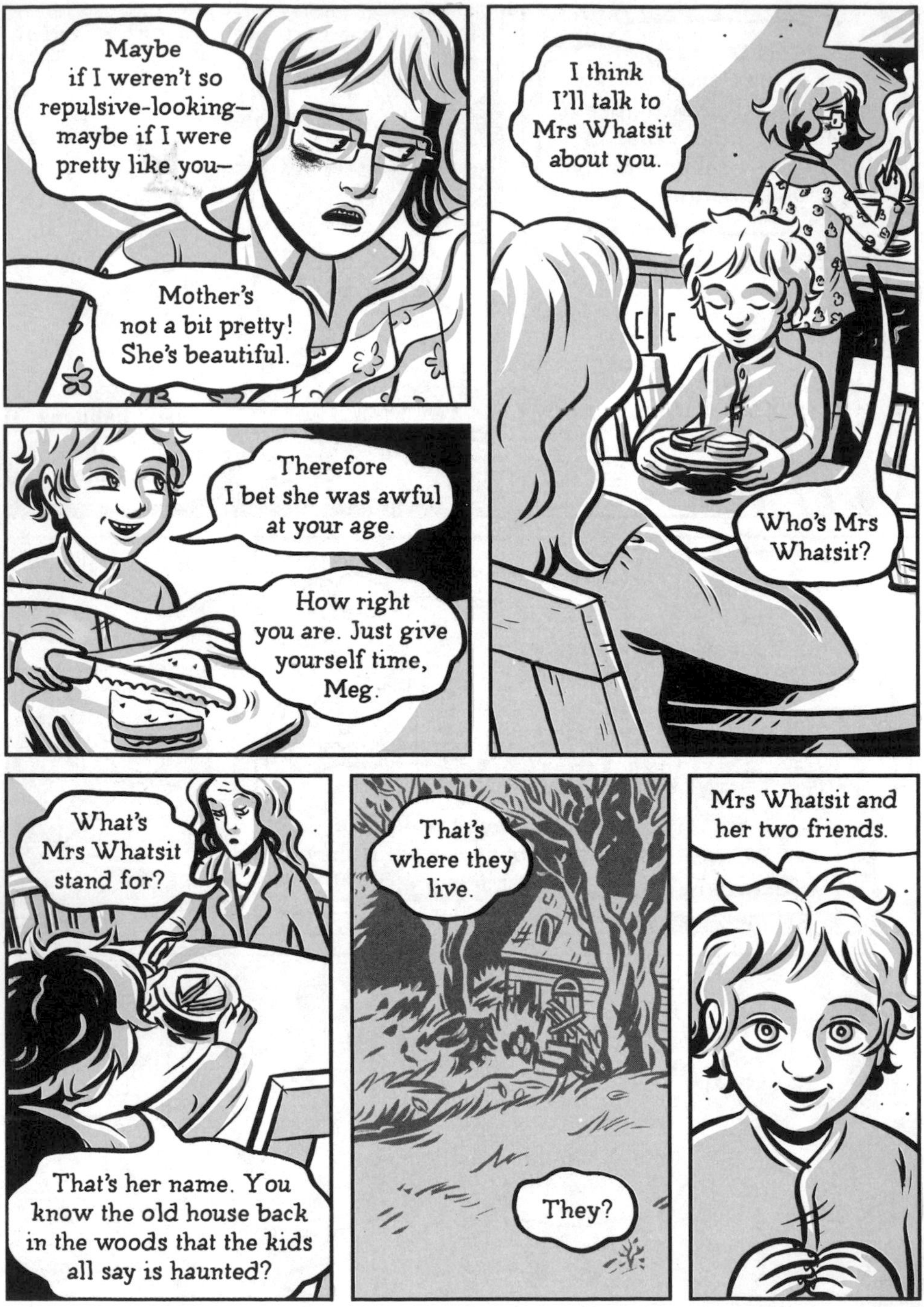
Maybe if I weren't so repulsive-looking—maybe if I were pretty like you—
Mother's not a bit pretty! She's beautiful.
Therefore I bet she was awful at your age.
How right you are. Just give yourself time, Meg.
I think I'll talk to Mrs Whatsit about you.
Who's Mrs Whatsit?
What's Mrs Whatsit stand for?
That's her name. You know the old house back in the woods that the kids all say is haunted?
That's where they live.
They?
Mrs Whatsit and her two friends.

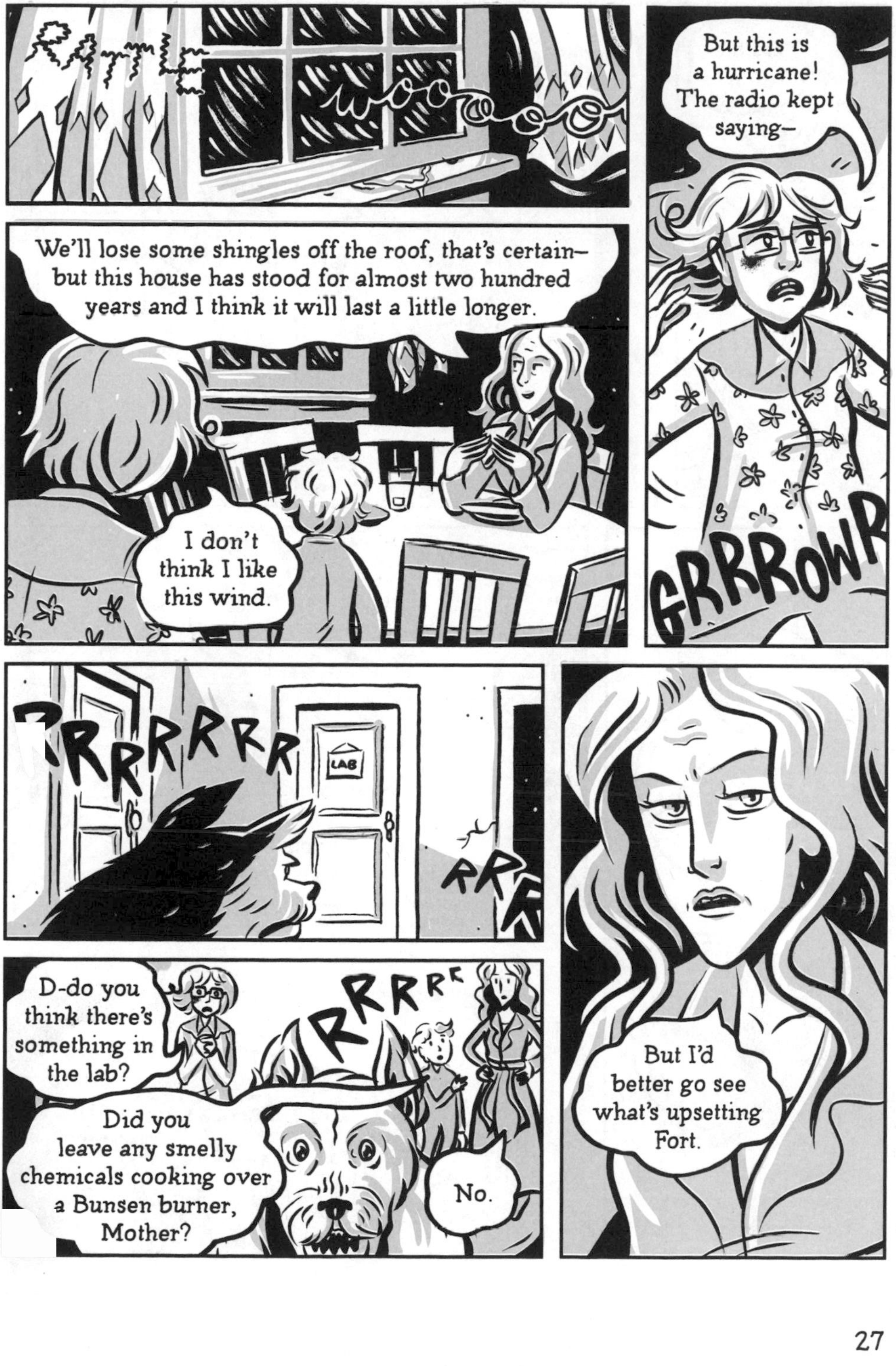
RATTLE
WOOOOOO
We'll lose some shingles off the roof, that's certain–but this house has stood for almost two hundred years and I think it will last a little longer.
I don't think I like this wind.
But this is a hurricane! The radio kept saying–
GRRROWR
RRRRRRR
LAB
RRR
But I'd better go see what's upsetting Fort.
D-do you think there's something in the lab?
RRRRR
Did you leave any smelly chemicals cooking over a Bunsen burner, Mother?
No.

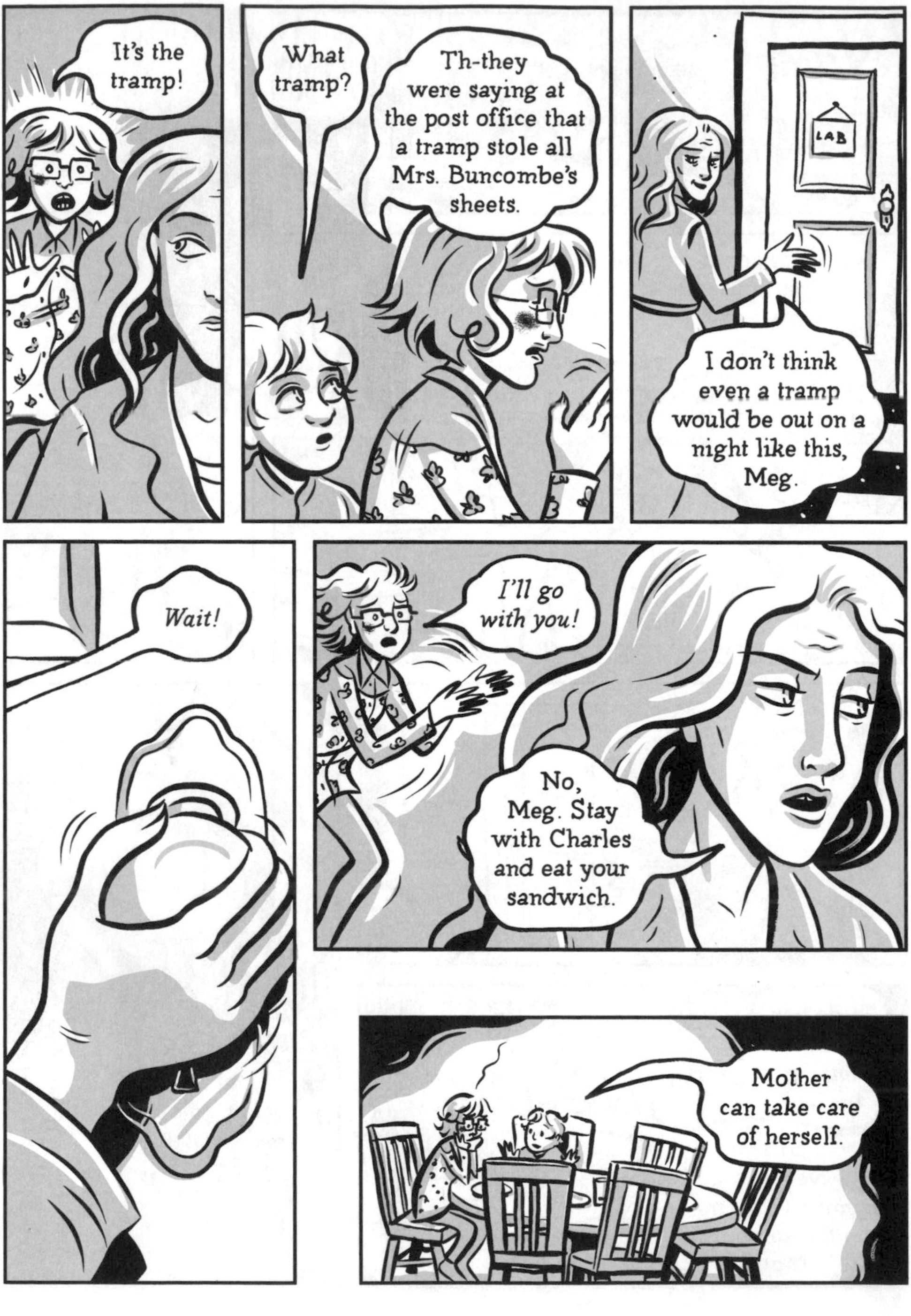
It's the tramp!
What tramp?
Th-they were saying at the post office that a tramp stole all Mrs. Buncombe's sheets.
LAB
I don't think even a tramp would be out on a night like this, Meg.
Wait!
I'll go with you!
No, Meg. Stay with Charles and eat your sandwich.
Mother can take care of herself.

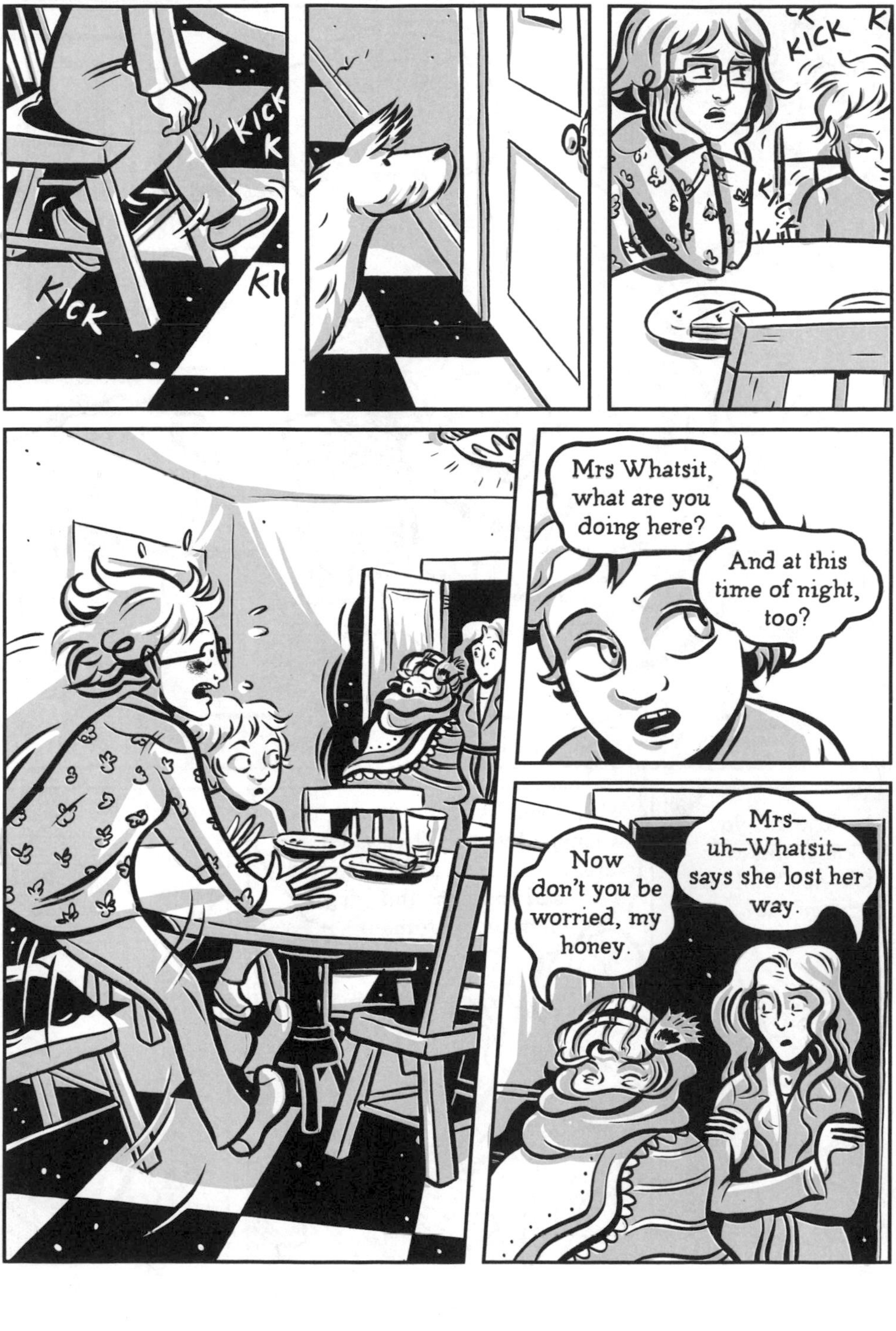
KICK
K
KICK
KI
KICK
KI
KICK
Mrs Whatsit, what are you doing here?
And at this time of night, too?
Mrs— uh—Whatsit— says she lost her way.
Now don't you be worried, my honey.

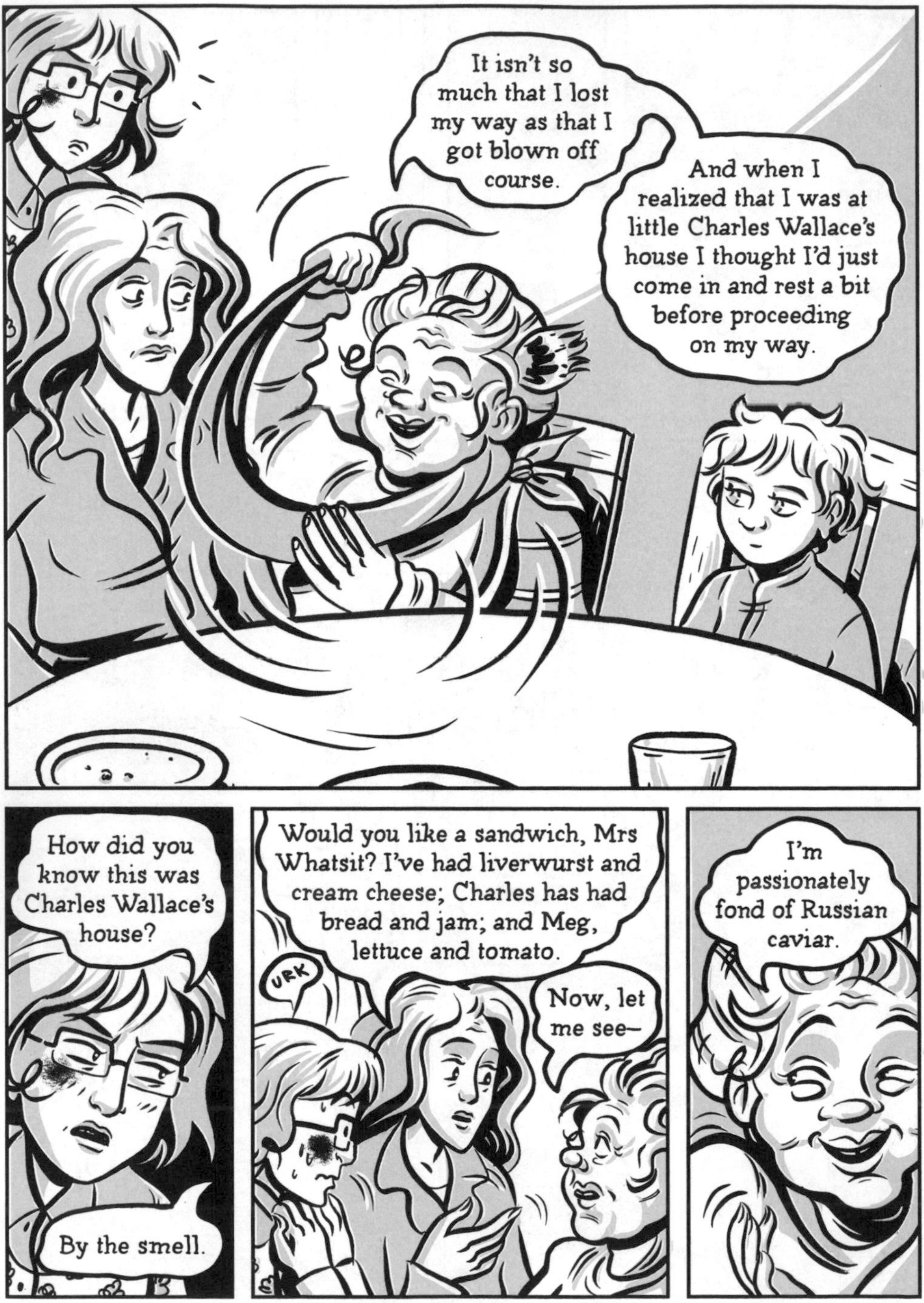
It isn't so much that I lost my way as that I got blown off course.
And when I realized that I was at little Charles Wallace's house I thought I'd just come in and rest a bit before proceeding on my way.
How did you know this was Charles Wallace's house?
By the smell.
Would you like a sandwich, Mrs Whatsit? I've had liverwurst and cream cheese; Charles has had bread and jam; and Meg, lettuce and tomato.
URK
Now, let me see–
I'm passionately fond of Russian caviar.

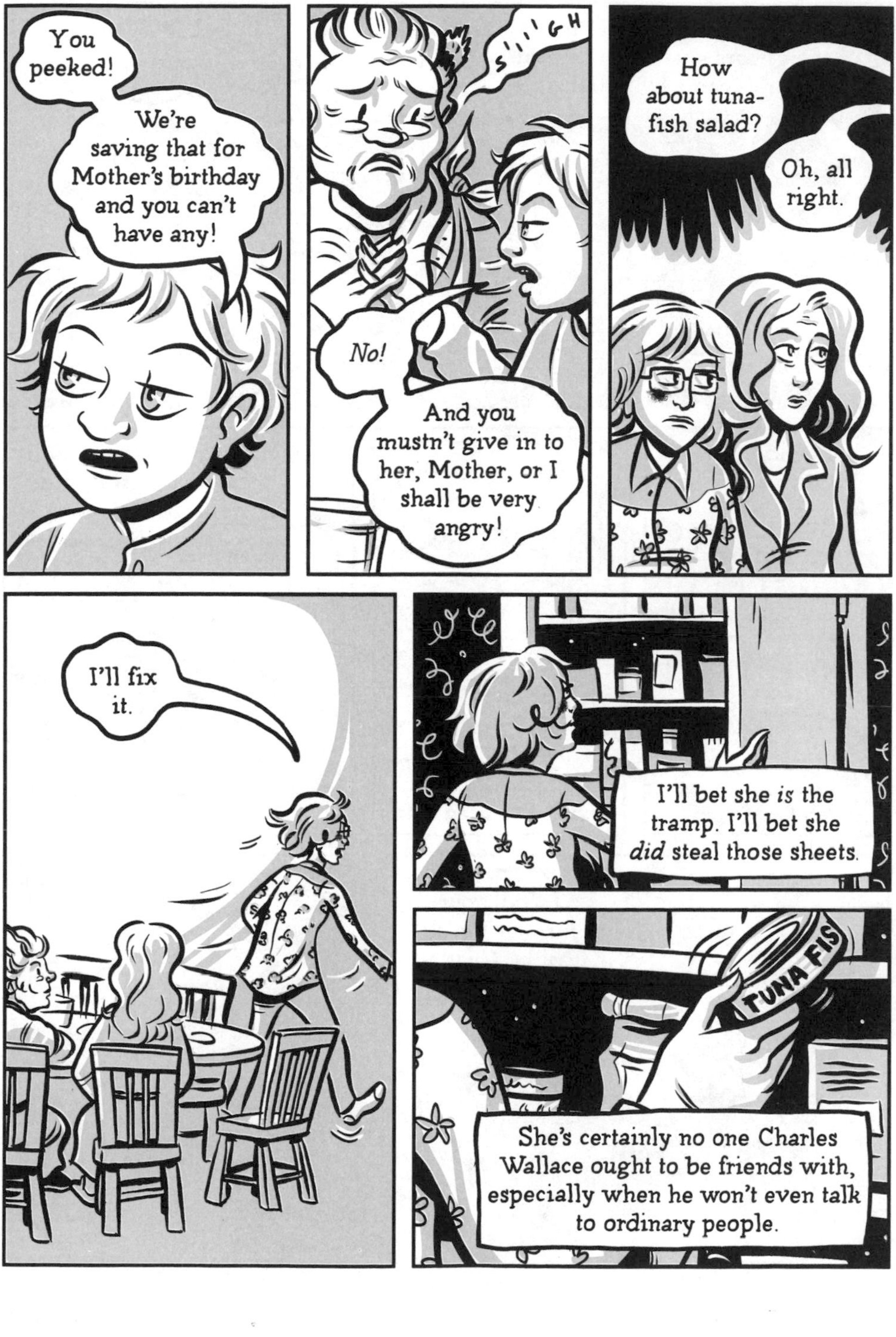
You peeked!
We're saving that for Mother's birthday and you can't have any!
S'I'GH
No!
And you mustn't give in to her, Mother, or I shall be very angry!
How about tuna-fish salad?
Oh, all right.
I'll fix it.
I'll bet she *is* the tramp. I'll bet she *did* steal those sheets.
TUNA FIS
She's certainly no one Charles Wallace ought to be friends with, especially when he won't even talk to ordinary people.

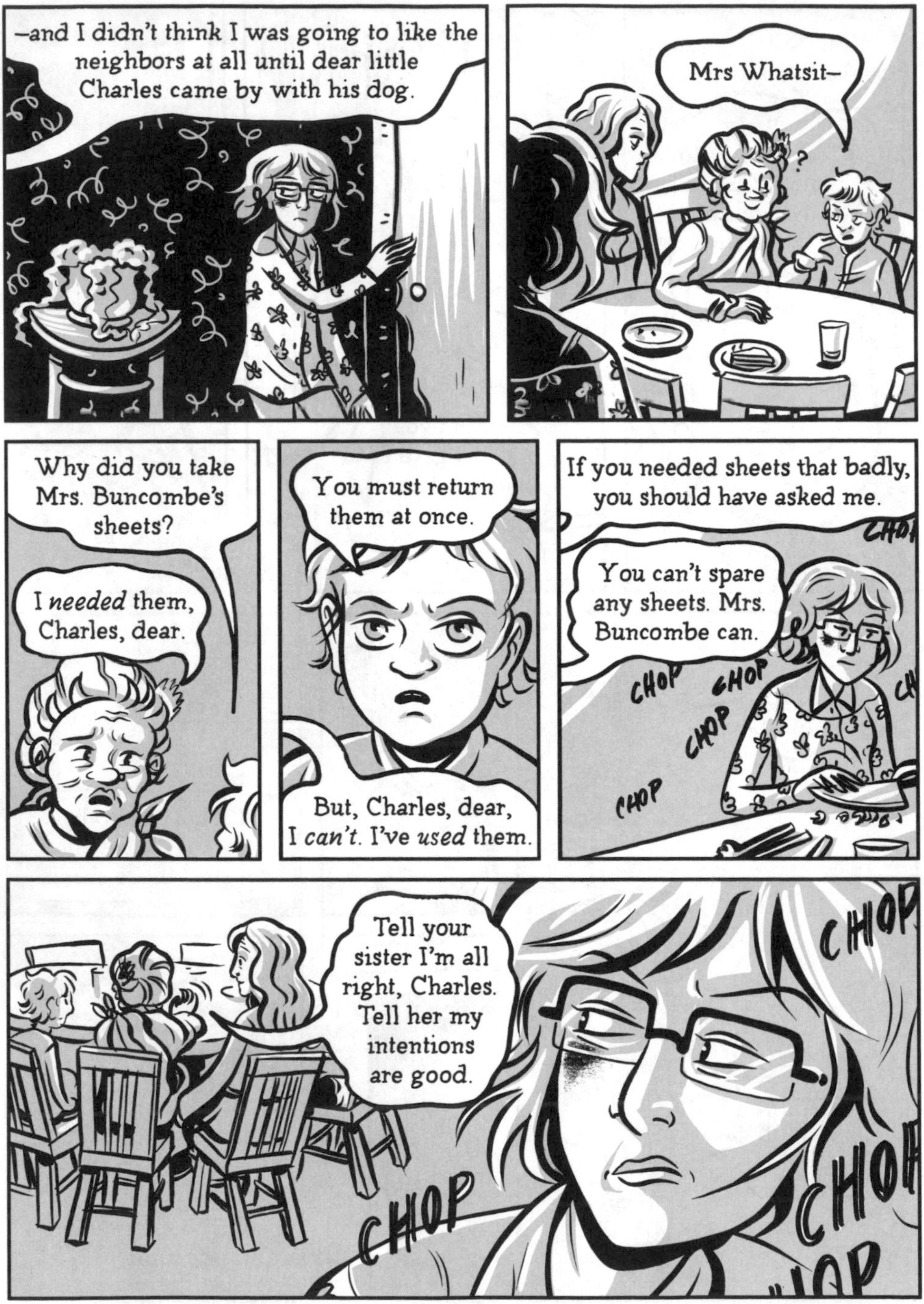

—and I didn't think I was going to like the neighbors at all until dear little Charles came by with his dog.
Mrs Whatsit—
?
Why did you take Mrs. Buncombe's sheets?
I *needed* them, Charles, dear.
You must return them at once.
But, Charles, dear, I *can't*. I've *used* them.
If you needed sheets that badly, you should have asked me.
You can't spare any sheets. Mrs. Buncombe can.
CHOP
CHOP
CHOP
CHOP
Tell your sister I'm all right, Charles. Tell her my intentions are good.
CHOP
CHOP

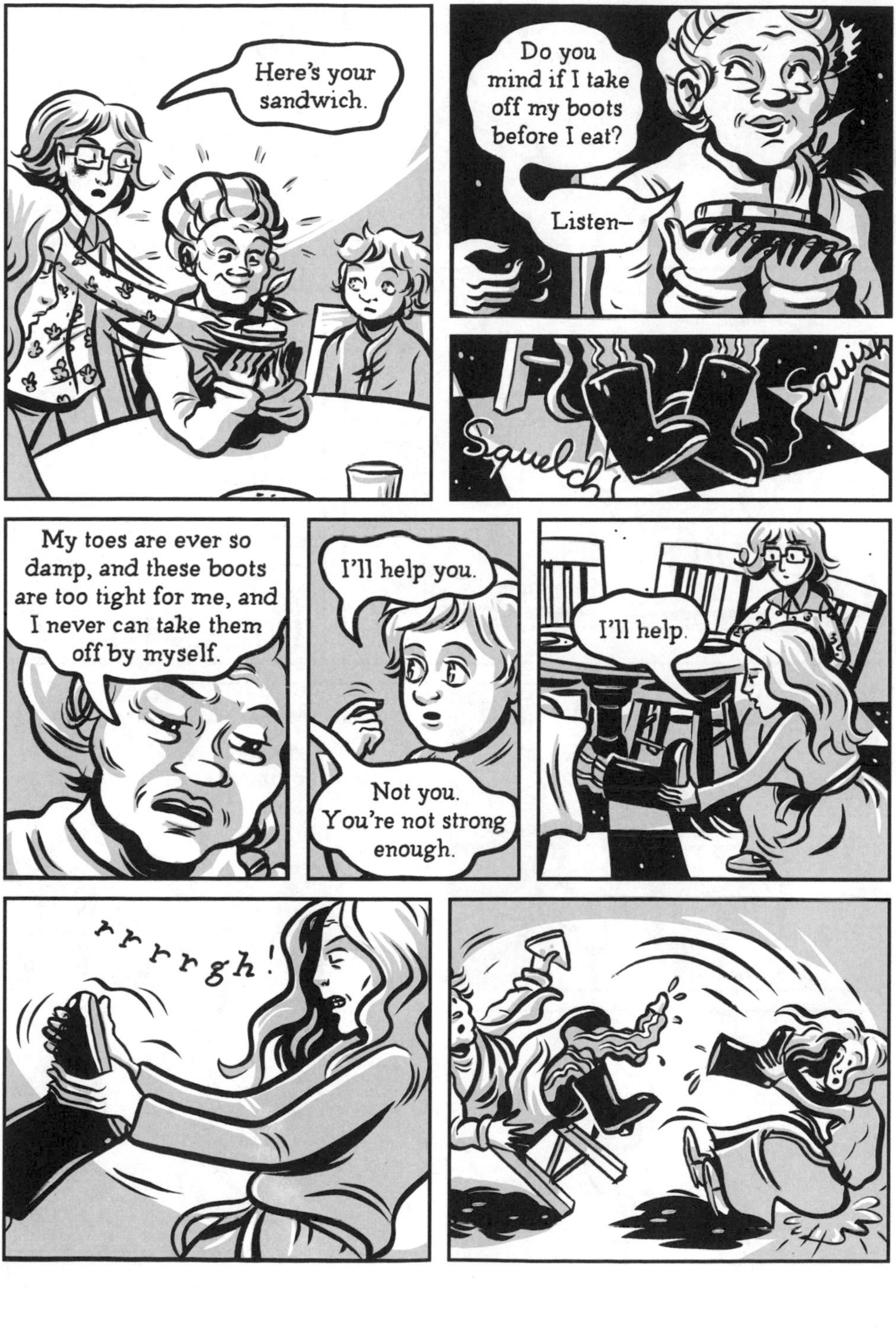
Here's your sandwich.
Do you mind if I take off my boots before I eat?
Listen—
Squelch
Squish
My toes are ever so damp, and these boots are too tight for me, and I never can take them off by myself.
I'll help you.
Not you. You're not strong enough.
I'll help.
rrrrgh!

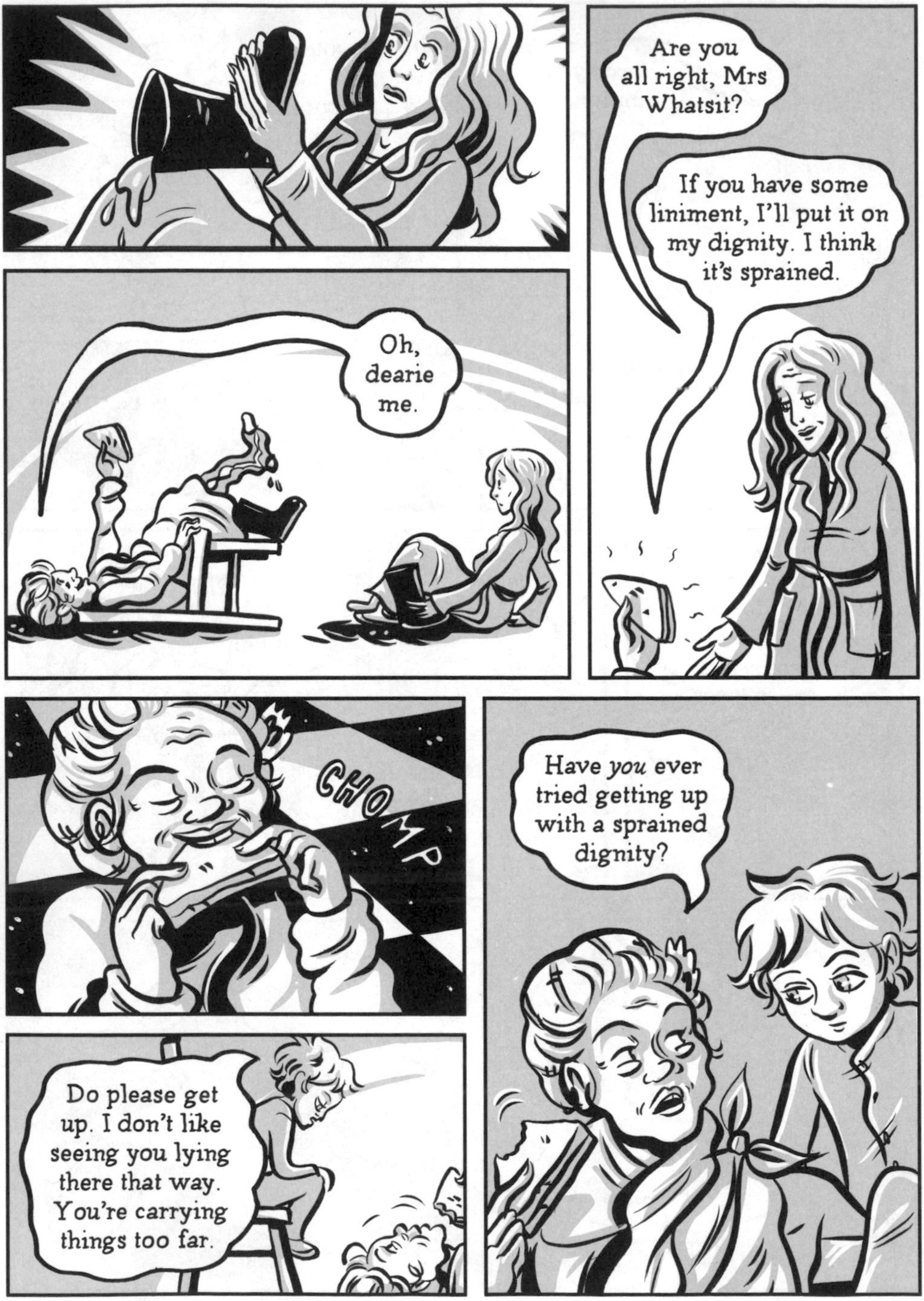

Oh, dearie me.
Are you all right, Mrs Whatsit?
If you have some liniment, I'll put it on my dignity. I think it's sprained.
CHOMP
Do please get up. I don't like seeing you lying there that way. You're carrying things too far.
Have *you* ever tried getting up with a sprained dignity?

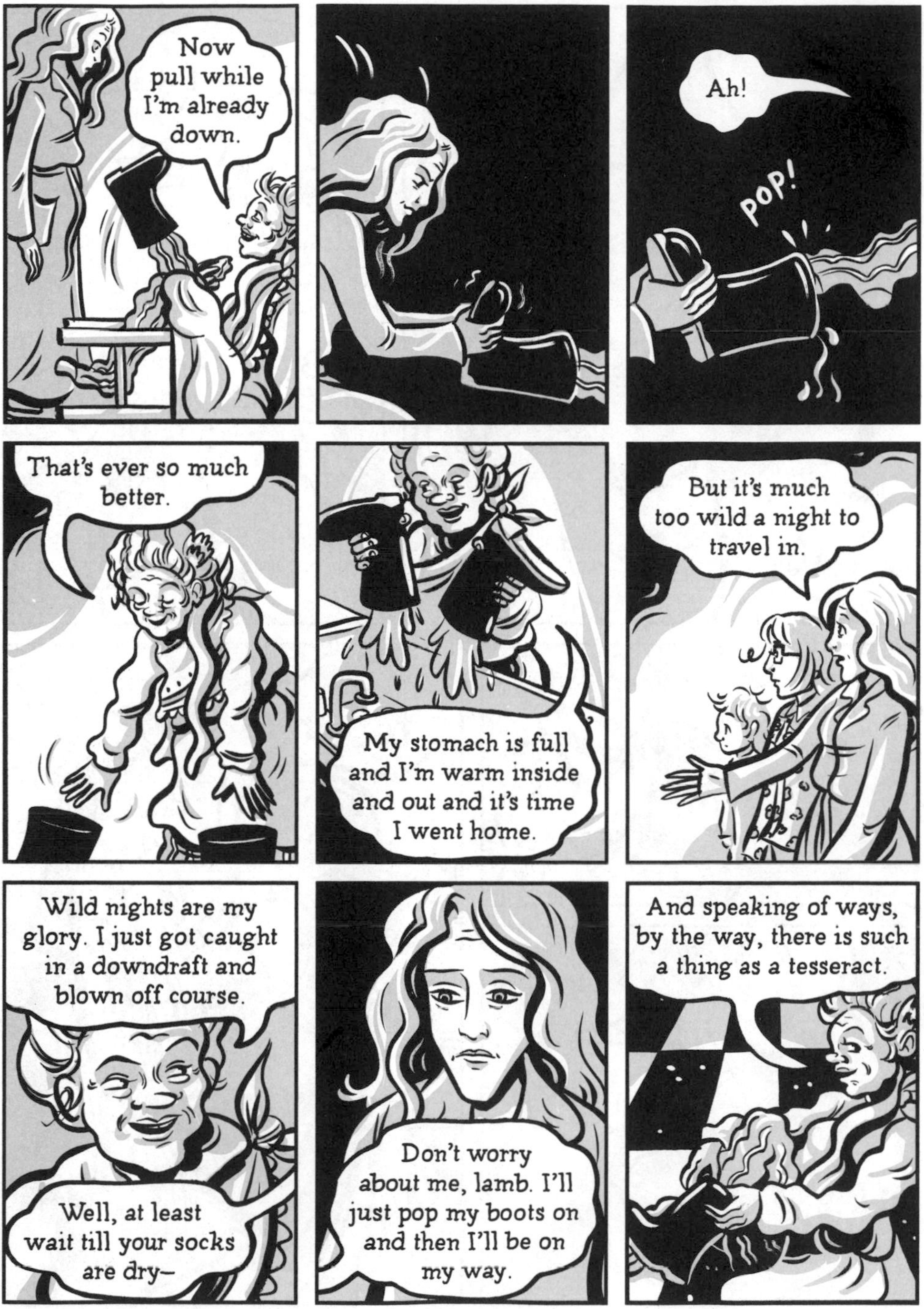
Now pull while I'm already down.
Ah!
POP!
That's ever so much better.
My stomach is full and I'm warm inside and out and it's time I went home.
But it's much too wild a night to travel in.
Wild nights are my glory. I just got caught in a downdraft and blown off course.
Well, at least wait till your socks are dry–
Don't worry about me, lamb. I'll just pop my boots on and then I'll be on my way.
And speaking of ways, by the way, there is such a thing as a tesseract.

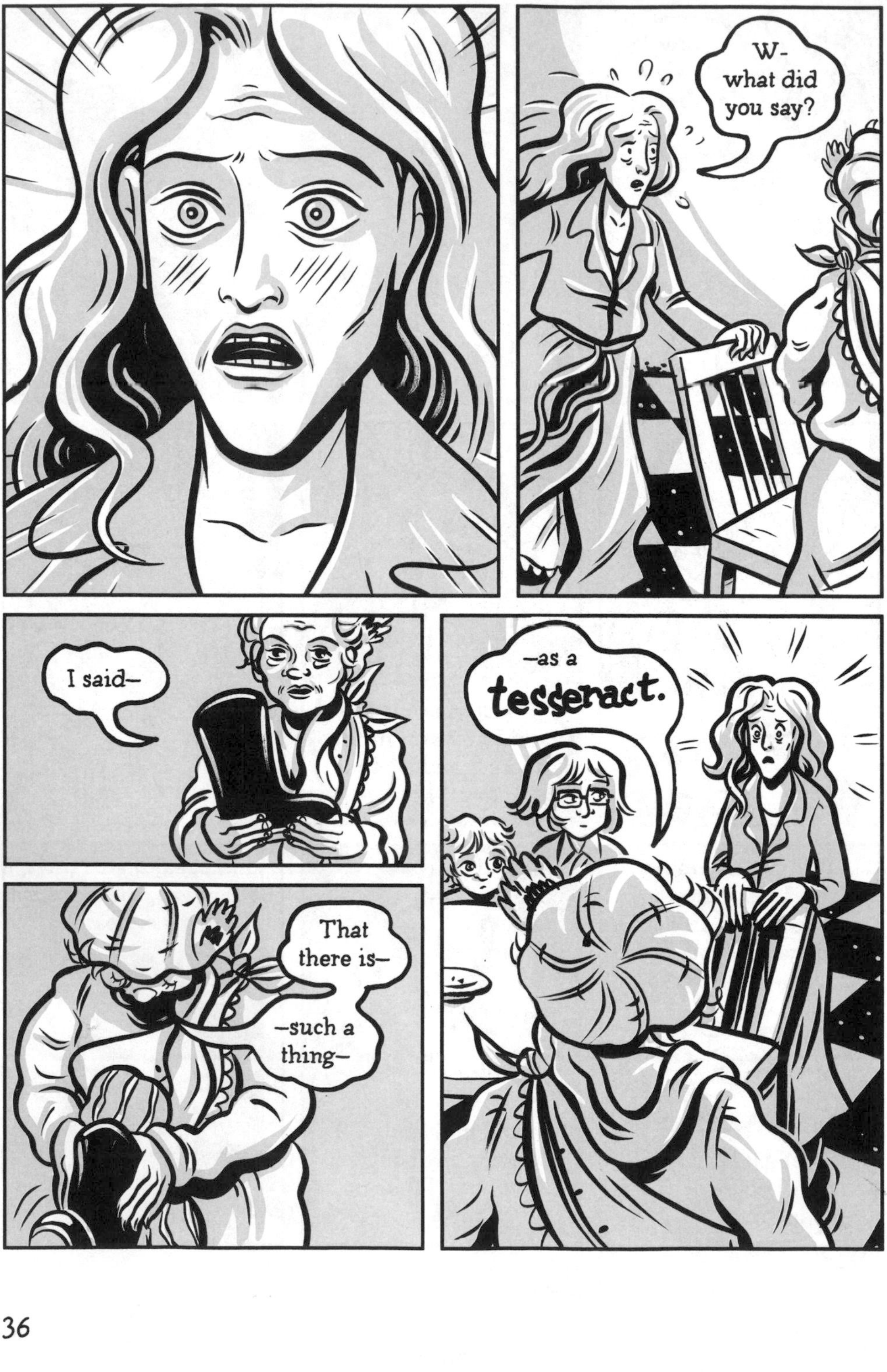
W- what did you say?
I said—
—as a tesseract.
That there is—
—such a thing—

2
Mrs Who

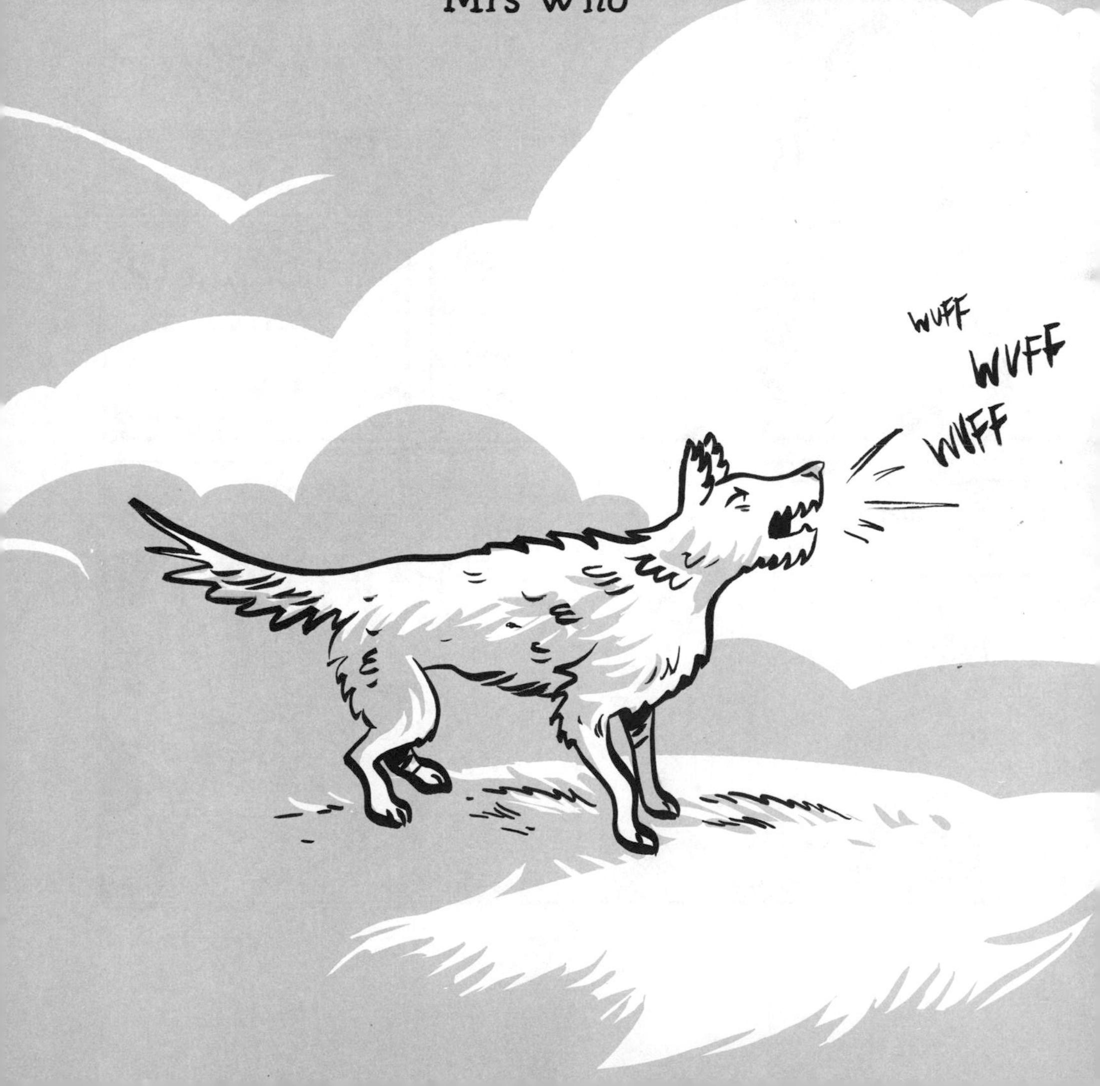
WUFF
WUFF
WUFF

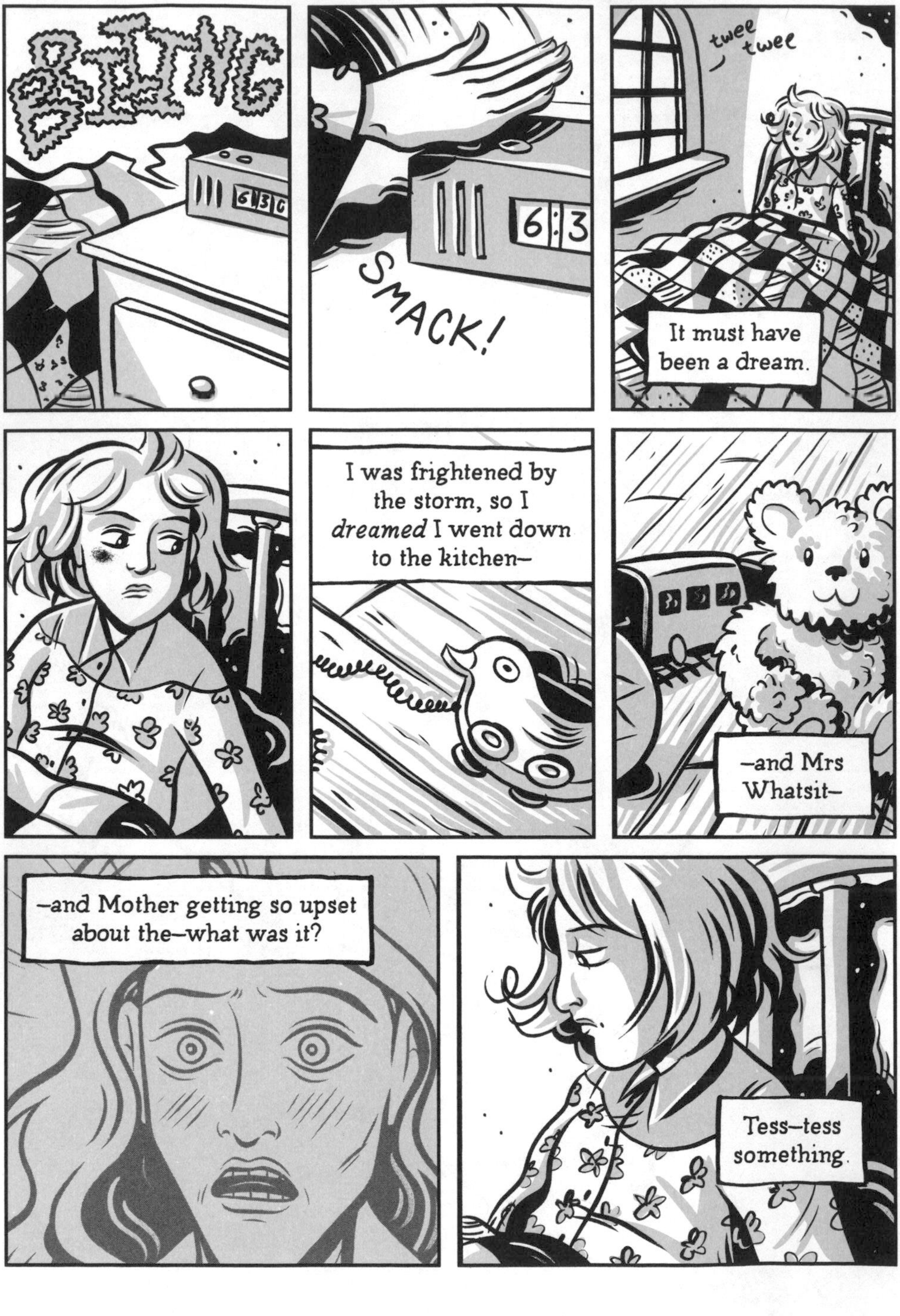
BRRING
6:30
SMACK!
6:3
twee
twee
It must have been a dream.
I was frightened by the storm, so I *dreamed* I went down to the kitchen–
–and Mrs Whatsit–
–and Mother getting so upset about the–what was it?
Tess–tess something.

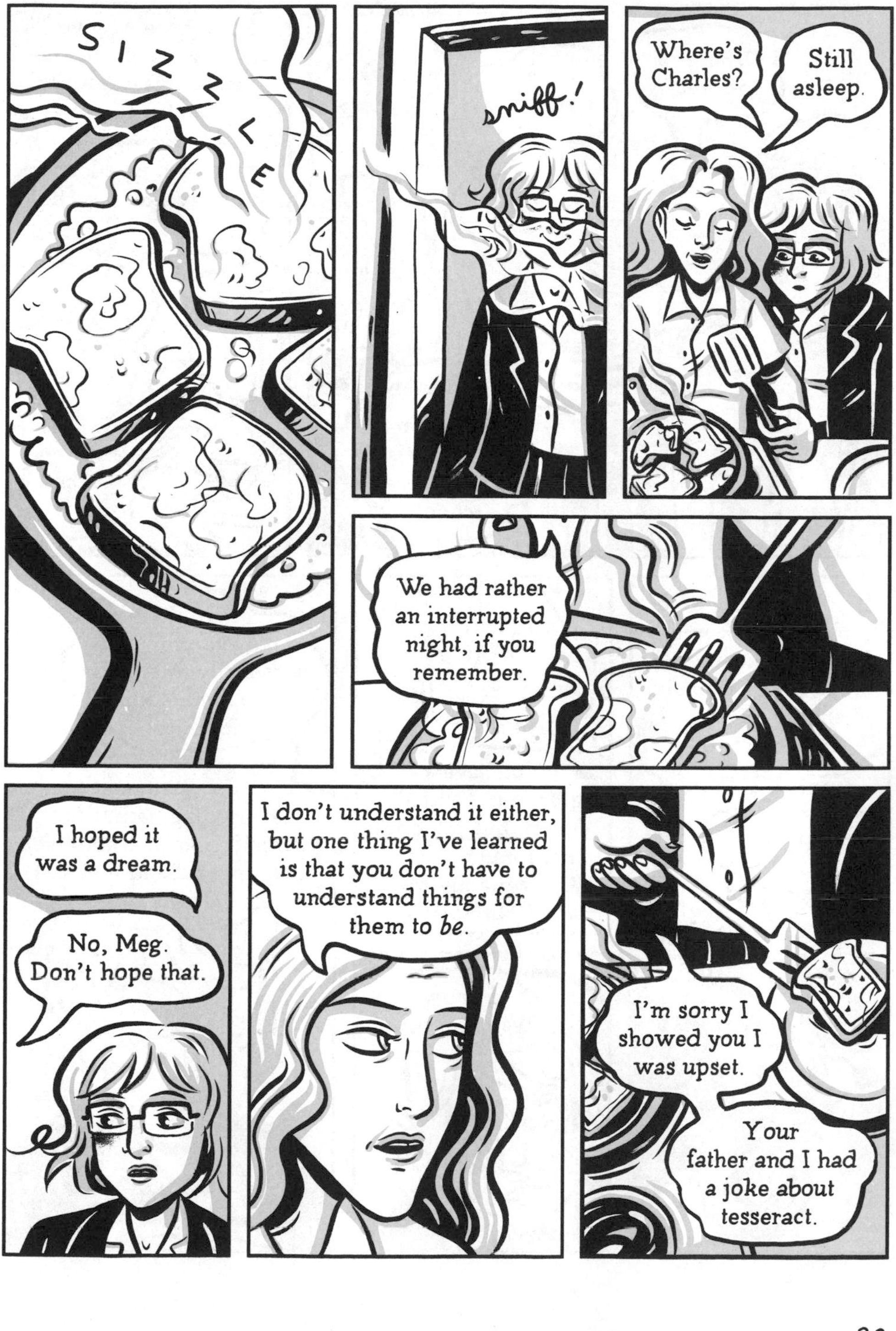
SIZZZLE
sniff!
Where's Charles?
Still asleep.
We had rather an interrupted night, if you remember.
I hoped it was a dream.
No, Meg. Don't hope that.
I don't understand it either, but one thing I've learned is that you don't have to understand things for them to *be*.
I'm sorry I showed you I was upset.
Your father and I had a joke about tesseract.

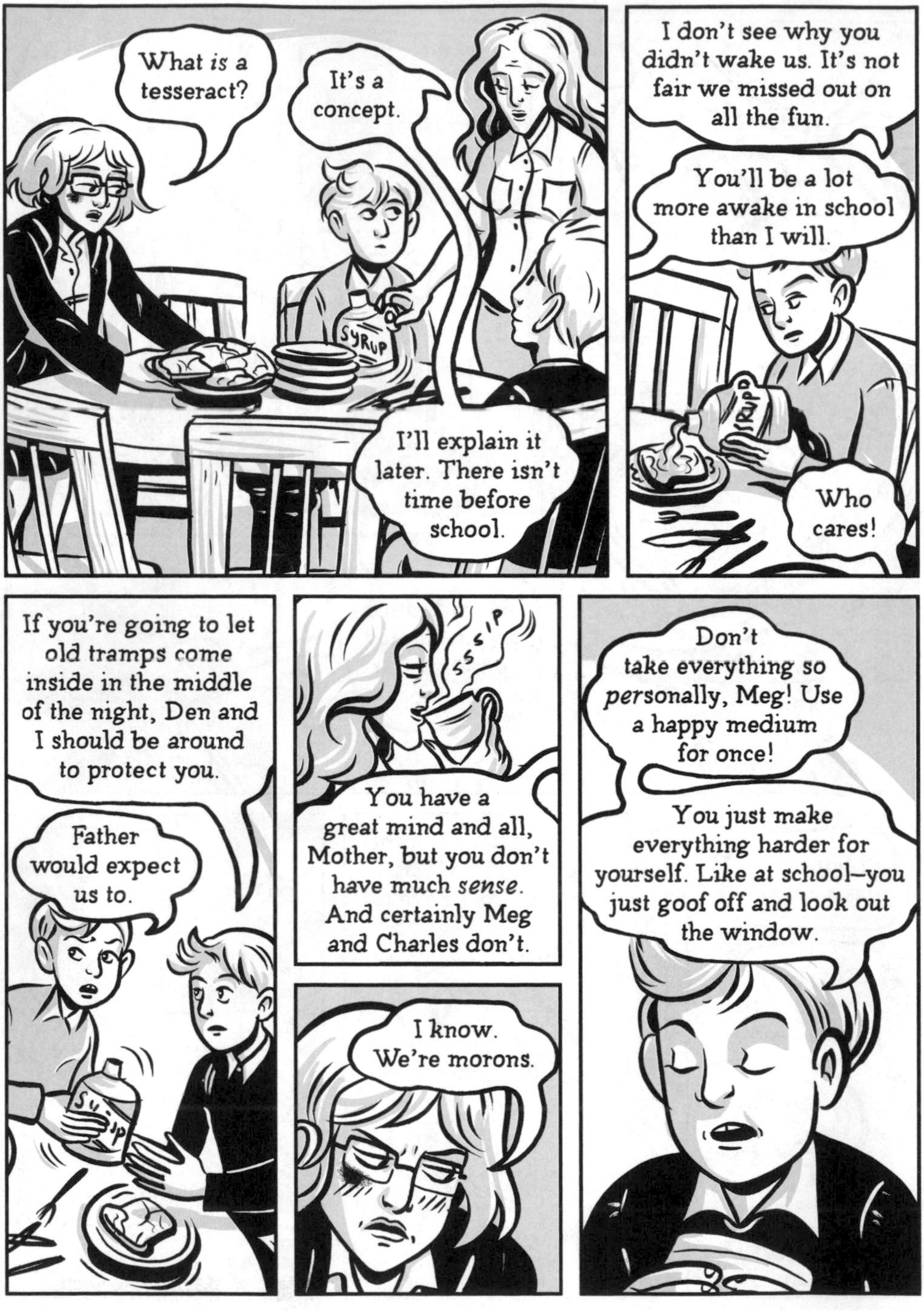
What *is* a tesseract?
It's a concept.
I'll explain it later. There isn't time before school.
I don't see why you didn't wake us. It's not fair we missed out on all the fun.
You'll be a lot more awake in school than I will.
Who cares!
SYRUP
If you're going to let old tramps come inside in the middle of the night, Den and I should be around to protect you.
Father would expect us to.
SSSIP
You have a great mind and all, Mother, but you don't have much *sense*. And certainly Meg and Charles don't.
I know. We're morons.
Don't take everything so *per*sonally, Meg! Use a happy medium for once!
You just make everything harder for yourself. Like at school–you just goof off and look out the window.

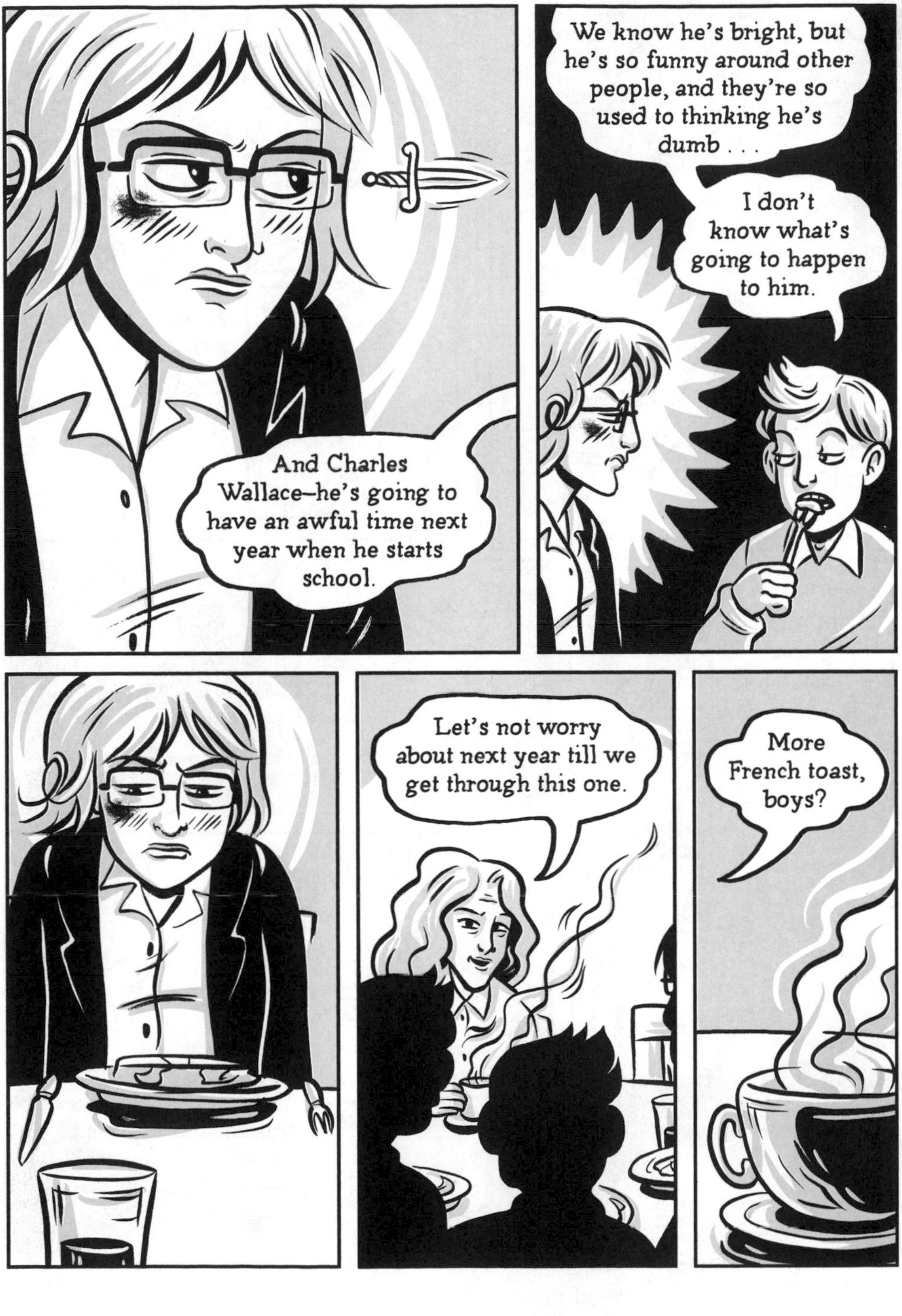
And Charles Wallace—he's going to have an awful time next year when he starts school.
We know he's bright, but he's so funny around other people, and they're so used to thinking he's dumb . . .
I don't know what's going to happen to him.
Let's not worry about next year till we get through this one.
More French toast, boys?

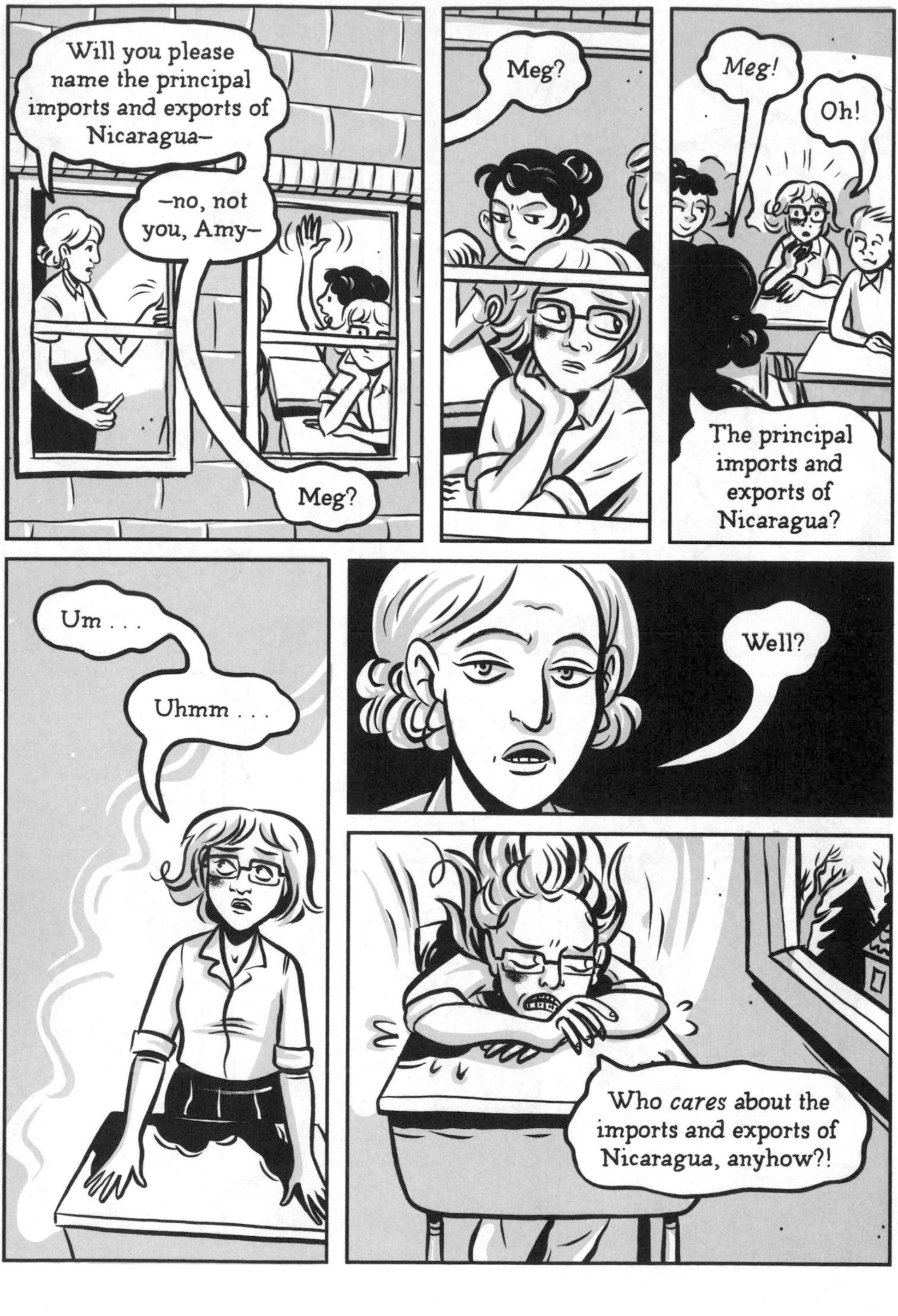
Will you please name the principal imports and exports of Nicaragua—
—no, not you, Amy—
Meg?
Meg?
Meg!
Oh!
The principal imports and exports of Nicaragua?
Um . . .
Uhmm . . .
Well?
Who *cares* about the imports and exports of Nicaragua, anyhow?!

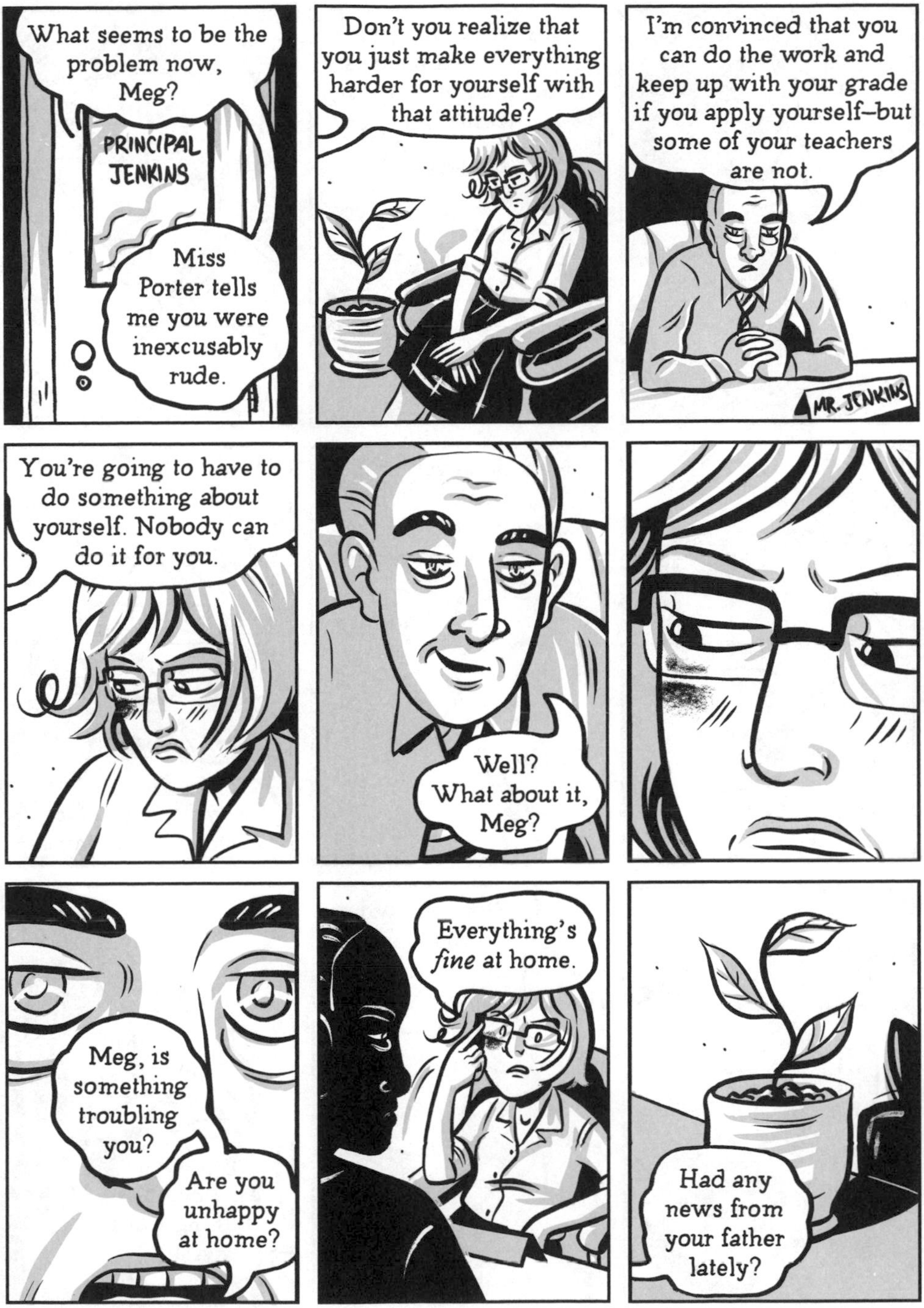
What seems to be the problem now, Meg?
PRINCIPAL JENKINS
Miss Porter tells me you were inexcusably rude.
Don't you realize that you just make everything harder for yourself with that attitude?
I'm convinced that you can do the work and keep up with your grade if you apply yourself—but some of your teachers are not.
MR. JENKINS
You're going to have to do something about yourself. Nobody can do it for you.
Well? What about it, Meg?
Meg, is something troubling you?
Are you unhappy at home?
Everything's *fine* at home.
Had any news from your father lately?

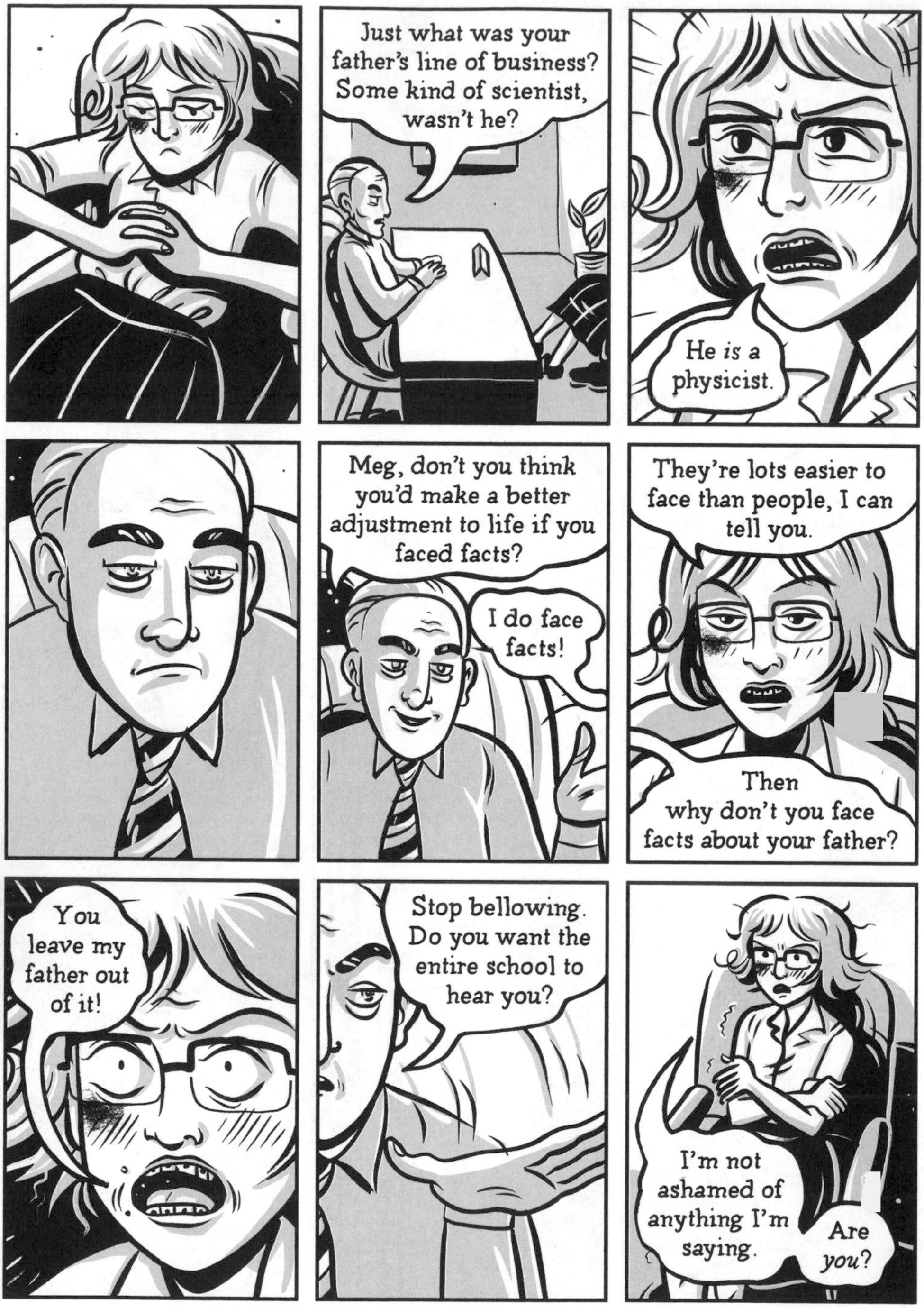
Just what was your father's line of business? Some kind of scientist, wasn't he?
He *is* a physicist.
Meg, don't you think you'd make a better adjustment to life if you faced facts?
I do face facts!
They're lots easier to face than people, I can tell you.
Then why don't you face facts about your father?
You leave my father out of it!
Stop bellowing. Do you want the entire school to hear you?
I'm not ashamed of anything I'm saying.
Are *you*?

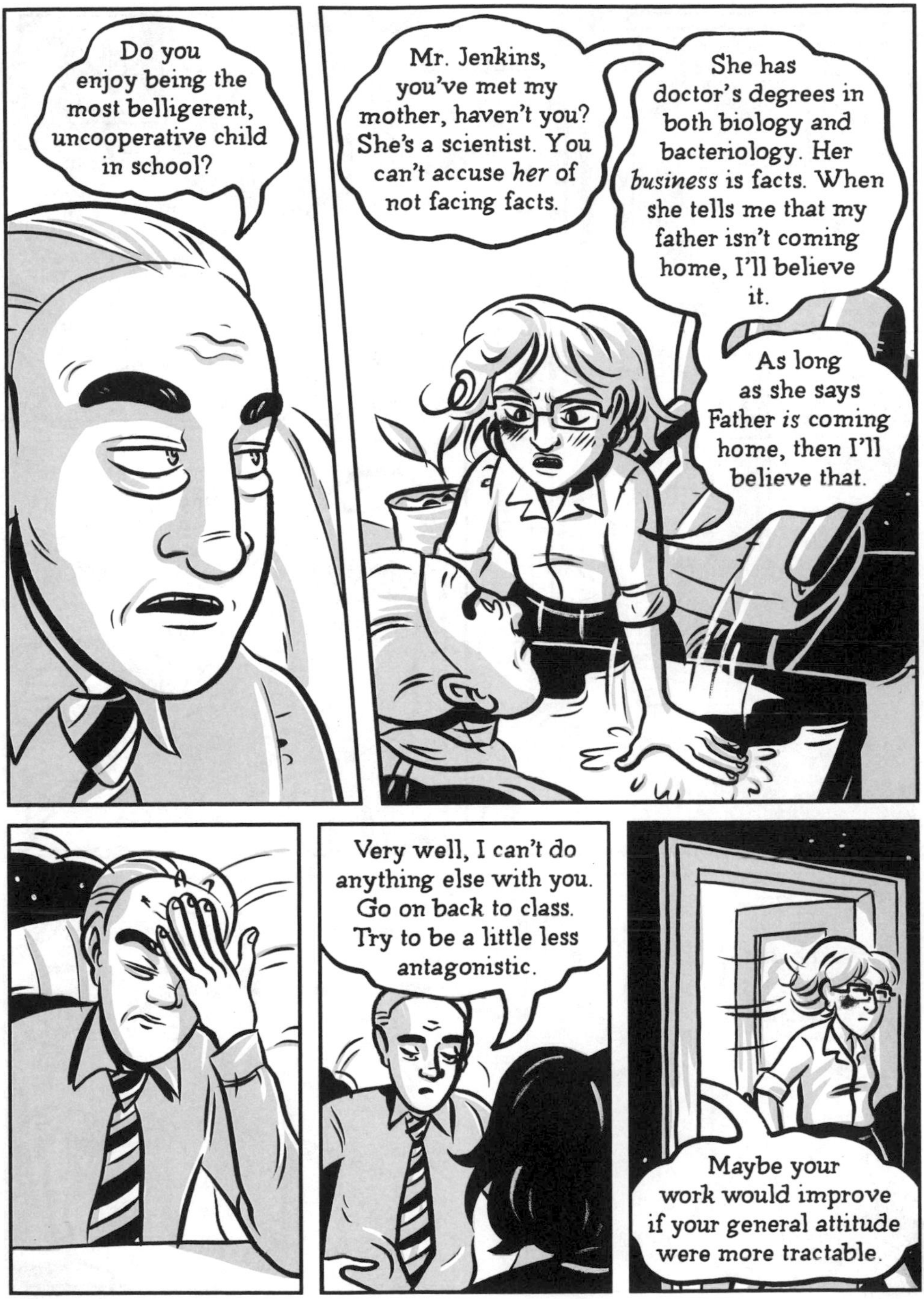
Do you enjoy being the most belligerent, uncooperative child in school?
Mr. Jenkins, you've met my mother, haven't you? She's a scientist. You can't accuse *her* of not facing facts.
She has doctor's degrees in both biology and bacteriology. Her *business* is facts. When she tells me that my father isn't coming home, I'll believe it.
As long as she says Father *is* coming home, then I'll believe that.
Very well, I can't do anything else with you. Go on back to class. Try to be a little less antagonistic.
Maybe your work would improve if your general attitude were more tractable.

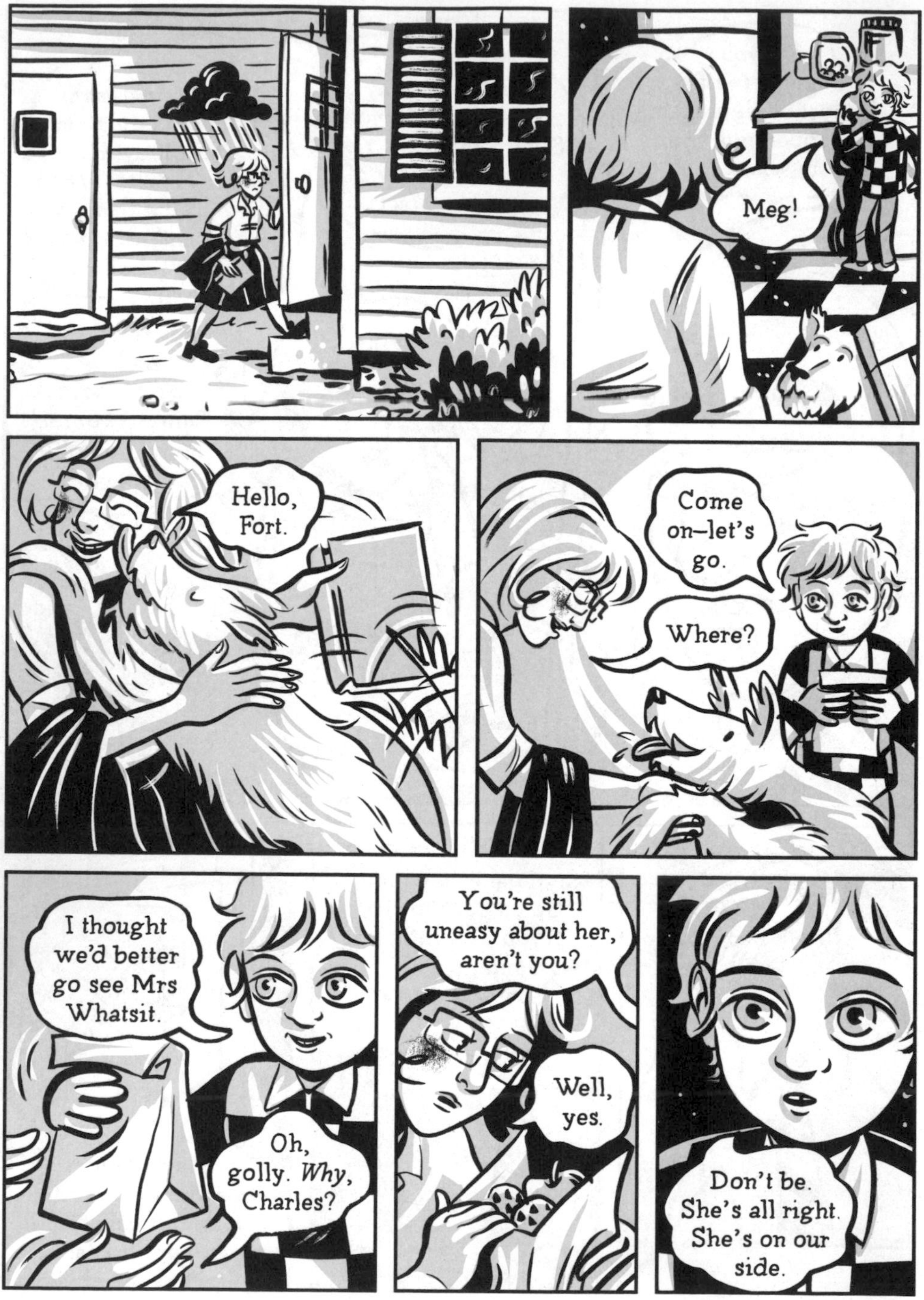
Meg!
Hello, Fort.
Come on–let's go.
Where?
I thought we'd better go see Mrs Whatsit.
Oh, golly. *Why*, Charles?
You're still uneasy about her, aren't you?
Well, yes.
Don't be. She's all right. She's on our side.

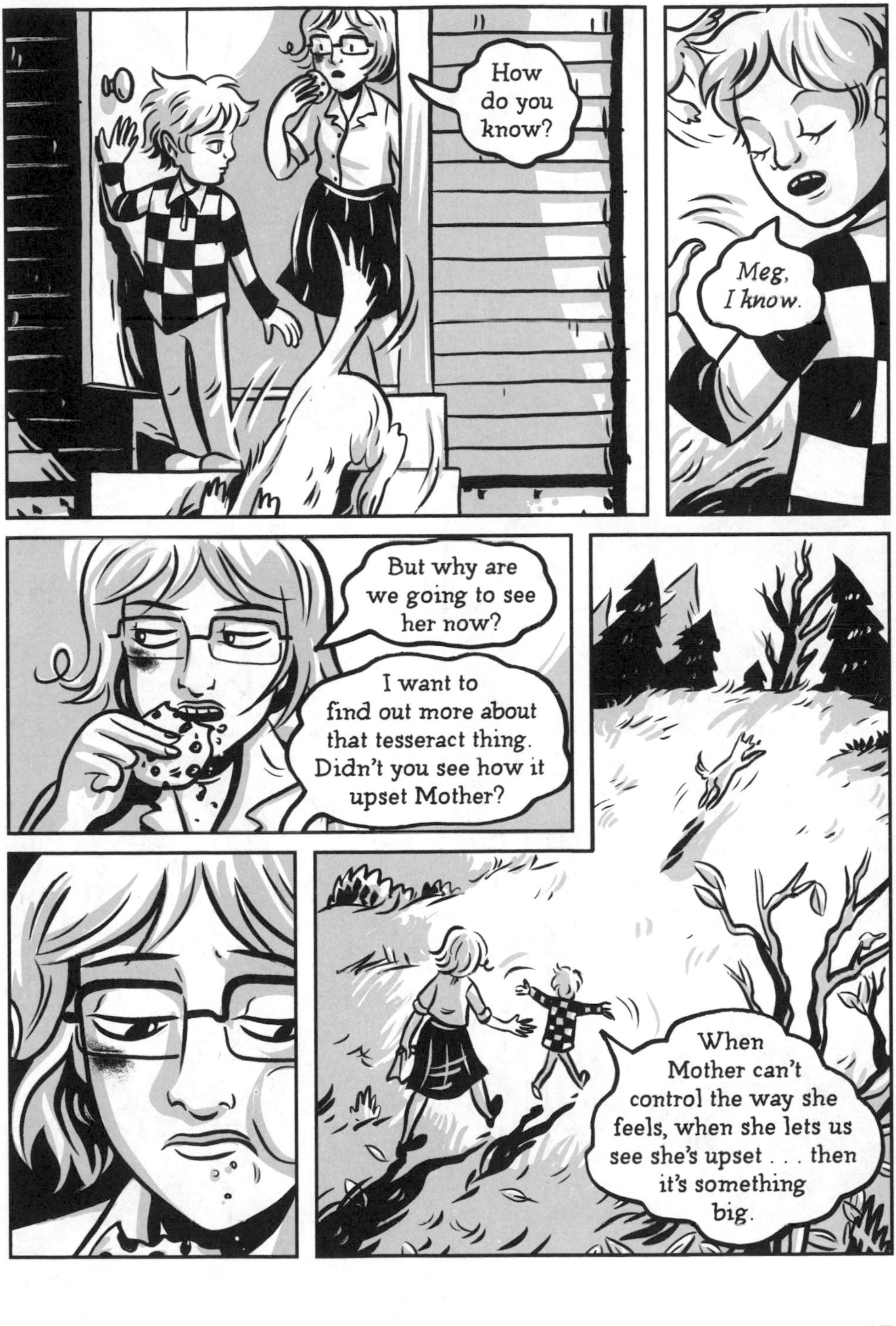
How do you know?
Meg, I know.
But why are we going to see her now?
I want to find out more about that tesseract thing. Didn't you see how it upset Mother?
When Mother can't control the way she feels, when she lets us see she's upset . . . then it's something big.

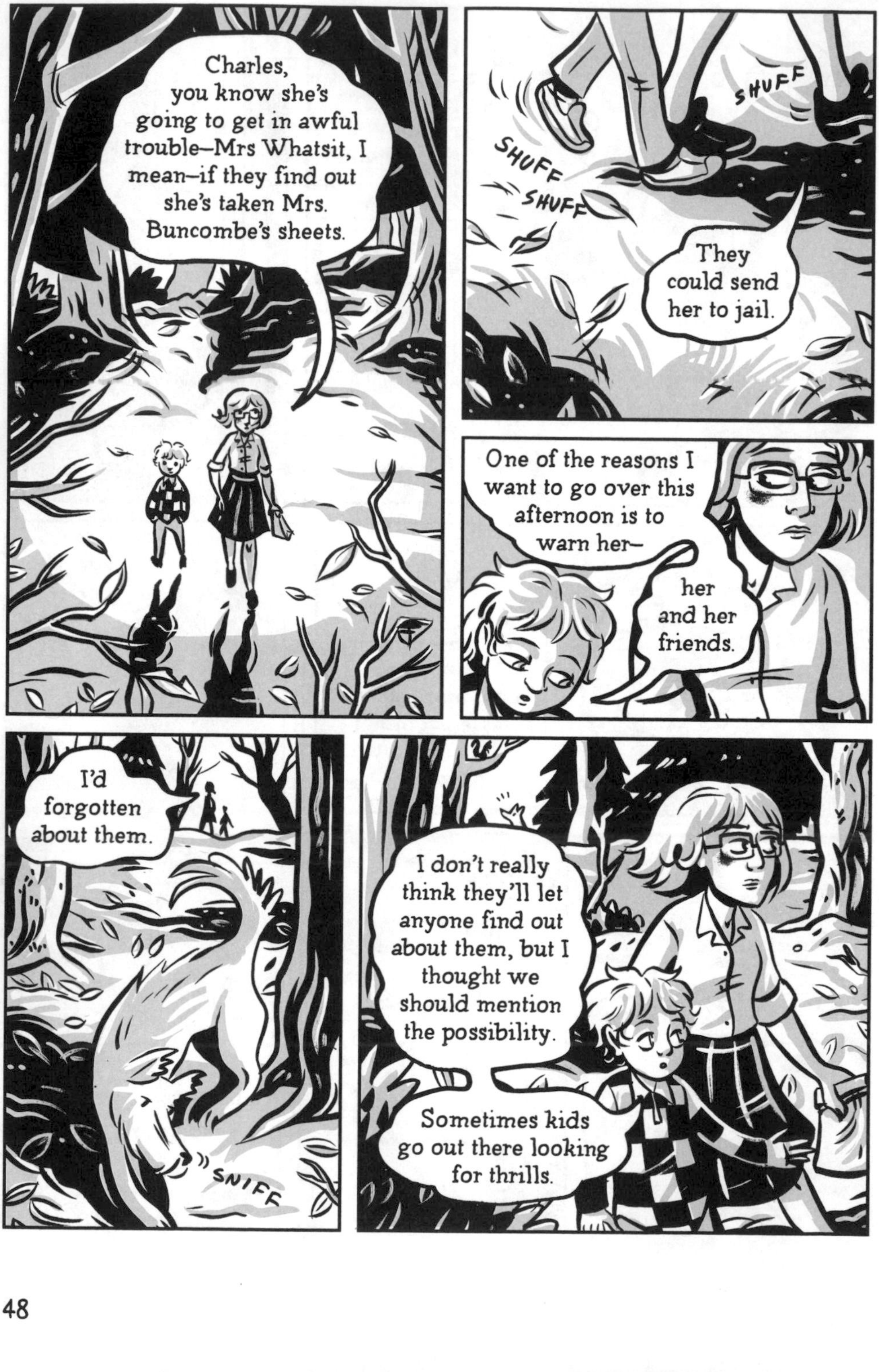
Charles, you know she's going to get in awful trouble—Mrs Whatsit, I mean—if they find out she's taken Mrs. Buncombe's sheets.
SHUFF
SHUFF
SHUFF
They could send her to jail.
One of the reasons I want to go over this afternoon is to warn her—
her and her friends.
I'd forgotten about them.
SNIFF
I don't really think they'll let anyone find out about them, but I thought we should mention the possibility.
Sometimes kids go out there looking for thrills.

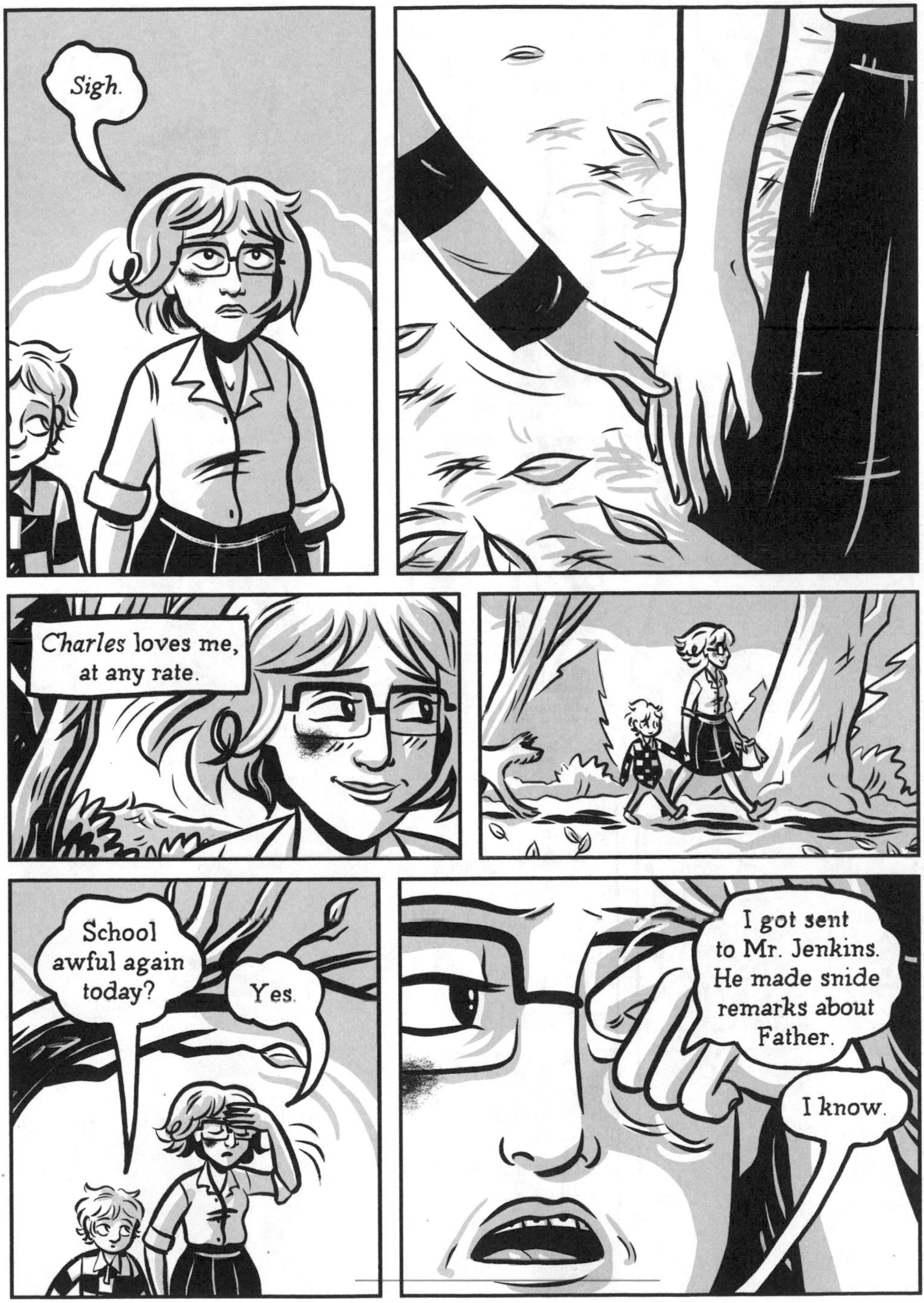

Sigh.
Charles loves me, at any rate.
School awful again today?
Yes.
I got sent to Mr. Jenkins. He made snide remarks about Father.
I know.

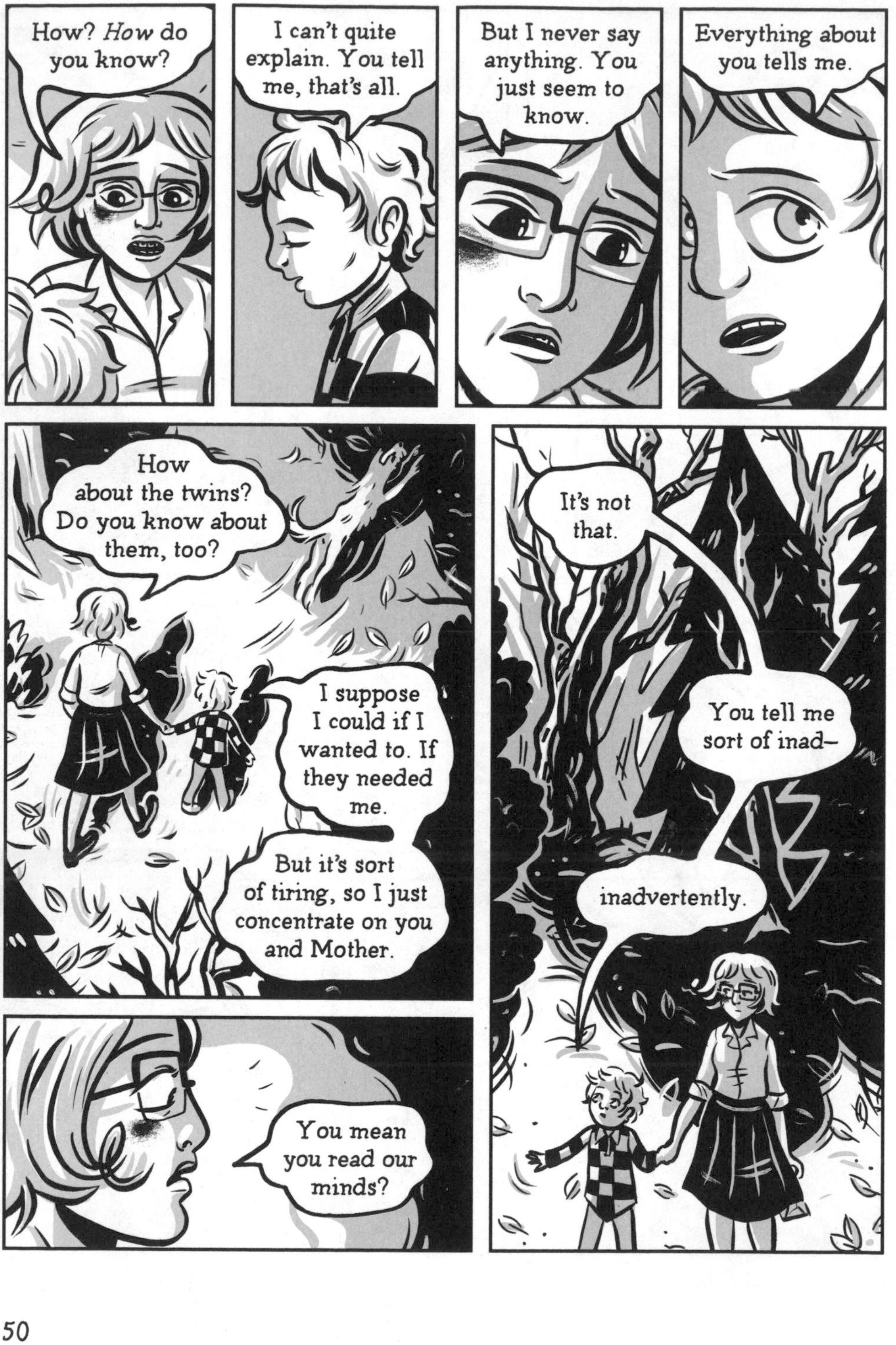
How? *How* do you know?
I can't quite explain. You tell me, that's all.
But I never say anything. You just seem to know.
Everything about you tells me.
How about the twins? Do you know about them, too?
I suppose I could if I wanted to. If they needed me.
But it's sort of tiring, so I just concentrate on you and Mother.
You mean you read our minds?
It's not that.
You tell me sort of inad–
inadvertently.

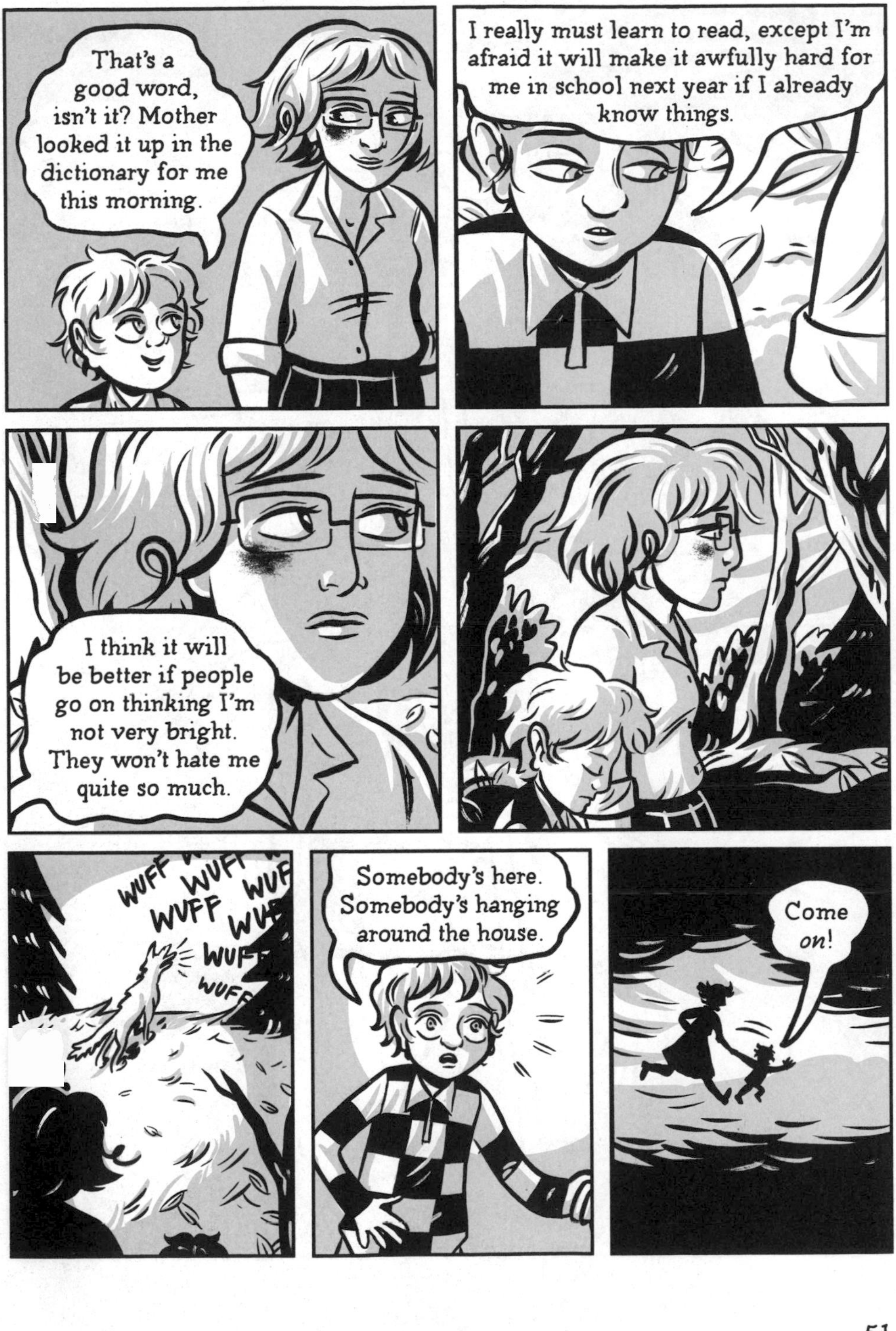
That's a good word, isn't it? Mother looked it up in the dictionary for me this morning.
I really must learn to read, except I'm afraid it will make it awfully hard for me in school next year if I already know things.
I think it will be better if people go on thinking I'm not very bright. They won't hate me quite so much.
WUFF WUFF WUFF WUFF WUFF WUFF WUFF
Somebody's here. Somebody's hanging around the house.
Come *on*!

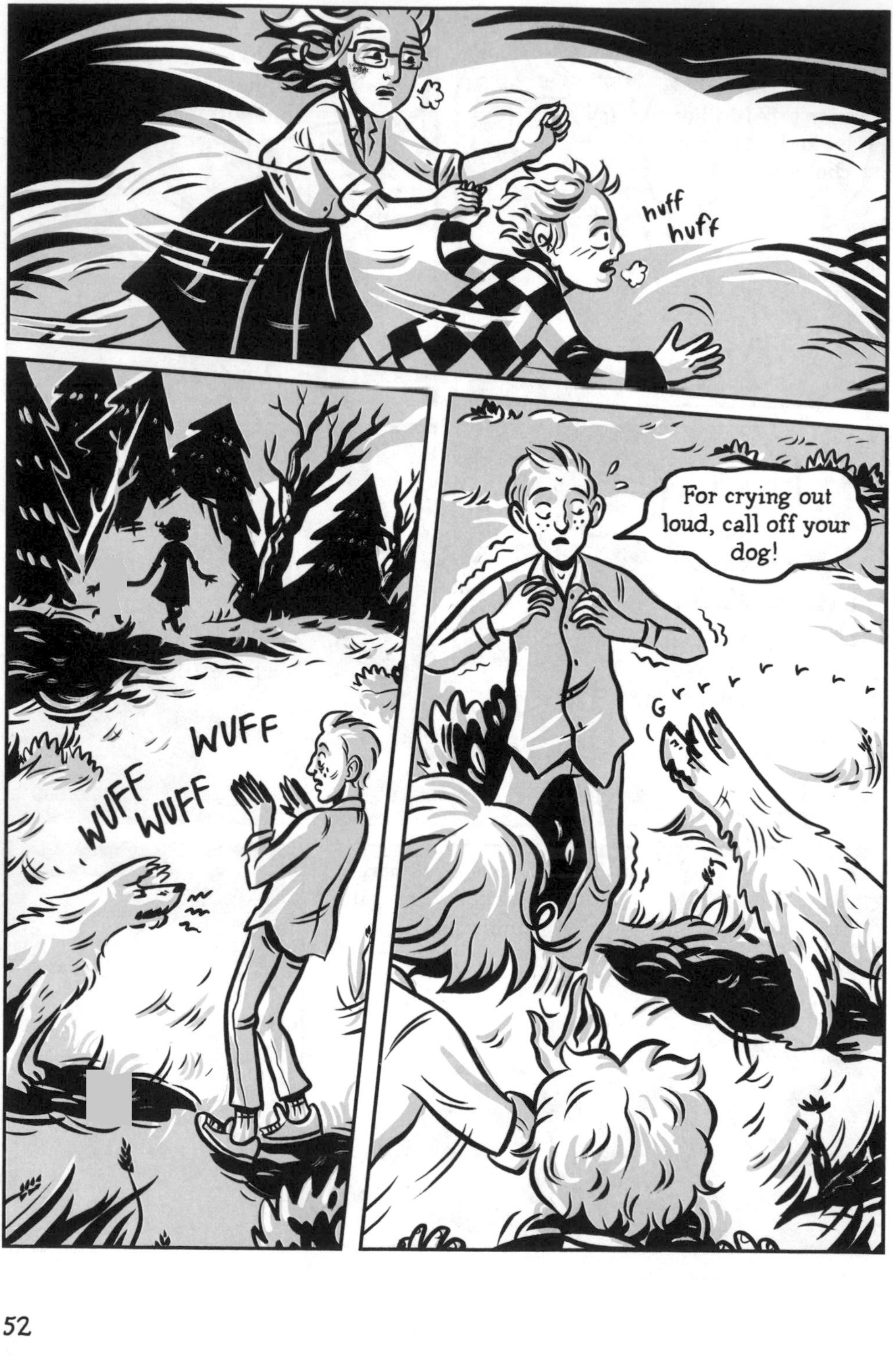
huff
huff
WUFF
WUFF
WUFF
For crying out loud, call off your dog!
Grrrrrrrrr

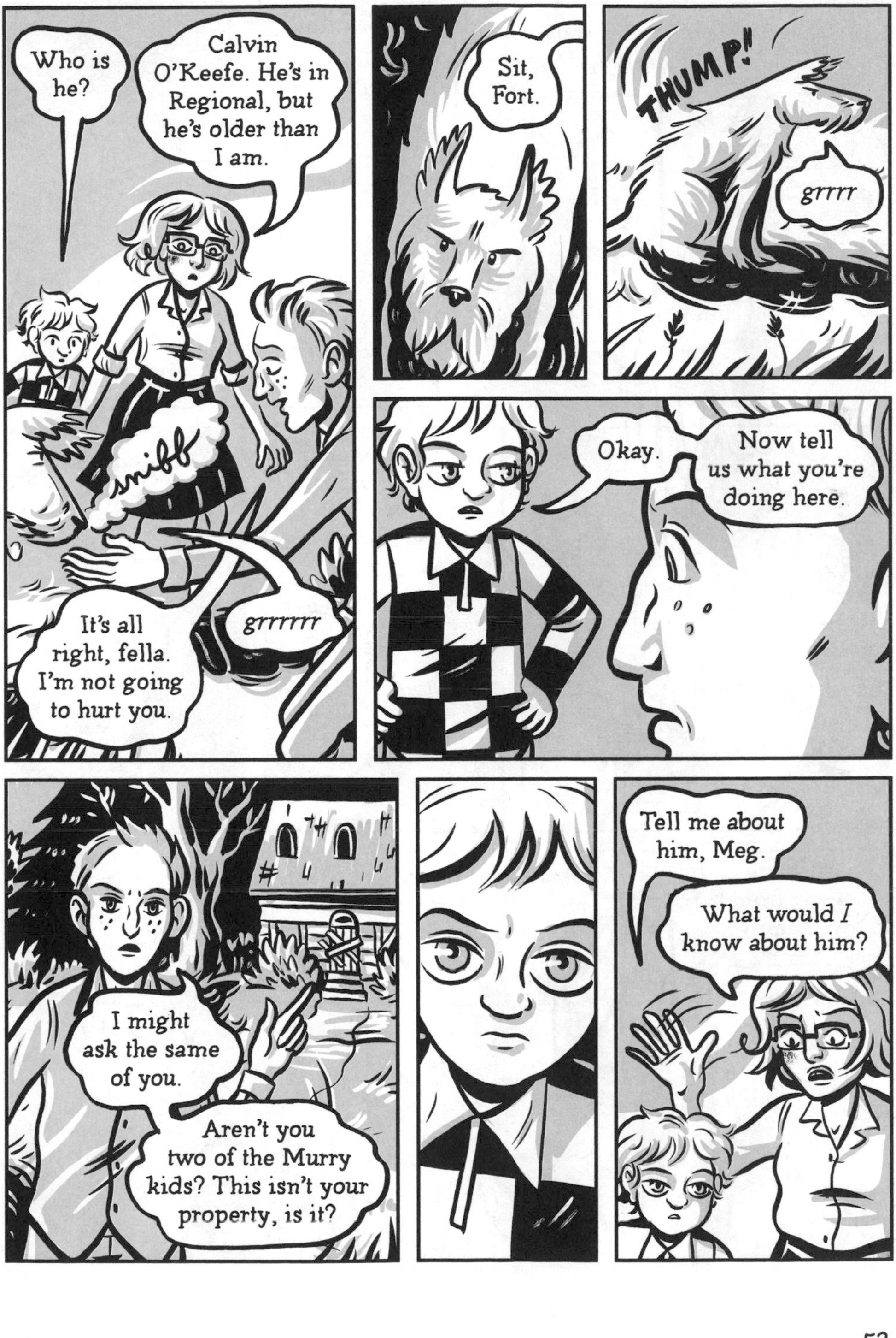
Who is he?
Calvin O'Keefe. He's in Regional, but he's older than I am.
sniff
It's all right, fella. I'm not going to hurt you.
grrrrrr
Sit, Fort.
THUMP!!
grrrr
Okay.
Now tell us what you're doing here.
I might ask the same of you.
Aren't you two of the Murry kids? This isn't your property, is it?
Tell me about him, Meg.
What would *I* know about him?

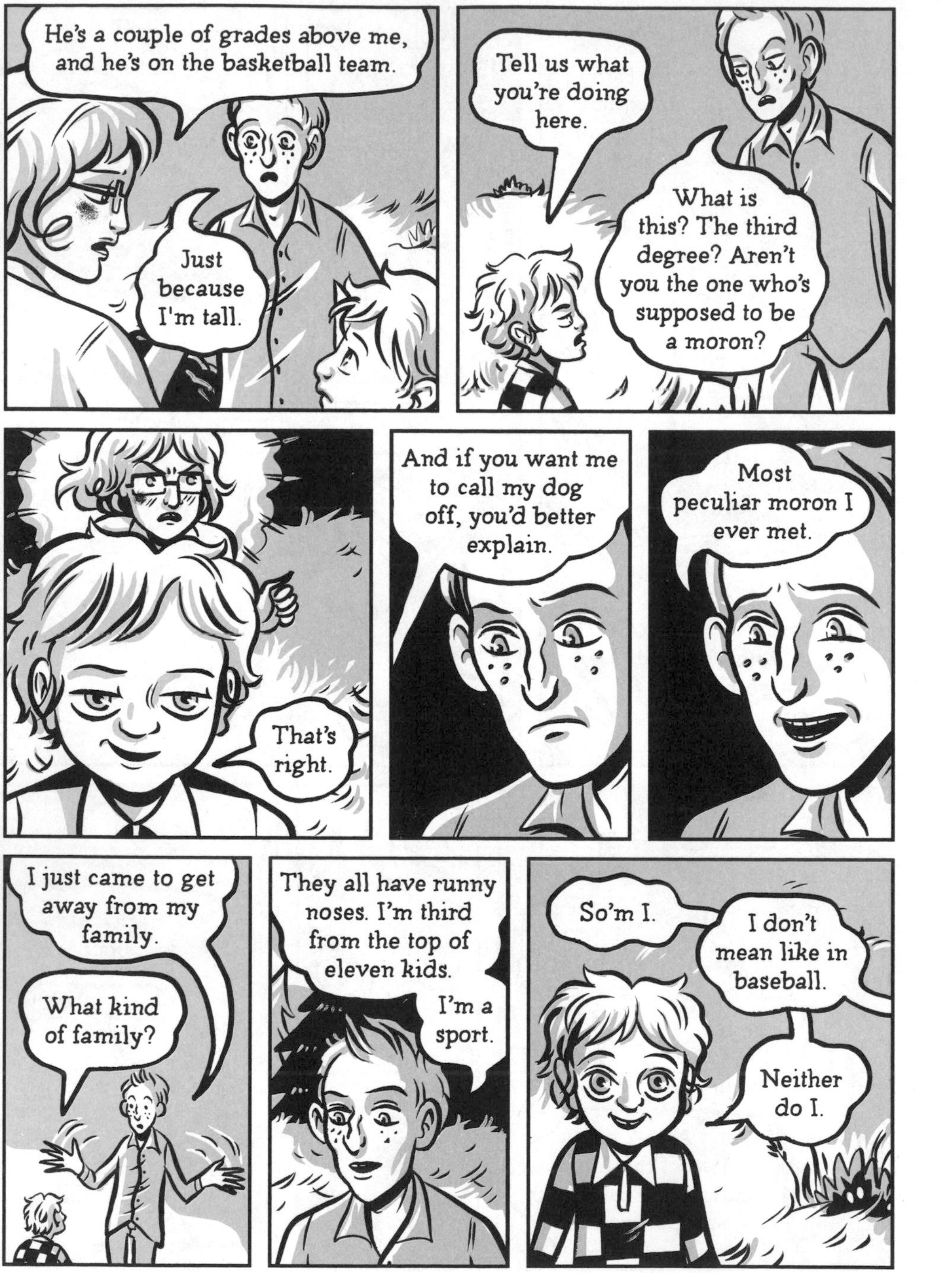
He's a couple of grades above me, and he's on the basketball team.
Just because I'm tall.
Tell us what you're doing here.
What is this? The third degree? Aren't you the one who's supposed to be a moron?
That's right.
And if you want me to call my dog off, you'd better explain.
Most peculiar moron I ever met.
I just came to get away from my family.
What kind of family?
They all have runny noses. I'm third from the top of eleven kids.
I'm a sport.
So'm I.
I don't mean like in baseball.
Neither do I.

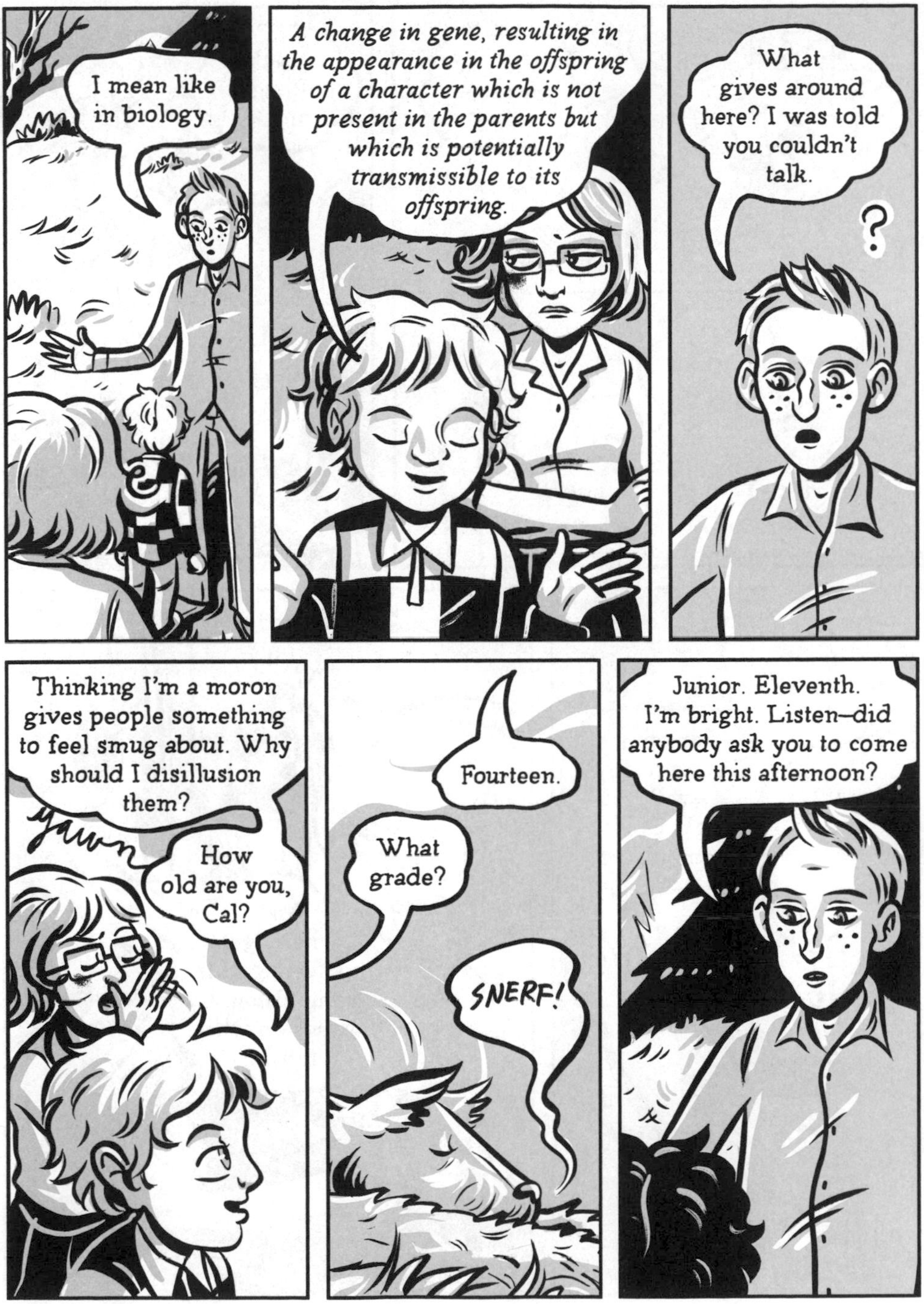
I mean like in biology.
A change in gene, resulting in the appearance in the offspring of a character which is not present in the parents but which is potentially transmissible to its offspring.
What gives around here? I was told you couldn't talk.
?
Thinking I'm a moron gives people something to feel smug about. Why should I disillusion them?
yawn
How old are you, Cal?
Fourteen.
What grade?
SNERF!
Junior. Eleventh. I'm bright. Listen—did anybody ask you to come here this afternoon?

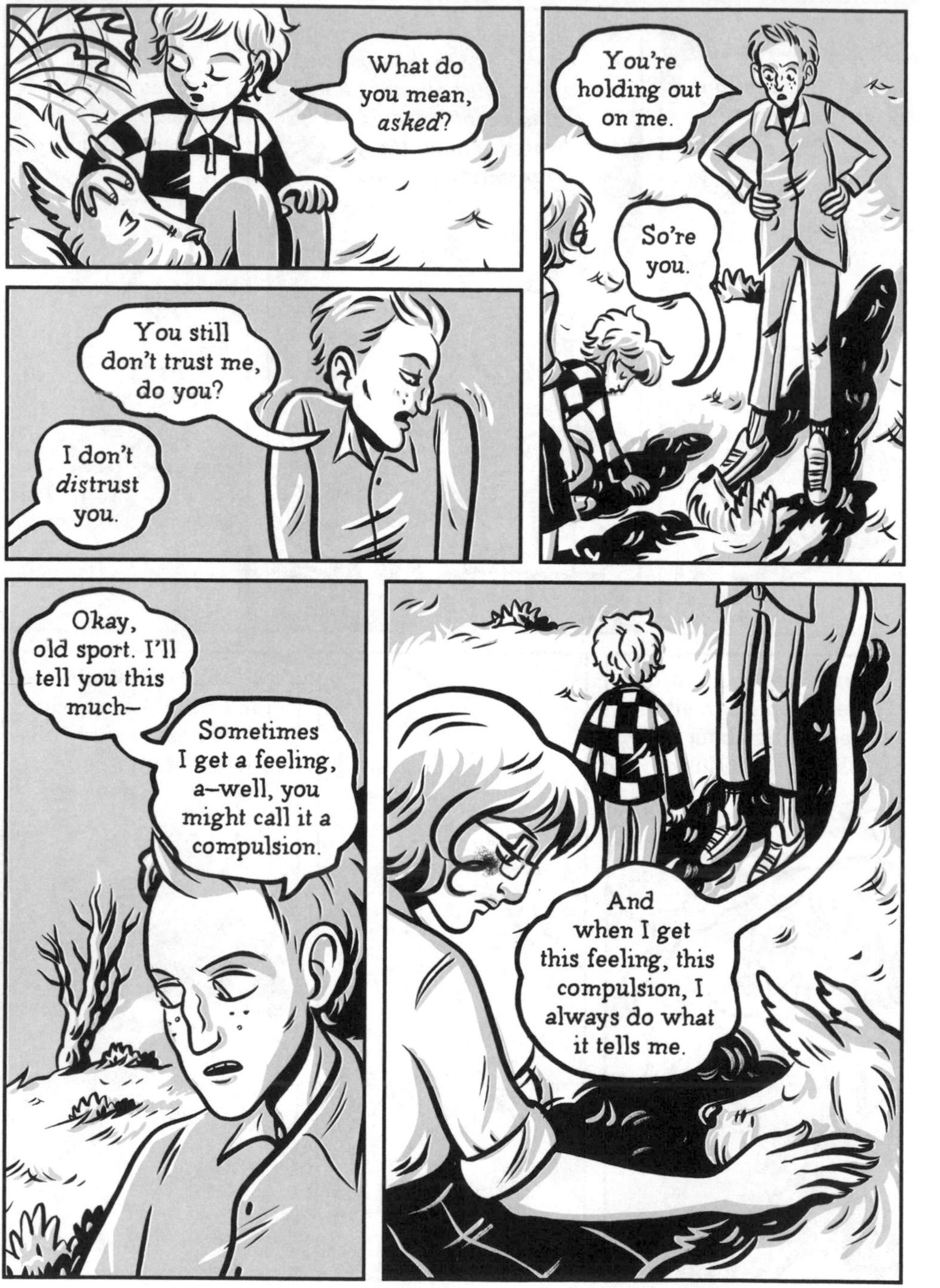
What do you mean, *asked*?
You're holding out on me.
So're you.
You still don't trust me, do you?
I don't *dis*trust you.
Okay, old sport. I'll tell you this much–
Sometimes I get a feeling, a–well, you might call it a compulsion.
And when I get this feeling, this compulsion, I always do what it tells me.

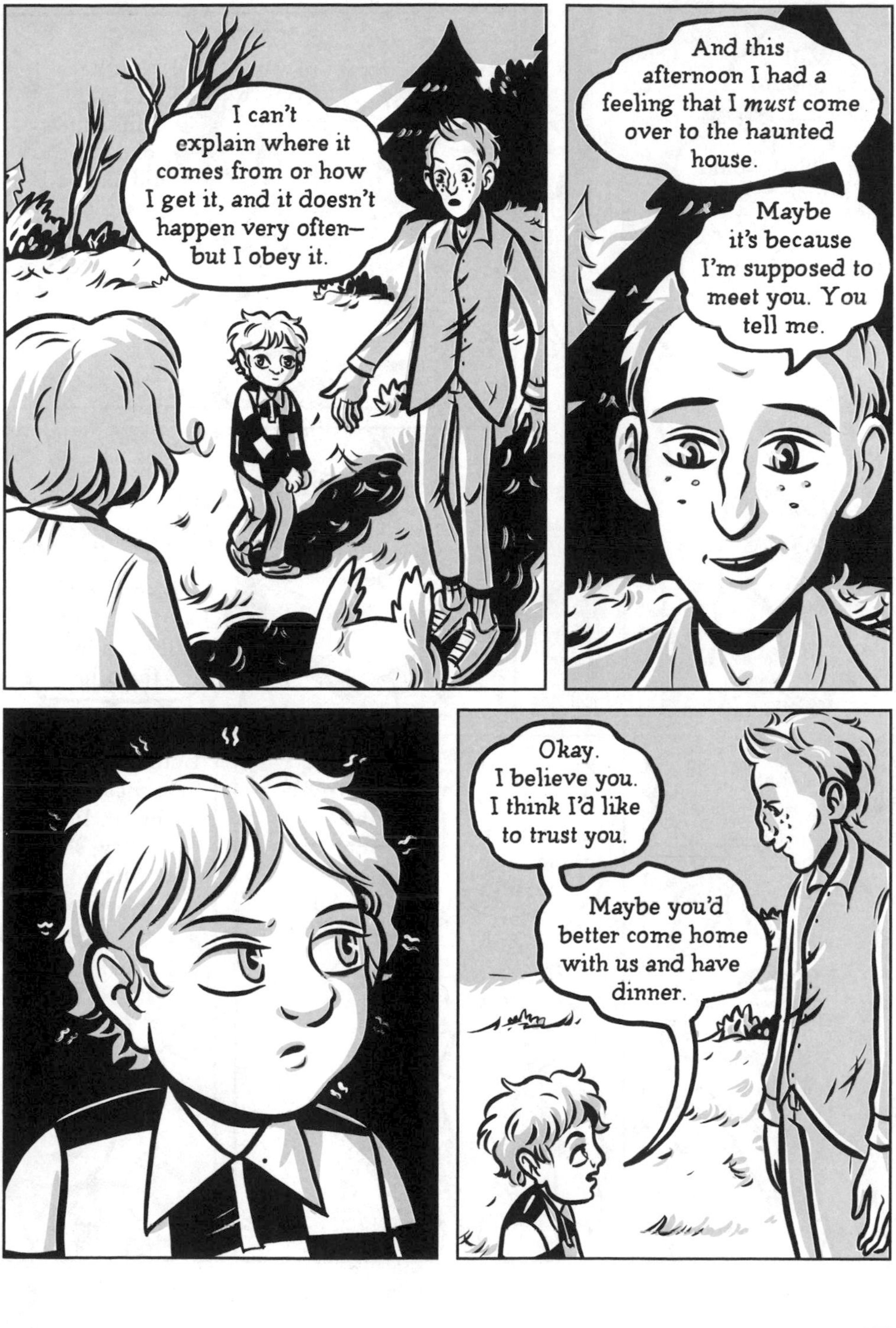
I can't explain where it comes from or how I get it, and it doesn't happen very often—but I obey it.
And this afternoon I had a feeling that I *must* come over to the haunted house.
Maybe it's because I'm supposed to meet you. You tell me.
Okay. I believe you. I think I'd like to trust you.
Maybe you'd better come home with us and have dinner.

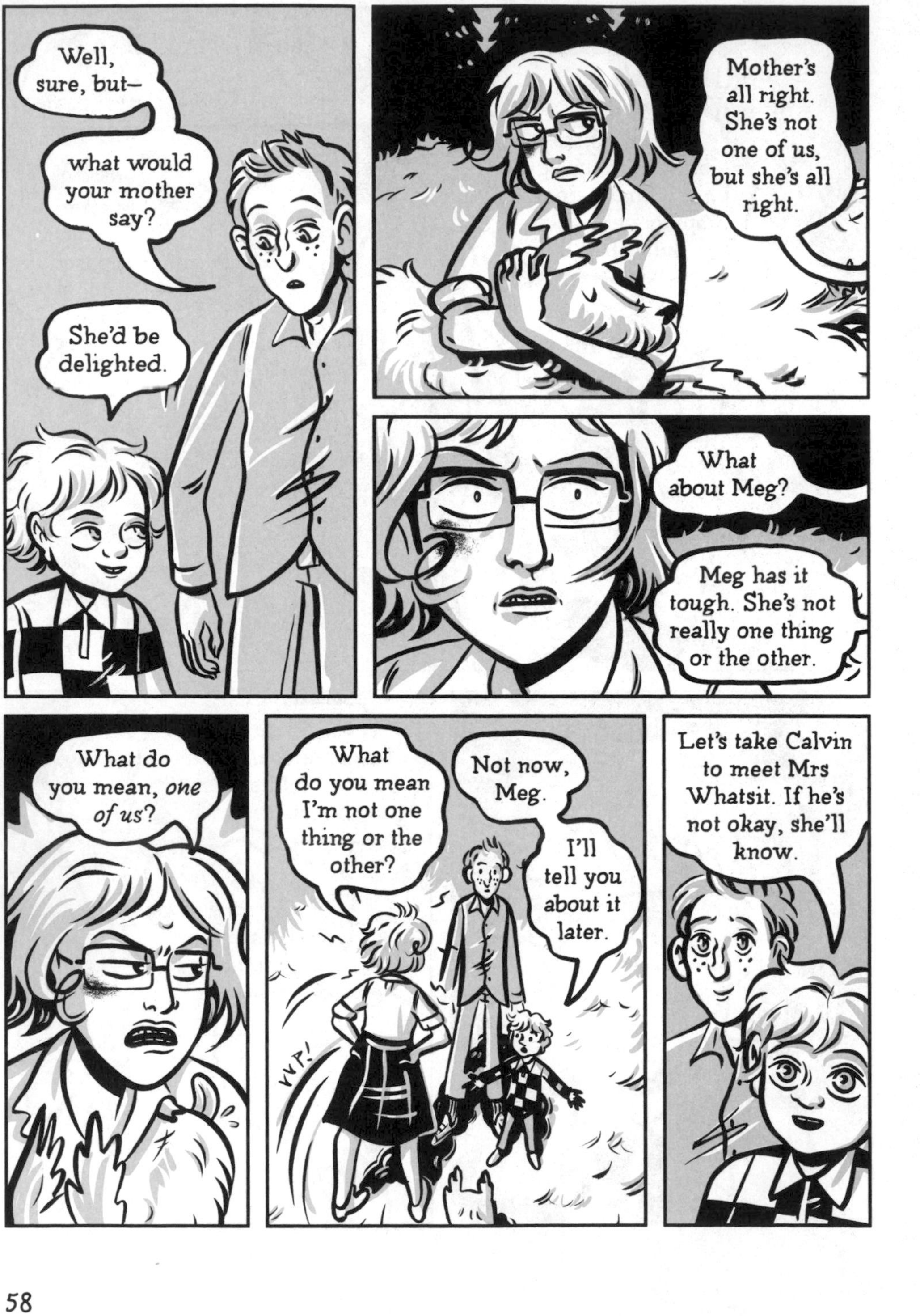

Well, sure, but—
what would your mother say?
She'd be delighted.
Mother's all right. She's not one of us, but she's all right.
What about Meg?
Meg has it tough. She's not really one thing or the other.
What do you mean, *one of us*?
What do you mean I'm not one thing or the other?
Not now, Meg.
I'll tell you about it later.
VVP!
Let's take Calvin to meet Mrs Whatsit. If he's not okay, she'll know.

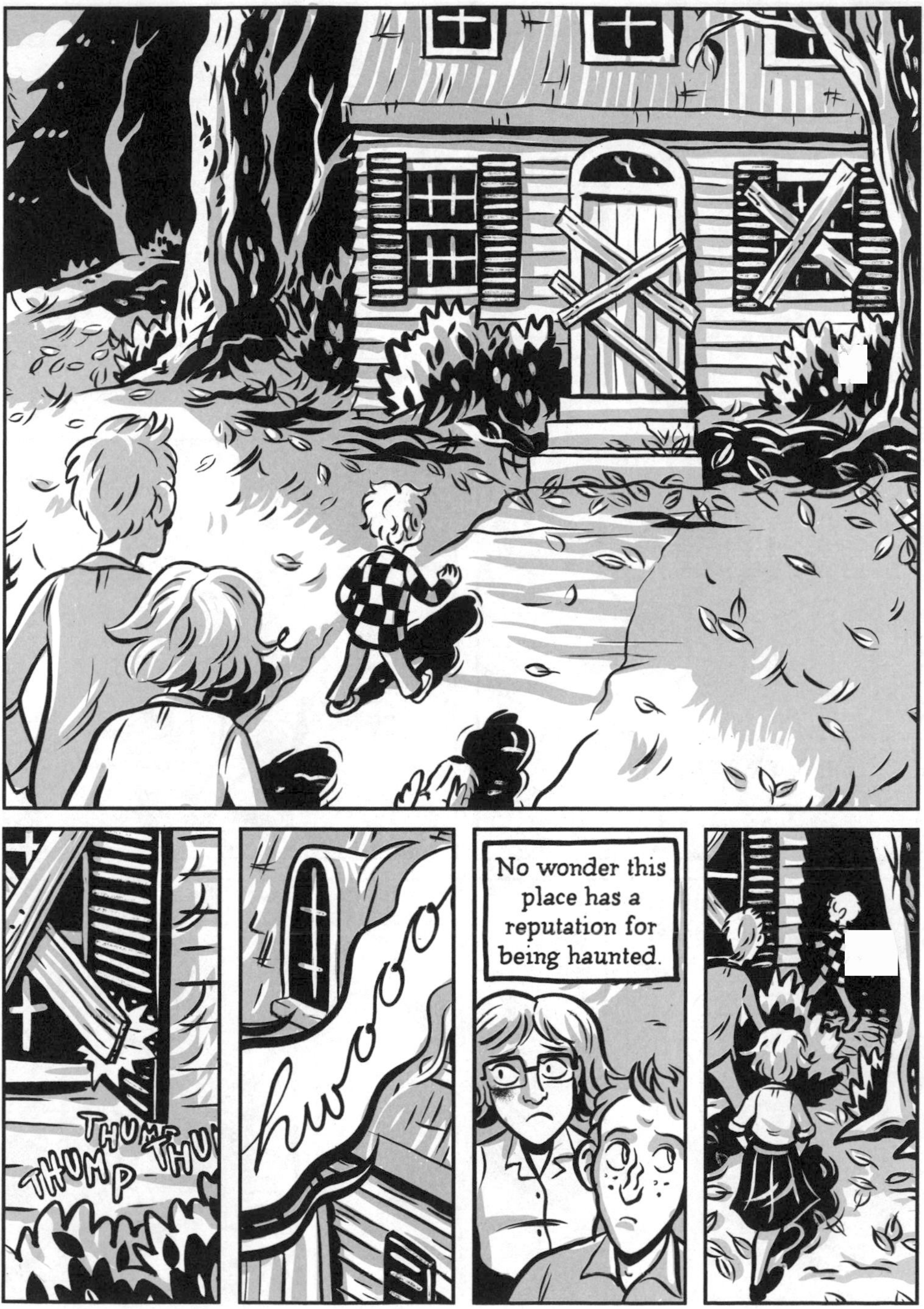
THUMP THUMP THU
hwoooo
No wonder this place has a reputation for being haunted.

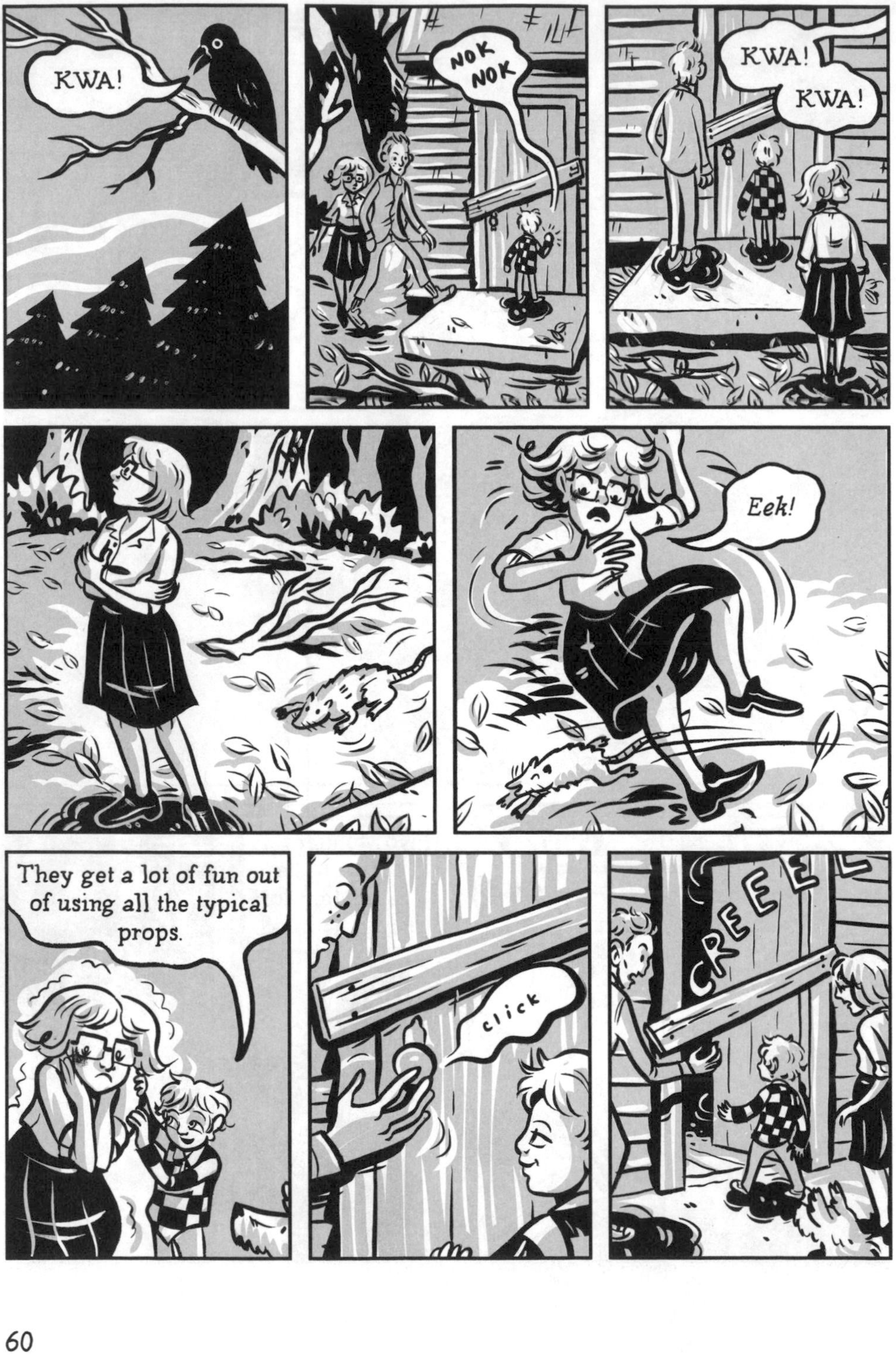
KWA!
NOK NOK
KWA!
KWA!
Eek!
They get a lot of fun out of using all the typical props.
click
CREEEE

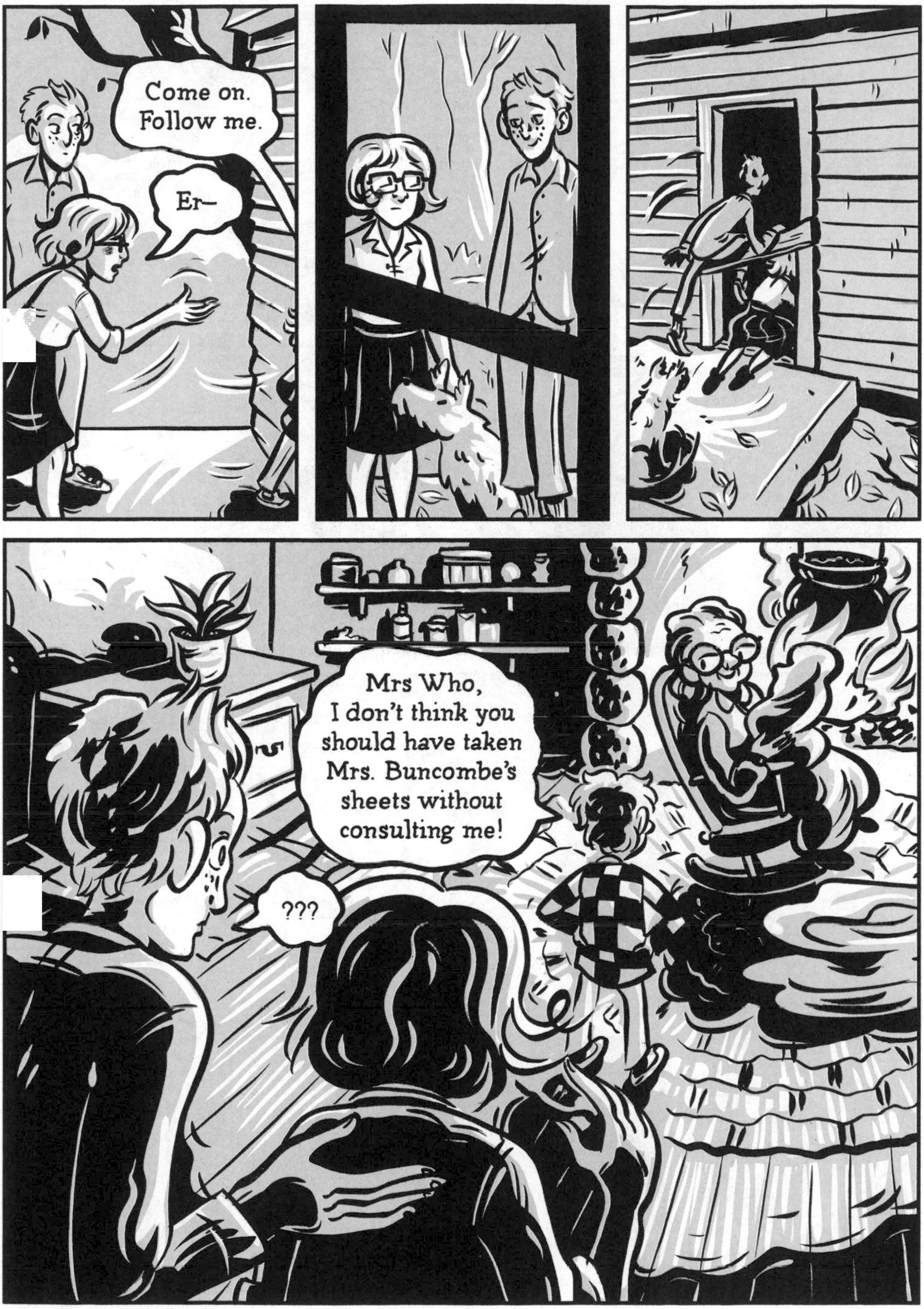
Come on. Follow me.
Er—
Mrs Who, I don't think you should have taken Mrs. Buncombe's sheets without consulting me!
???

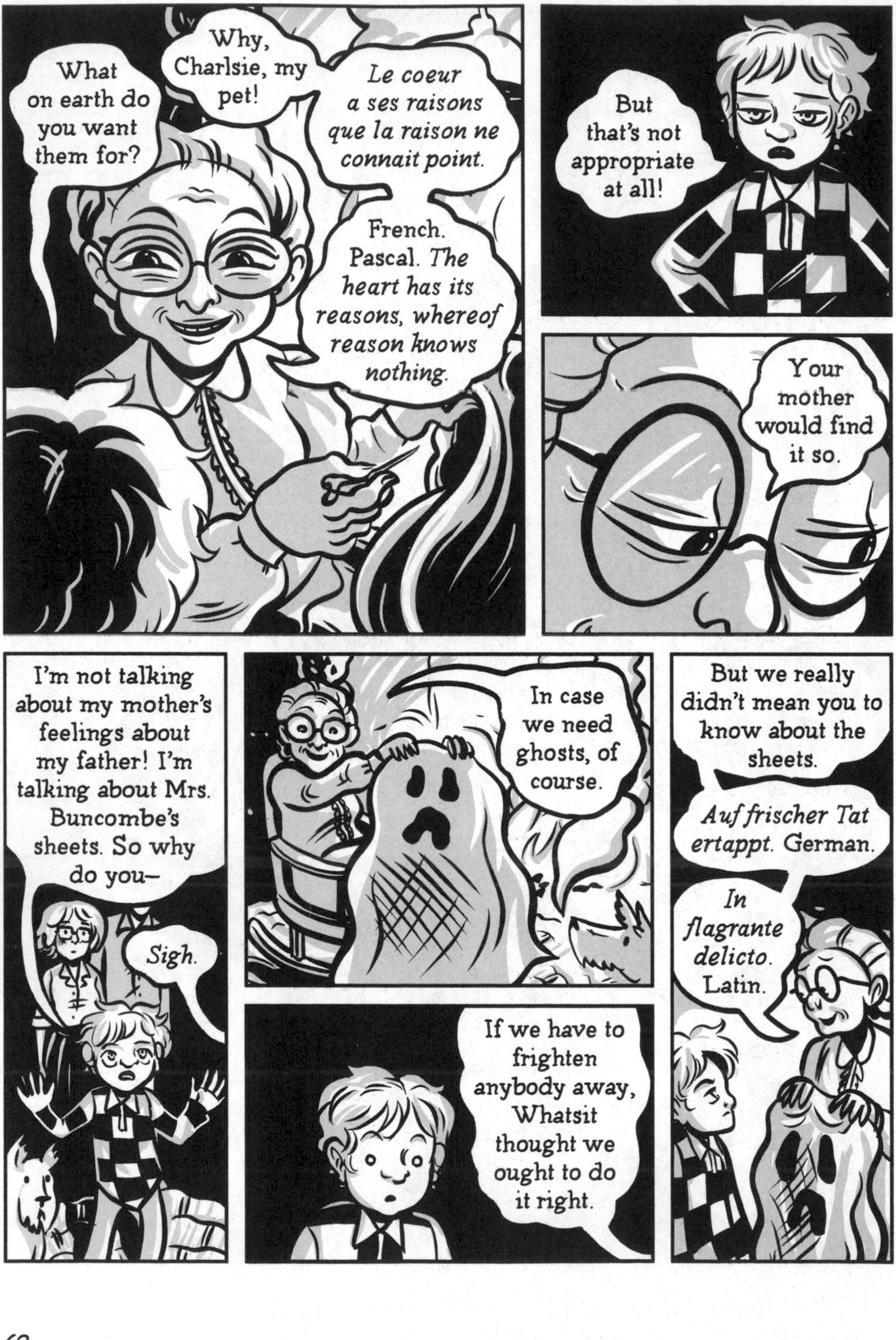
What on earth do you want them for?
Why, Charlsie, my pet!
Le coeur a ses raisons que la raison ne connait point.
French. Pascal. *The heart has its reasons, whereof reason knows nothing.*
But that's not appropriate at all!
Your mother would find it so.
I'm not talking about my mother's feelings about my father! I'm talking about Mrs. Buncombe's sheets. So why do you–
Sigh.
In case we need ghosts, of course.
If we have to frighten anybody away, Whatsit thought we ought to do it right.
But we really didn't mean you to know about the sheets.
Auf frischer Tat ertappt. German.
In flagrante delicto. Latin.

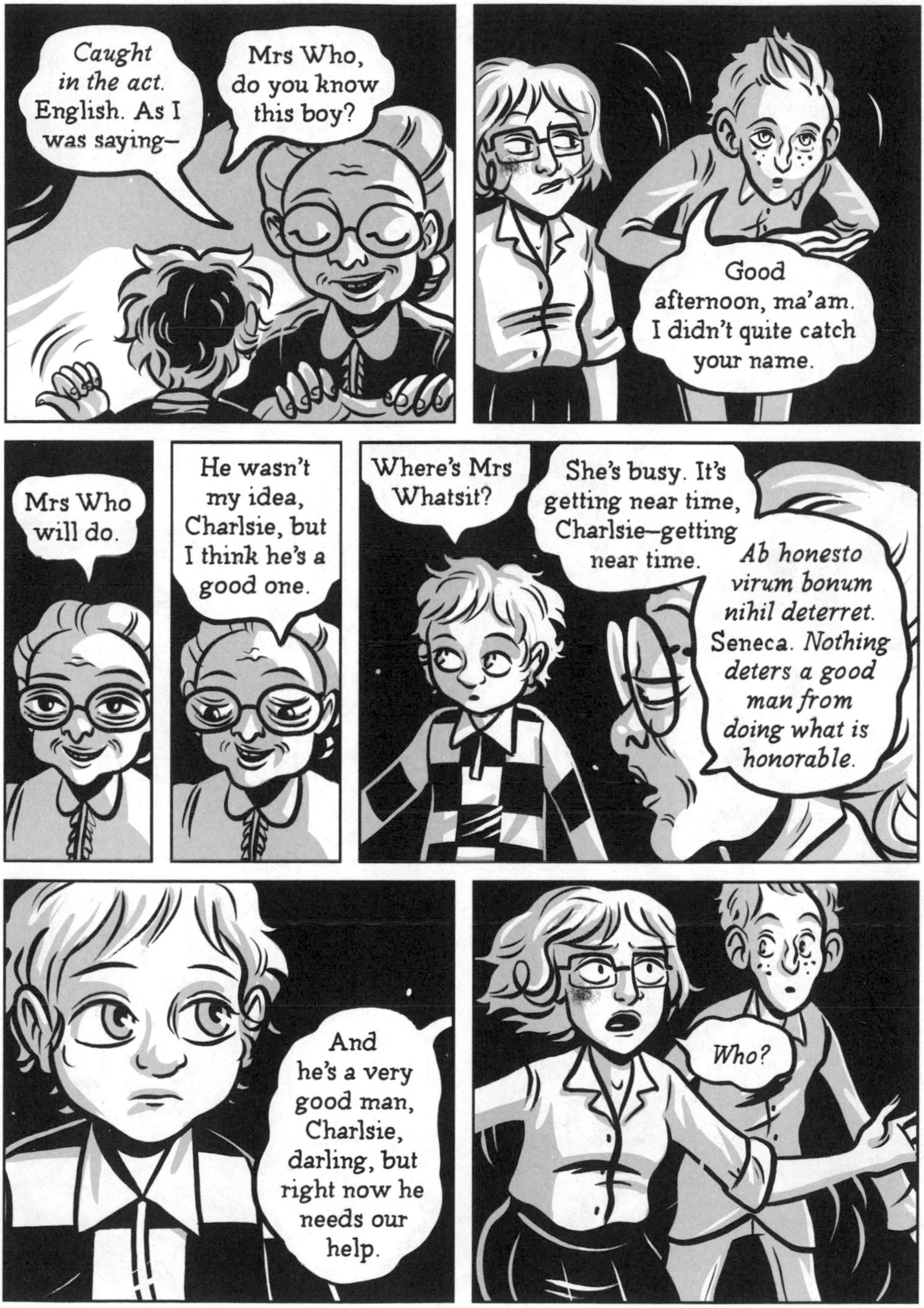

Caught in the act. English. As I was saying–
Mrs Who, do you know this boy?
Good afternoon, ma'am. I didn't quite catch your name.
Mrs Who will do.
He wasn't my idea, Charlsie, but I think he's a good one.
Where's Mrs Whatsit?
She's busy. It's getting near time, Charlsie–getting near time.
Ab honesto virum bonum nihil deterret. Seneca. *Nothing deters a good man from doing what is honorable.*
And he's a very good man, Charlsie, darling, but right now he needs our help.
Who?

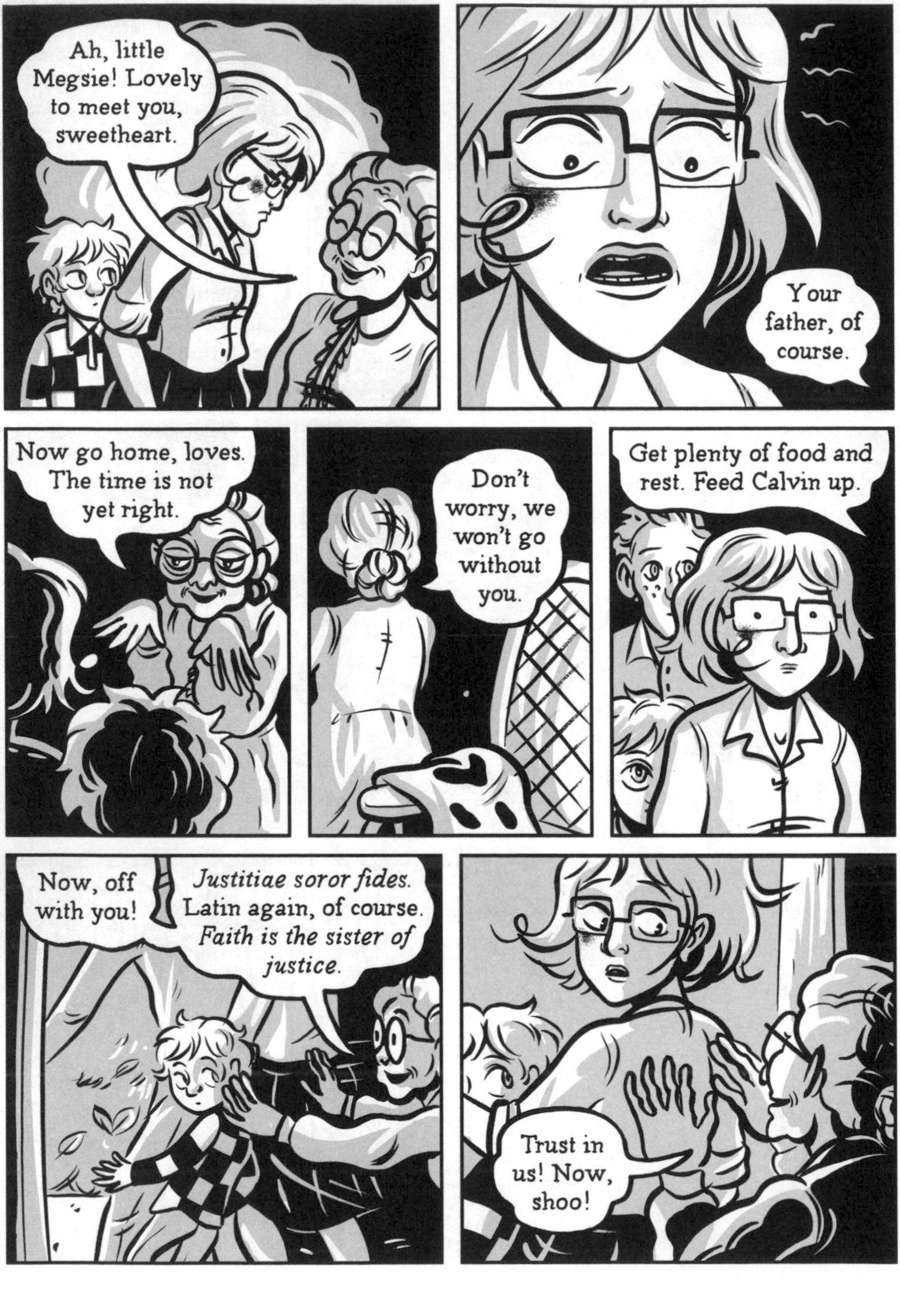
Ah, little Megsie! Lovely to meet you, sweetheart.
Your father, of course.
Now go home, loves. The time is not yet right.
Don't worry, we won't go without you.
Get plenty of food and rest. Feed Calvin up.
Now, off with you!
Justitiae soror fides. Latin again, of course. *Faith is the sister of justice.*
Trust in us! Now, shoo!

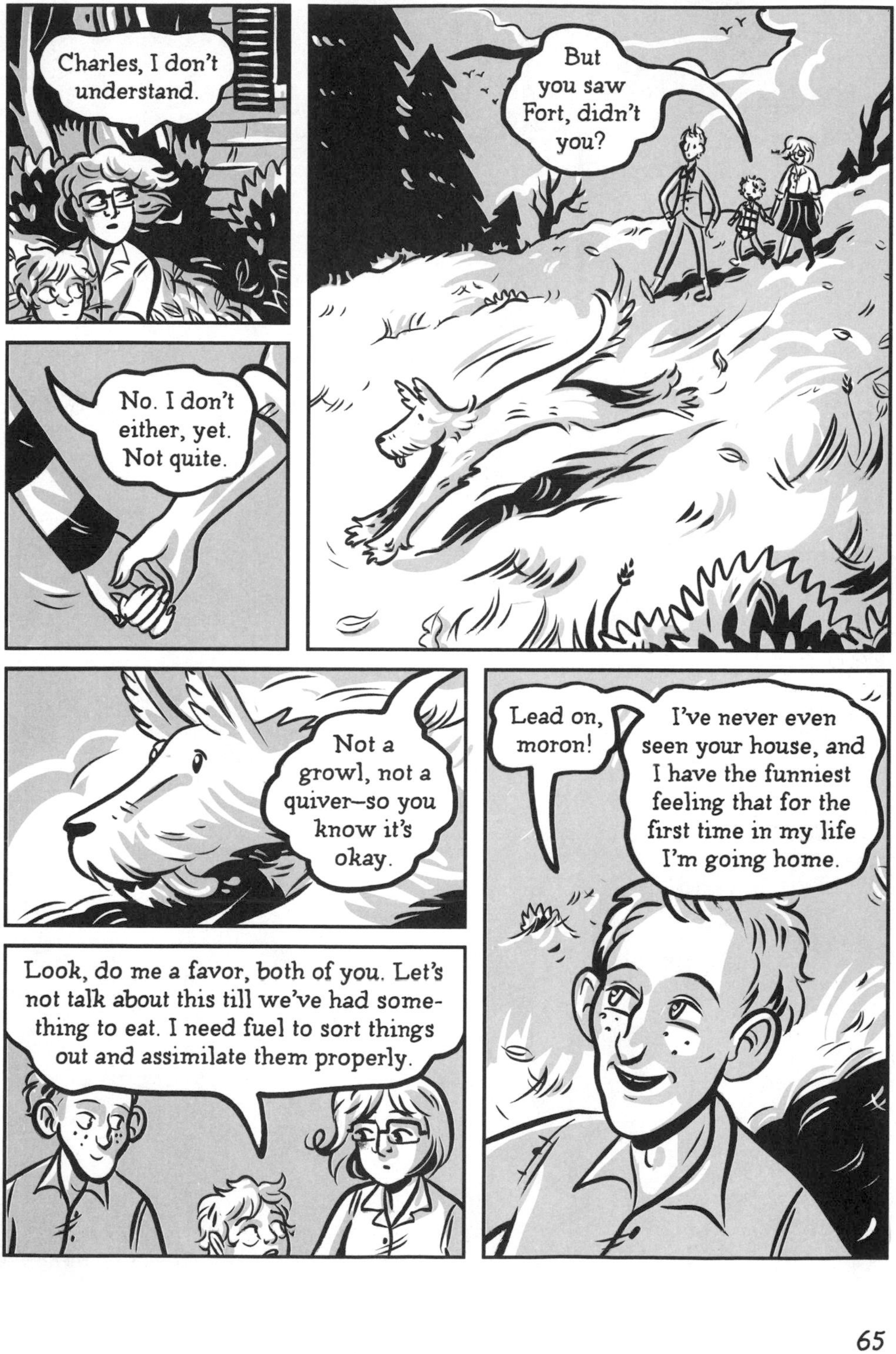
Charles, I don't understand.
But you saw Fort, didn't you?
No. I don't either, yet. Not quite.
Not a growl, not a quiver—so you know it's okay.
Lead on, moron!
I've never even seen your house, and I have the funniest feeling that for the first time in my life I'm going home.
Look, do me a favor, both of you. Let's not talk about this till we've had something to eat. I need fuel to sort things out and assimilate them properly.

3
Mrs Which

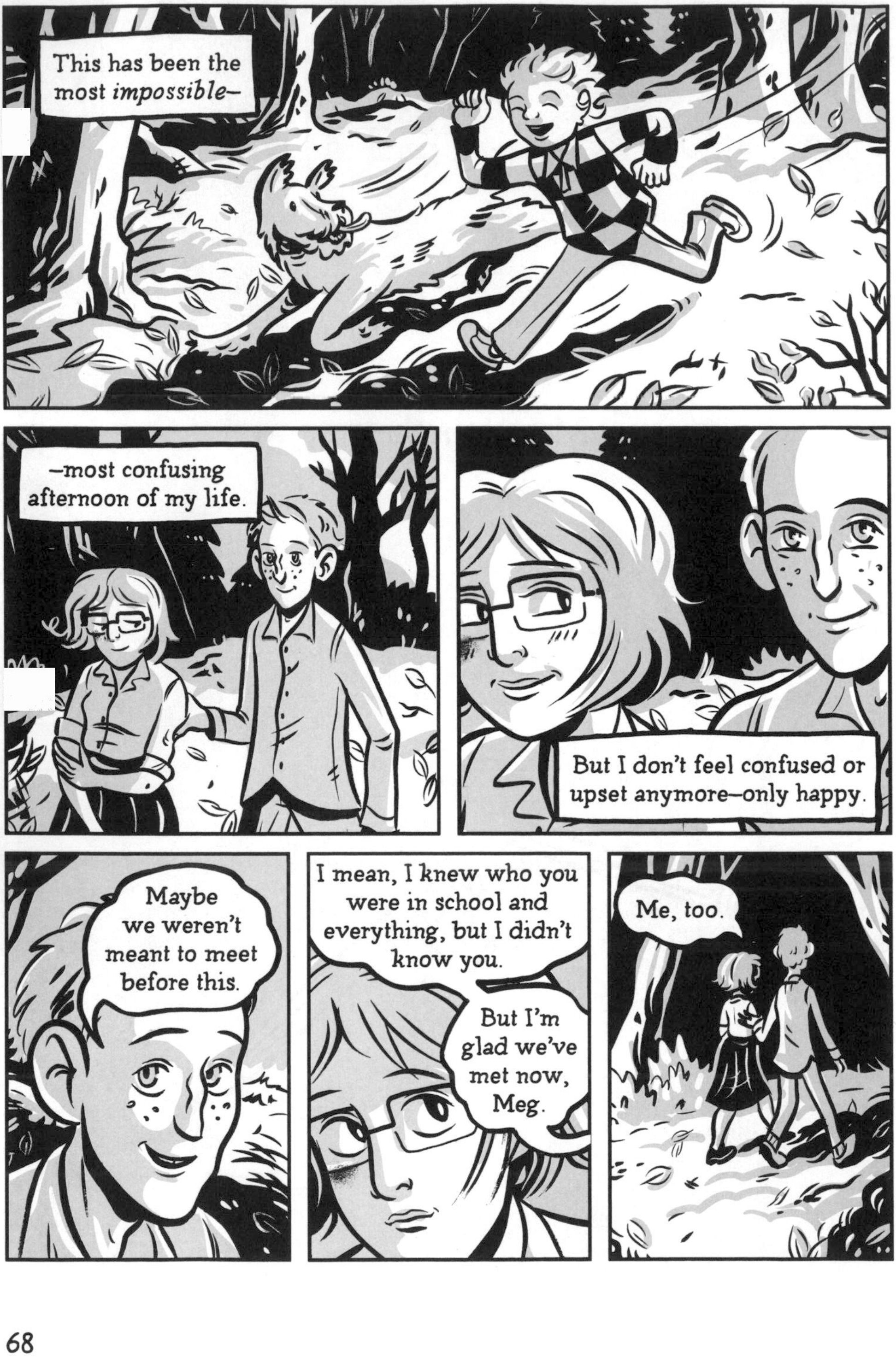
This has been the most *impossible*–
–most confusing afternoon of my life.
But I don't feel confused or upset anymore–only happy.
Maybe we weren't meant to meet before this.
I mean, I knew who you were in school and everything, but I didn't know you.
But I'm glad we've met now, Meg.
Me, too.

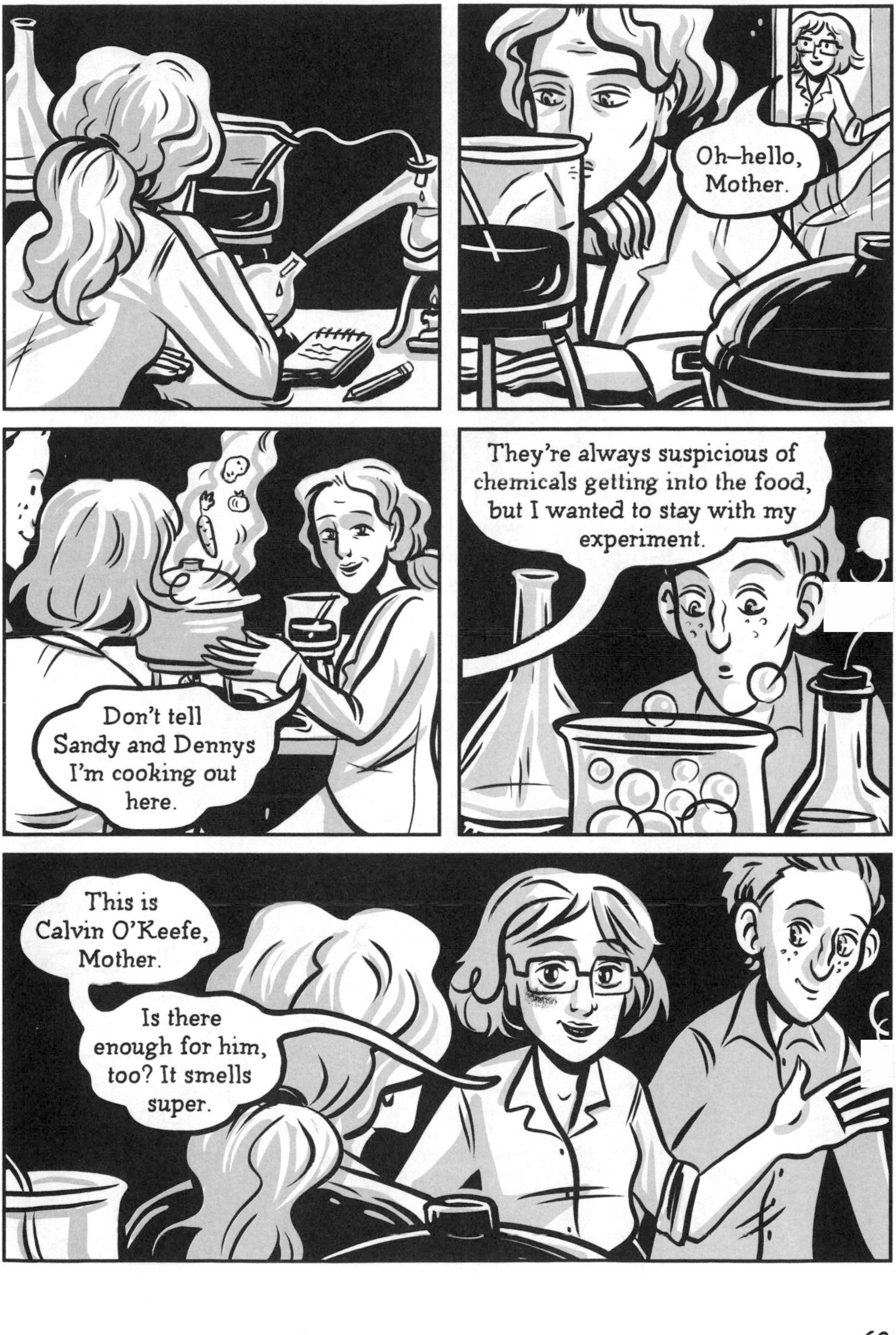
Oh—hello, Mother.
Don't tell Sandy and Dennys I'm cooking out here.
They're always suspicious of chemicals getting into the food, but I wanted to stay with my experiment.
This is Calvin O'Keefe, Mother.
Is there enough for him, too? It smells super.

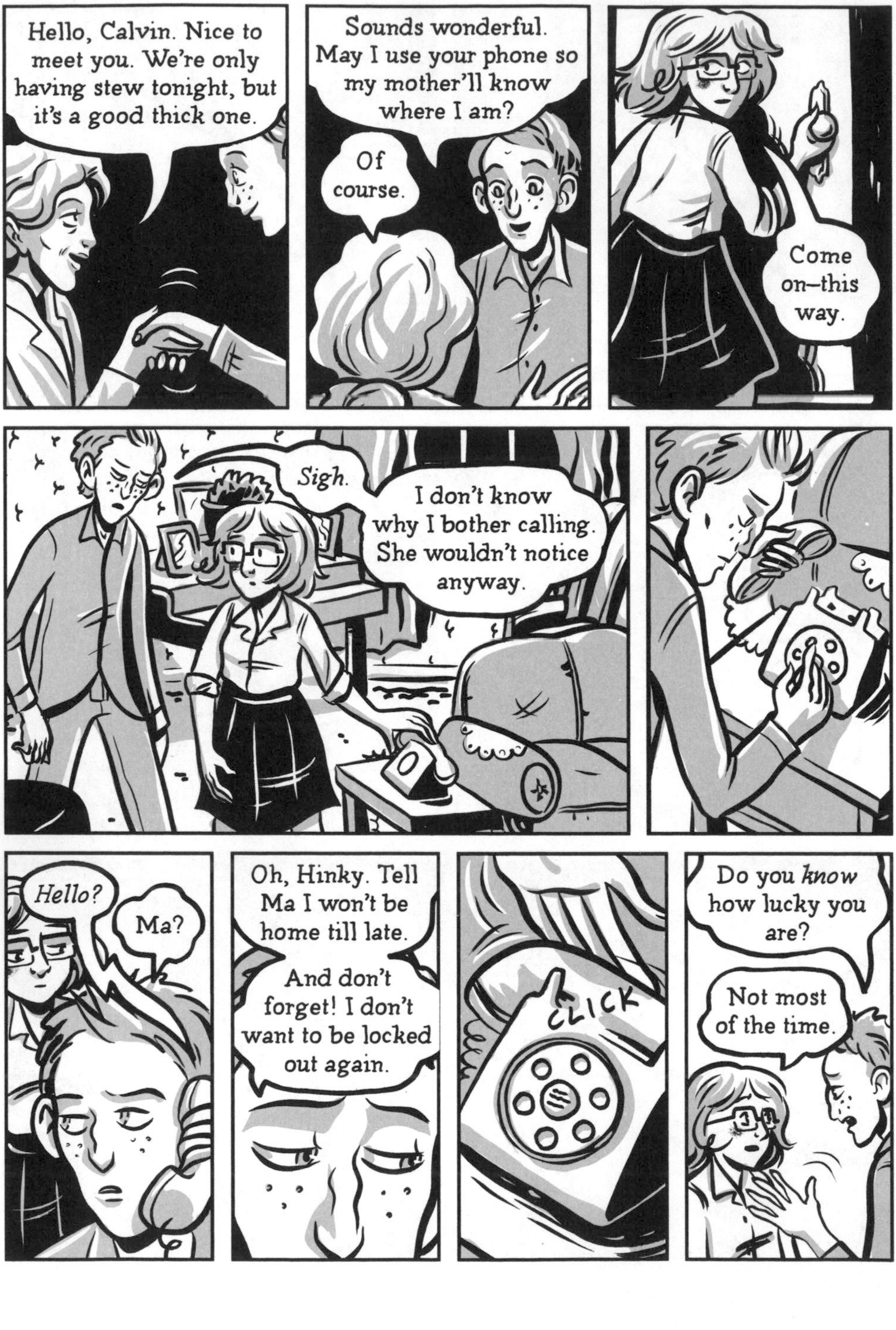
Hello, Calvin. Nice to meet you. We're only having stew tonight, but it's a good thick one.
Sounds wonderful. May I use your phone so my mother'll know where I am?
Of course.
Come on—this way.
Sigh.
I don't know why I bother calling. She wouldn't notice anyway.
Hello?
Ma?
Oh, Hinky. Tell Ma I won't be home till late.
And don't forget! I don't want to be locked out again.
CLICK
Do you *know* how lucky you are?
Not most of the time.

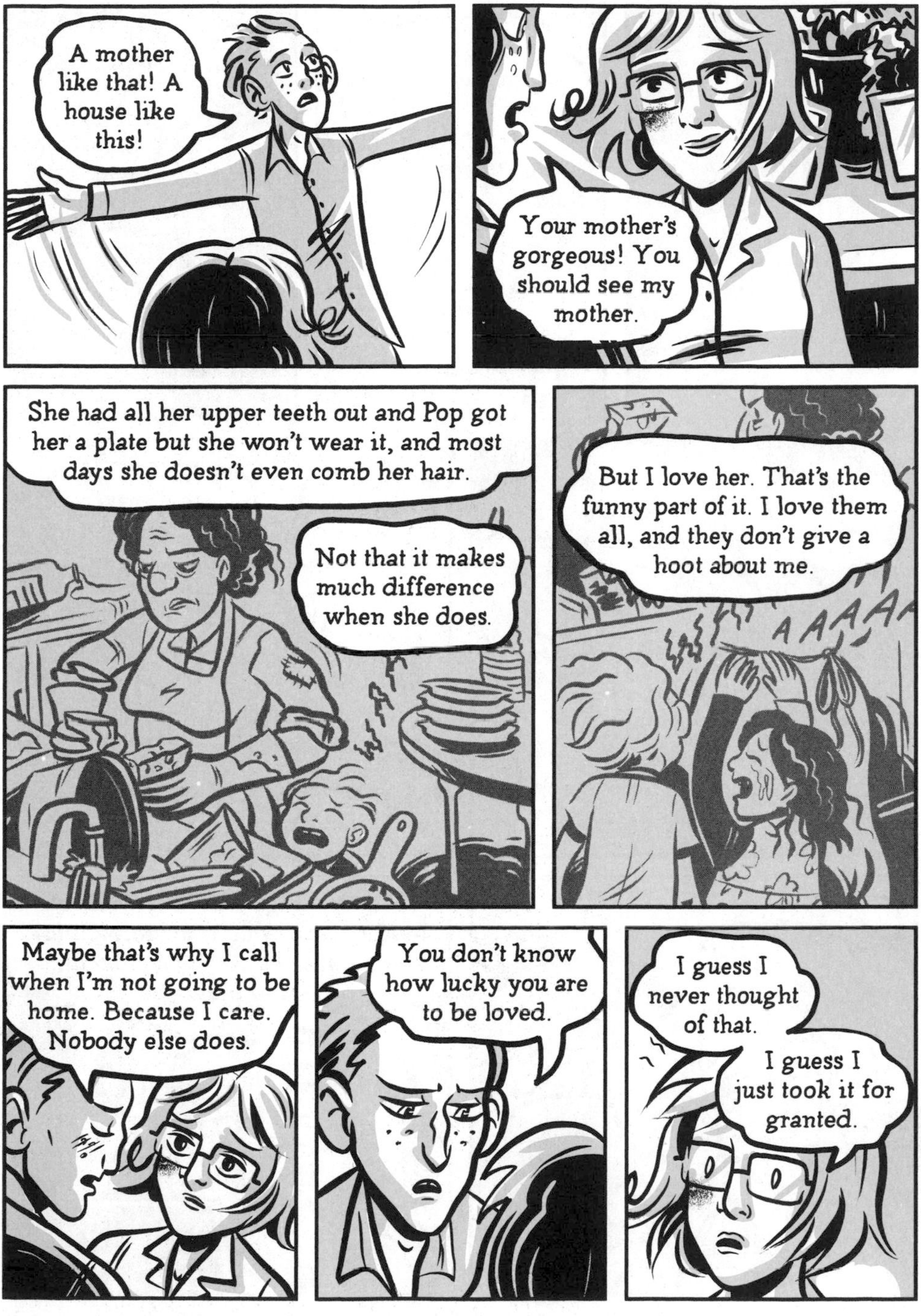
A mother like that! A house like this!
Your mother's gorgeous! You should see my mother.
She had all her upper teeth out and Pop got her a plate but she won't wear it, and most days she doesn't even comb her hair.
Not that it makes much difference when she does.
But I love her. That's the funny part of it. I love them all, and they don't give a hoot about me.
AAAA
Maybe that's why I call when I'm not going to be home. Because I care. Nobody else does.
You don't know how lucky you are to be loved.
I guess I never thought of that.
I guess I just took it for granted.

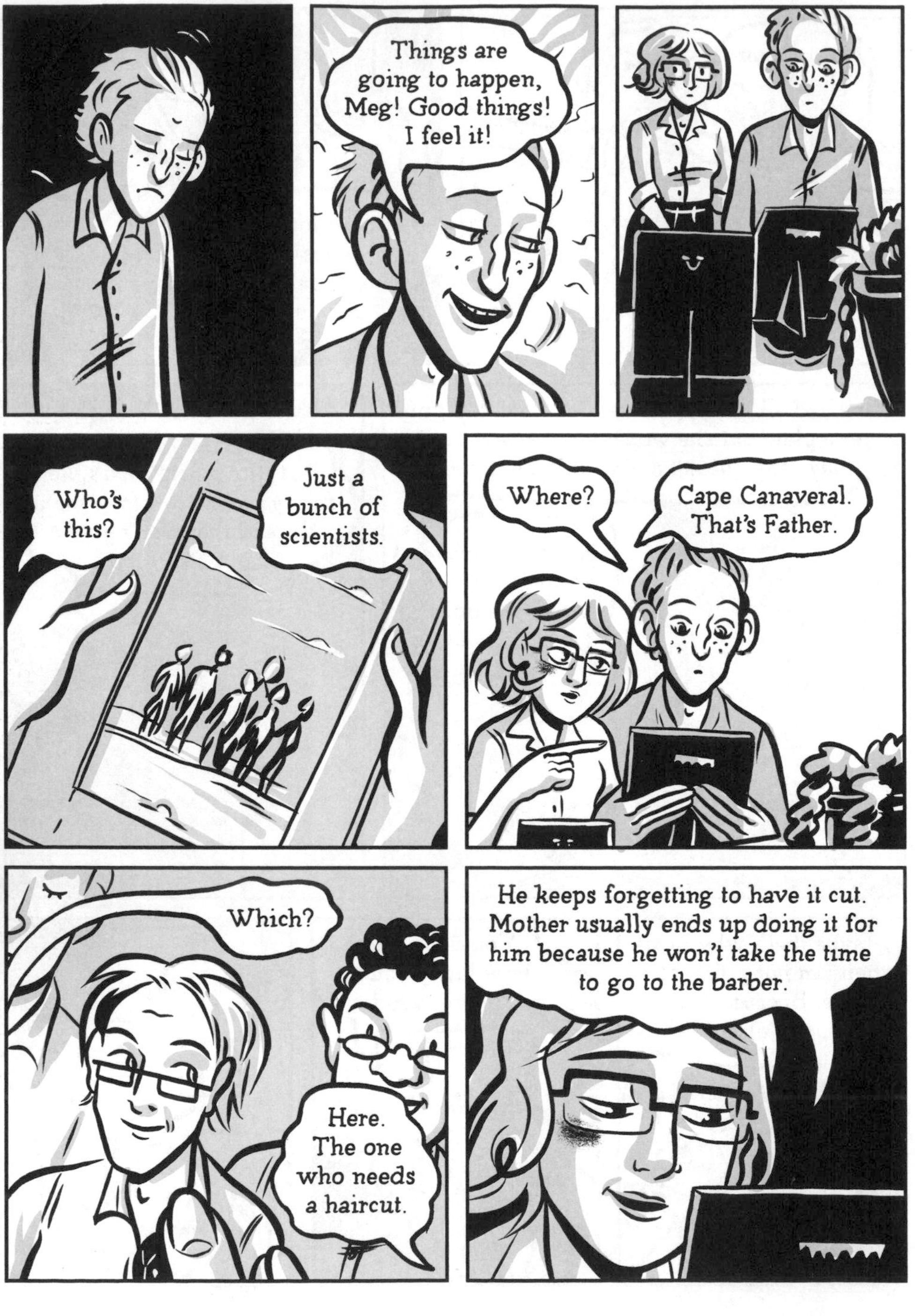

Things are going to happen, Meg! Good things! I feel it!
Who's this?
Just a bunch of scientists.
Where?
Cape Canaveral. That's Father.
Which?
Here. The one who needs a haircut.
He keeps forgetting to have it cut. Mother usually ends up doing it for him because he won't take the time to go to the barber.

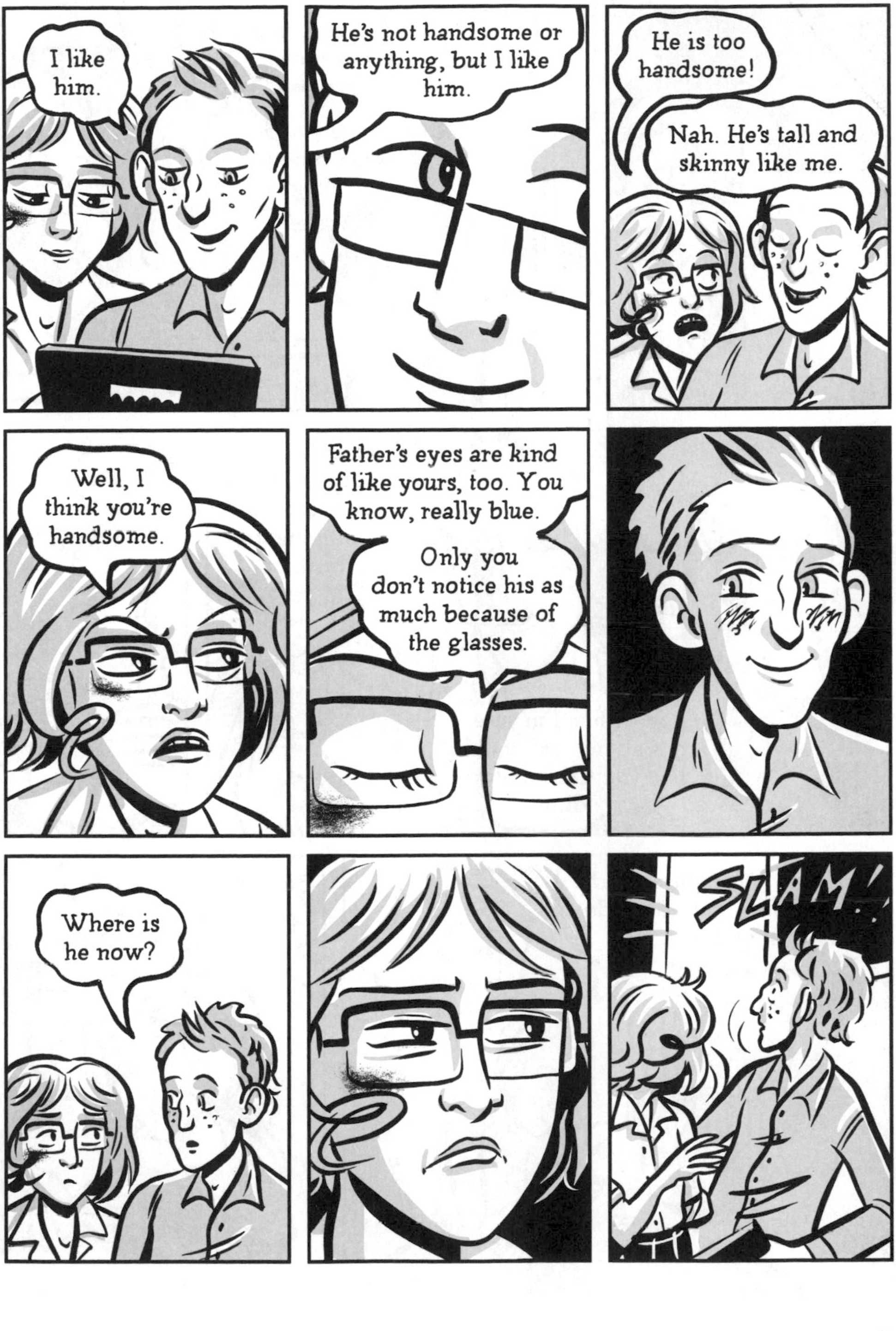
I like him.
He's not handsome or anything, but I like him.
He is too handsome!
Nah. He's tall and skinny like me.
Well, I think you're handsome.
Father's eyes are kind of like yours, too. You know, really blue.
Only you don't notice his as much because of the glasses.
Where is he now?
SLAM!

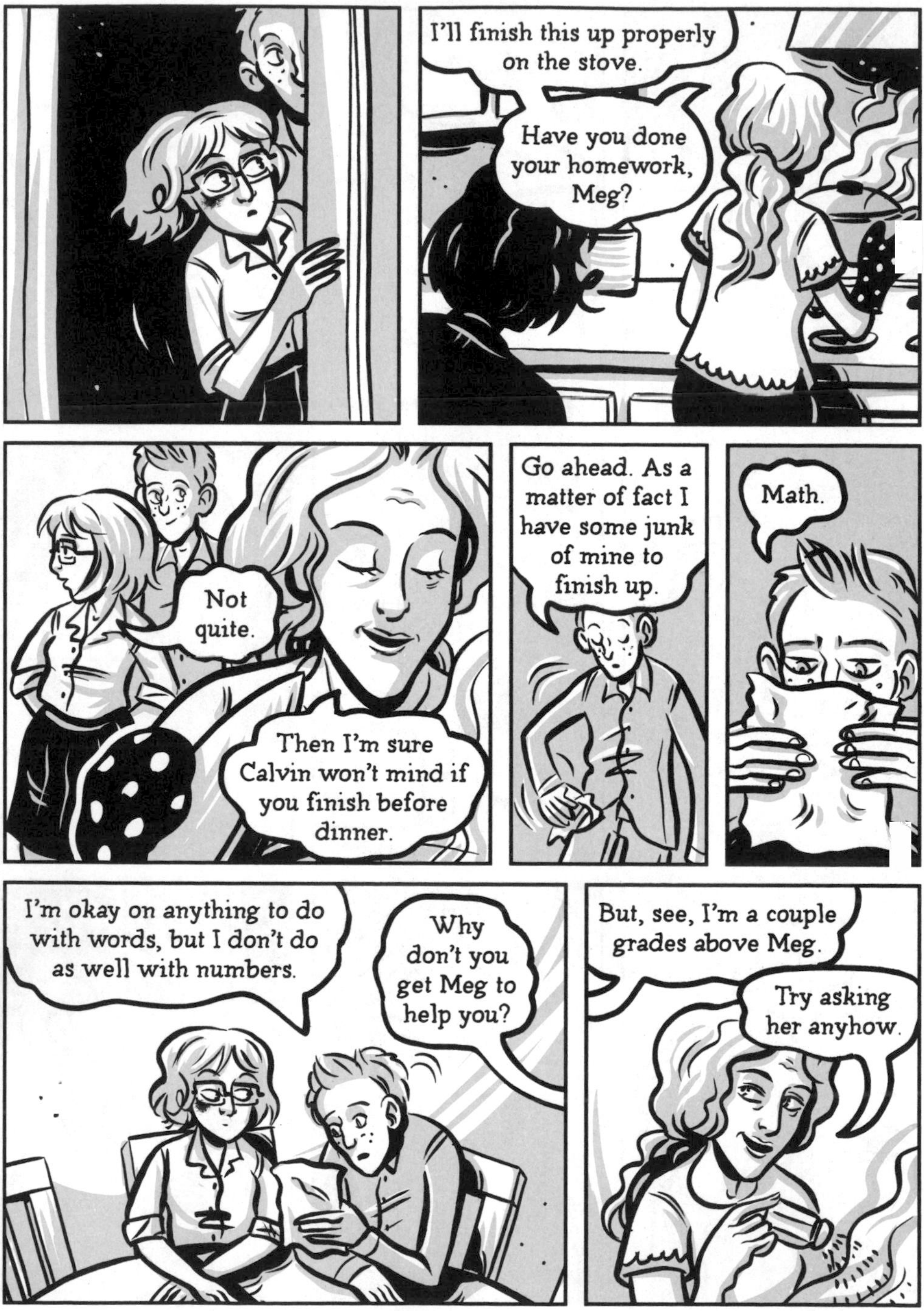
I'll finish this up properly on the stove.
Have you done your homework, Meg?
Not quite.
Then I'm sure Calvin won't mind if you finish before dinner.
Go ahead. As a matter of fact I have some junk of mine to finish up.
Math.
I'm okay on anything to do with words, but I don't do as well with numbers.
Why don't you get Meg to help you?
But, see, I'm a couple grades above Meg.
Try asking her anyhow.

Here. But it's pretty complicated.

Do they care *how* you do it? I mean, can you work it out your own way?

Sure, as long as I understand it and get the answers right.

Lucky. *We* have to do it *their* way.

Now, look. See how much easier it would be if you did it *this* way?

Hey—

Hey! I think I get it!

Show me once more on another one.

All you have to remember . . .

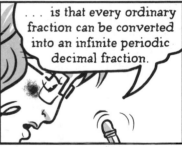

. . . is that every ordinary fraction can be converted into an infinite periodic decimal fraction.

See? So 3/7 is 0.428571.

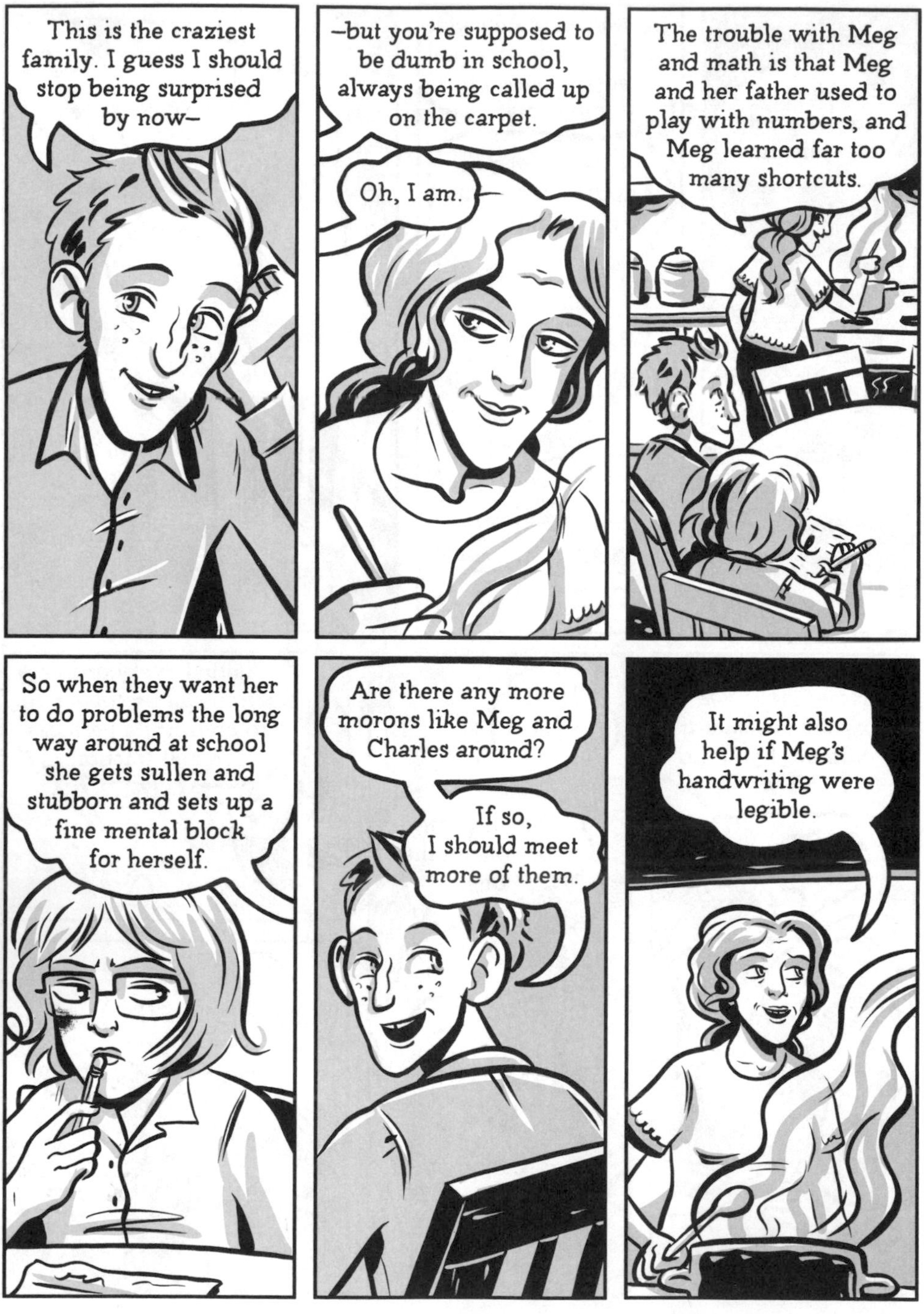
This is the craziest family. I guess I should stop being surprised by now–
–but you're supposed to be dumb in school, always being called up on the carpet.
Oh, I am.
The trouble with Meg and math is that Meg and her father used to play with numbers, and Meg learned far too many shortcuts.
So when they want her to do problems the long way around at school she gets sullen and stubborn and sets up a fine mental block for herself.
Are there any more morons like Meg and Charles around?
If so, I should meet more of them.
It might also help if Meg's handwriting were legible.

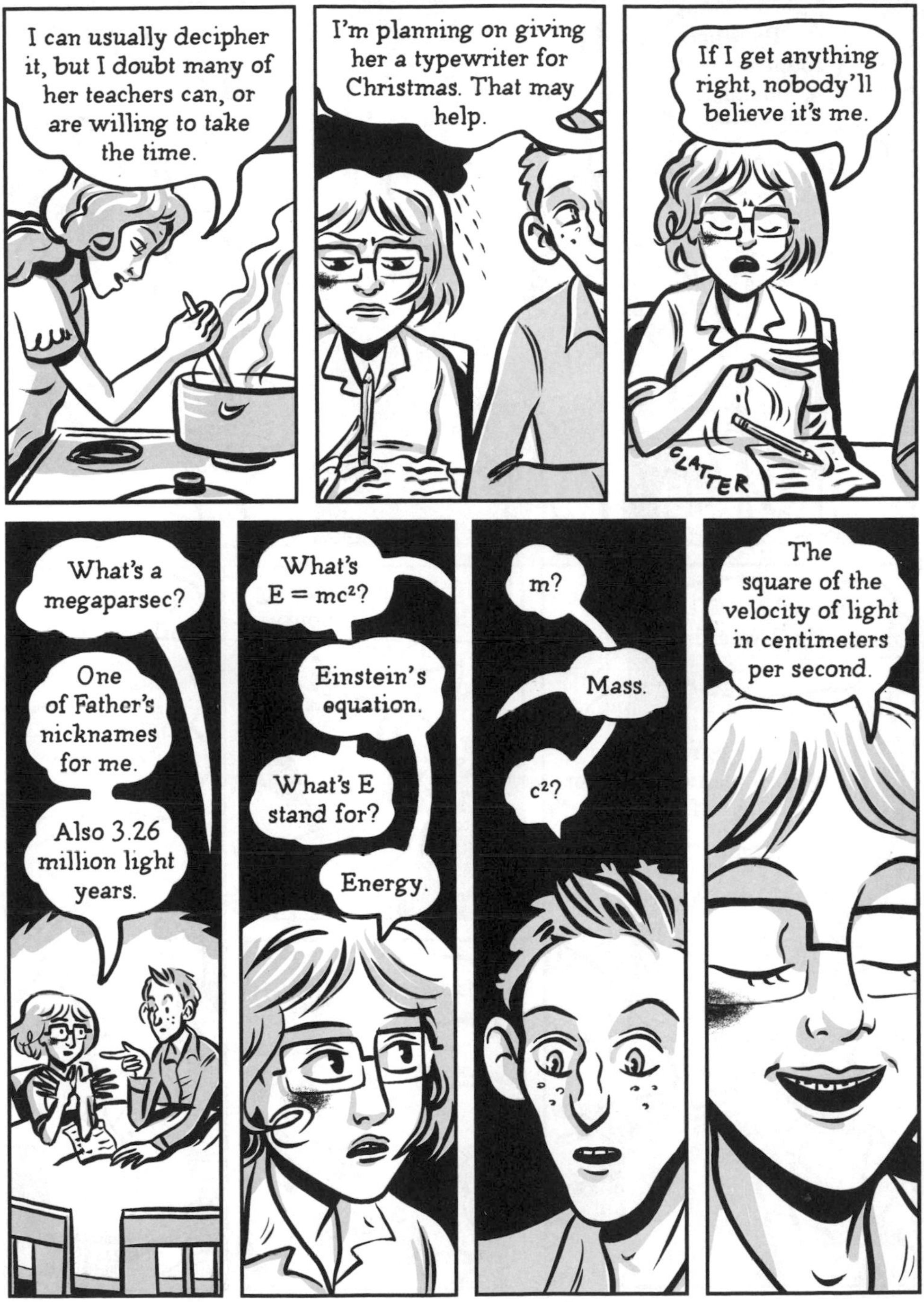
I can usually decipher it, but I doubt many of her teachers can, or are willing to take the time.
I'm planning on giving her a typewriter for Christmas. That may help.
If I get anything right, nobody'll believe it's me.
CLATTER
What's a megaparsec?
One of Father's nicknames for me.
Also 3.26 million light years.
What's E = mc²?
Einstein's equation.
What's E stand for?
Energy.
m?
Mass.
c²?
The square of the velocity of light in centimeters per second.

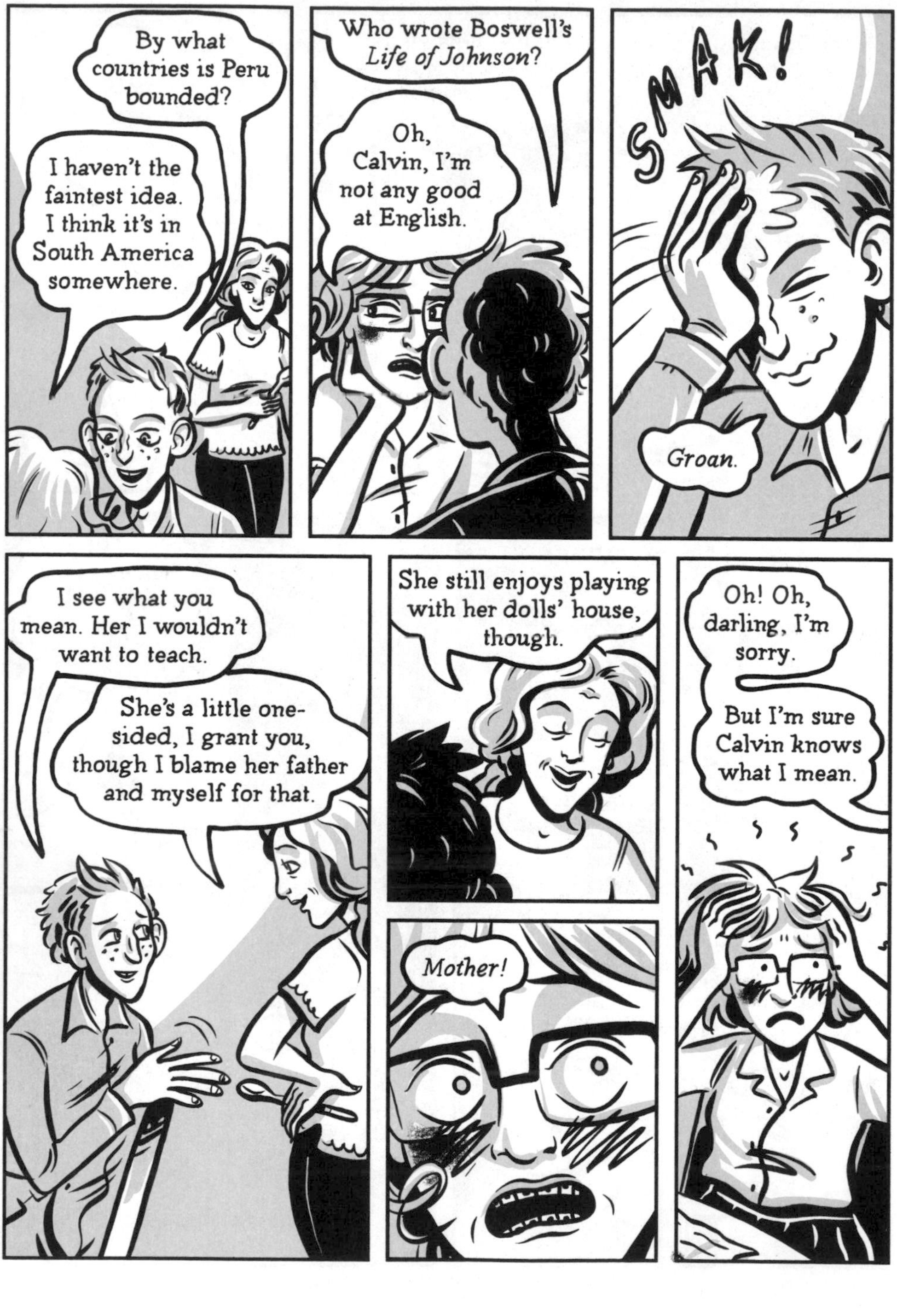
By what countries is Peru bounded?
I haven't the faintest idea. I think it's in South America somewhere.
Who wrote Boswell's *Life of Johnson*?
Oh, Calvin, I'm not any good at English.
SMAK!
Groan.
I see what you mean. Her I wouldn't want to teach.
She's a little one-sided, I grant you, though I blame her father and myself for that.
She still enjoys playing with her dolls' house, though.
Mother!
Oh! Oh, darling, I'm sorry.
But I'm sure Calvin knows what I mean.

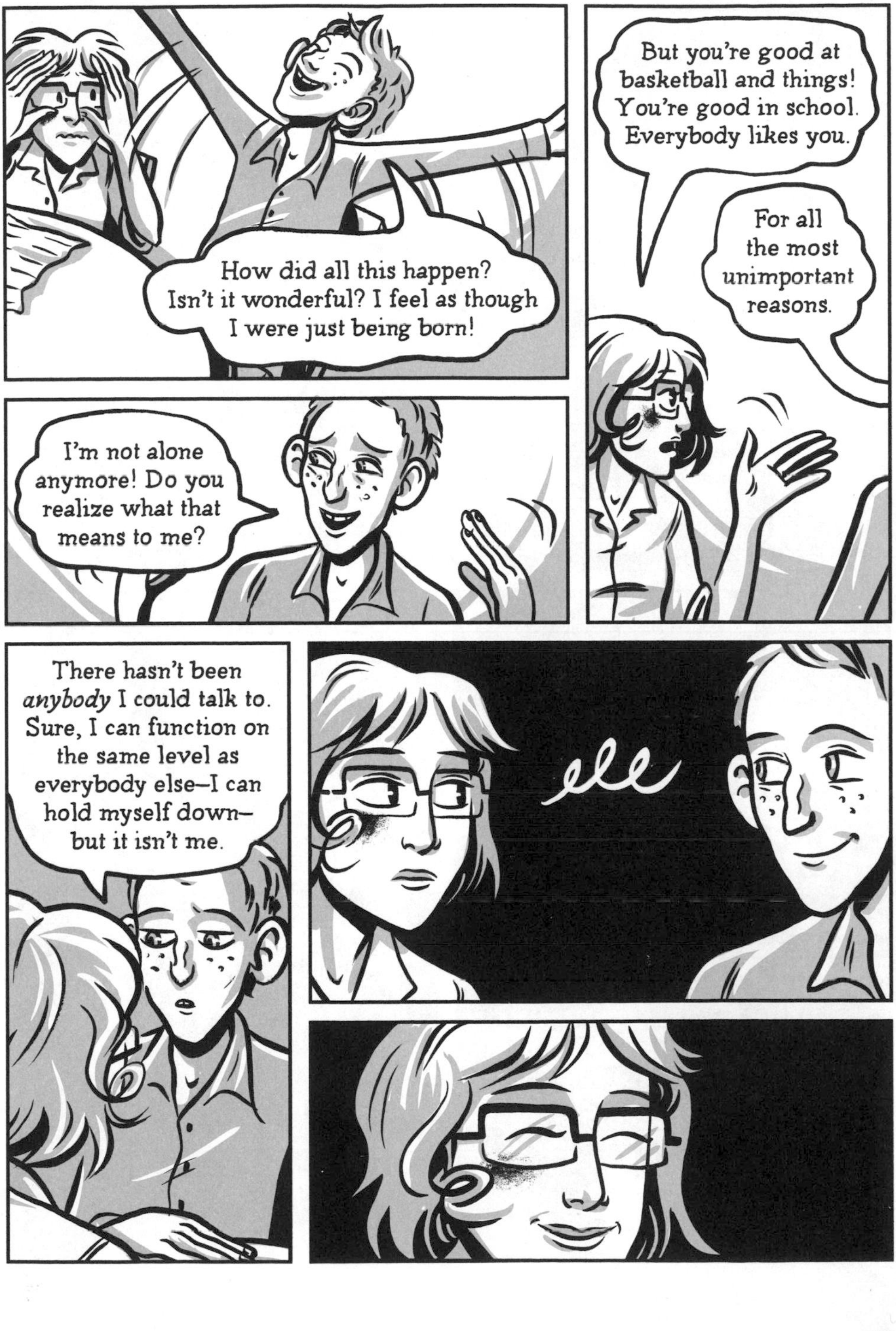
How did all this happen? Isn't it wonderful? I feel as though I were just being born!
But you're good at basketball and things! You're good in school. Everybody likes you.
For all the most unimportant reasons.
I'm not alone anymore! Do you realize what that means to me?
There hasn't been *anybody* I could talk to. Sure, I can function on the same level as everybody else—I can hold myself down—but it isn't me.

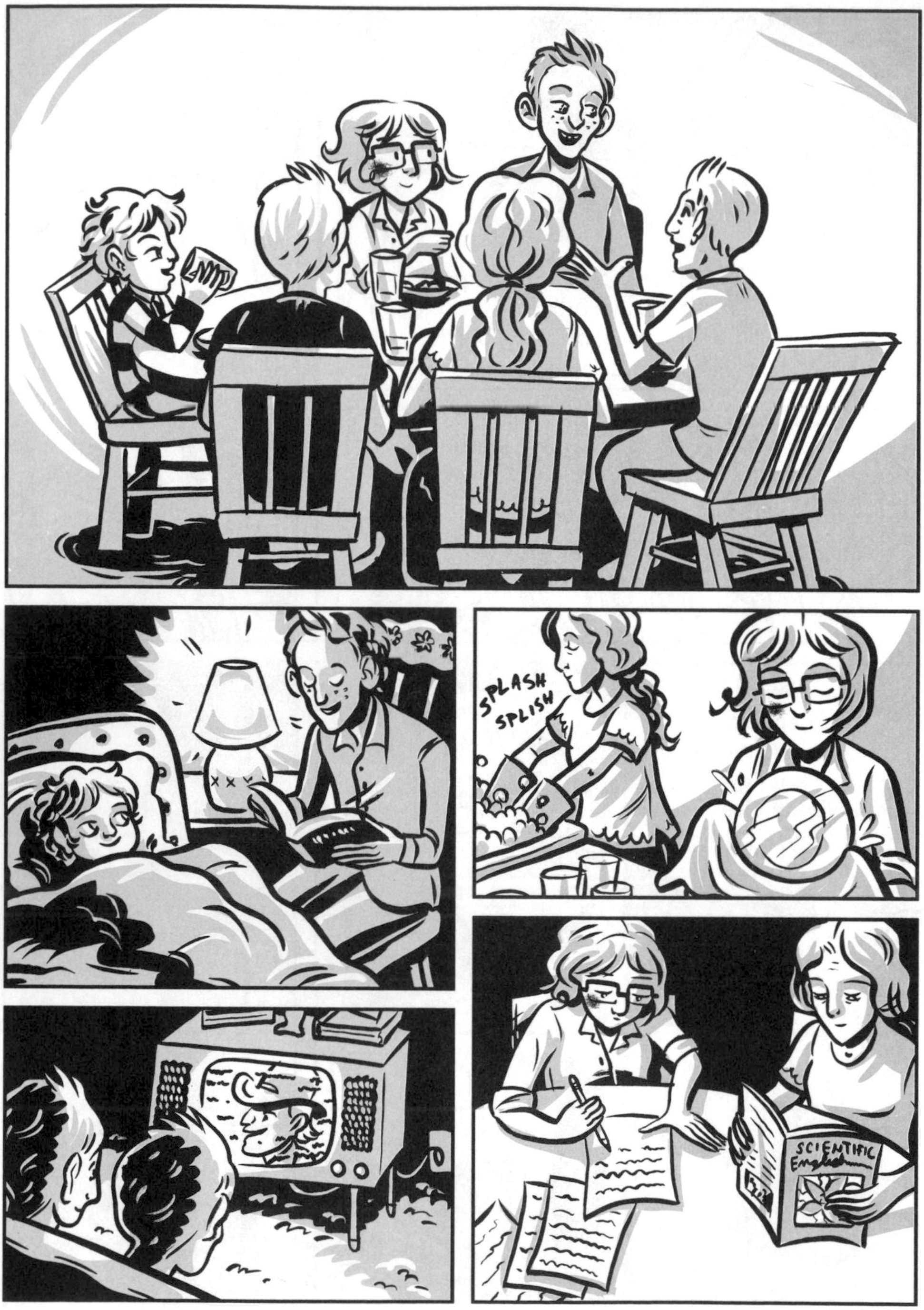
SPLASH
SPLISH
SCIENTIFIC

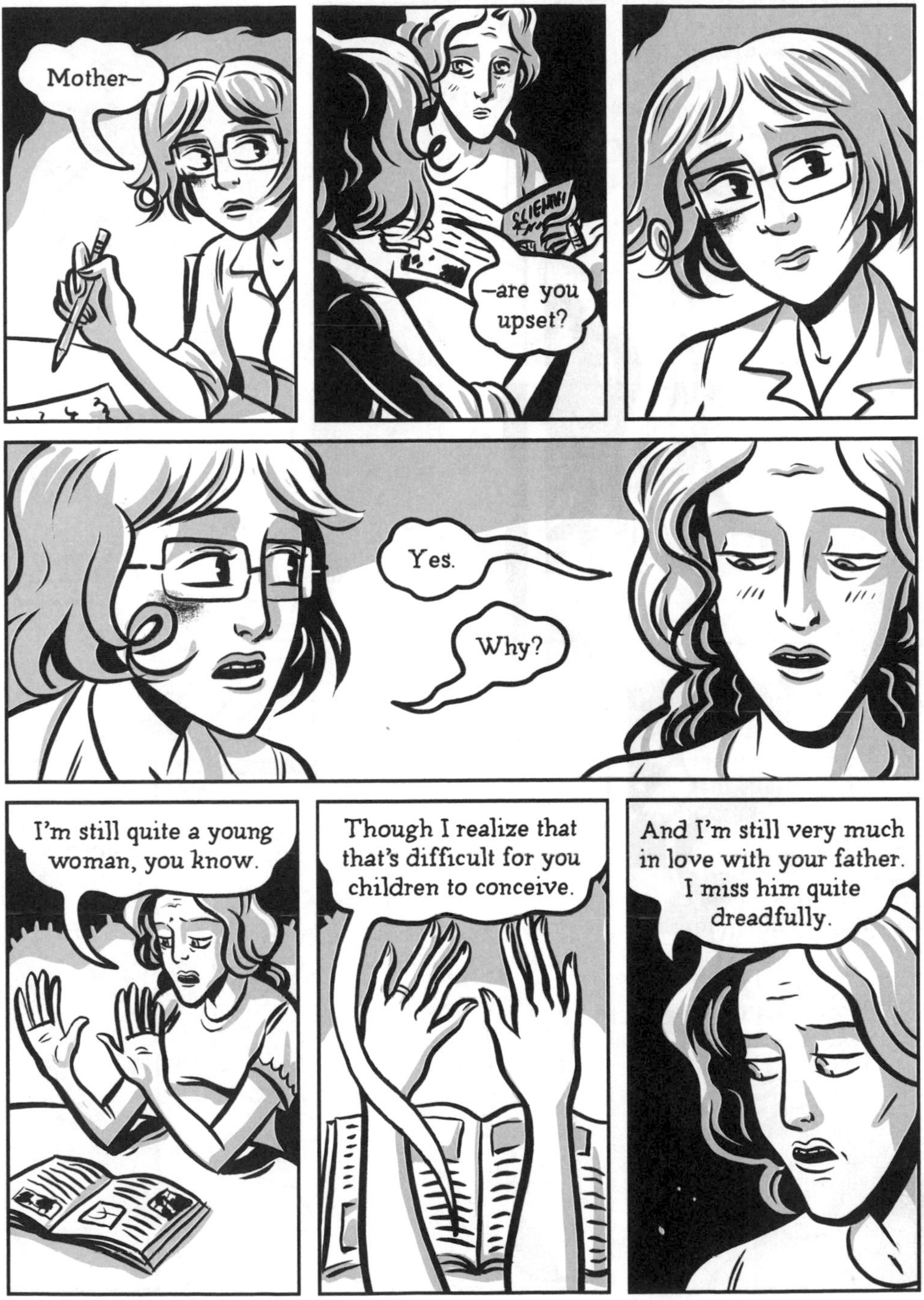
Mother–
–are you upset?
Yes.
Why?
I'm still quite a young woman, you know.
Though I realize that that's difficult for you children to conceive.
And I'm still very much in love with your father. I miss him quite dreadfully.

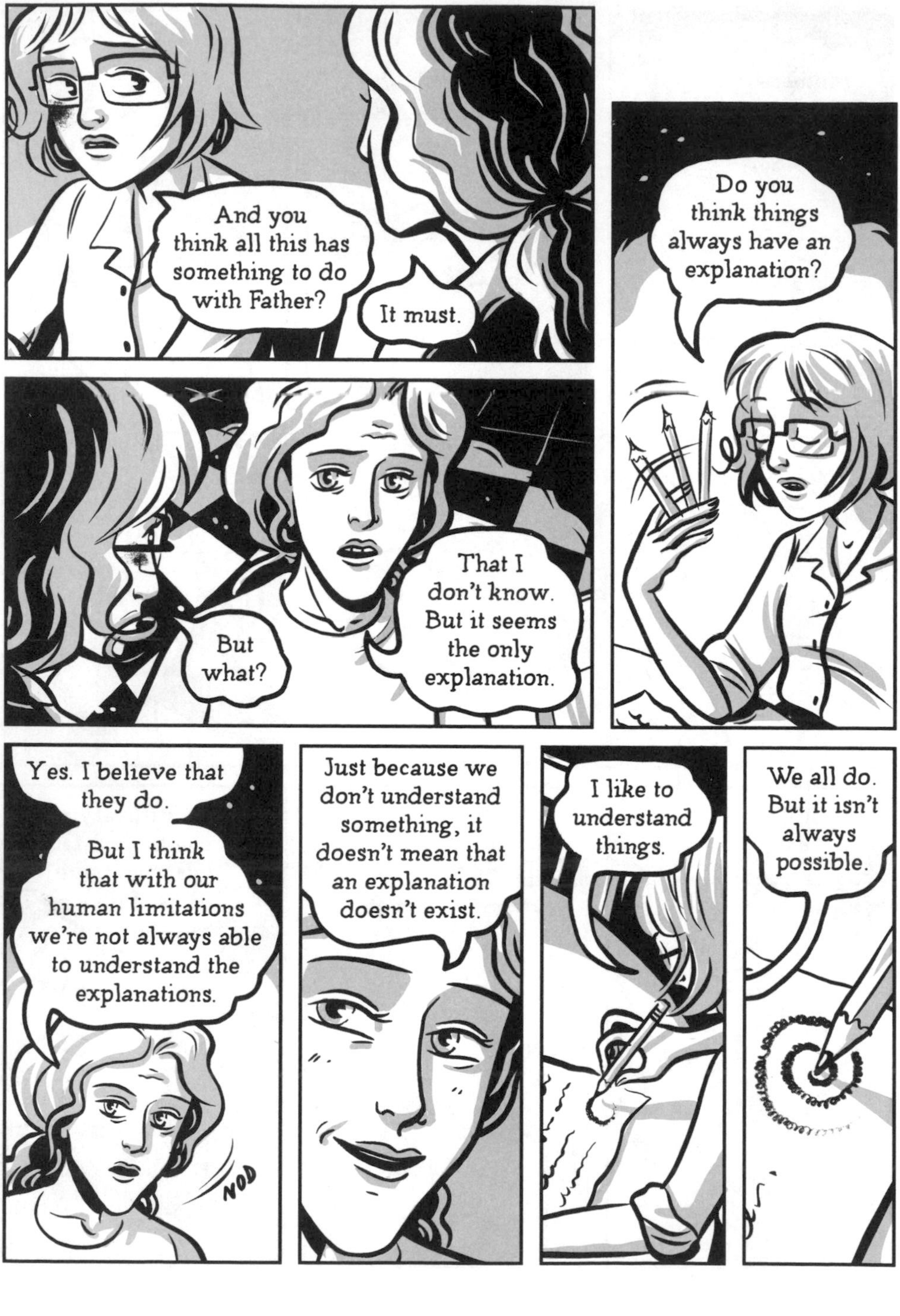
And you think all this has something to do with Father?
It must.
Do you think things always have an explanation?
But what?
That I don't know. But it seems the only explanation.
Yes. I believe that they do.
But I think that with our human limitations we're not always able to understand the explanations.
NOD
Just because we don't understand something, it doesn't mean that an explanation doesn't exist.
I like to understand things.
We all do. But it isn't always possible.

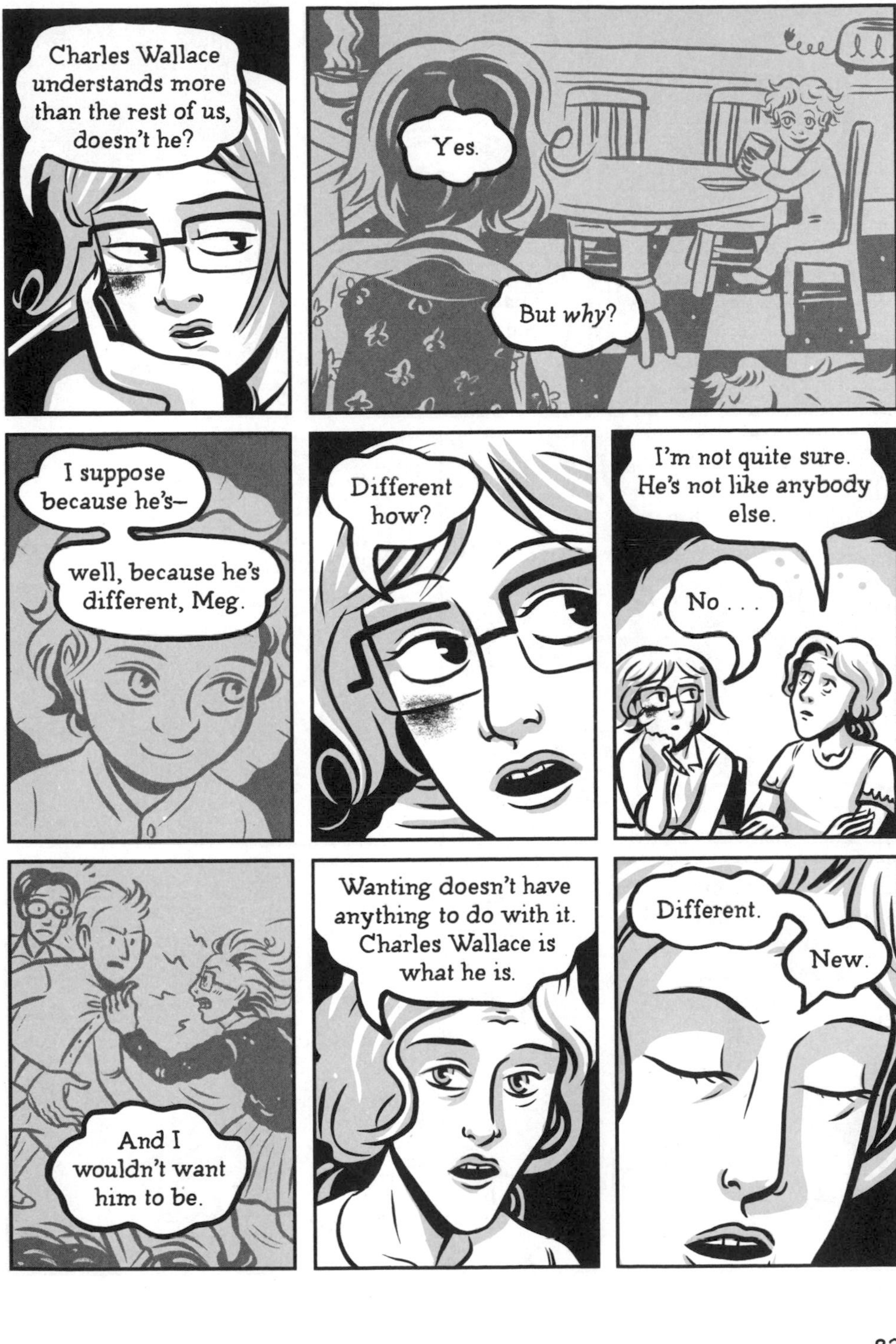
Charles Wallace understands more than the rest of us, doesn't he?
Yes.
But *why*?
I suppose because he's—
well, because he's different, Meg.
Different how?
I'm not quite sure. He's not like anybody else.
No . . .
And I wouldn't want him to be.
Wanting doesn't have anything to do with it. Charles Wallace is what he is.
Different.
New.

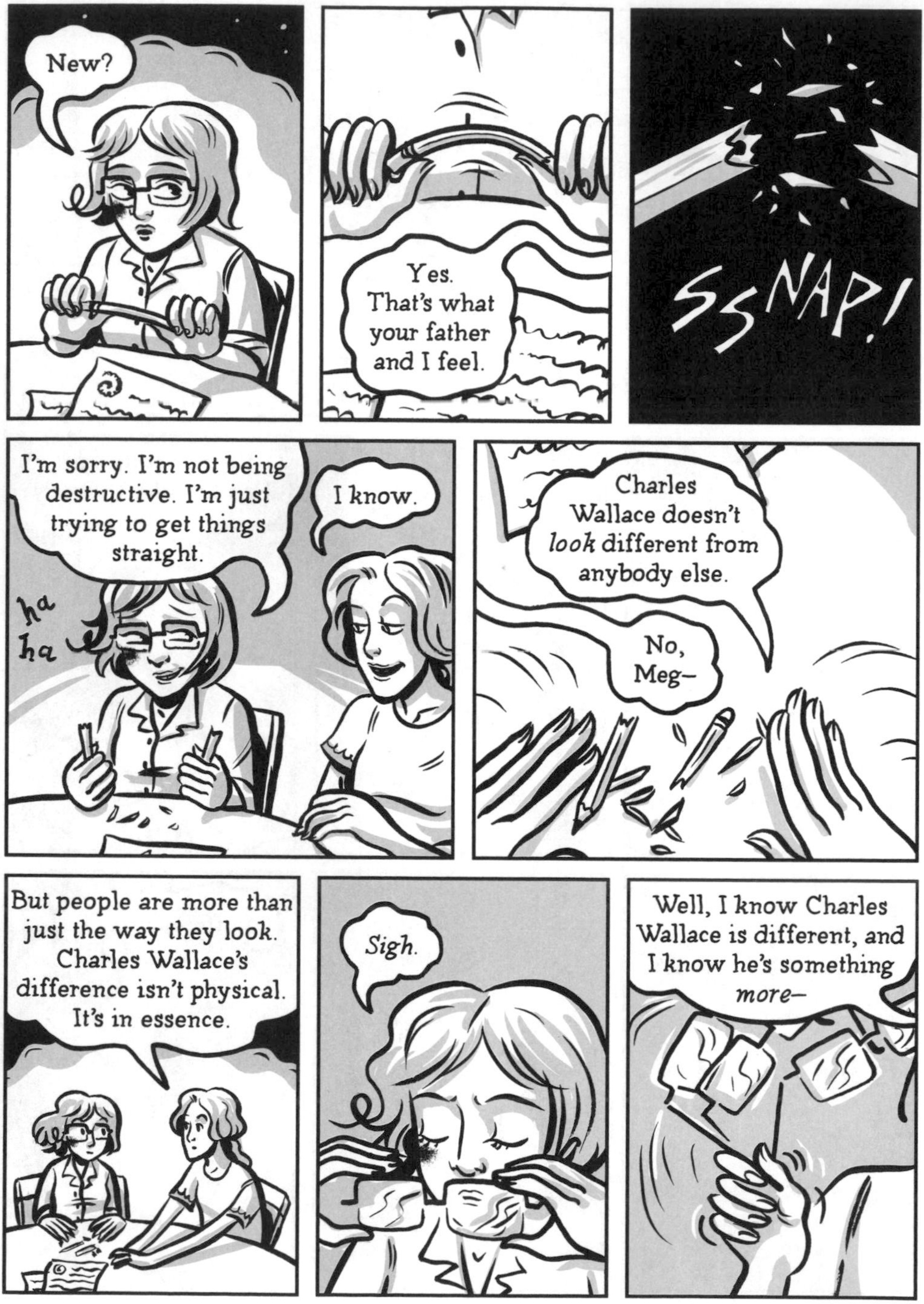
New?
Yes. That's what your father and I feel.
SSNAP!
I'm sorry. I'm not being destructive. I'm just trying to get things straight.
ha ha
I know.
Charles Wallace doesn't *look* different from anybody else.
No, Meg–
But people are more than just the way they look. Charles Wallace's difference isn't physical. It's in essence.
Sigh.
Well, I know Charles Wallace is different, and I know he's something *more*–

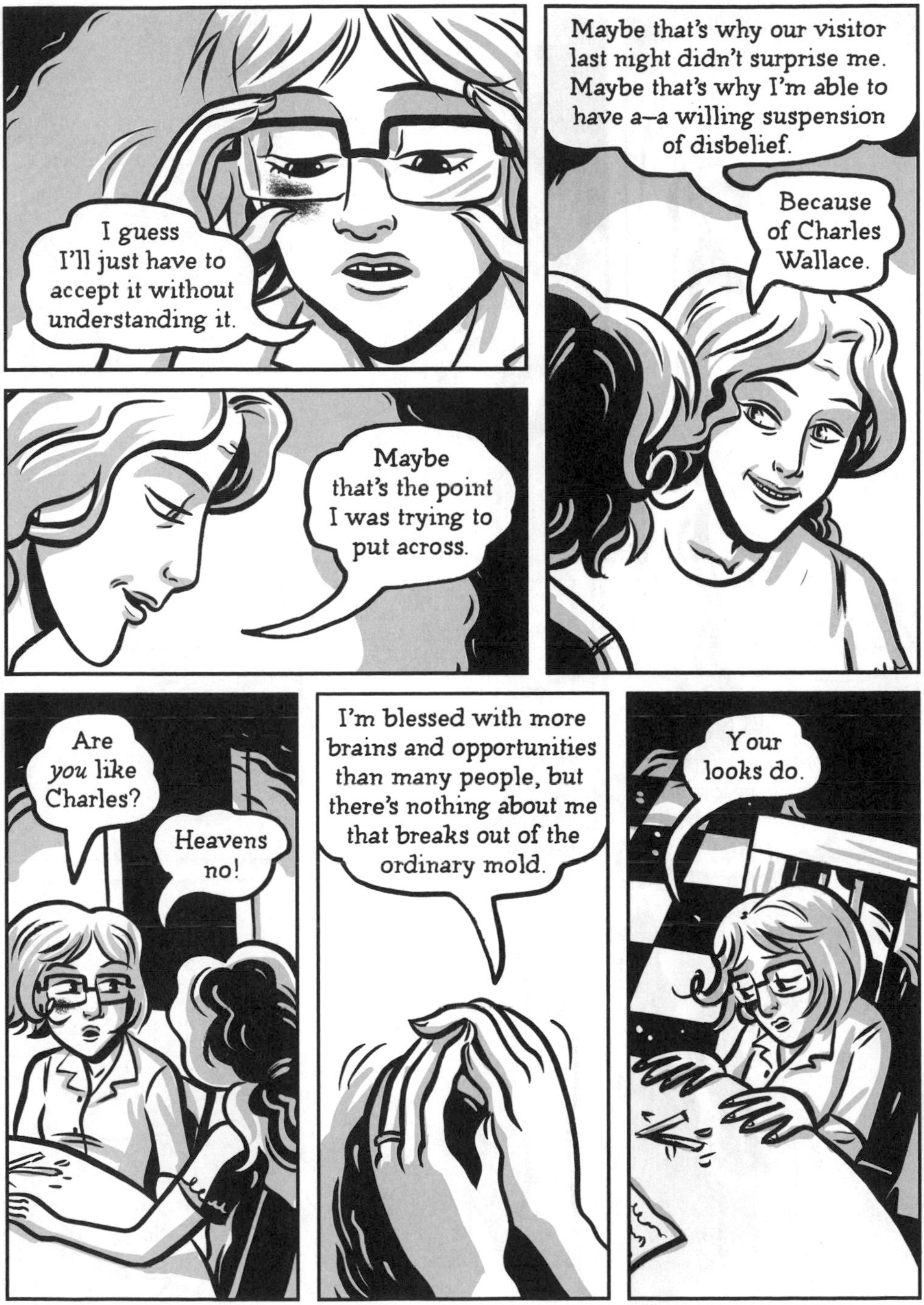
I guess I'll just have to accept it without understanding it.
Maybe that's the point I was trying to put across.
Maybe that's why our visitor last night didn't surprise me. Maybe that's why I'm able to have a—a willing suspension of disbelief.
Because of Charles Wallace.
Are *you* like Charles?
Heavens no!
I'm blessed with more brains and opportunities than many people, but there's nothing about me that breaks out of the ordinary mold.
Your looks do.

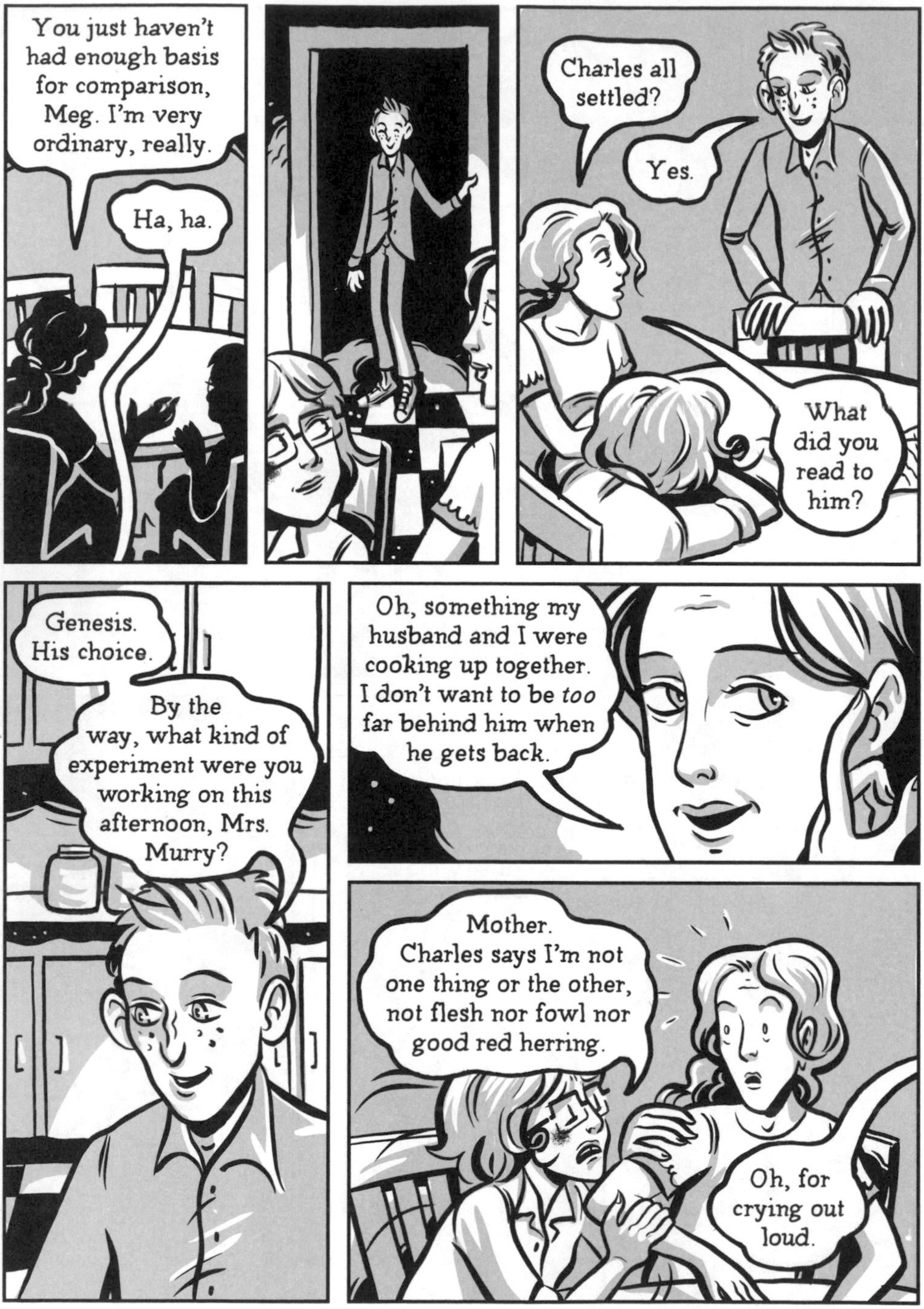
You just haven't had enough basis for comparison, Meg. I'm very ordinary, really.
Ha, ha.
Charles all settled?
Yes.
What did you read to him?
Genesis. His choice.
By the way, what kind of experiment were you working on this afternoon, Mrs. Murry?
Oh, something my husband and I were cooking up together. I don't want to be *too* far behind him when he gets back.
Mother. Charles says I'm not one thing or the other, not flesh nor fowl nor good red herring.
Oh, for crying out loud.

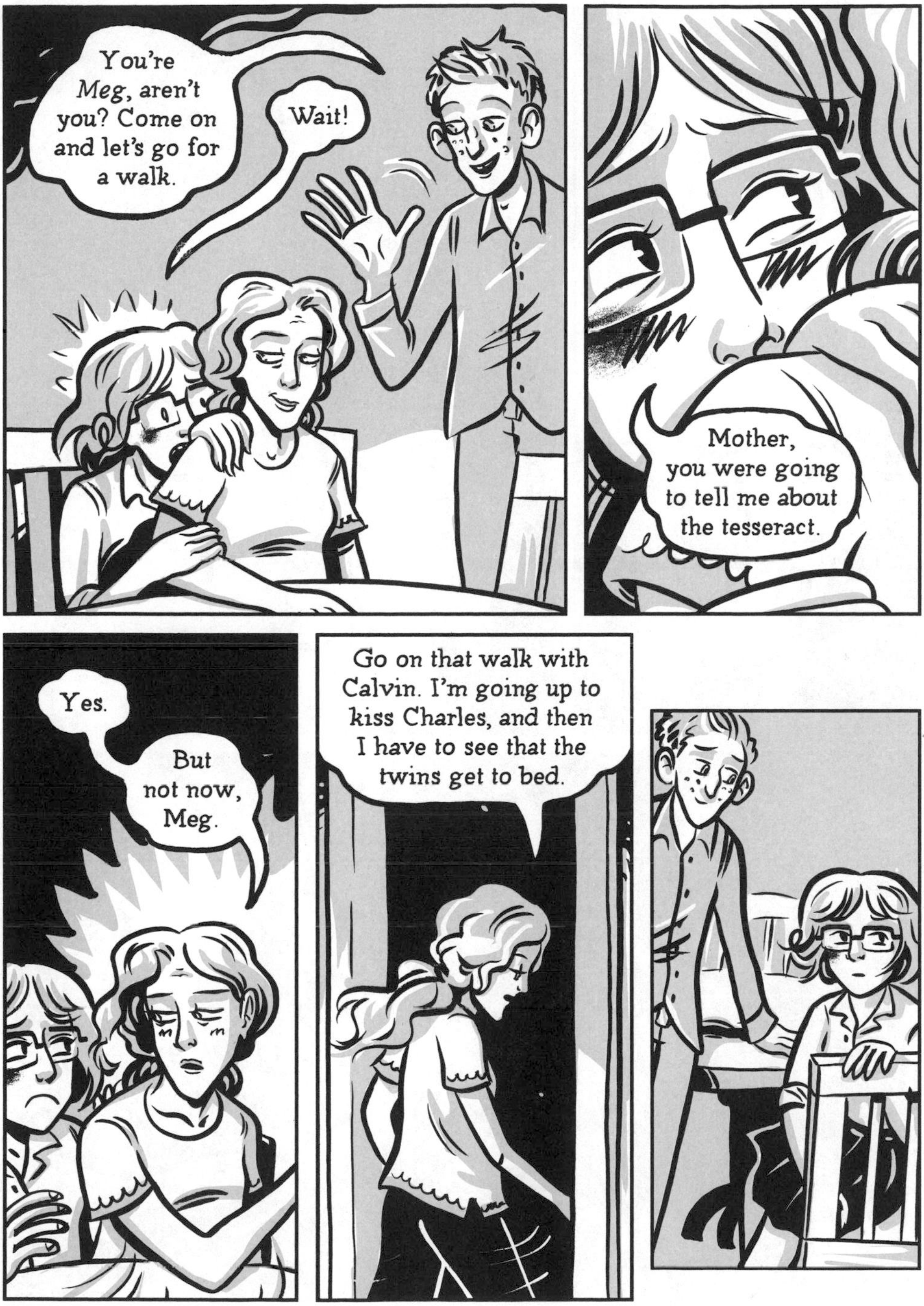
You're *Meg*, aren't you? Come on and let's go for a walk.
Wait!
Mother, you were going to tell me about the tesseract.
Yes.
But not now, Meg.
Go on that walk with Calvin. I'm going up to kiss Charles, and then I have to see that the twins get to bed.

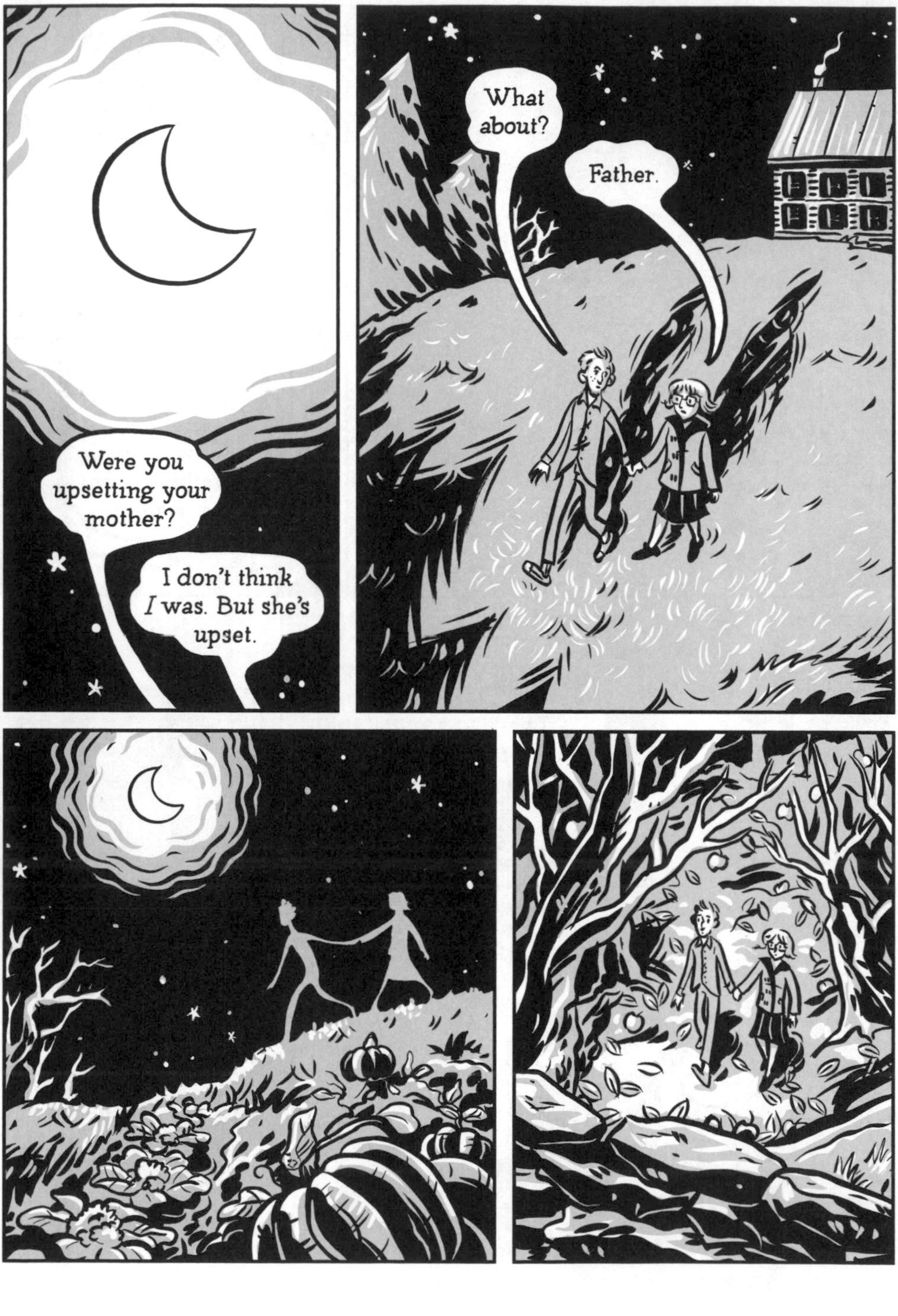
Were you upsetting your mother?
I don't think *I* was. But she's upset.
What about?
Father.

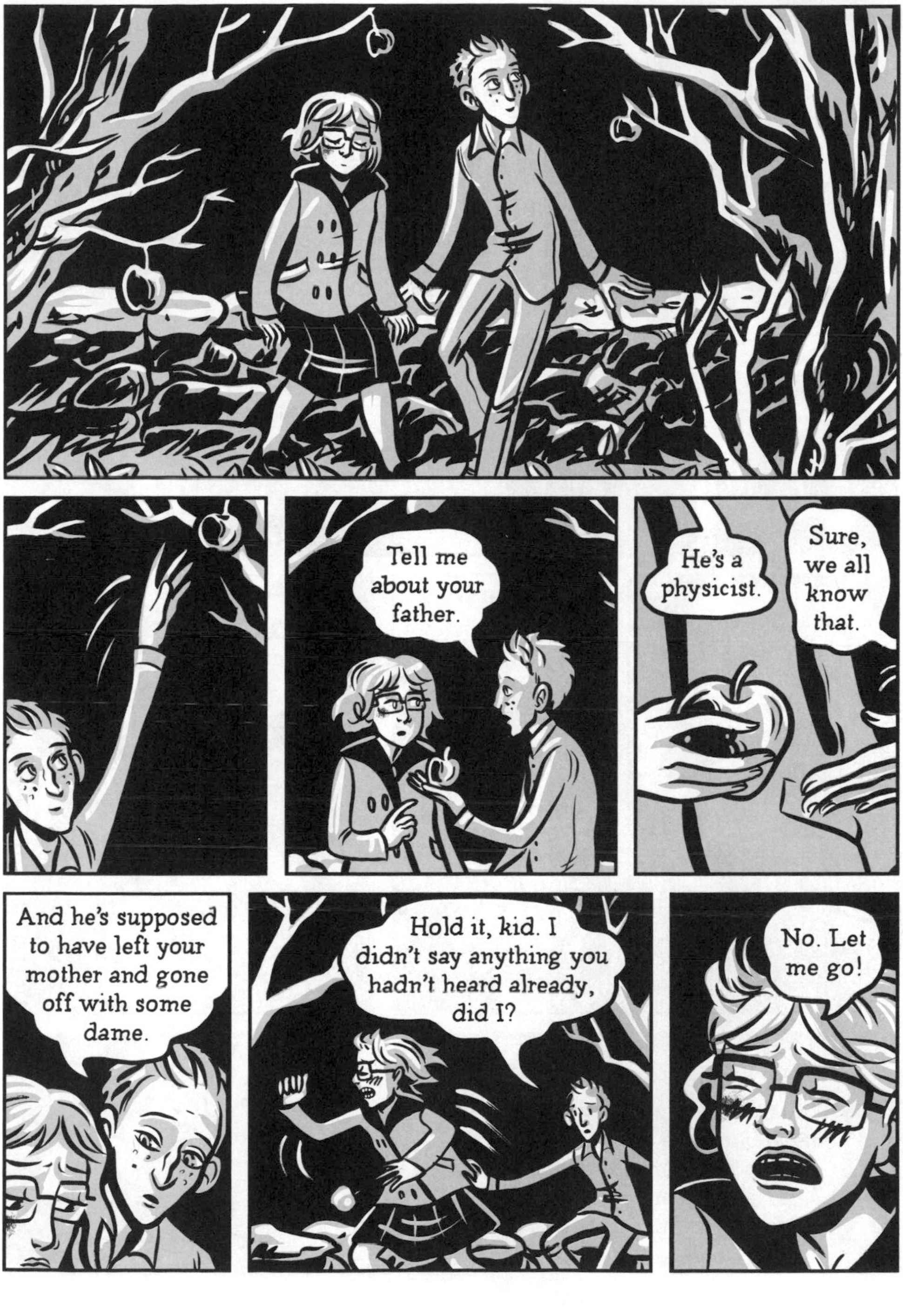
Tell me about your father.
He's a physicist.
Sure, we all know that.
And he's supposed to have left your mother and gone off with some dame.
Hold it, kid. I didn't say anything you hadn't heard already, did I?
No. Let me go!

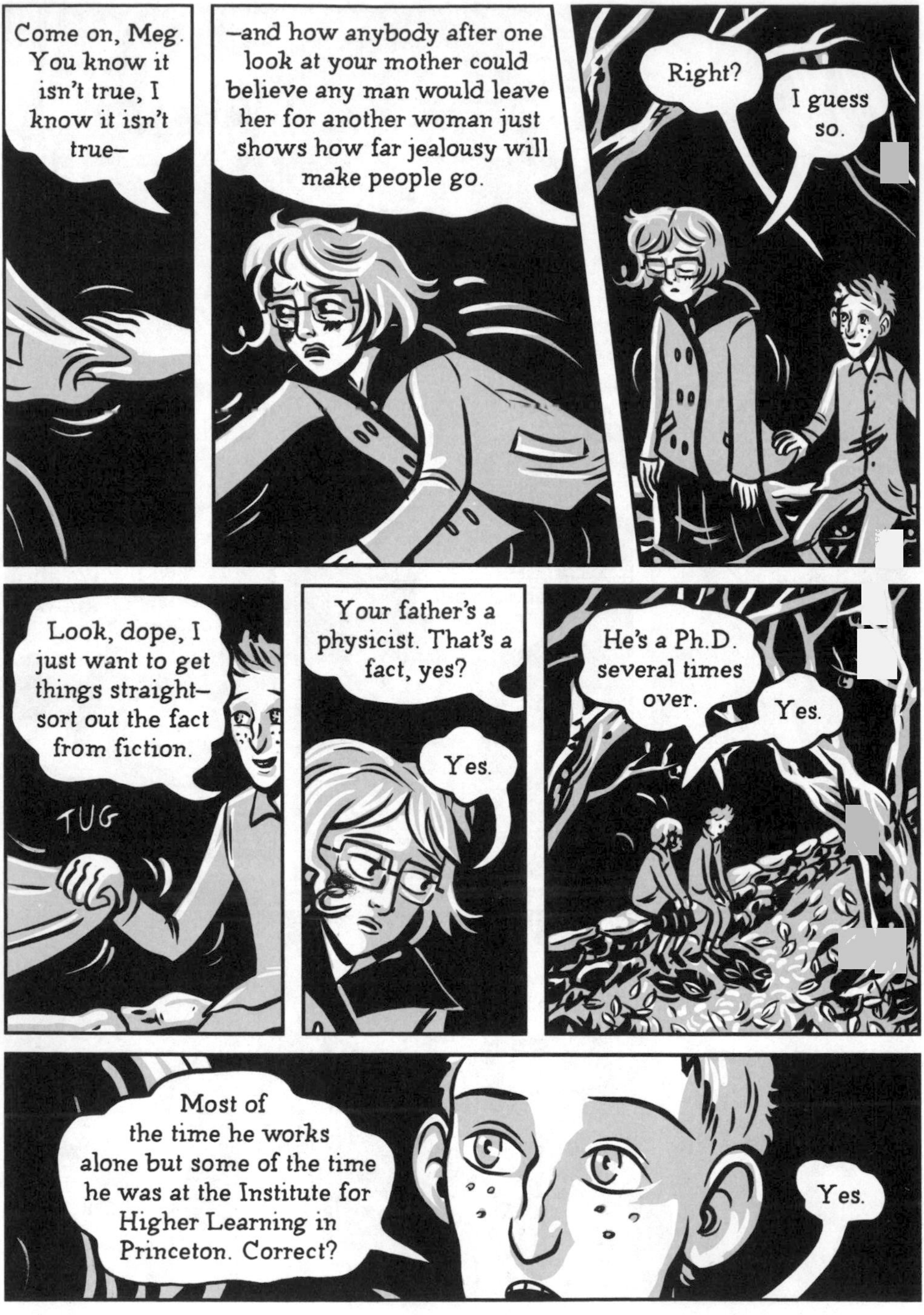
Come on, Meg. You know it isn't true, I know it isn't true–
–and how anybody after one look at your mother could believe any man would leave her for another woman just shows how far jealousy will make people go.
Right?
I guess so.
Look, dope, I just want to get things straight– sort out the fact from fiction.
TUG
Your father's a physicist. That's a fact, yes?
Yes.
He's a Ph.D. several times over.
Yes.
Most of the time he works alone but some of the time he was at the Institute for Higher Learning in Princeton. Correct?
Yes.

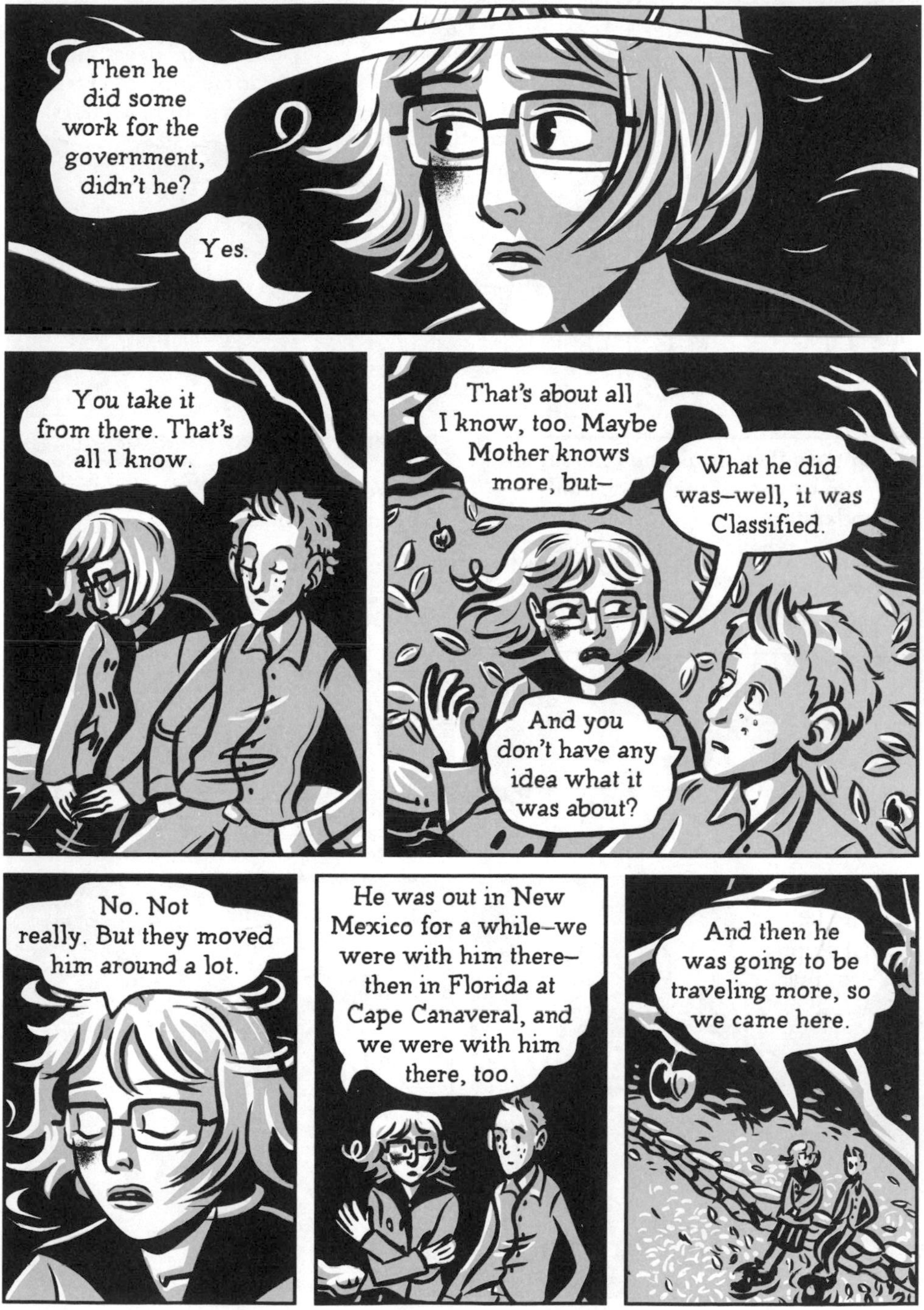
Then he did some work for the government, didn't he?
Yes.
You take it from there. That's all I know.
That's about all I know, too. Maybe Mother knows more, but–
What he did was–well, it was Classified.
And you don't have any idea what it was about?
No. Not really. But they moved him around a lot.
He was out in New Mexico for a while–we were with him there–then in Florida at Cape Canaveral, and we were with him there, too.
And then he was going to be traveling more, so we came here.

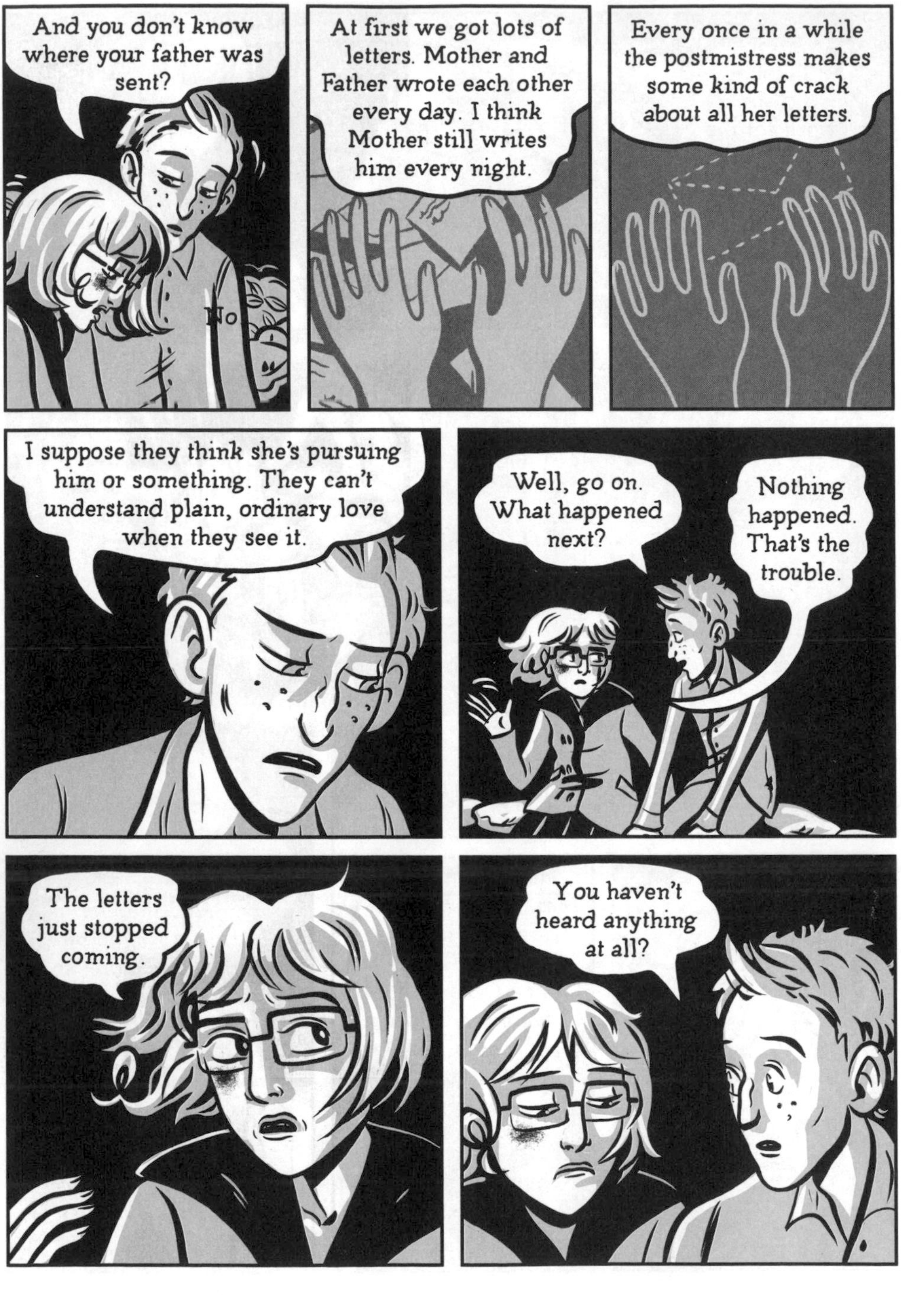
And you don't know where your father was sent?
At first we got lots of letters. Mother and Father wrote each other every day. I think Mother still writes him every night.
Every once in a while the postmistress makes some kind of crack about all her letters.
I suppose they think she's pursuing him or something. They can't understand plain, ordinary love when they see it.
Well, go on. What happened next?
Nothing happened. That's the trouble.
The letters just stopped coming.
You haven't heard anything at all?

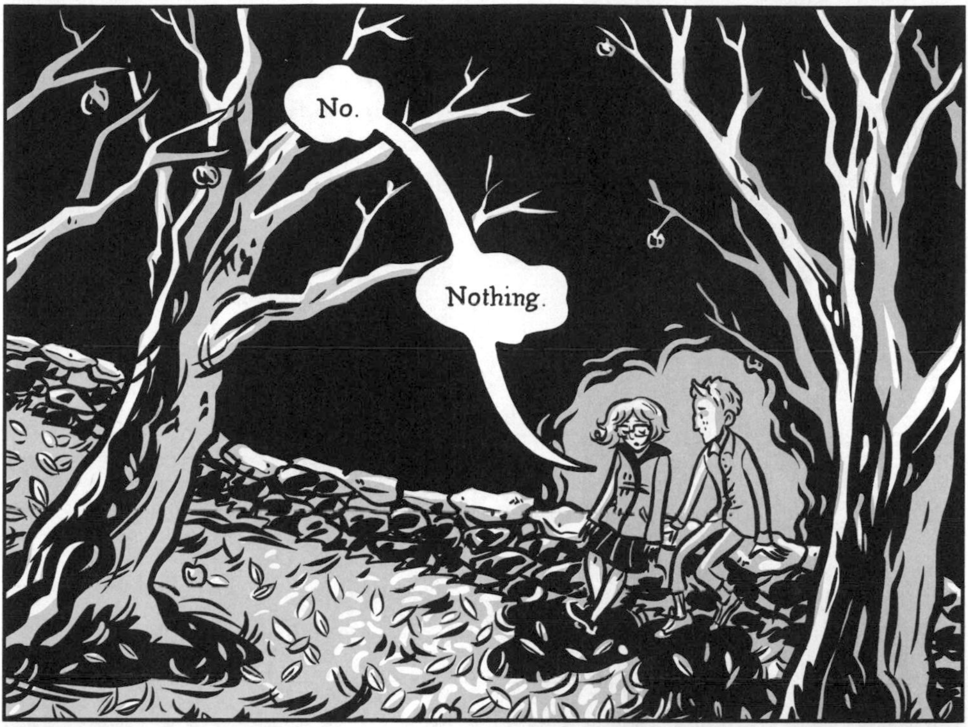
No.
Nothing.

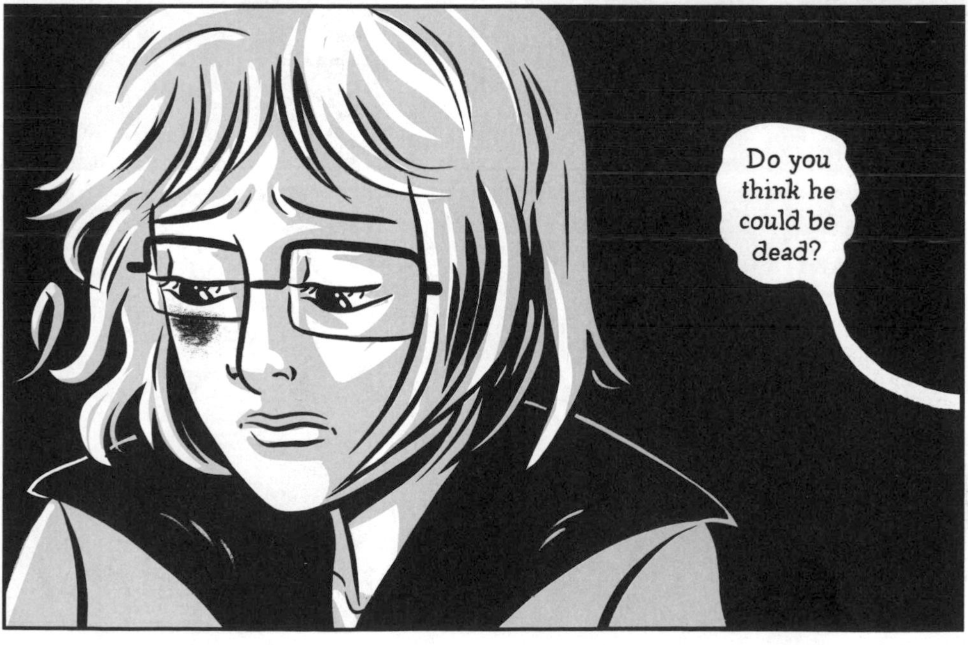
Do you think he could be dead?

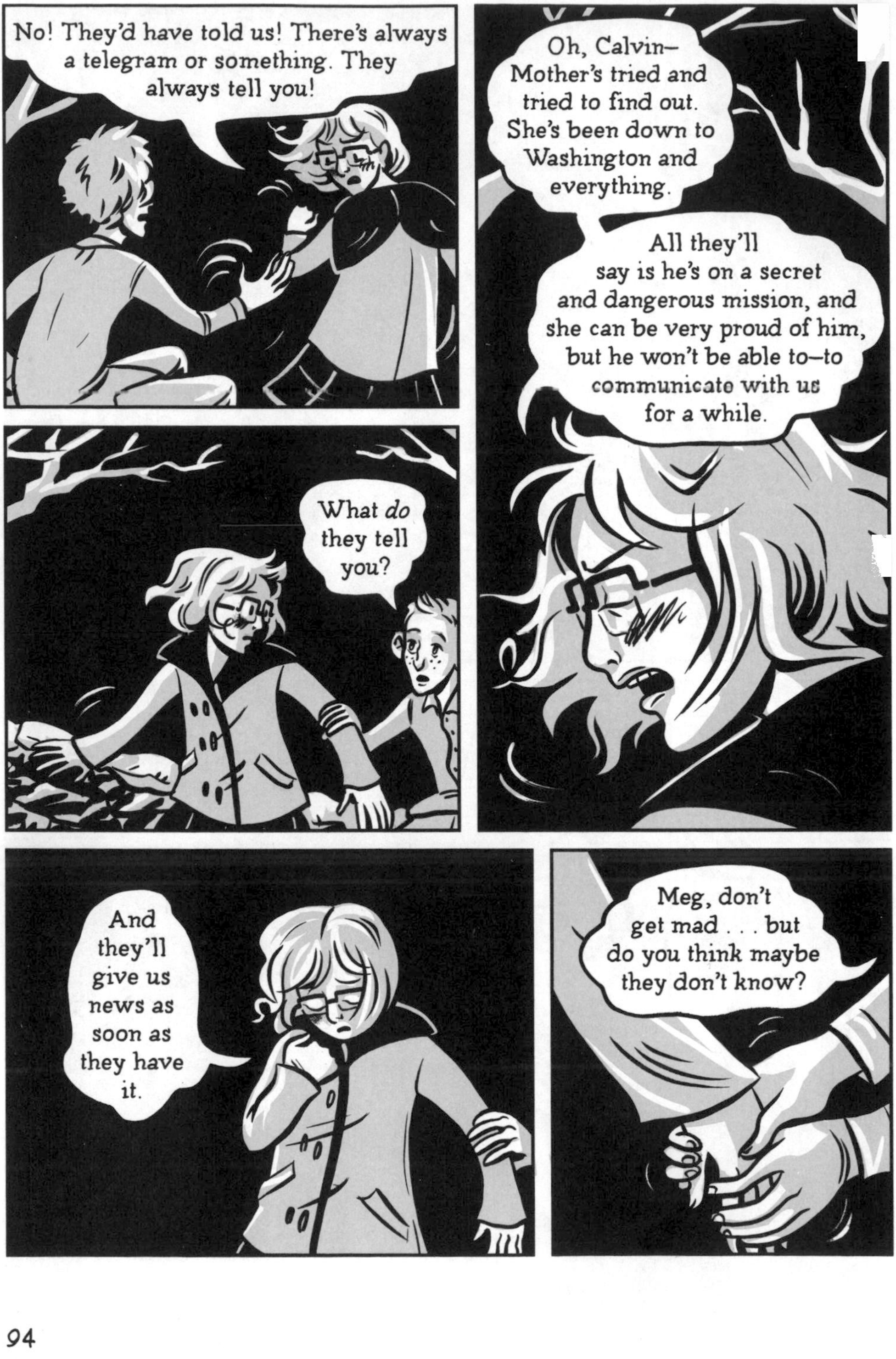
No! They'd have told us! There's always a telegram or something. They always tell you!
Oh, Calvin– Mother's tried and tried to find out. She's been down to Washington and everything.
All they'll say is he's on a secret and dangerous mission, and she can be very proud of him, but he won't be able to–to communicate with us for a while.
What *do* they tell you?
And they'll give us news as soon as they have it.
Meg, don't get mad . . . but do you think maybe they don't know?

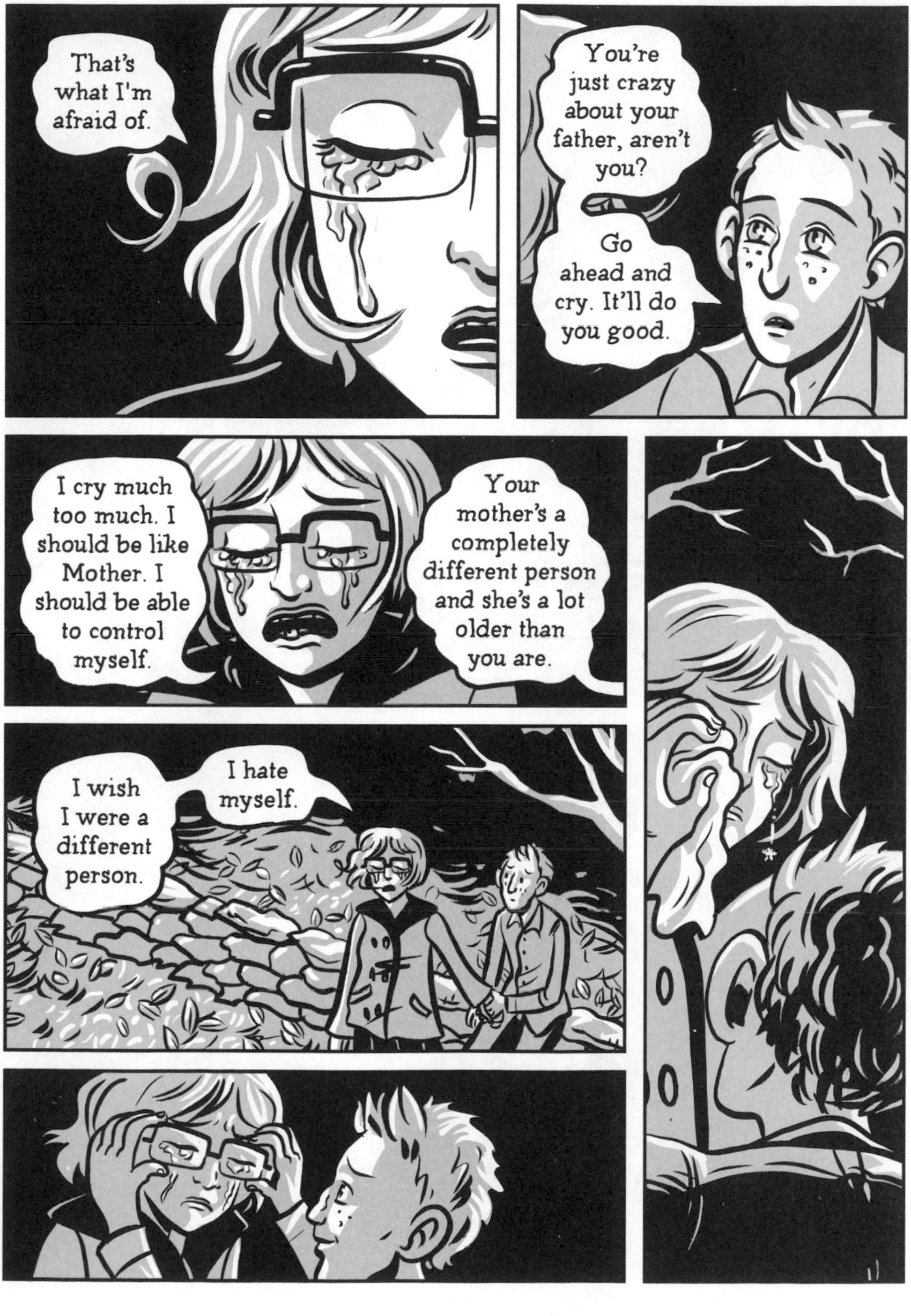

That's what I'm afraid of.
You're just crazy about your father, aren't you?
Go ahead and cry. It'll do you good.
I cry much too much. I should be like Mother. I should be able to control myself.
Your mother's a completely different person and she's a lot older than you are.
I hate myself.
I wish I were a different person.

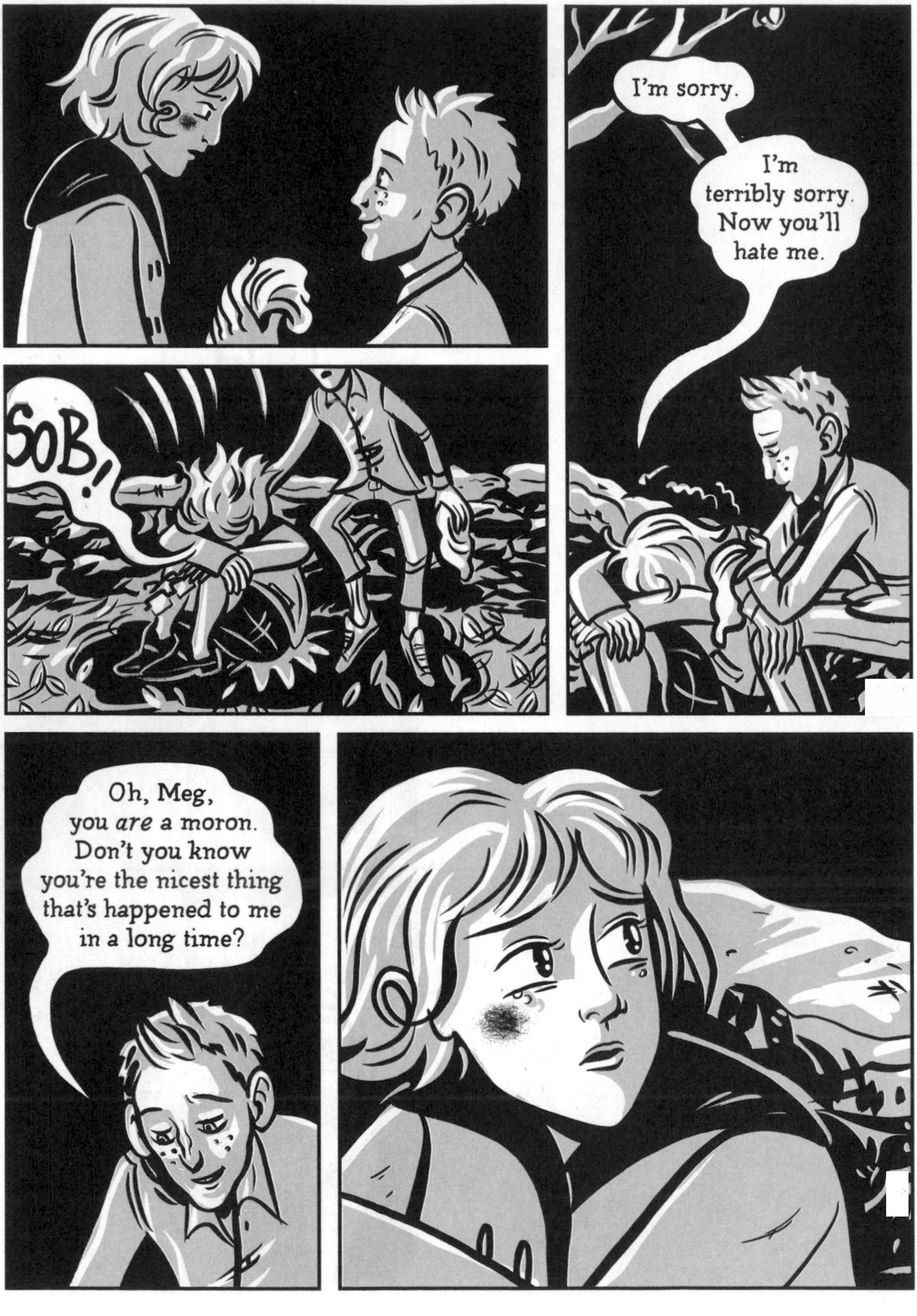
I'm sorry.
I'm terribly sorry. Now you'll hate me.
SOB!
Oh, Meg, you *are* a moron. Don't you know you're the nicest thing that's happened to me in a long time?

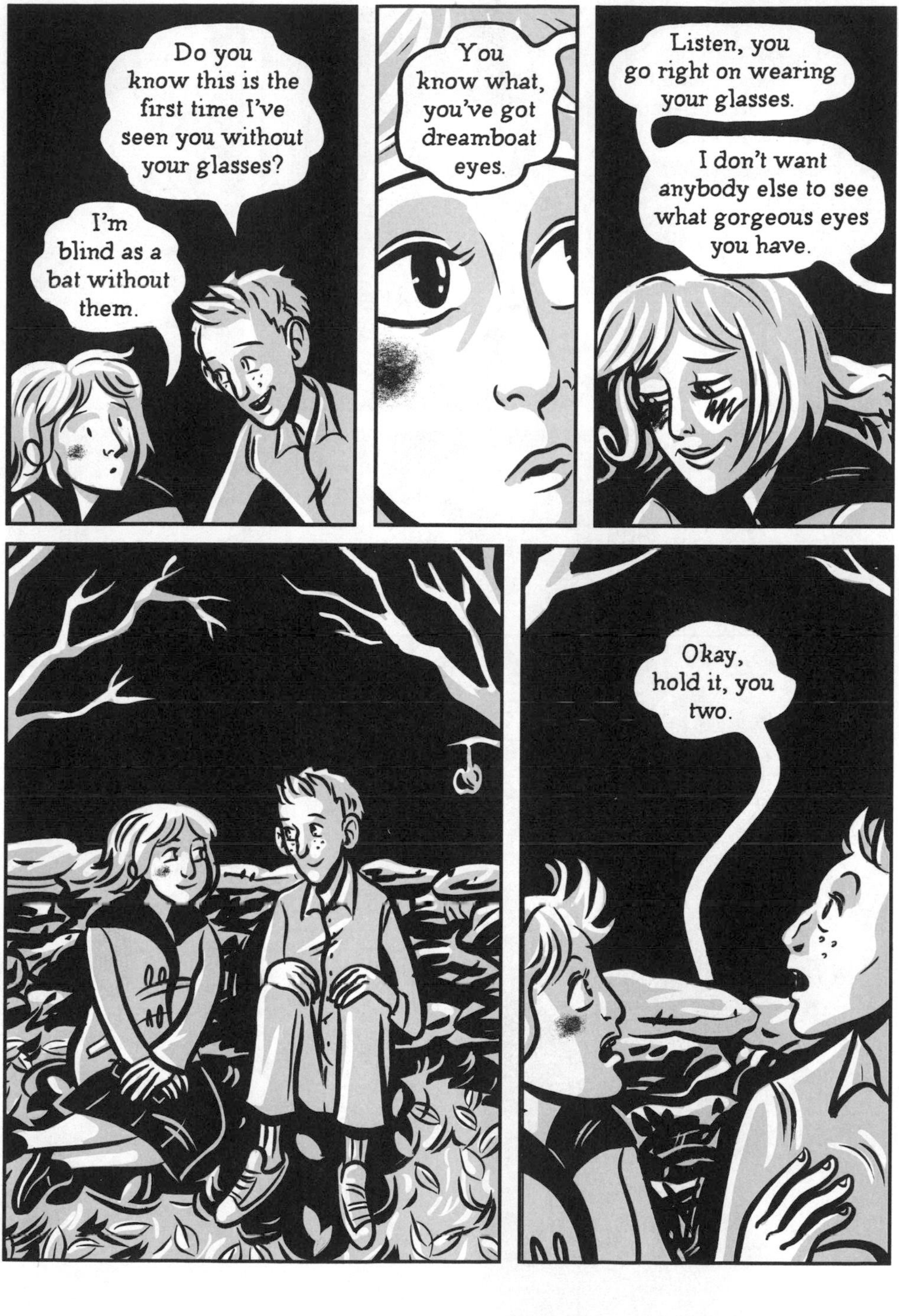
Do you know this is the first time I've seen you without your glasses?
I'm blind as a bat without them.
You know what, you've got dreamboat eyes.
Listen, you go right on wearing your glasses.
I don't want anybody else to see what gorgeous eyes you have.
Okay, hold it, you two.

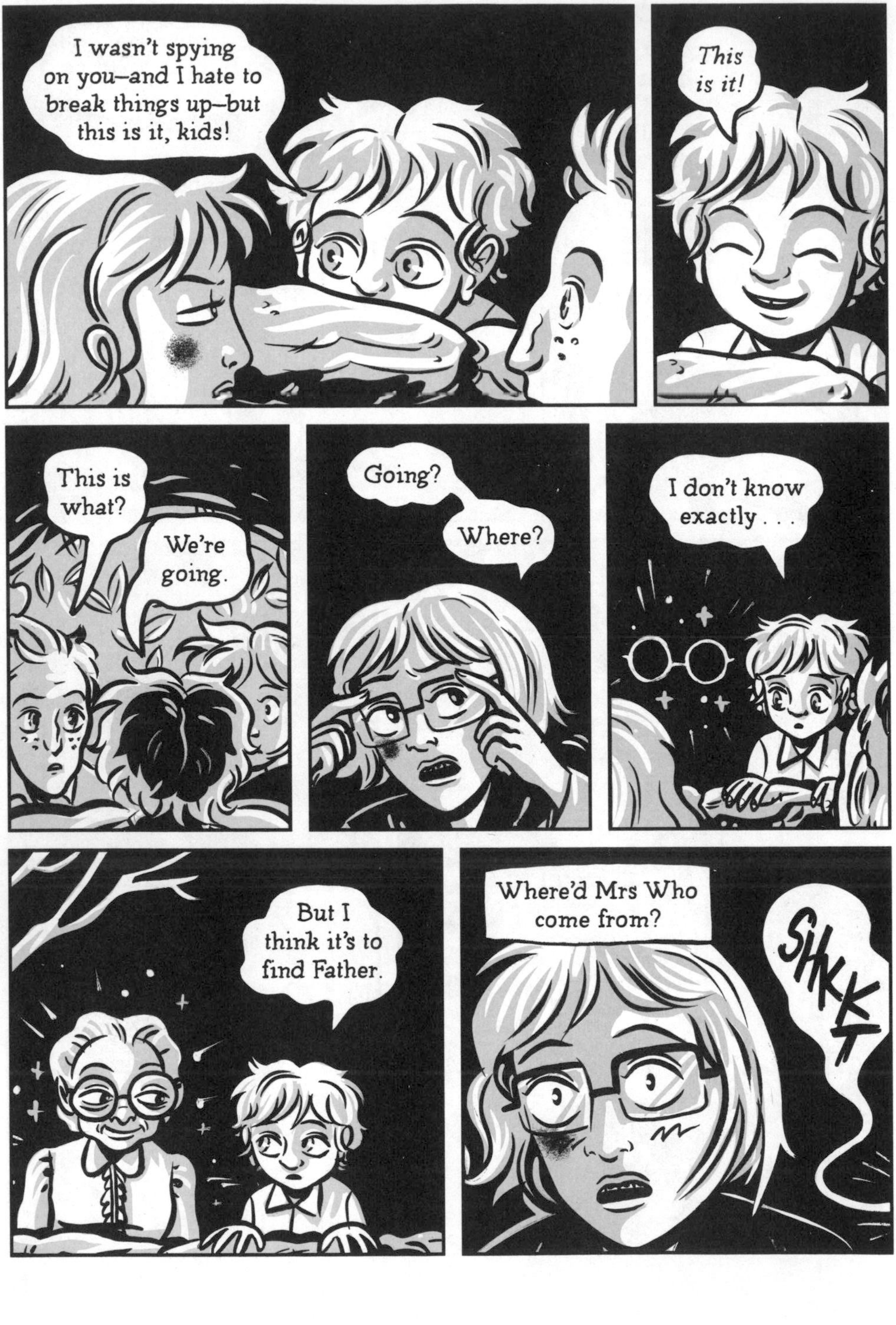
I wasn't spying on you—and I hate to break things up—but this is it, kids!
This is it!
This is what?
We're going.
Going?
Where?
I don't know exactly . . .
But I think it's to find Father.
Where'd Mrs Who come from?
SHKKT

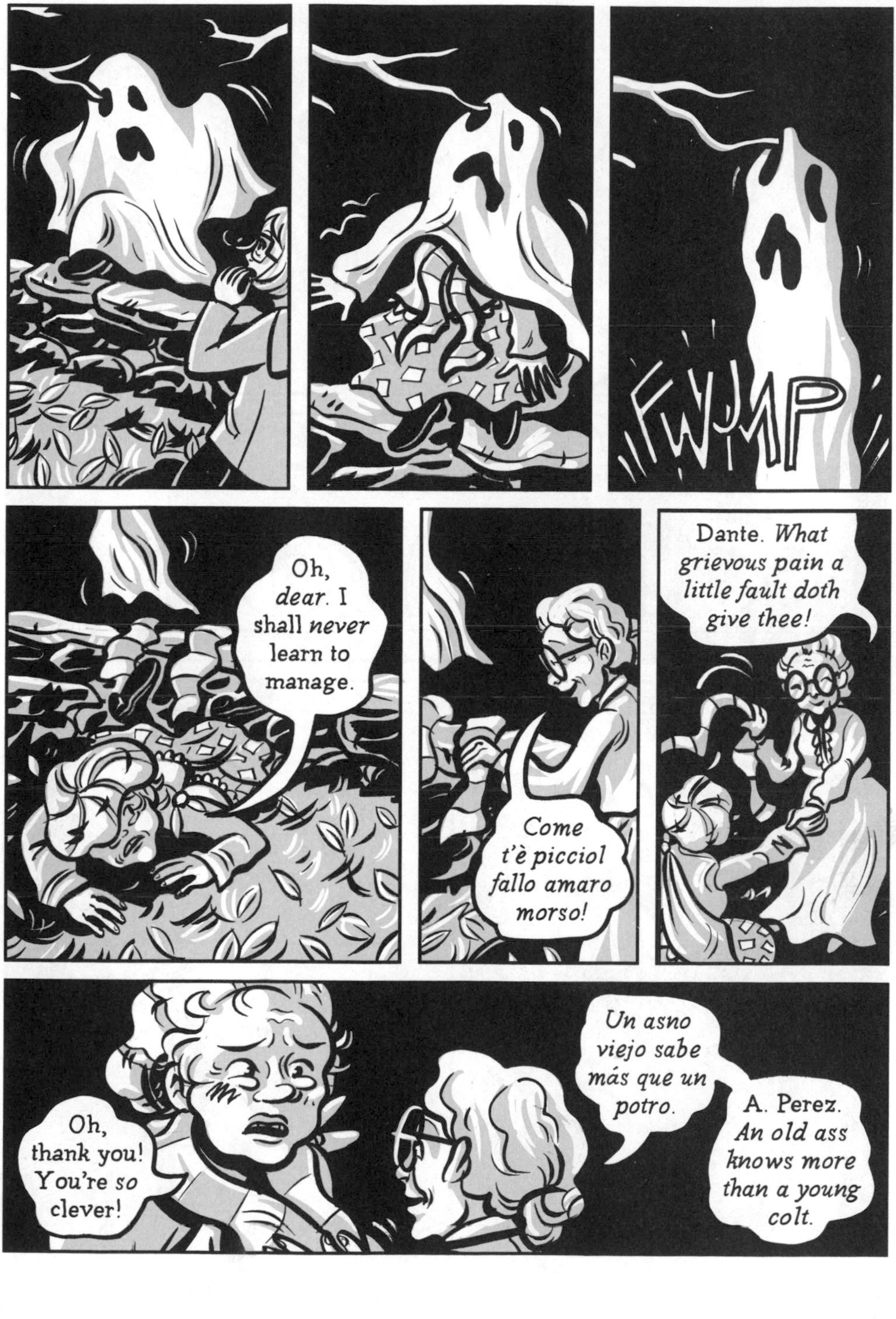
FWUMP
Oh, *dear*. I shall *never* learn to manage.
Come t'è picciol fallo amaro morso!
Dante. *What grievous pain a little fault doth give thee!*
Oh, thank you! You're so clever!
Un asno viejo sabe más que un potro.
A. Perez. *An old ass knows more than a young colt.*

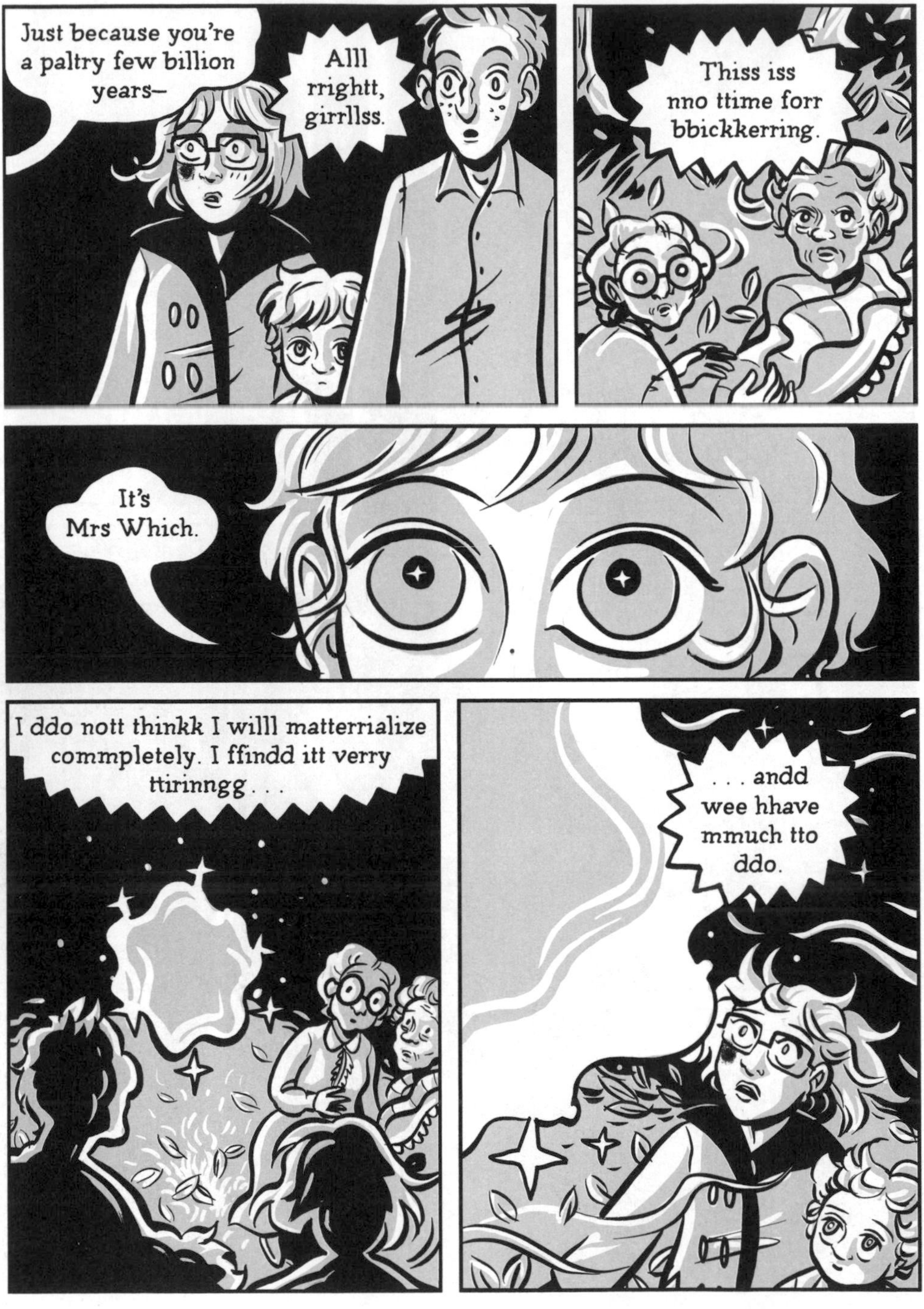
Just because you're a paltry few billion years–
Alll rrightt, girrllss.
Thiss iss nno ttime forr bbickkerring.
It's Mrs Which.
I ddo nott thinkk I willl matterrialize commpletely. I ffindd itt verry ttirinngg . . .
. . . andd wee hhave mmuch tto ddo.

4

The Black Thing

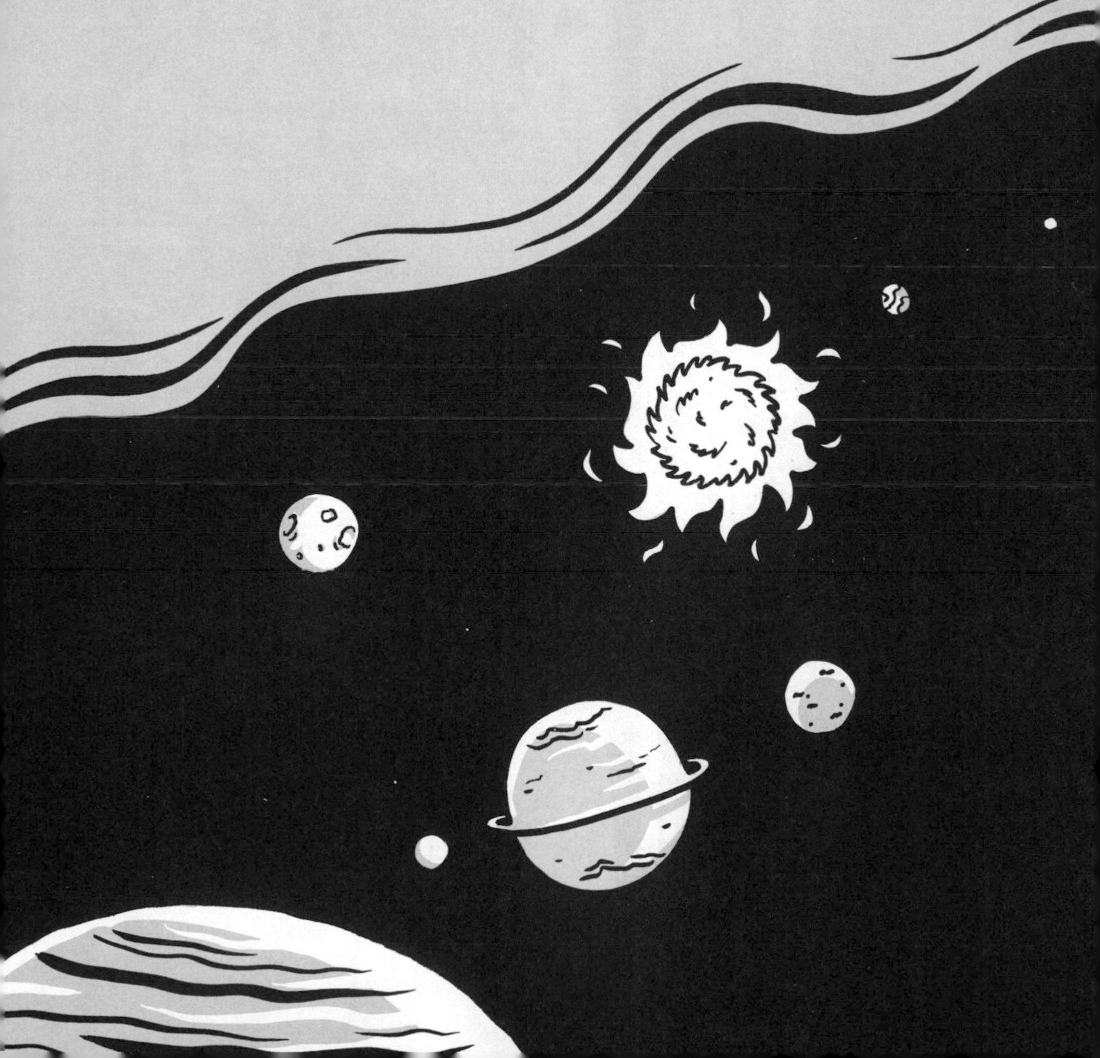

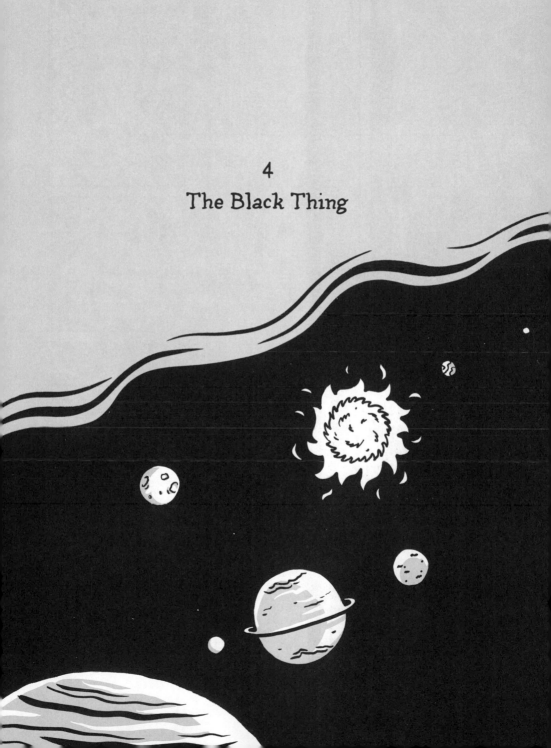

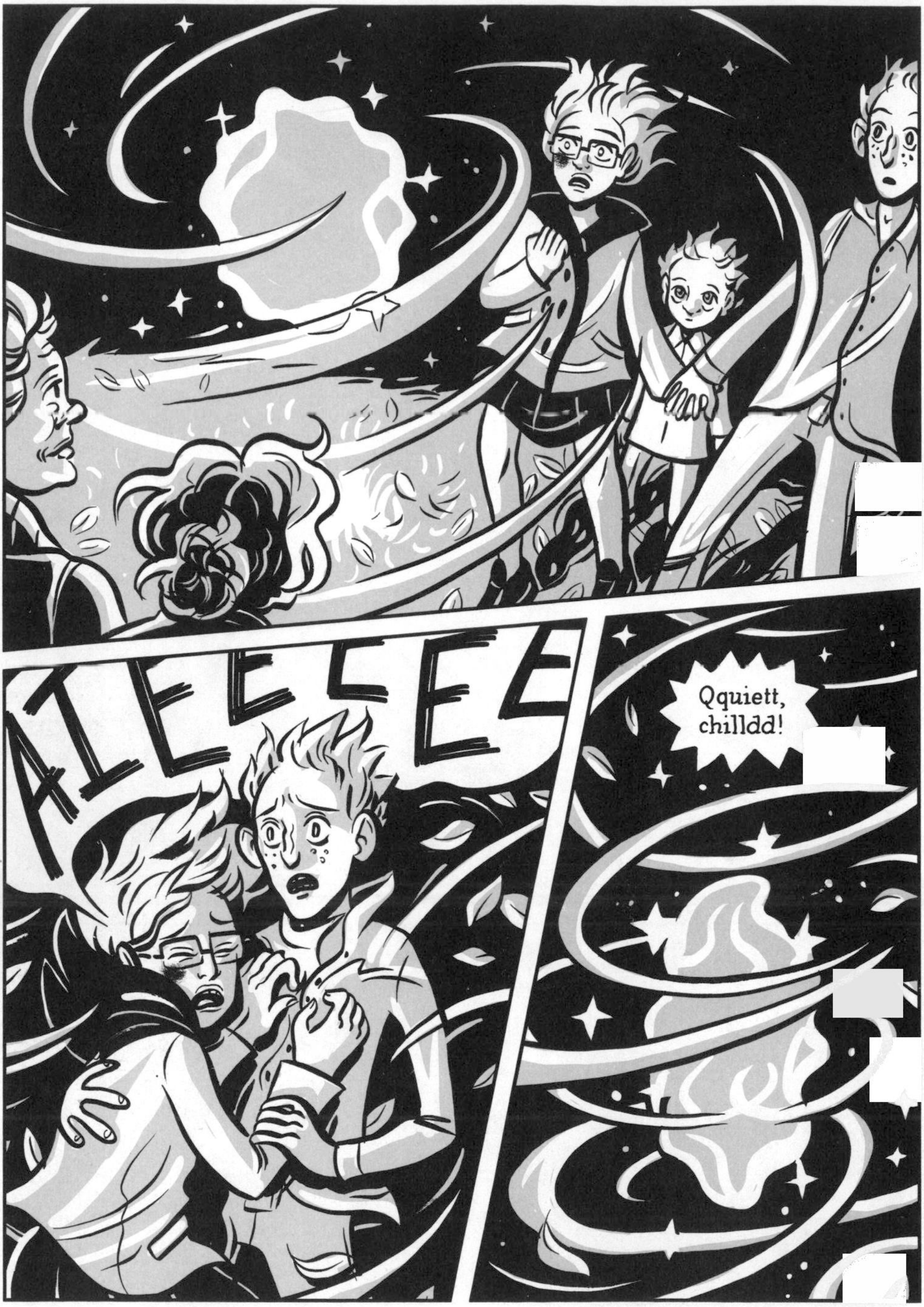
AIEEEE
Qquiett, chilldd!

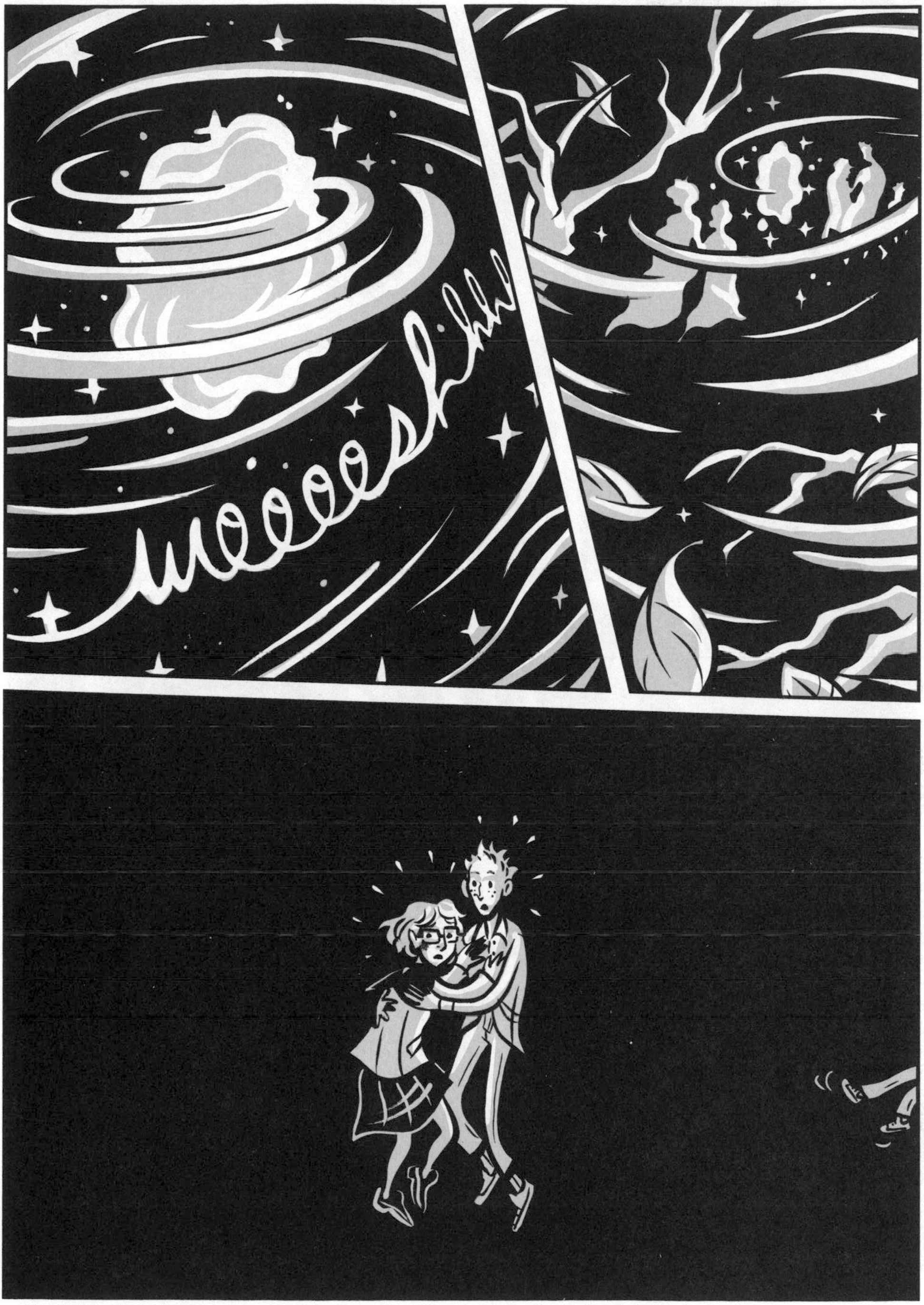
wooooshhhh

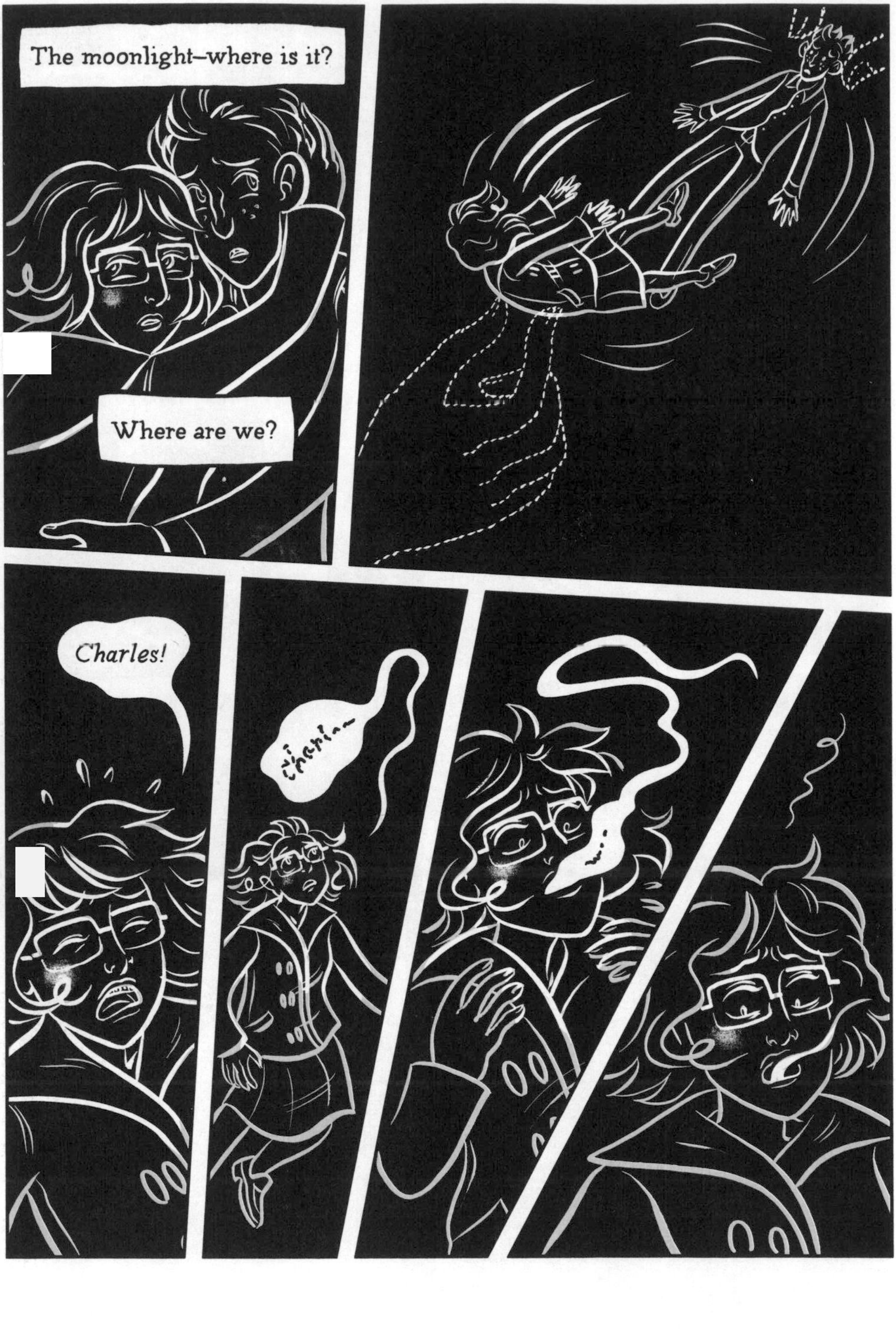
The moonlight—where is it?
Where are we?
Charles!
Charl–

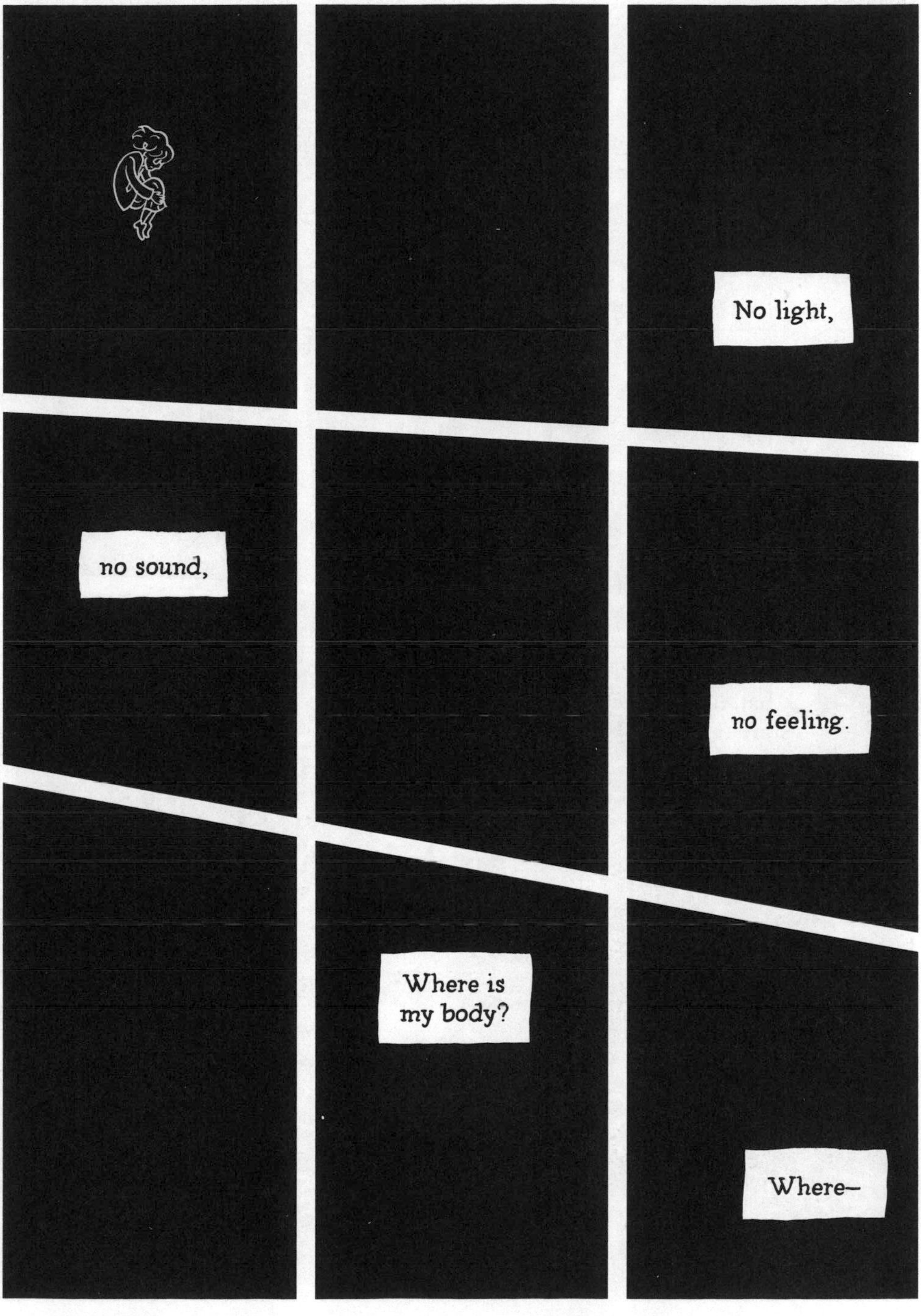
No light,
no sound,
no feeling.
Where is my body?
Where–

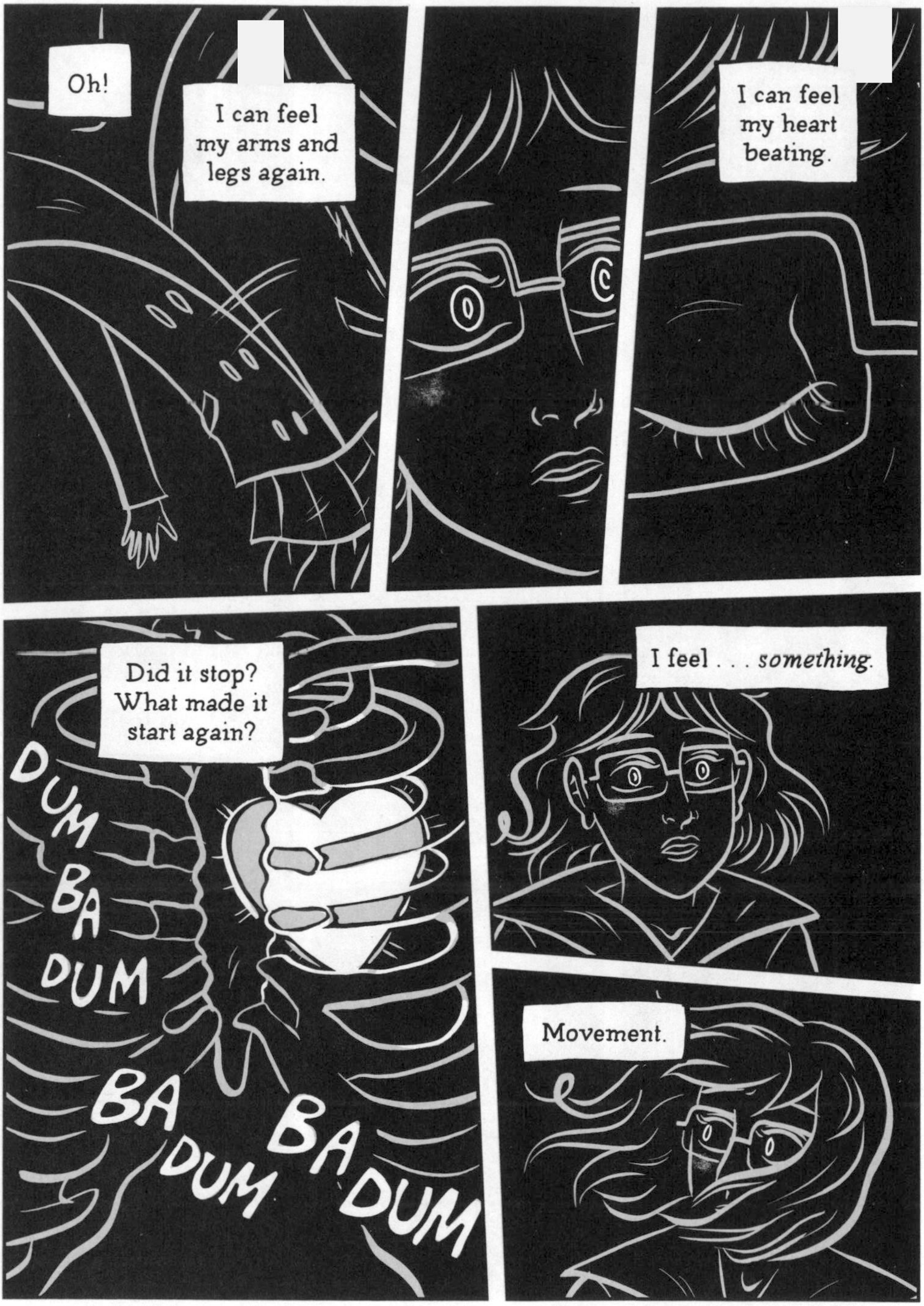
Oh!
I can feel my arms and legs again.
I can feel my heart beating.
Did it stop? What made it start again?
DUM BA DUM
BA DUM
BA DUM
I feel . . . *something.*
Movement.

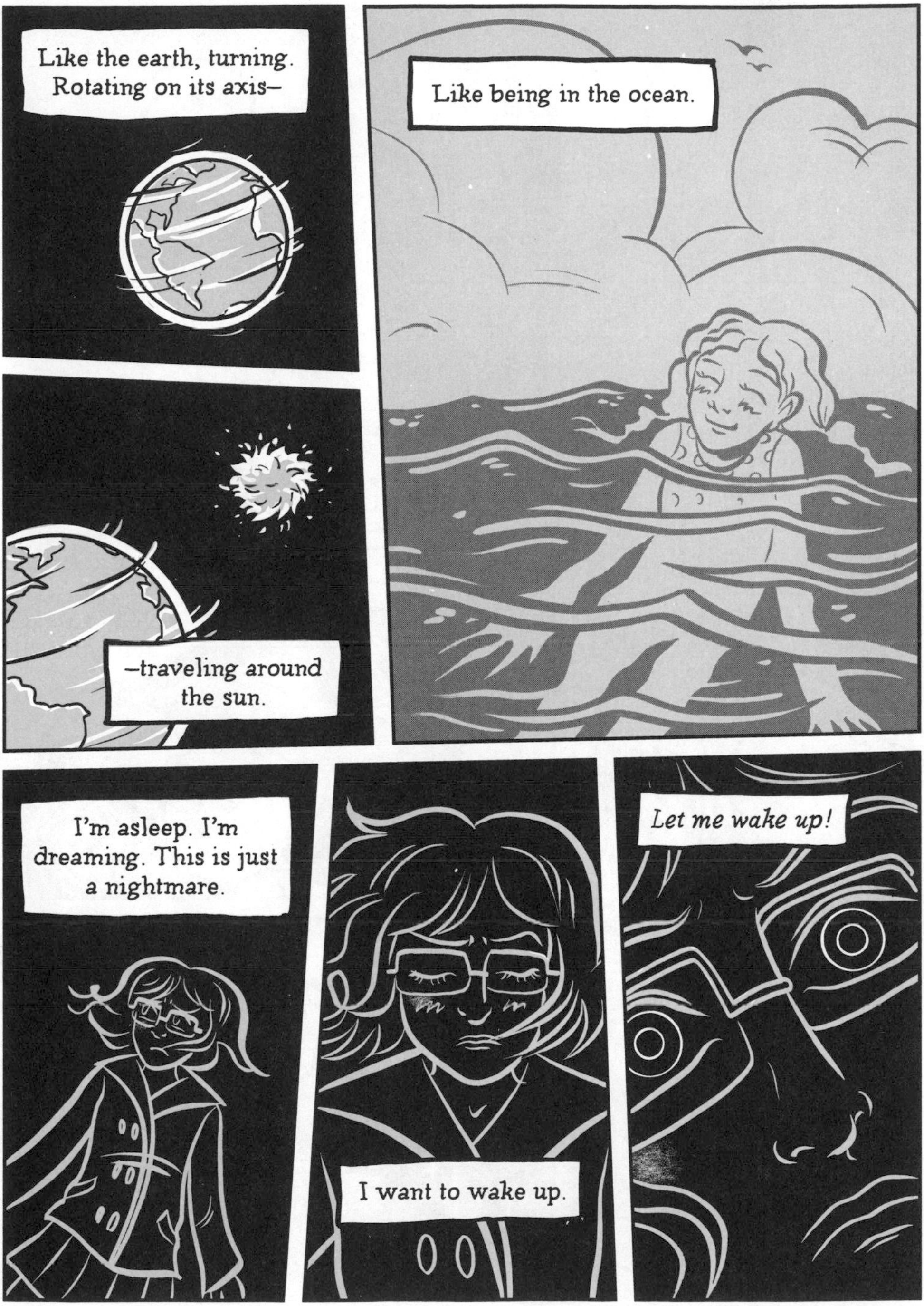
Like the earth, turning. Rotating on its axis–
Like being in the ocean.
–traveling around the sun.
I'm asleep. I'm dreaming. This is just a nightmare.
I want to wake up.
Let me wake up!

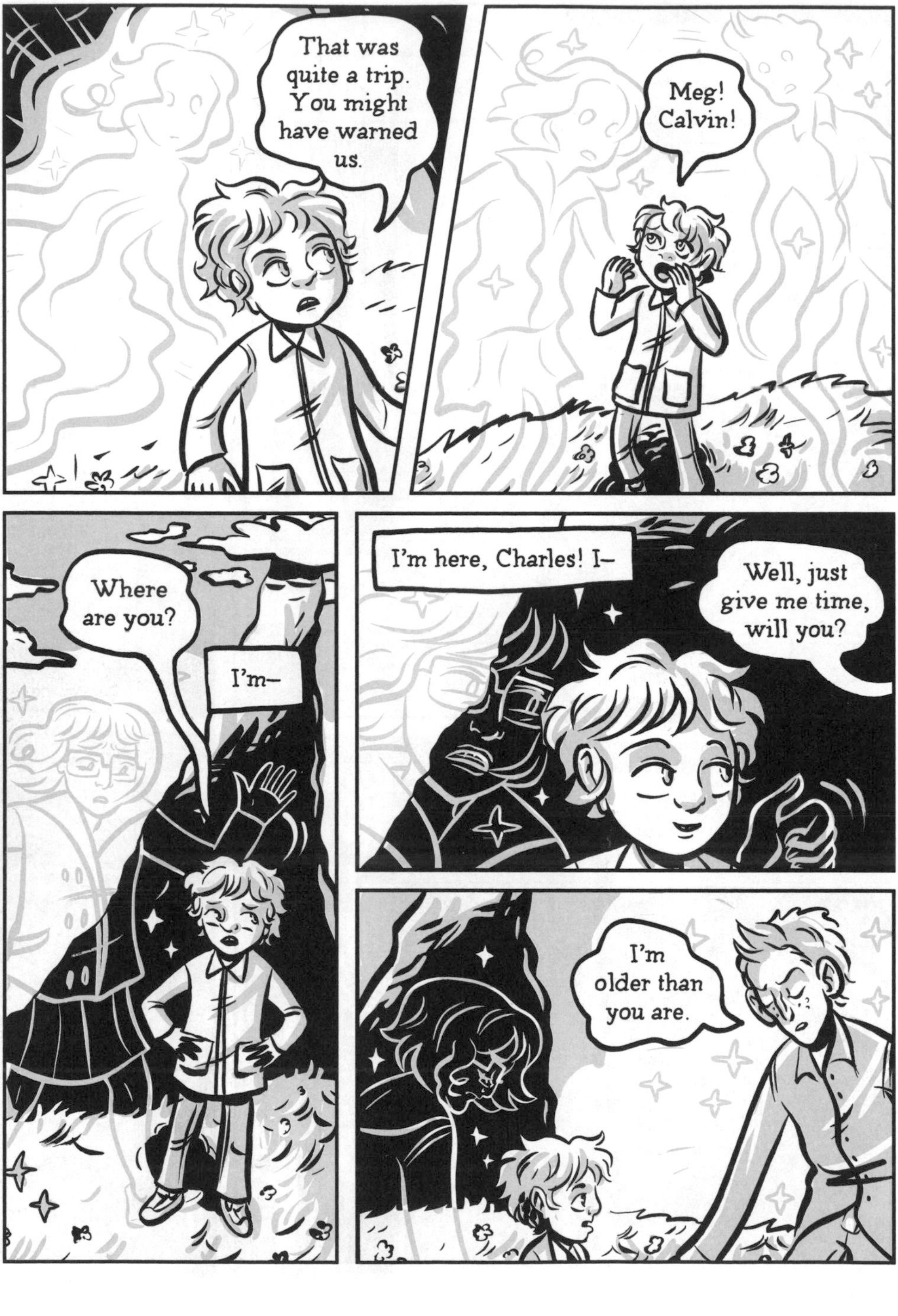
That was quite a trip. You might have warned us.
Meg! Calvin!
Where are you?
I'm—
I'm here, Charles! I—
Well, just give me time, will you?
I'm older than you are.

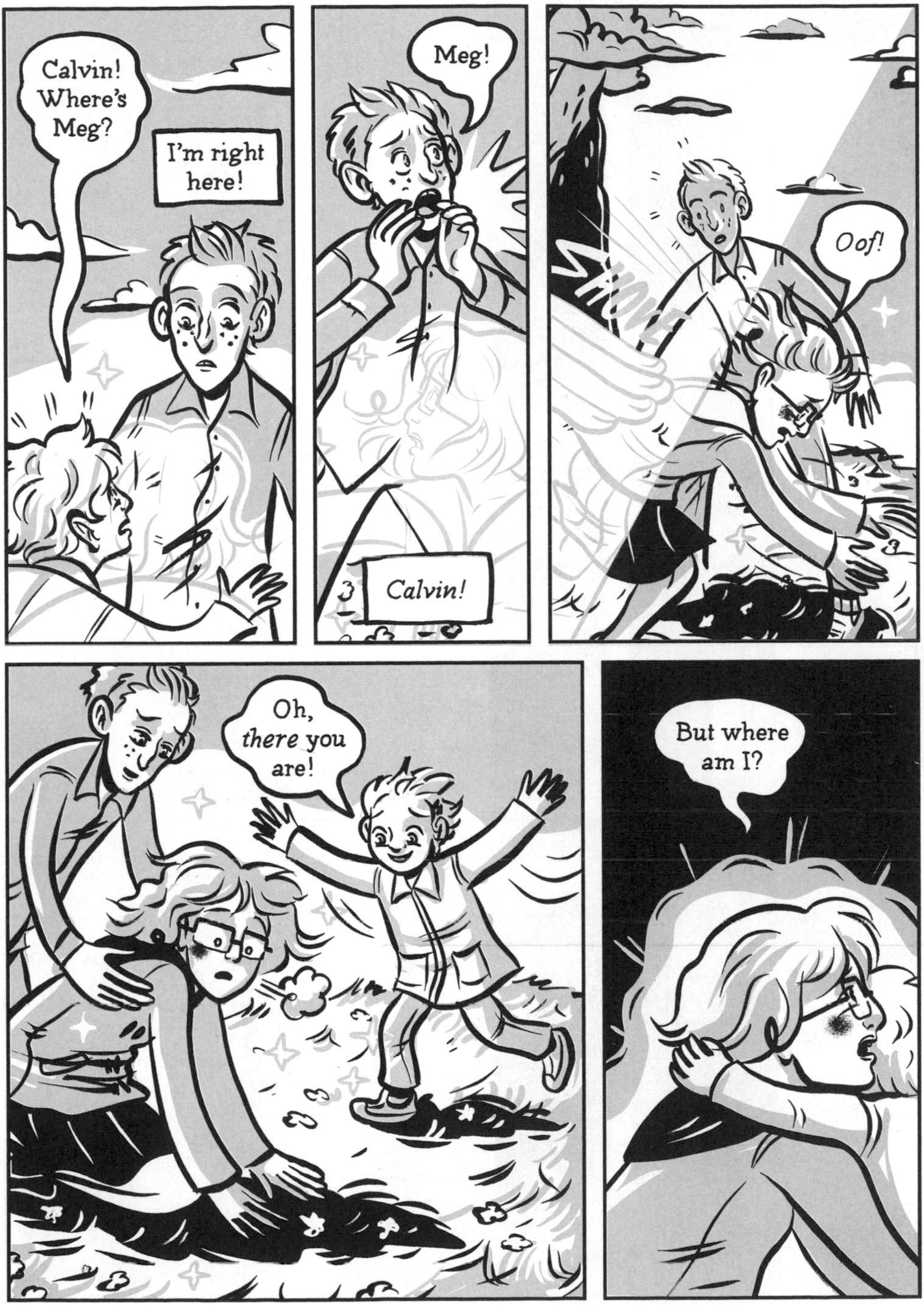
Calvin! Where's Meg?
I'm right here!
Meg!
Calvin!
SHOVE
Oof!
Oh, *there* you are!
But where am I?

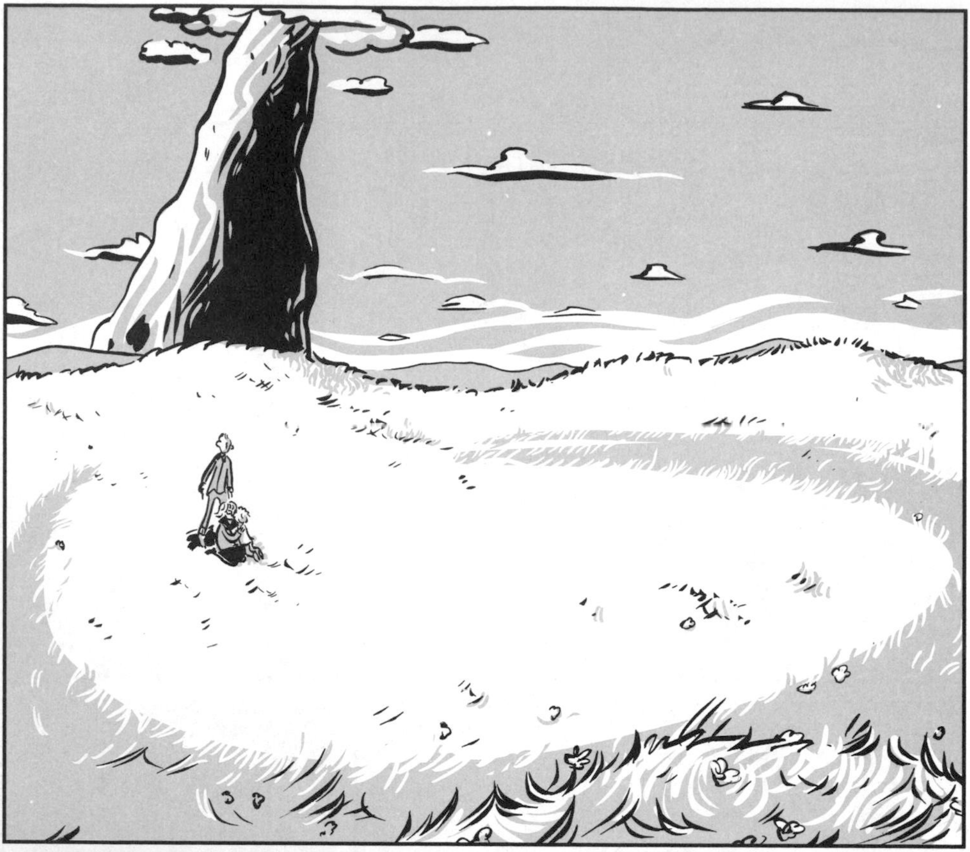

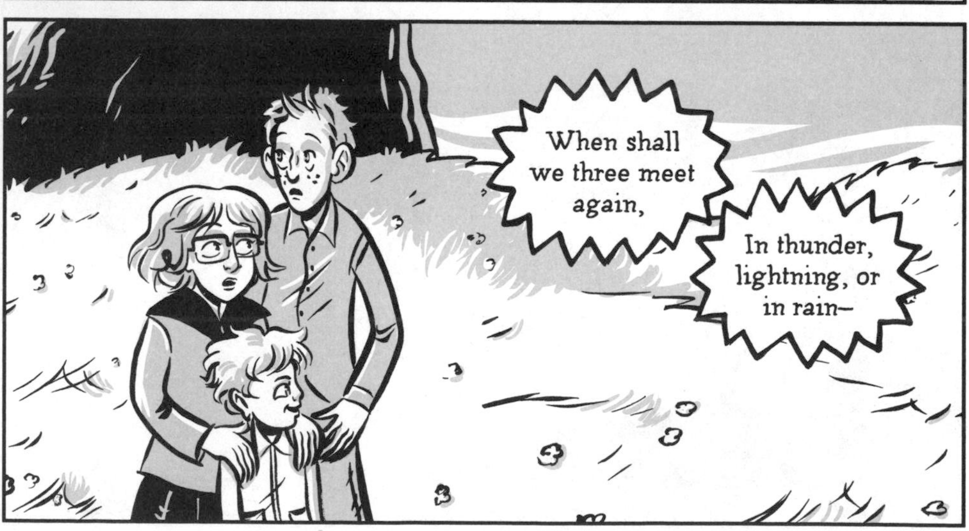
When shall we three meet again,
In thunder, lightning, or in rain–

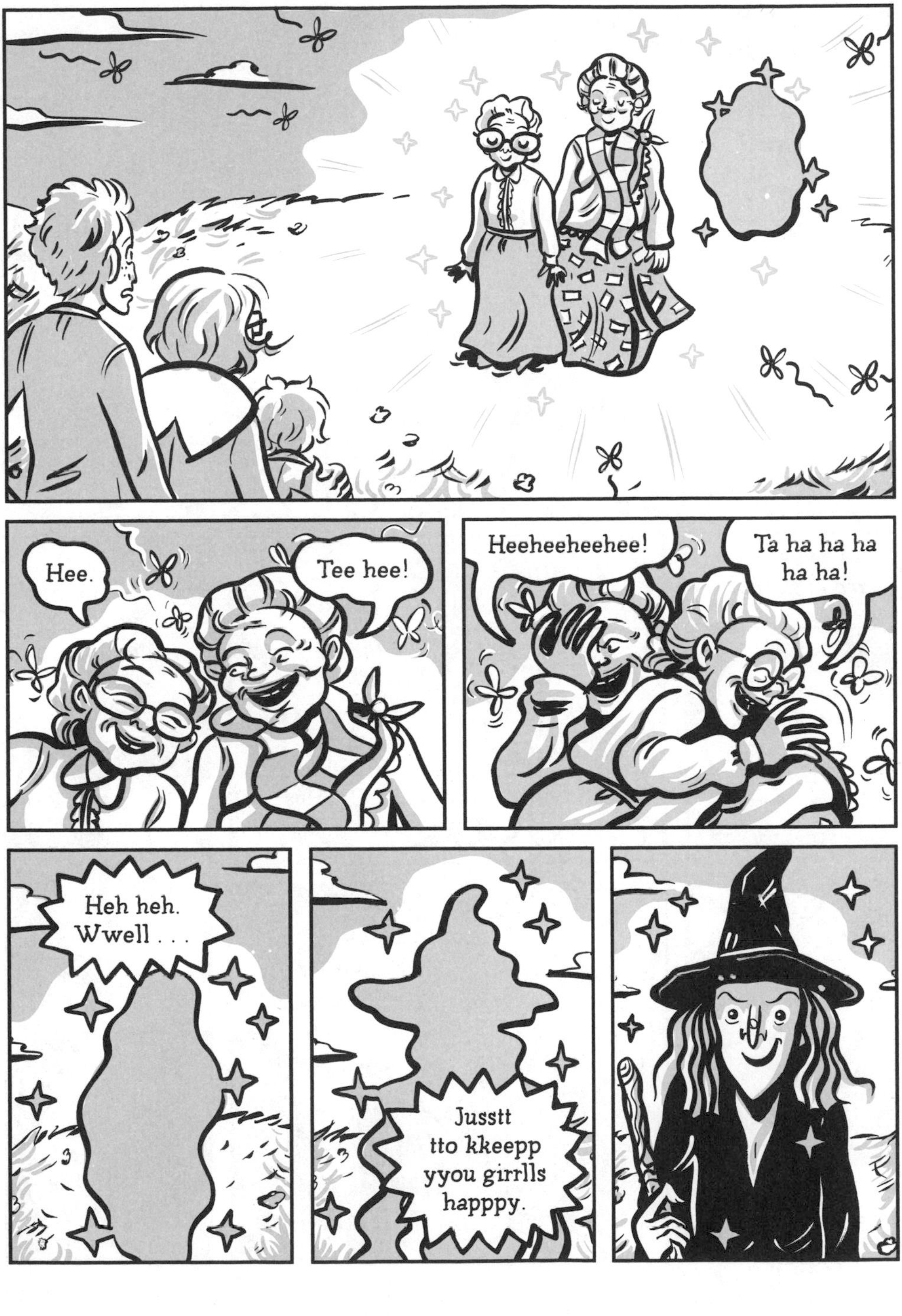
Hee.
Tee hee!
Heeheeheehee!
Ta ha ha ha ha ha!
Heh heh. Wwell . . .
Jusstt tto kkeepp yyou girrlls happpy.

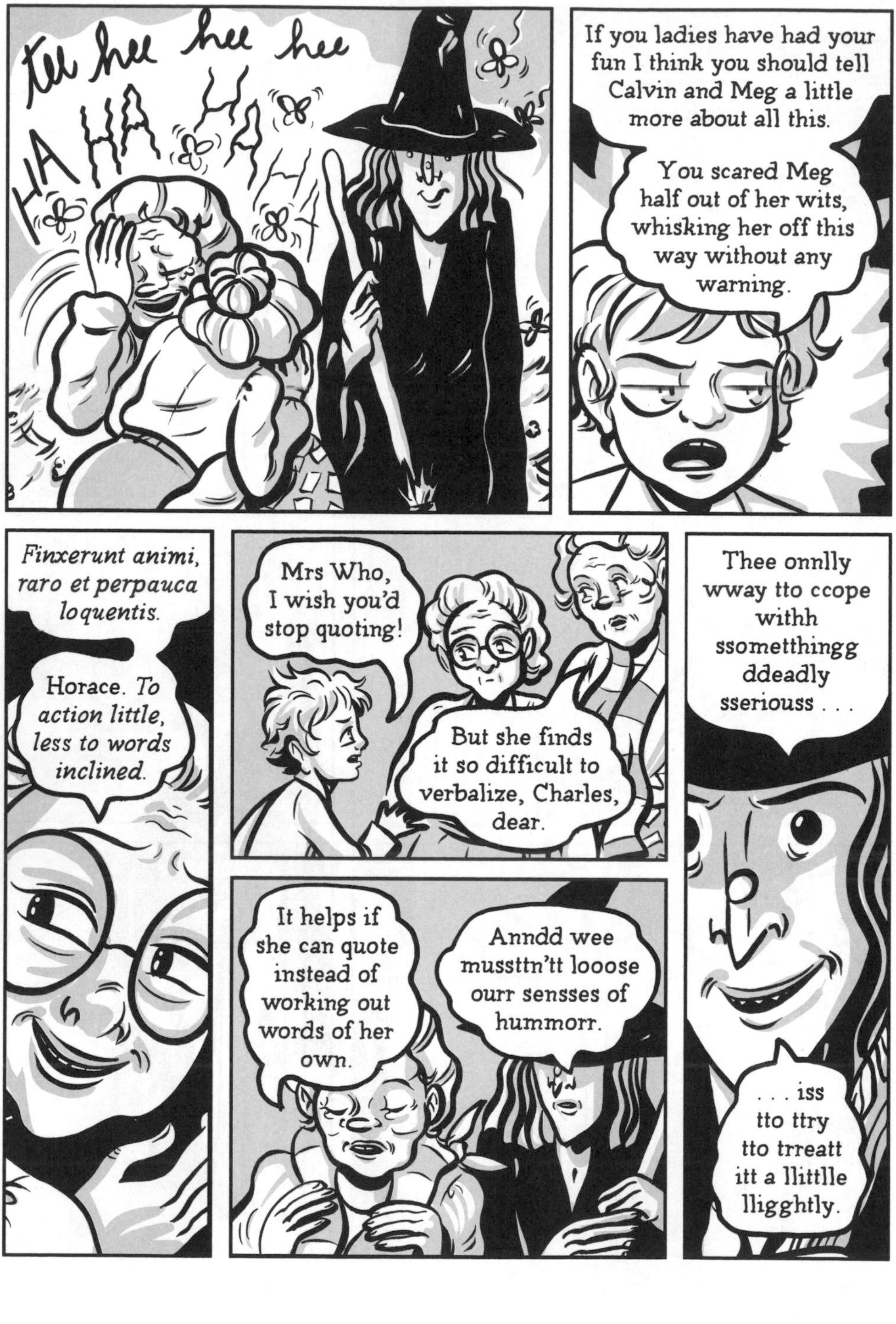
Tee hee hee hee
HA HA HA HA HA
If you ladies have had your fun I think you should tell Calvin and Meg a little more about all this.
You scared Meg half out of her wits, whisking her off this way without any warning.
Finxerunt animi, raro et perpauca loquentis.
Horace. *To action little, less to words inclined.*
Mrs Who, I wish you'd stop quoting!
But she finds it so difficult to verbalize, Charles, dear.
It helps if she can quote instead of working out words of her own.
Anndd wee mussttn'tt looose ourr sensses of hummorr.
Thee onnlly wway tto ccope withh ssomethingg ddeadly sseriouss . . .
. . . iss tto ttry tto trreatt itt a llittlle lligghtly.

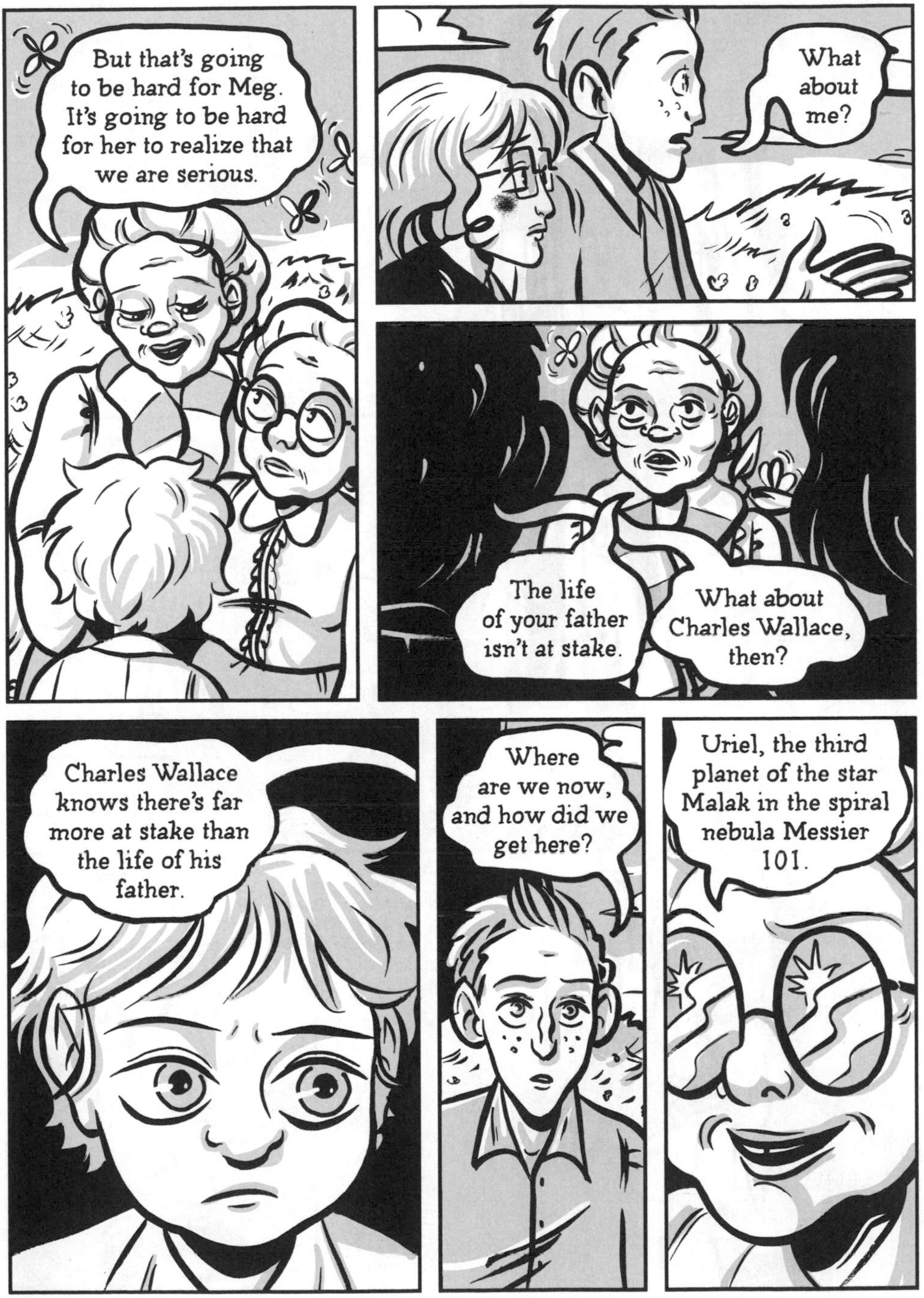
But that's going to be hard for Meg. It's going to be hard for her to realize that we are serious.
What about me?
The life of your father isn't at stake.
What about Charles Wallace, then?
Charles Wallace knows there's far more at stake than the life of his father.
Where are we now, and how did we get here?
Uriel, the third planet of the star Malak in the spiral nebula Messier 101.

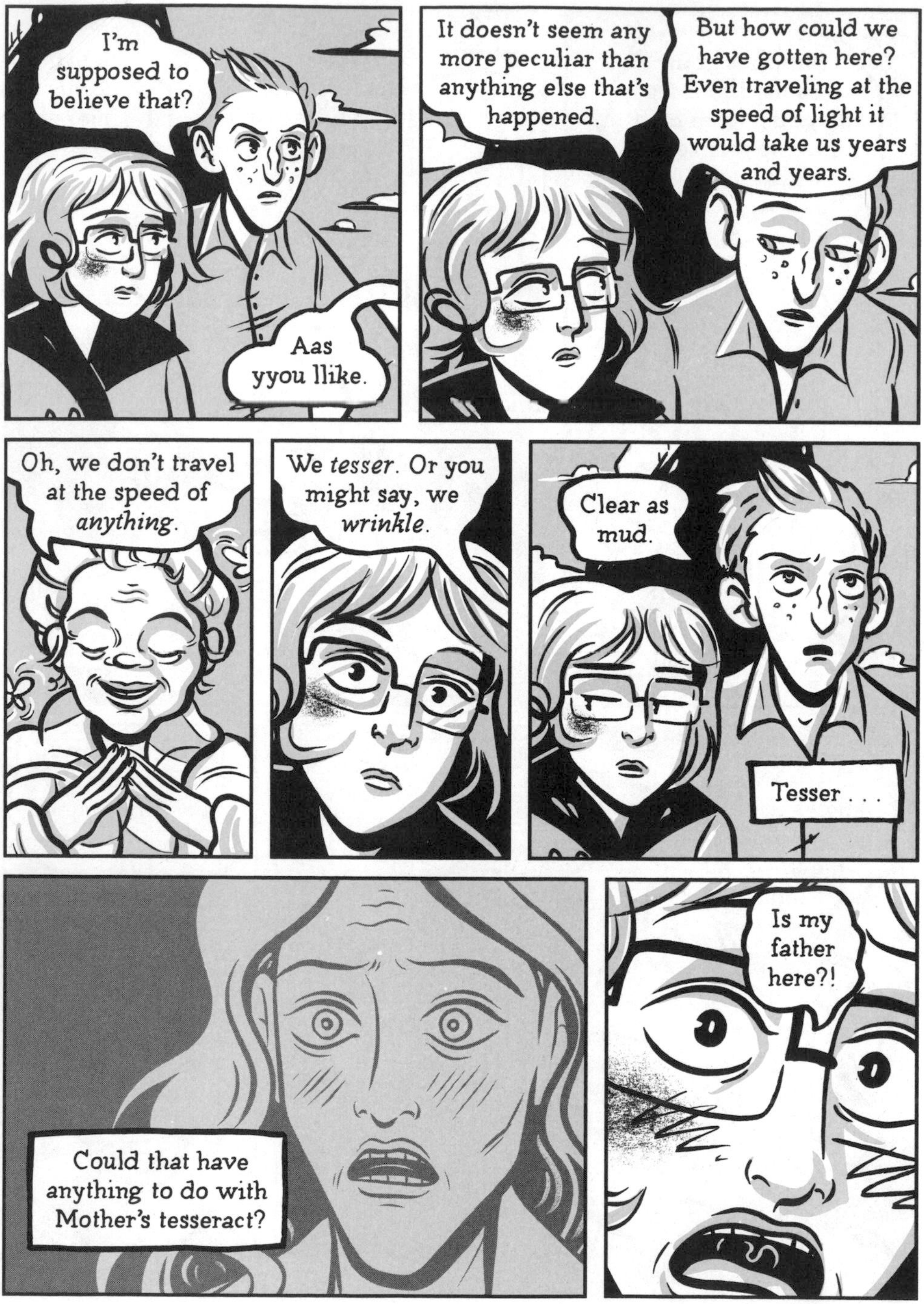
I'm supposed to believe that?
Aas yyou llike.
It doesn't seem any more peculiar than anything else that's happened.
But how could we have gotten here? Even traveling at the speed of light it would take us years and years.
Oh, we don't travel at the speed of *anything*.
We *tesser*. Or you might say, we *wrinkle*.
Clear as mud.
Tesser . . .
Could that have anything to do with Mother's tesseract?
Is my father here?!

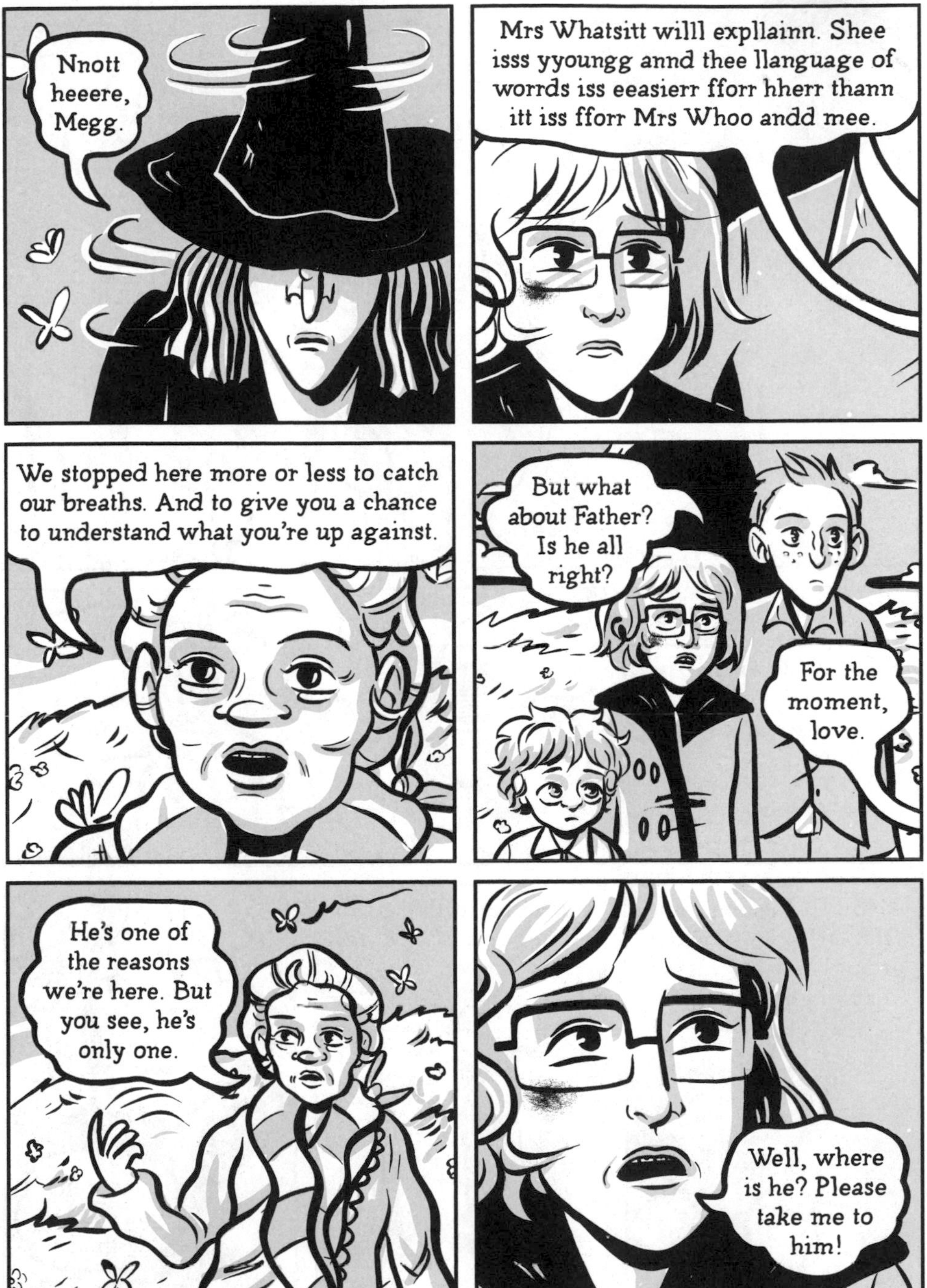
Nnott heeere, Megg.
Mrs Whatsitt willl expllainn. Shee isss yyoungg annd thee llanguage of worrds iss eeasierr fforr hherr thann itt iss fforr Mrs Whoo andd mee.
We stopped here more or less to catch our breaths. And to give you a chance to understand what you're up against.
But what about Father? Is he all right?
For the moment, love.
He's one of the reasons we're here. But you see, he's only one.
Well, where is he? Please take me to him!

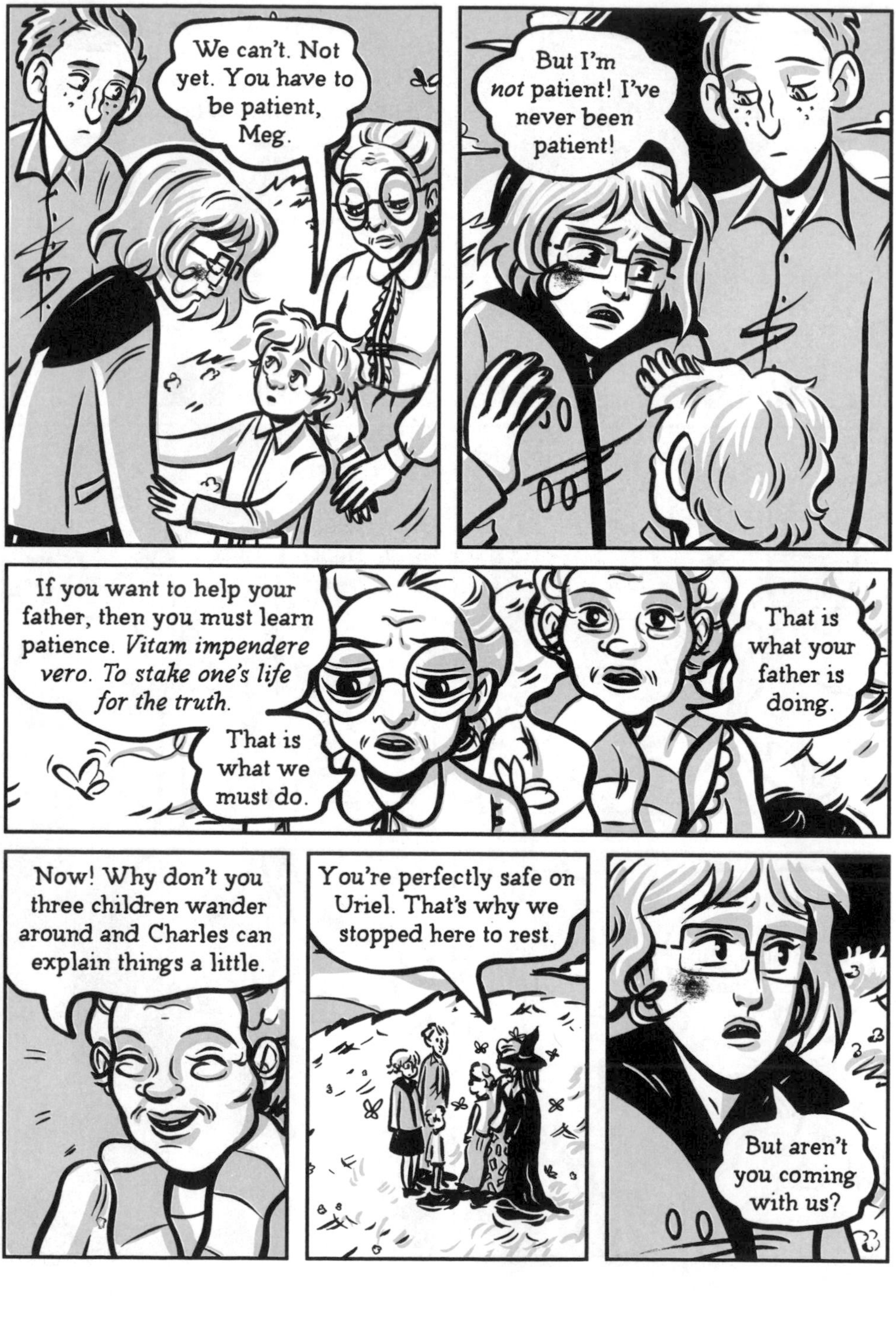
We can't. Not yet. You have to be patient, Meg.
But I'm *not* patient! I've never been patient!
If you want to help your father, then you must learn patience. *Vitam impendere vero. To stake one's life for the truth.*
That is what we must do.
That is what your father is doing.
Now! Why don't you three children wander around and Charles can explain things a little.
You're perfectly safe on Uriel. That's why we stopped here to rest.
But aren't you coming with us?

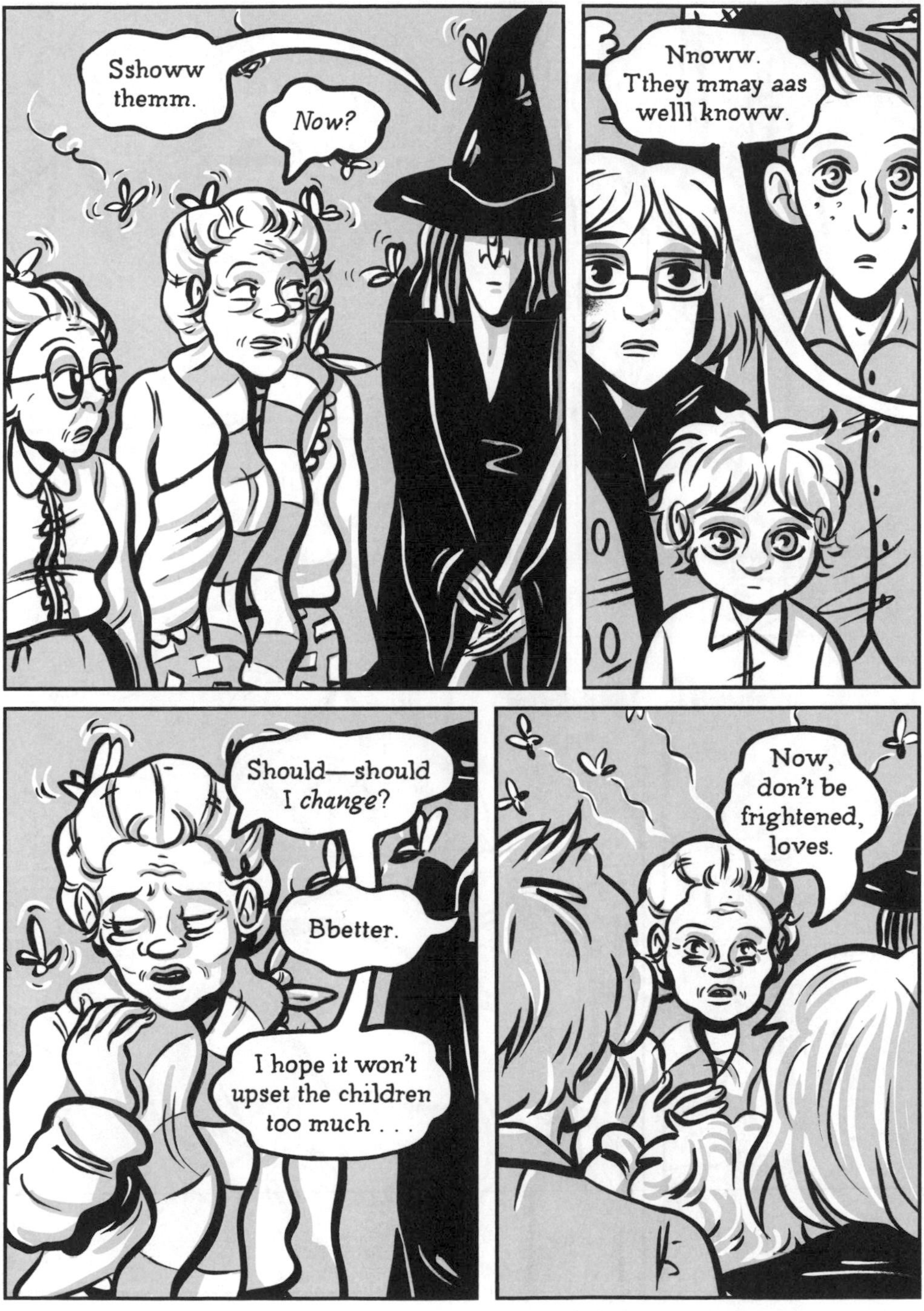
Sshoww themm.
Now?
Nnoww. Tthey mmay aas welll knoww.
Should—should I *change*?
Bbetter.
I hope it won't upset the children too much . . .
Now, don't be frightened, loves.

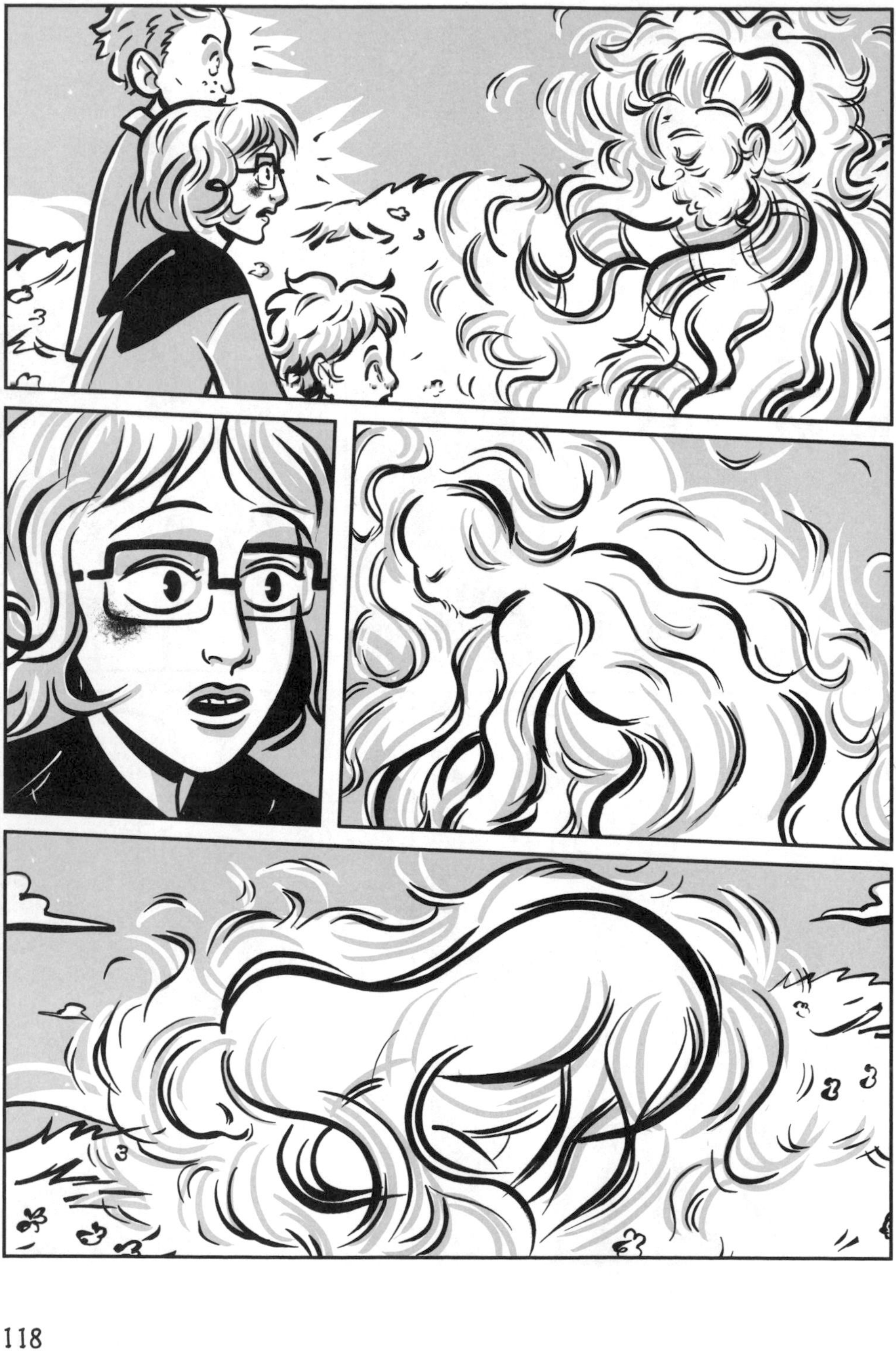

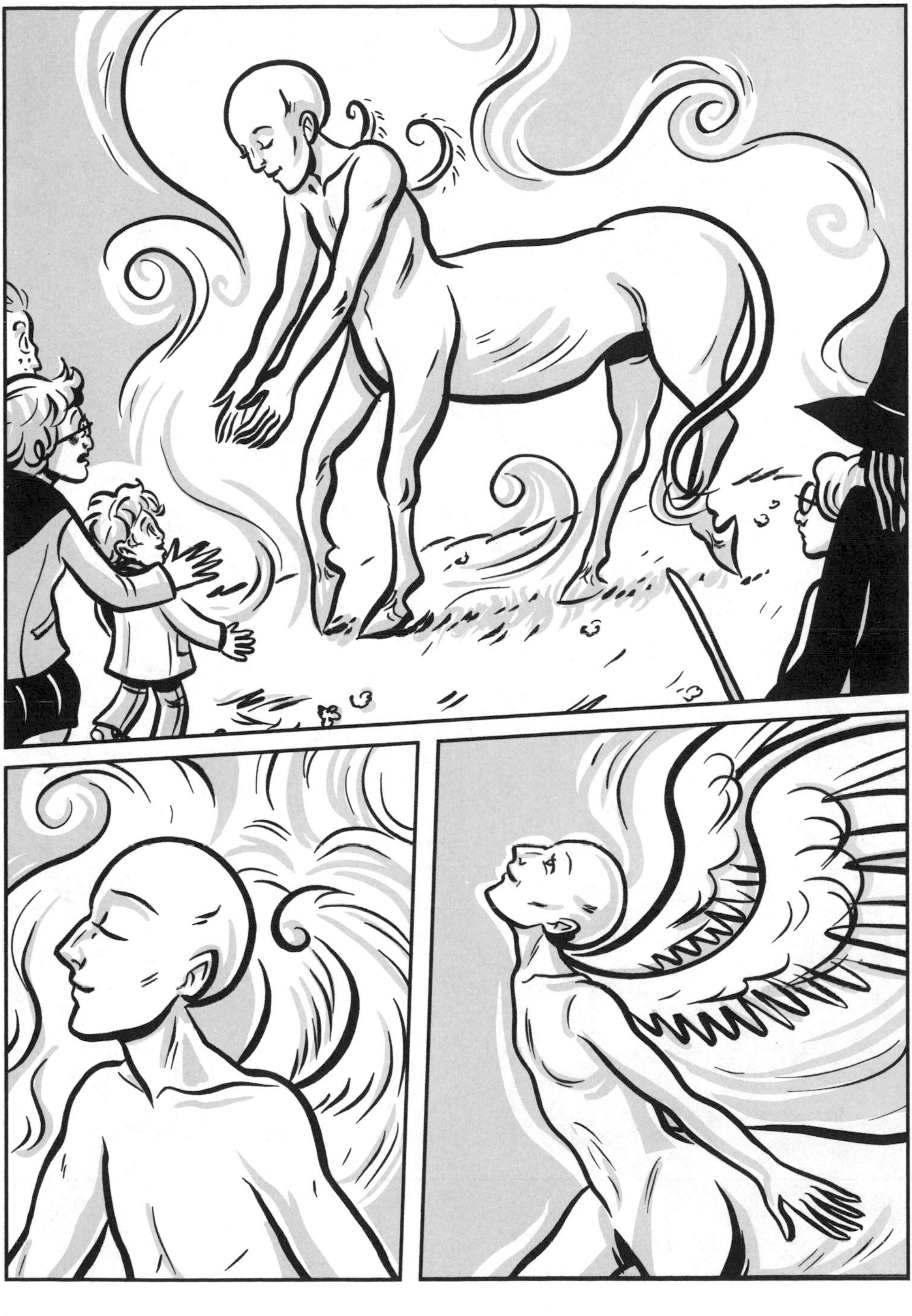

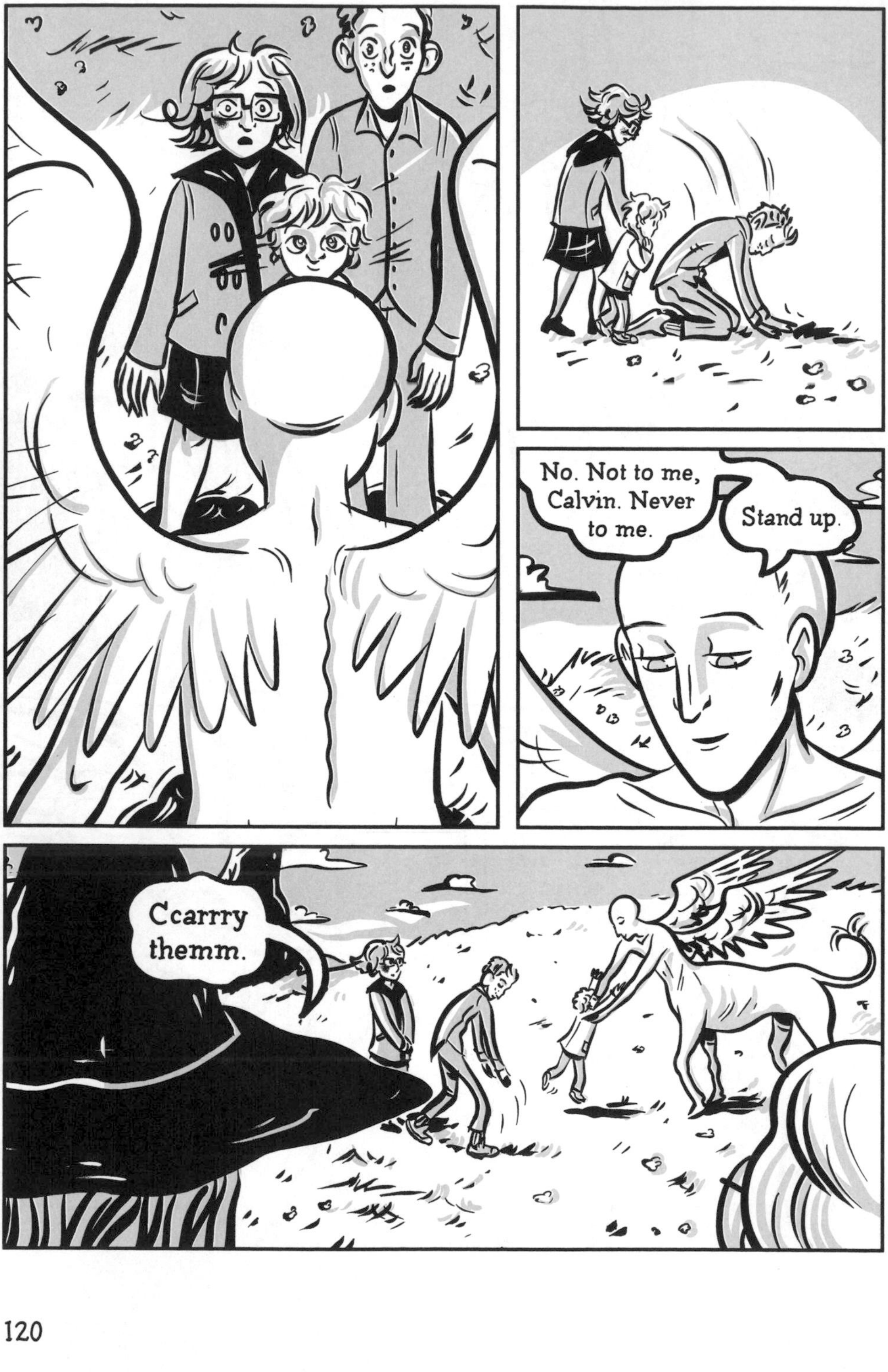
No. Not to me, Calvin. Never to me.
Stand up.
Ccarrry themm.

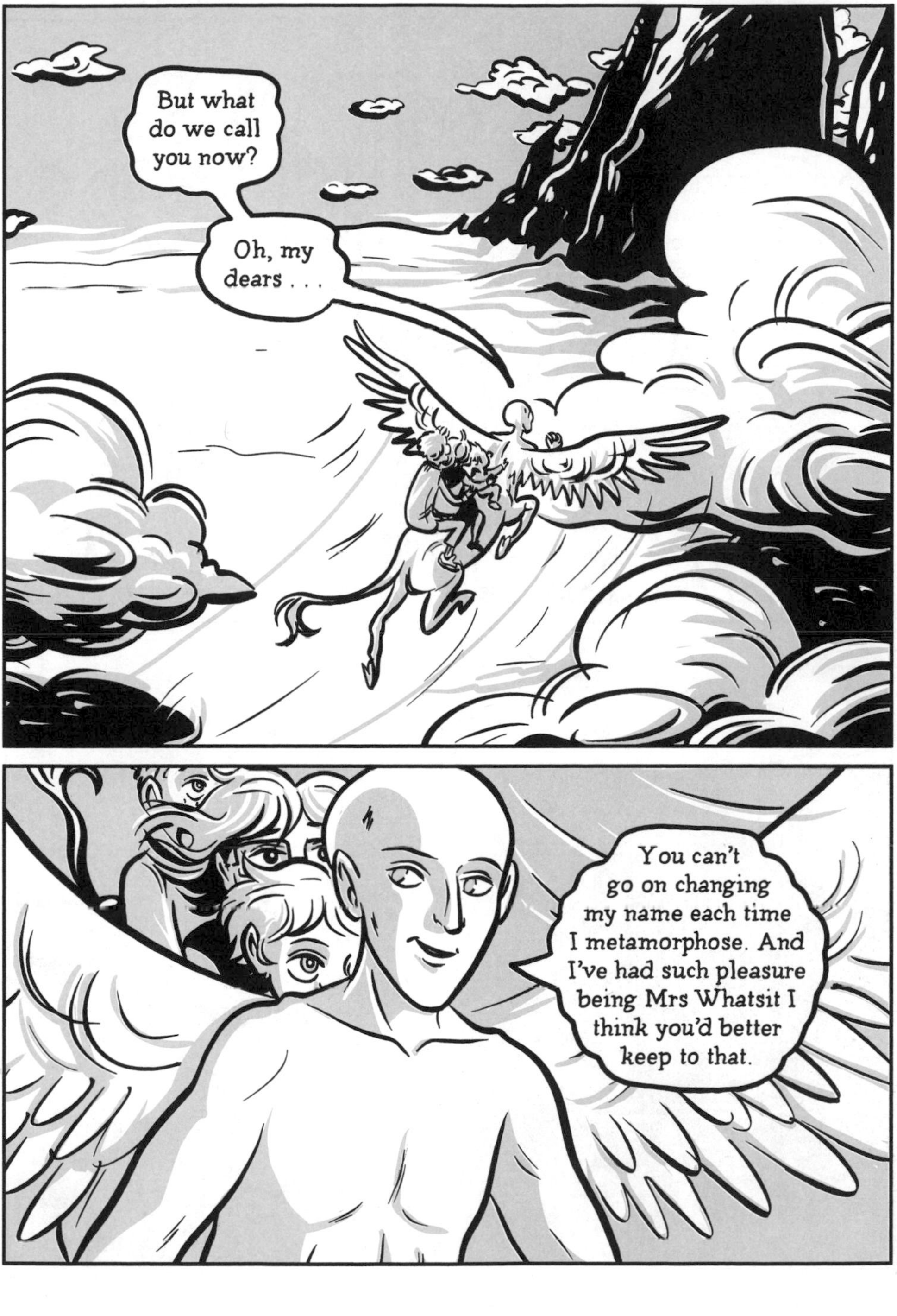
But what do we call you now?
Oh, my dears . . .
You can't go on changing my name each time I metamorphose. And I've had such pleasure being Mrs Whatsit I think you'd better keep to that.

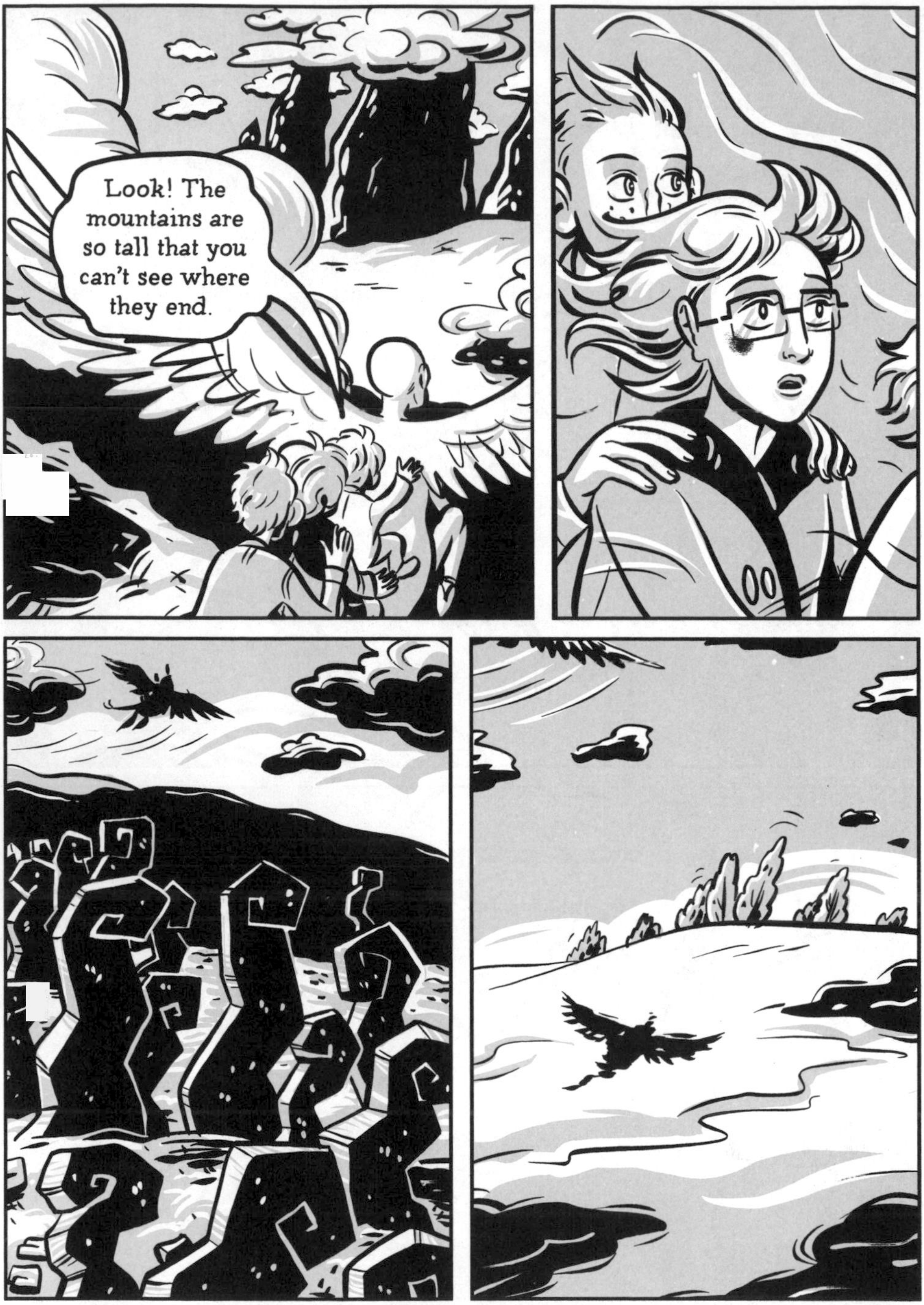
Look! The mountains are so tall that you can't see where they end.

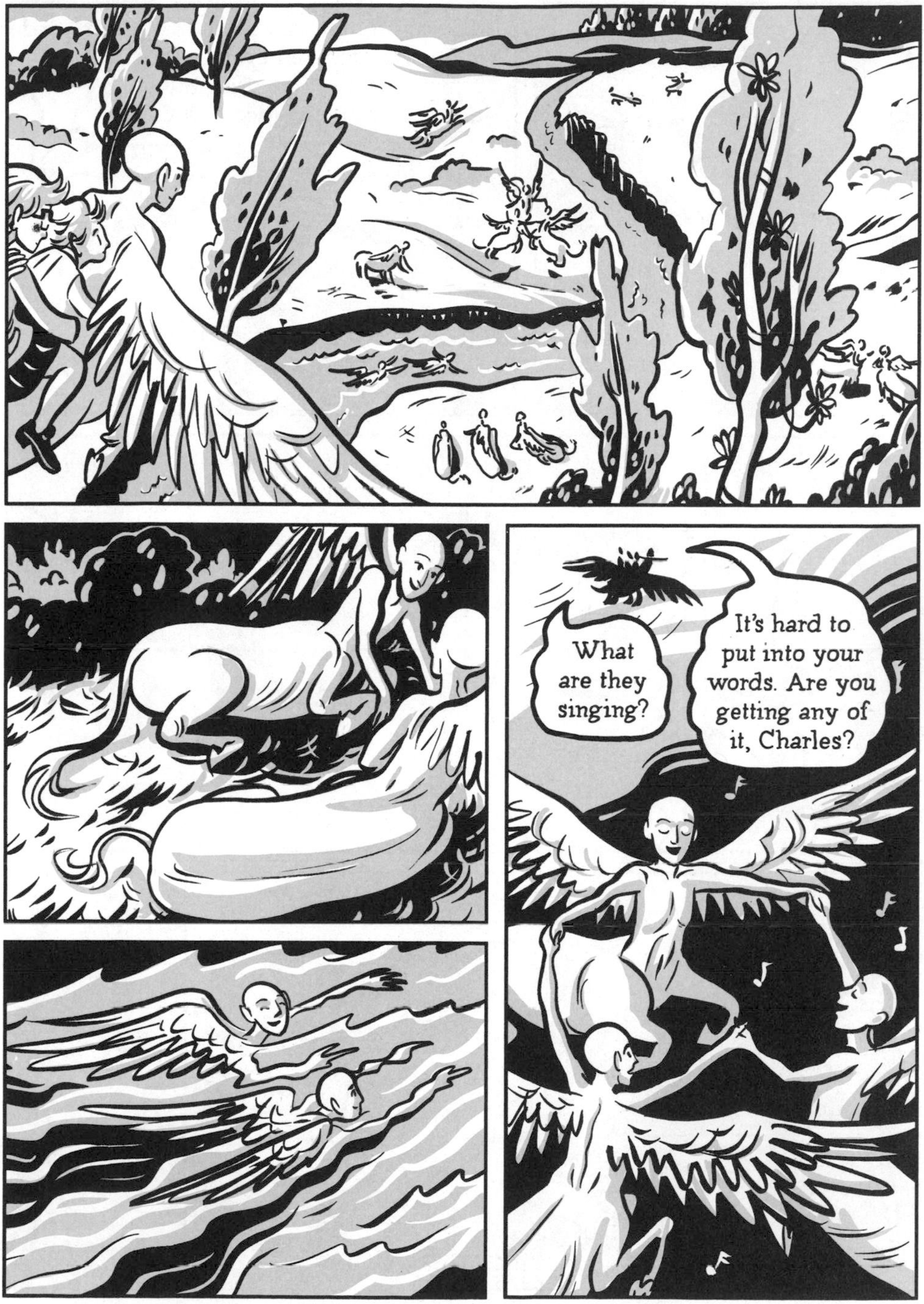
What are they singing?
It's hard to put into your words. Are you getting any of it, Charles?

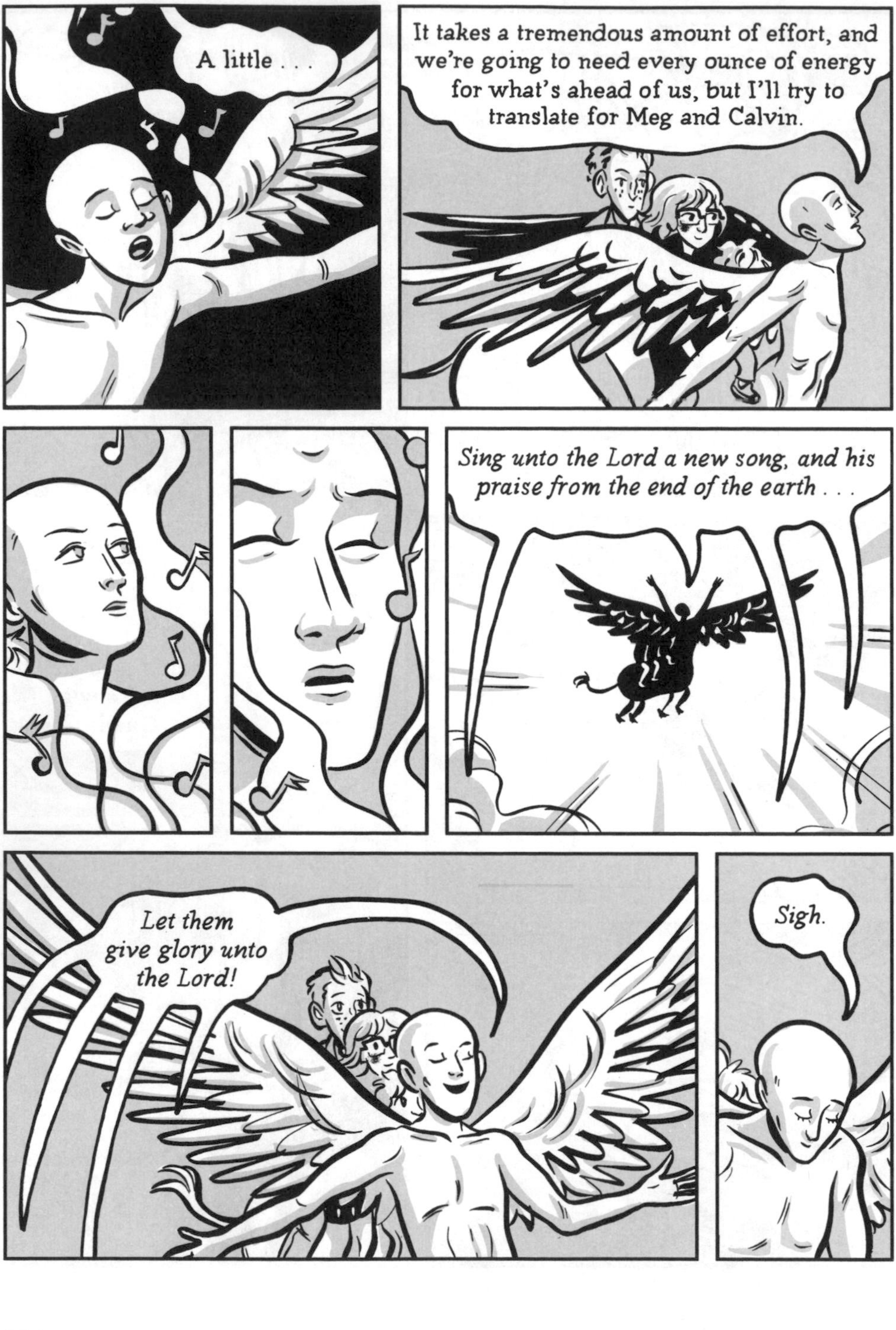
A little . . .
It takes a tremendous amount of effort, and we're going to need every ounce of energy for what's ahead of us, but I'll try to translate for Meg and Calvin.
Sing unto the Lord a new song, and his praise from the end of the earth . . .
Let them give glory unto the Lord!
Sigh.

We must go now, children. But first—

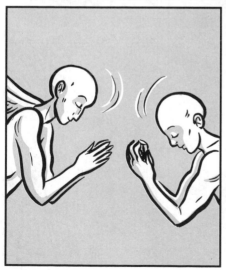

Each of you take one.

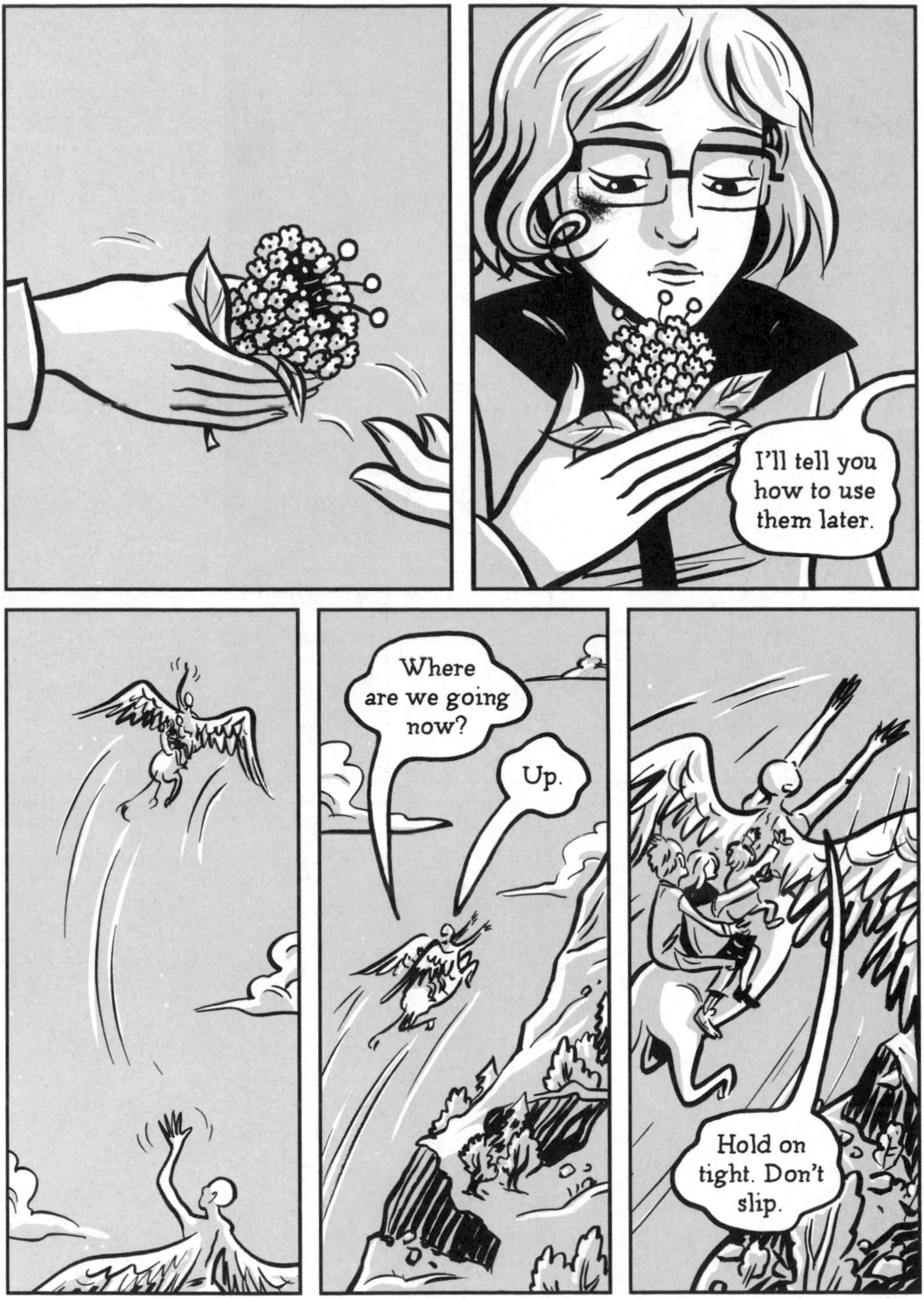
I'll tell you how to use them later.
Where are we going now?
Up.
Hold on tight. Don't slip.

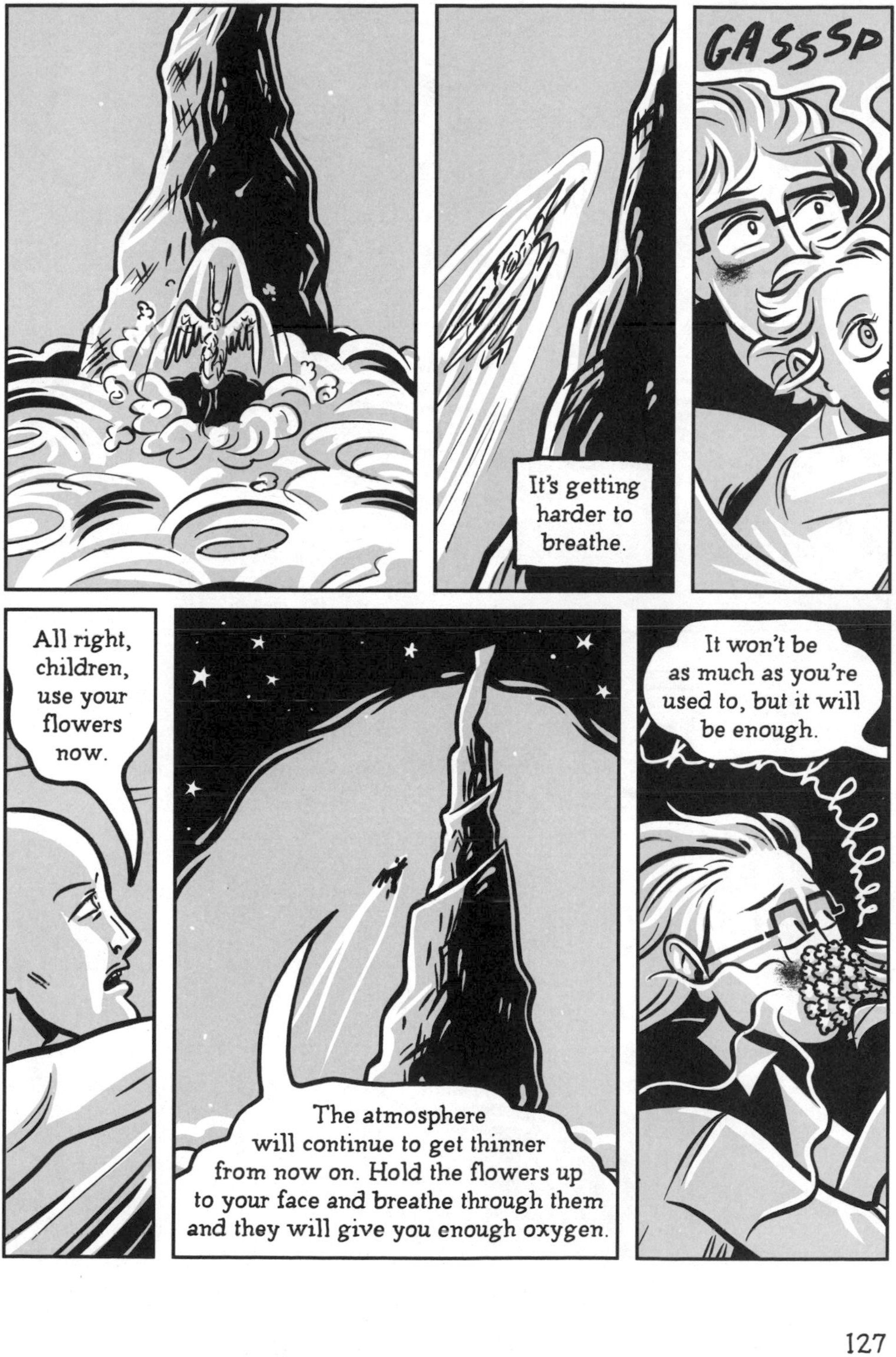

It's getting harder to breathe.
GASSSP
All right, children, use your flowers now.
The atmosphere will continue to get thinner from now on. Hold the flowers up to your face and breathe through them and they will give you enough oxygen.
It won't be as much as you're used to, but it will be enough.

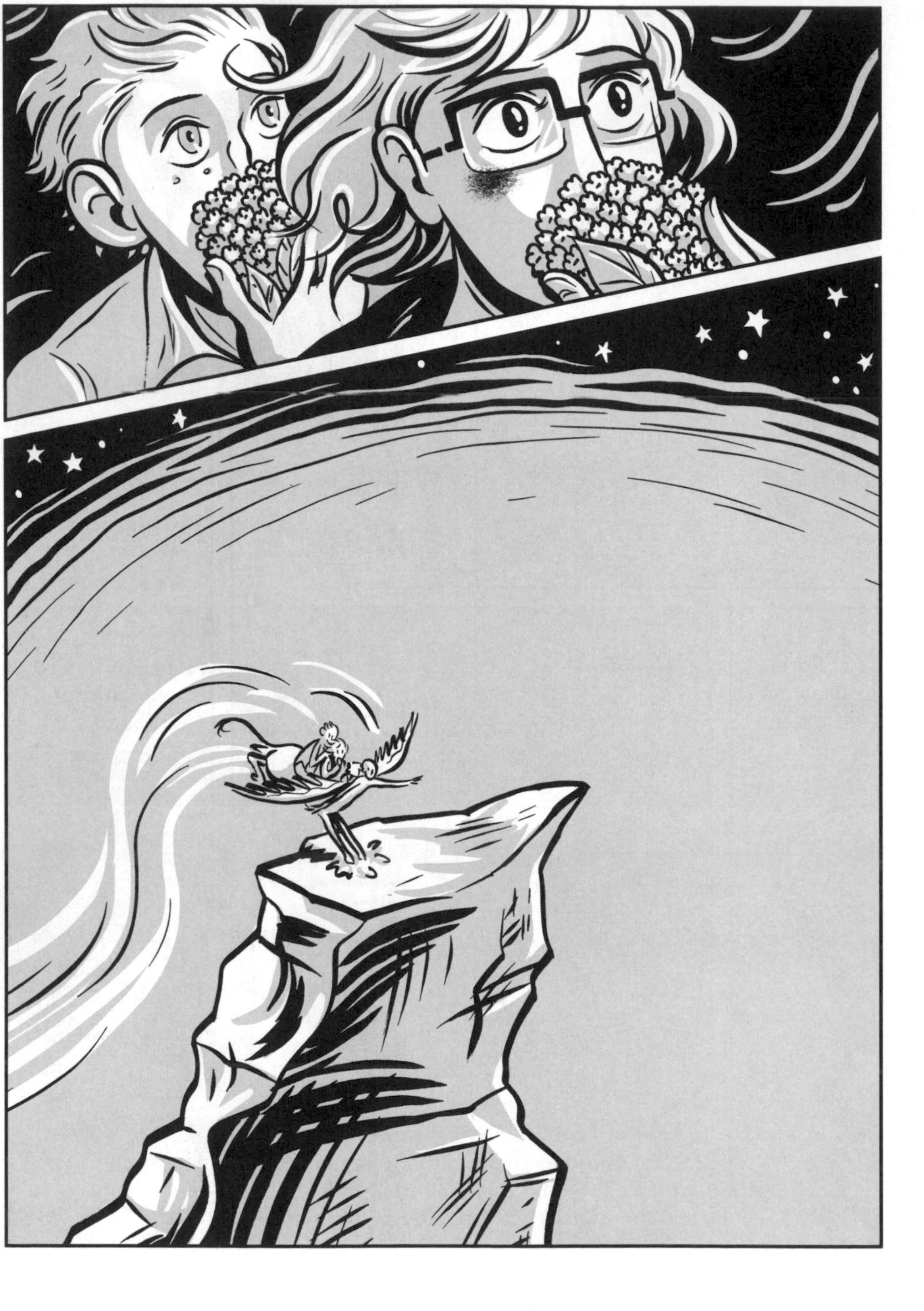

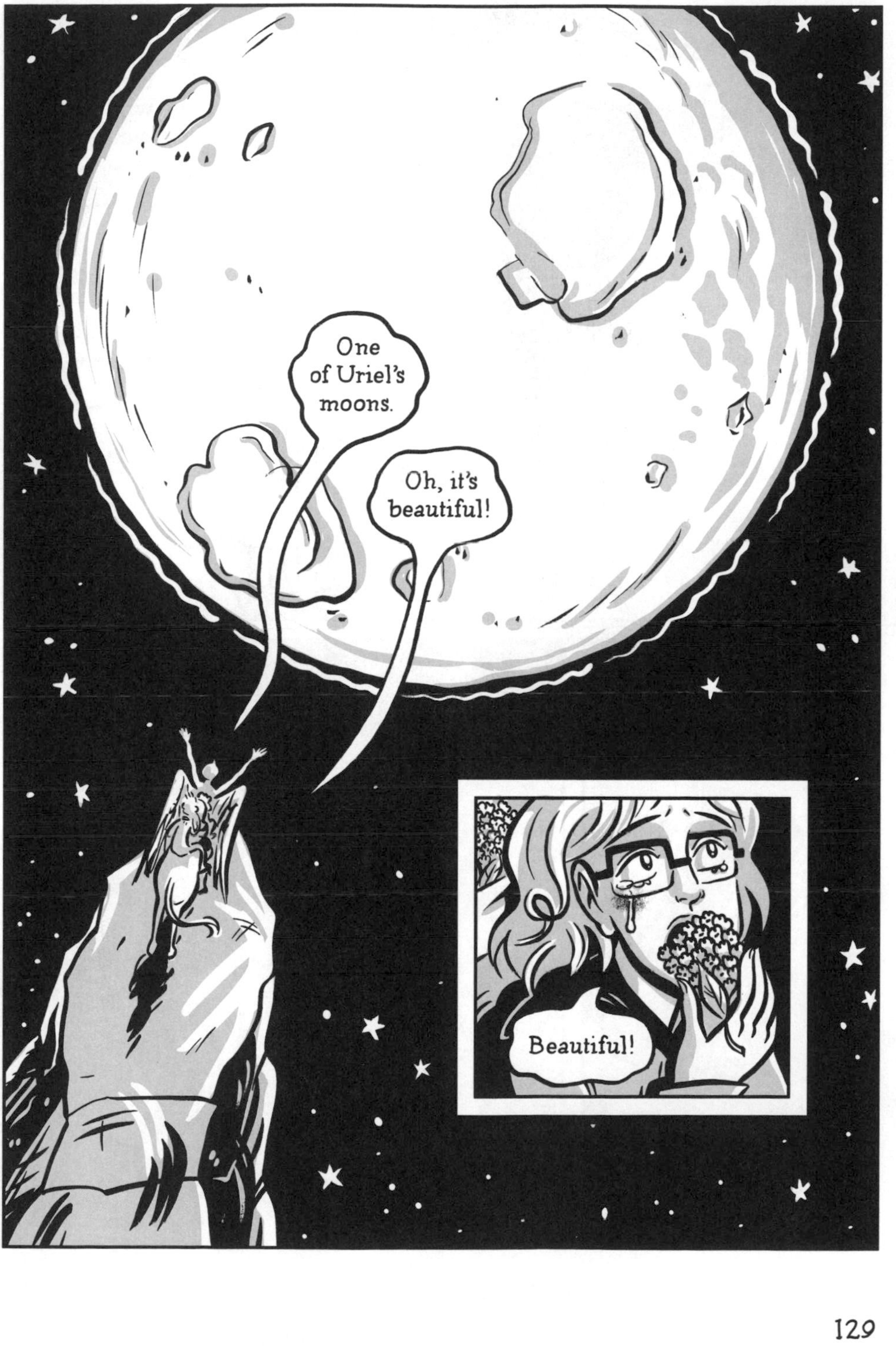
One of Uriel's moons.
Oh, it's beautiful!
Beautiful!

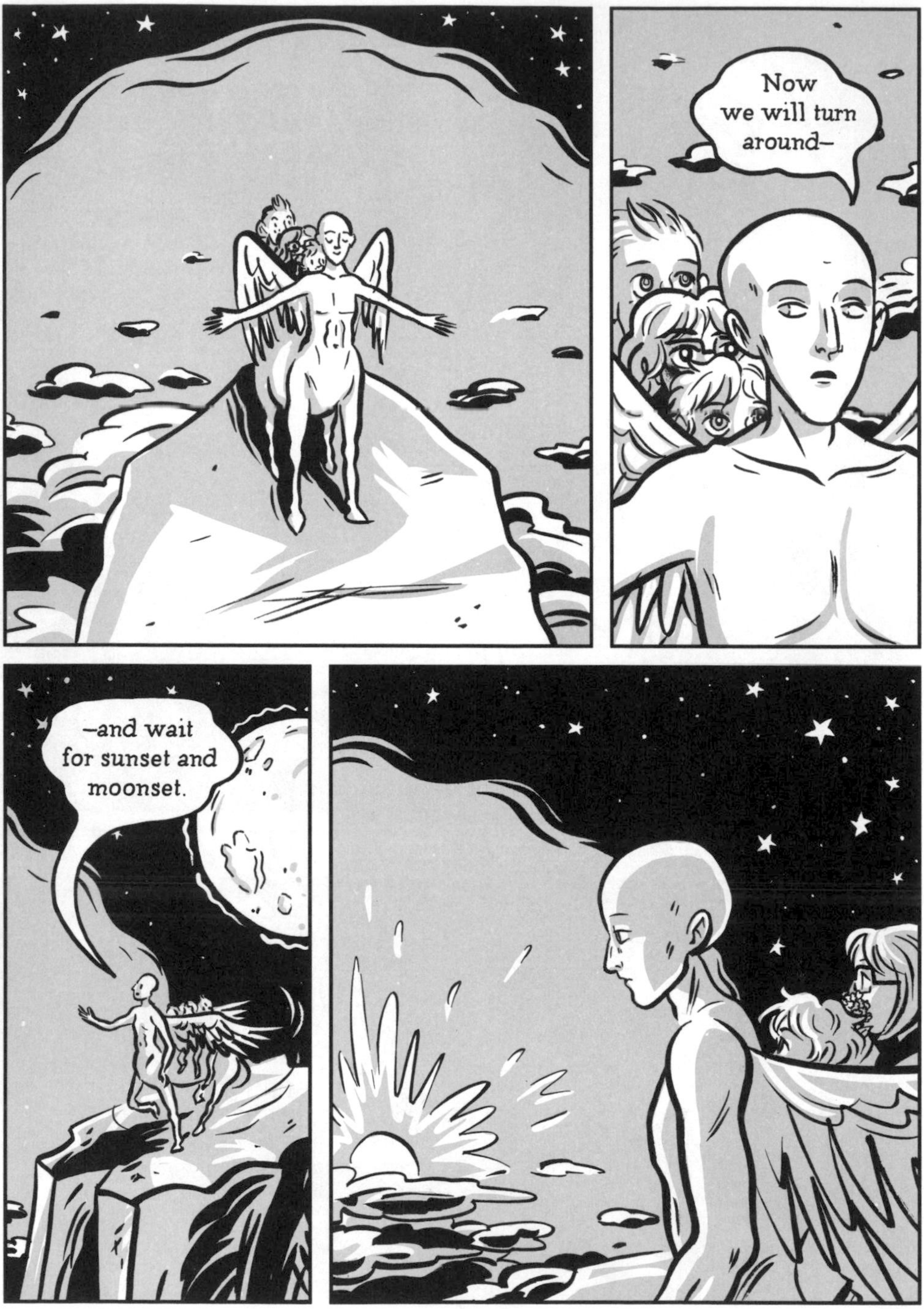
Now we will turn around–
–and wait for sunset and moonset.

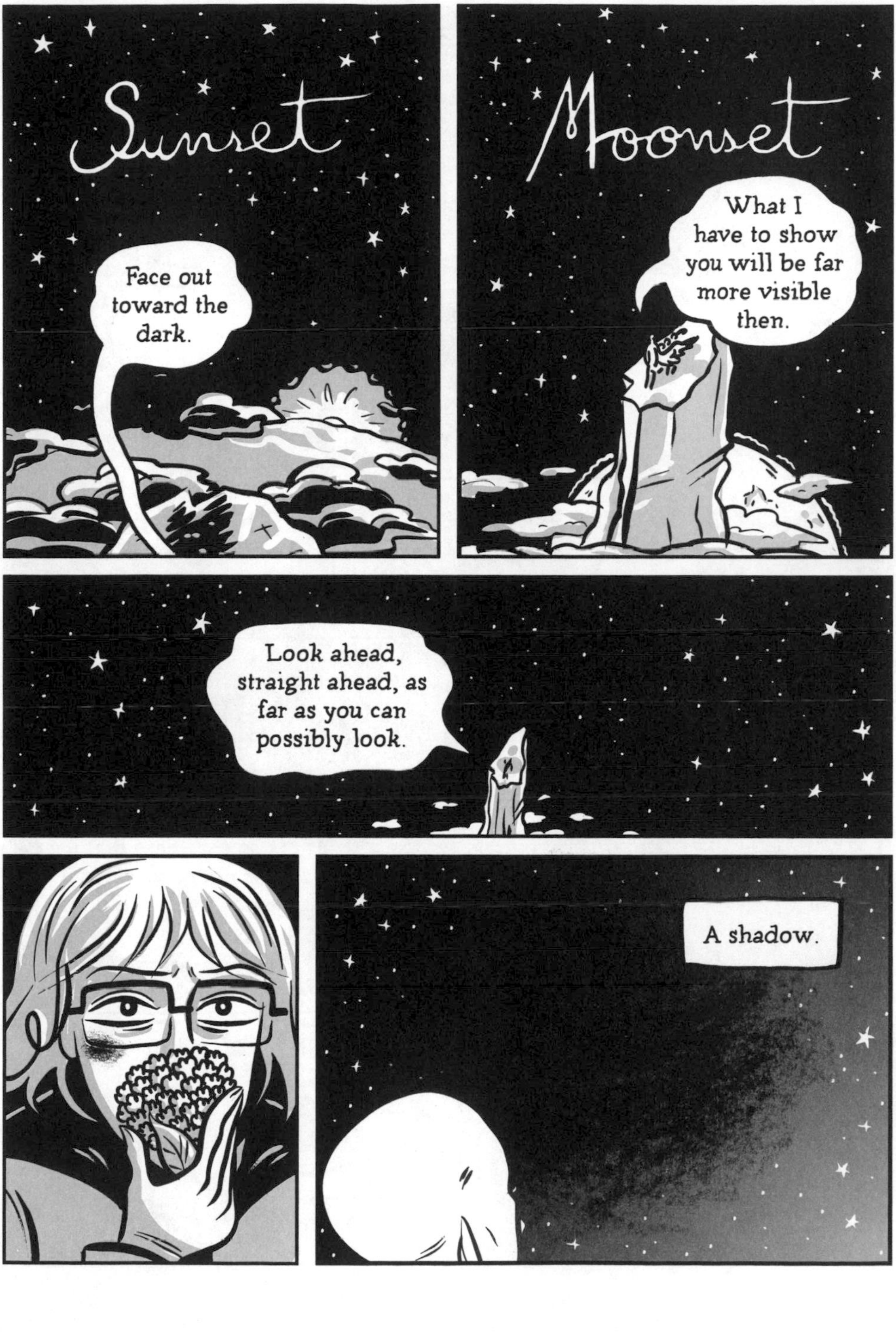
Sunset
Face out toward the dark.
Moonset
What I have to show you will be far more visible then.
Look ahead, straight ahead, as far as you can possibly look.
A shadow.

Is it really there? It's so faint, I can't be sure—

What's that?

That sort of thing out there—what is it?

Watch.

Is the shadow cast by something?

Is the shadow a Thing in itself?

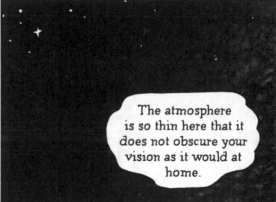

The atmosphere is so thin here that it does not obscure your vision as it would at home.

Now look. Look straight ahead.

Terrible. It's terrible.

Looking at it makes me feel I could never be happy again.

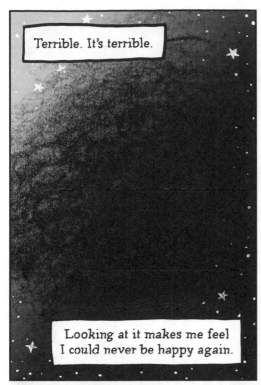

Make it go away, Mrs Whatsit. Make it go away. It's evil.

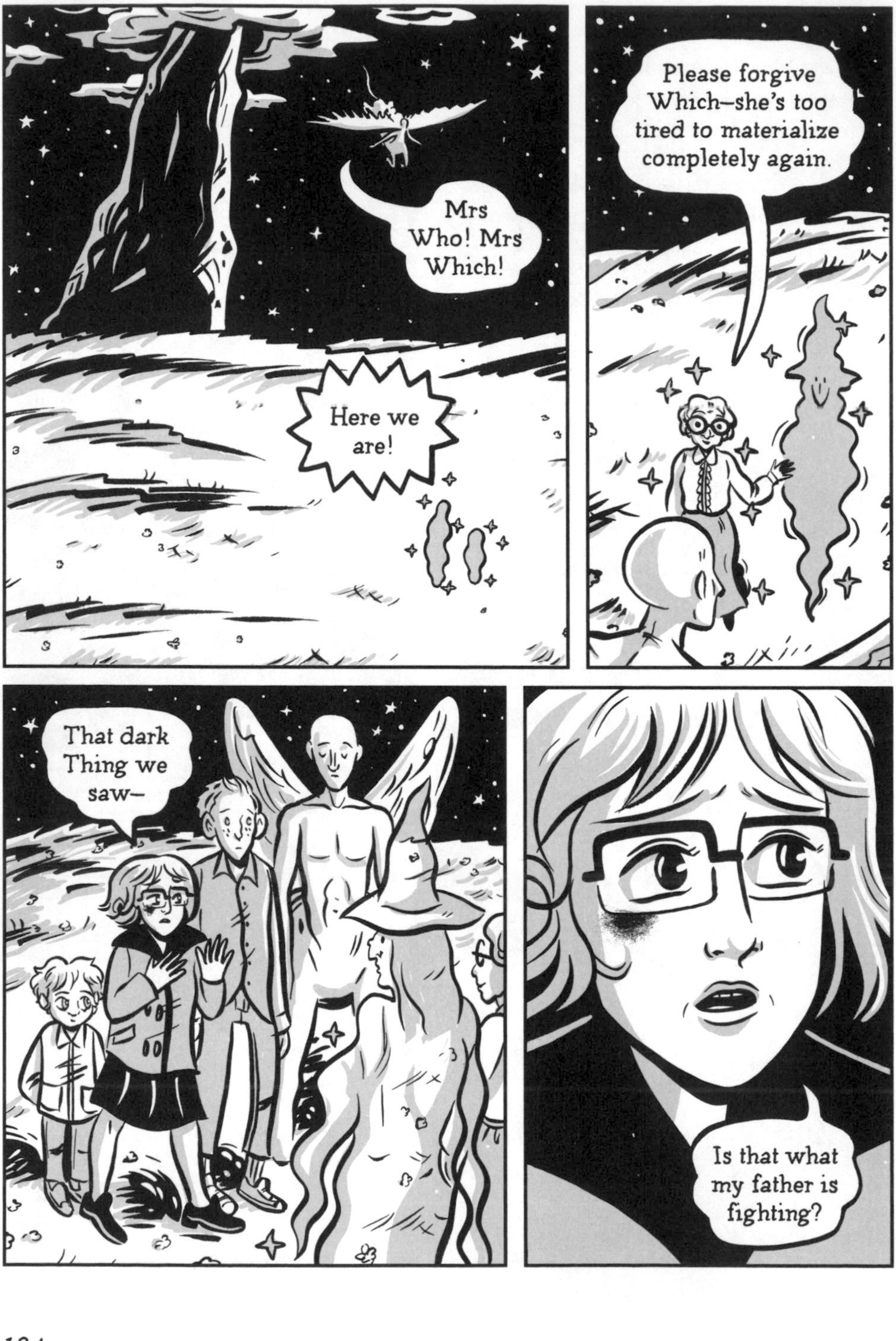
Mrs Who! Mrs Which!
Here we are!
Please forgive Which–she's too tired to materialize completely again.
That dark Thing we saw–
Is that what my father is fighting?

5
The Tesseract

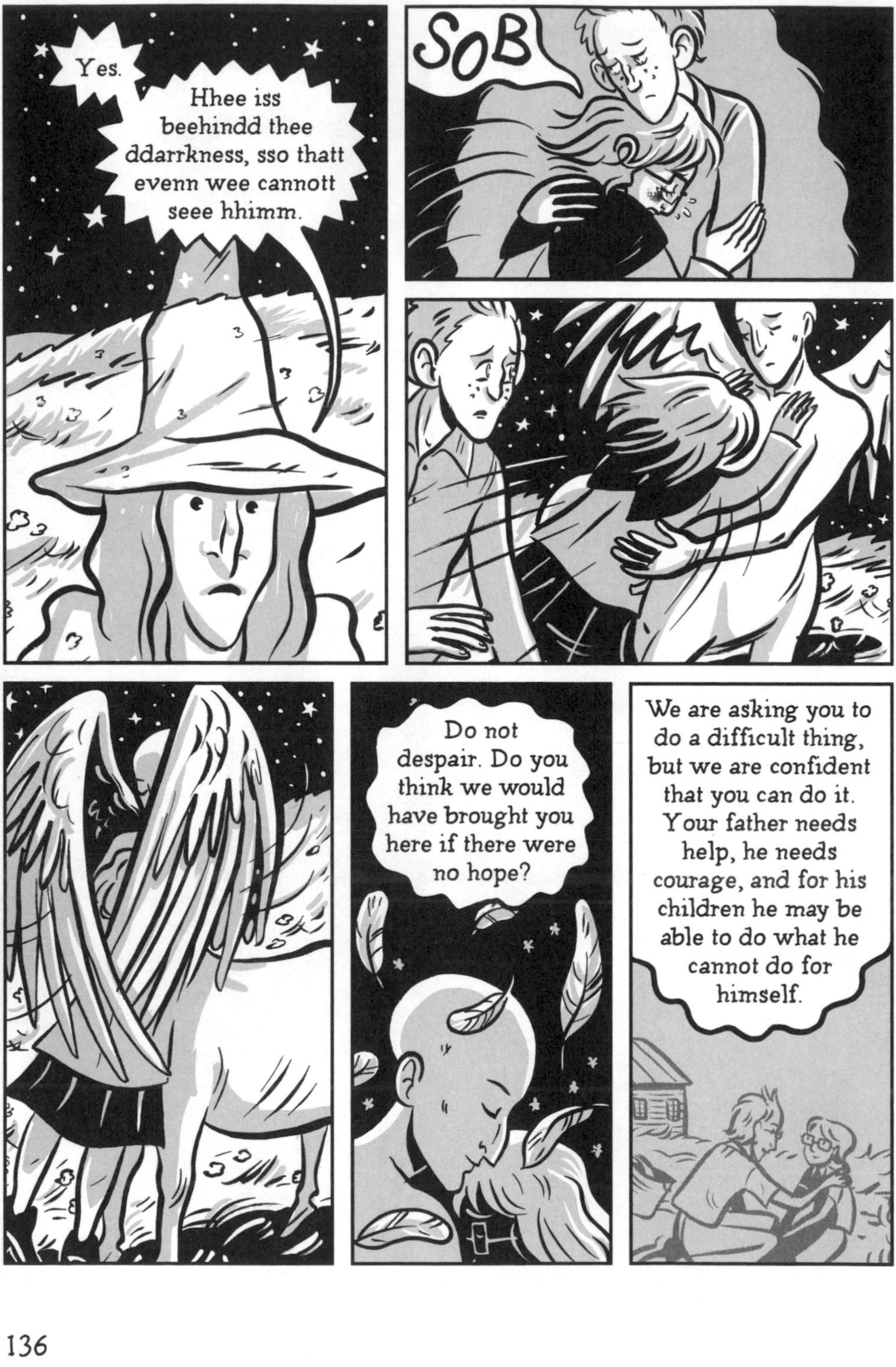
Yes.
Hhee iss beehindd thee ddarrkness, sso thatt evenn wee cannott seee hhimm.
SOB
Do not despair. Do you think we would have brought you here if there were no hope?
We are asking you to do a difficult thing, but we are confident that you can do it. Your father needs help, he needs courage, and for his children he may be able to do what he cannot do for himself.

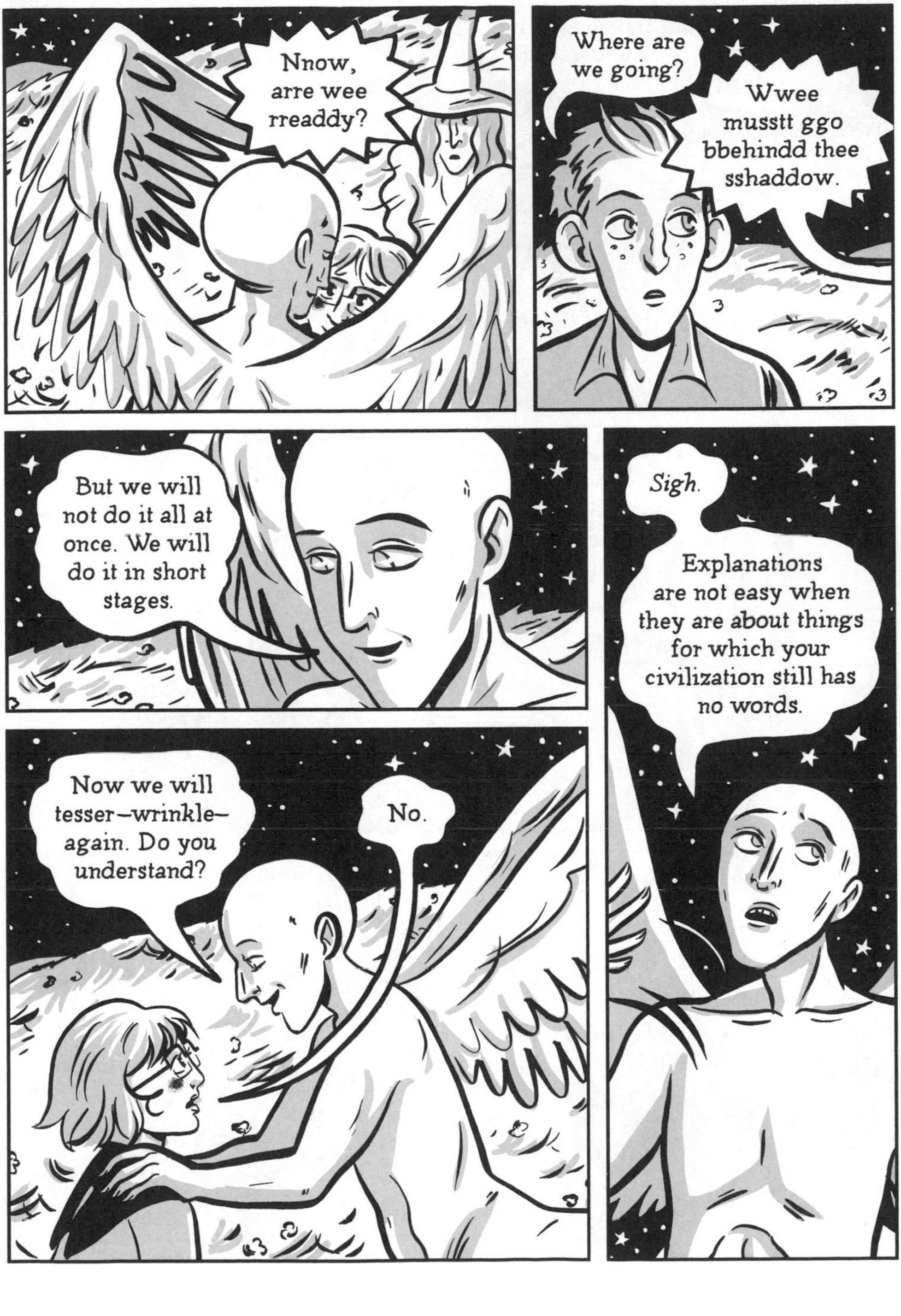

Nnow, arre wee rreaddy?
Where are we going?
Wwee musstt ggo bbehindd thee sshaddow.
But we will not do it all at once. We will do it in short stages.
Sigh.
Explanations are not easy when they are about things for which your civilization still has no words.
Now we will tesser—wrinkle—again. Do you understand?
No.

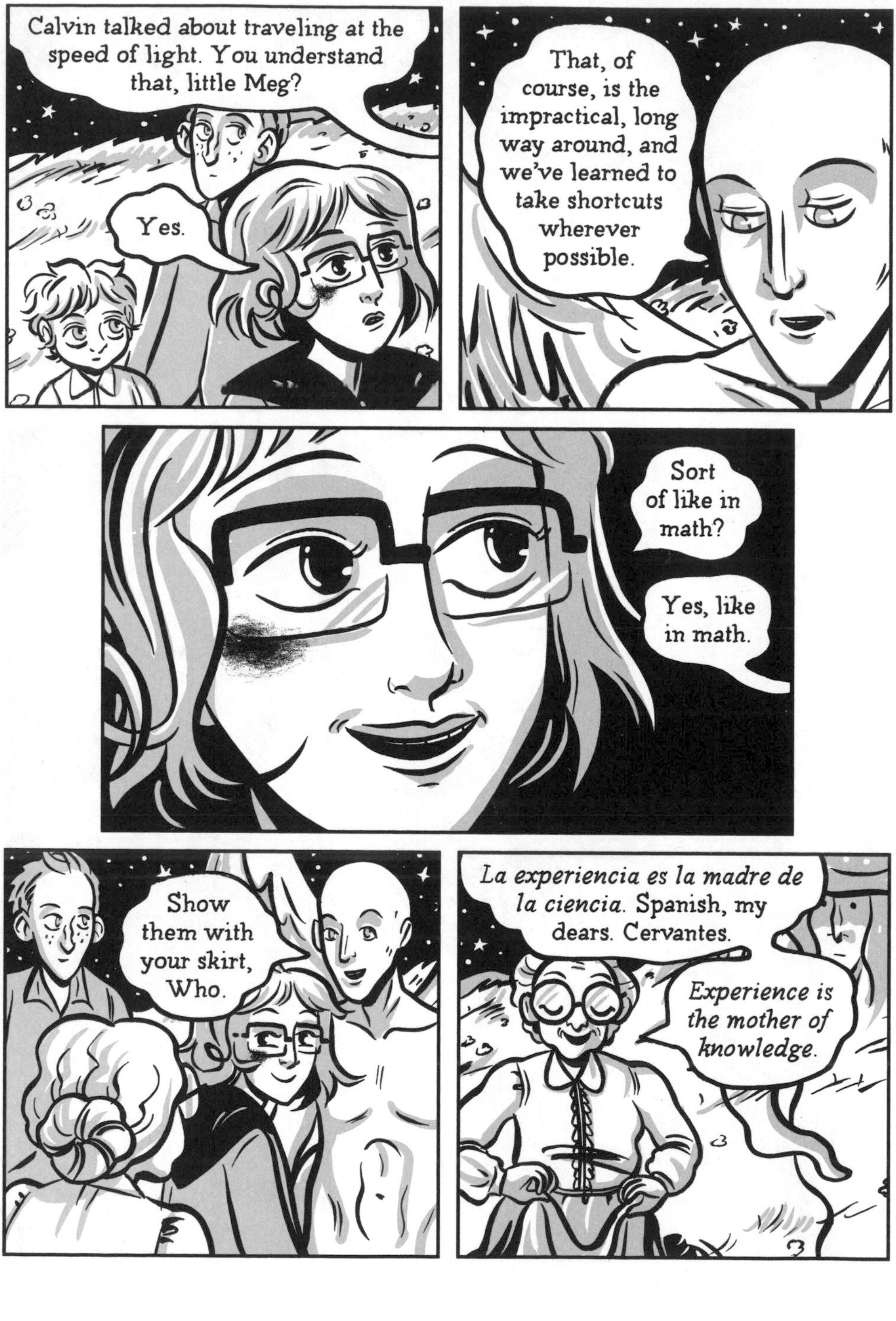
Calvin talked about traveling at the speed of light. You understand that, little Meg?
Yes.
That, of course, is the impractical, long way around, and we've learned to take shortcuts wherever possible.
Sort of like in math?
Yes, like in math.
Show them with your skirt, Who.
La experiencia es la madre de la ciencia. Spanish, my dears. Cervantes.
Experience is the mother of knowledge.

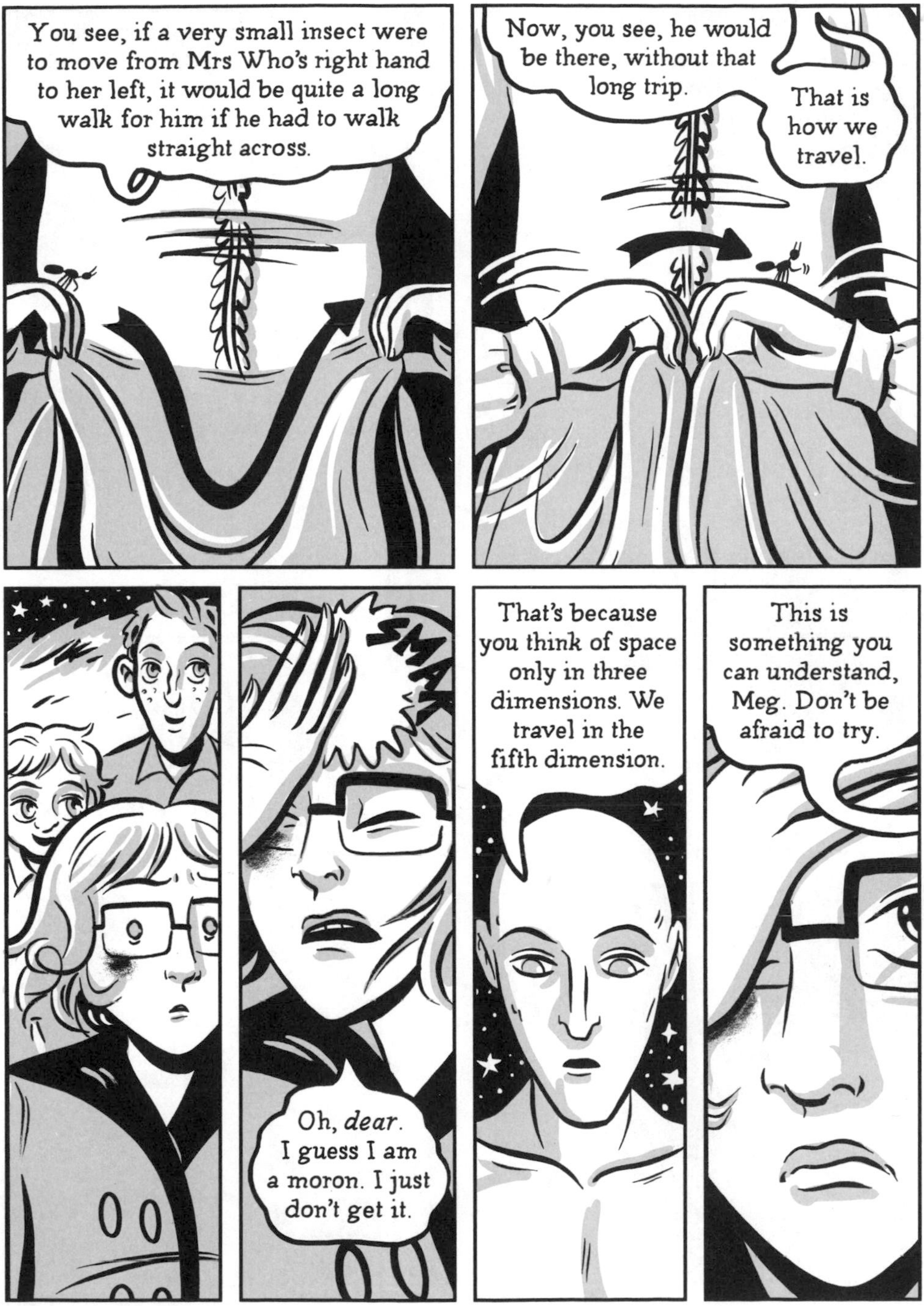
You see, if a very small insect were to move from Mrs Who's right hand to her left, it would be quite a long walk for him if he had to walk straight across.
Now, you see, he would be there, without that long trip.
That is how we travel.
SMAK
Oh, *dear*. I guess I am a moron. I just don't get it.
That's because you think of space only in three dimensions. We travel in the fifth dimension.
This is something you can understand, Meg. Don't be afraid to try.

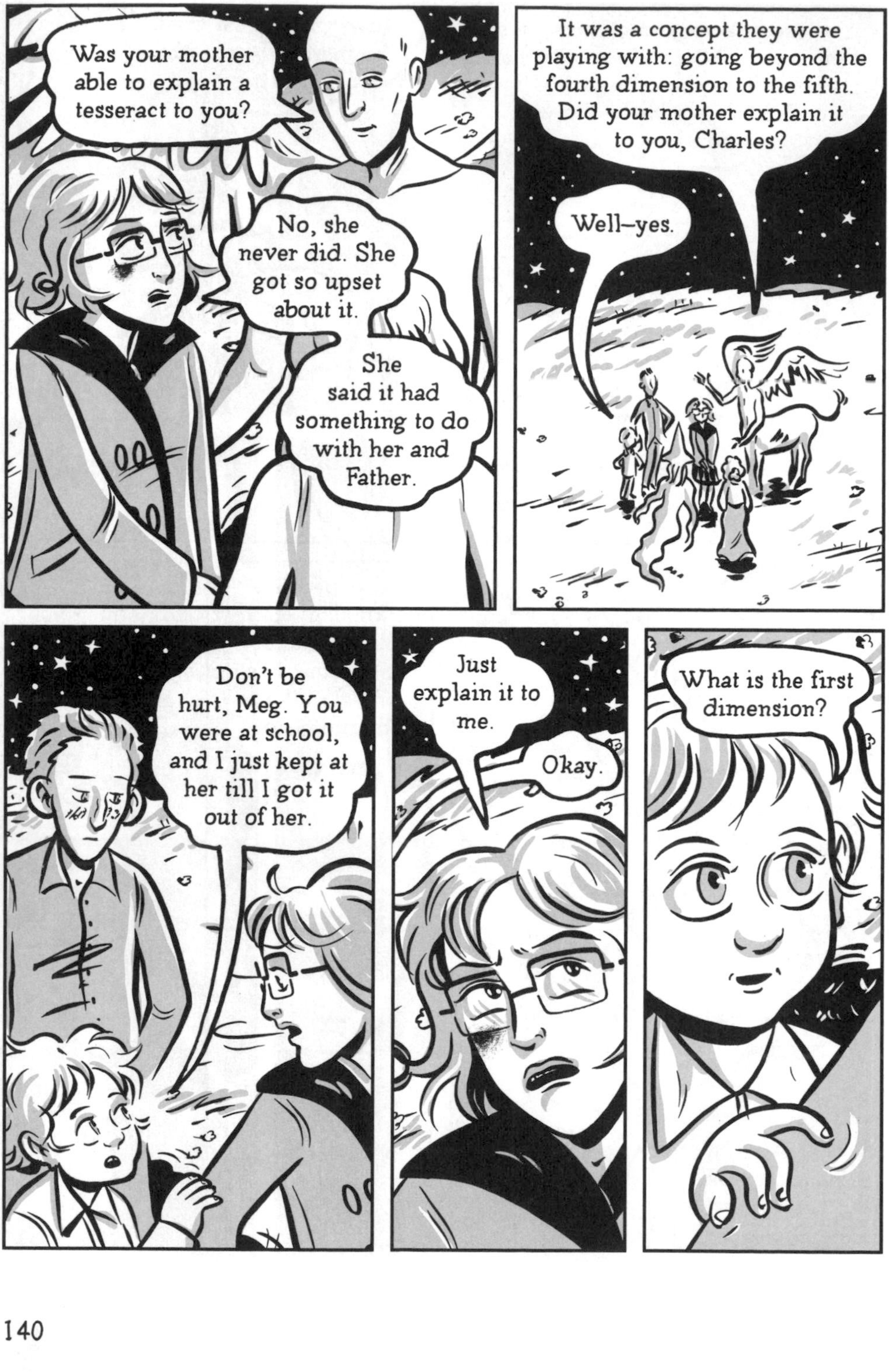
Was your mother able to explain a tesseract to you?
No, she never did. She got so upset about it.
She said it had something to do with her and Father.
It was a concept they were playing with: going beyond the fourth dimension to the fifth. Did your mother explain it to you, Charles?
Well—yes.
Don't be hurt, Meg. You were at school, and I just kept at her till I got it out of her.
Just explain it to me.
Okay.
What is the first dimension?

Well—
a line.
Okay. And the second dimension?
A
B
Well, you'd square the line. A flat square would be in the second dimension.
And the third?
You'd square the second dimension.
Then the square wouldn't be flat anymore. It would have a bottom, and sides, and a top.
And the fourth?
Well, in mathematical terms you'd square the square.
But you can't take a pencil and draw that the way you can the first three.
I know it's got something to do with Einstein and time. I guess maybe you could call the fourth dimension Time.

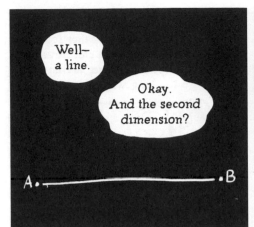

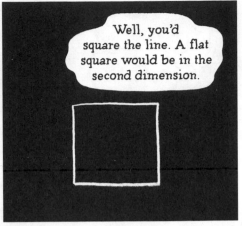

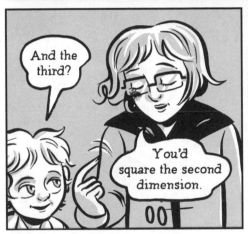

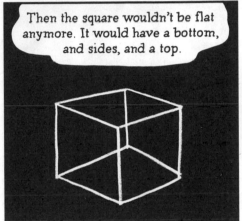

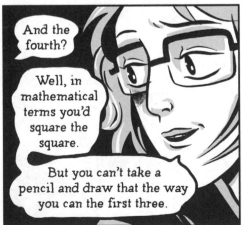

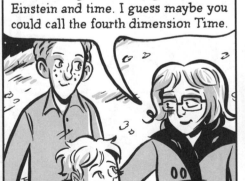

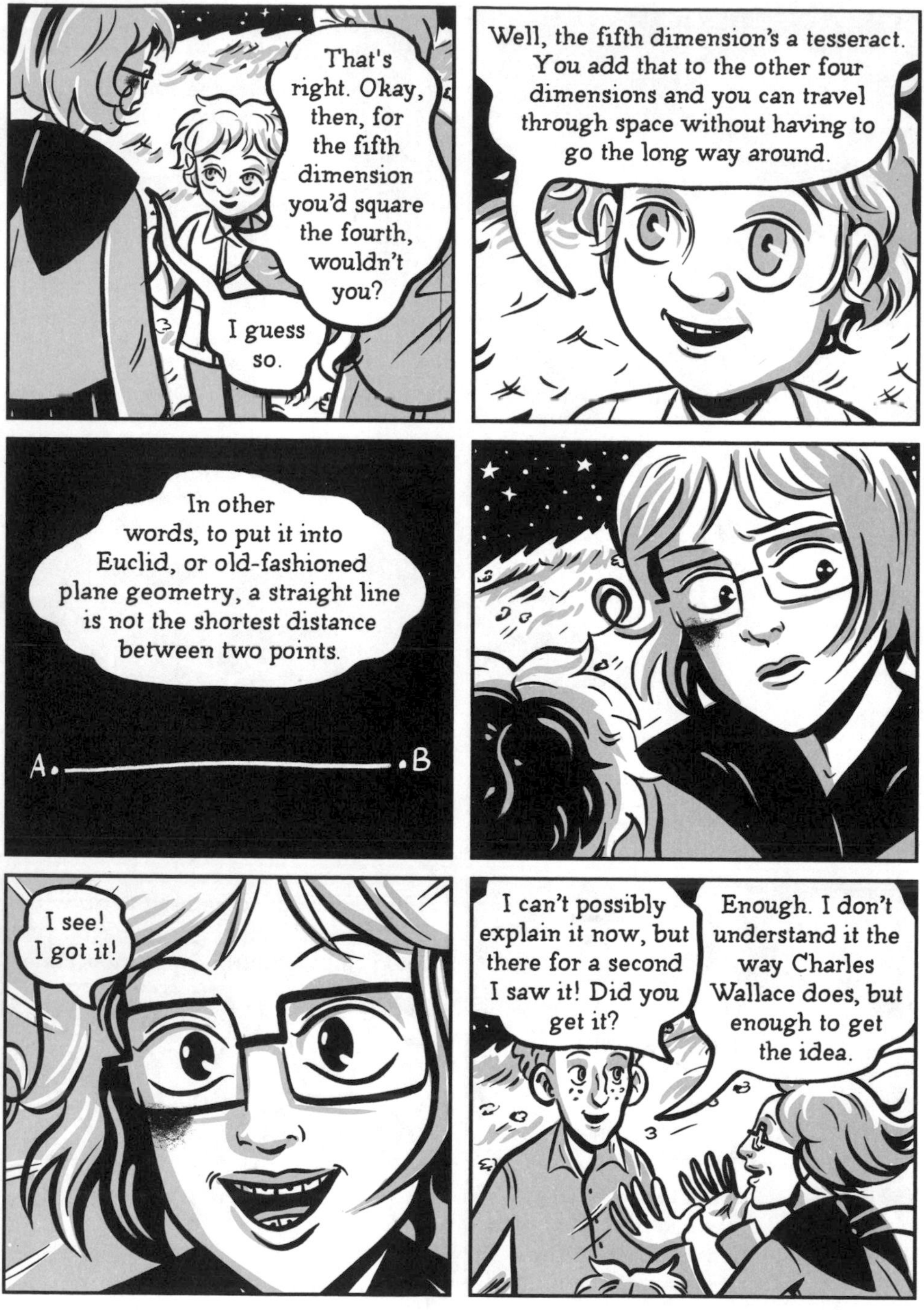
That's right. Okay, then, for the fifth dimension you'd square the fourth, wouldn't you?
I guess so.
Well, the fifth dimension's a tesseract. You add that to the other four dimensions and you can travel through space without having to go the long way around.
In other words, to put it into Euclid, or old-fashioned plane geometry, a straight line is not the shortest distance between two points.
A.
.B
I see! I got it!
I can't possibly explain it now, but there for a second I saw it! Did you get it?
Enough. I don't understand it the way Charles Wallace does, but enough to get the idea.

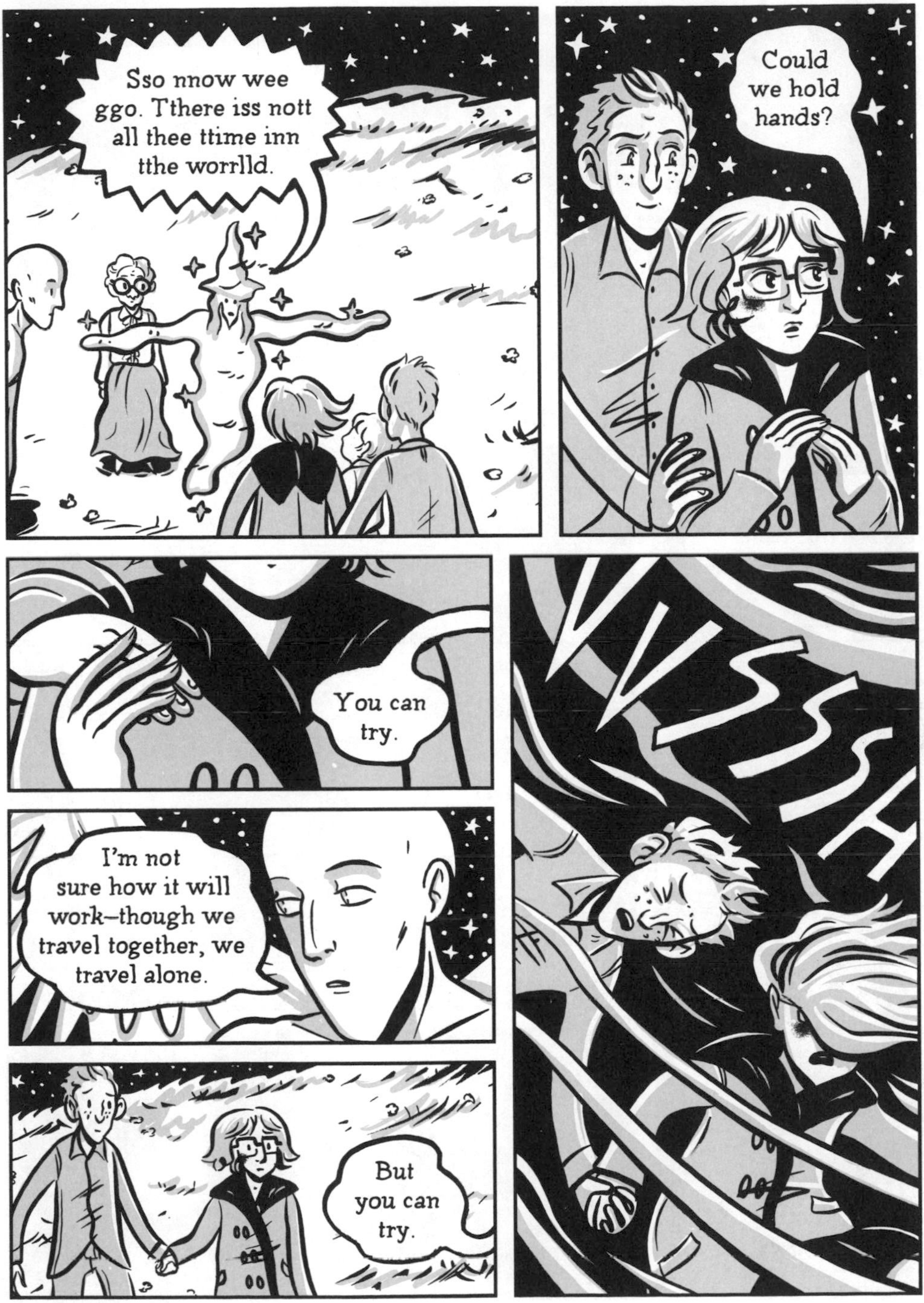
Sso nnow wee ggo. Tthere iss nott all thee ttime inn tthe worrlld.
Could we hold hands?
You can try.
I'm not sure how it will work—though we travel together, we travel alone.
But you can try.
VVSSSH

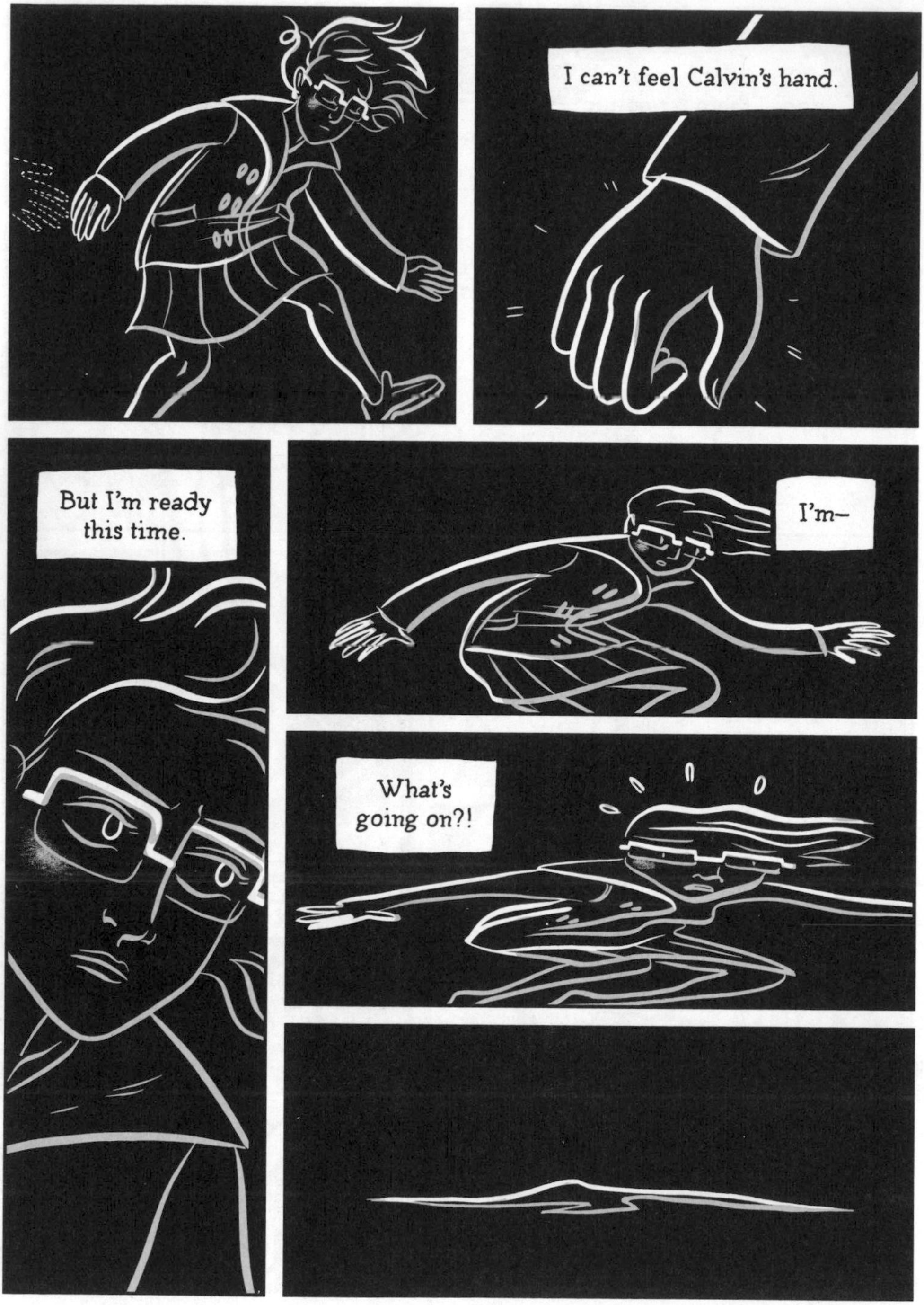
I can't feel Calvin's hand.
But I'm ready this time.
I'm–
What's going on?!

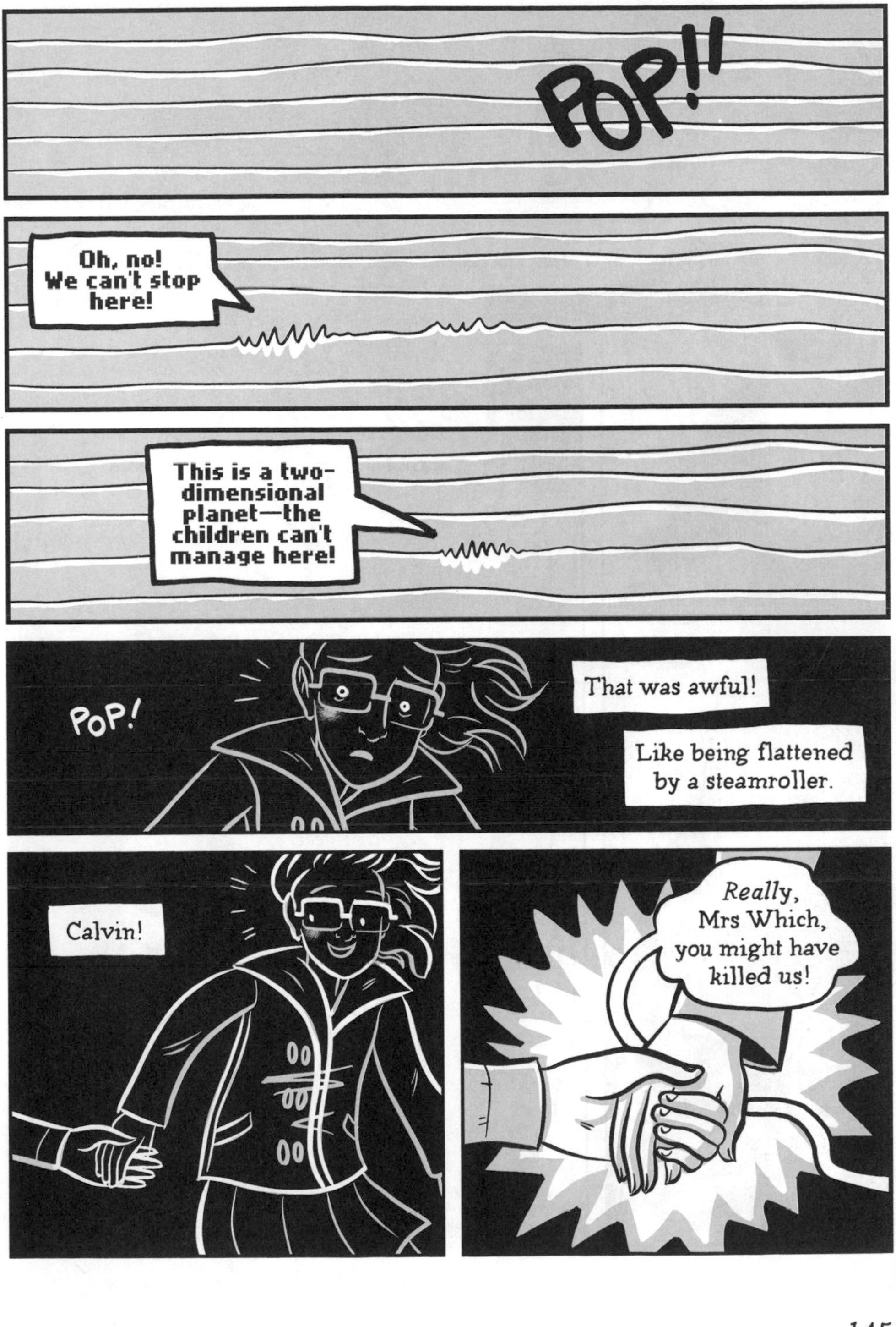
POP!!
Oh, no! We can't stop here!
This is a two-dimensional planet—the children can't manage here!
POP!
That was awful!
Like being flattened by a steamroller.
Calvin!
Really, Mrs Which, you might have killed us!

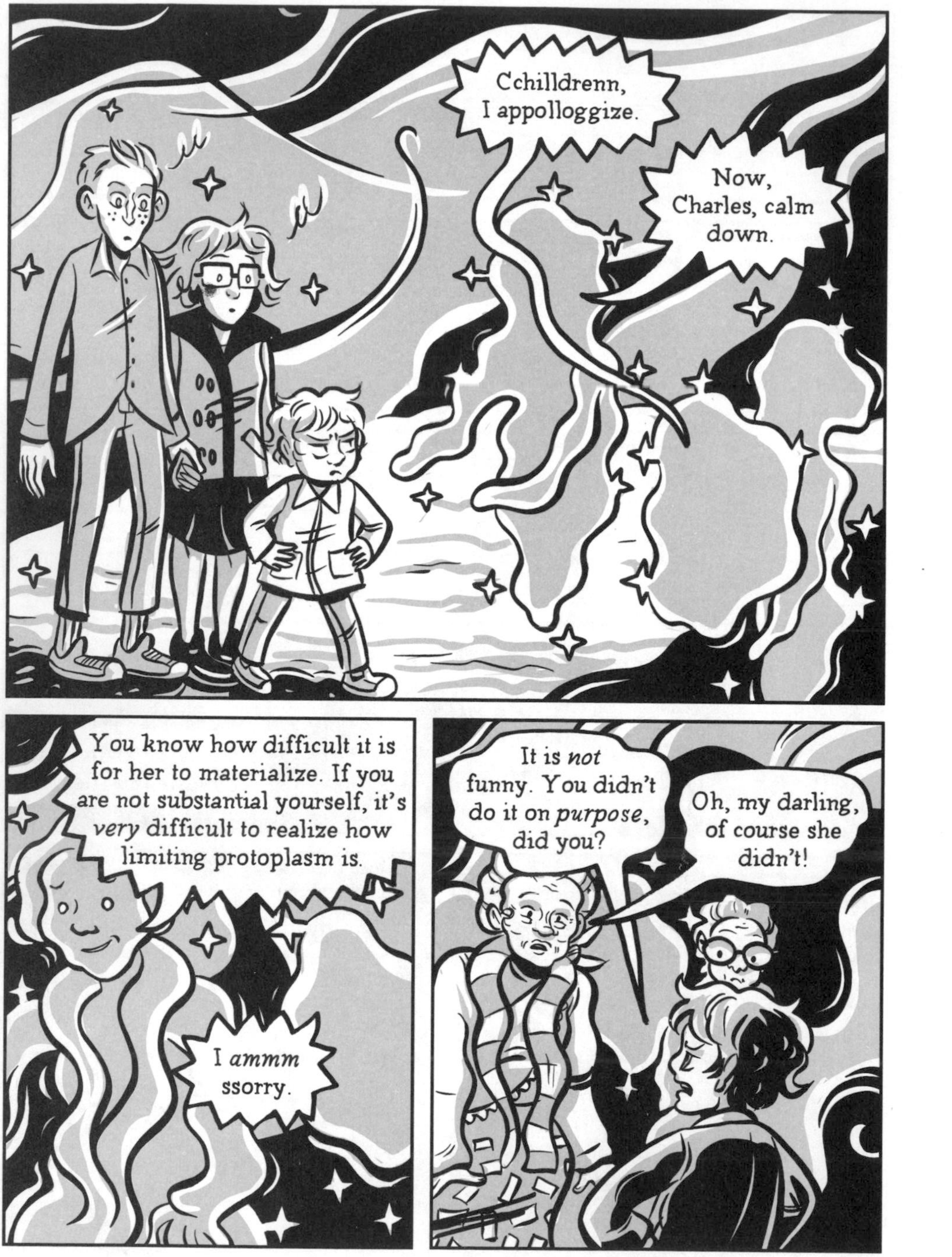
Cchilldrenn, I appolloggize.
Now, Charles, calm down.
You know how difficult it is for her to materialize. If you are not substantial yourself, it's *very* difficult to realize how limiting protoplasm is.
I *ammm* ssorry.
It is *not* funny. You didn't do it on *purpose*, did you?
Oh, my darling, of course she didn't!

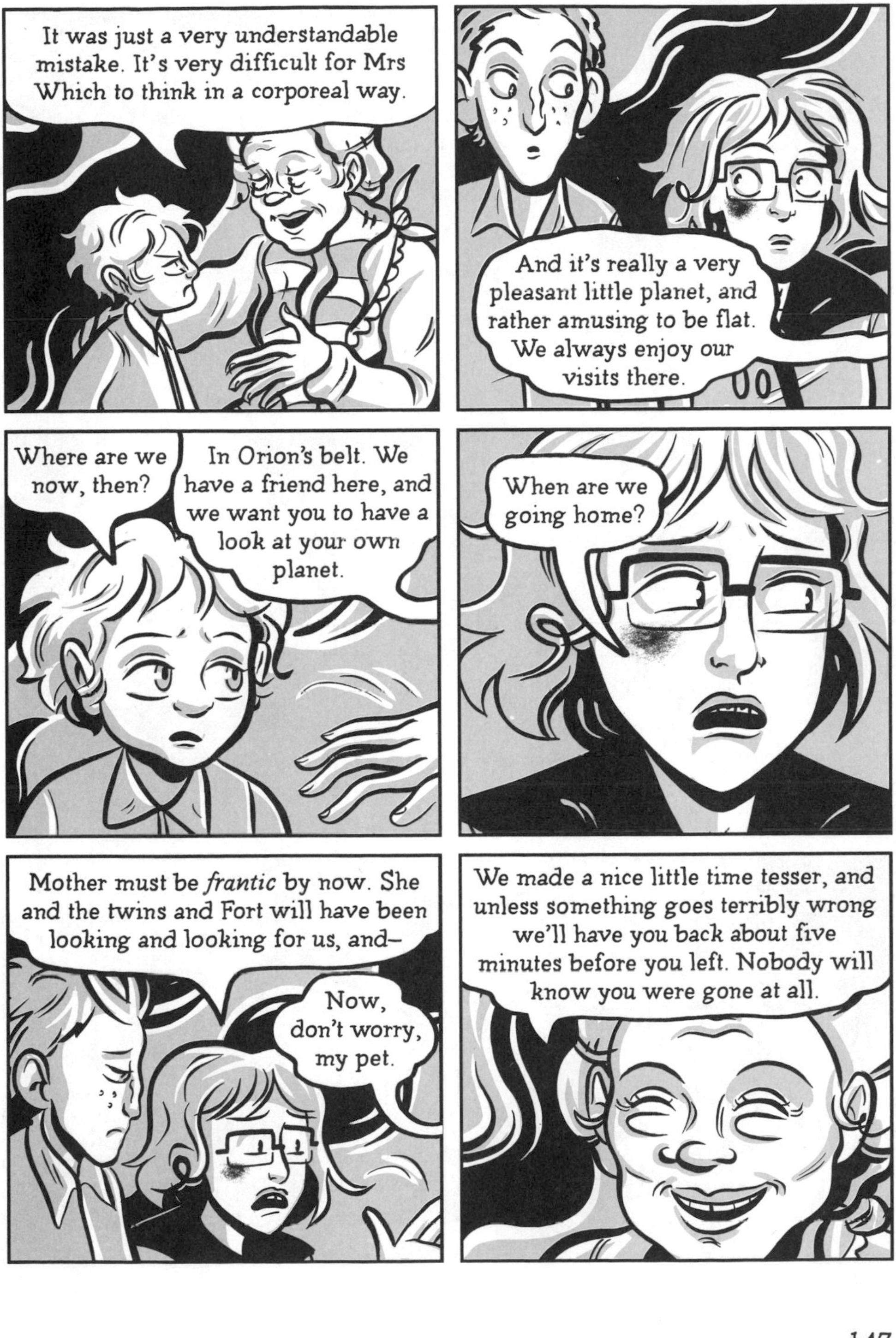
It was just a very understandable mistake. It's very difficult for Mrs Which to think in a corporeal way.
And it's really a very pleasant little planet, and rather amusing to be flat. We always enjoy our visits there.
Where are we now, then?
In Orion's belt. We have a friend here, and we want you to have a look at your own planet.
When are we going home?
Mother must be *frantic* by now. She and the twins and Fort will have been looking and looking for us, and–
Now, don't worry, my pet.
We made a nice little time tesser, and unless something goes terribly wrong we'll have you back about five minutes before you left. Nobody will know you were gone at all.

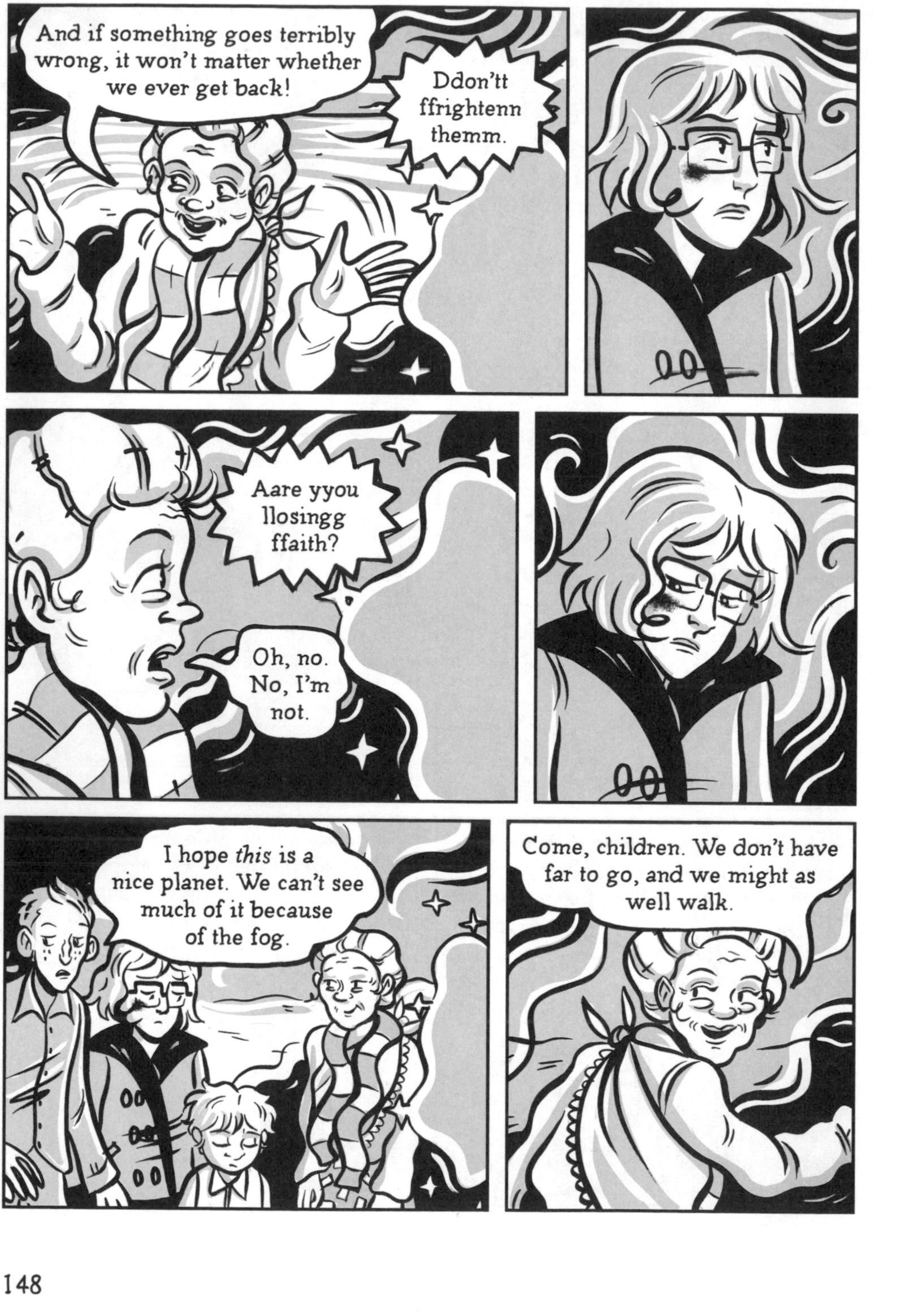
And if something goes terribly wrong, it won't matter whether we ever get back!
Ddon'tt ffrightenn themm.
Aare yyou llosingg ffaith?
Oh, no. No, I'm not.
I hope *this* is a nice planet. We can't see much of it because of the fog.
Come, children. We don't have far to go, and we might as well walk.

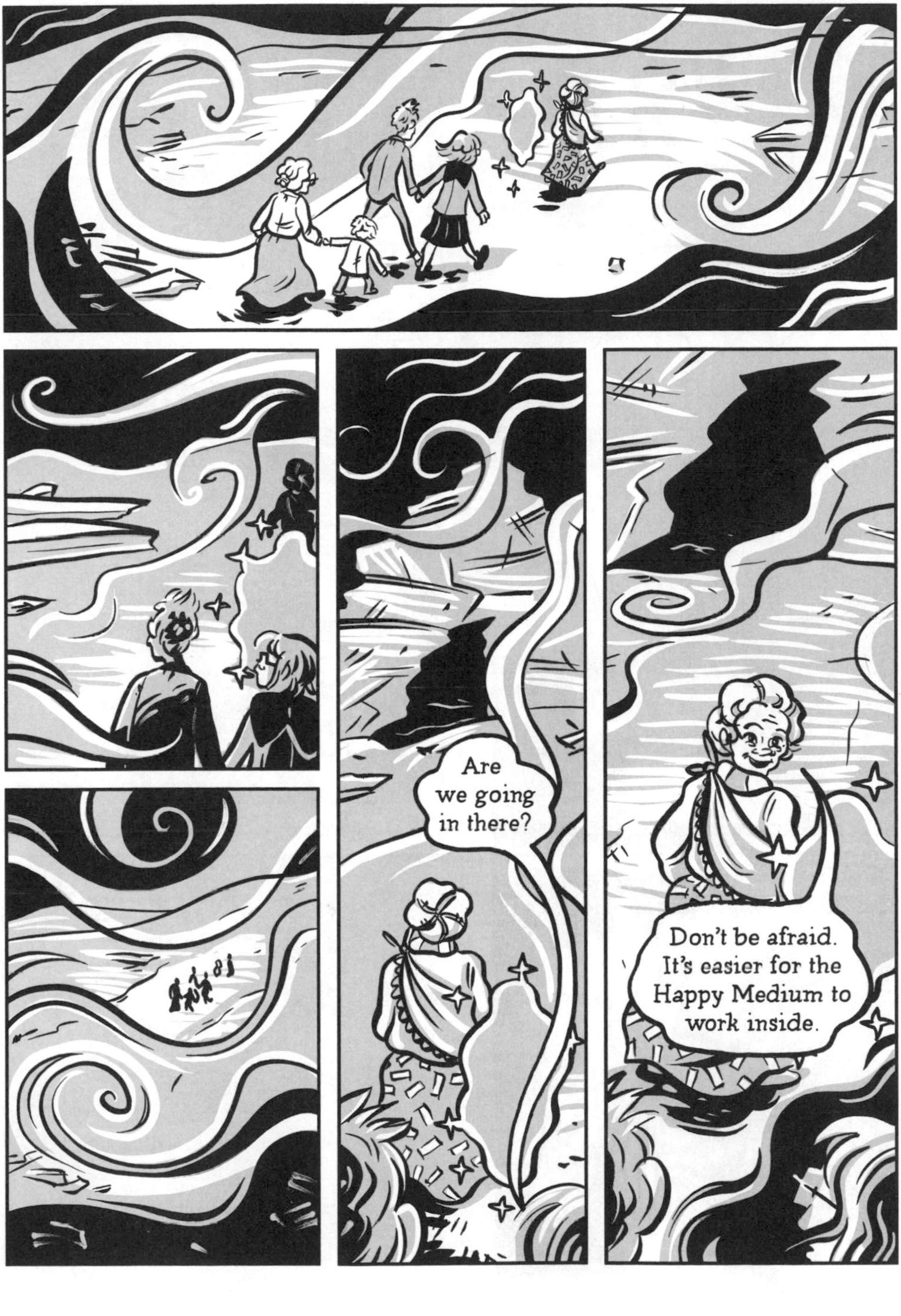
Are we going in there?
Don't be afraid. It's easier for the Happy Medium to work inside.

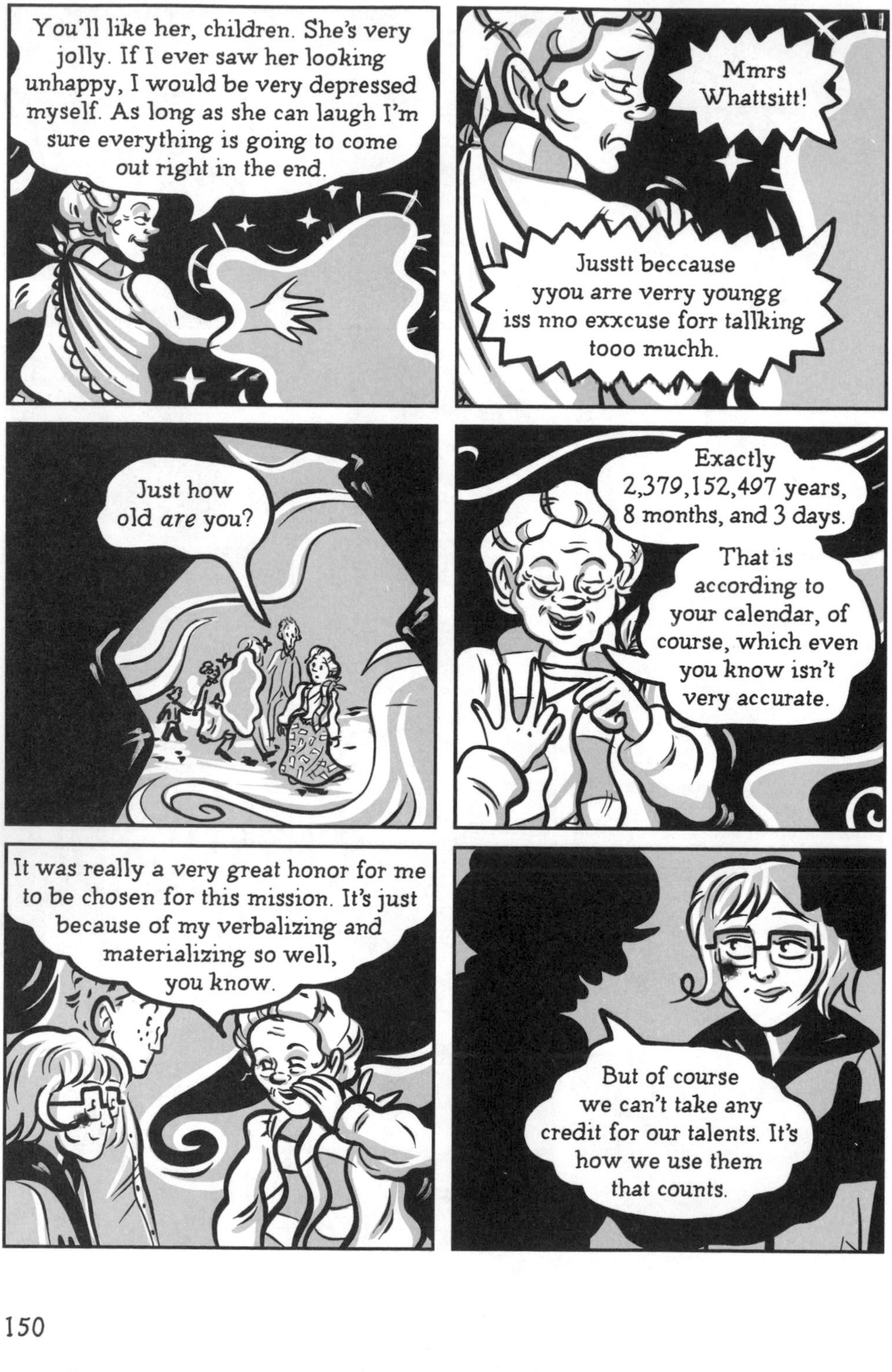
You'll like her, children. She's very jolly. If I ever saw her looking unhappy, I would be very depressed myself. As long as she can laugh I'm sure everything is going to come out right in the end.
Mmrs Whattsitt!
Jusstt beccause yyou arre verry youngg iss nno exxcuse forr tallking tooo muchh.
Just how old *are* you?
Exactly 2,379,152,497 years, 8 months, and 3 days.
That is according to your calendar, of course, which even you know isn't very accurate.
It was really a very great honor for me to be chosen for this mission. It's just because of my verbalizing and materializing so well, you know.
But of course we can't take any credit for our talents. It's how we use them that counts.

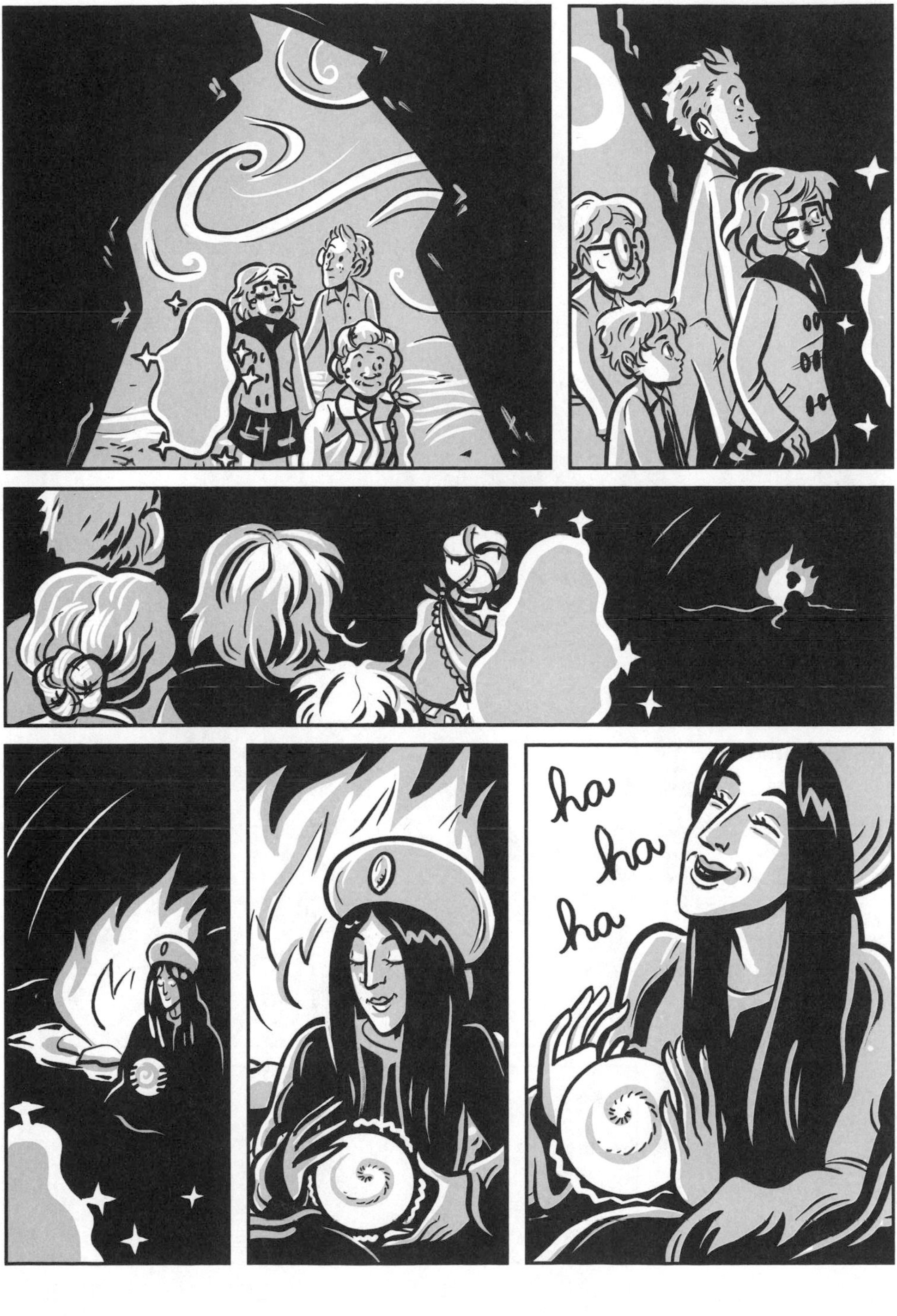
ha
ha
ha

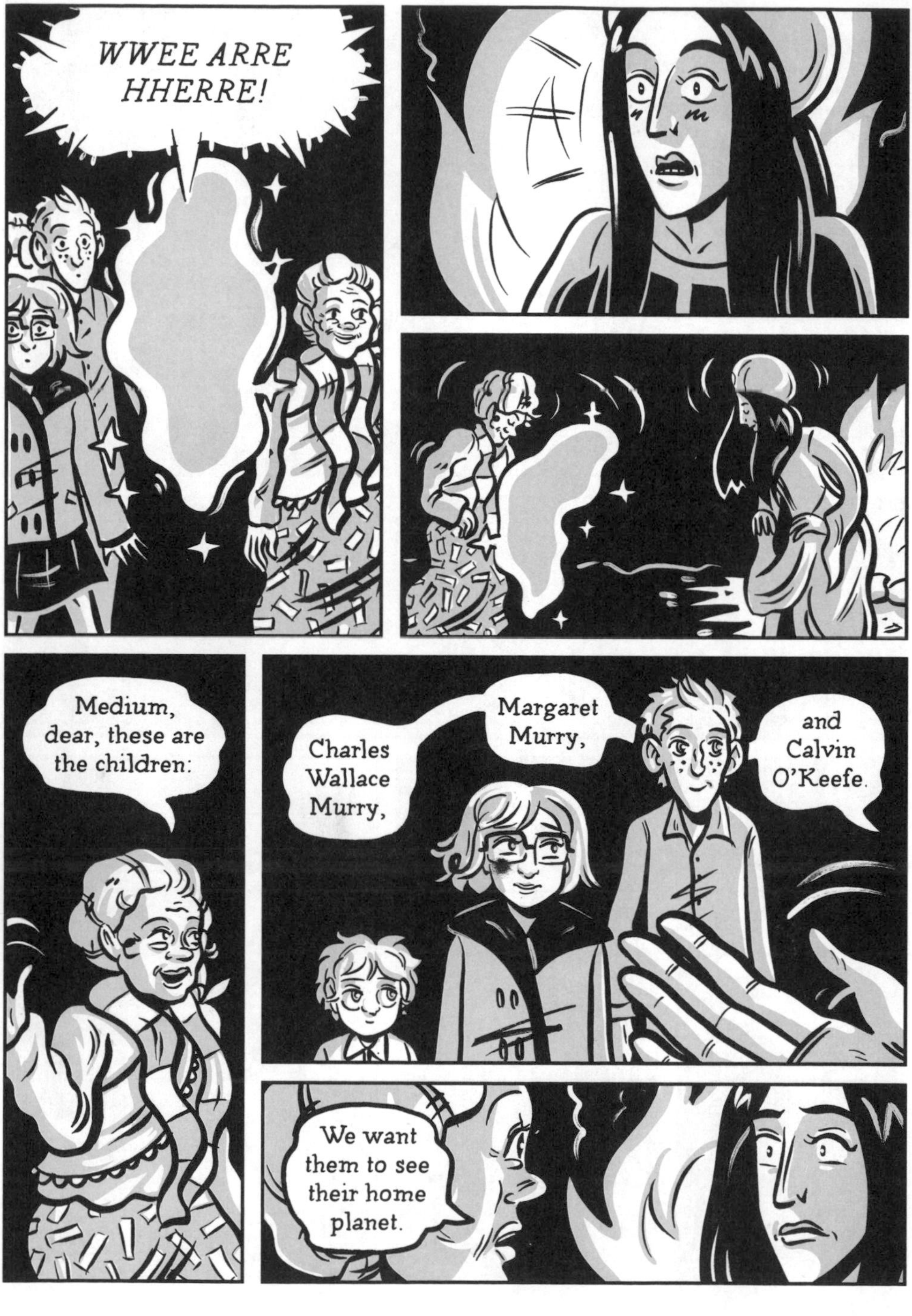
WWEE ARRE HHERRE!
Medium, dear, these are the children:
Charles Wallace Murry,
Margaret Murry,
and Calvin O'Keefe.
We want them to see their home planet.

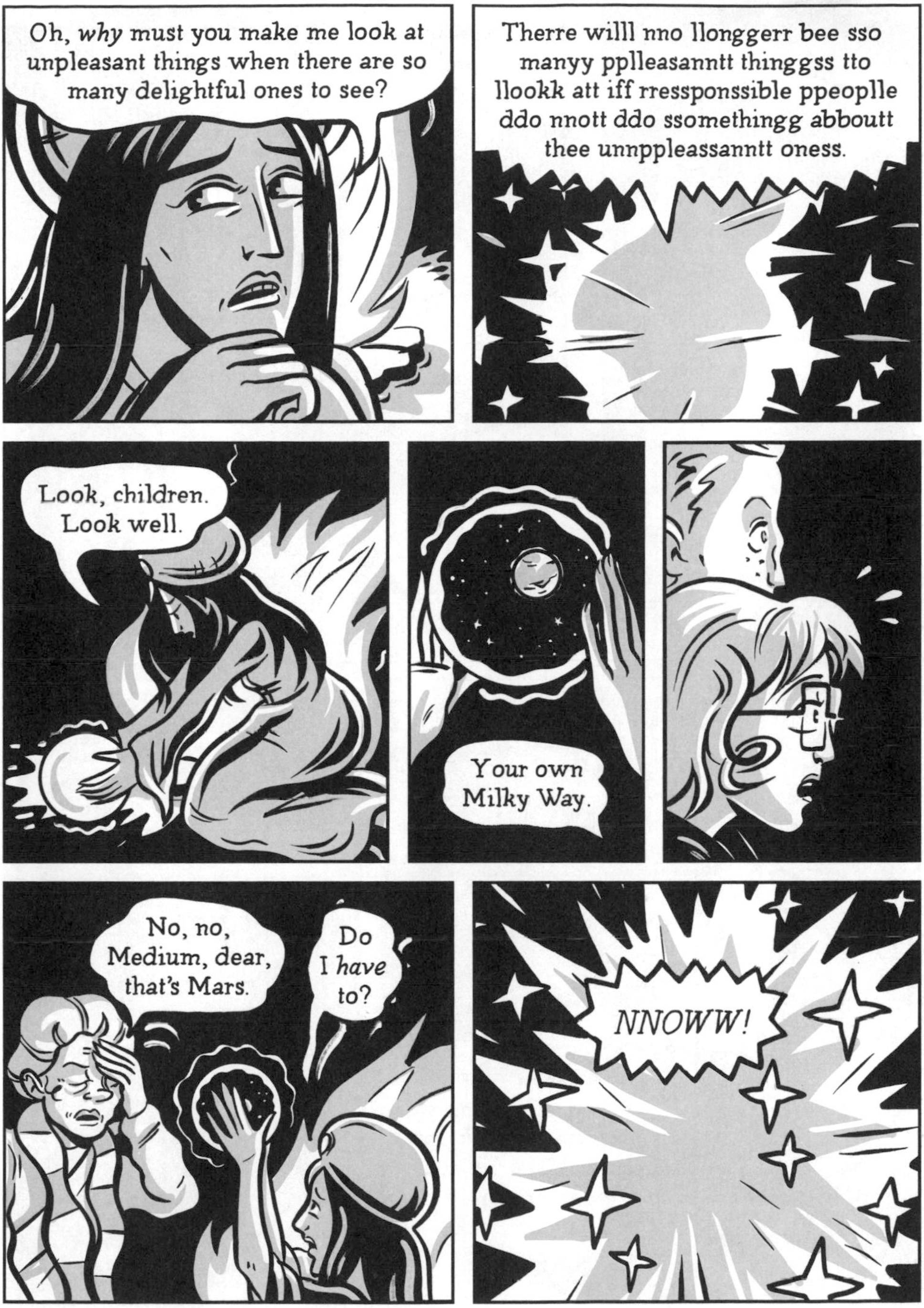

Oh, *why* must you make me look at unpleasant things when there are so many delightful ones to see?
Therre willl nno llonggerr bee sso manyy pplleasanntt thinggss tto llookk att iff rressponssible ppeopllle ddo nnott ddo ssomethingg abboutt thee unnppleassanntt oness.
Look, children. Look well.
Your own Milky Way.
No, no, Medium, dear, that's Mars.
Do I *have* to?
NNOWW!

Is it because of our atmosphere that we can't see properly?

Nno, Mmegg, yyou knnoww thatt itt iss nnott tthee attmosspheeere.

Yyou mmusstt bee brrave.

It's the Thing!

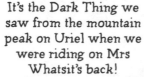

It's the Dark Thing we saw from the mountain peak on Uriel when we were riding on Mrs Whatsit's back!

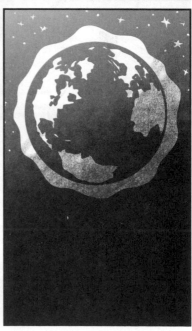

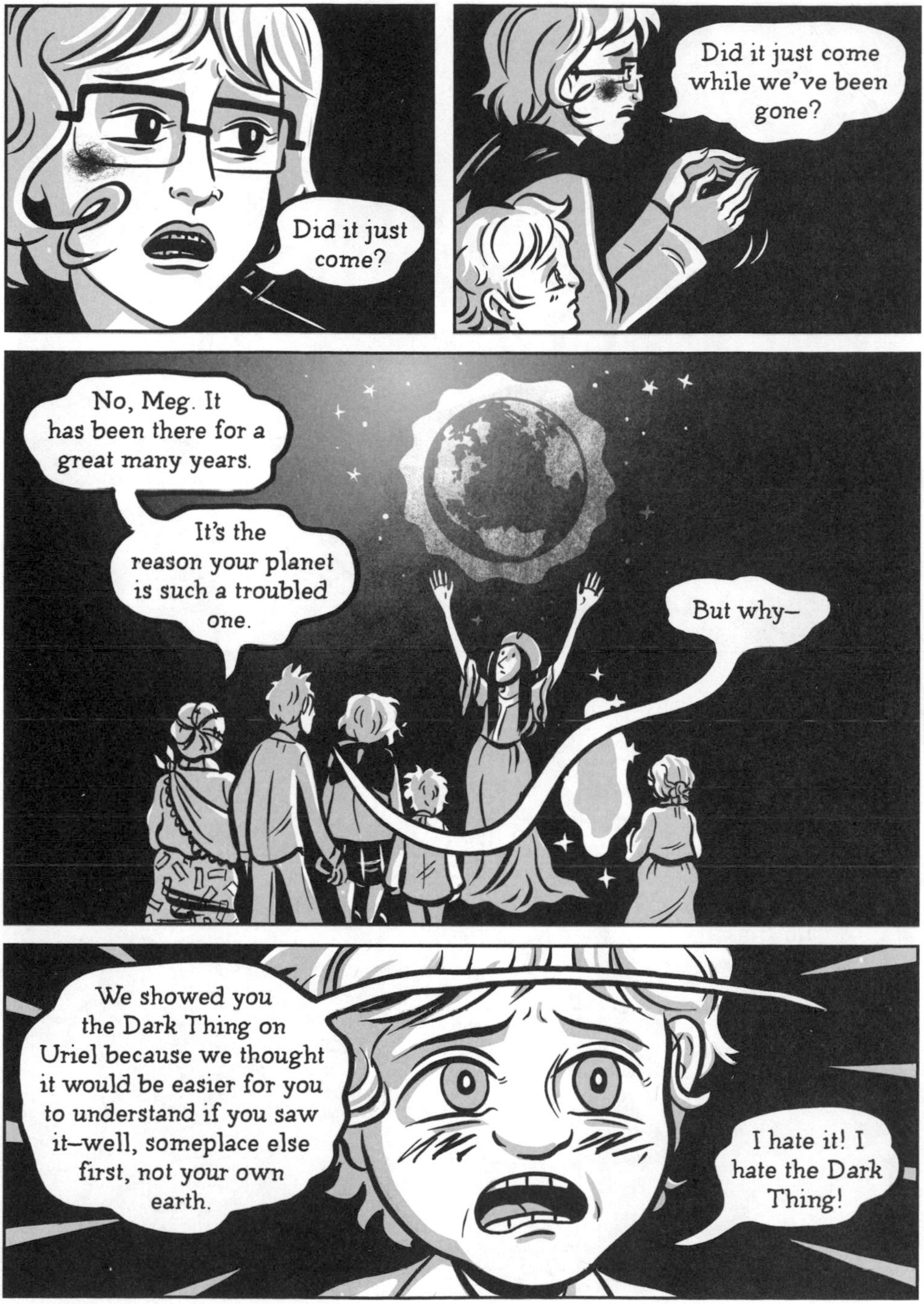
Did it just come?
Did it just come while we've been gone?
No, Meg. It has been there for a great many years.
It's the reason your planet is such a troubled one.
But why–
We showed you the Dark Thing on Uriel because we thought it would be easier for you to understand if you saw it–well, someplace else first, not your own earth.
I hate it! I hate the Dark Thing!

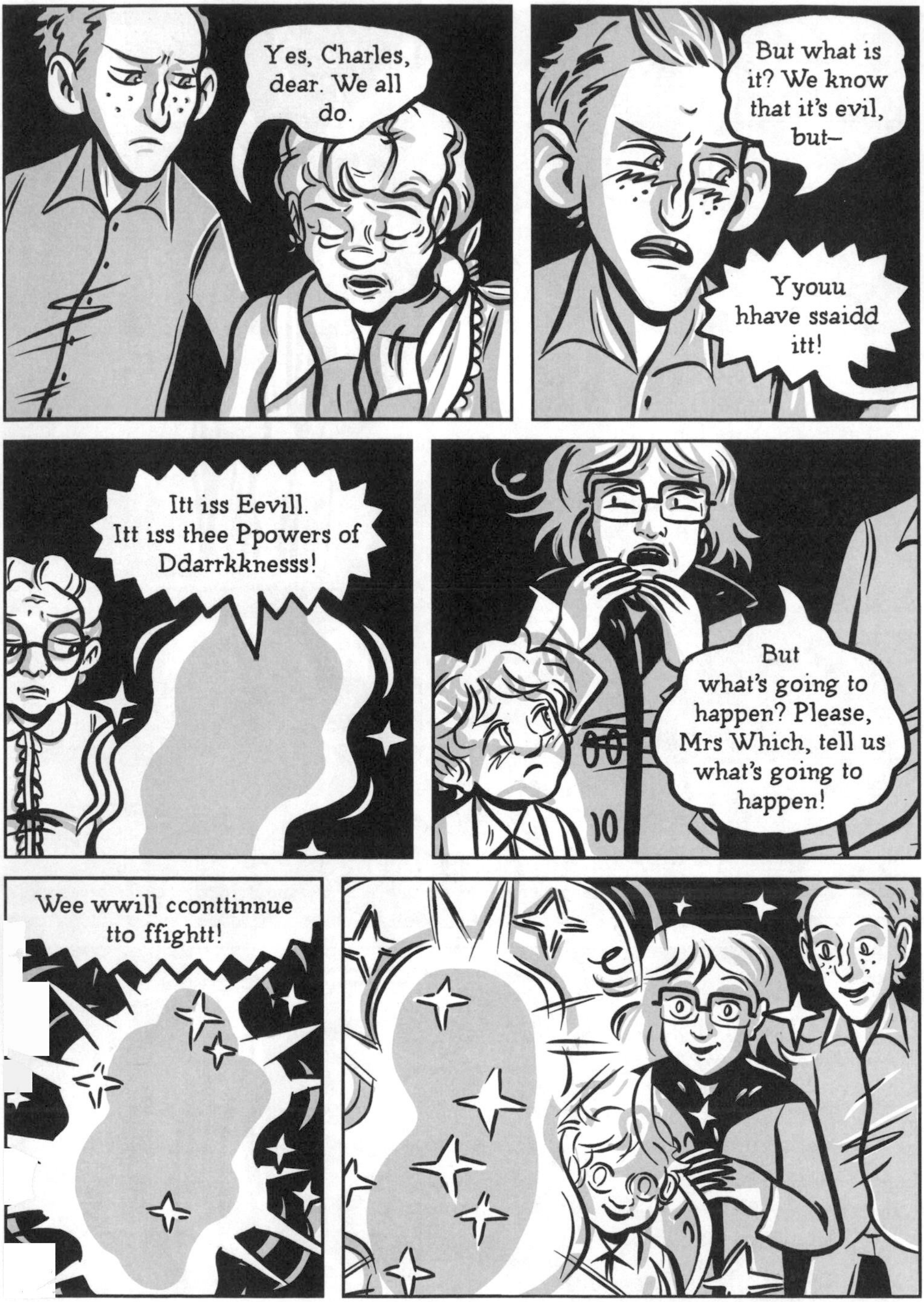
Yes, Charles, dear. We all do.
But what is it? We know that it's evil, but–
Yyouu hhave ssaidd itt!
Itt iss Eevill. Itt iss thee Ppowers of Ddarrkknesss!
But what's going to happen? Please, Mrs Which, tell us what's going to happen!
Wee wwill ccontinnue tto ffightt!

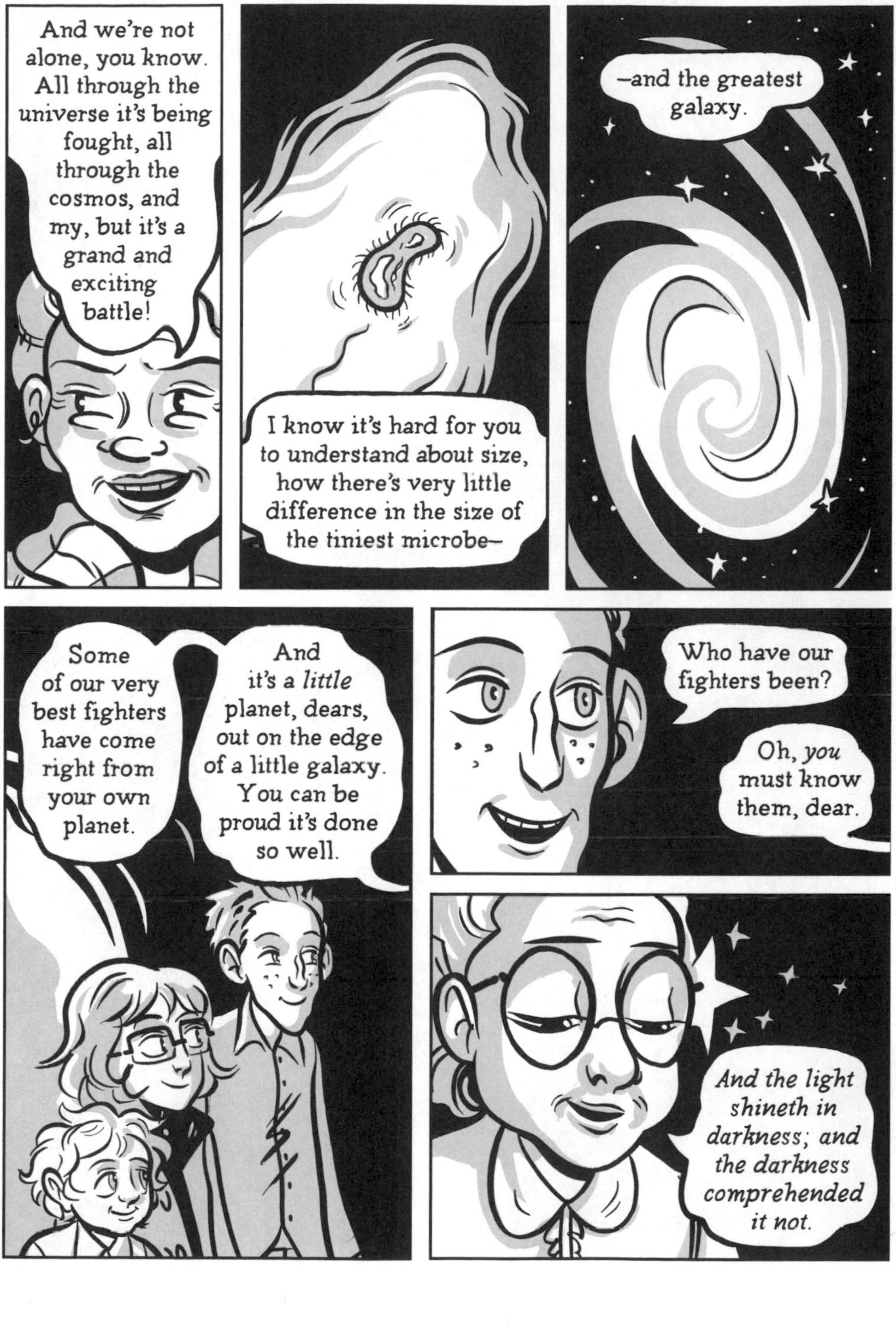

And we're not alone, you know. All through the universe it's being fought, all through the cosmos, and my, but it's a grand and exciting battle!
I know it's hard for you to understand about size, how there's very little difference in the size of the tiniest microbe—
—and the greatest galaxy.
Some of our very best fighters have come right from your own planet.
And it's a *little* planet, dears, out on the edge of a little galaxy. You can be proud it's done so well.
Who have our fighters been?
Oh, *you* must know them, dear.
And the light shineth in darkness; and the darkness comprehended it not.

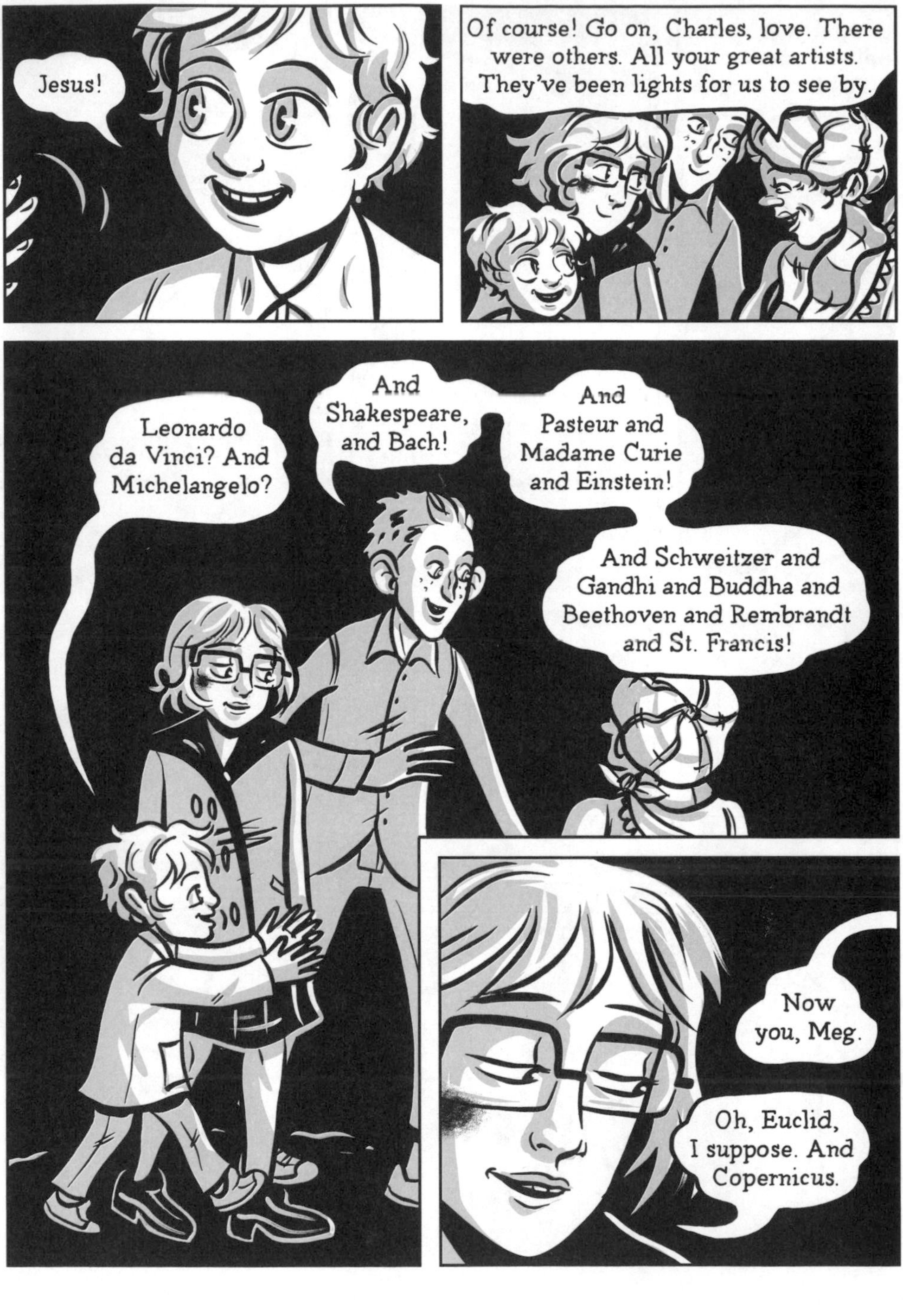
Jesus!
Of course! Go on, Charles, love. There were others. All your great artists. They've been lights for us to see by.
Leonardo da Vinci? And Michelangelo?
And Shakespeare, and Bach!
And Pasteur and Madame Curie and Einstein!
And Schweitzer and Gandhi and Buddha and Beethoven and Rembrandt and St. Francis!
Now you, Meg.
Oh, Euclid, I suppose. And Copernicus.

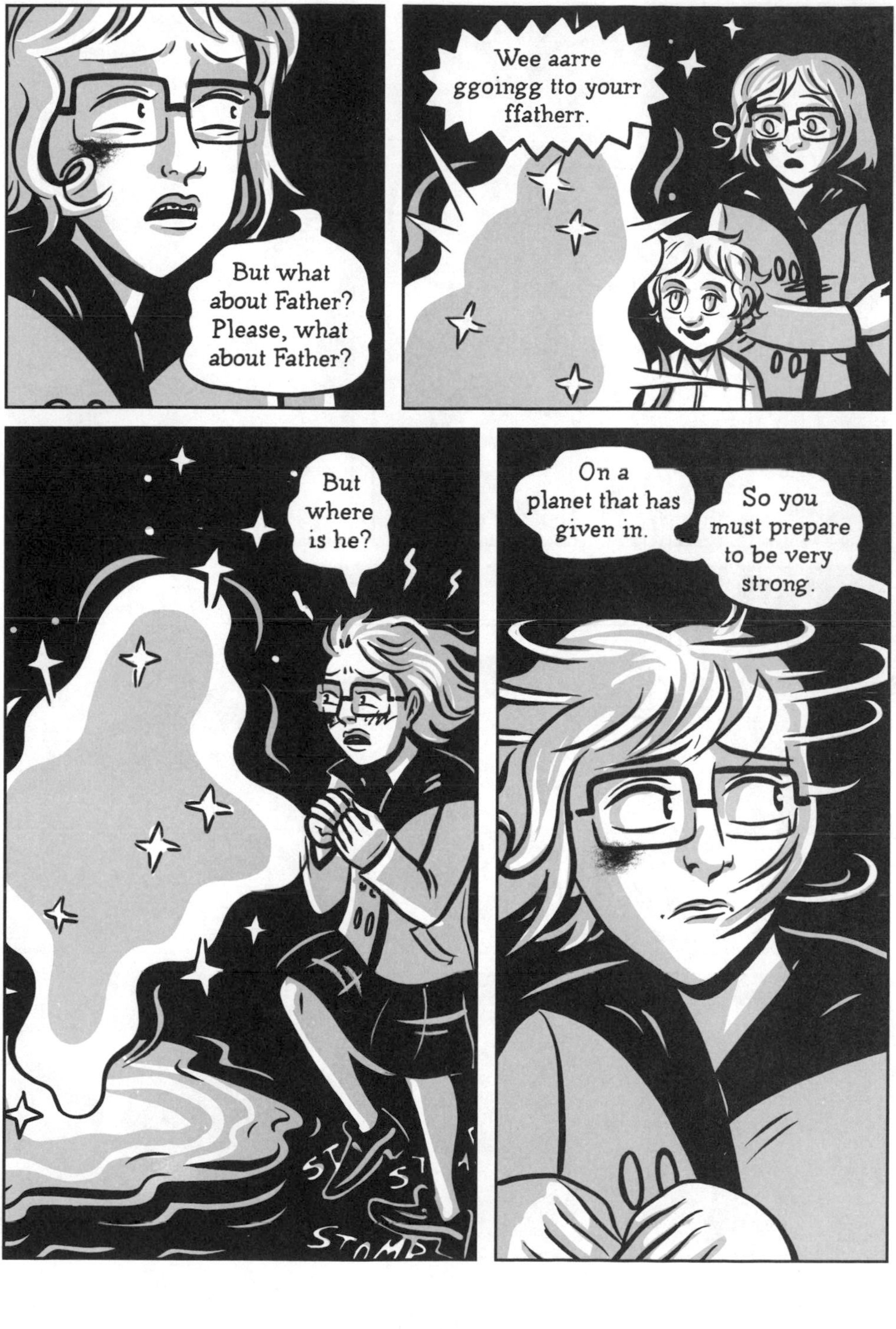

But what about Father? Please, what about Father?
Wee aarre ggoingg tto yourr ffatherr.
But where is he?
STOMP
On a planet that has given in.
So you must prepare to be very strong.

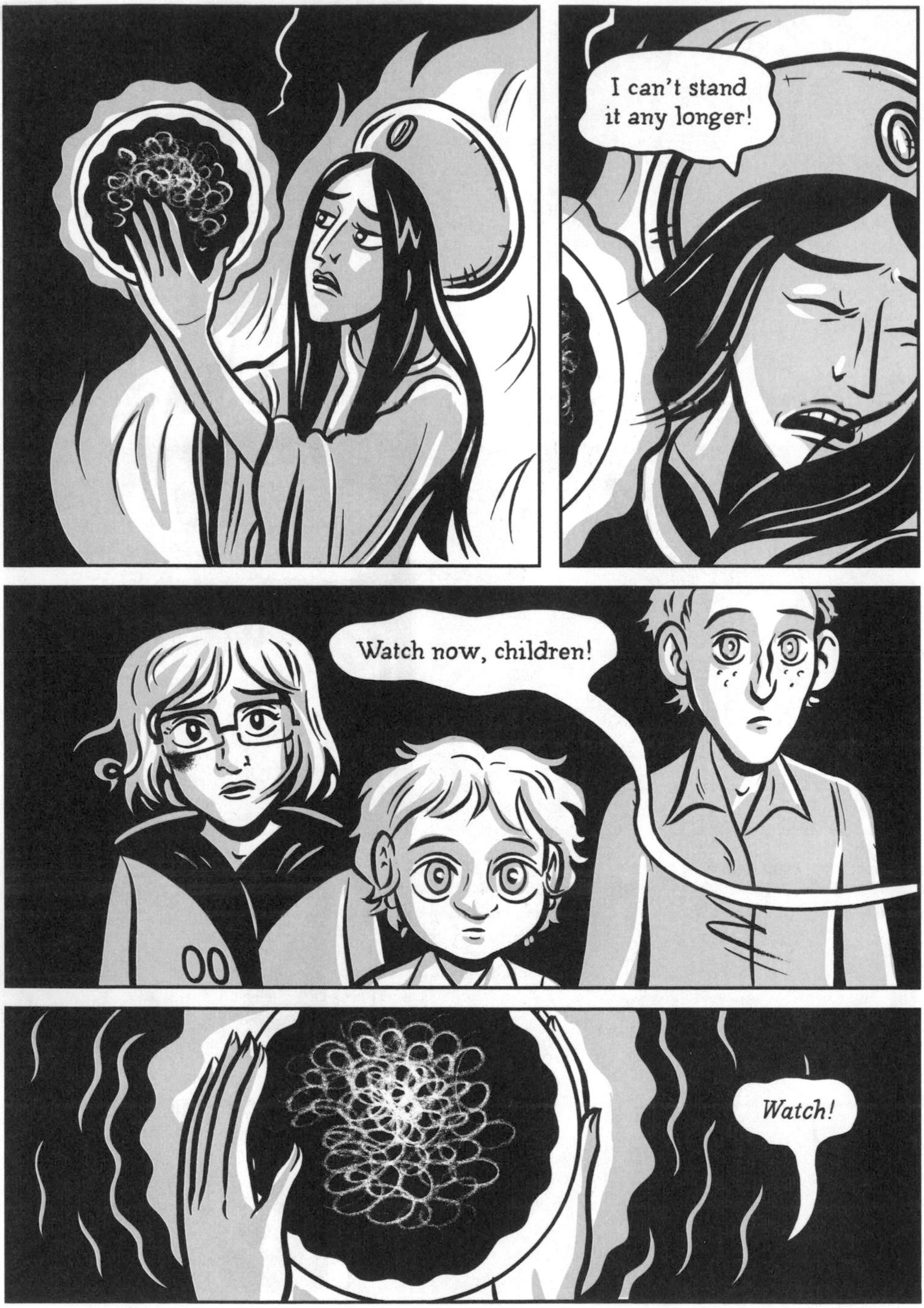
I can't stand it any longer!
Watch now, children!
Watch!

6
The Happy Medium

Watch!

This is supposed to *comfort* us?

PING!

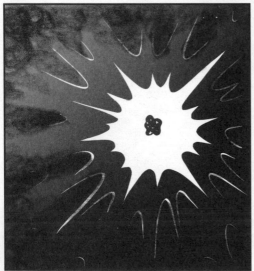

You see! It can be overcome! It is being overcome all the time!

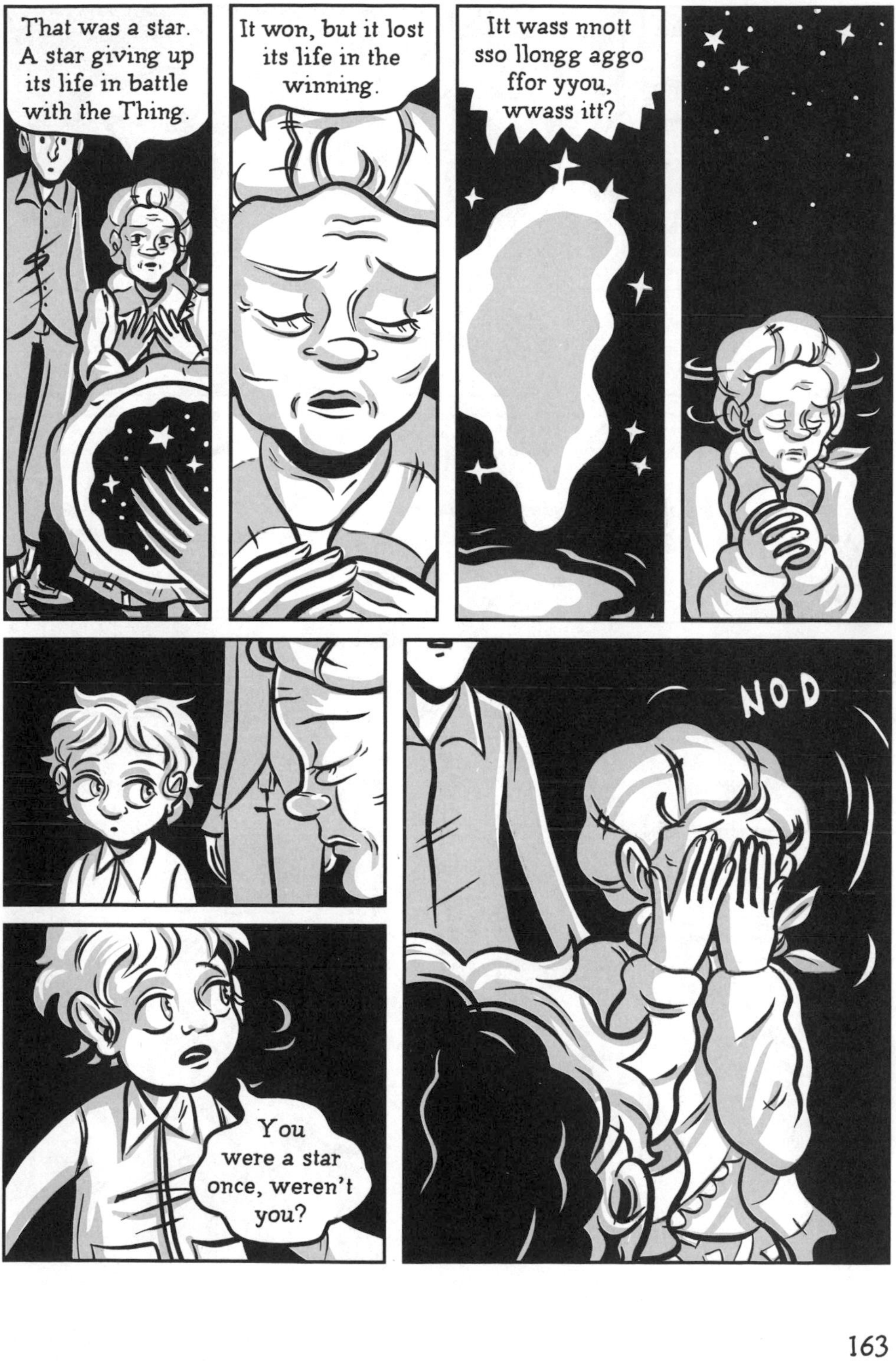
That was a star. A star giving up its life in battle with the Thing.
It won, but it lost its life in the winning.
Itt wass nnott sso llongg aggo ffor yyou, wwass itt?
NOD
You were a star once, weren't you?

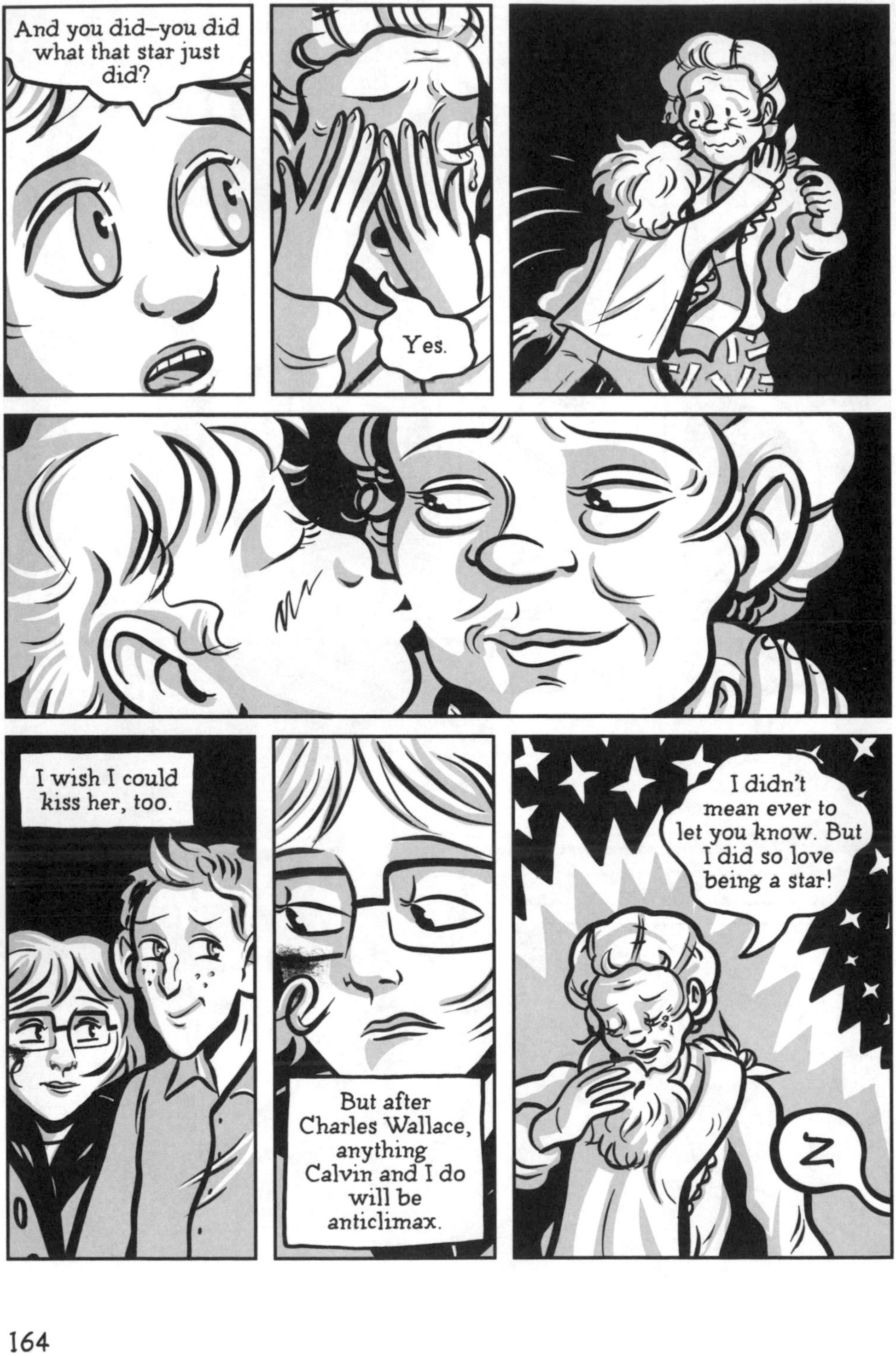
And you did—you did what that star just did?
Yes.
I wish I could kiss her, too.
But after Charles Wallace, anything Calvin and I do will be anticlimax.
I didn't mean ever to let you know. But I did so love being a star!
Z

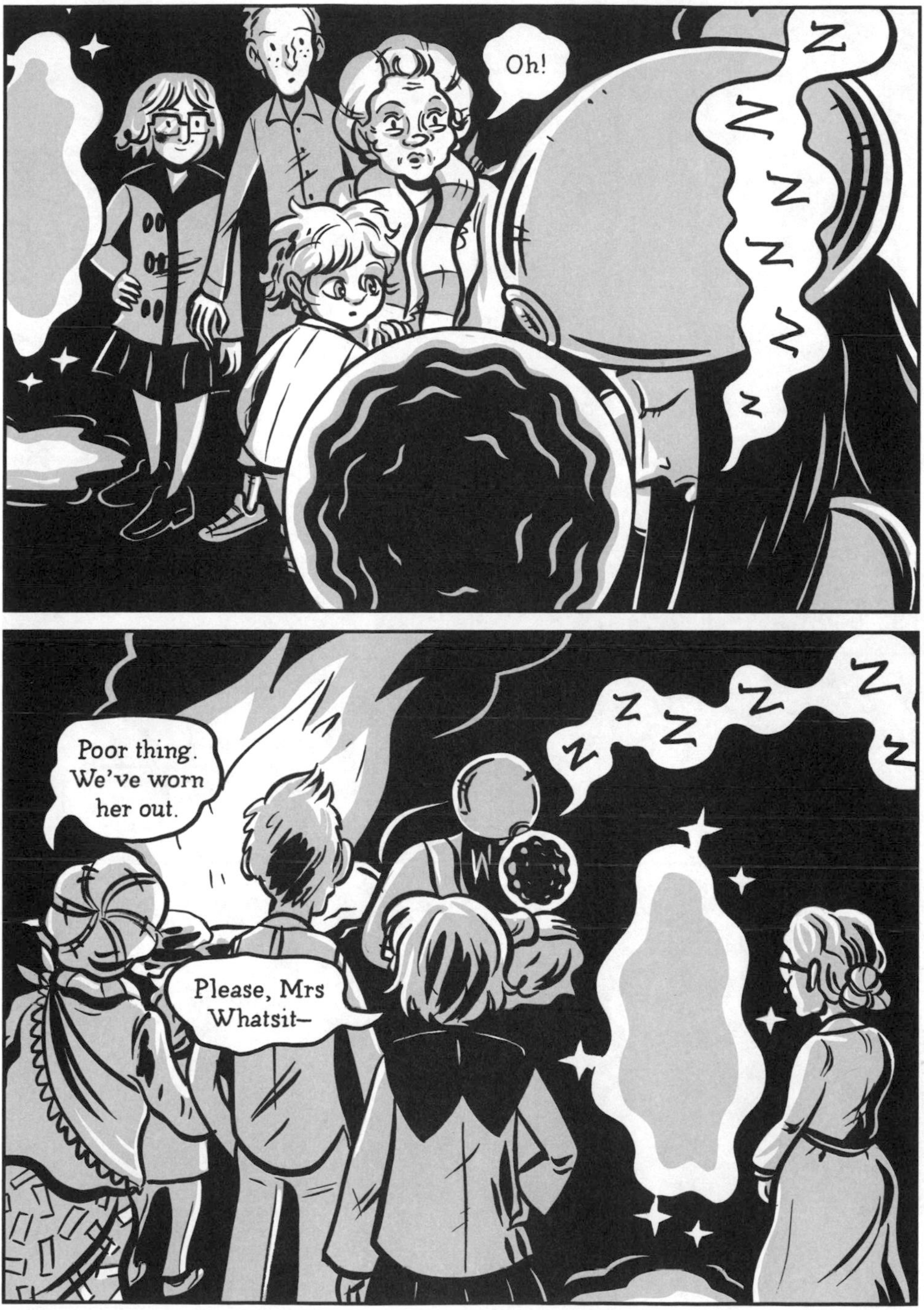
Oh!
Z Z Z Z Z Z Z
Poor thing. We've worn her out.
Z Z Z Z Z Z
Please, Mrs Whatsit–

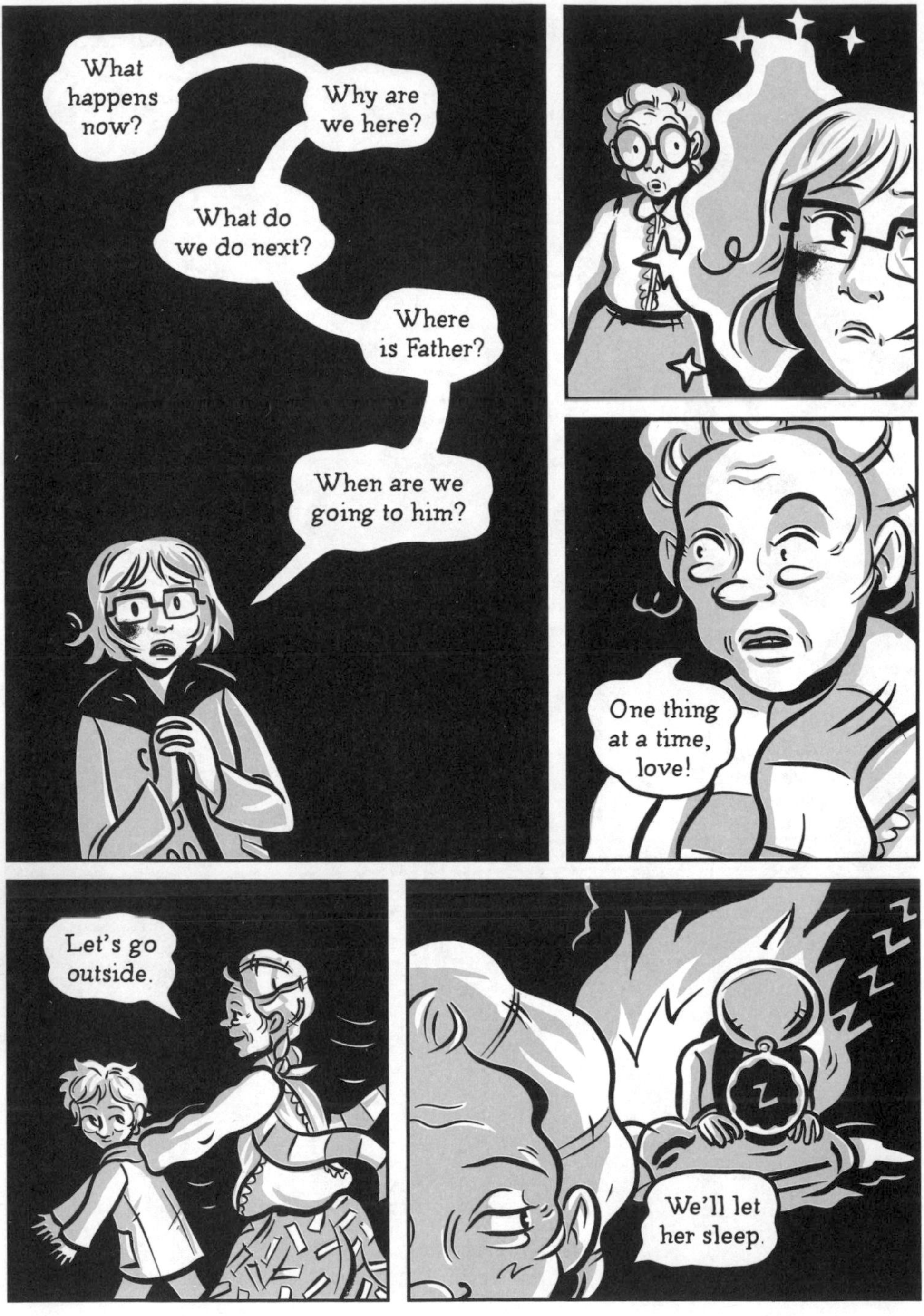
What happens now?
Why are we here?
What do we do next?
Where is Father?
When are we going to him?
One thing at a time, love!
Let's go outside.
We'll let her sleep.

You weren't going to go without saying good-bye?

I was going to give you some ambrosia or nectar or at least some tea.

Gurrrgle

How long has it been since we ate those bowls of stew?

Thank you, dear, but I think we'd better be going.

They don't need to eat, you know. Not food, anyway. As soon as we get organized I'll remind them they have to feed us sooner or later.

But I should do something nice for you, after showing you such horrible things.

Would you like to see your mothers before you go?

Could we see Father?

Nno. Wwee aare ggoingg tto yourr ffatherr, Mmegg. Ddo nnott bbee immpatientt.

But she *could* see her mother, couldn't she?

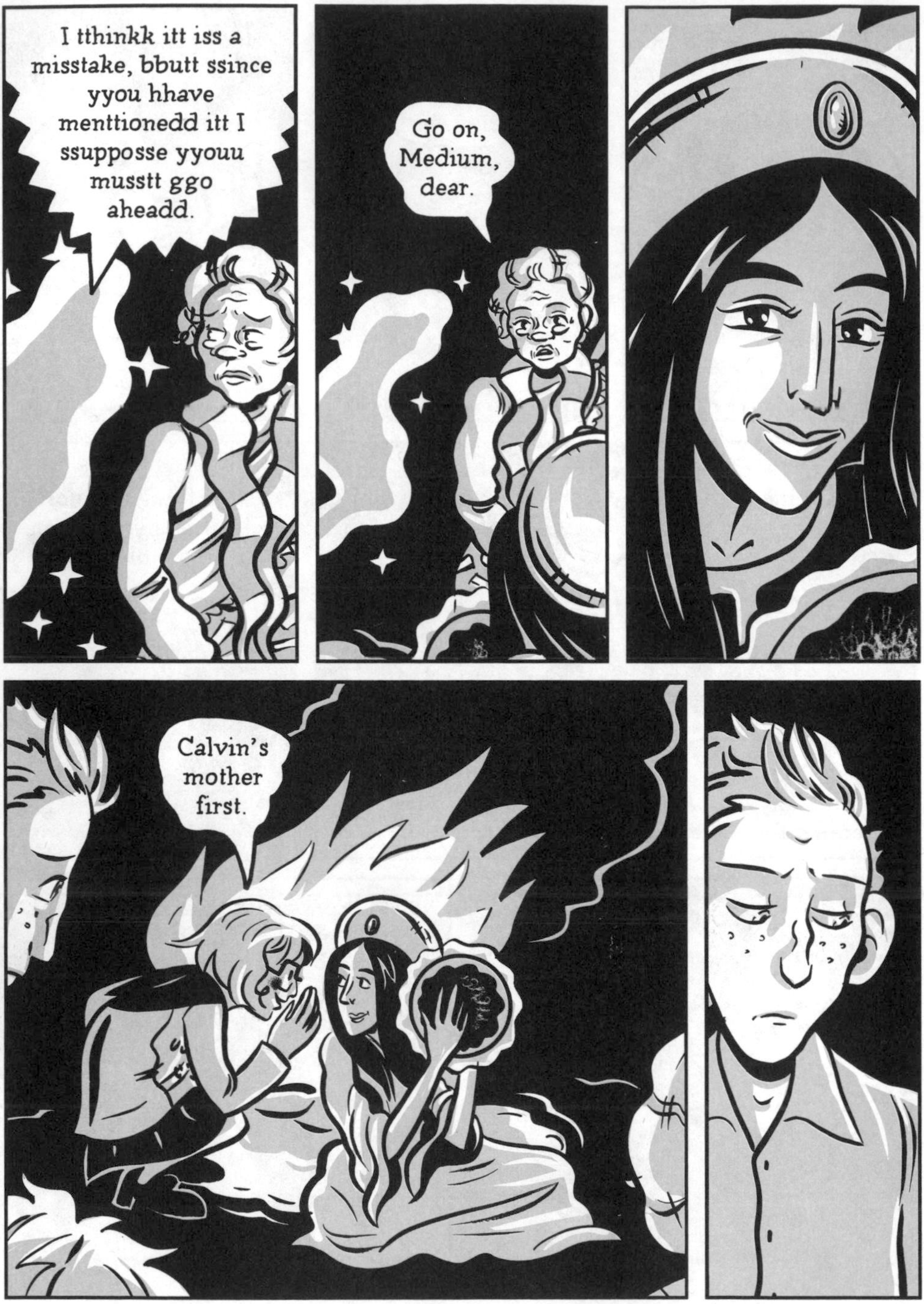
I tthinkk itt iss a misstake, bbutt ssince yyou hhave menttionedd itt I ssupposse yyouu musstt ggo aheadd.
Go on, Medium, dear.
Calvin's mother first.

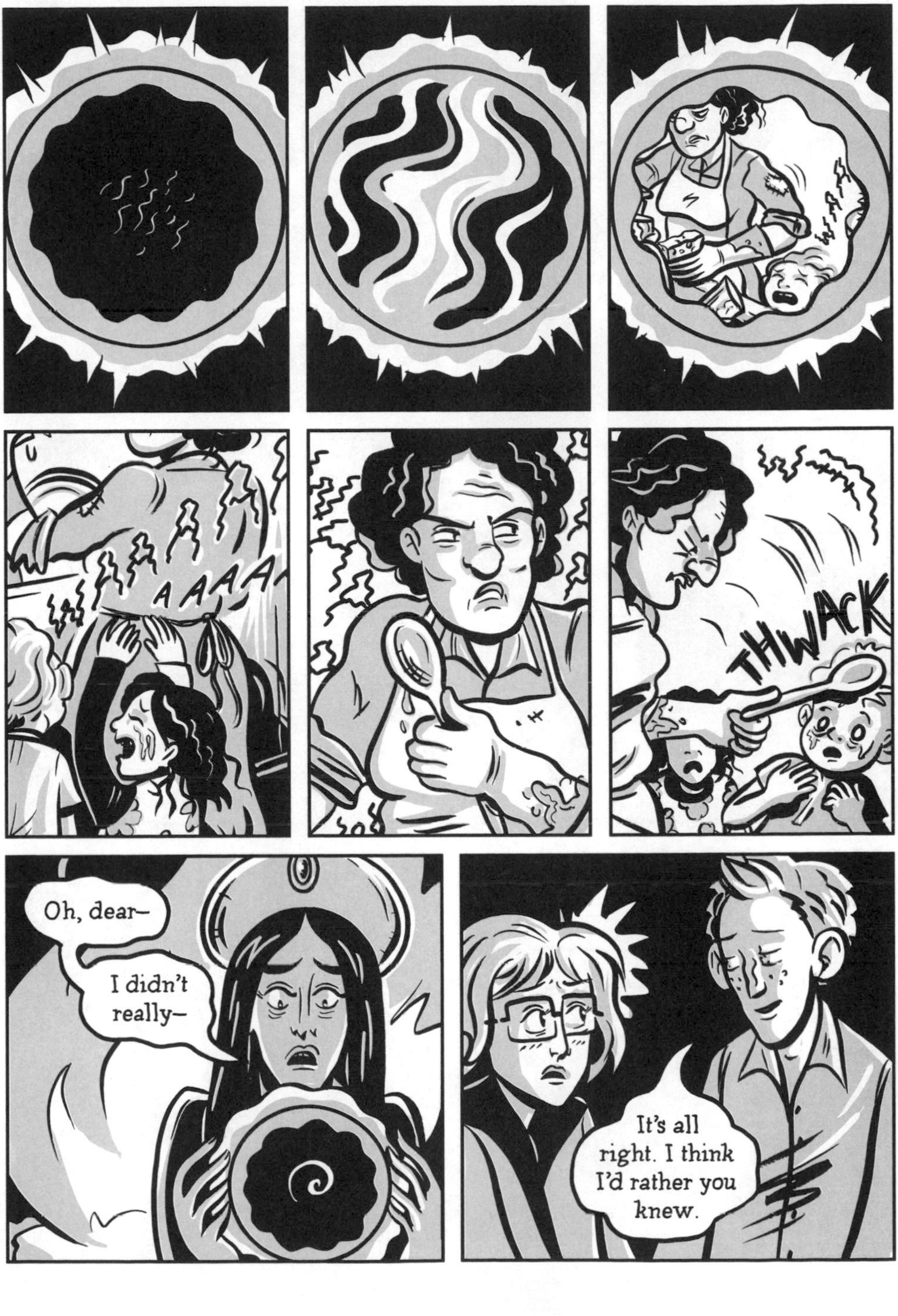
AAAA
THWACK
Oh, dear—
I didn't really—
It's all right. I think I'd rather you knew.

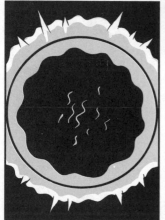

She's writing Father, like she does every night.

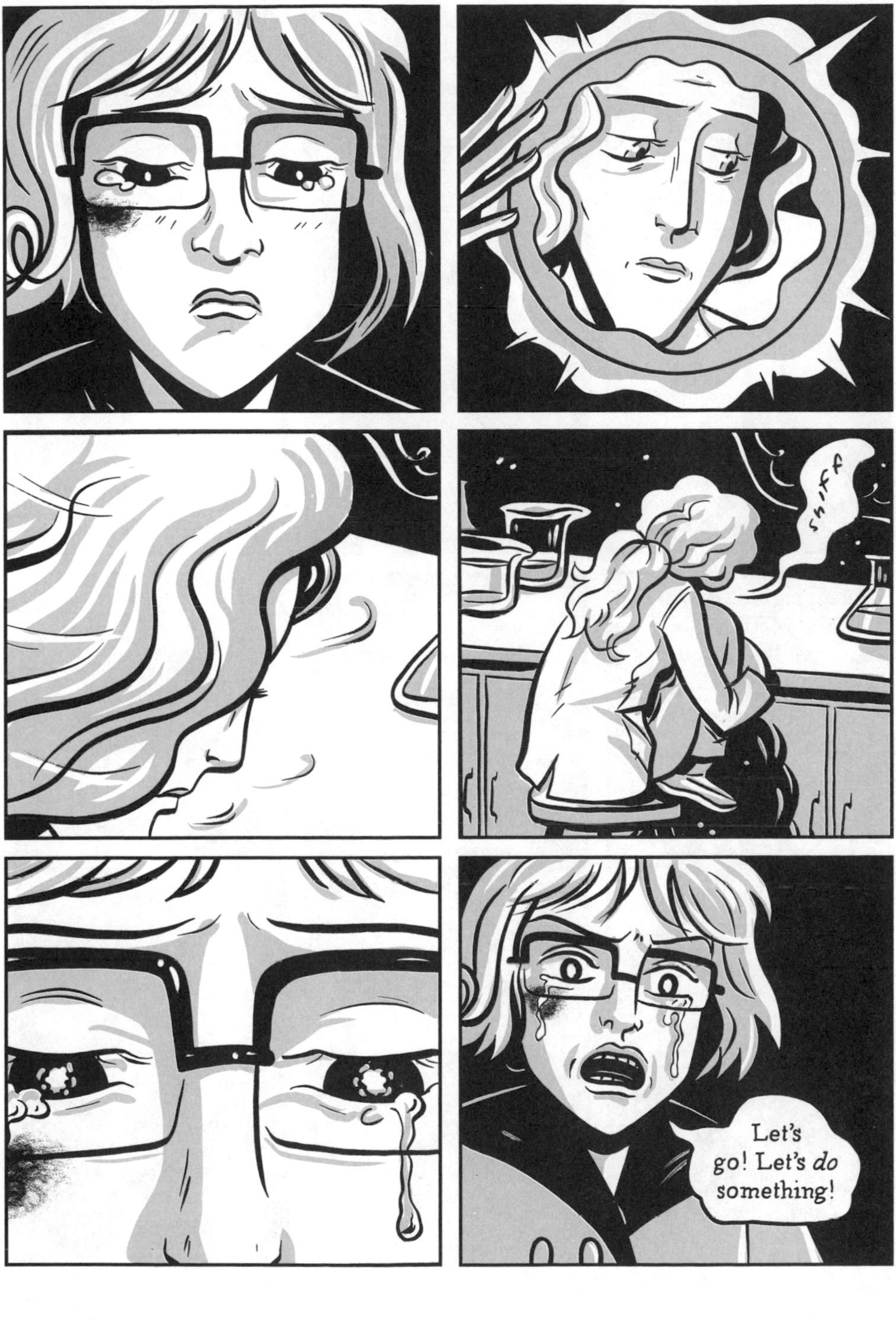
sniff
Let's go! Let's *do* something!

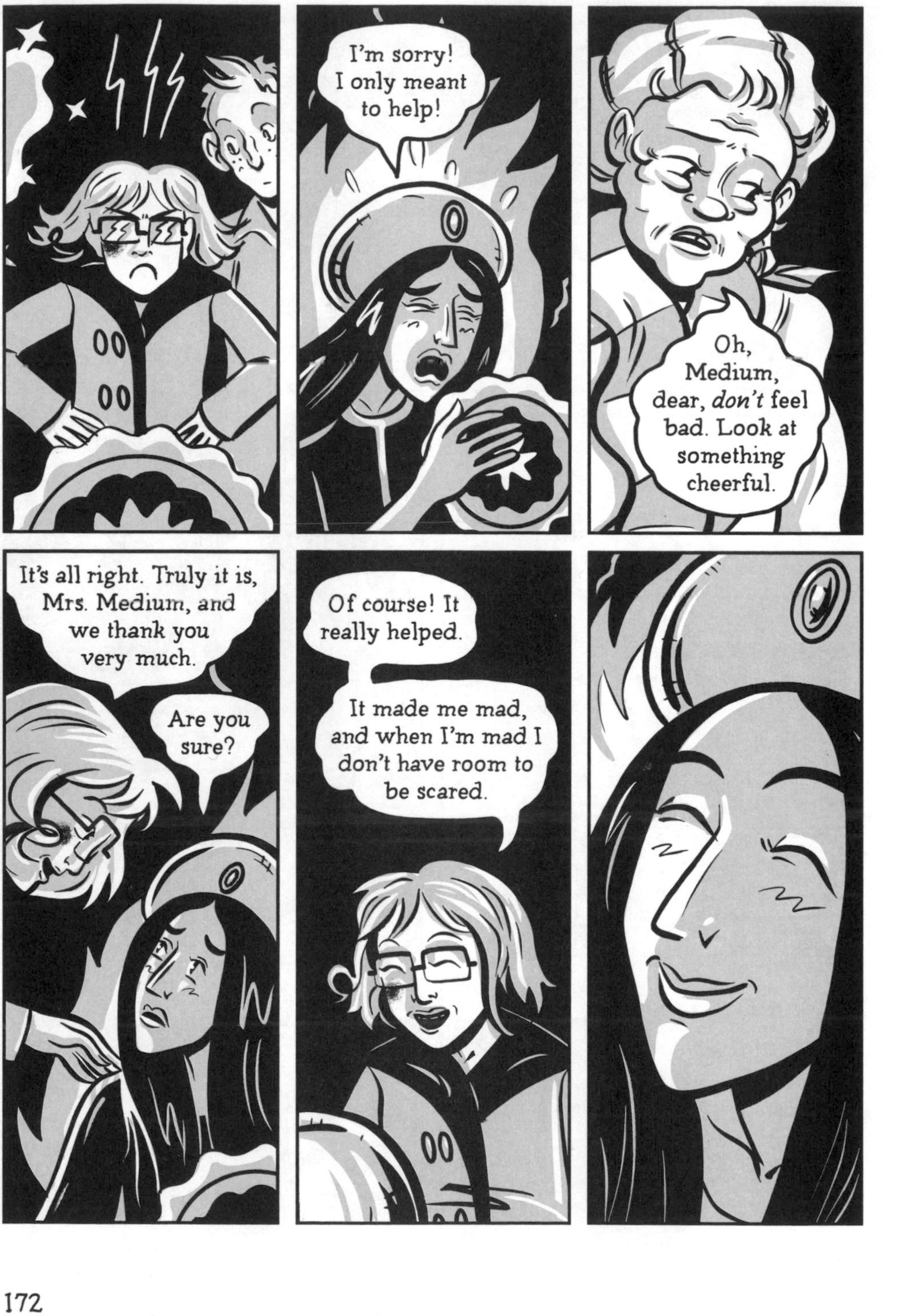
I'm sorry! I only meant to help!
Oh, Medium, dear, *don't* feel bad. Look at something cheerful.
It's all right. Truly it is, Mrs. Medium, and we thank you very much.
Are you sure?
Of course! It really helped.
It made me mad, and when I'm mad I don't have room to be scared.

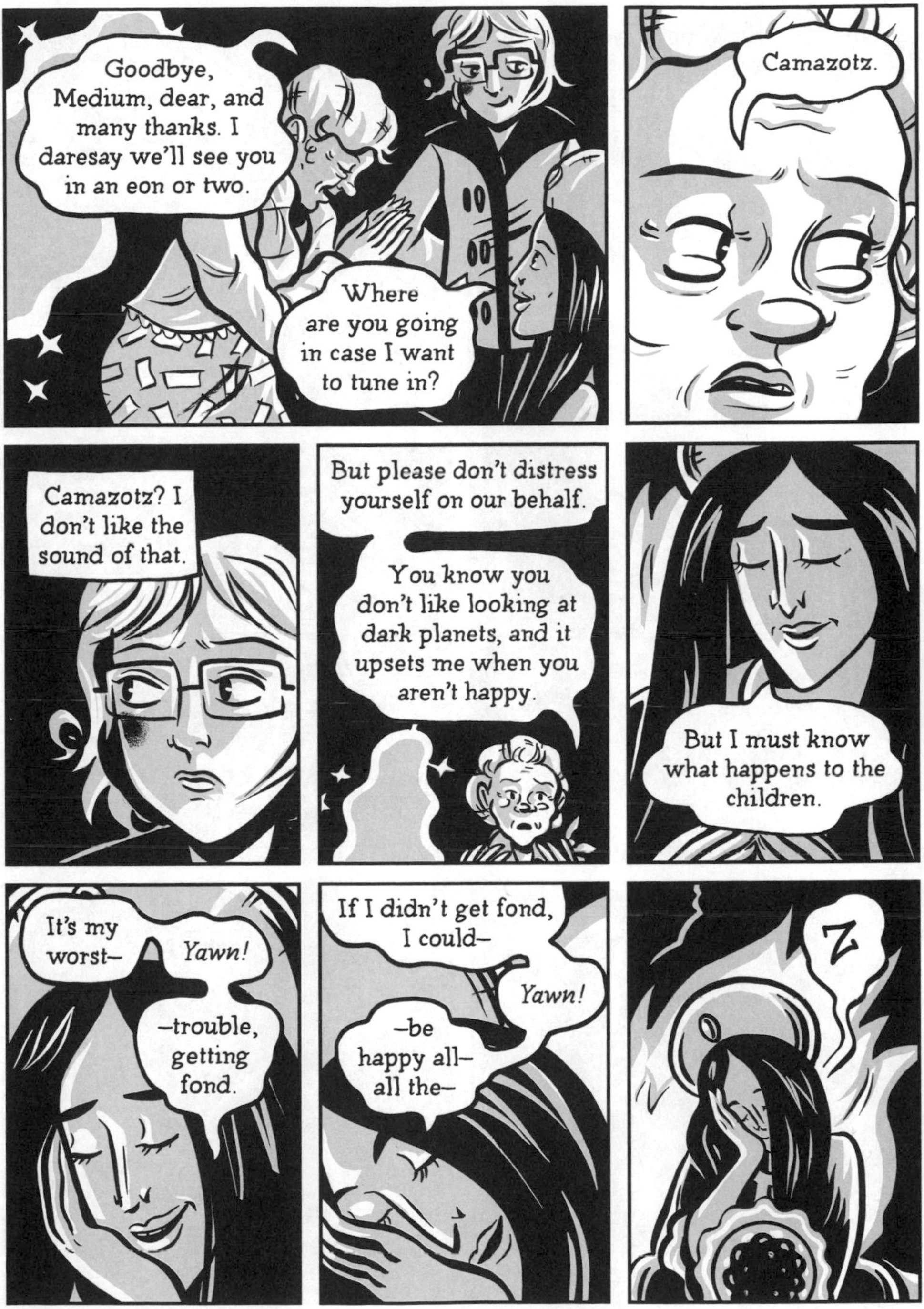
Goodbye, Medium, dear, and many thanks. I daresay we'll see you in an eon or two.
Where are you going in case I want to tune in?
Camazotz.
Camazotz? I don't like the sound of that.
But please don't distress yourself on our behalf.
You know you don't like looking at dark planets, and it upsets me when you aren't happy.
But I *must* know what happens to the children.
It's my worst–
Yawn!
–trouble, getting fond.
If I didn't get fond, I could–
Yawn!
–be happy all– all the–
Z

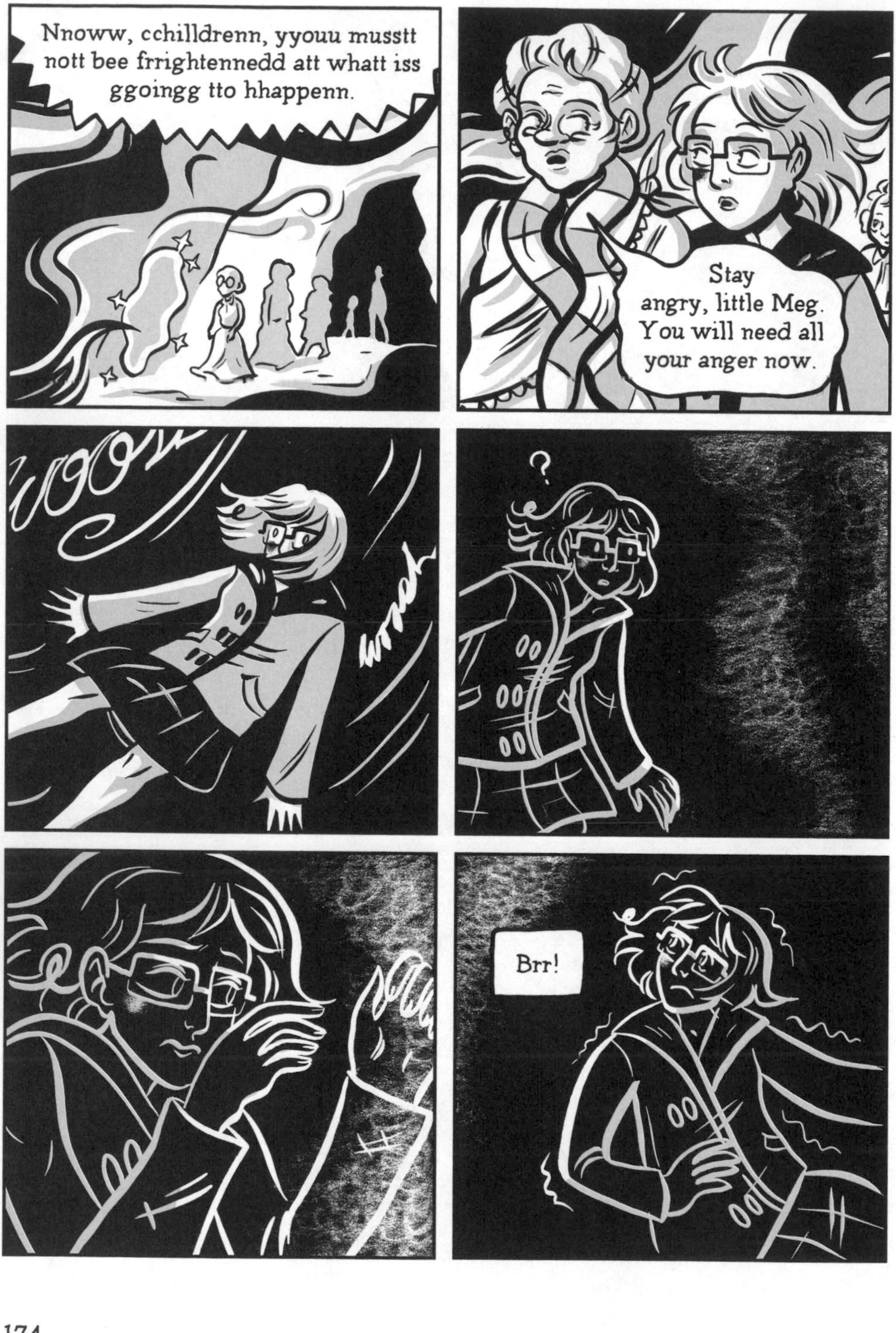
Nnoww, cchilldrenn, yyouu musstt nott bee frrightennedd att whatt iss ggoingg tto hhappenn.
Stay angry, little Meg. You will need all your anger now.
?
Brr!

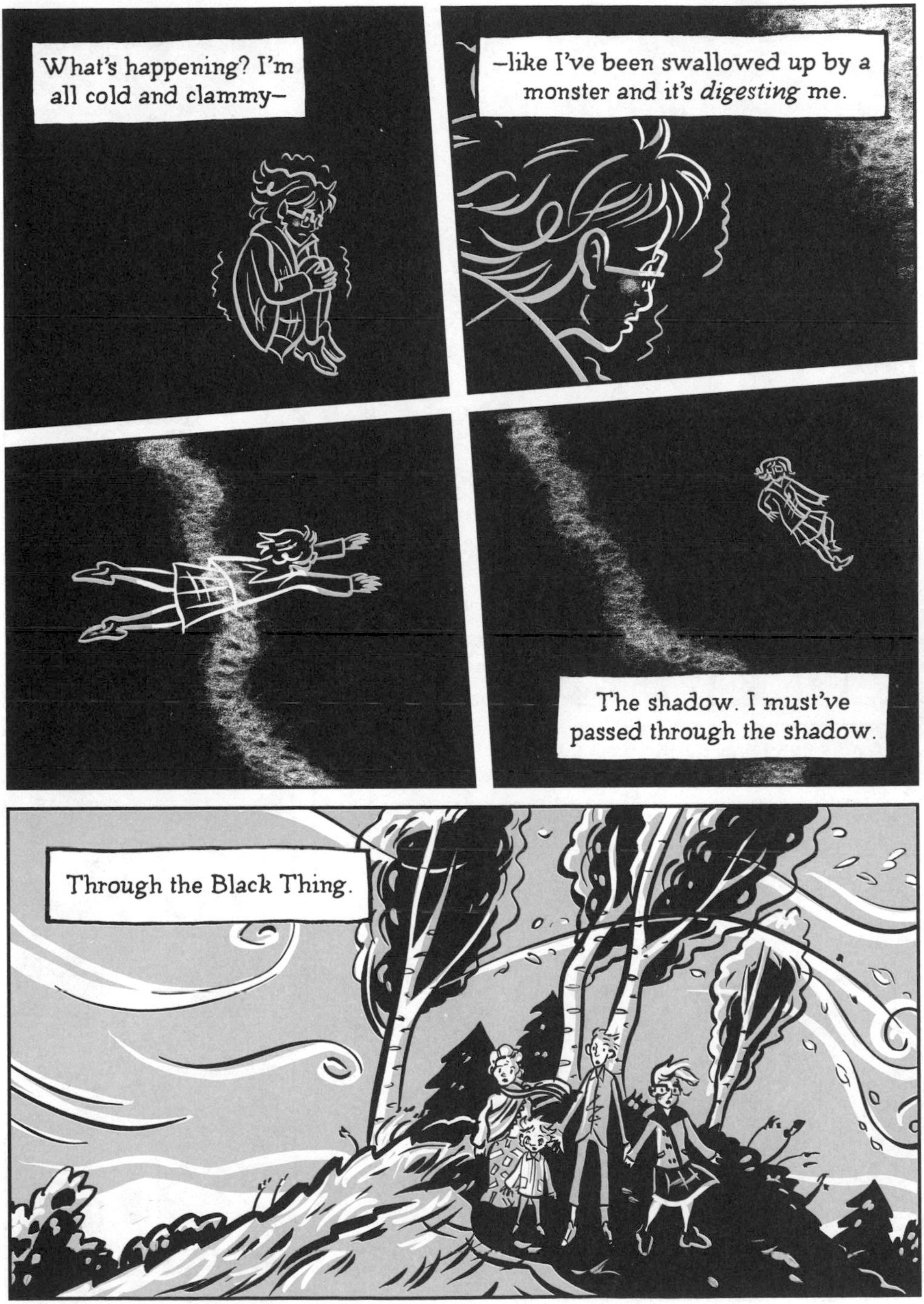
What's happening? I'm all cold and clammy—
—like I've been swallowed up by a monster and it's *digesting* me.
The shadow. I must've passed through the shadow.
Through the Black Thing.

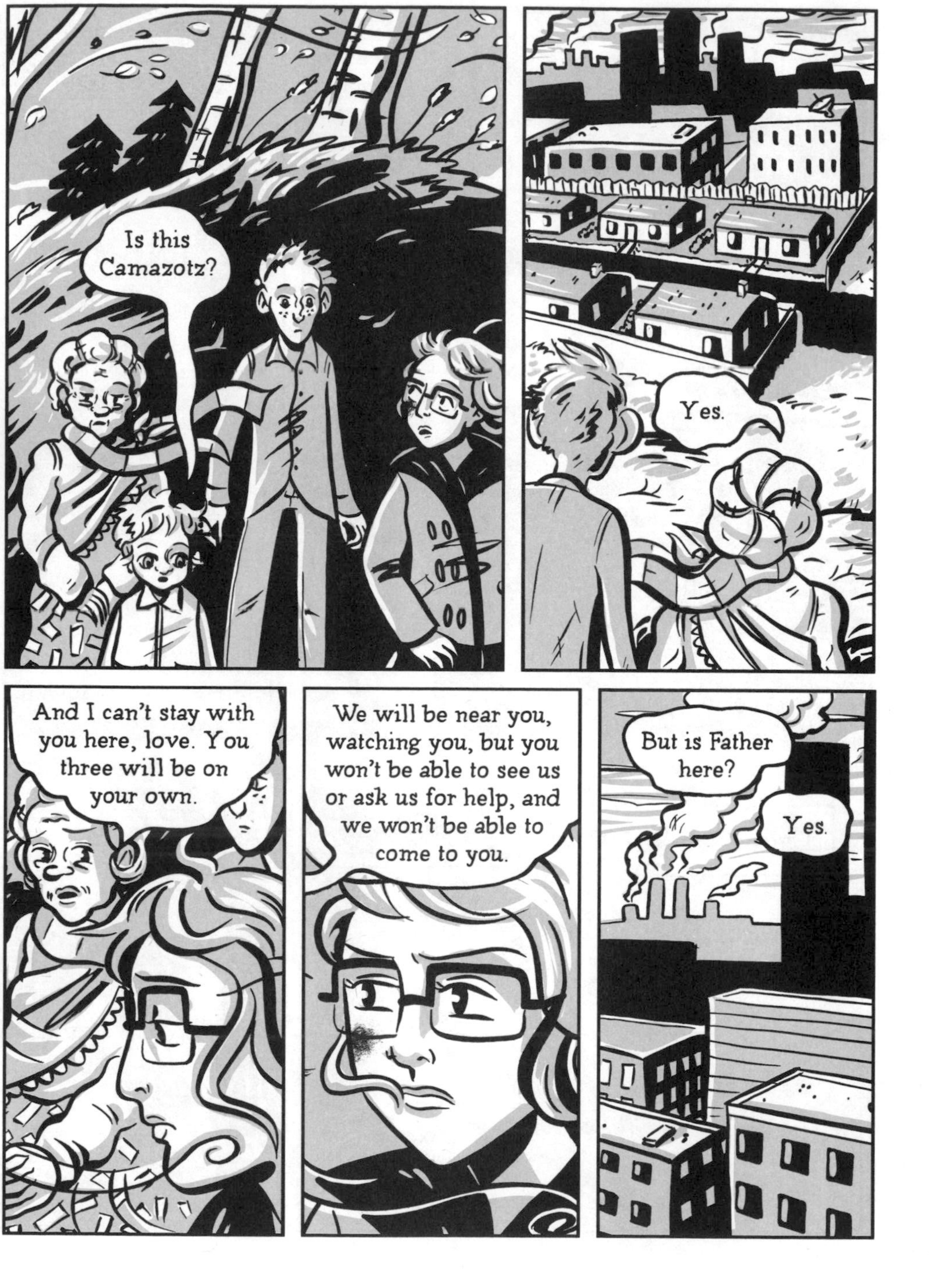
Is this Camazotz?
Yes.
And I can't stay with you here, love. You three will be on your own.
We will be near you, watching you, but you won't be able to see us or ask us for help, and we won't be able to come to you.
But is Father here?
Yes.

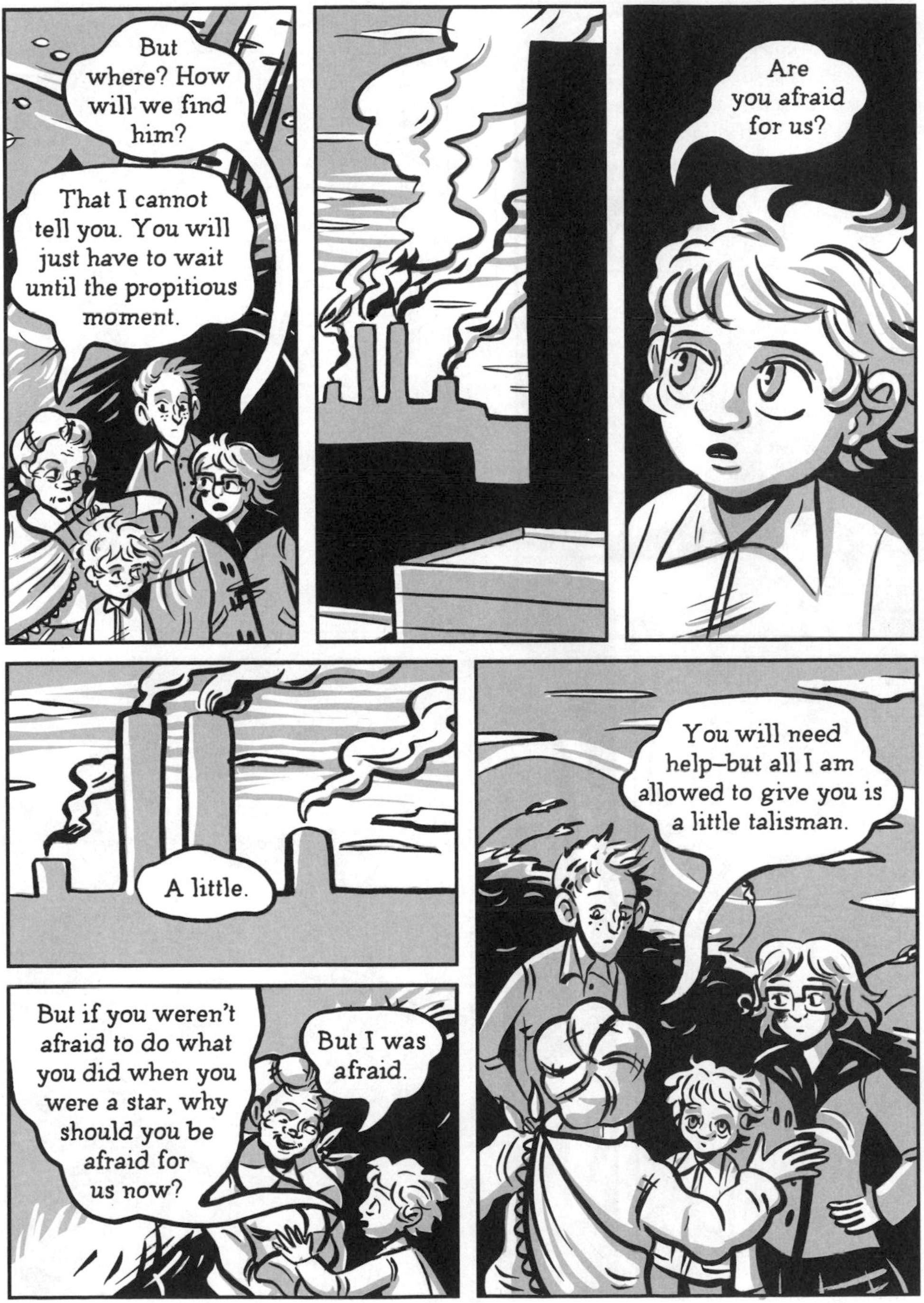
But where? How will we find him?
That I cannot tell you. You will just have to wait until the propitious moment.
Are you afraid for us?
A little.
You will need help—but all I am allowed to give you is a little talisman.
But if you weren't afraid to do what you did when you were a star, why should you be afraid for us now?
But I was afraid.

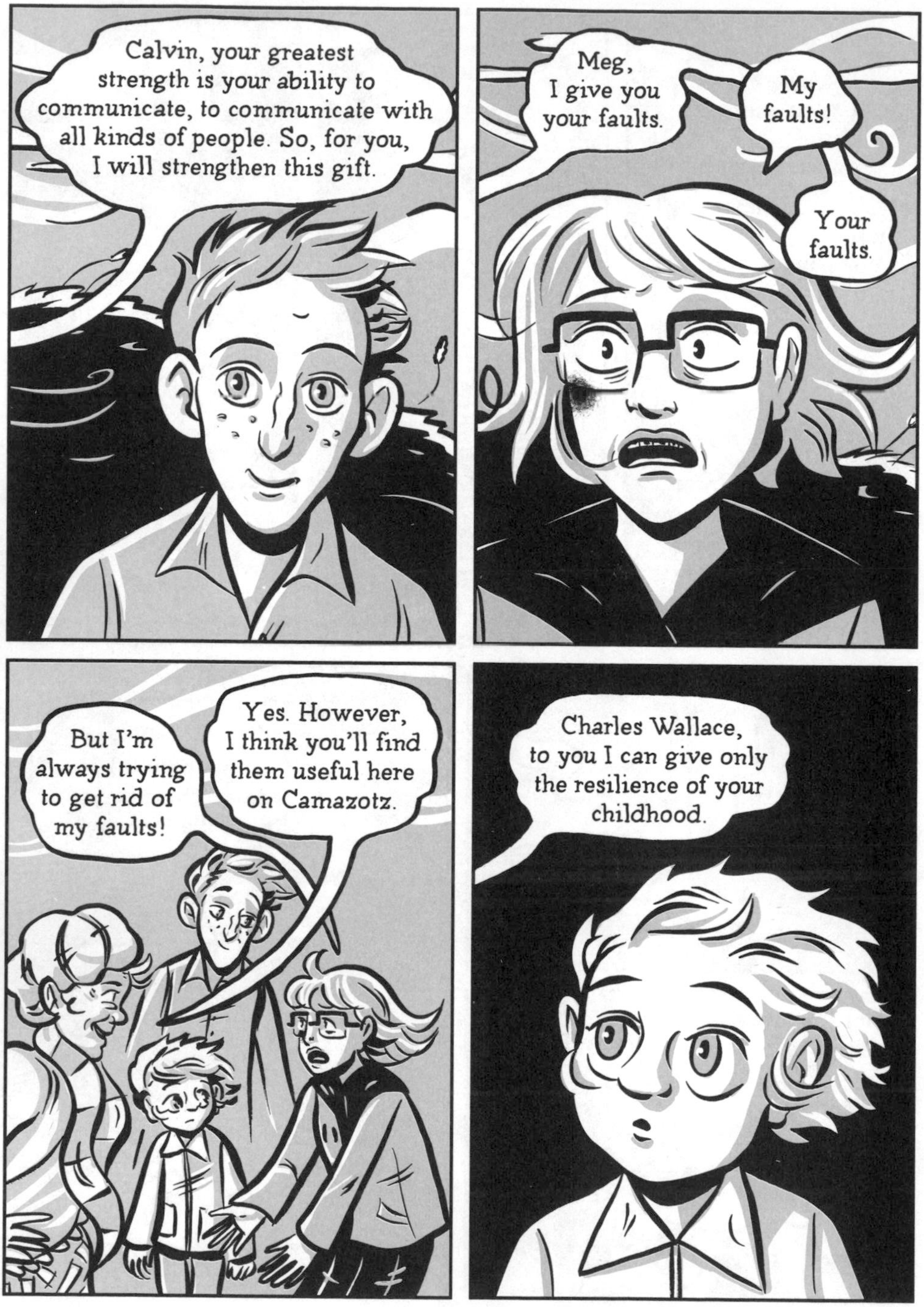
Calvin, your greatest strength is your ability to communicate, to communicate with all kinds of people. So, for you, I will strengthen this gift.
Meg, I give you your faults.
My faults!
Your faults.
But I'm always trying to get rid of my faults!
Yes. However, I think you'll find them useful here on Camazotz.
Charles Wallace, to you I can give only the resilience of your childhood.

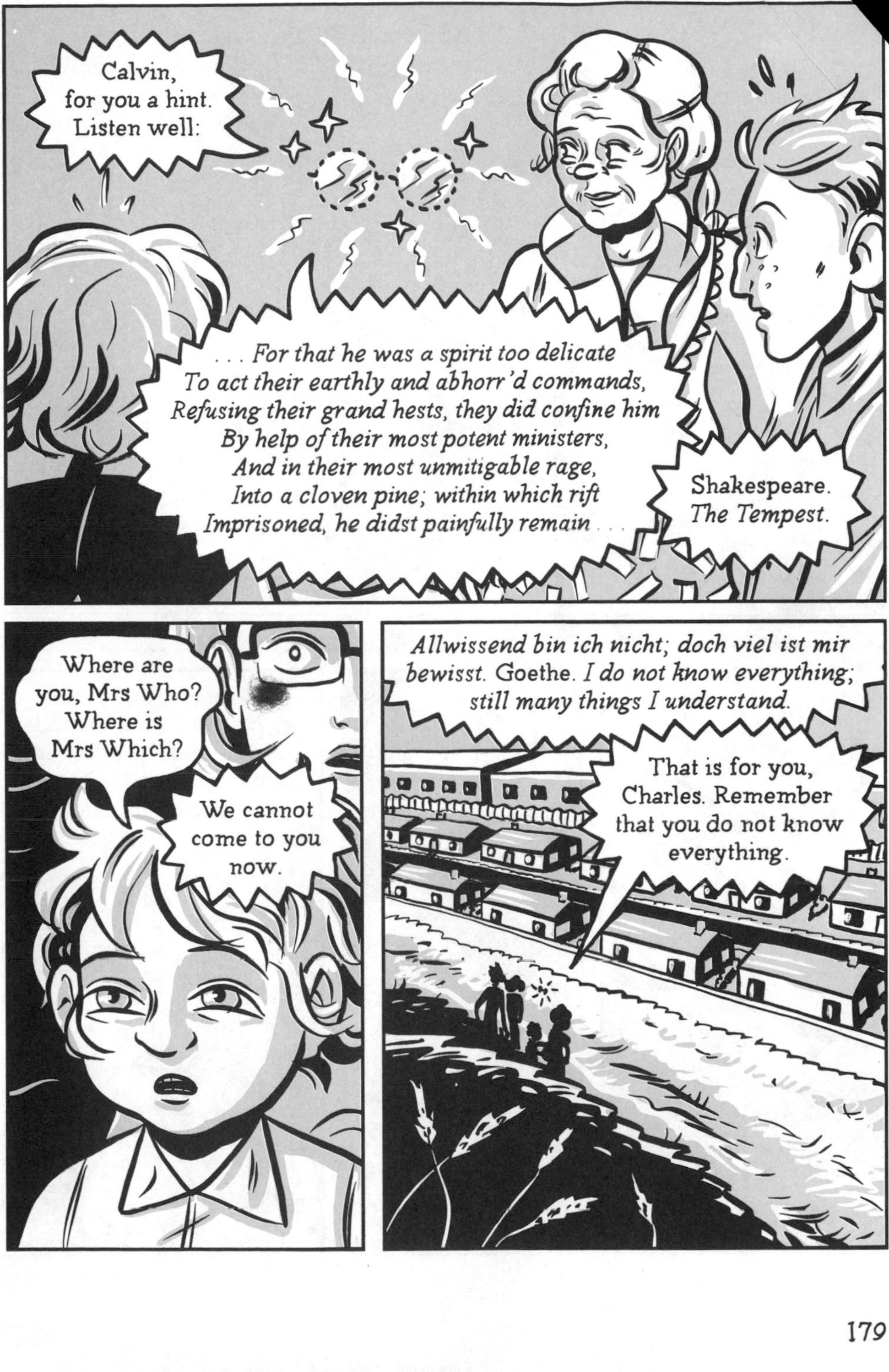
Calvin, for you a hint. Listen well:
. . . For that he was a spirit too delicate
To act their earthly and abhorr'd commands,
Refusing their grand hests, they did confine him
By help of their most potent ministers,
And in their most unmitigable rage,
Into a cloven pine; within which rift
Imprisoned, he didst painfully remain . . .
Shakespeare. *The Tempest.*
Where are you, Mrs Who? Where is Mrs Which?
We cannot come to you now.
Allwissend bin ich nicht; doch viel ist mir bewisst. Goethe. *I do not know everything; still many things I understand.*
That is for you, Charles. Remember that you do not know everything.

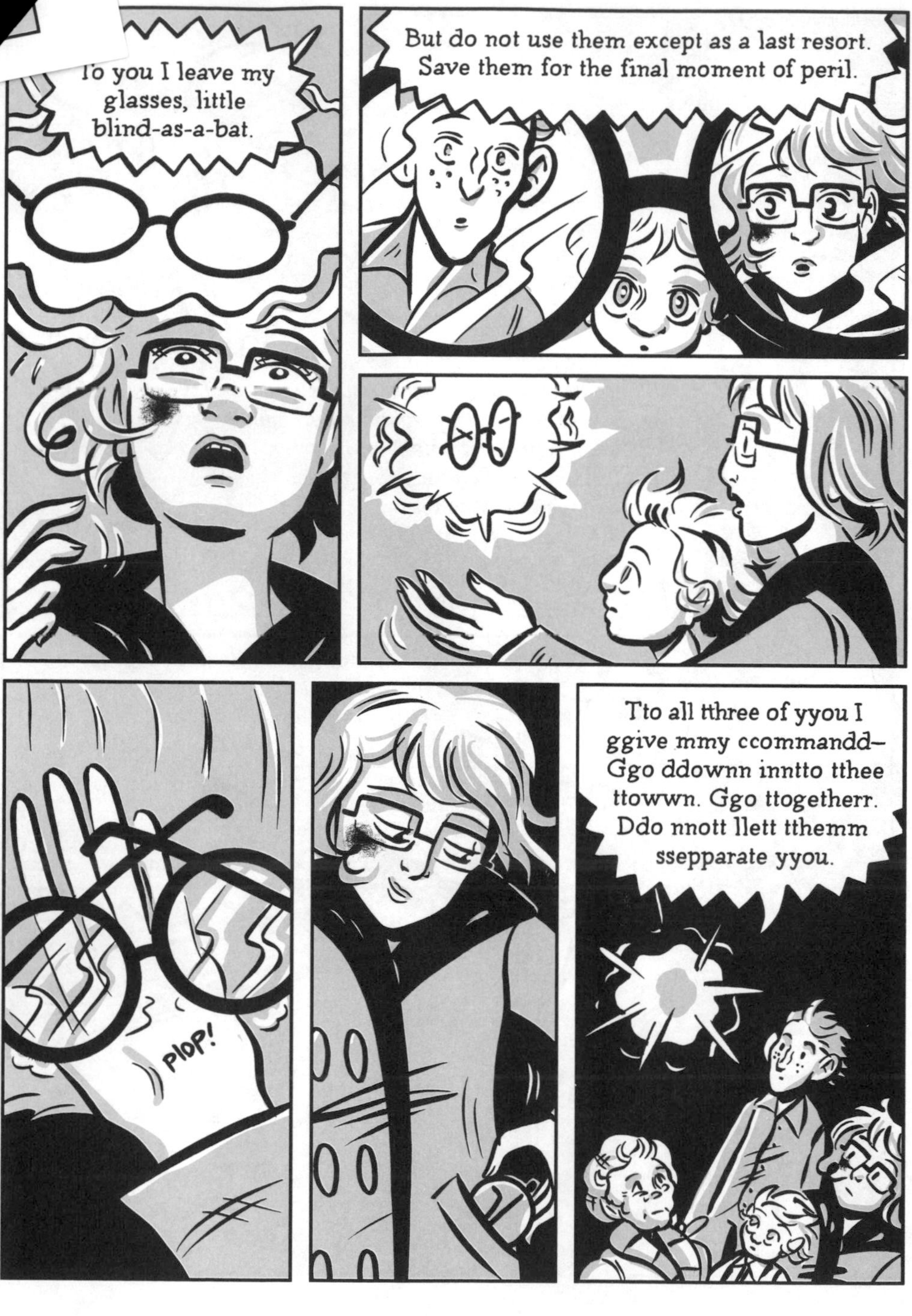

To you I leave my glasses, little blind-as-a-bat.
But do not use them except as a last resort. Save them for the final moment of peril.
PLOP!
Tto all tthree of yyou I ggive mmy ccommandd– Ggo ddownn inntto tthee ttowwn. Ggo ttogetherr. Ddo nnott llett tthemm ssepparate yyou.

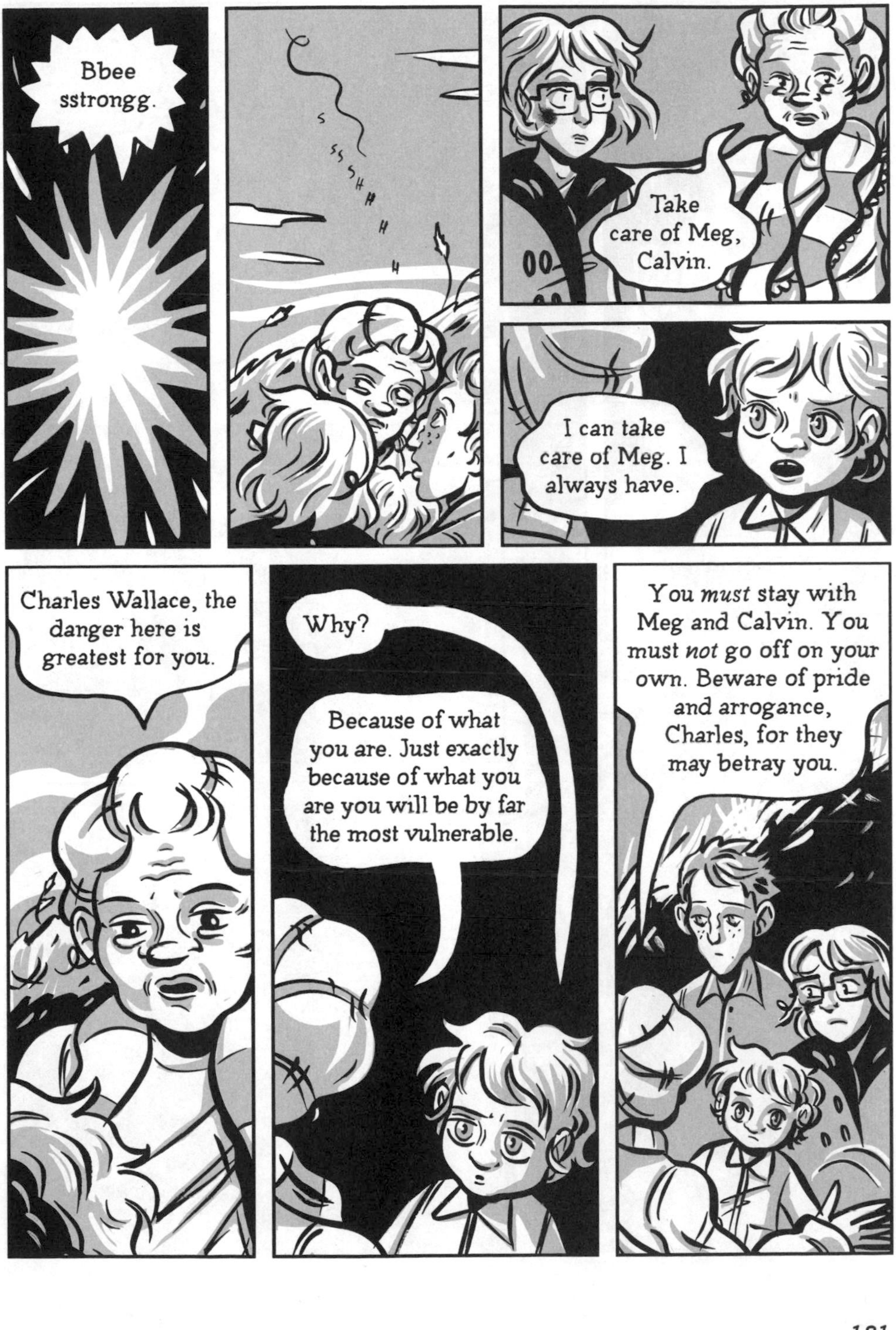
Bbee sstrongg.
SSSHHHH
Take care of Meg, Calvin.
I can take care of Meg. I always have.
Charles Wallace, the danger here is greatest for you.
Why?
Because of what you are. Just exactly because of what you are you will be by far the most vulnerable.
You *must* stay with Meg and Calvin. You must *not* go off on your own. Beware of pride and arrogance, Charles, for they may betray you.

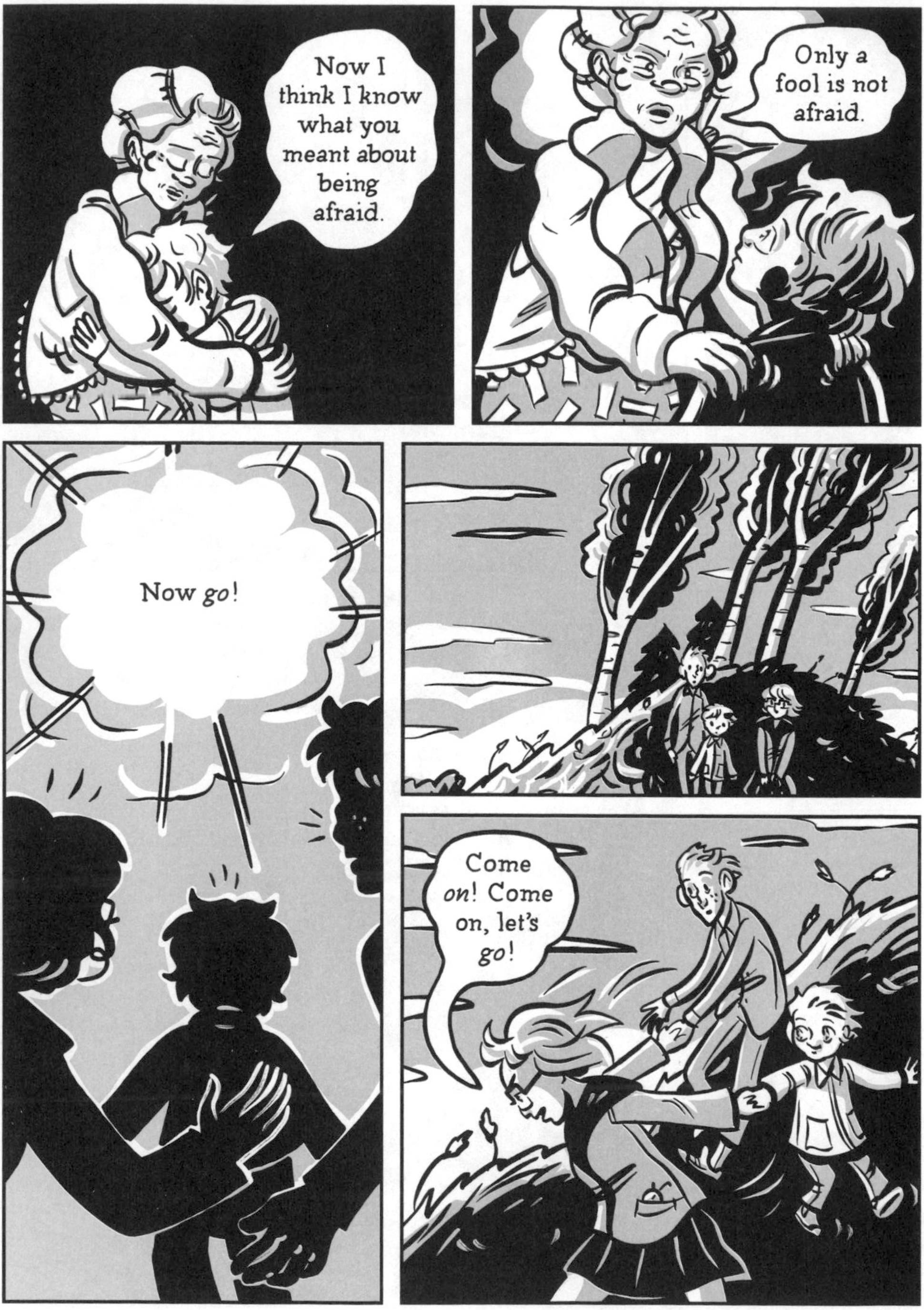
Now I think I know what you meant about being afraid.
Only a fool is not afraid.
Now *go*!
Come *on*! Come on, let's *go*!

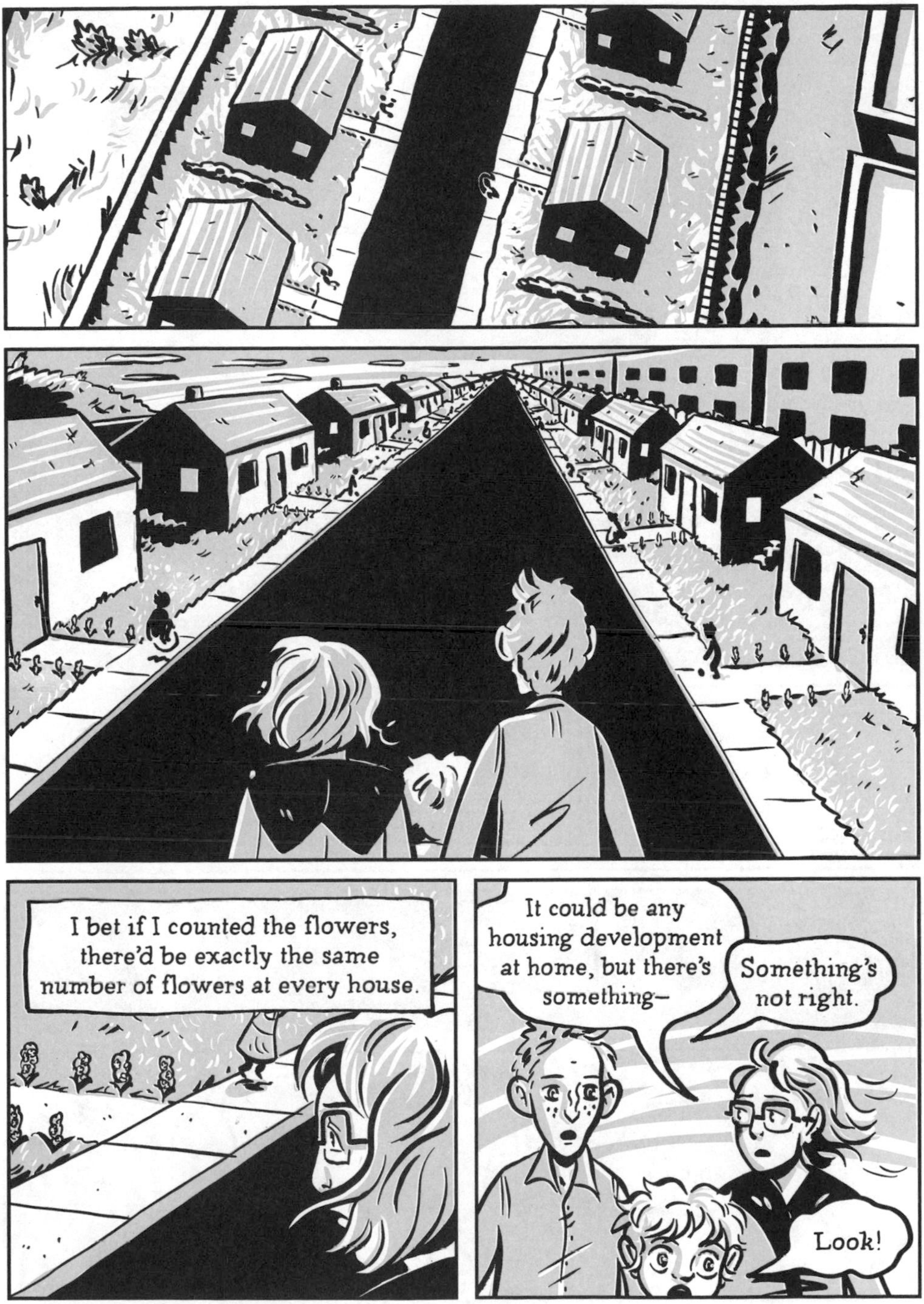
I bet if I counted the flowers, there'd be exactly the same number of flowers at every house.
It could be any housing development at home, but there's something–
Something's not right.
Look!

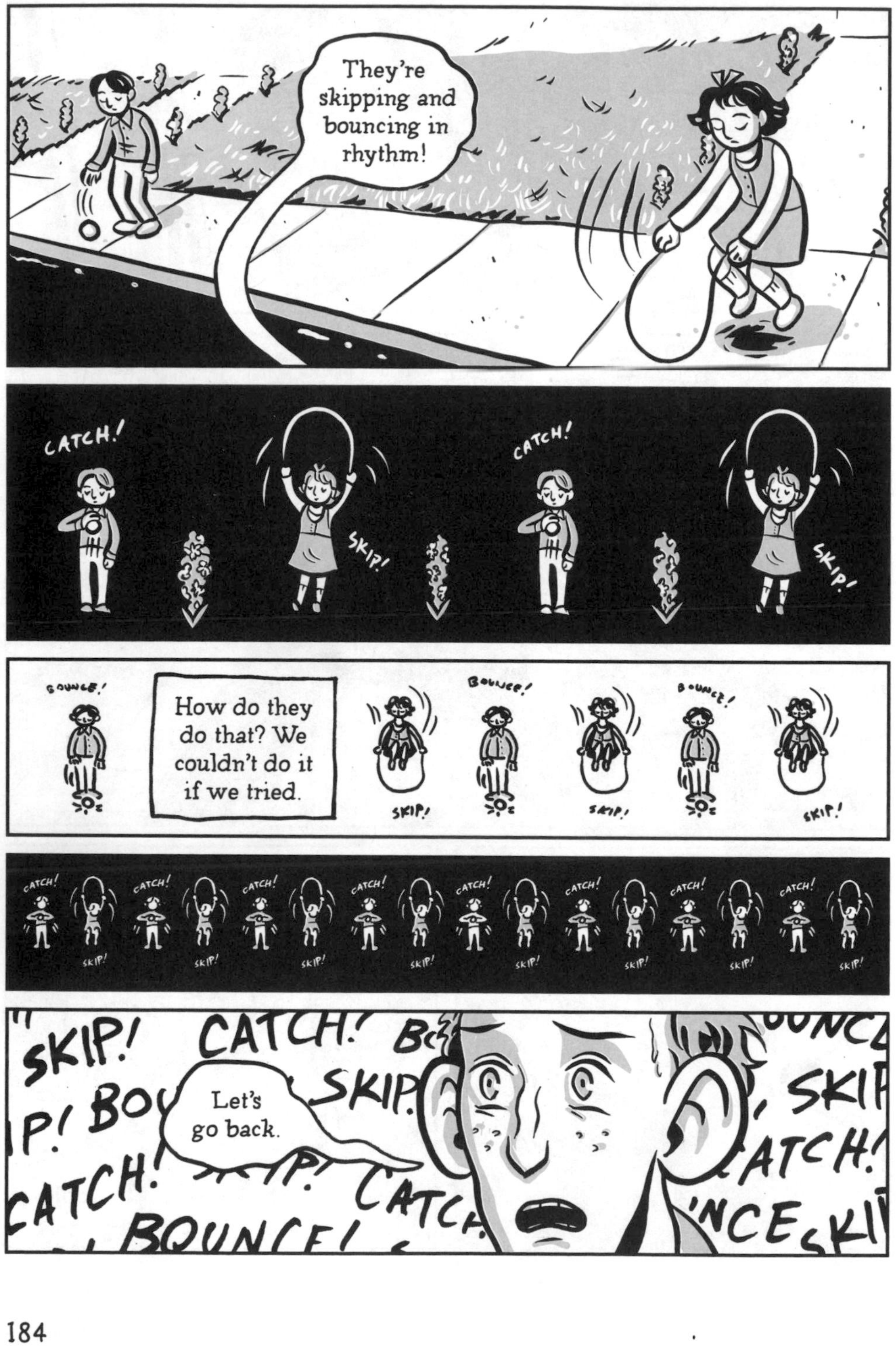
They're skipping and bouncing in rhythm!
CATCH!
SKIP!
CATCH!
SKIP!
BOUNCE!
How do they do that? We couldn't do it if we tried.
SKIP!
BOUNCE!
SKIP!
BOUNCE!
SKIP!
CATCH!
SKIP!
SKIP!
CATCH!
SKIP
Let's go back.
CATCH!
BOUNCE!

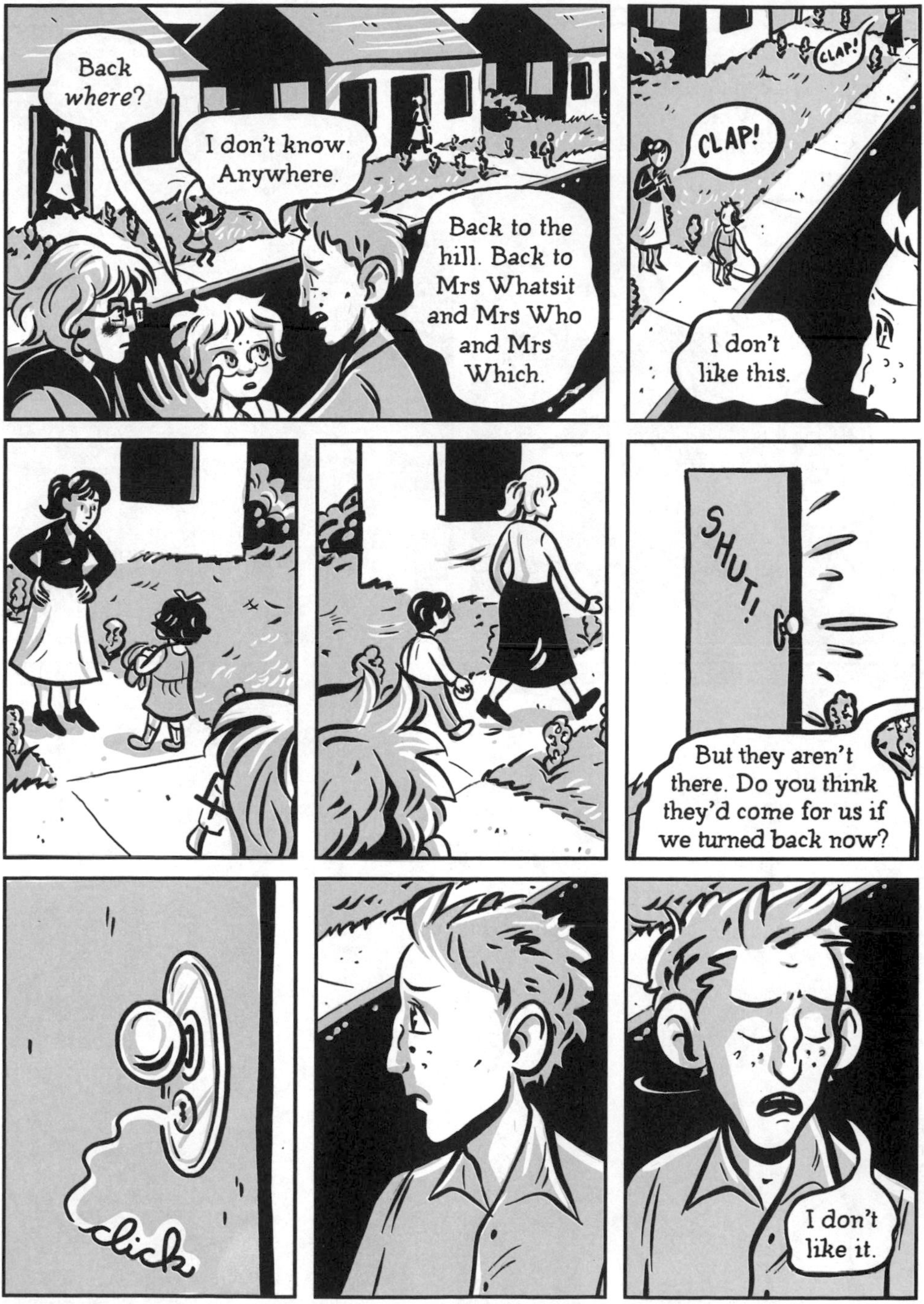
Back *where*?
I don't know. Anywhere.
Back to the hill. Back to Mrs Whatsit and Mrs Who and Mrs Which.
CLAP!
CLAP!
I don't like this.
SHUT!
But they aren't there. Do you think they'd come for us if we turned back now?
click
I don't like it.

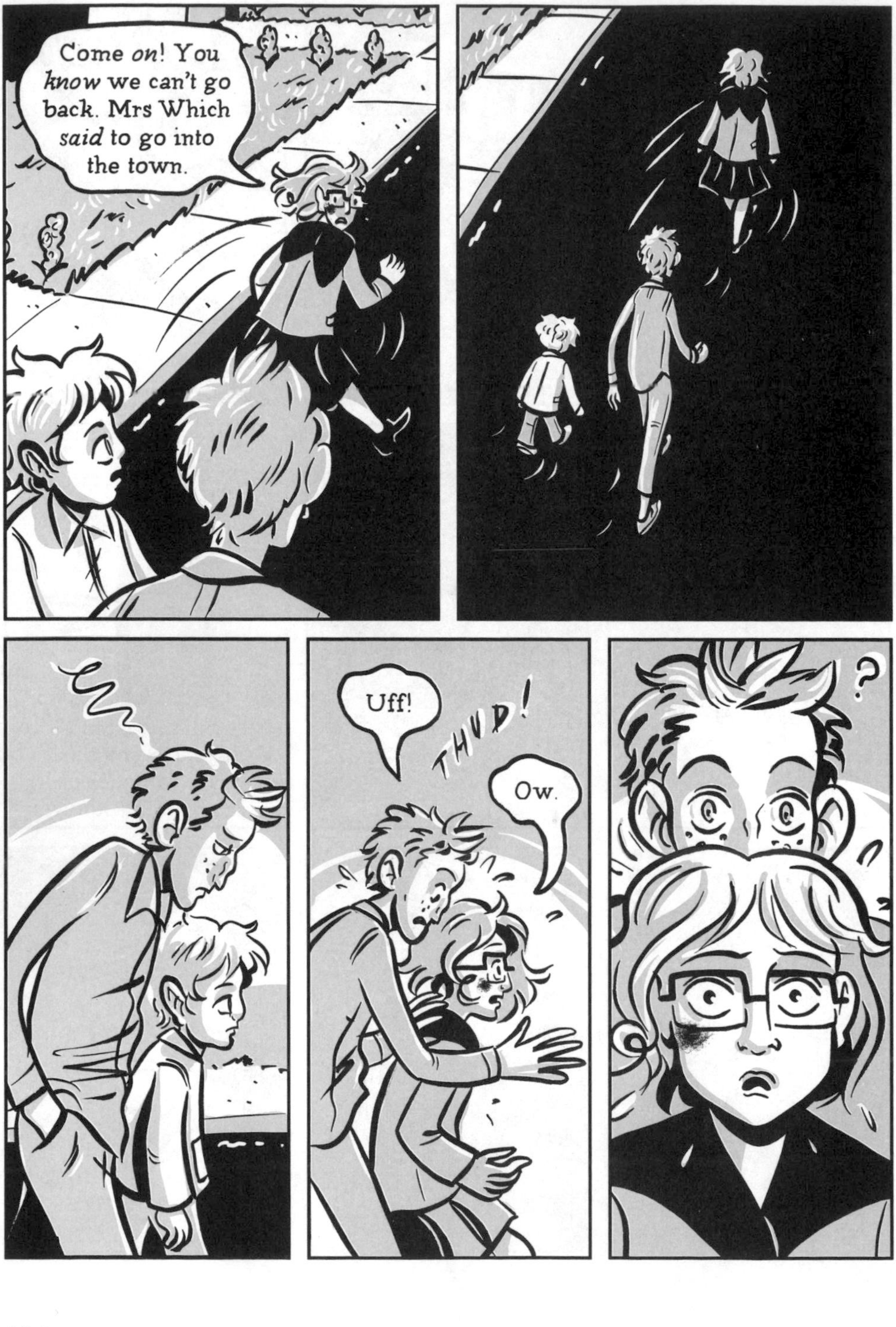
Come *on*! You *know* we can't go back. Mrs Which *said* to go into the town.
Uff!
THUD!
Ow.
?

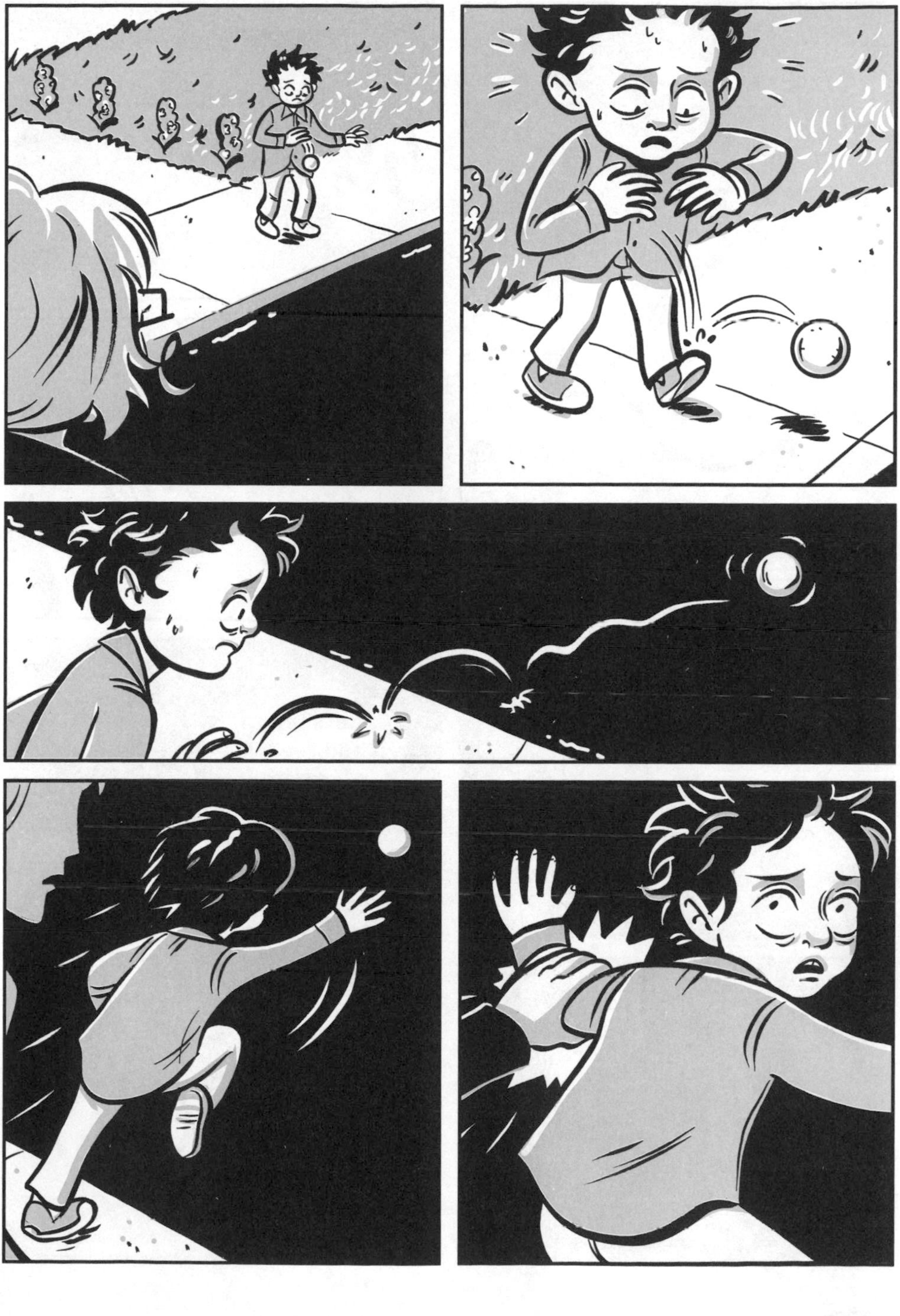

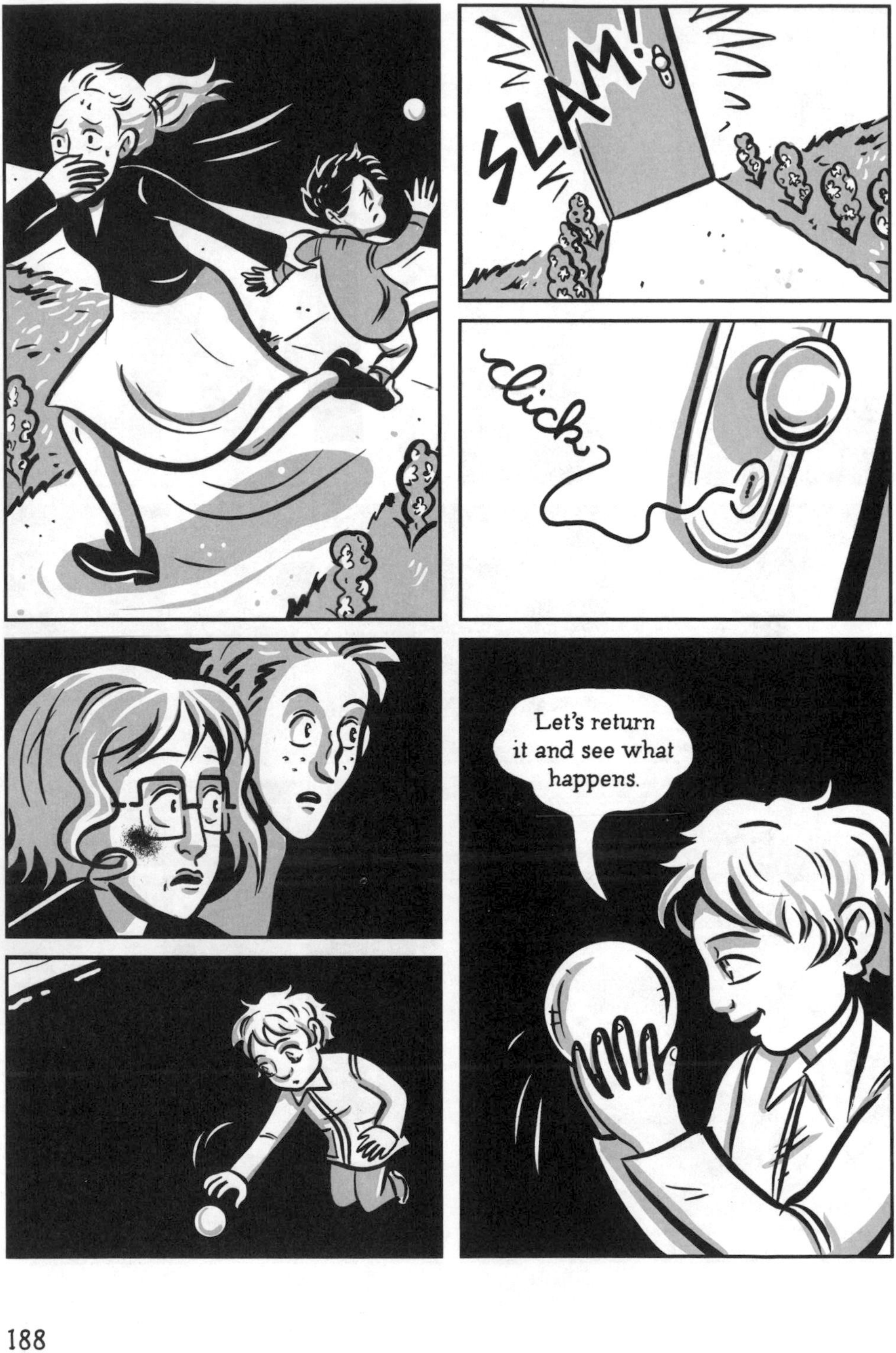
SLAM!
click
Let's return it and see what happens.

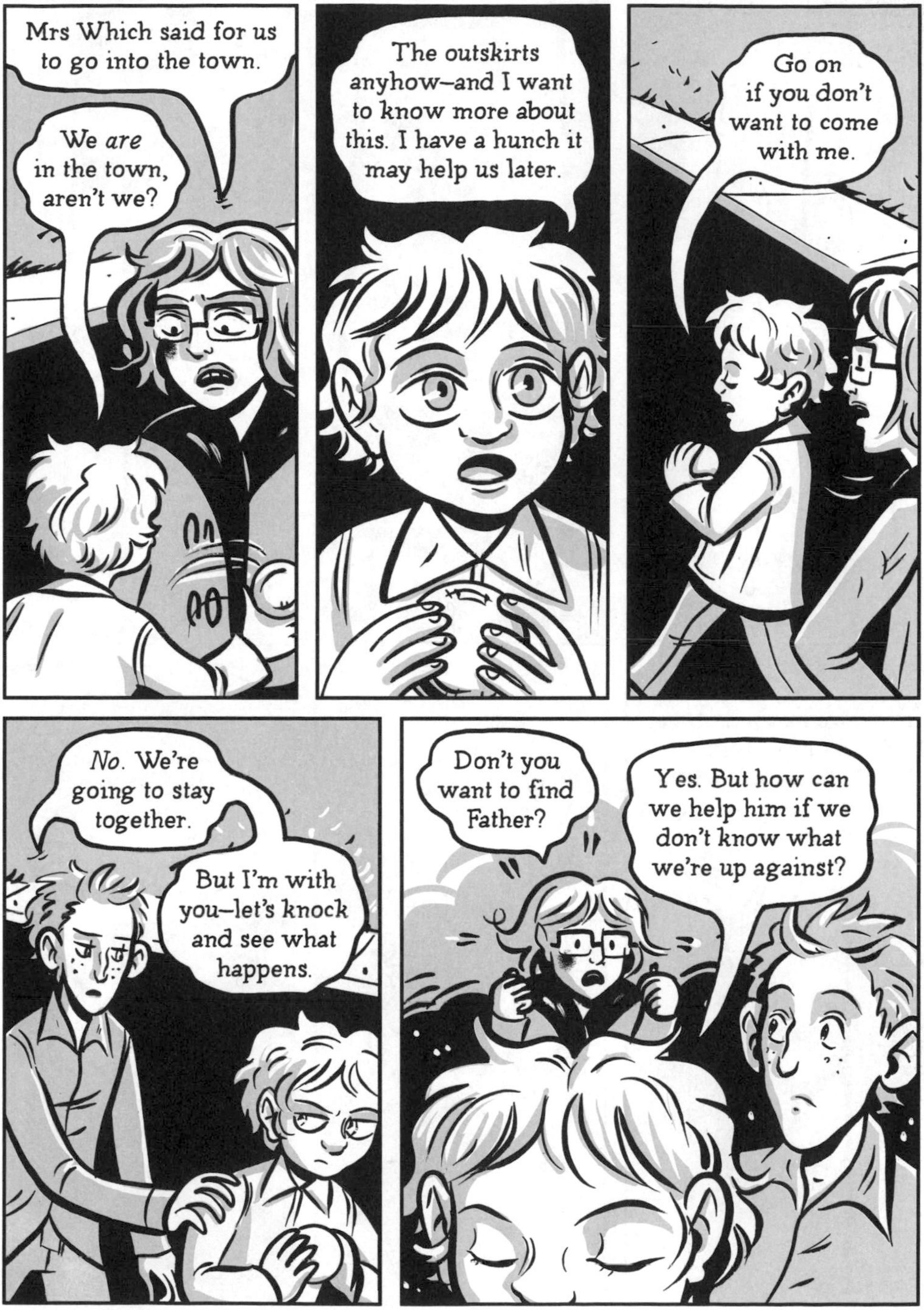
Mrs Which said for us to go into the town.
We *are* in the town, aren't we?
The outskirts anyhow—and I want to know more about this. I have a hunch it may help us later.
Go on if you don't want to come with me.
No. We're going to stay together.
But I'm with you—let's knock and see what happens.
Don't you want to find Father?
Yes. But how can we help him if we don't know what we're up against?

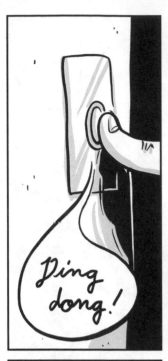

Ding dong!

KA-
CHUNK

creeeee

What do you want?

It isn't paper time yet; we've had milk time; and I've given my Decency Donations regularly. All my papers are in order.

I think your little boy dropped his ball.

Oh, no! The children in our section *never* drop balls!

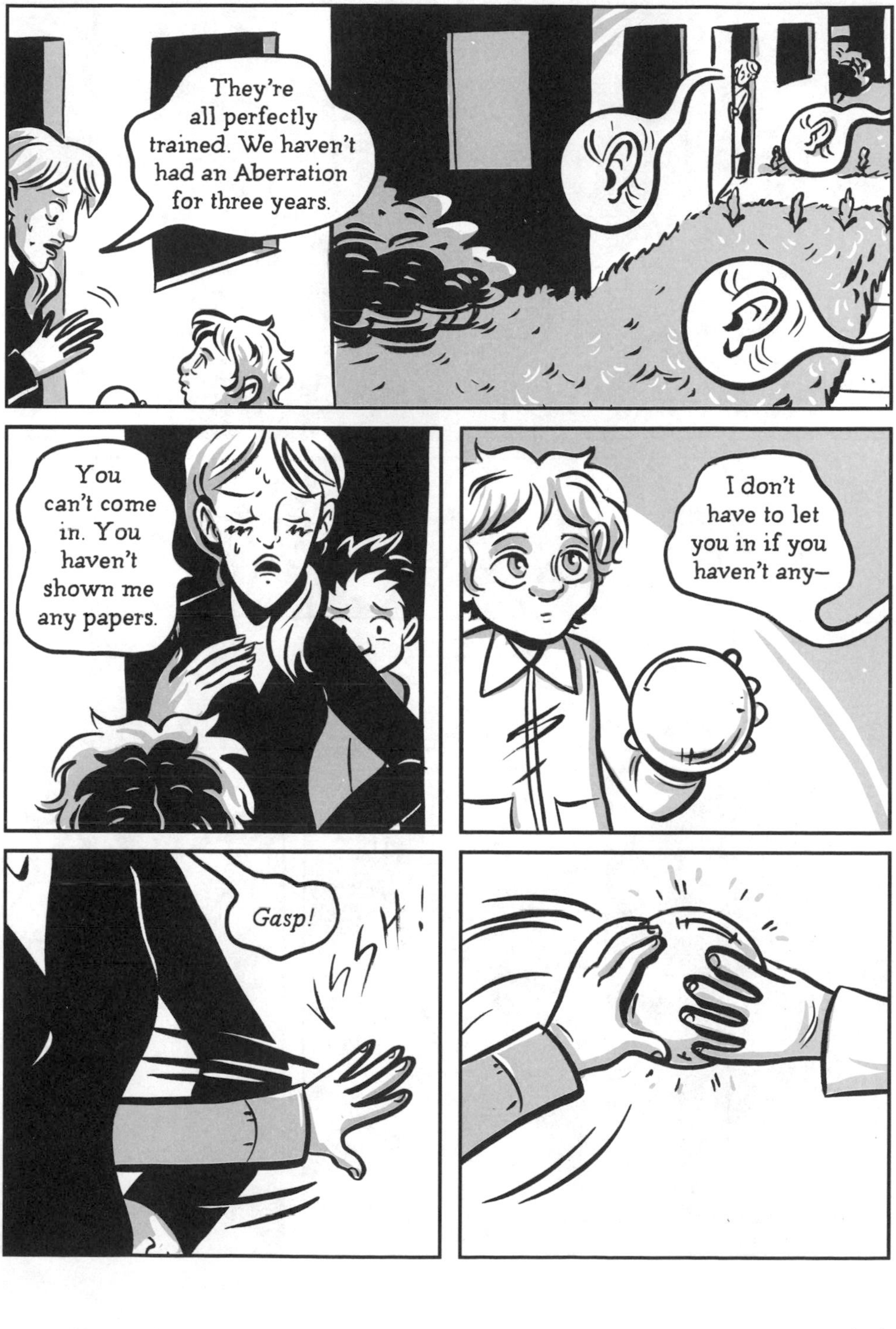
They're all perfectly trained. We haven't had an Aberration for three years.
You can't come in. You haven't shown me any papers.
I don't have to let you in if you haven't any—
Gasp!
VSSH!

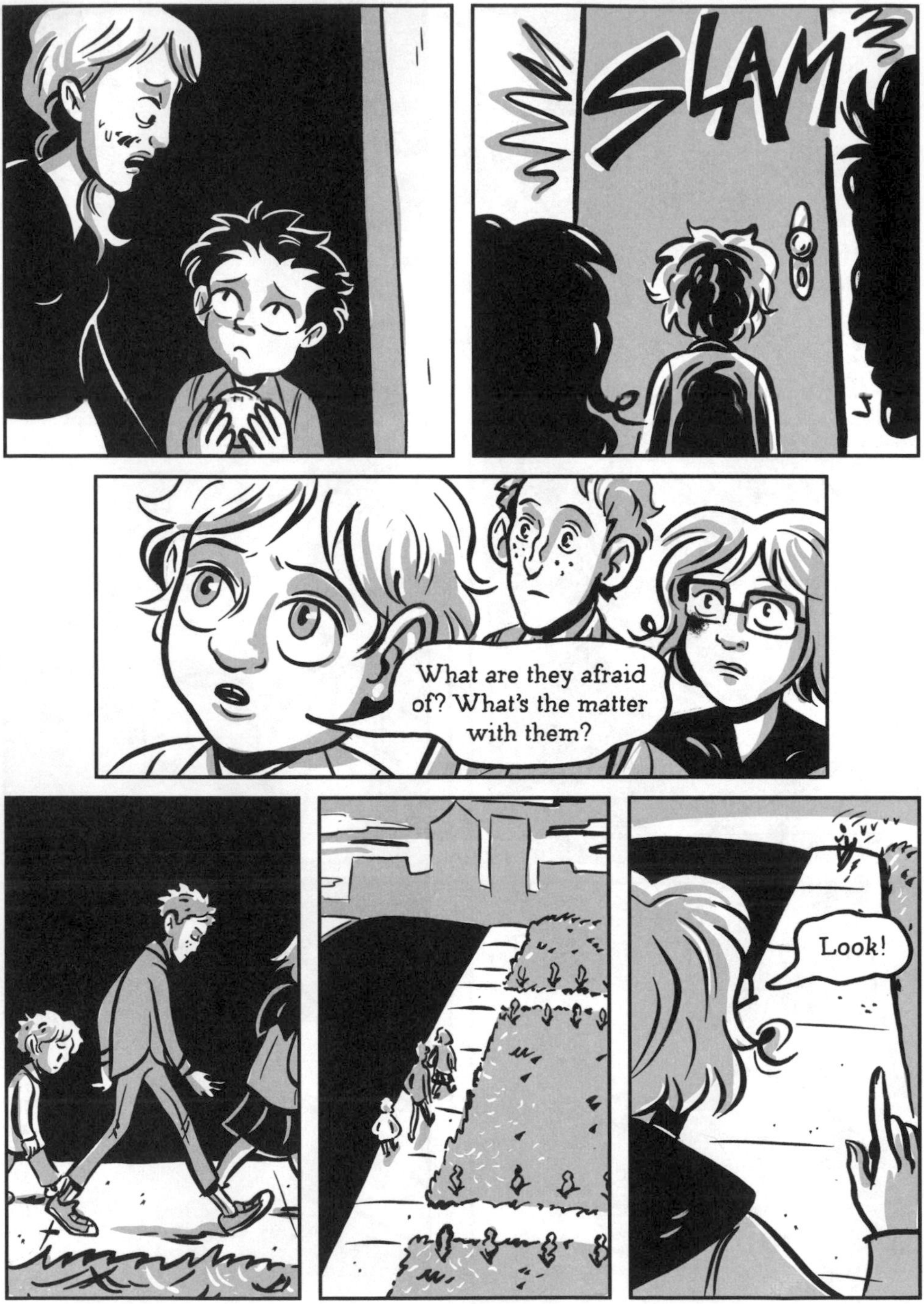
SLAM
What are they afraid of? What's the matter with them?
Look!

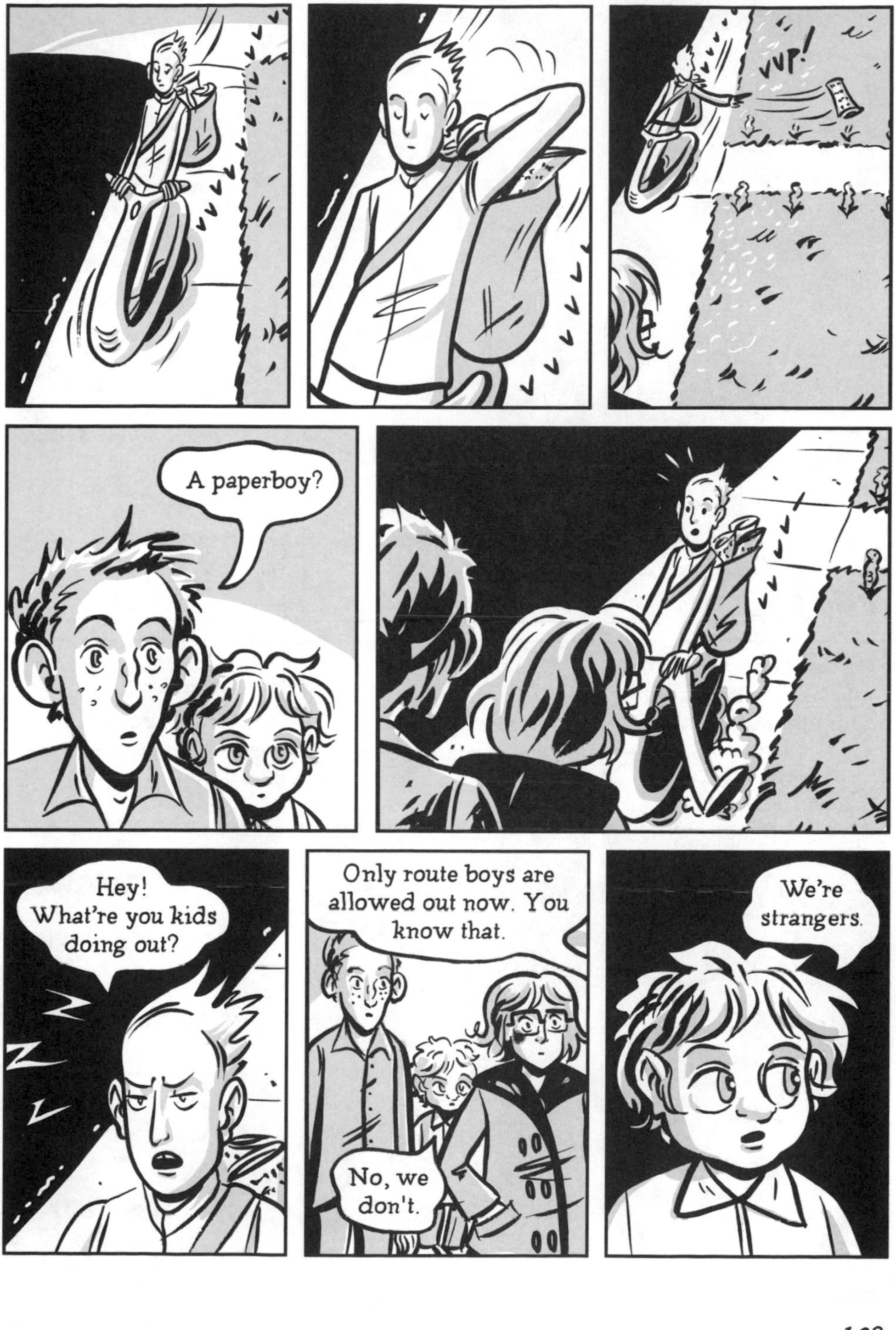
VVP!
A paperboy?
Hey!
What're you kids
doing out?
Only route boys are
allowed out now. You
know that.
No, we
don't.
We're
strangers.

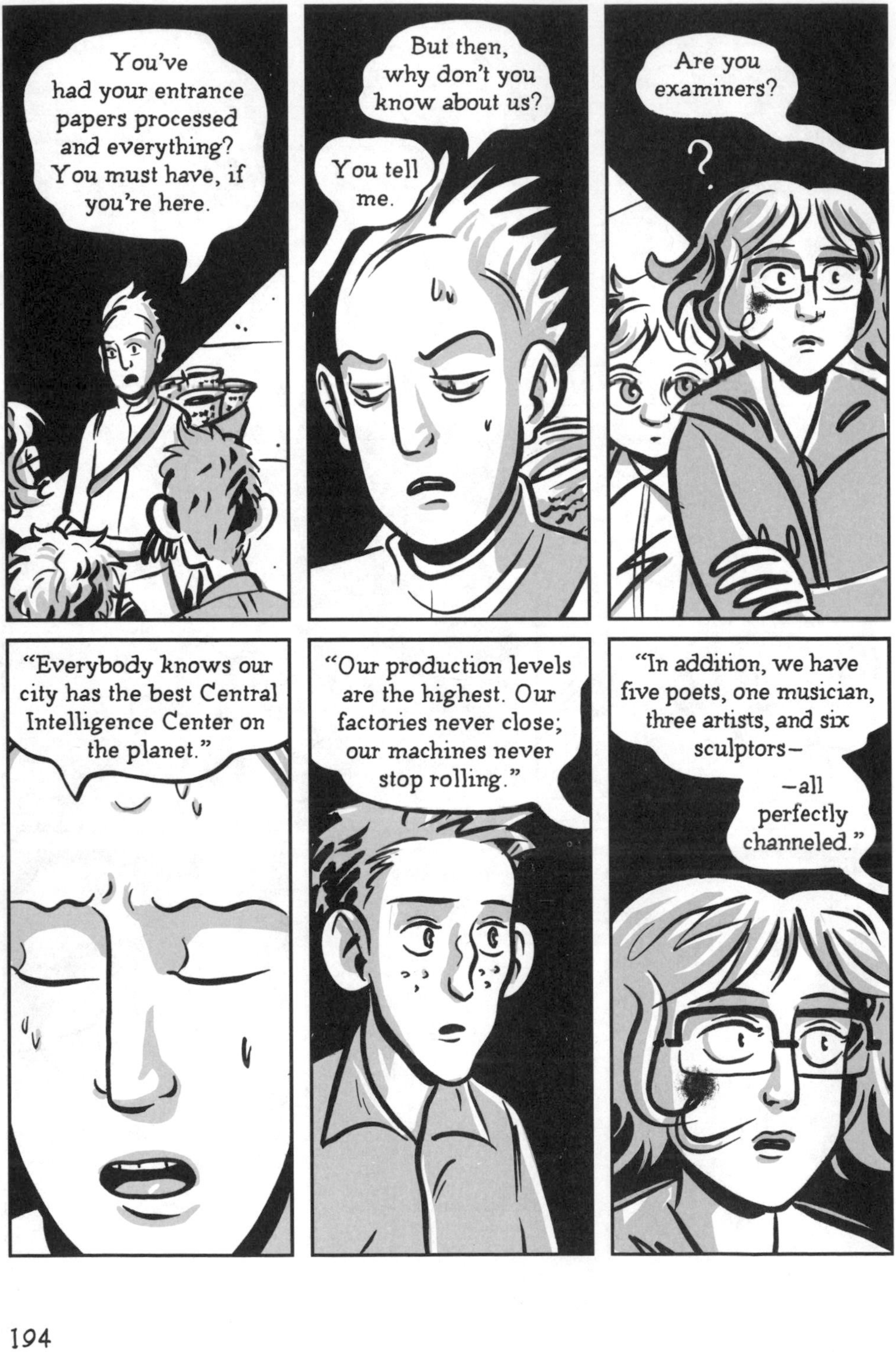
You've had your entrance papers processed and everything? You must have, if you're here.
But then, why don't you know about us?
You tell me.
Are you examiners?
?
"Everybody knows our city has the best Central Intelligence Center on the planet."
"Our production levels are the highest. Our factories never close; our machines never stop rolling."
"In addition, we have five poets, one musician, three artists, and six sculptors—
—all perfectly channeled."

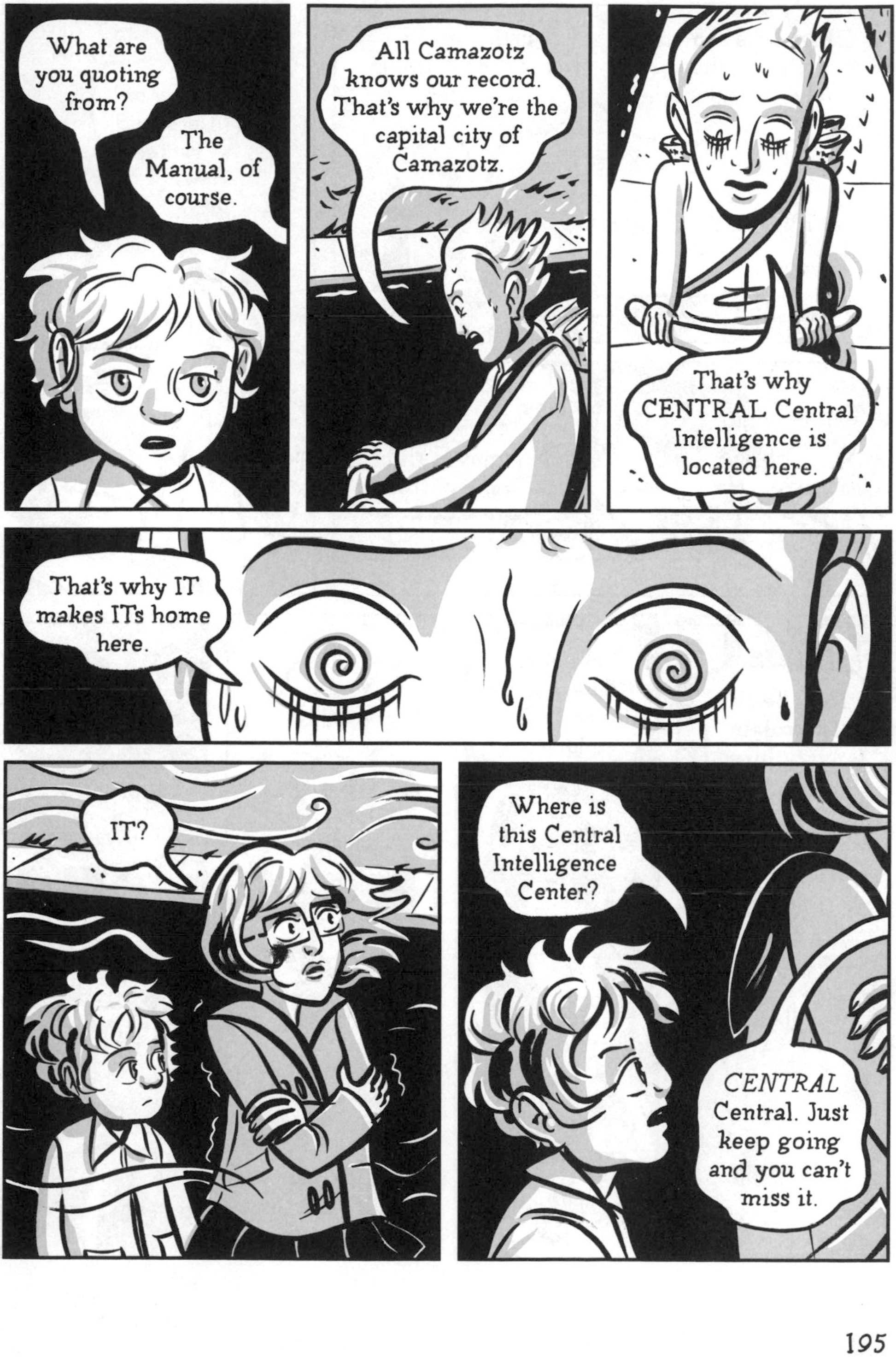
What are you quoting from?
The Manual, of course.
All Camazotz knows our record. That's why we're the capital city of Camazotz.
That's why CENTRAL Central Intelligence is located here.
That's why IT makes ITs home here.
IT?
Where is this Central Intelligence Center?
CENTRAL Central. Just keep going and you can't miss it.

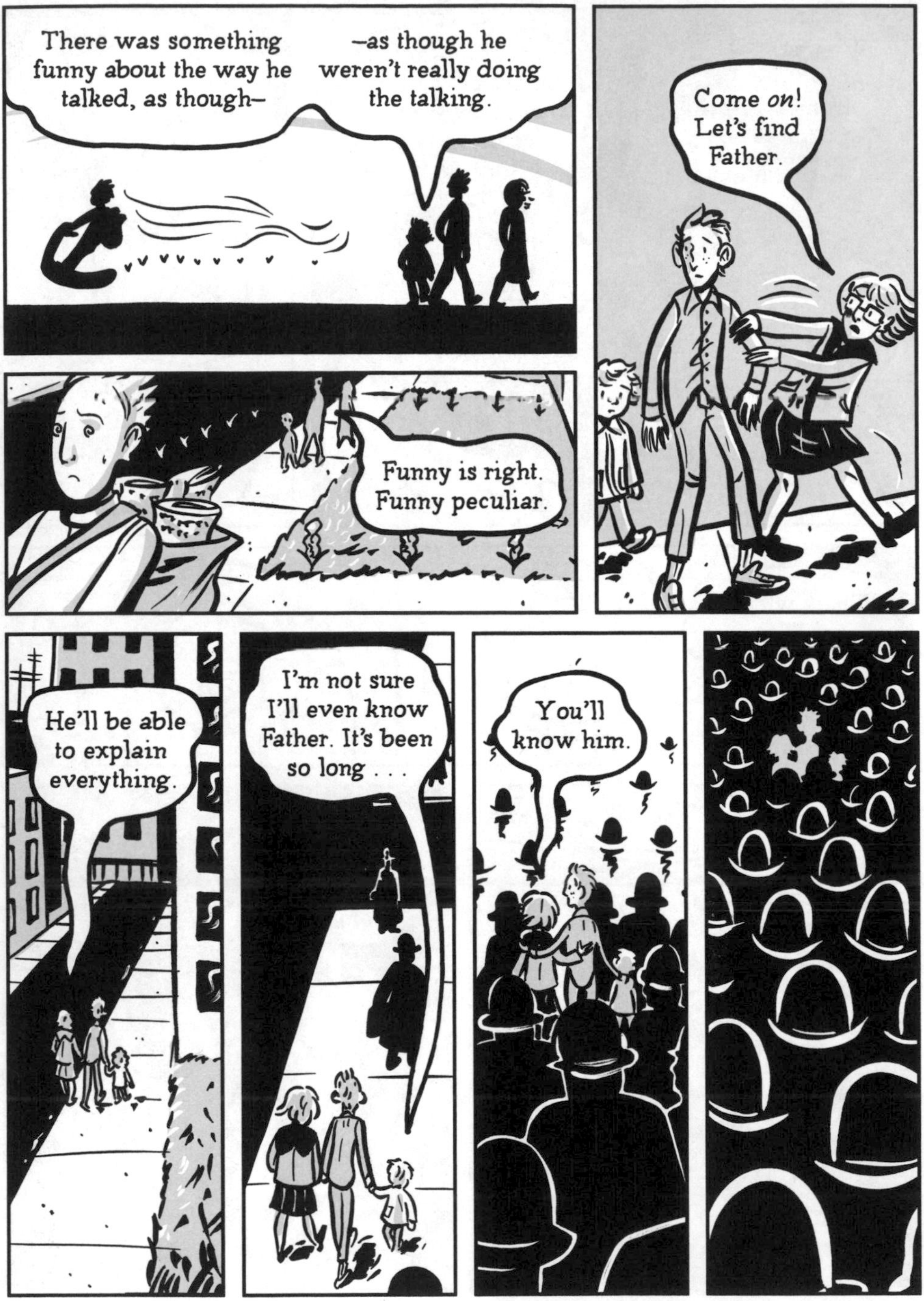
There was something funny about the way he talked, as though–
–as though he weren't really doing the talking.
Come *on*! Let's find Father.
Funny is right. Funny peculiar.
He'll be able to explain everything.
I'm not sure I'll even know Father. It's been so long . . .
You'll know him.

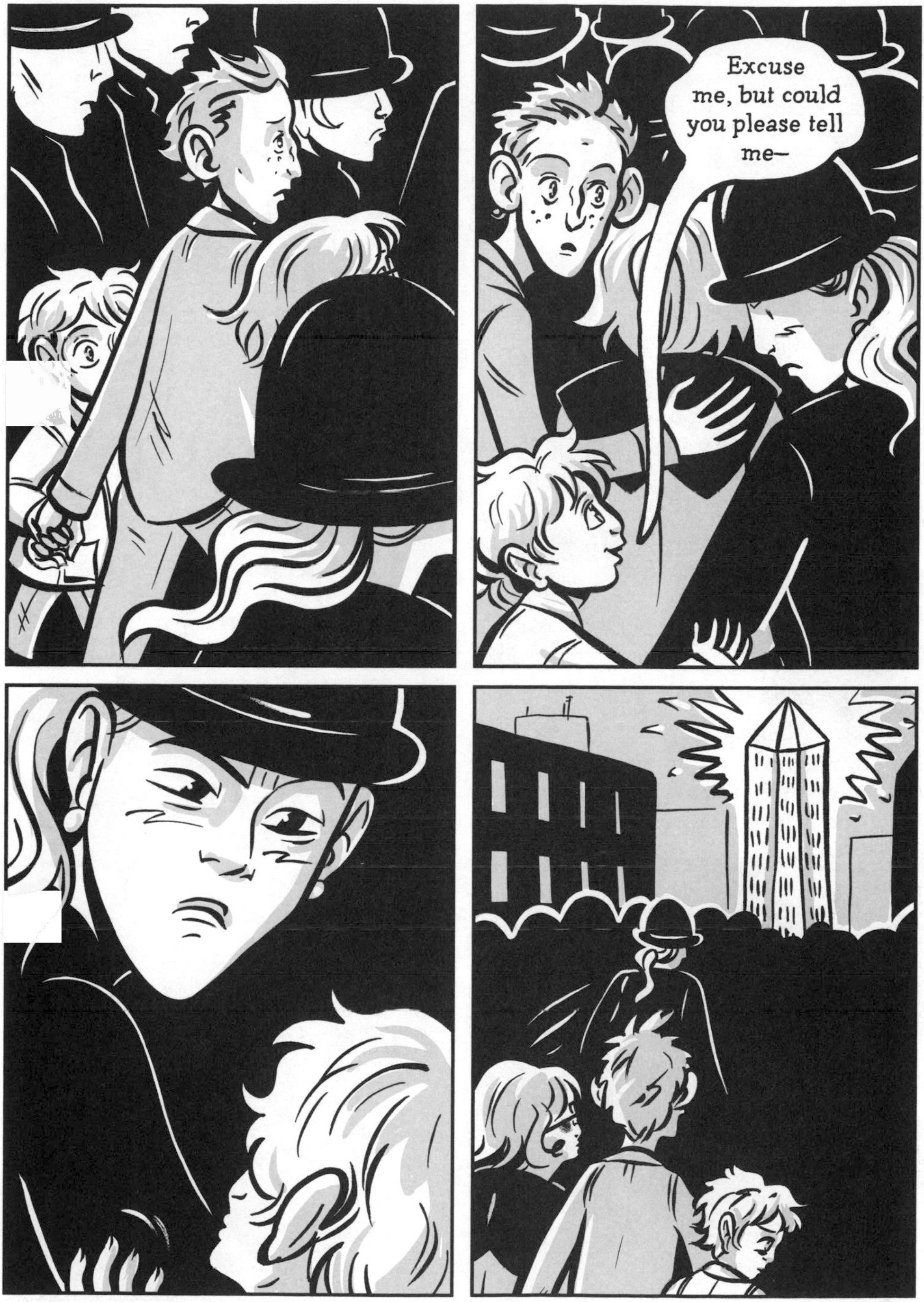
Excuse me, but could you please tell me–

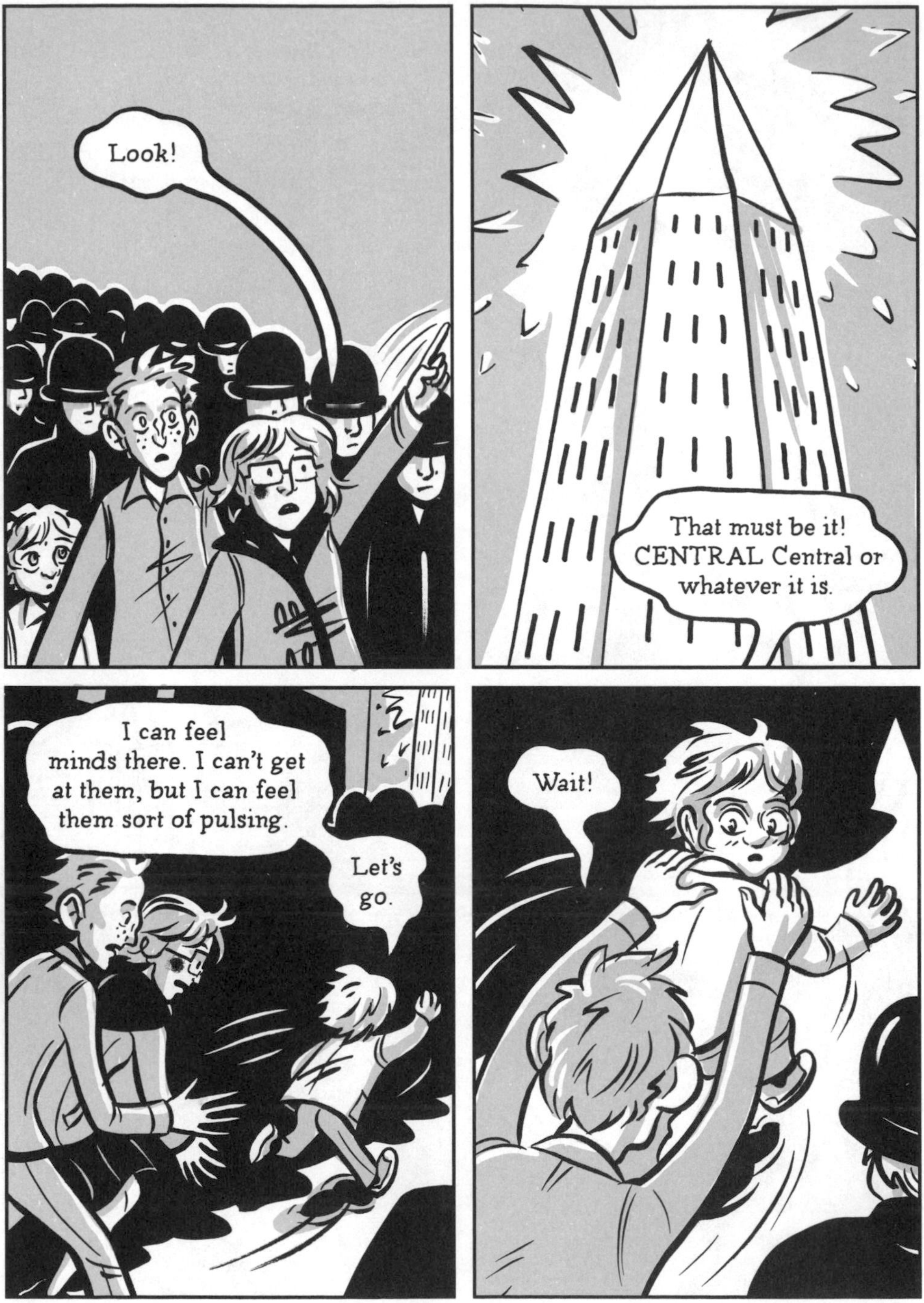
Look!
That must be it! CENTRAL Central or whatever it is.
I can feel minds there. I can't get at them, but I can feel them sort of pulsing.
Let's go.
Wait!

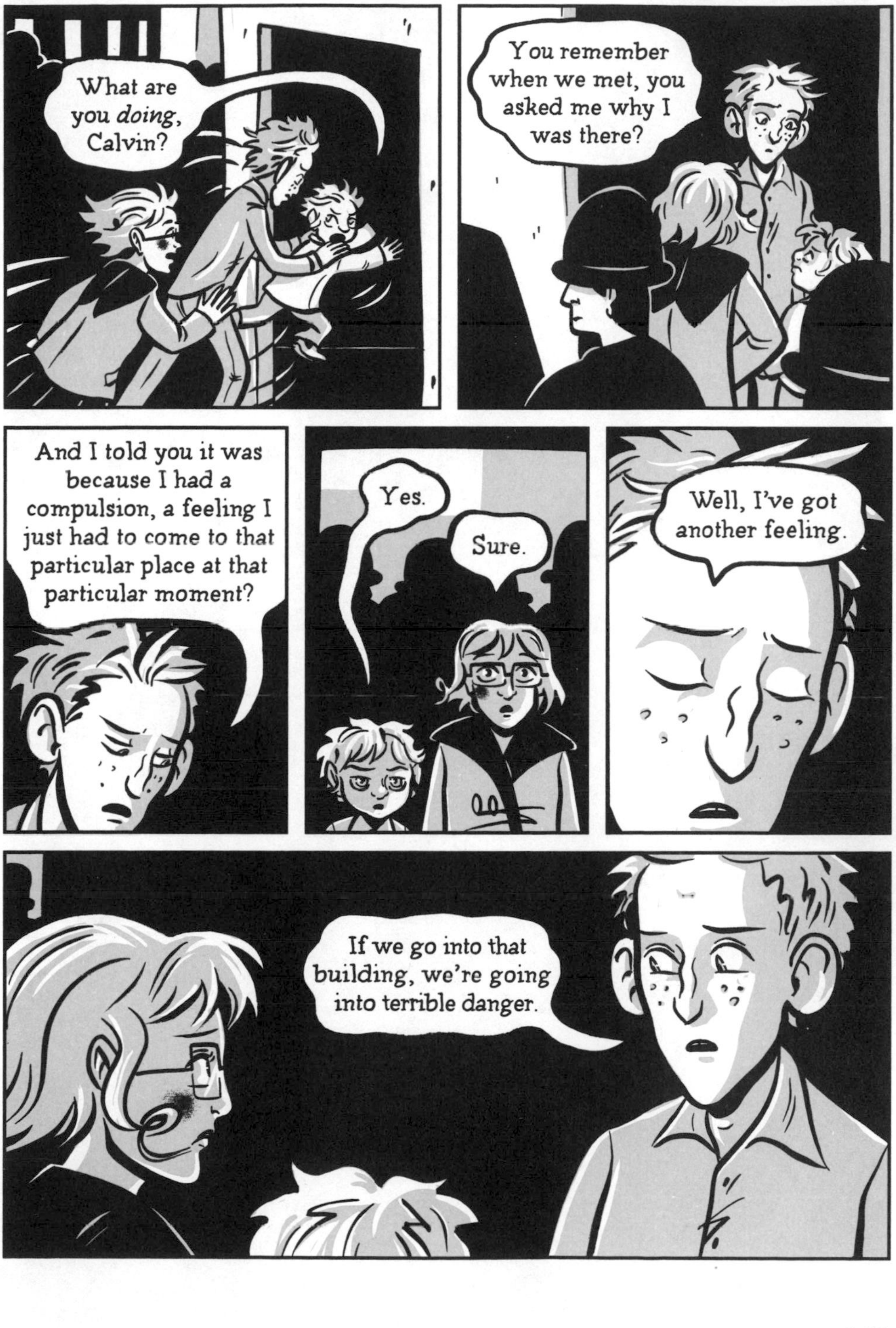
What are you *doing*, Calvin?
You remember when we met, you asked me why I was there?
And I told you it was because I had a compulsion, a feeling I just had to come to that particular place at that particular moment?
Yes.
Sure.
Well, I've got another feeling.
If we go into that building, we're going into terrible danger.

7
The Man with Red Eyes

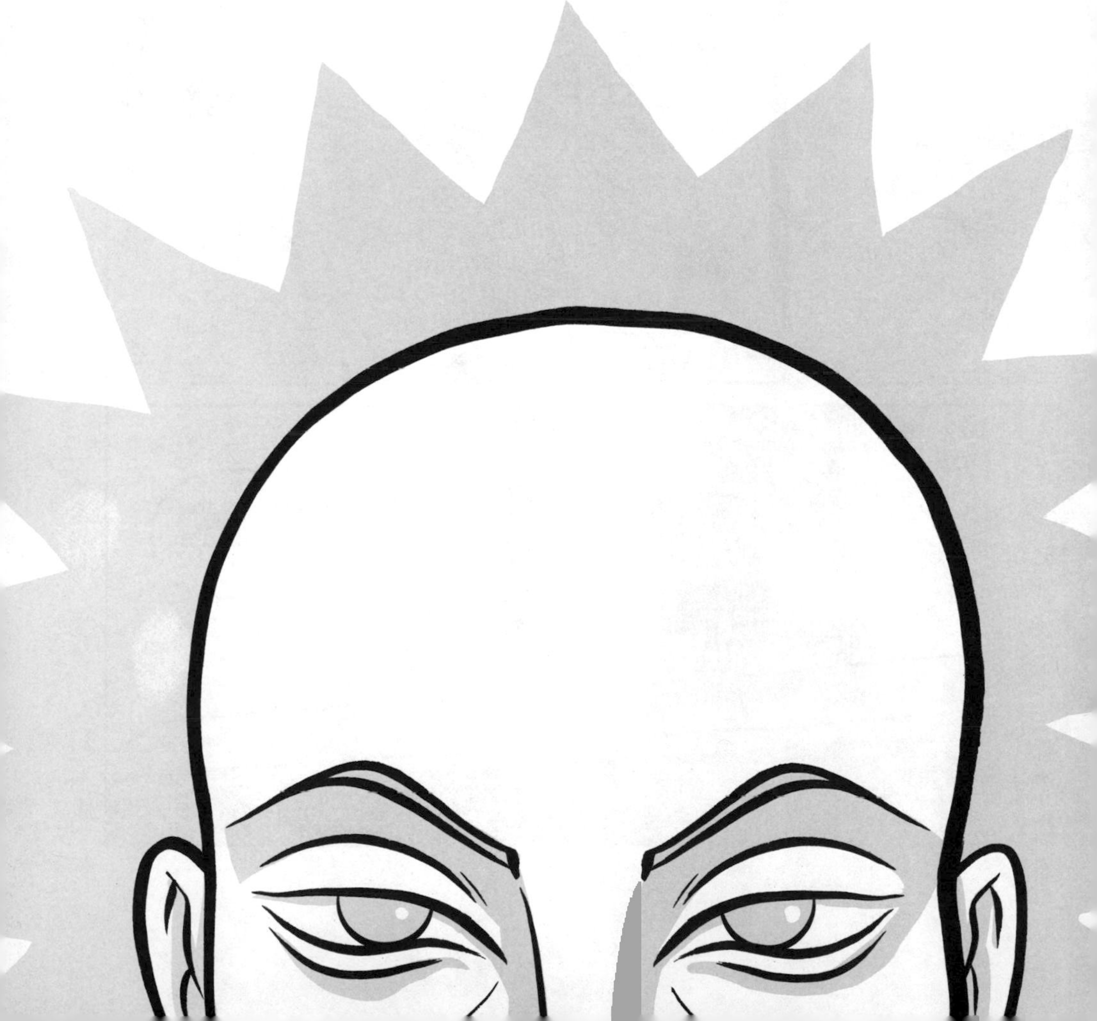

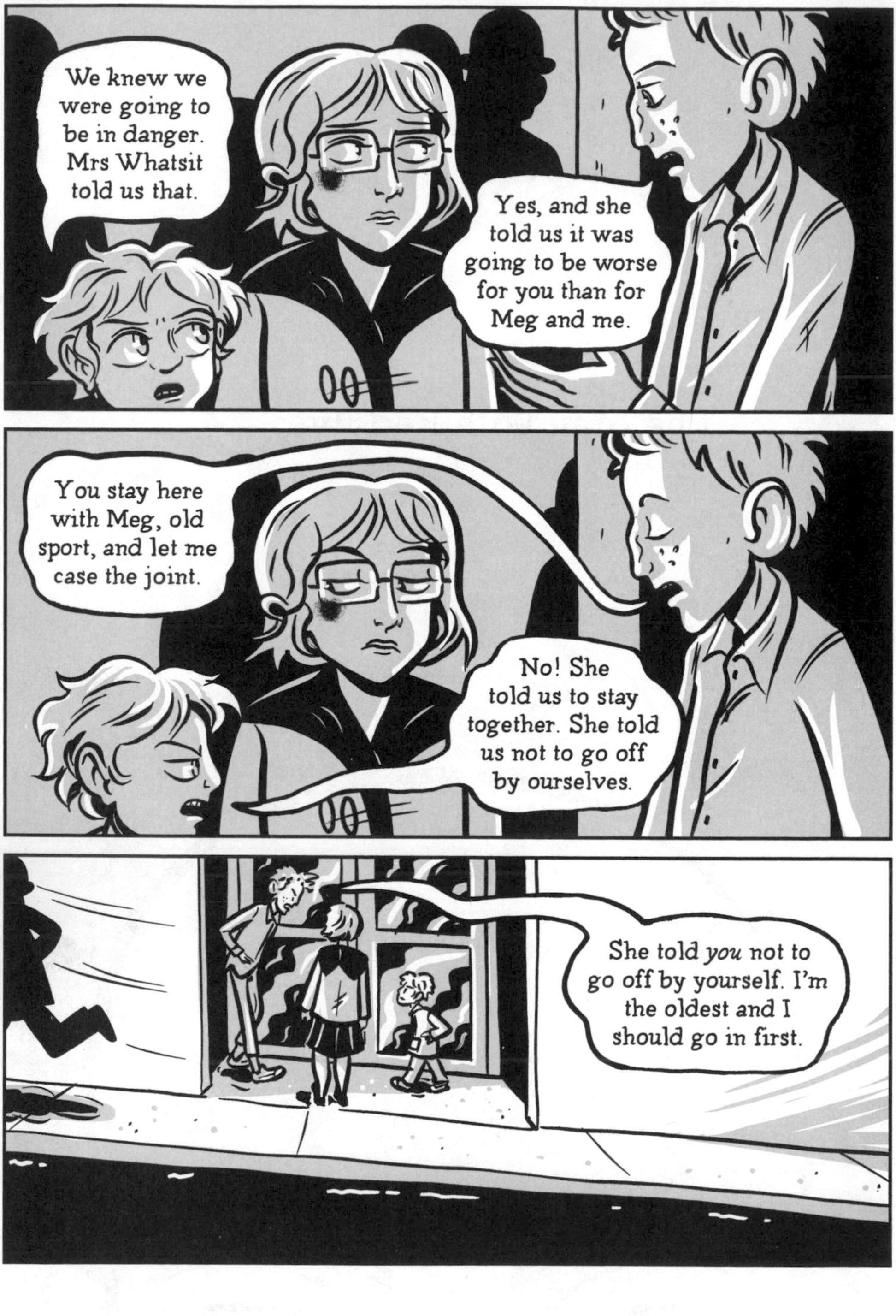
We knew we were going to be in danger. Mrs Whatsit told us that.
Yes, and she told us it was going to be worse for you than for Meg and me.
You stay here with Meg, old sport, and let me case the joint.
No! She told us to stay together. She told us not to go off by ourselves.
She told *you* not to go off by yourself. I'm the oldest and I should go in first.

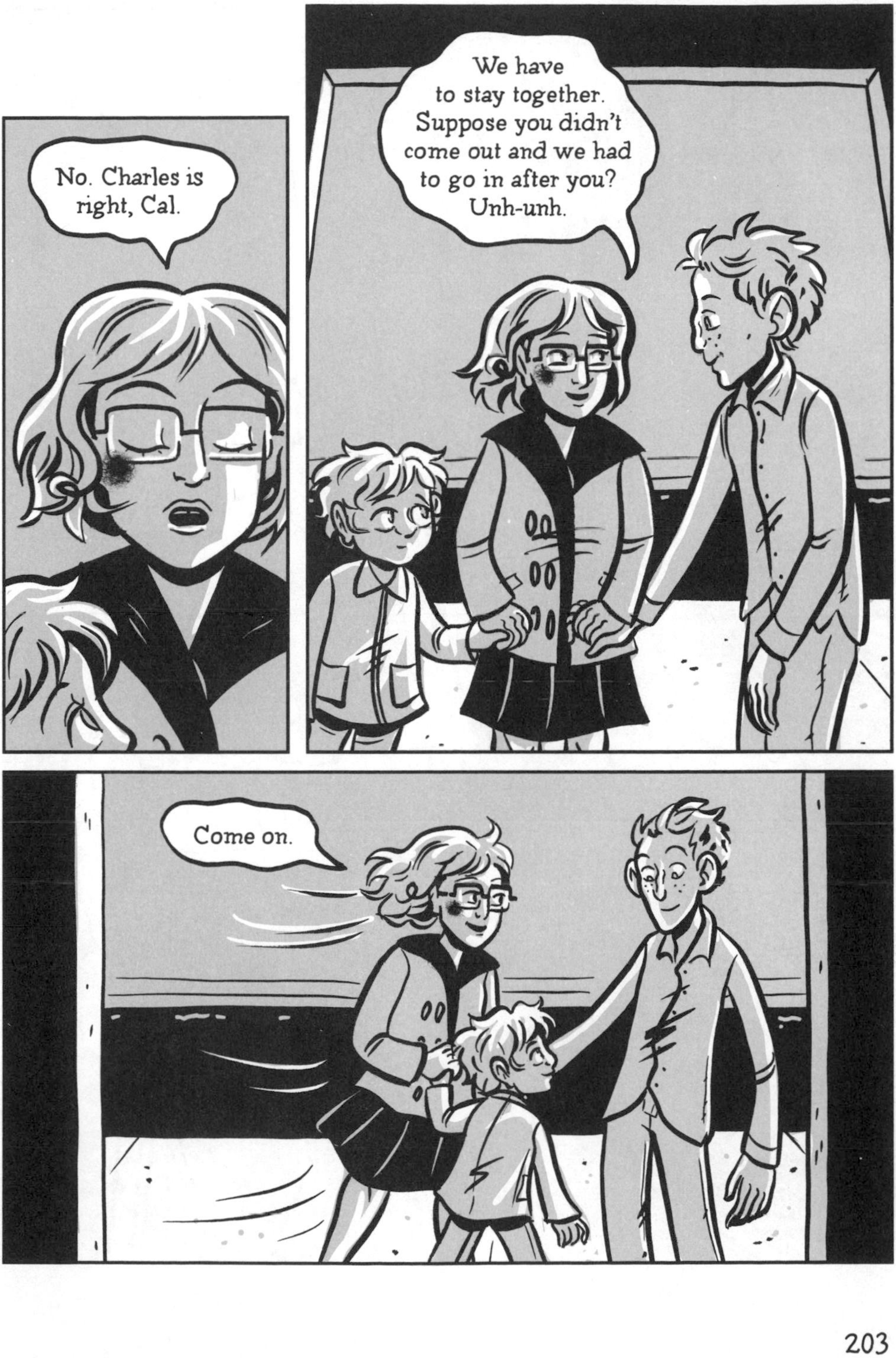
No. Charles is right, Cal.
We have to stay together. Suppose you didn't come out and we had to go in after you? Unh-unh.
Come on.

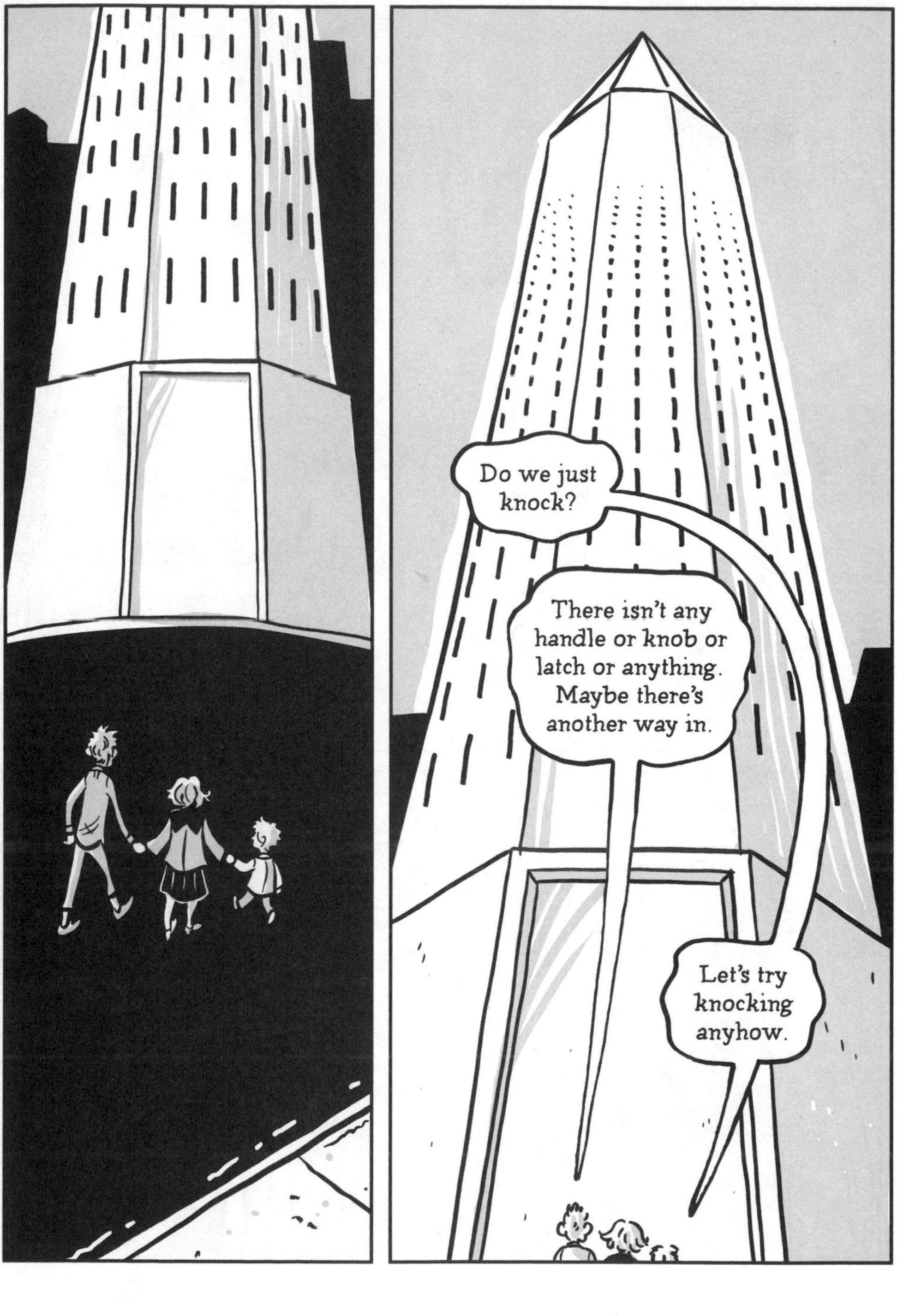
Do we just knock?
There isn't any handle or knob or latch or anything. Maybe there's another way in.
Let's try knocking anyhow.

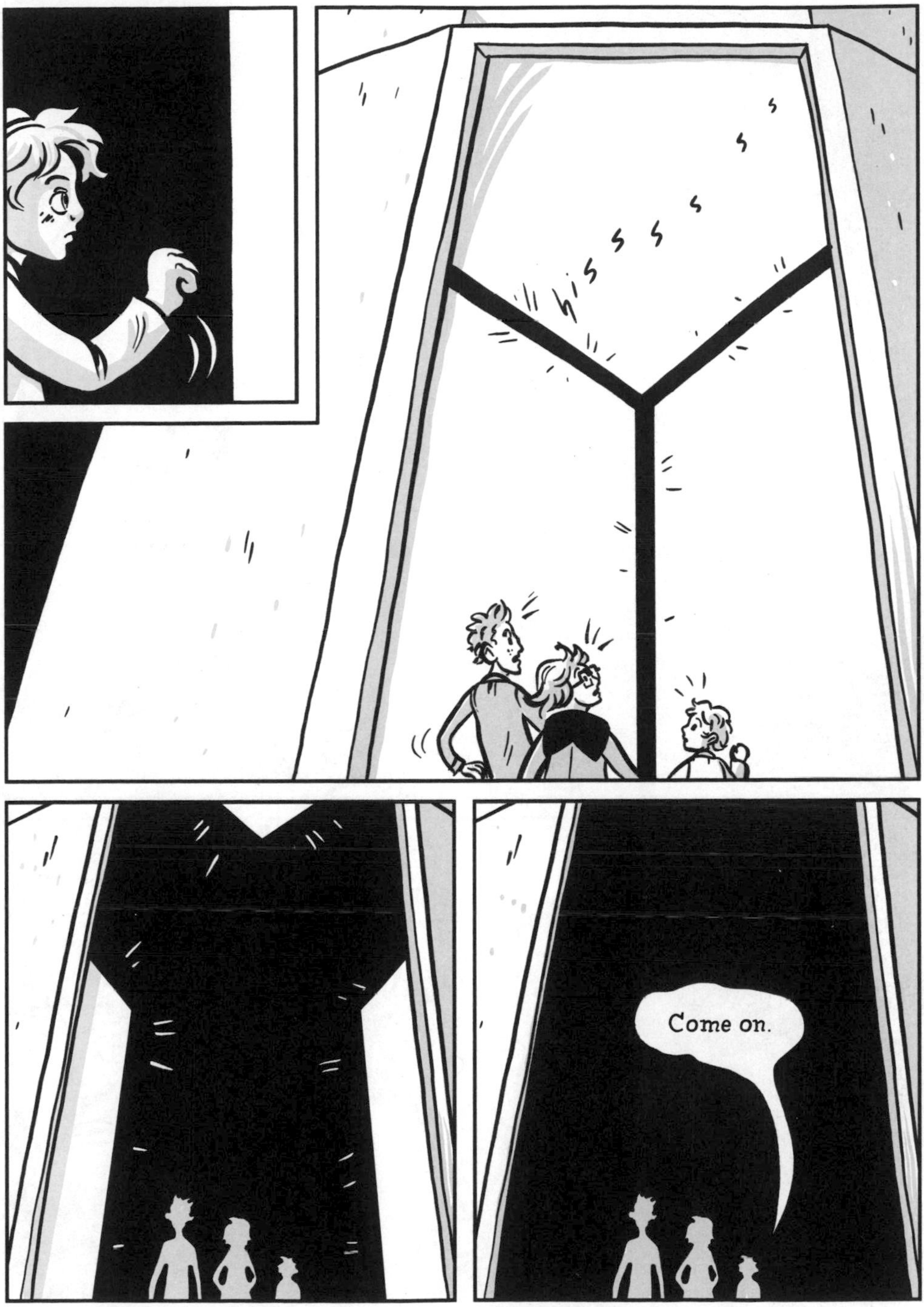
hissssss
Come on.

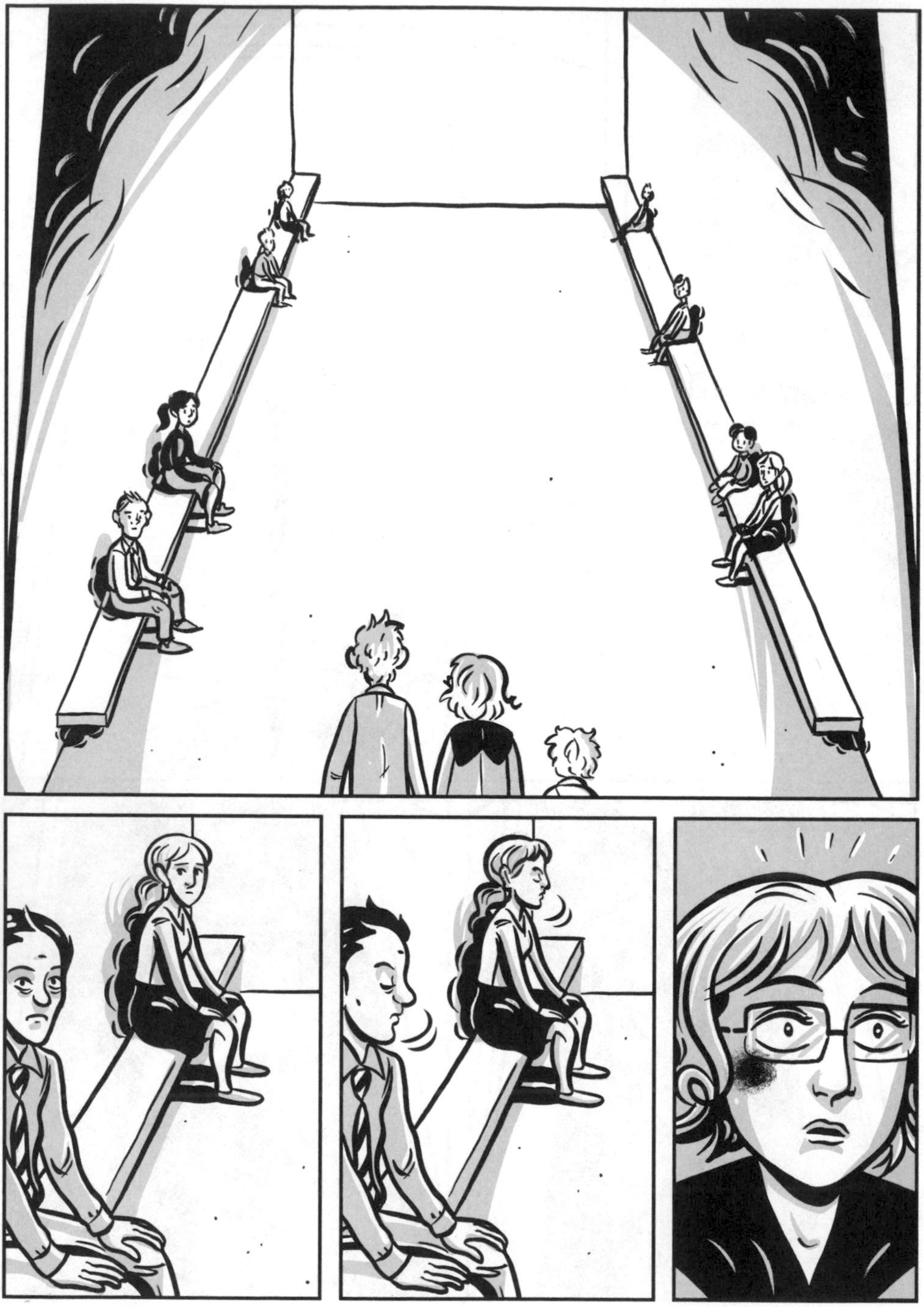

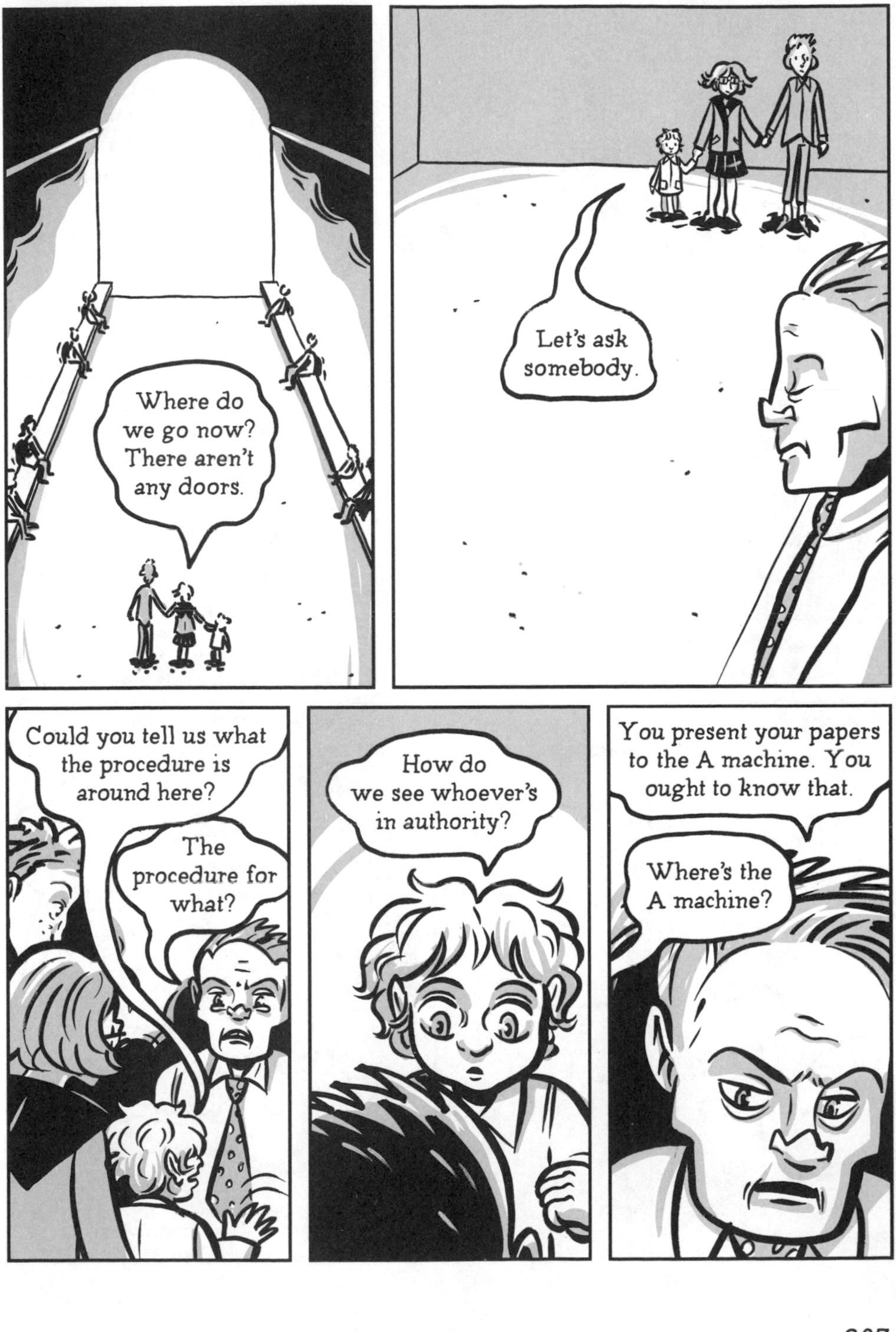
Where do we go now? There aren't any doors.
Let's ask somebody.
Could you tell us what the procedure is around here?
The procedure for what?
How do we see whoever's in authority?
You present your papers to the A machine. You ought to know that.
Where's the A machine?

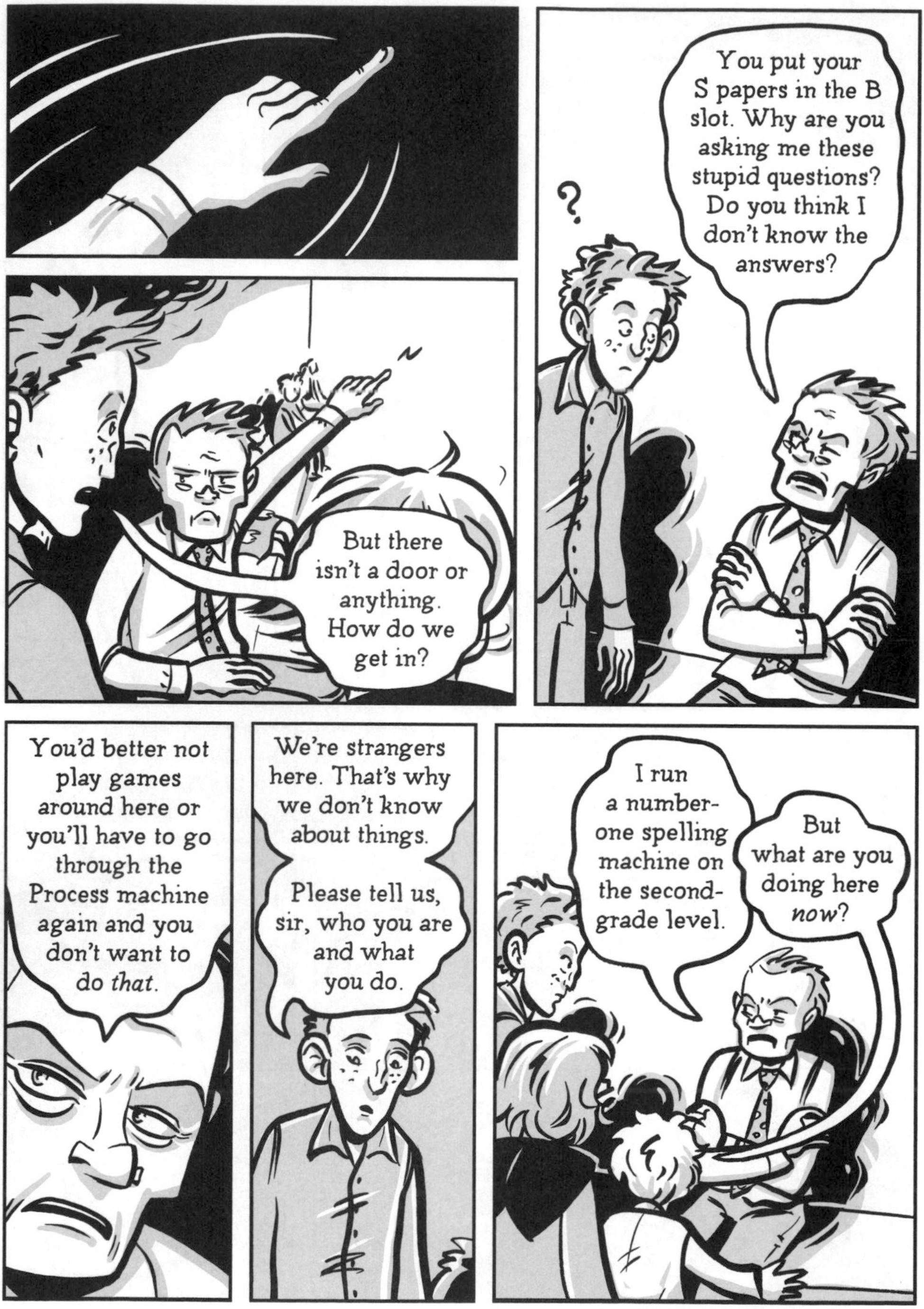
?
You put your S papers in the B slot. Why are you asking me these stupid questions? Do you think I don't know the answers?
But there isn't a door or anything. How do we get in?
You'd better not play games around here or you'll have to go through the Process machine again and you don't want to do *that*.
We're strangers here. That's why we don't know about things.
Please tell us, sir, who you are and what you do.
I run a number-one spelling machine on the second-grade level.
But what are you doing here *now*?

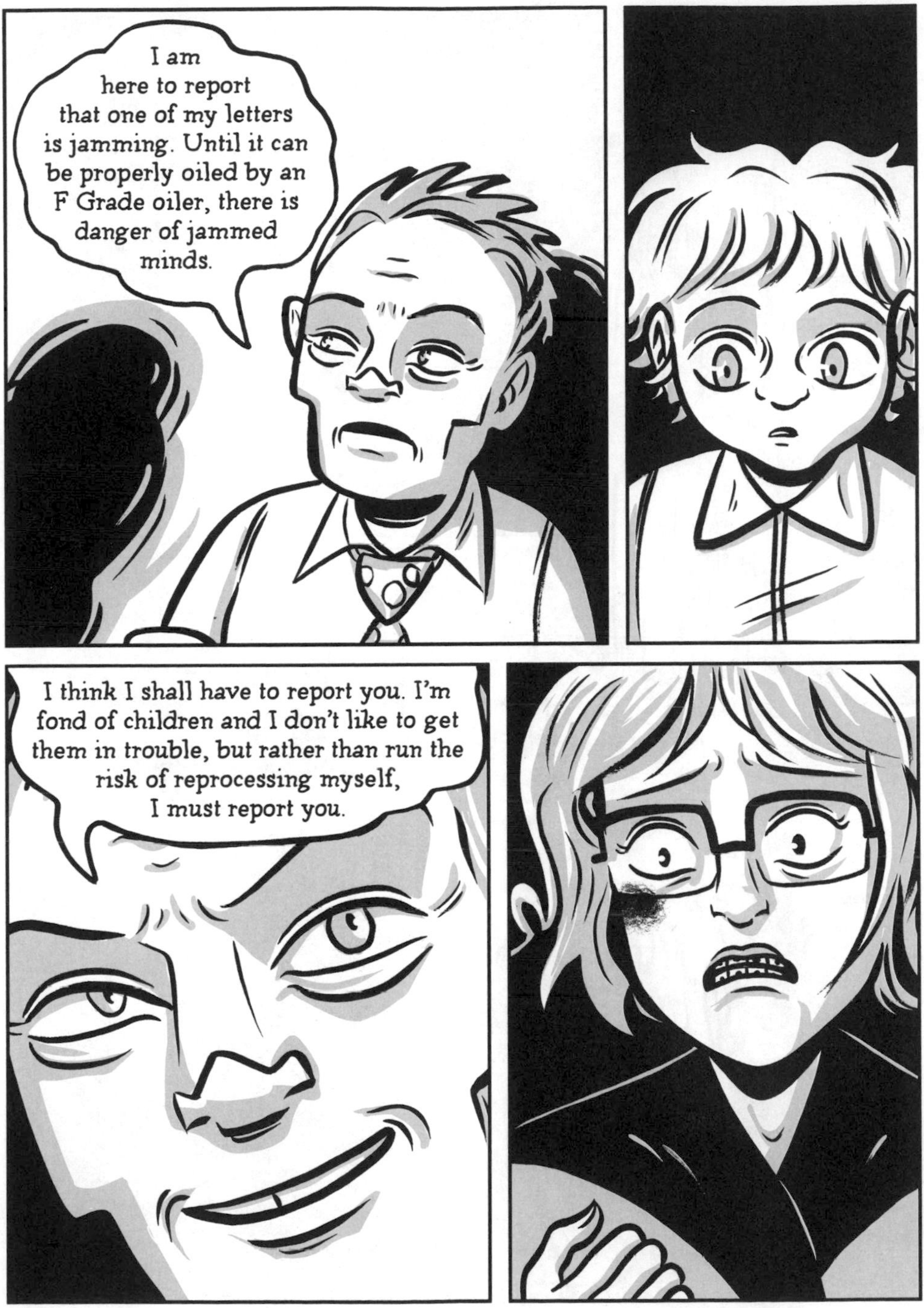
I am here to report that one of my letters is jamming. Until it can be properly oiled by an F Grade oiler, there is danger of jammed minds.
I think I shall have to report you. I'm fond of children and I don't like to get them in trouble, but rather than run the risk of reprocessing myself, I must report you.

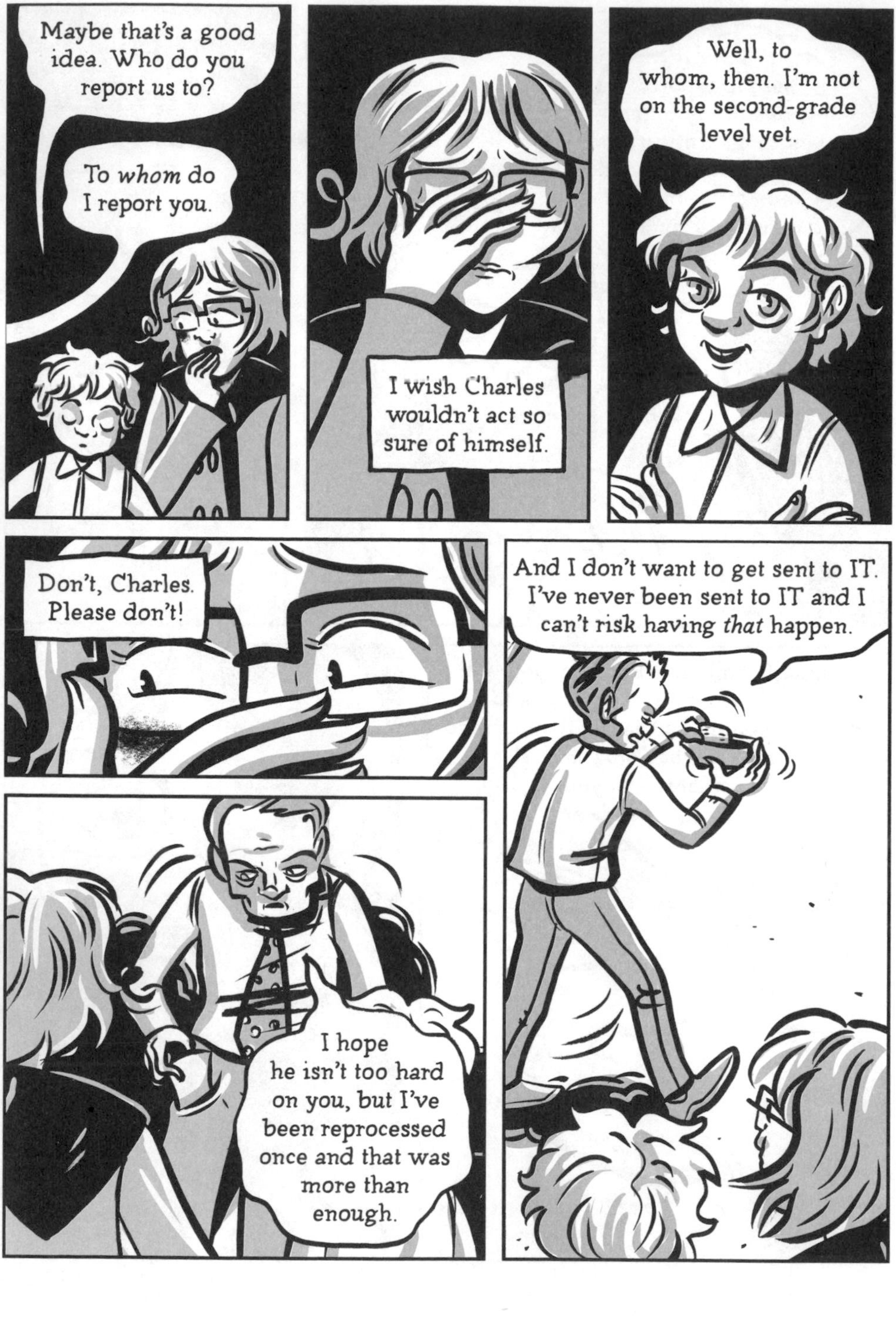

Maybe that's a good idea. Who do you report us to?
To *whom* do I report you.
I wish Charles wouldn't act so sure of himself.
Well, to whom, then. I'm not on the second-grade level yet.
Don't, Charles. Please don't!
And I don't want to get sent to IT. I've never been sent to IT and I can't risk having *that* happen.
I hope he isn't too hard on you, but I've been reprocessed once and that was more than enough.

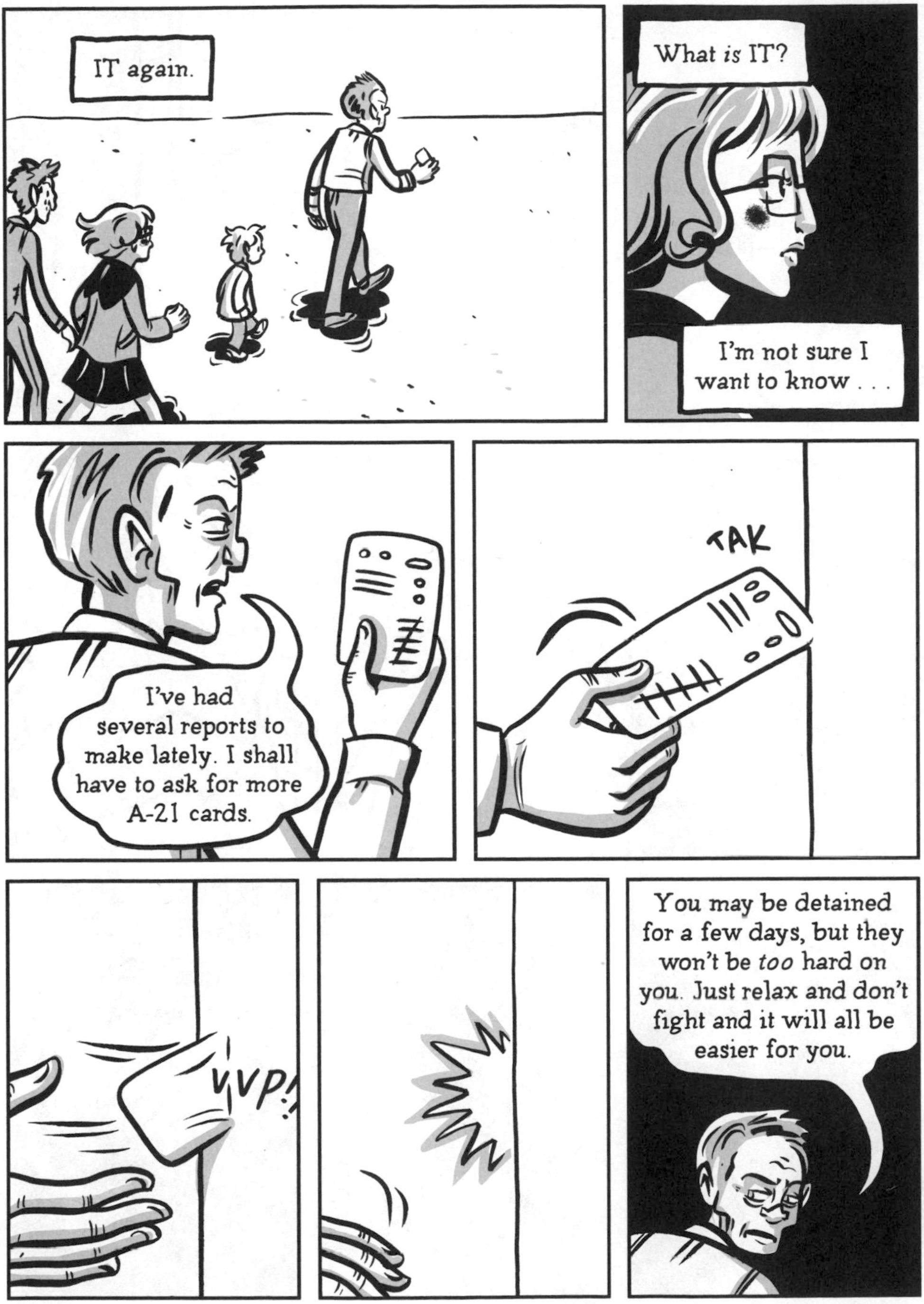
IT again.
What *is* IT?
I'm not sure I want to know . . .
I've had several reports to make lately. I shall have to ask for more A-21 cards.
TAK
VVP!
You may be detained for a few days, but they won't be *too* hard on you. Just relax and don't fight and it will all be easier for you.

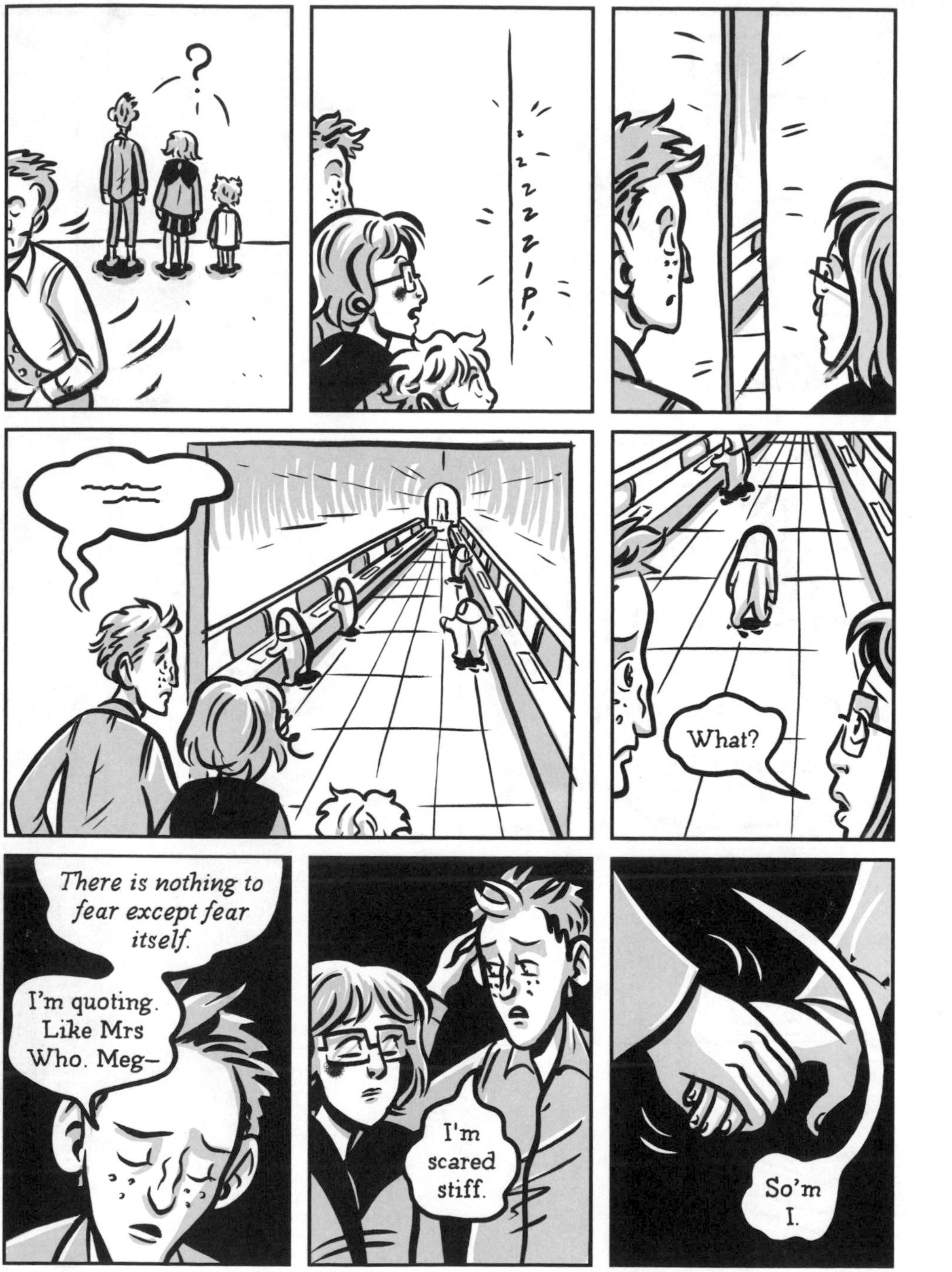
?
ZZZZZIP!
What?
There is nothing to fear except fear itself.
I'm quoting. Like Mrs Who. Meg–
I'm scared stiff.
So'm I.

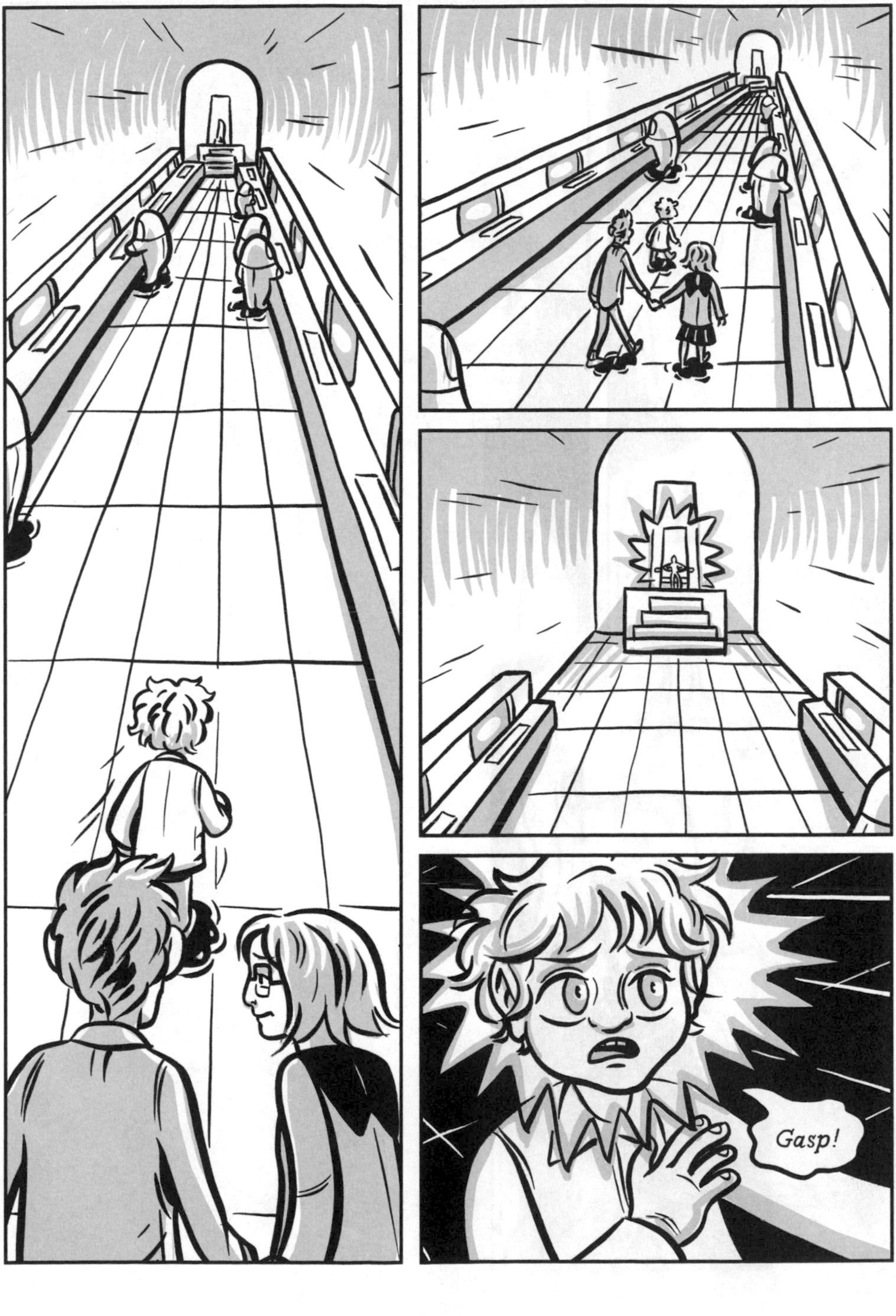
Gasp!

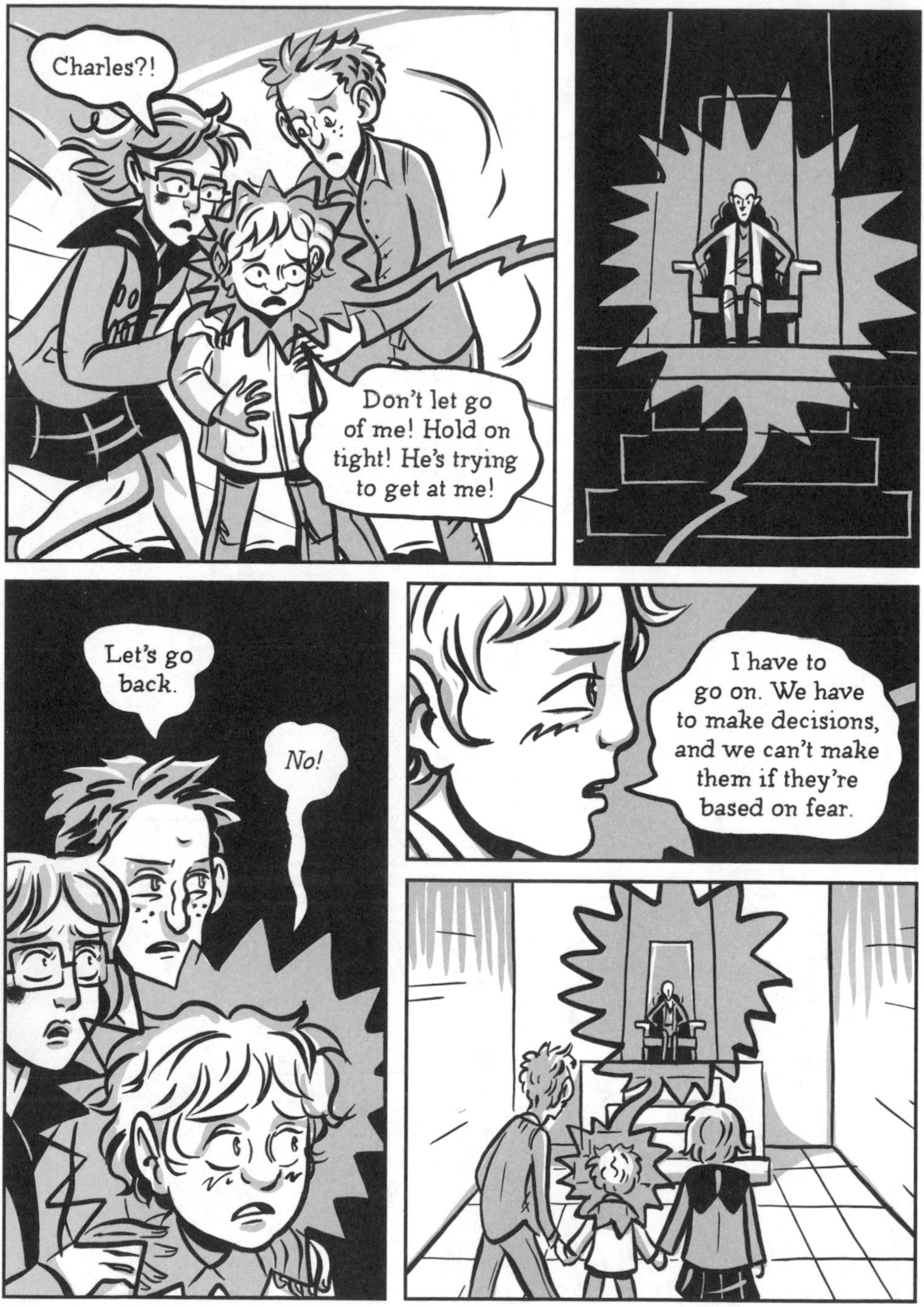
Charles?!
Don't let go of me! Hold on tight! He's trying to get at me!
Let's go back.
No!
I have to go on. We have to make decisions, and we can't make them if they're based on fear.

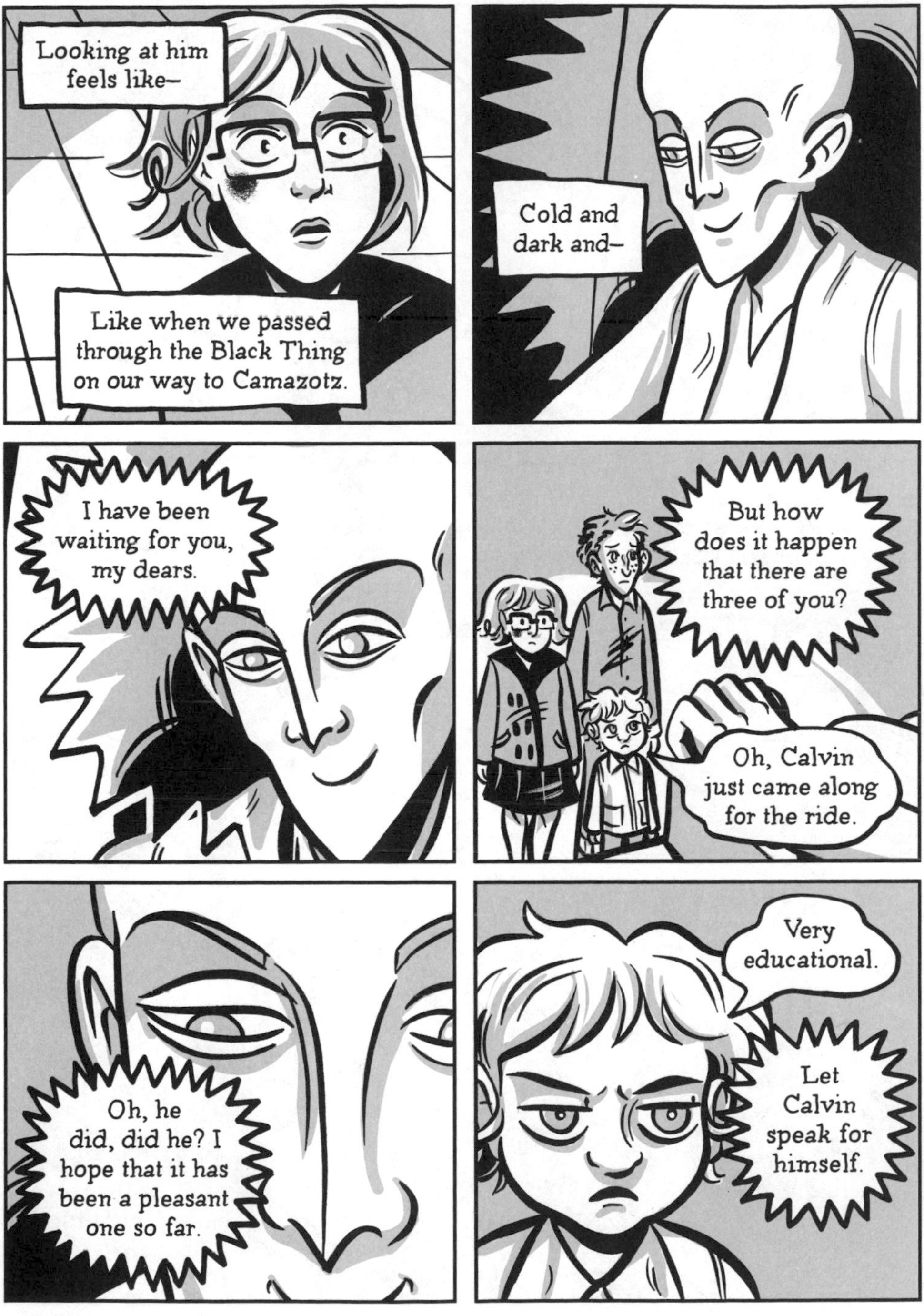
Looking at him feels like–
Like when we passed through the Black Thing on our way to Camazotz.
Cold and dark and–
I have been waiting for you, my dears.
But how does it happen that there are three of you?
Oh, Calvin just came along for the ride.
Oh, he did, did he? I hope that it has been a pleasant one so far.
Very educational.
Let Calvin speak for himself.

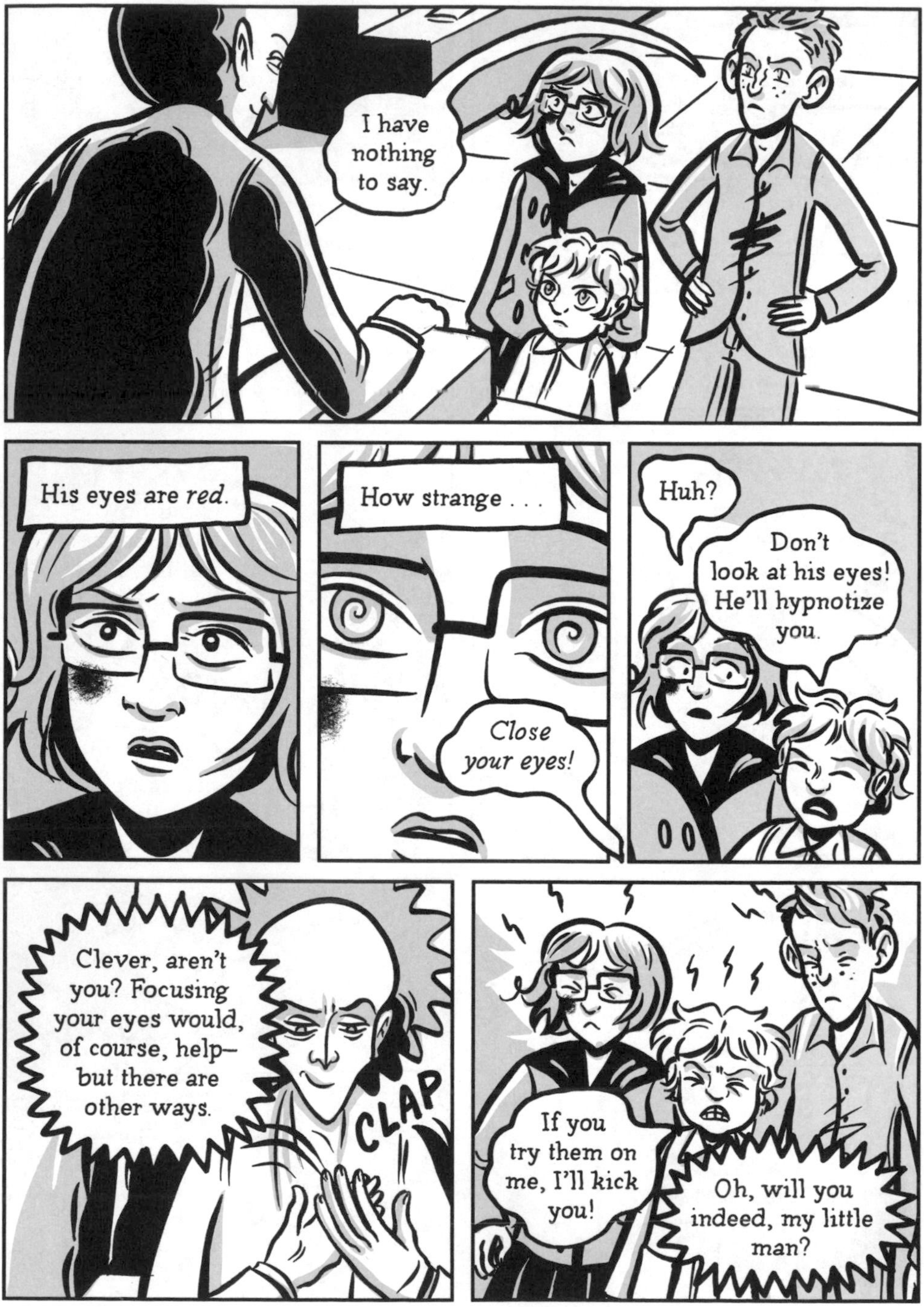
I have nothing to say.
His eyes are *red*.
How strange . . .
Close your eyes!
Huh?
Don't look at his eyes! He'll hypnotize you.
Clever, aren't you? Focusing your eyes would, of course, help—but there are other ways.
CLAP
If you try them on me, I'll kick you!
Oh, will you indeed, my little man?

It's no good to try to oppose me.

And you will soon realize there is no need to fight me.

Not only is there no need, but you will not have the slightest desire to do so.

For why should you wish to fight someone who is here only to save you pain and trouble?

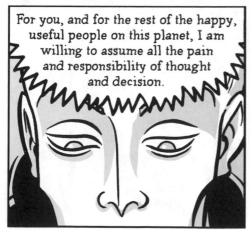

For you, and for the rest of the happy, useful people on this planet, I am willing to assume all the pain and responsibility of thought and decision.

We'll make our own decisions, thank you!

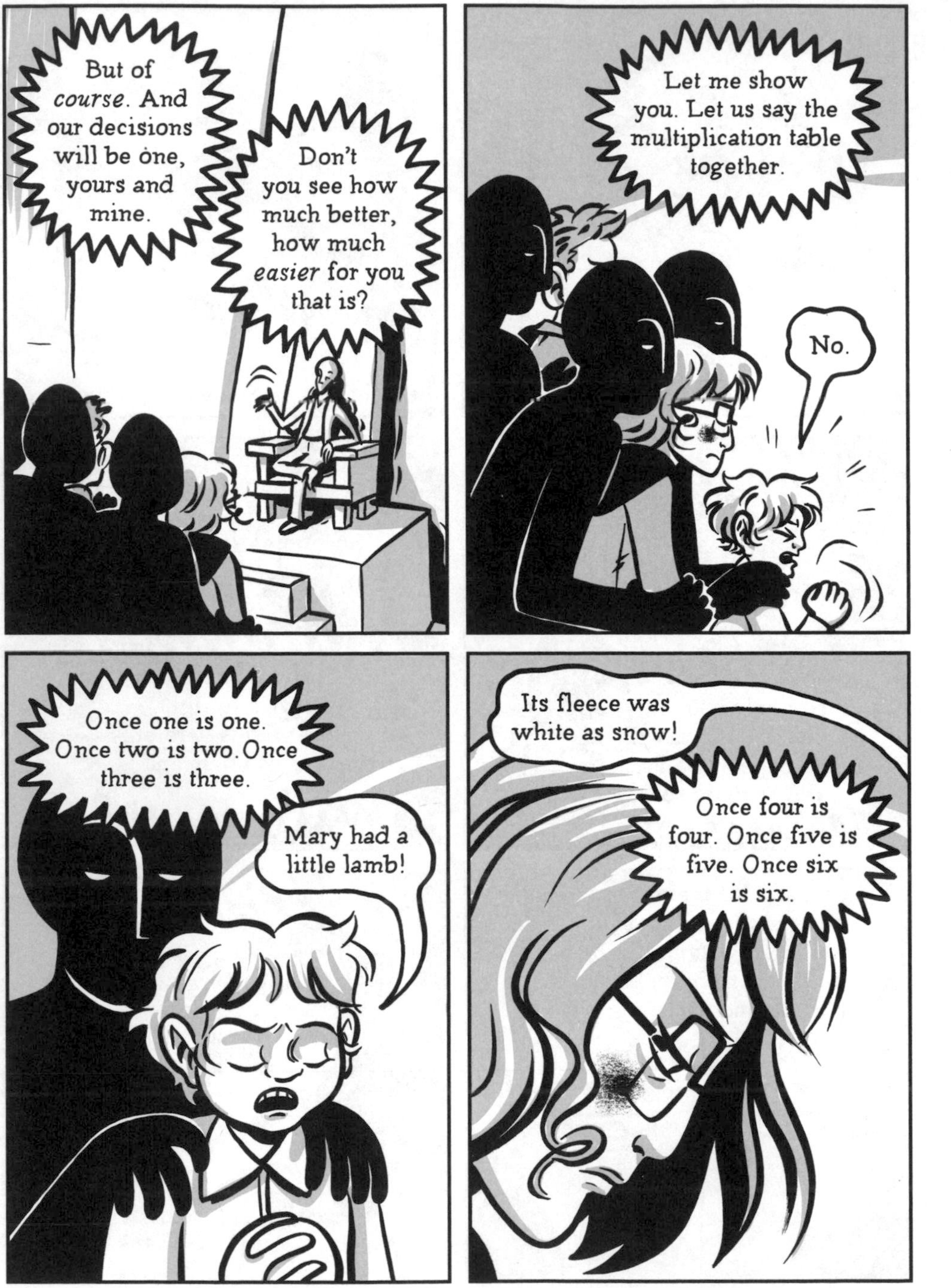
But of *course*. And our decisions will be one, yours and mine.
Don't you see how much better, how much *easier* for you that is?
Let me show you. Let us say the multiplication table together.
No.
Once one is one. Once two is two. Once three is three.
Mary had a little lamb!
Its fleece was white as snow!
Once four is four. Once five is five. Once six is six.

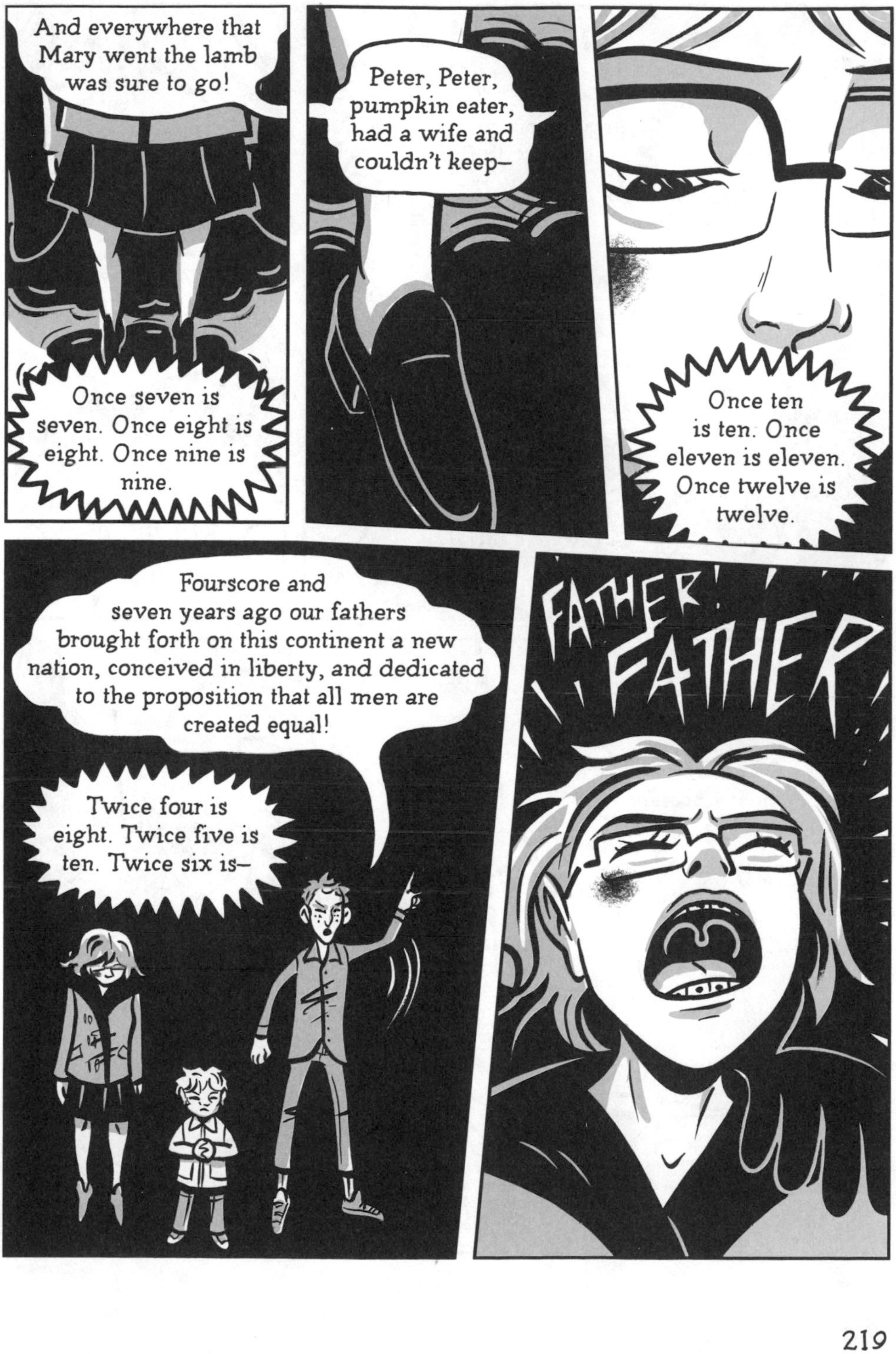

And everywhere that Mary went the lamb was sure to go!
Once seven is seven. Once eight is eight. Once nine is nine.
Peter, Peter, pumpkin eater, had a wife and couldn't keep–
Once ten is ten. Once eleven is eleven. Once twelve is twelve.
Fourscore and seven years ago our fathers brought forth on this continent a new nation, conceived in liberty, and dedicated to the proposition that all men are created equal!
Twice four is eight. Twice five is ten. Twice six is–
FATHER!
FATHER

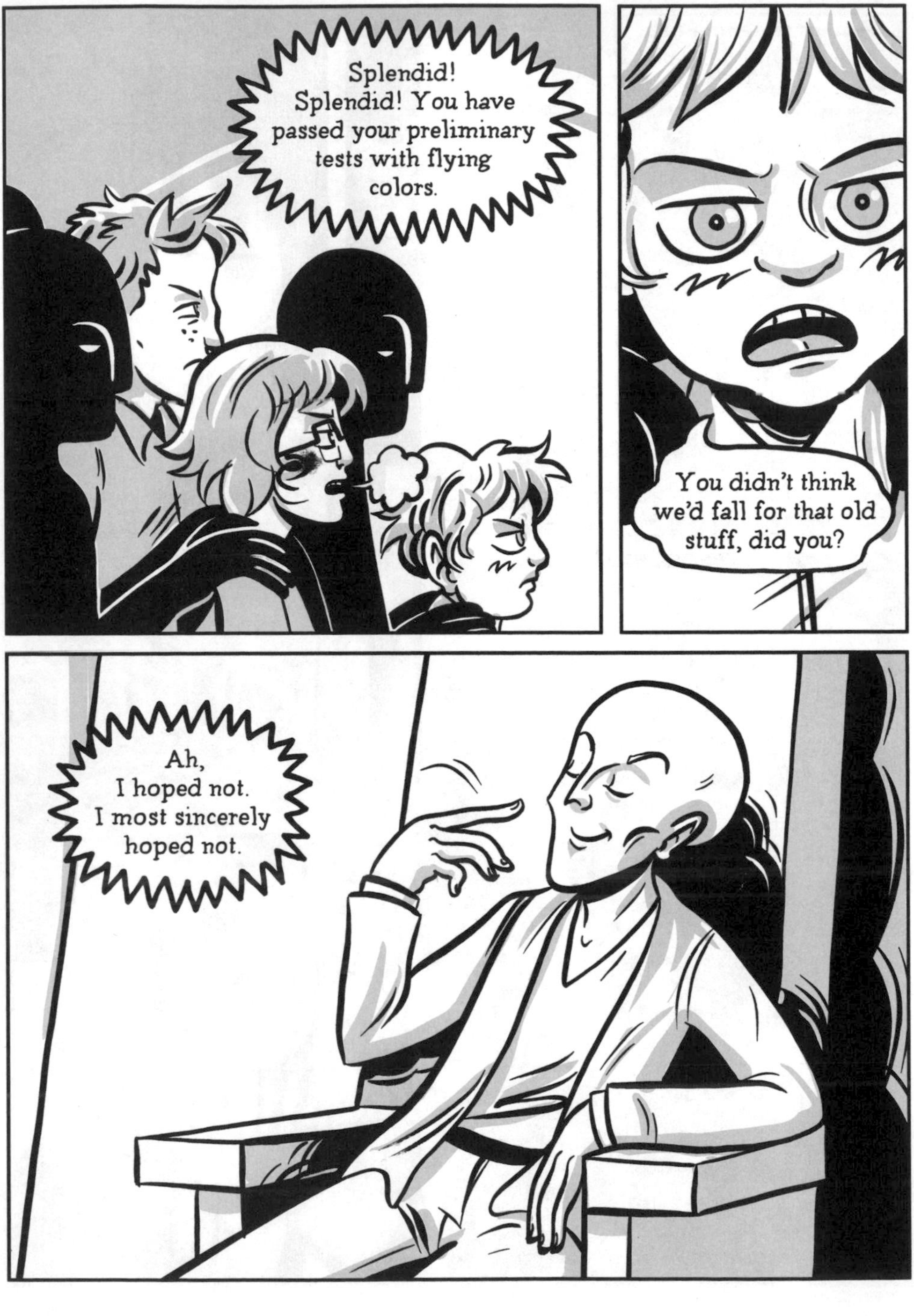
Splendid! Splendid! You have passed your preliminary tests with flying colors.
You didn't think we'd fall for that old stuff, did you?
Ah, I hoped not. I most sincerely hoped not.

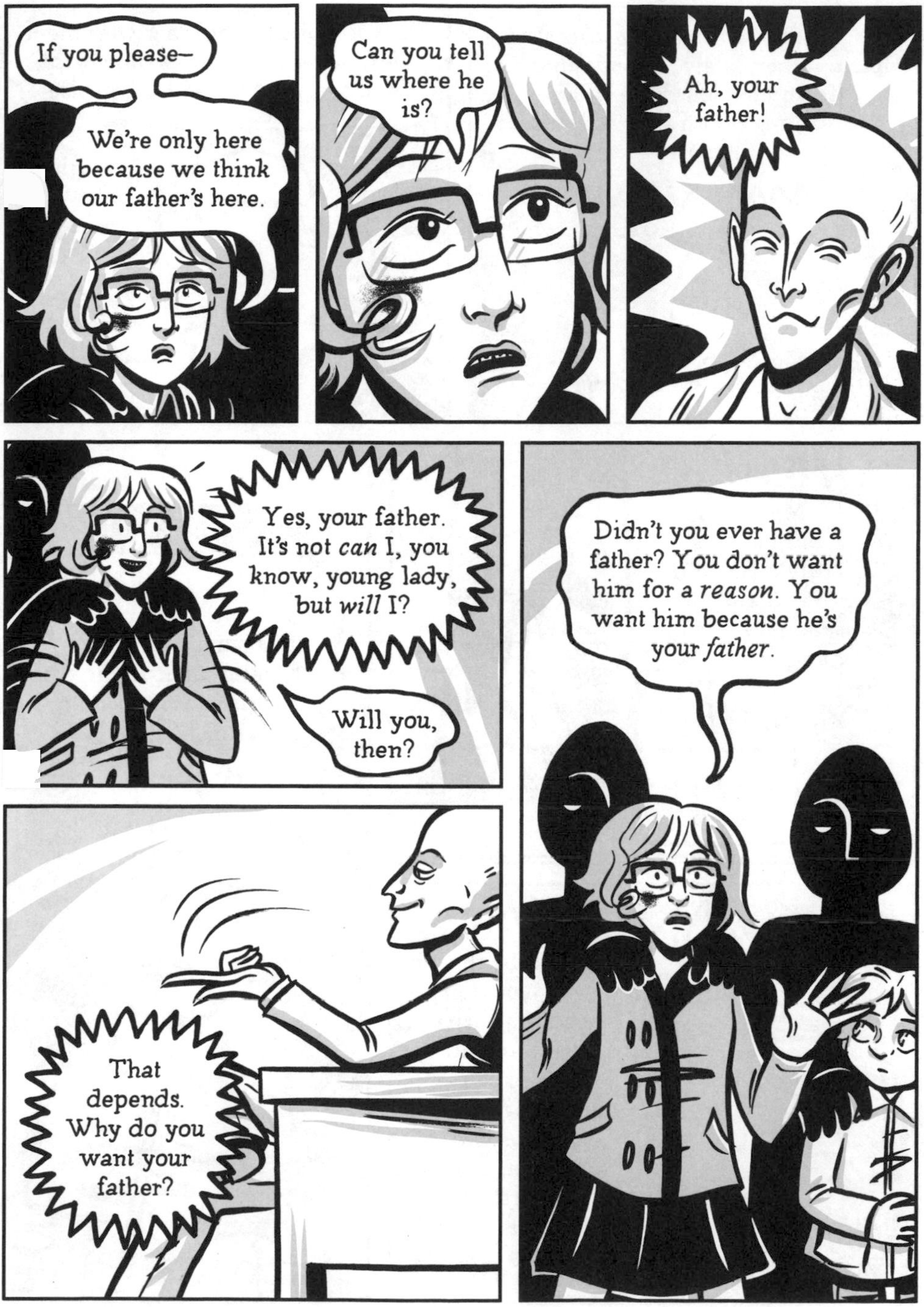
If you please—
We're only here because we think our father's here.
Can you tell us where he is?
Ah, your father!
Yes, your father. It's not *can* I, you know, young lady, but *will* I?
Will you, then?
Didn't you ever have a father? You don't want him for a *reason*. You want him because he's your *father*.
That depends. Why do you want your father?

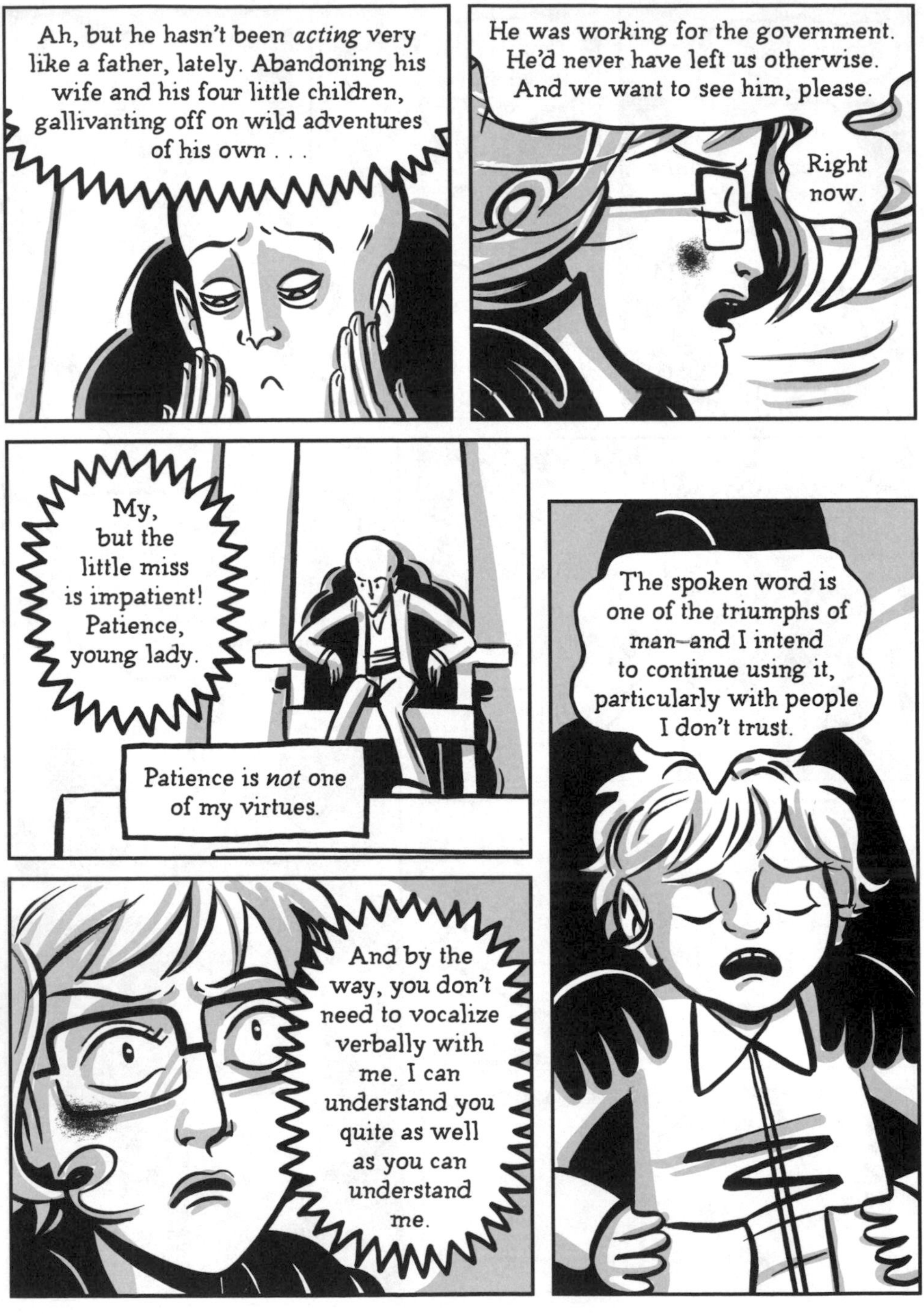
Ah, but he hasn't been *acting* very like a father, lately. Abandoning his wife and his four little children, gallivanting off on wild adventures of his own . . .
He was working for the government. He'd never have left us otherwise. And we want to see him, please.
Right now.
My, but the little miss is impatient! Patience, young lady.
Patience is *not* one of my virtues.
The spoken word is one of the triumphs of man—and I intend to continue using it, particularly with people I don't trust.
And by the way, you don't need to vocalize verbally with me. I can understand you quite as well as you can understand me.

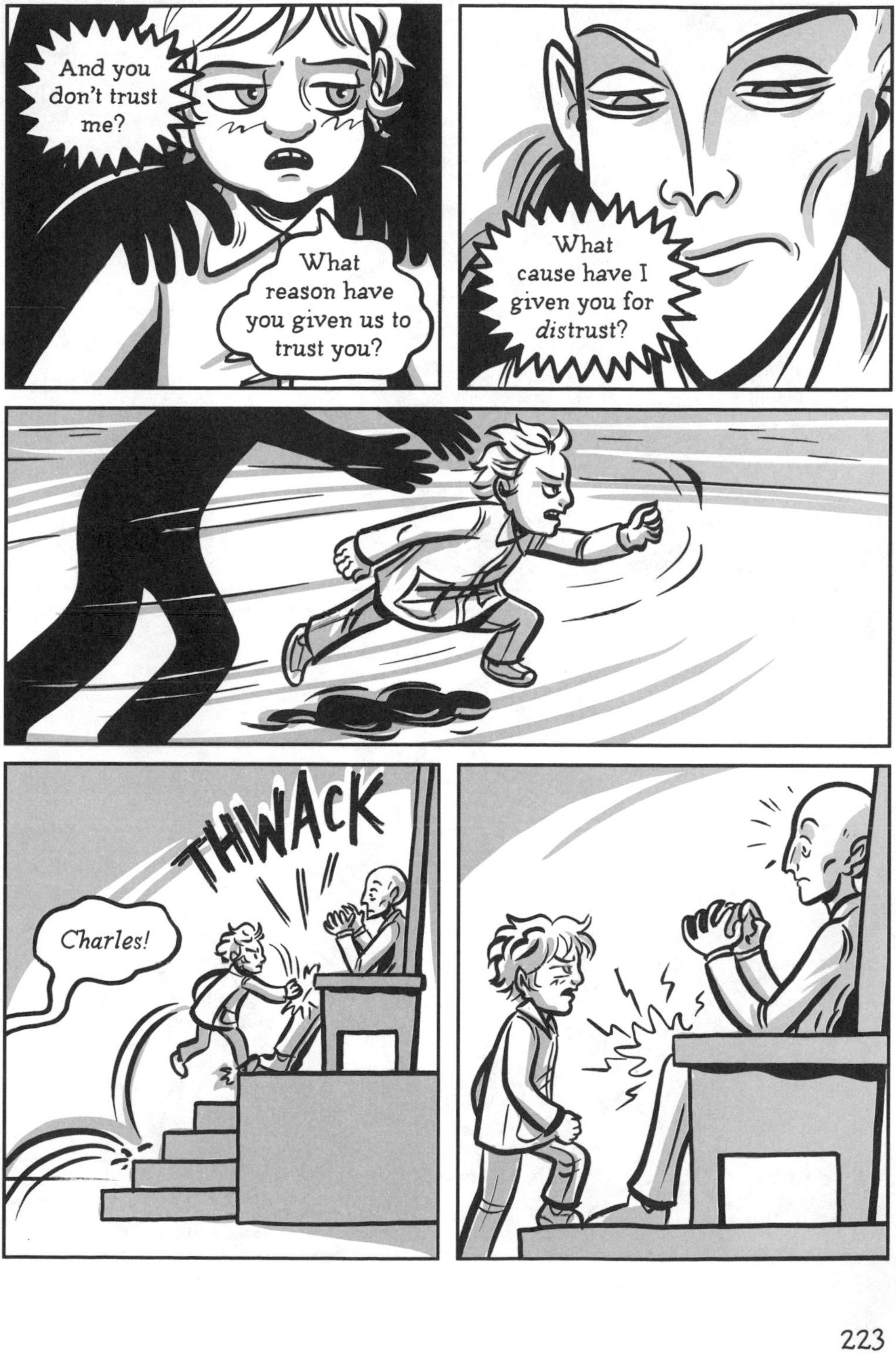
And you don't trust me?
What reason have you given us to trust you?
What cause have I given you for *dis*trust?
THWACK
Charles!

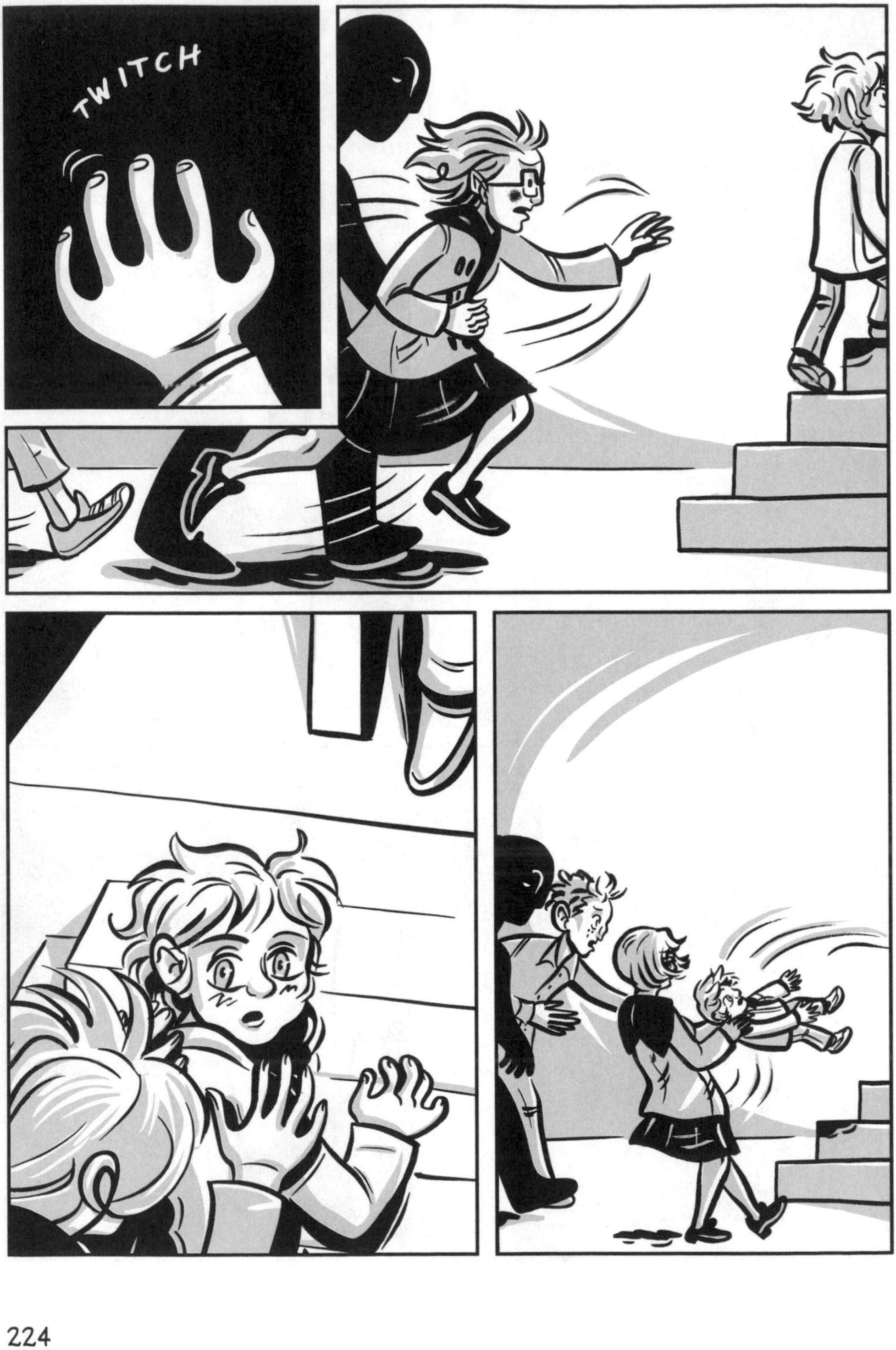
TWITCH

May I—*hah*— ask why you—*hah*— did that?

Because you aren't you.

I'm not sure what you are, but you . . . You aren't what's talking to us. I'm sorry if I hurt you. I didn't think you were real.

I thought perhaps you were a robot, because I don't feel anything coming directly from you.

I'm not sure where it's coming from, but it's coming *through* you. It isn't you.

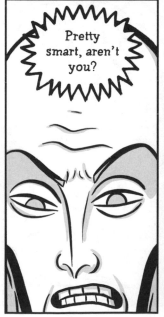

Pretty smart, aren't you?

It's not that I'm smart.

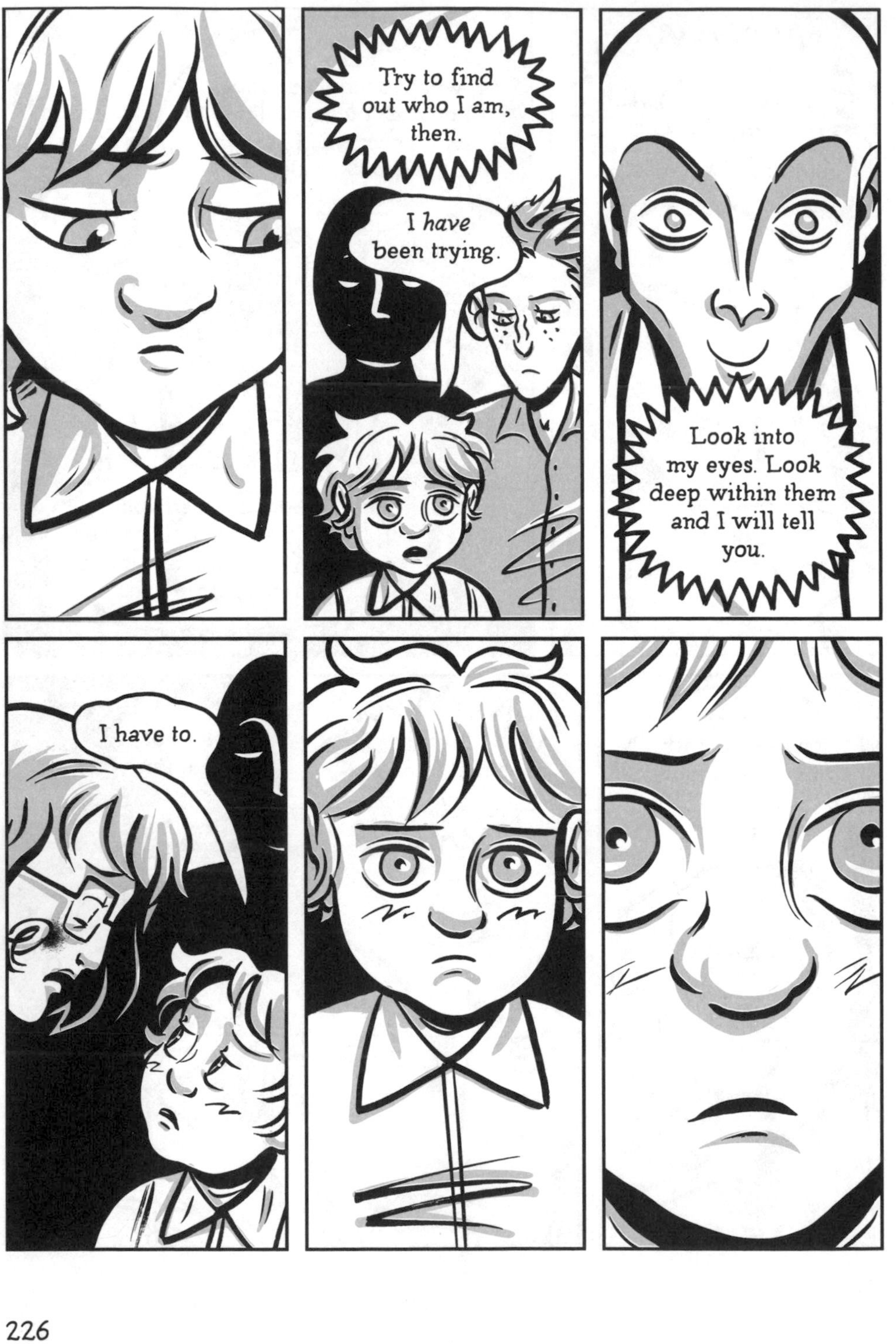
Try to find out who I am, then.
I *have* been trying.
Look into my eyes. Look deep within them and I will tell you.
I have to.

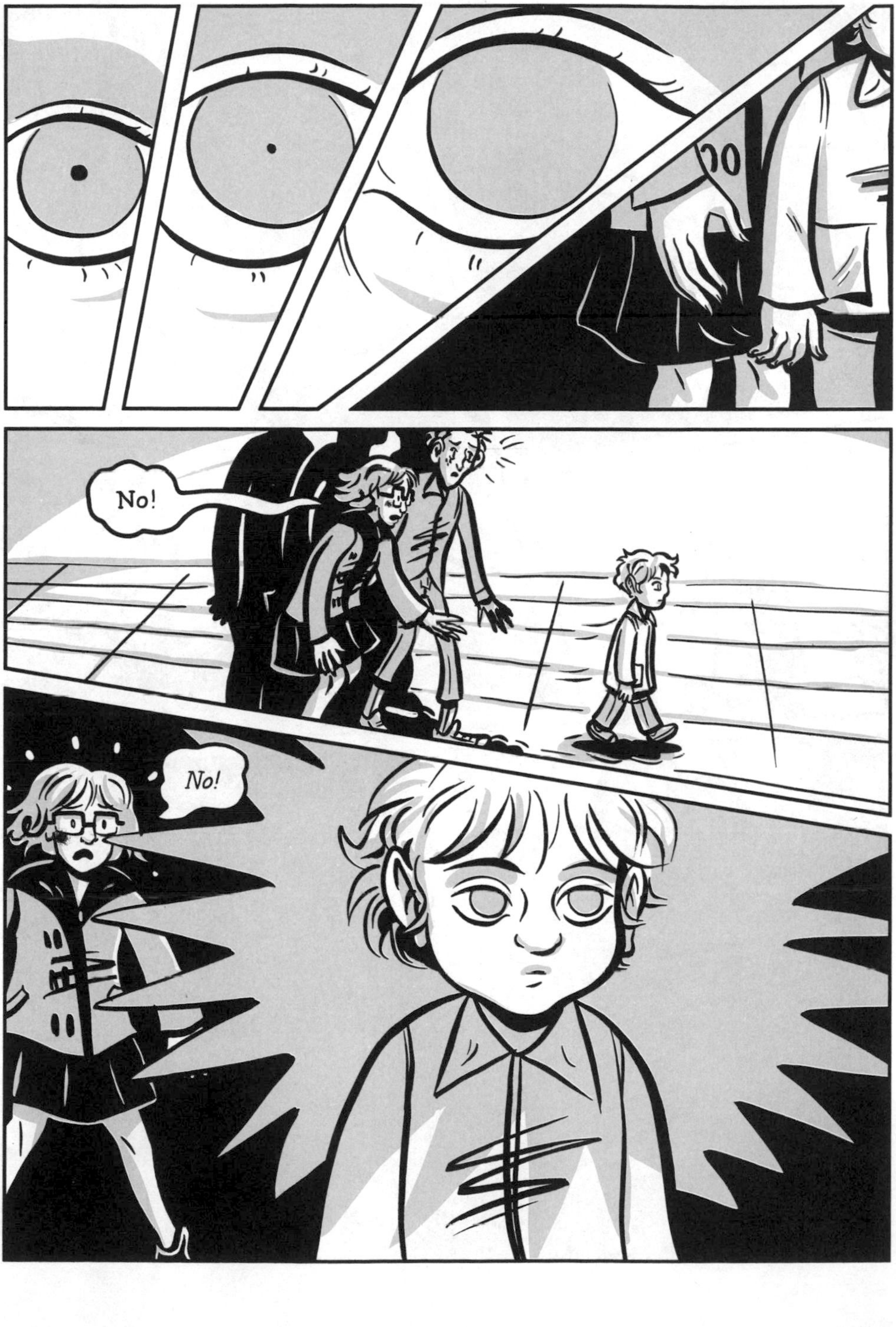
No!
No!

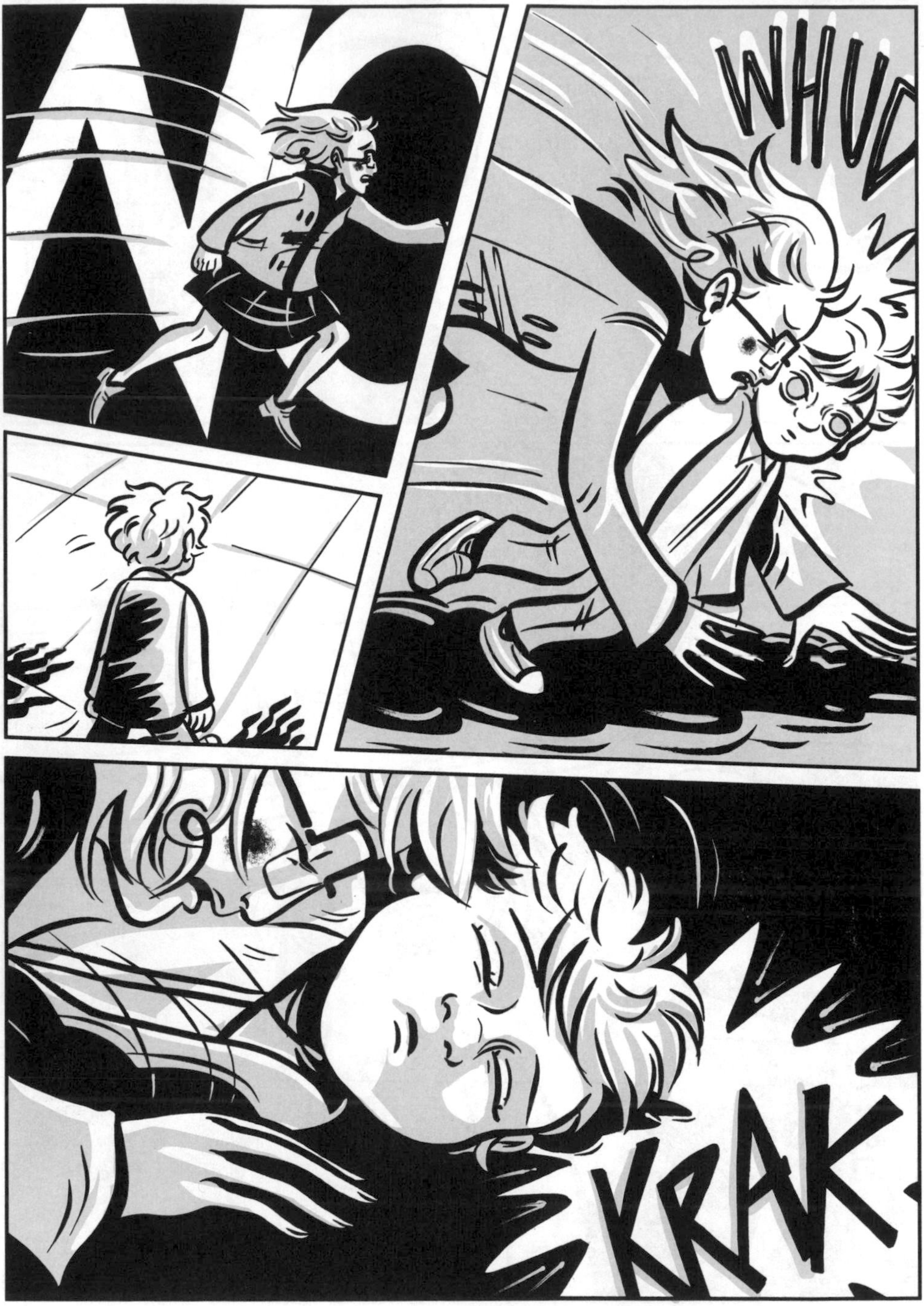
WHUD
KRAK

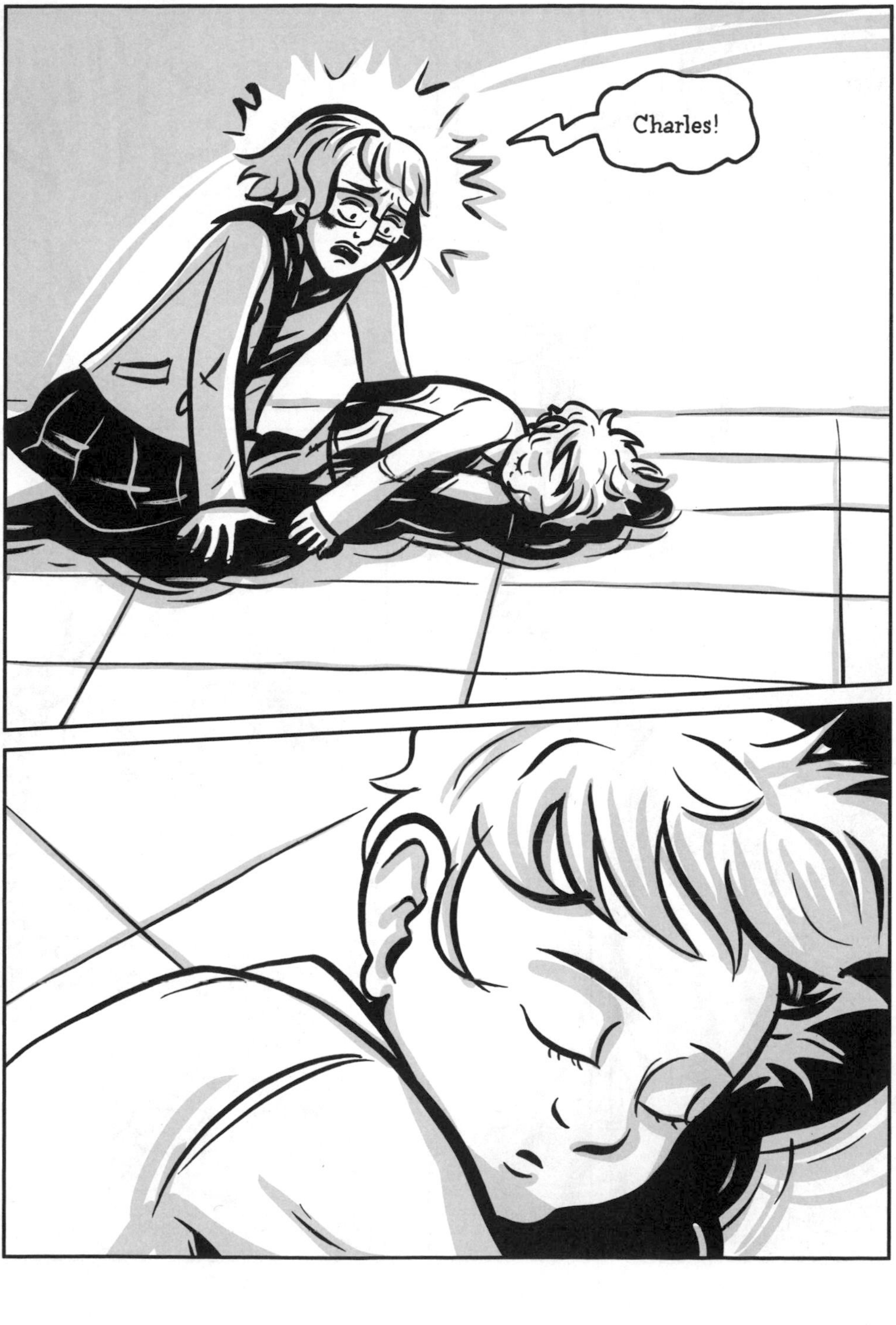
Charles!

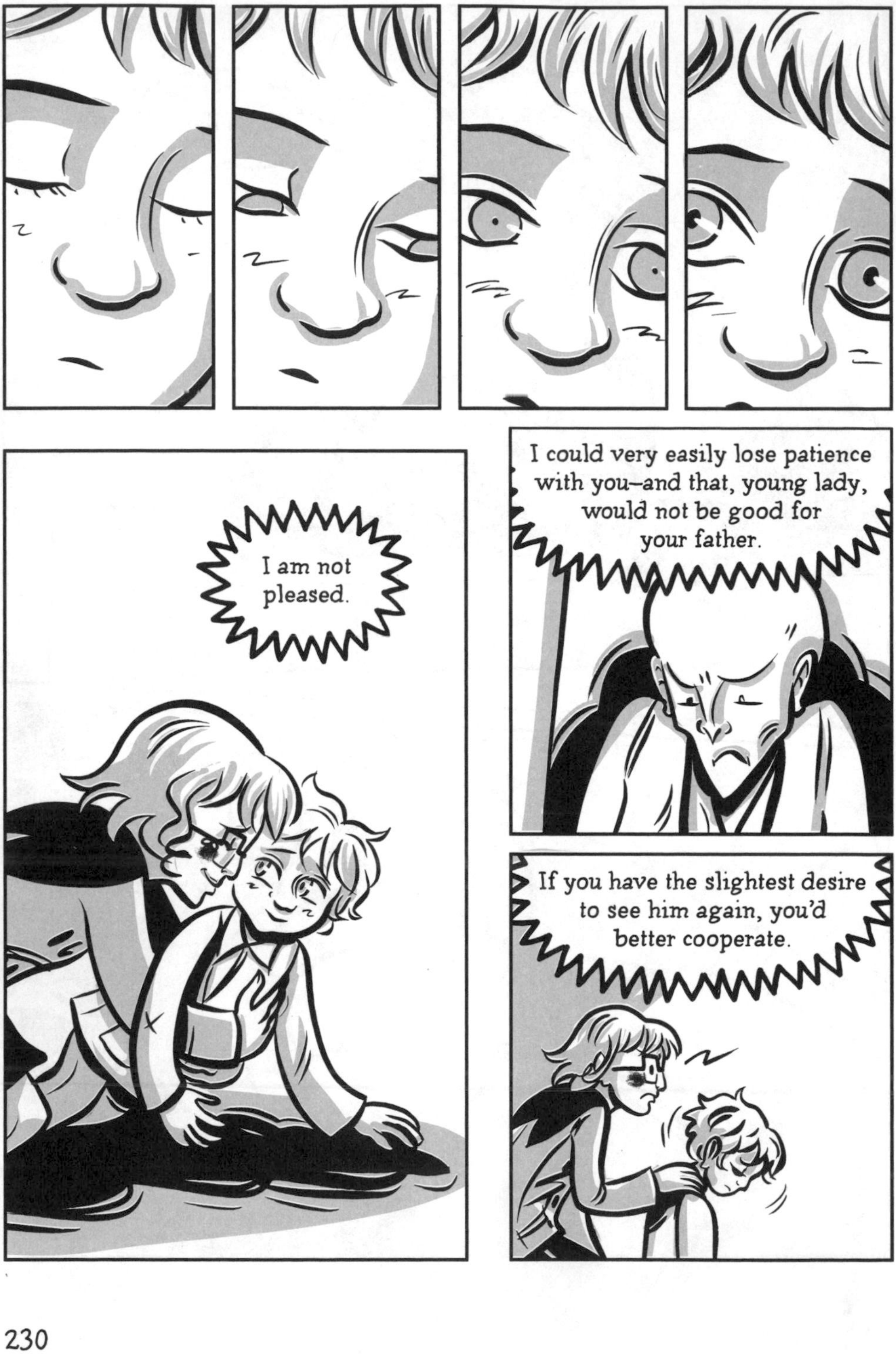
I am not pleased.
I could very easily lose patience with you—and that, young lady, would not be good for your father.
If you have the slightest desire to see him again, you'd better cooperate.

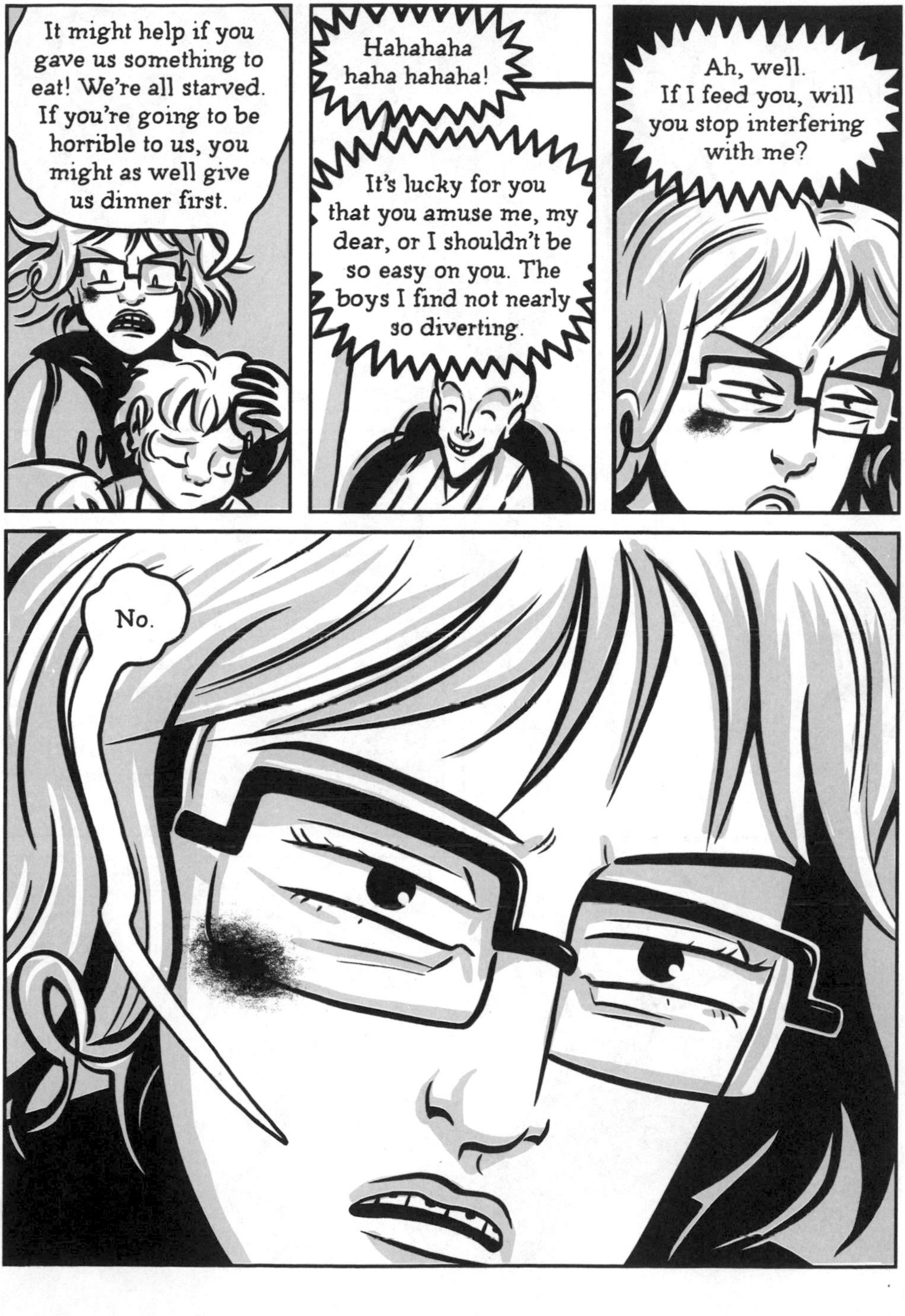
It might help if you gave us something to eat! We're all starved. If you're going to be horrible to us, you might as well give us dinner first.
Hahahaha haha hahaha!
It's lucky for you that you amuse me, my dear, or I shouldn't be so easy on you. The boys I find not nearly so diverting.
Ah, well. If I feed you, will you stop interfering with me?
No.

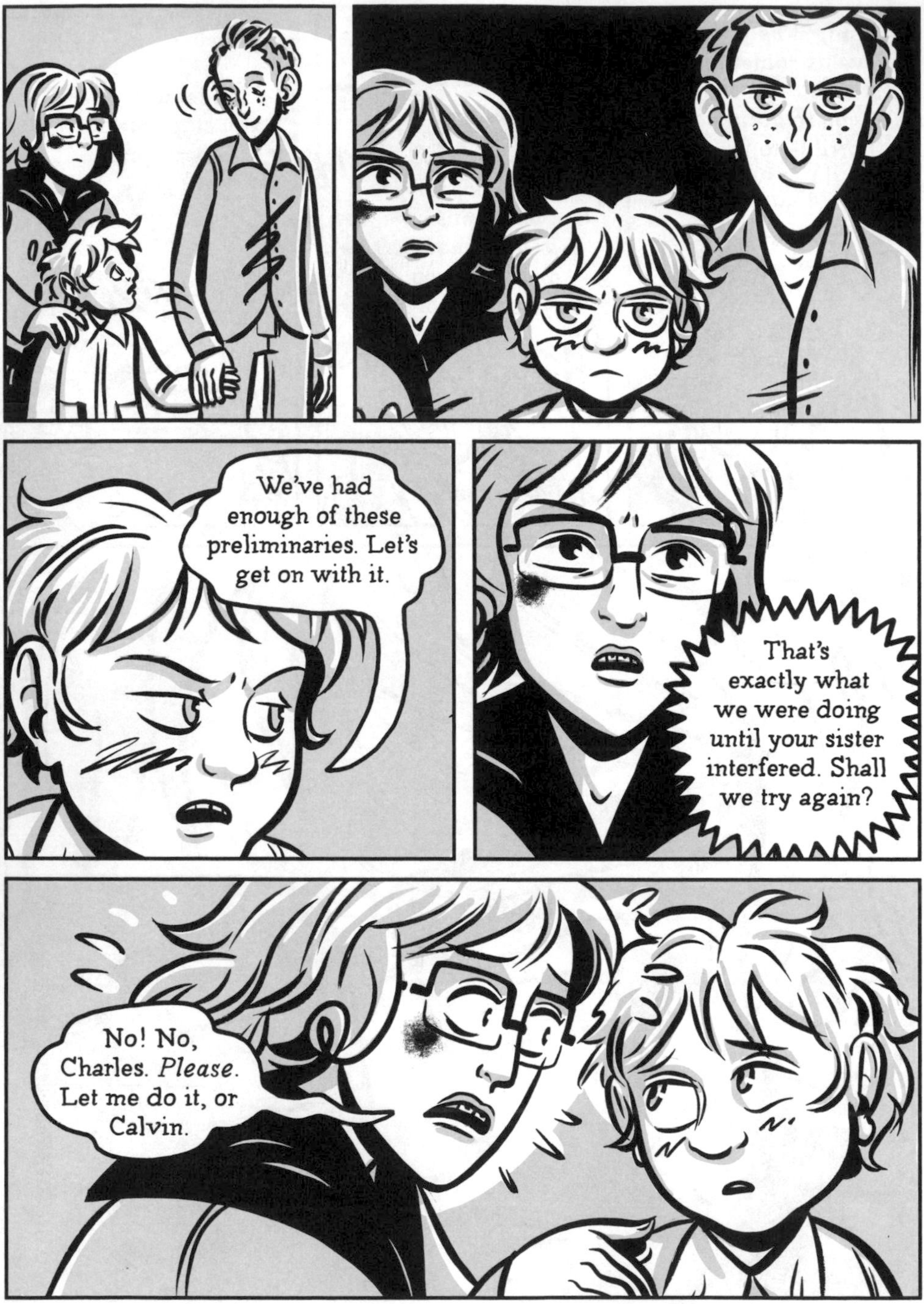
We've had enough of these preliminaries. Let's get on with it.
That's exactly what we were doing until your sister interfered. Shall we try again?
No! No, Charles. *Please*. Let me do it, or Calvin.

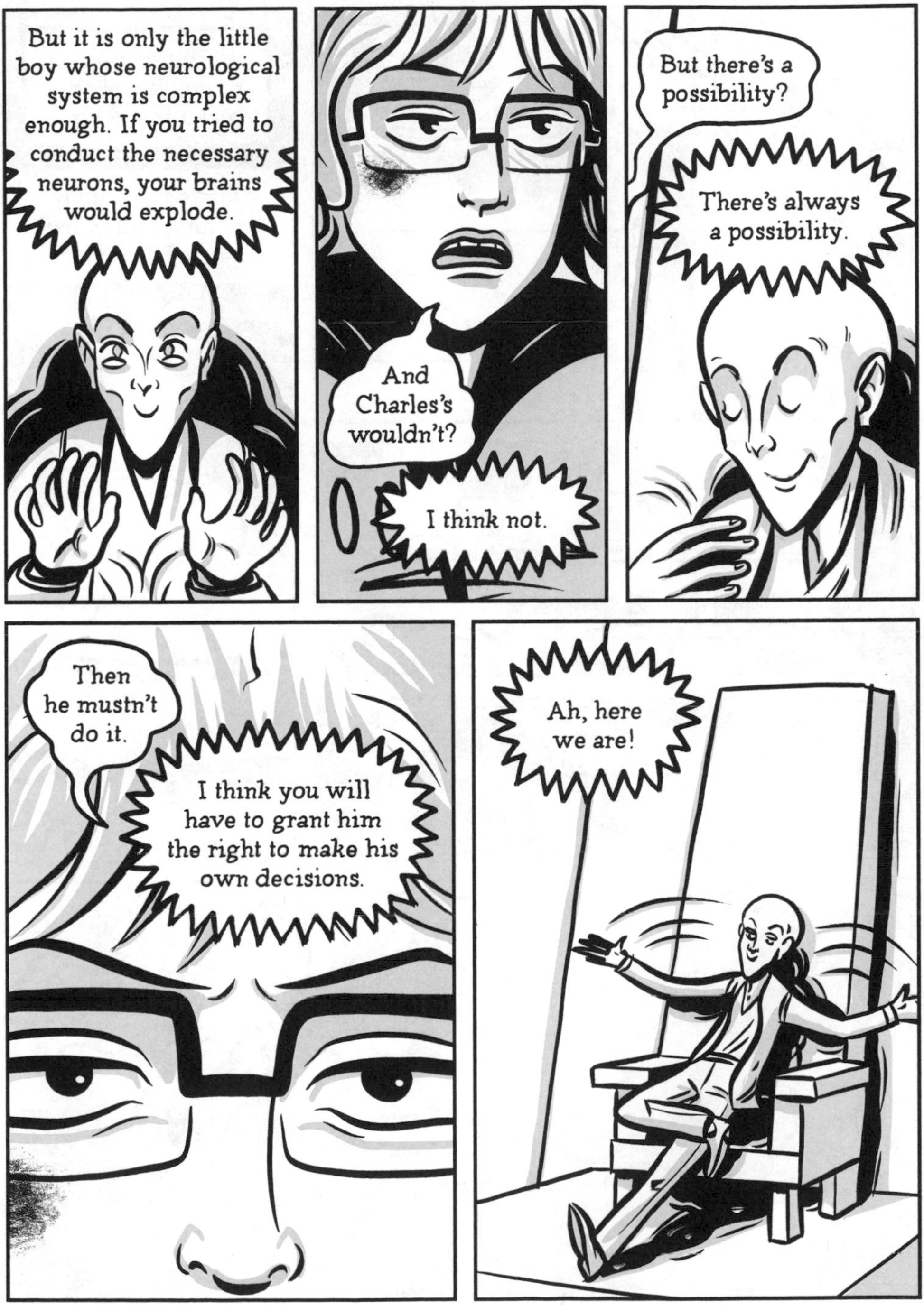
But it is only the little boy whose neurological system is complex enough. If you tried to conduct the necessary neurons, your brains would explode.
And Charles's wouldn't?
I think not.
But there's a possibility?
There's always a possibility.
Then he mustn't do it.
I think you will have to grant him the right to make his own decisions.
Ah, here we are!

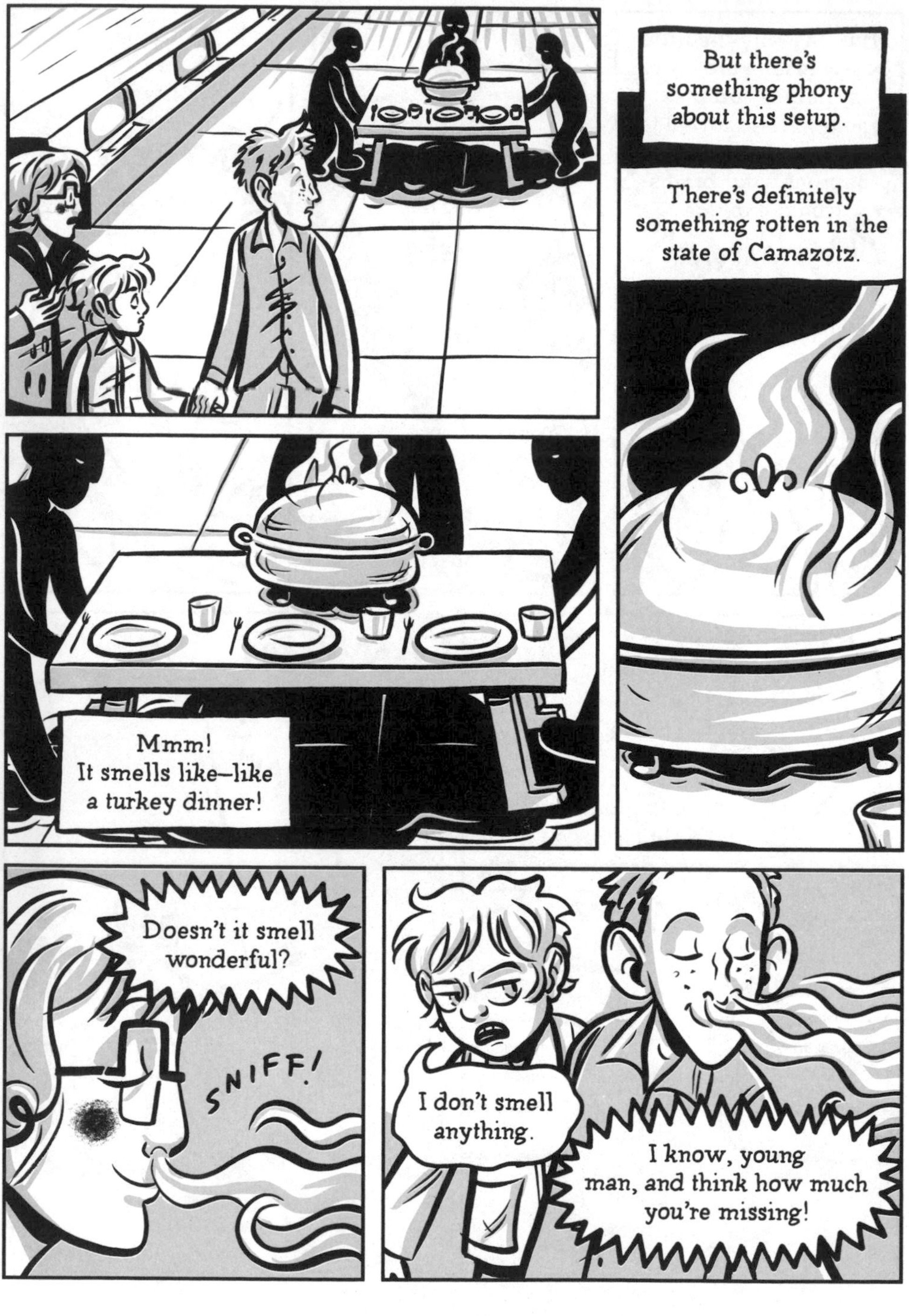

But there's something phony about this setup.
There's definitely something rotten in the state of Camazotz.
Mmm! It smells like—like a turkey dinner!
Doesn't it smell wonderful?
SNIFF!
I don't smell anything.
I know, young man, and think how much you're missing!

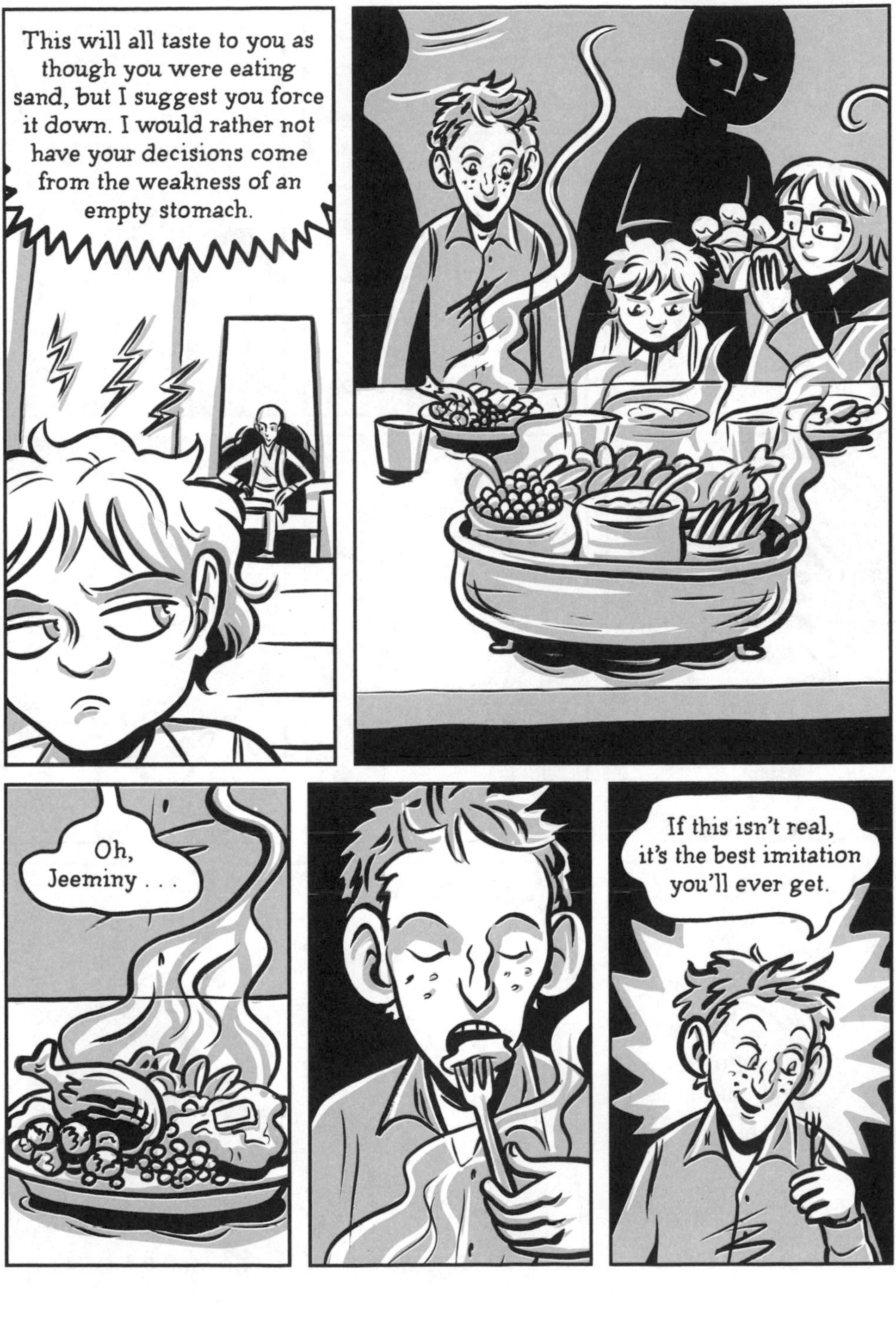
This will all taste to you as though you were eating sand, but I suggest you force it down. I would rather not have your decisions come from the weakness of an empty stomach.
Oh, Jeeminy . . .
If this isn't real, it's the best imitation you'll ever get.

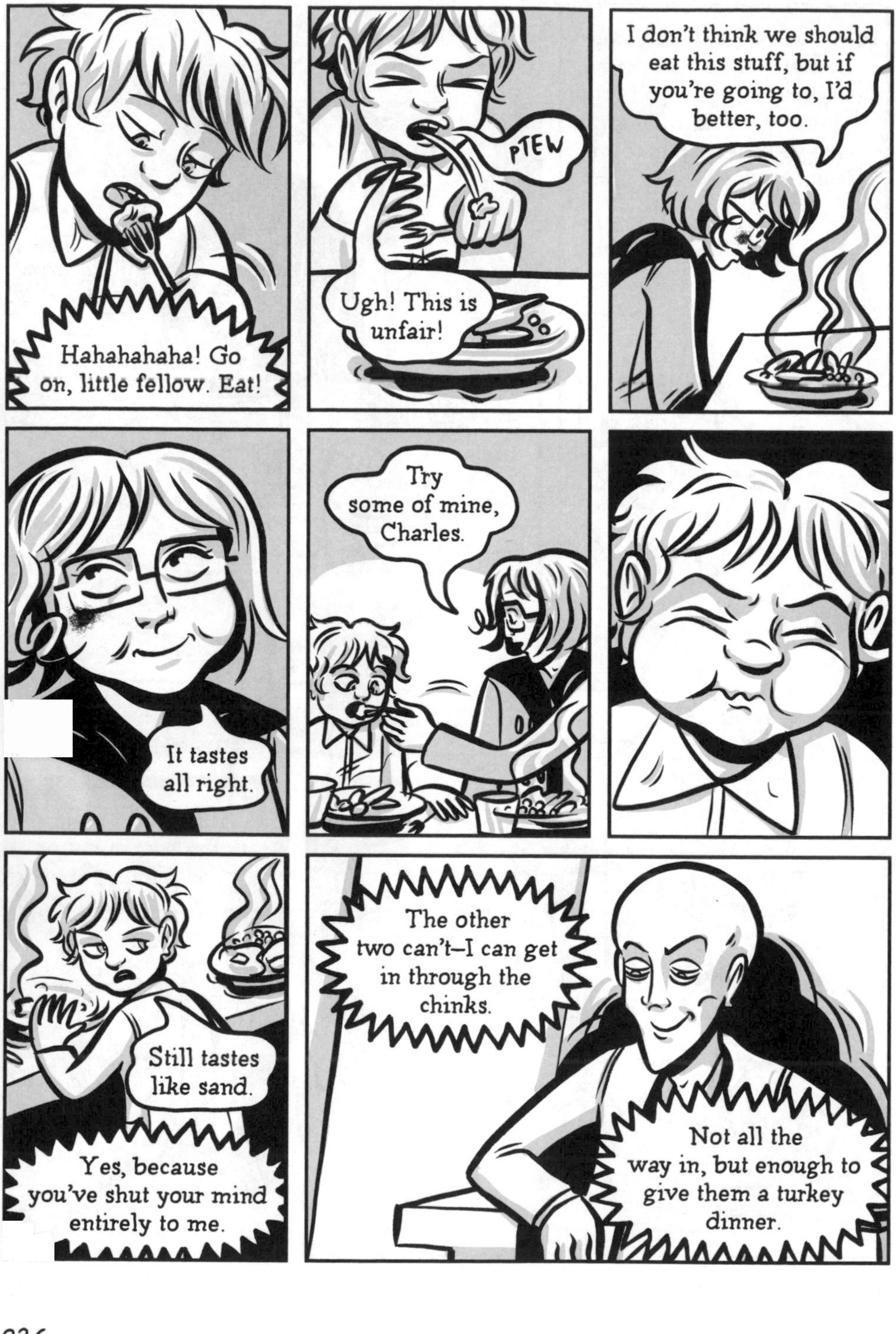

Hahahahaha! Go on, little fellow. Eat!
PTEW
Ugh! This is unfair!
I don't think we should eat this stuff, but if you're going to, I'd better, too.
It tastes all right.
Try some of mine, Charles.
Still tastes like sand.
Yes, because you've shut your mind entirely to me.
The other two can't—I can get in through the chinks.
Not all the way in, but enough to give them a turkey dinner.

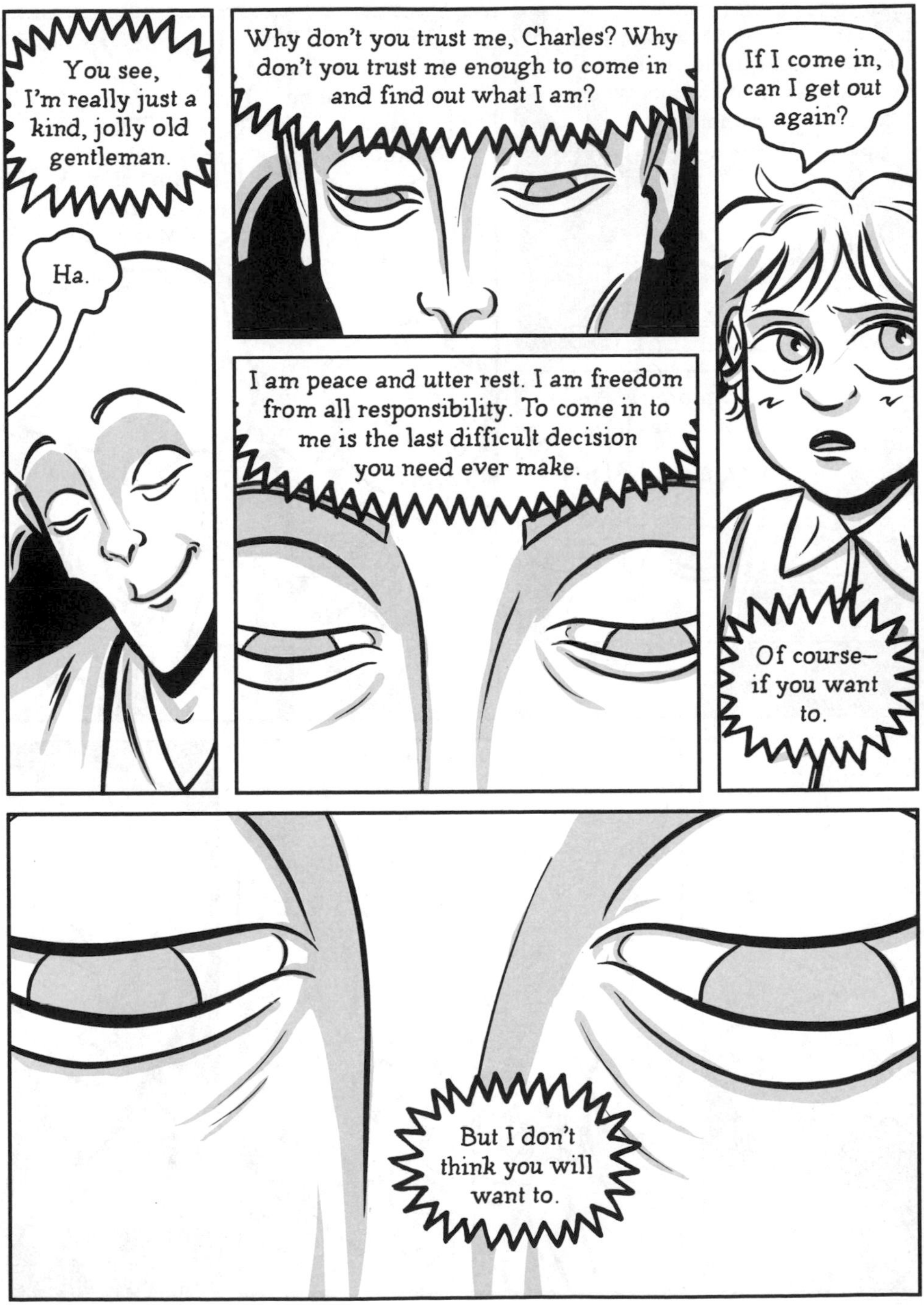

You see, I'm really just a kind, jolly old gentleman.
Ha.
Why don't you trust me, Charles? Why don't you trust me enough to come in and find out what I am?
I am peace and utter rest. I am freedom from all responsibility. To come in to me is the last difficult decision you need ever make.
If I come in, can I get out again?
Of course— if you want to.
But I don't think you will want to.

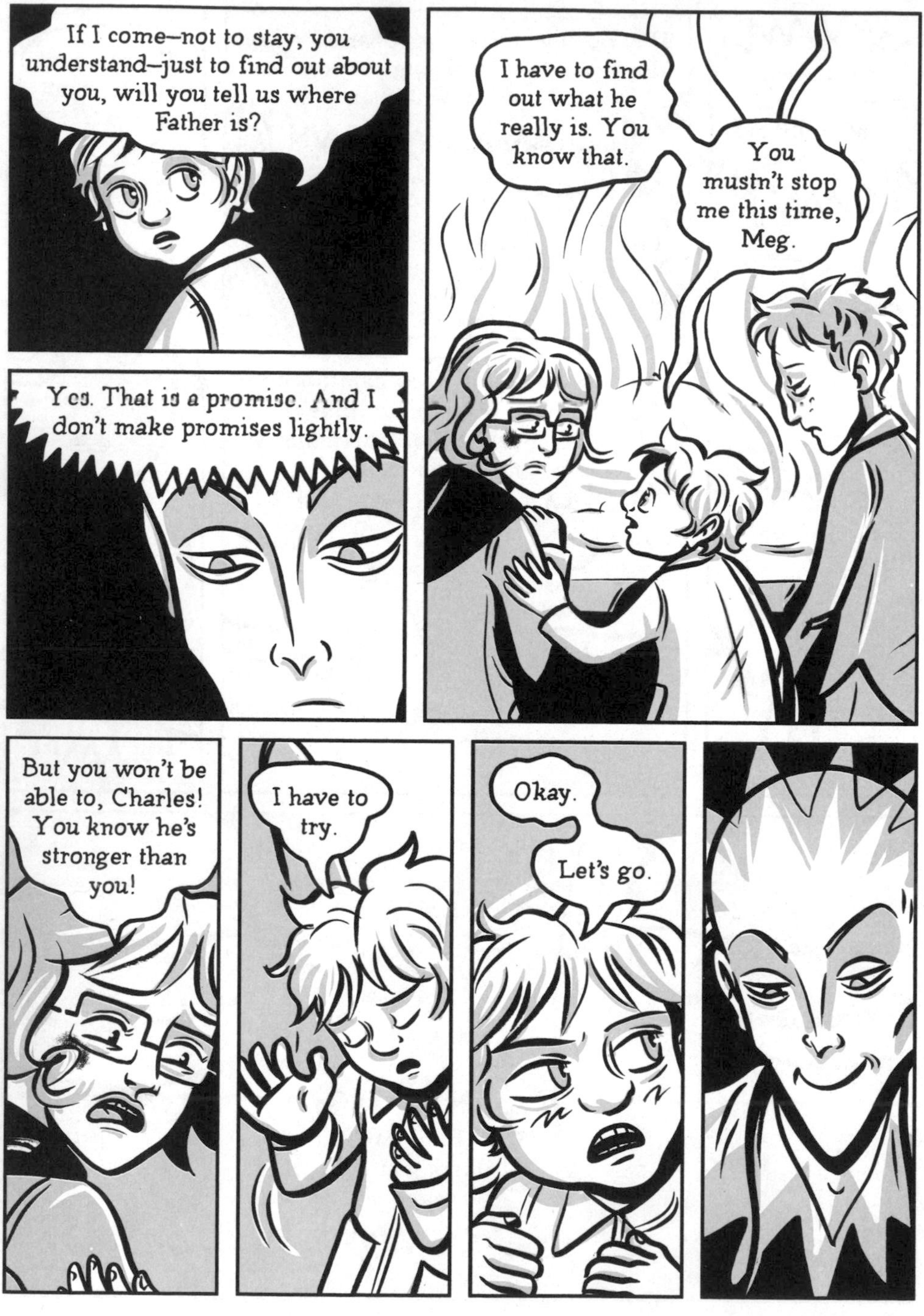
If I come—not to stay, you understand—just to find out about you, will you tell us where Father is?
Yes. That is a promise. And I don't make promises lightly.
I have to find out what he really is. You know that.
You mustn't stop me this time, Meg.
But you won't be able to, Charles! You know he's stronger than you!
I have to try.
Okay.
Let's go.

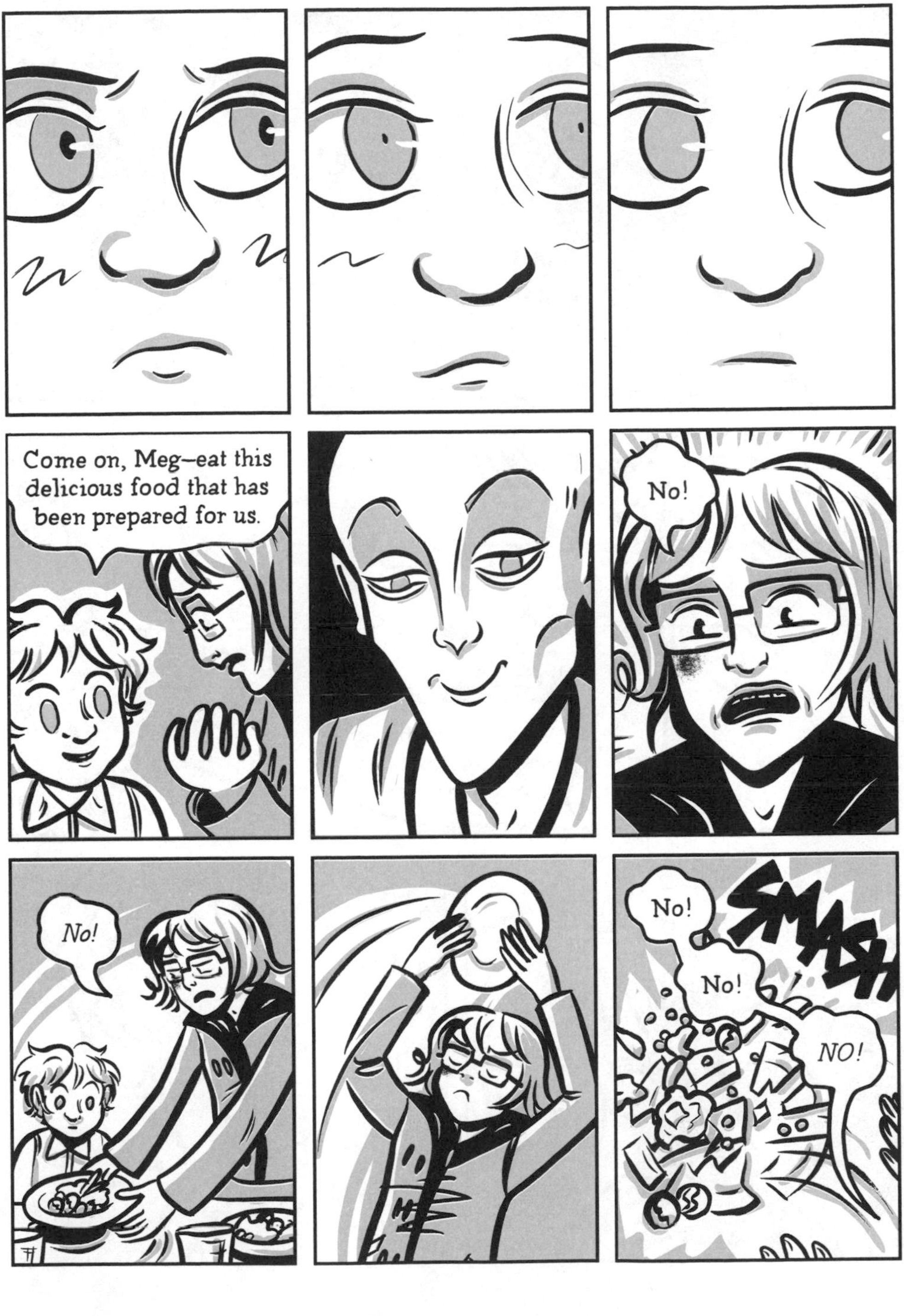
Come on, Meg—eat this delicious food that has been prepared for us.
No!
No!
No!
SMASH
No!
NO!

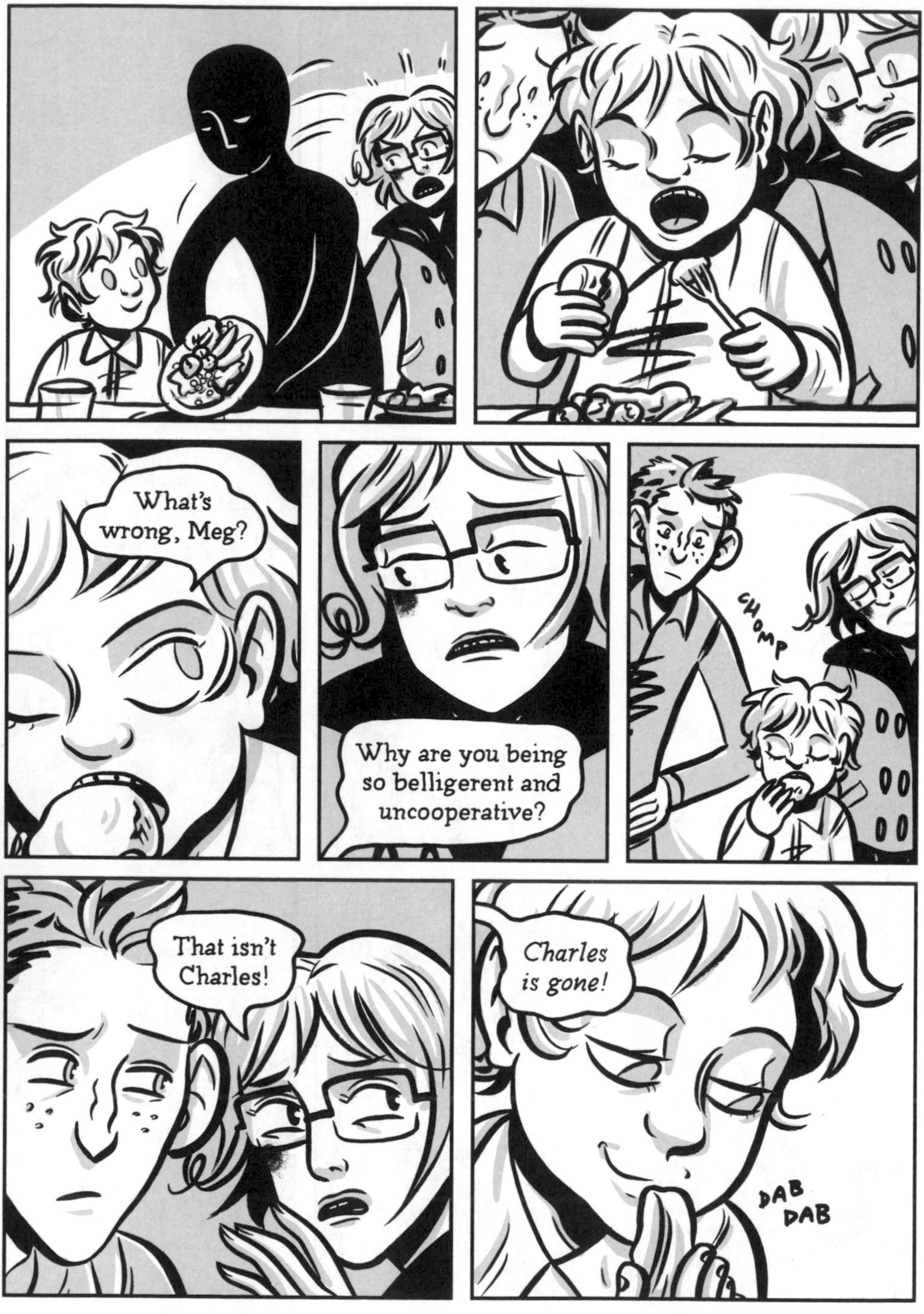
What's wrong, Meg?
Why are you being so belligerent and uncooperative?
CHOMP
That isn't Charles!
Charles is gone!
DAB DAB

8
The Transparent Column

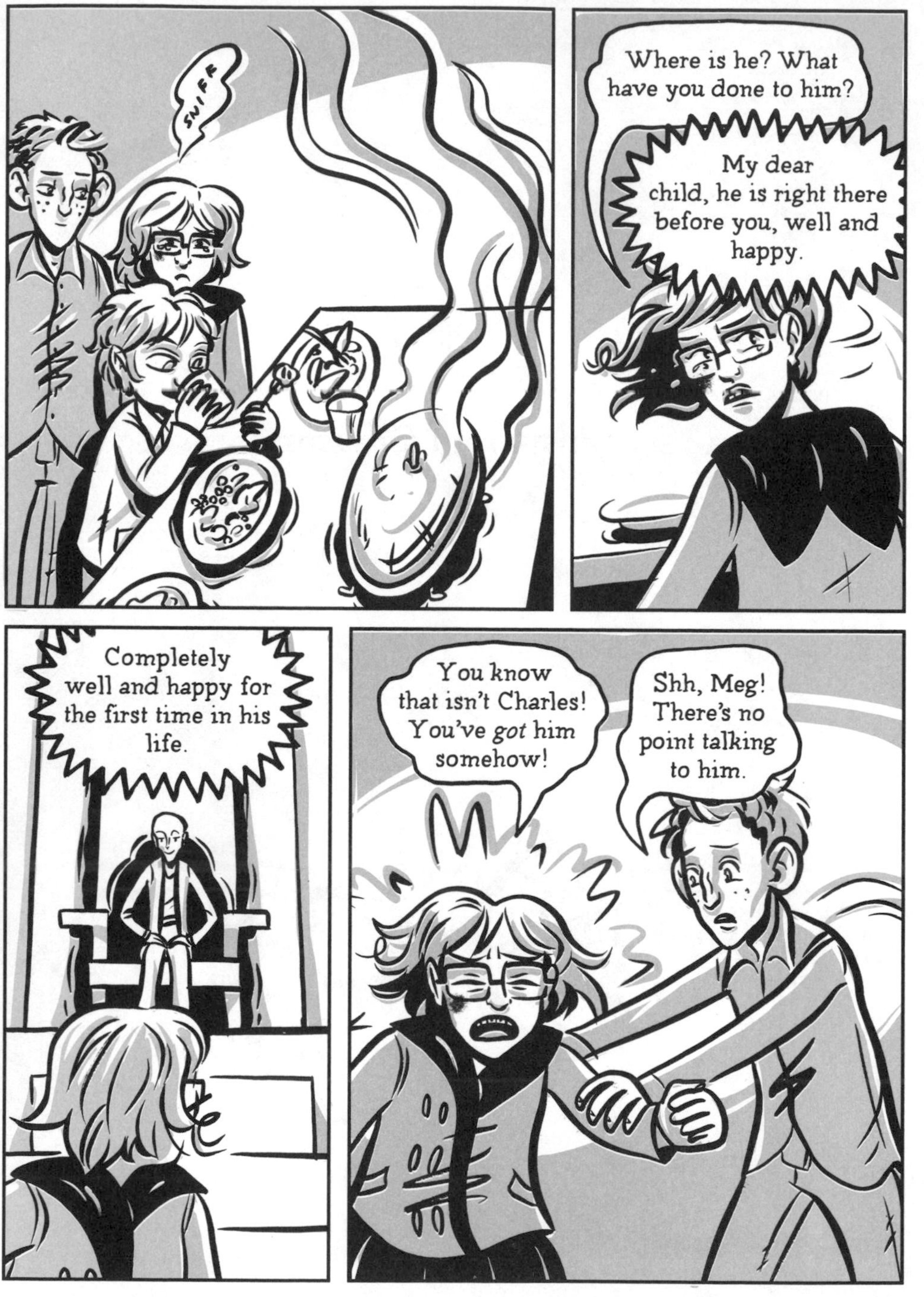
SNIFF
Where is he? What have you done to him?
My dear child, he is right there before you, well and happy.
Completely well and happy for the first time in his life.
You know that isn't Charles! You've *got* him somehow!
Shh, Meg! There's no point talking to him.

What we have to do is hold Charles Wallace tight. He's in there, somewhere, and we can't let them take him away.

Help me hold him, Meg. Don't lose control of yourself—not now.

You're *hurting* me, Meg! Let go!

No.

But listen, Meg—we've all been wrong.

He isn't an enemy at all. He's our friend.

Nuts.

You don't understand, Calvin.

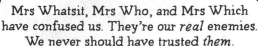

Mrs Whatsit, Mrs Who, and Mrs Which have confused us. They're our *real* enemies. We never should have trusted *them.*

Meg, let go. I'll explain everything, but you must let go.

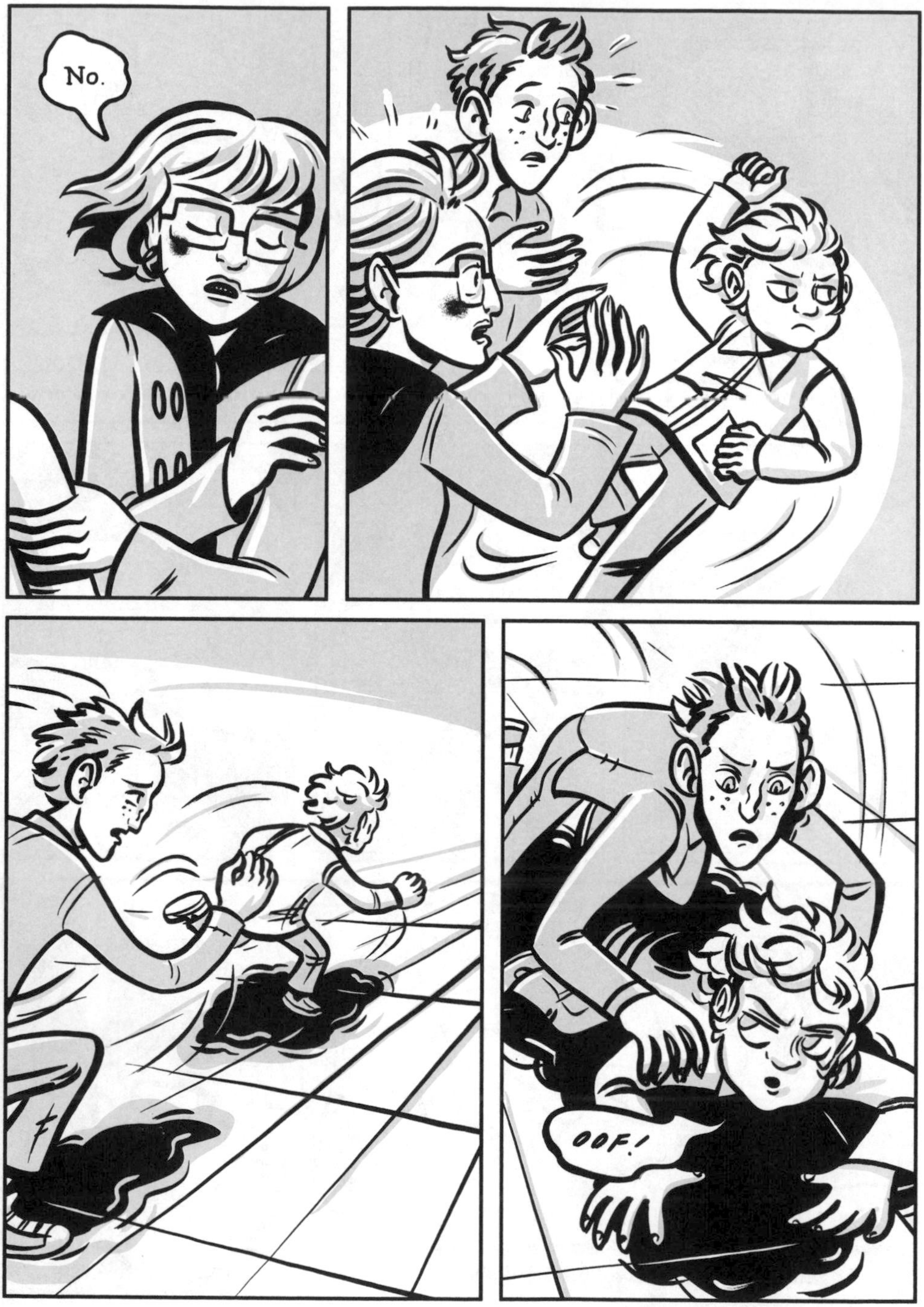
No.
OOF!

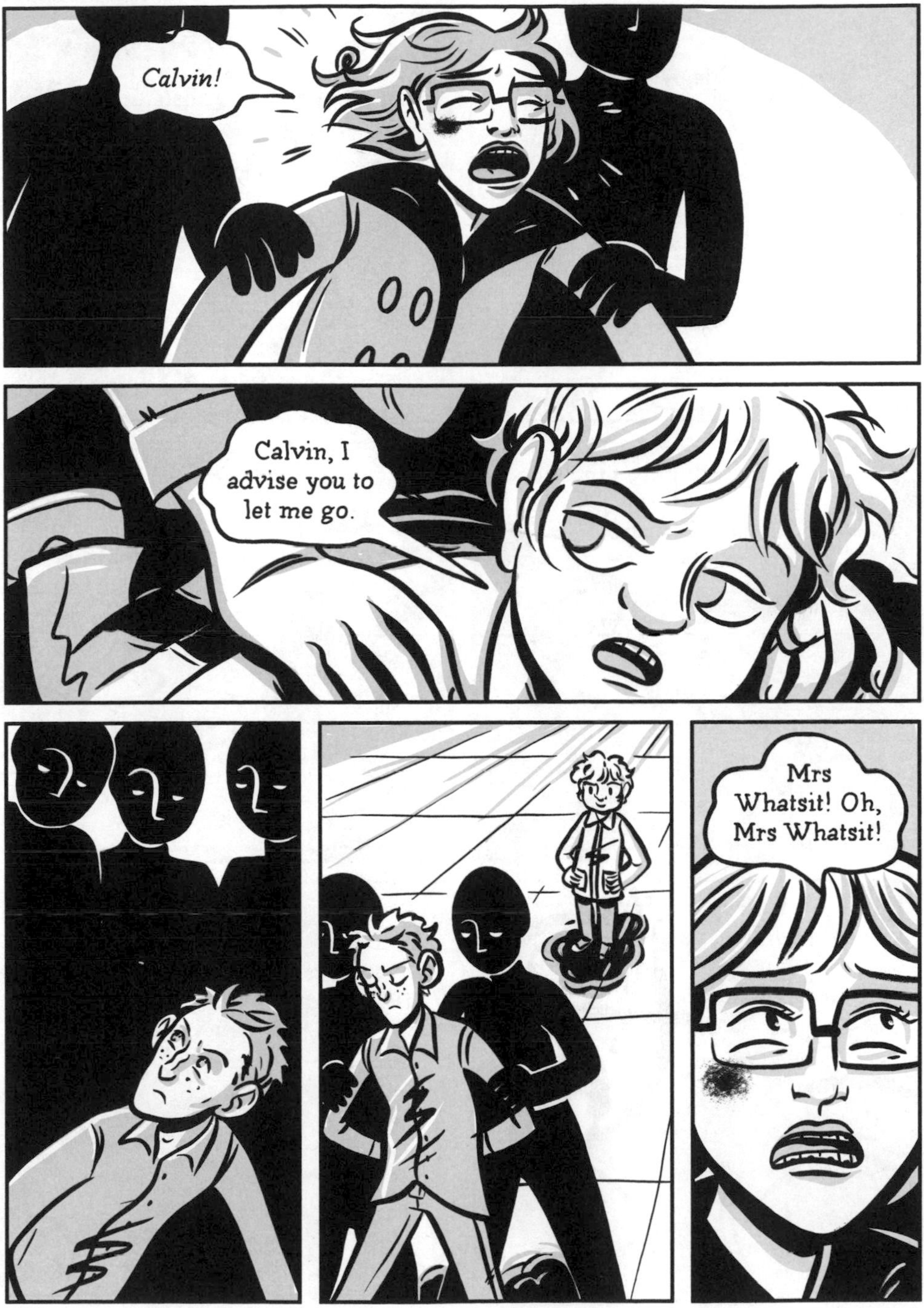
Calvin!
Calvin, I advise you to let me go.
Mrs Whatsit! Oh, Mrs Whatsit!

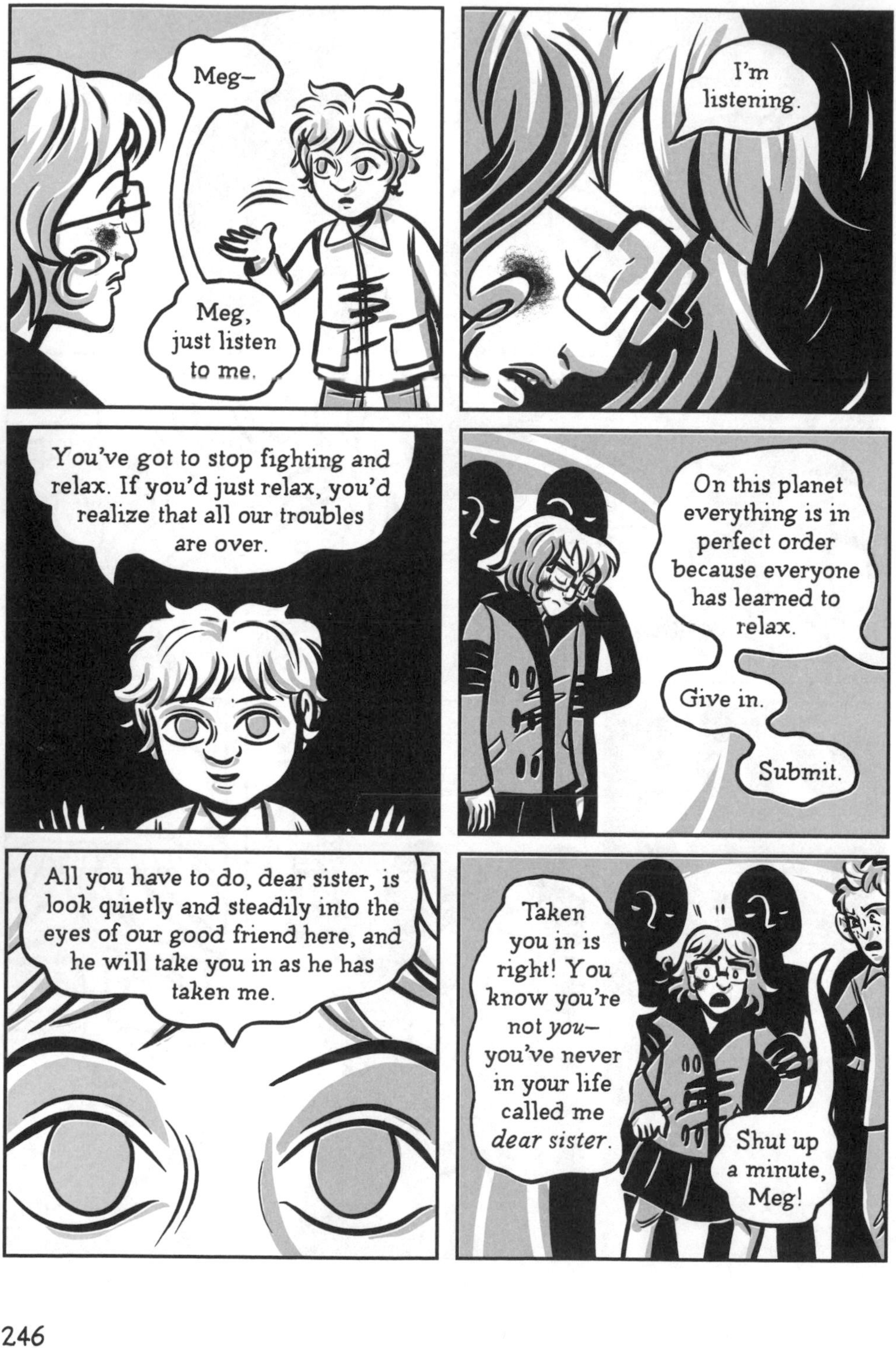
Meg–
Meg, just listen to me.
I'm listening.
You've got to stop fighting and relax. If you'd just relax, you'd realize that all our troubles are over.
On this planet everything is in perfect order because everyone has learned to relax.
Give in.
Submit.
All you have to do, dear sister, is look quietly and steadily into the eyes of our good friend here, and he will take you in as he has taken me.
Taken you in is right! You know you're not *you*– you've never in your life called me *dear sister*.
Shut up a minute, Meg!

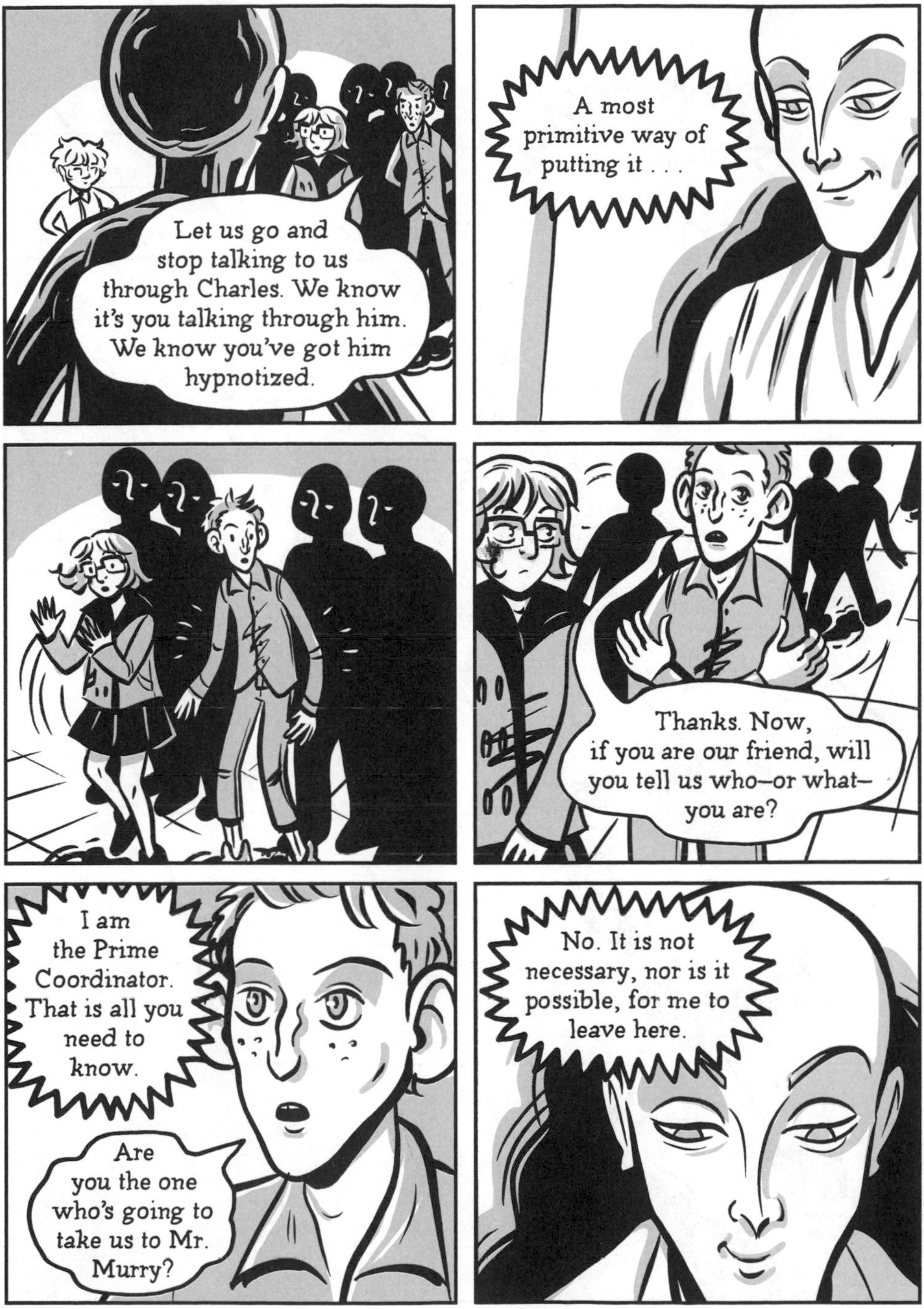
Let us go and stop talking to us through Charles. We know it's you talking through him. We know you've got him hypnotized.
A most primitive way of putting it . . .
Thanks. Now, if you are our friend, will you tell us who—or what—you are?
I am the Prime Coordinator. That is all you need to know.
Are you the one who's going to take us to Mr. Murry?
No. It is not necessary, nor is it possible, for me to leave here.

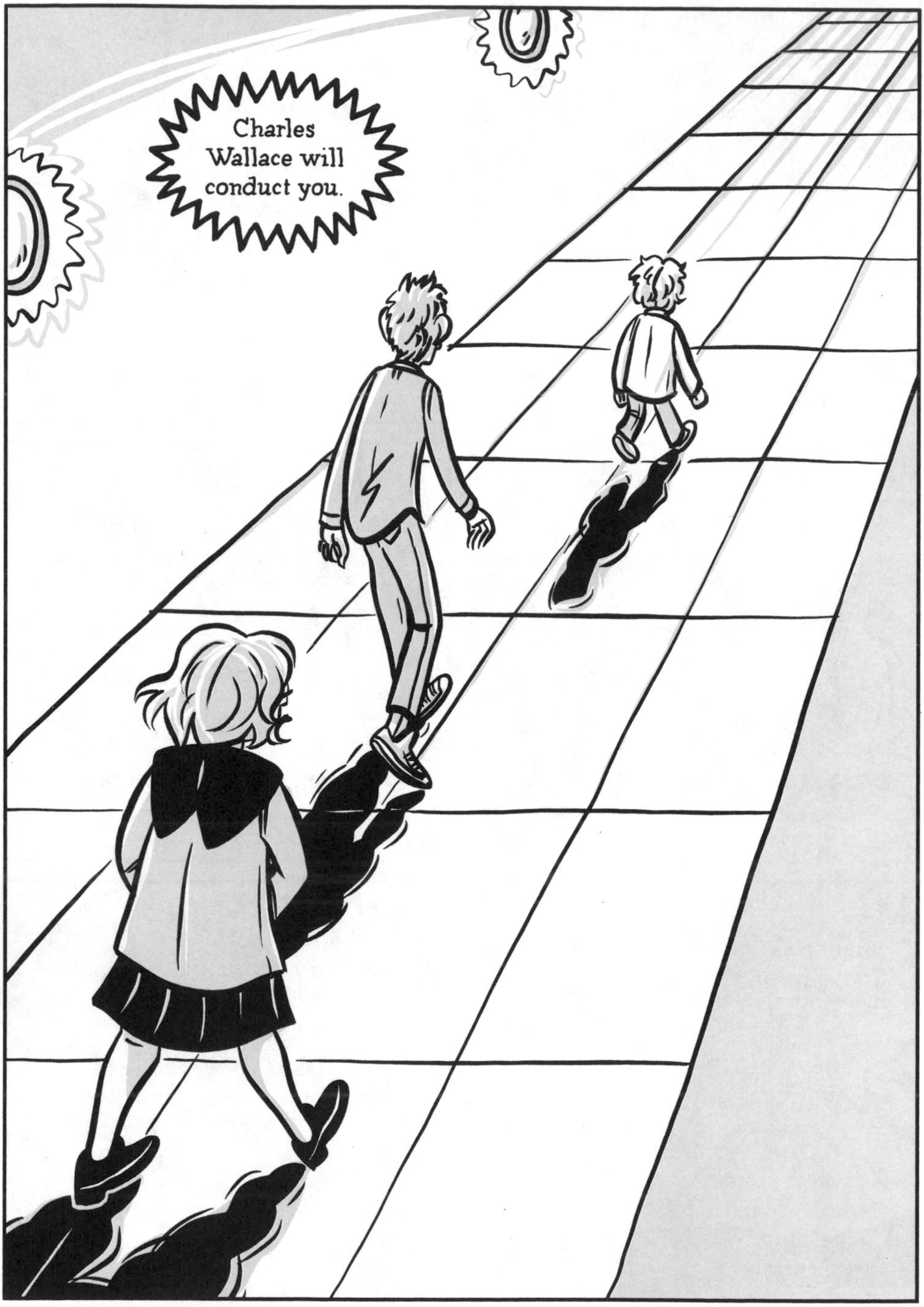
Charles Wallace will conduct you.

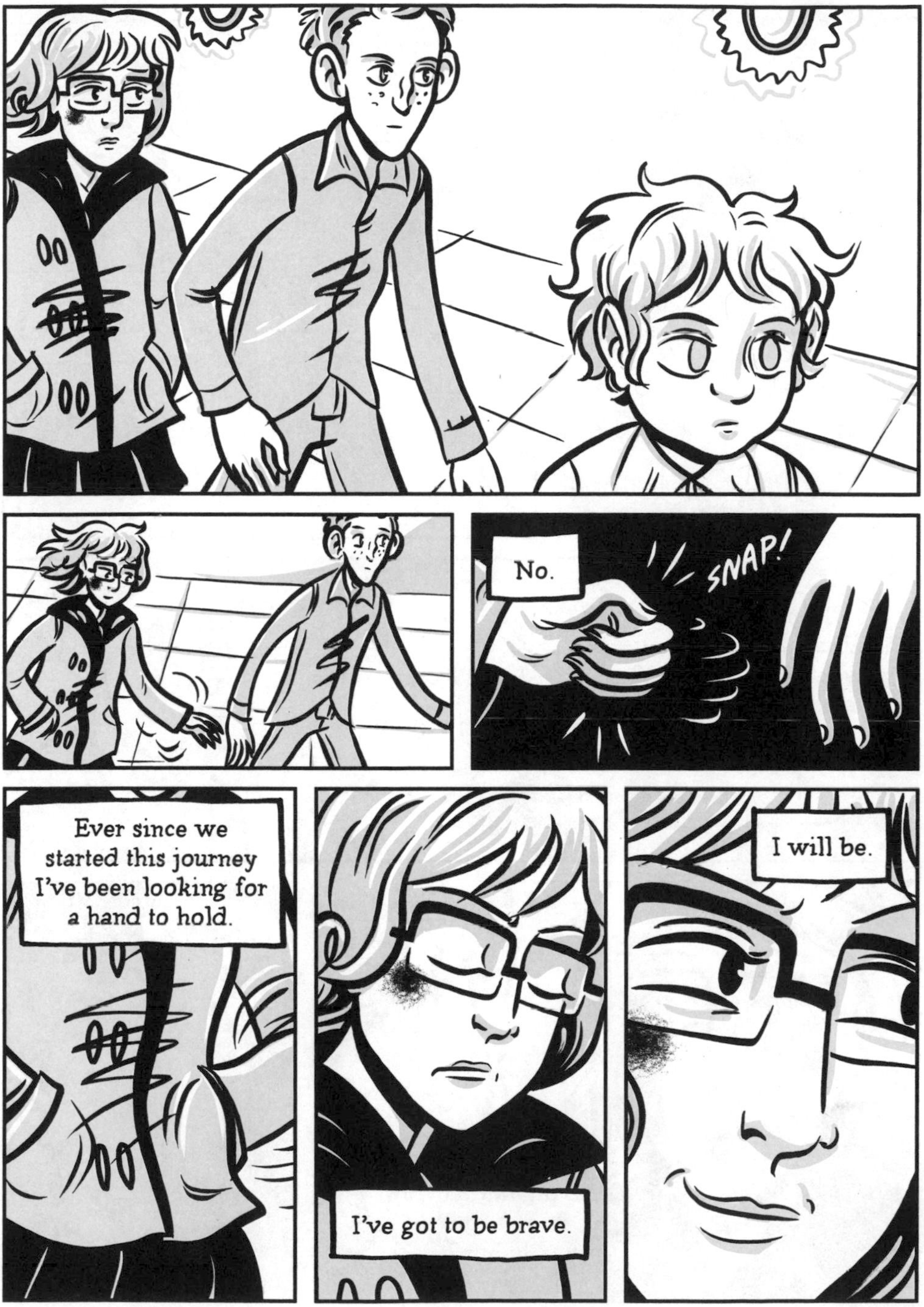
No.
SNAP!
Ever since we started this journey I've been looking for a hand to hold.
I've got to be brave.
I will be.

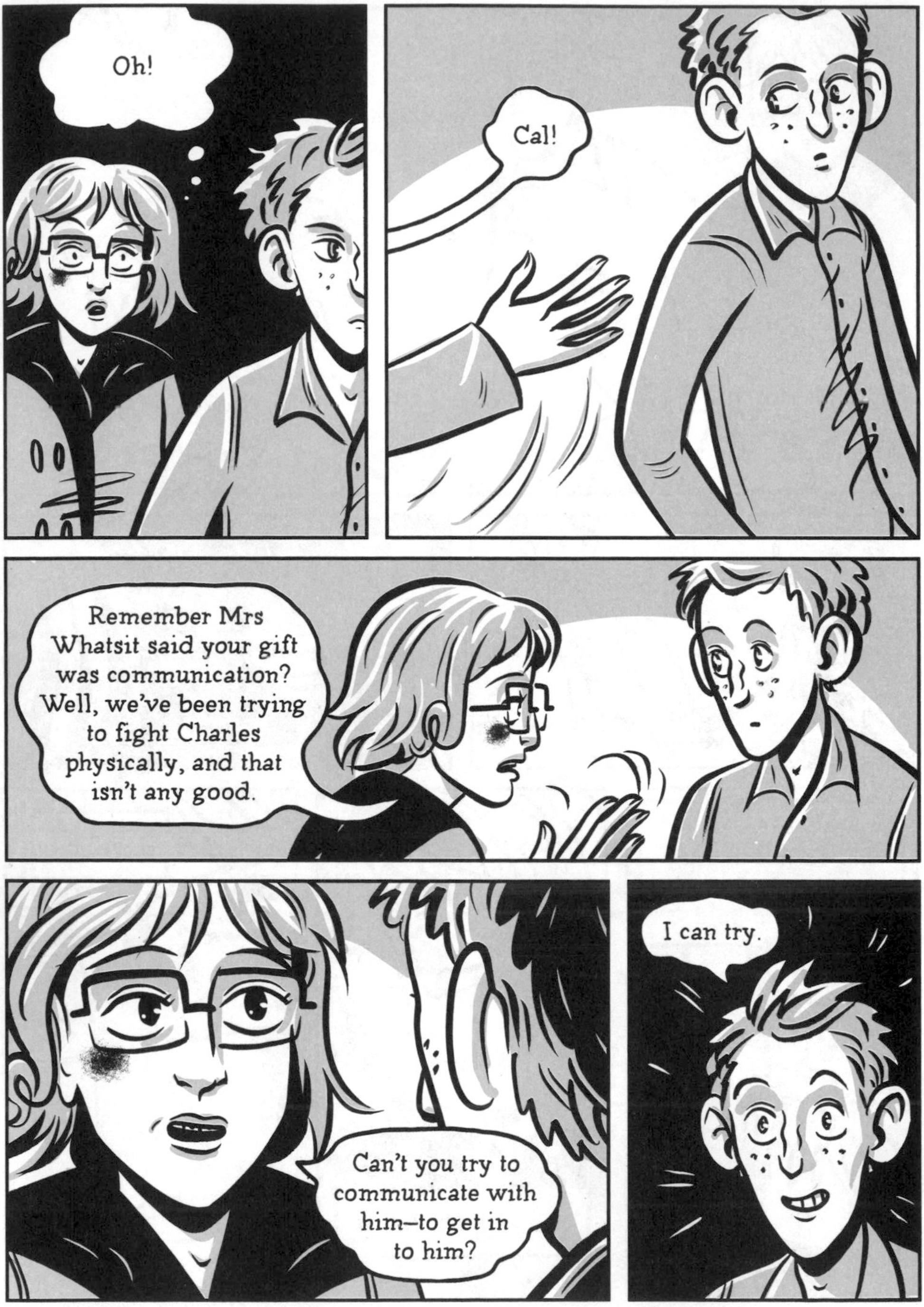
Oh!
Cal!
Remember Mrs Whatsit said your gift was communication? Well, we've been trying to fight Charles physically, and that isn't any good.
Can't you try to communicate with him—to get in to him?
I can try.

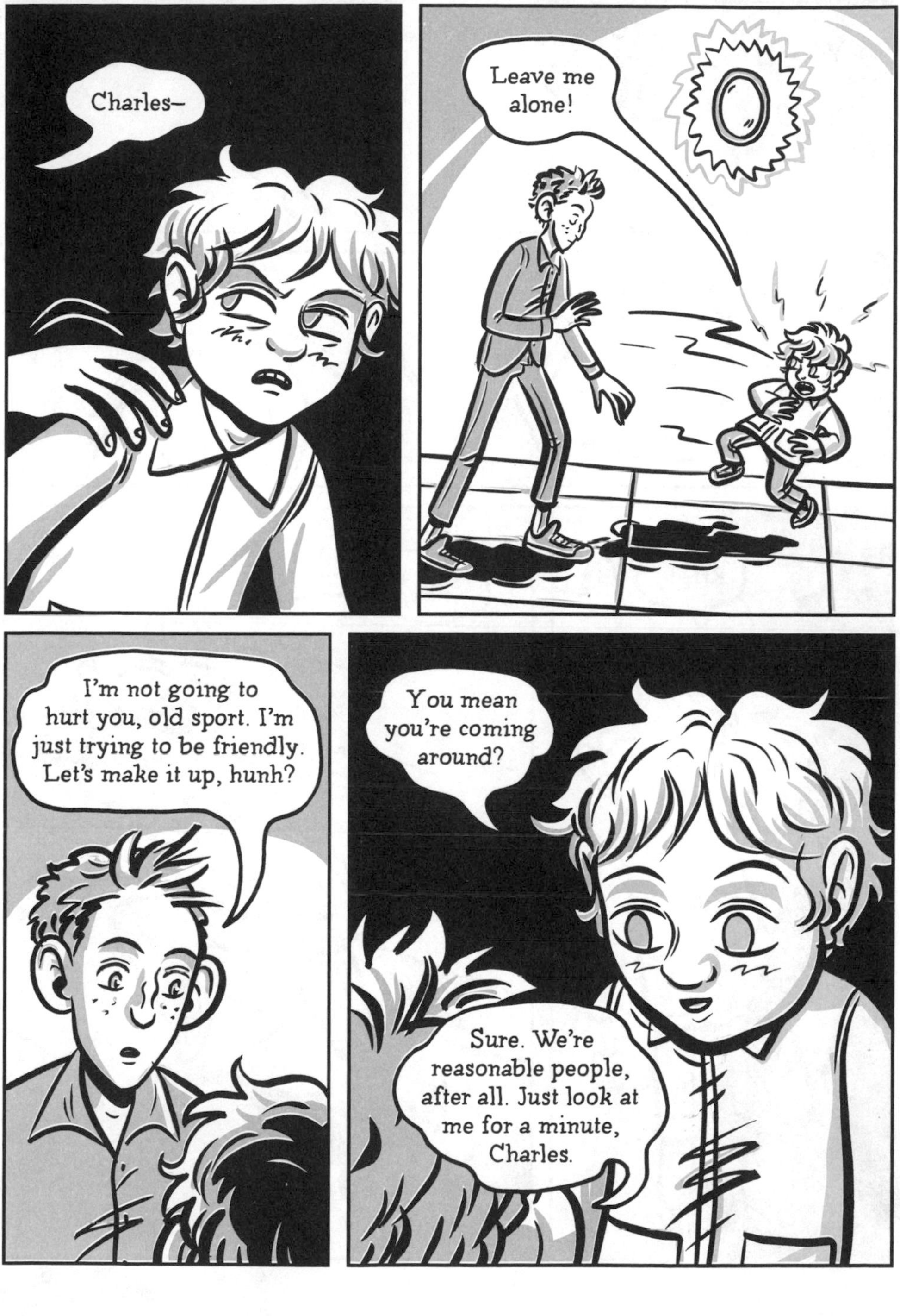

Charles–
Leave me alone!
I'm not going to hurt you, old sport. I'm just trying to be friendly. Let's make it up, hunh?
You mean you're coming around?
Sure. We're reasonable people, after all. Just look at me for a minute, Charles.

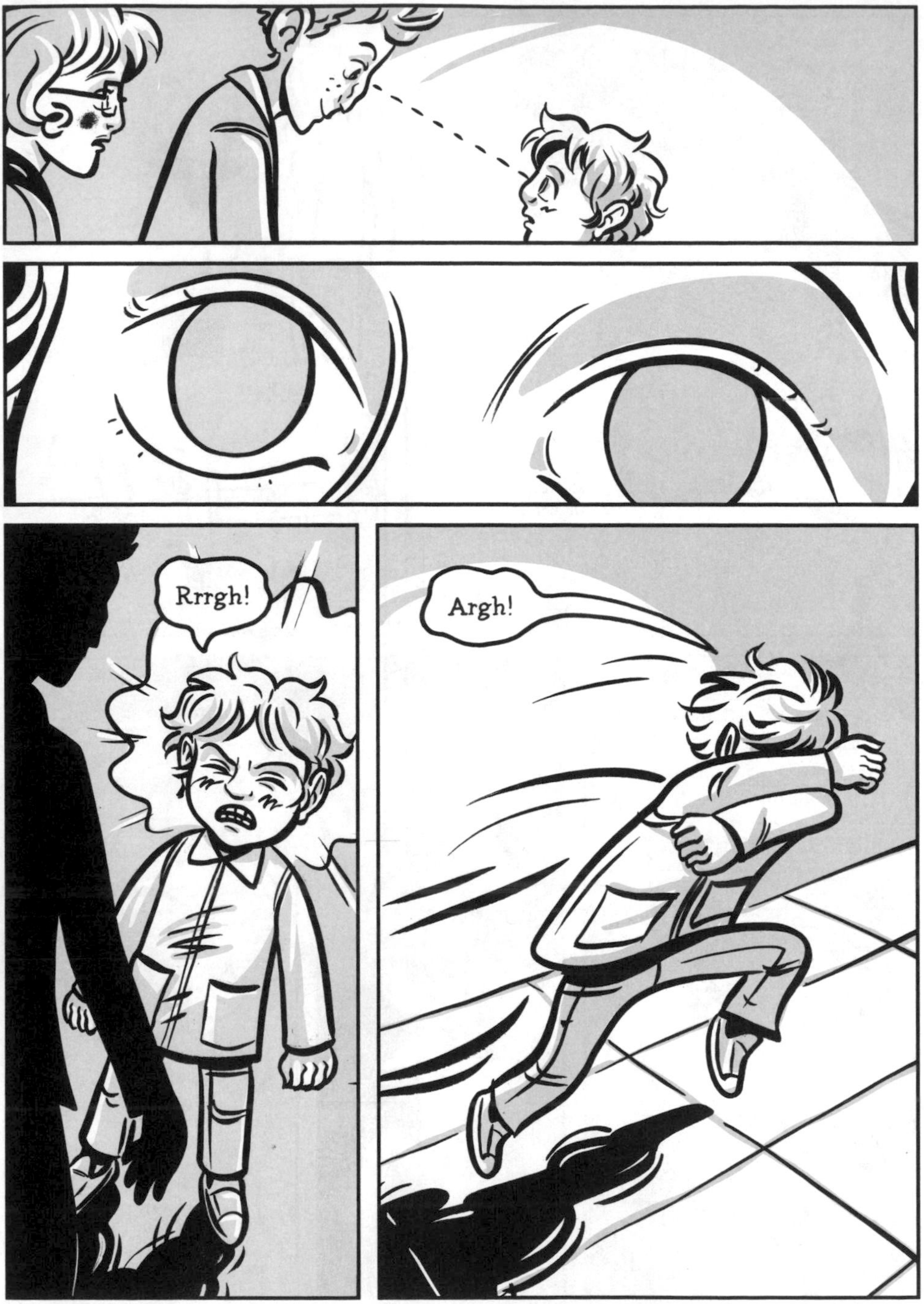
Rrrgh!
Argh!

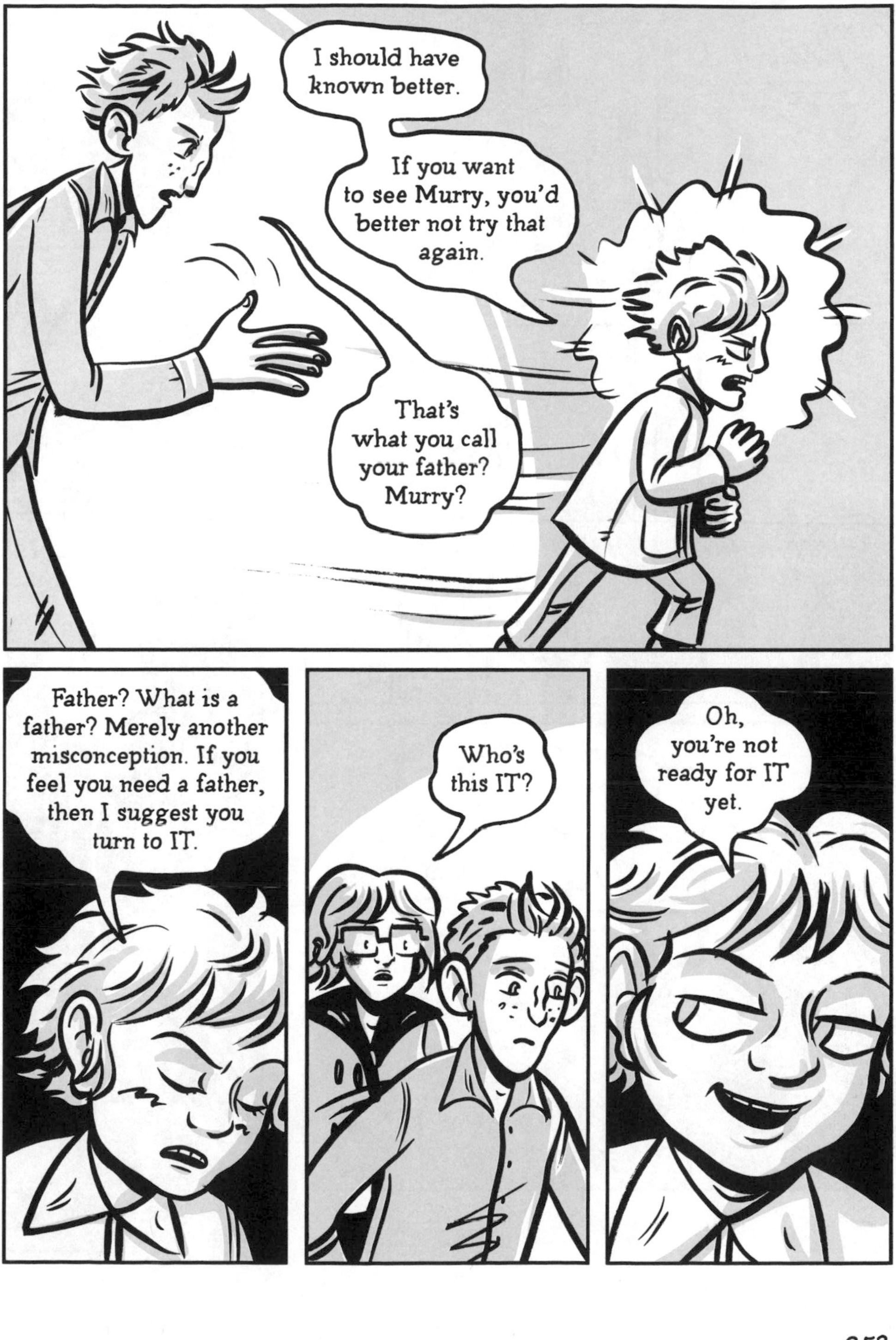
I should have known better.
If you want to see Murry, you'd better not try that again.
That's what you call your father? Murry?
Father? What is a father? Merely another misconception. If you feel you need a father, then I suggest you turn to IT.
Who's this IT?
Oh, you're not ready for IT yet.

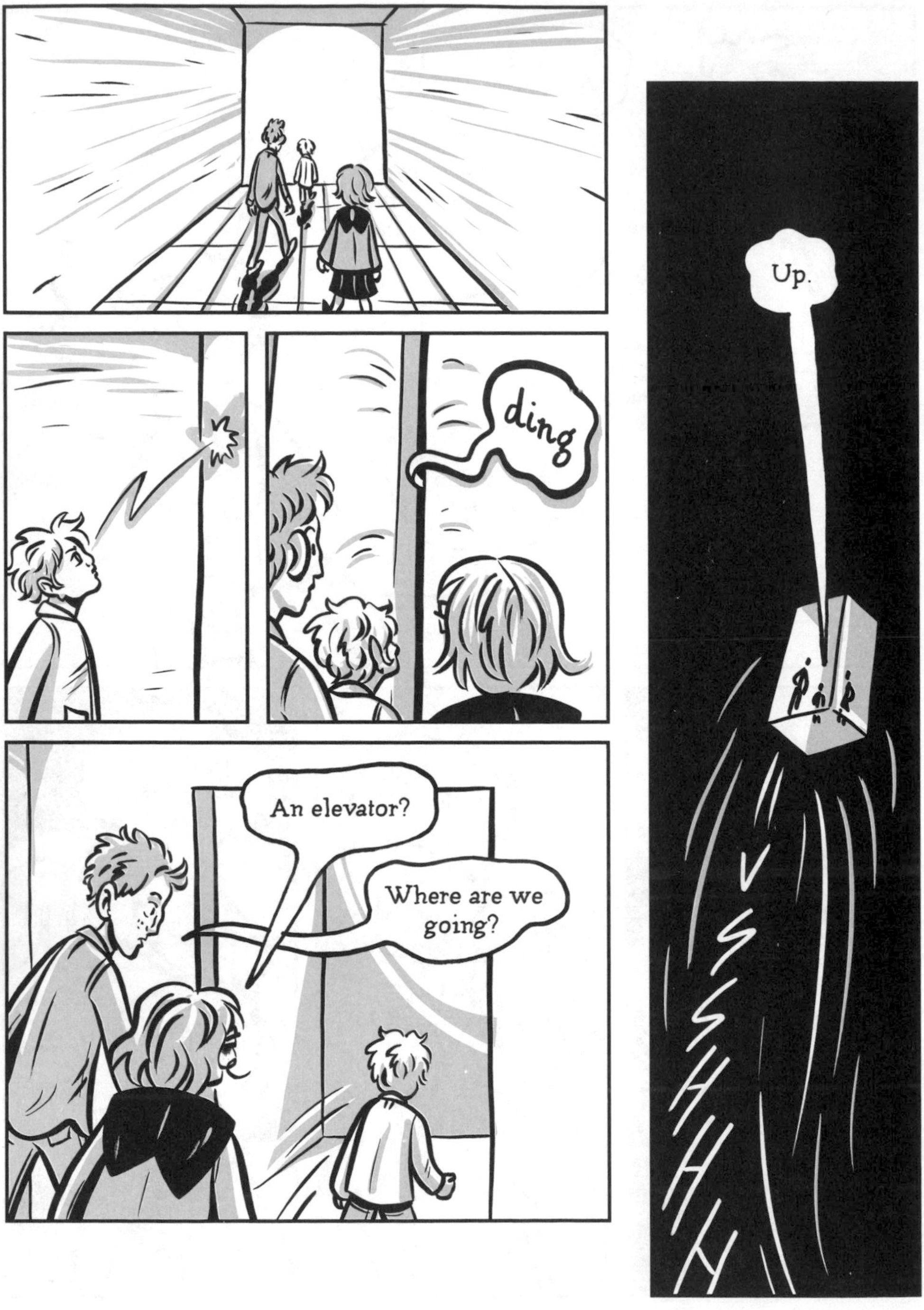
ding
An elevator?
Where are we going?
Up.
VSSHHHH

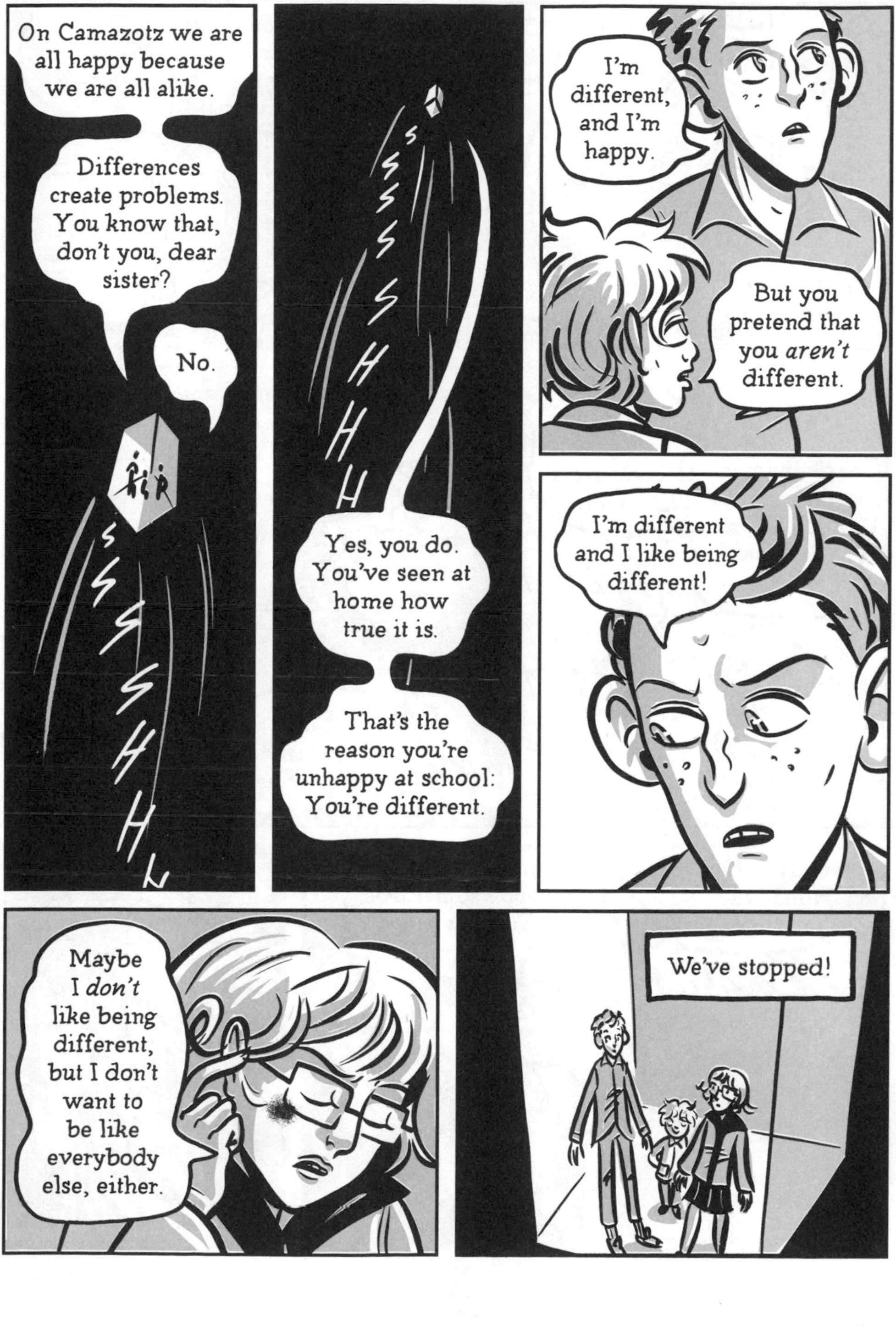
On Camazotz we are all happy because we are all alike.
Differences create problems. You know that, don't you, dear sister?
No.
Yes, you do. You've seen at home how true it is.
That's the reason you're unhappy at school: You're different.
I'm different, and I'm happy.
But you pretend that you *aren't* different.
I'm different and I like being different!
Maybe I *don't* like being different, but I don't want to be like everybody else, either.
We've stopped!

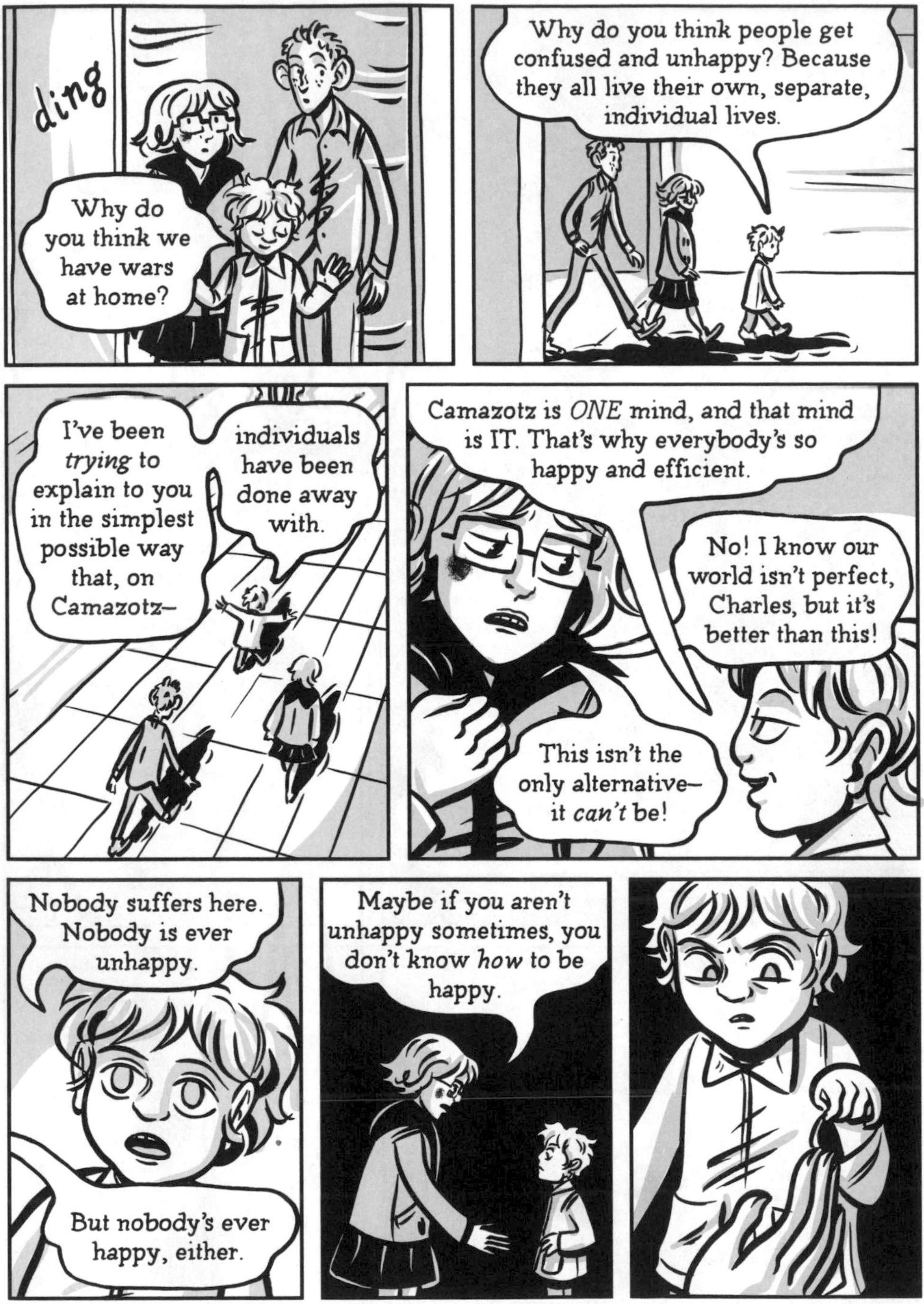
ding
Why do you think we have wars at home?
Why do you think people get confused and unhappy? Because they all live their own, separate, individual lives.
I've been *trying* to explain to you in the simplest possible way that, on Camazotz–
individuals have been done away with.
Camazotz is *ONE* mind, and that mind is IT. That's why everybody's so happy and efficient.
No! I know our world isn't perfect, Charles, but it's better than this!
This isn't the only alternative– it *can't* be!
Nobody suffers here. Nobody is ever unhappy.
But nobody's ever happy, either.
Maybe if you aren't unhappy sometimes, you don't know *how* to be happy.

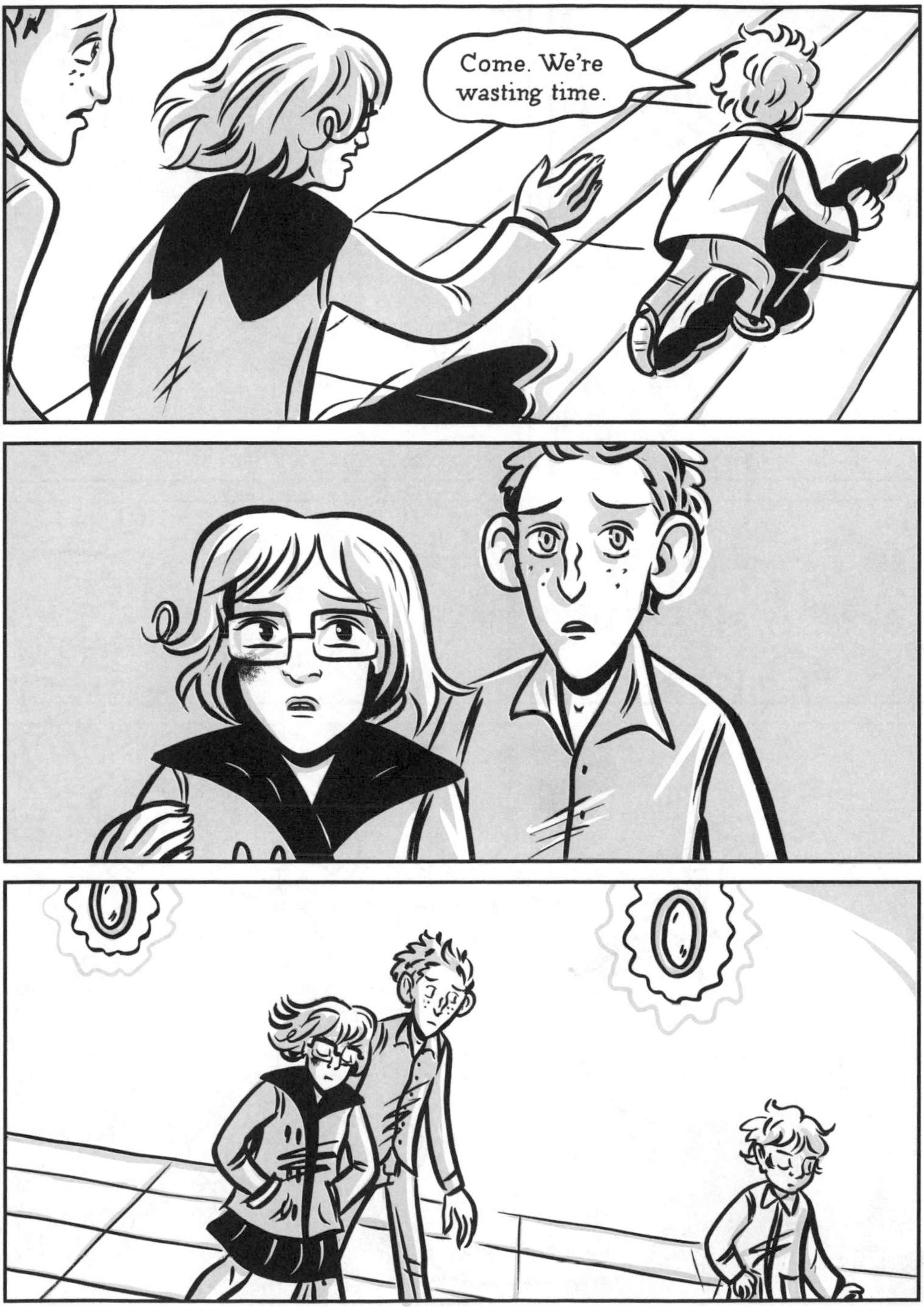
Come. We're wasting time.

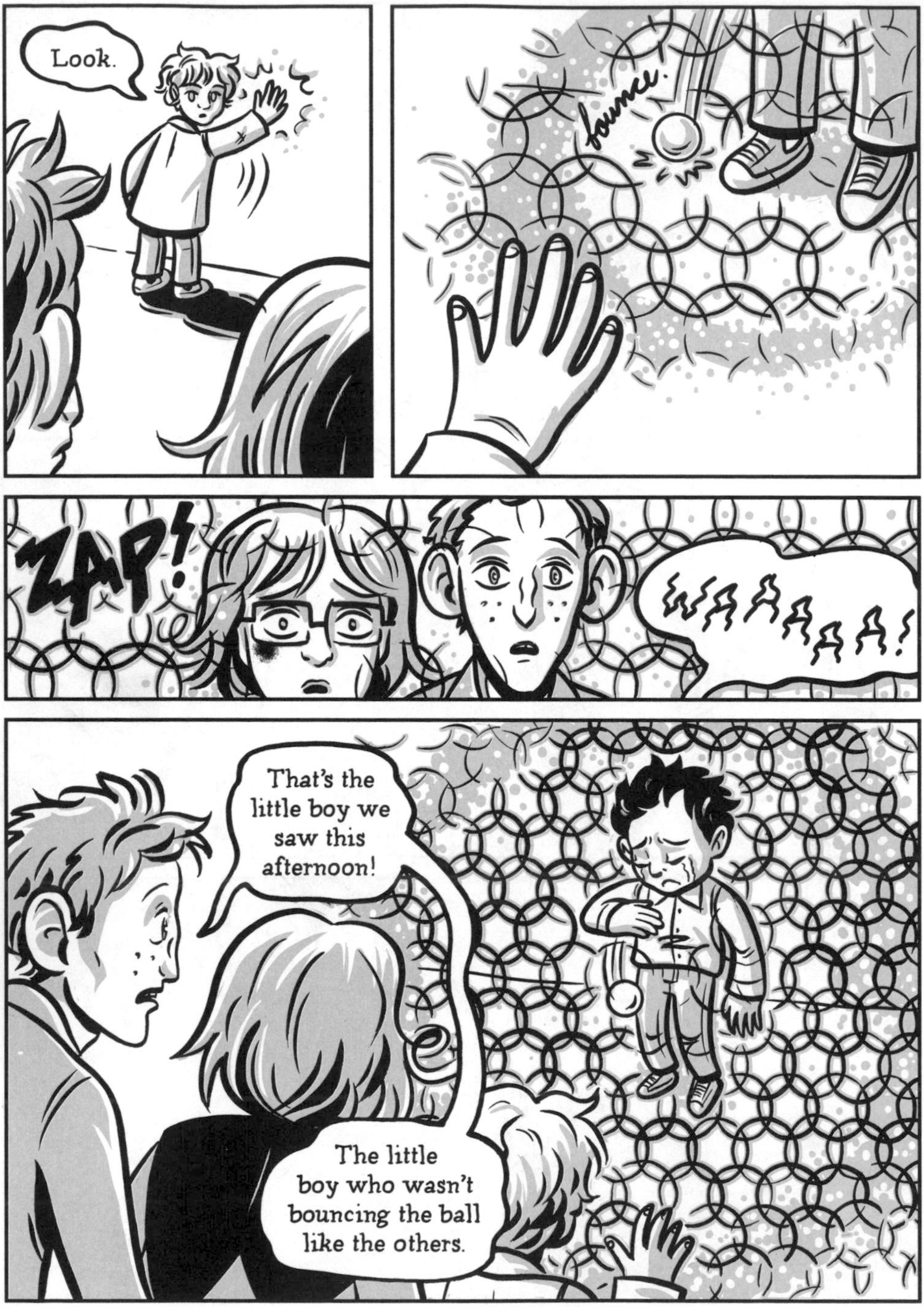
Look.
founce.
ZAP!
WAAAAA!
That's the little boy we saw this afternoon!
The little boy who wasn't bouncing the ball like the others.

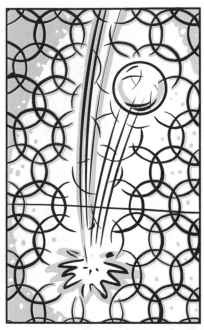

ZAP!

WAAAA!

giggle!

Yes.

Every once in a while there's a little trouble with cooperation, but it's easily taken care of. After today he'll never desire to deviate again.

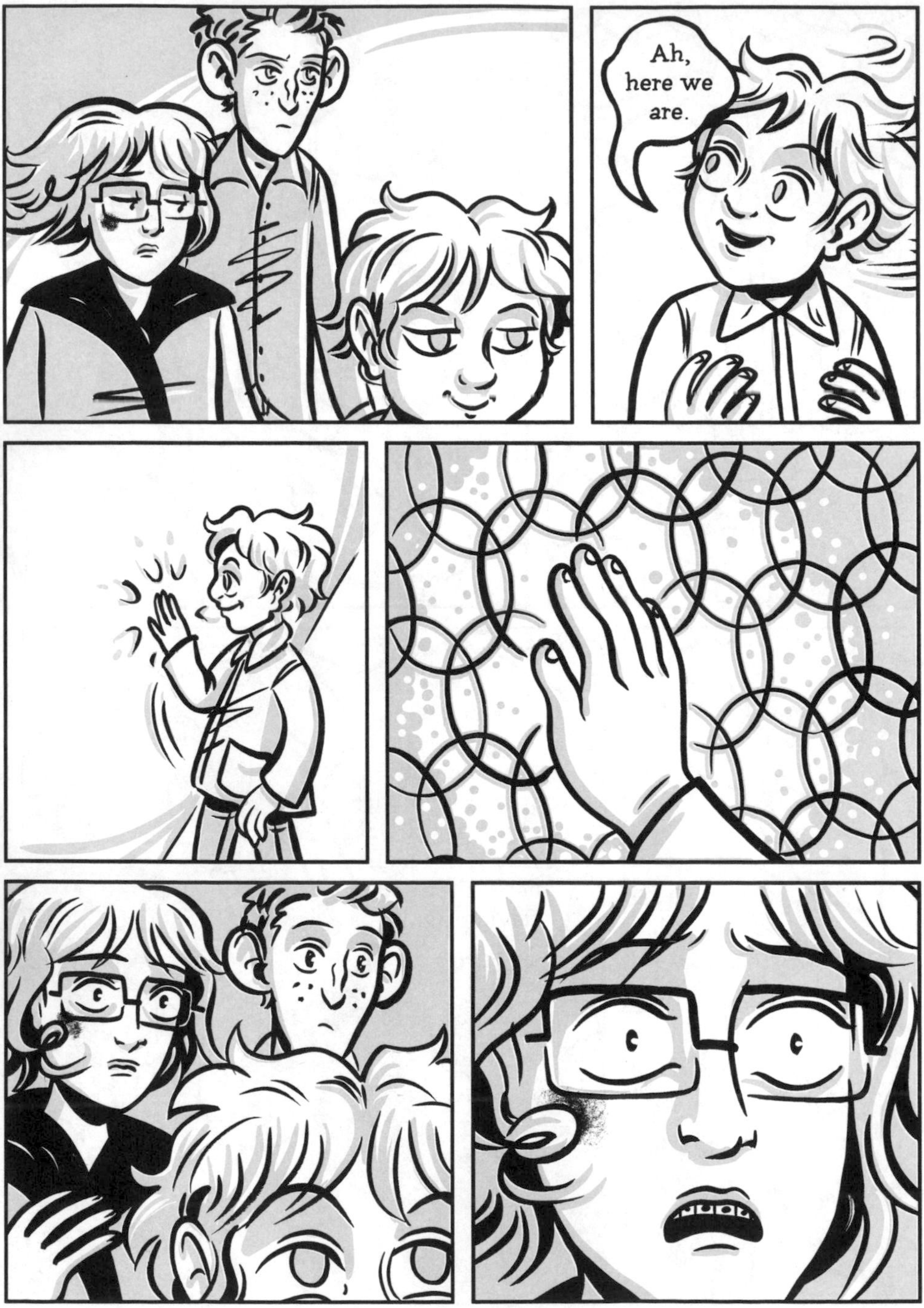
Ah, here we are.

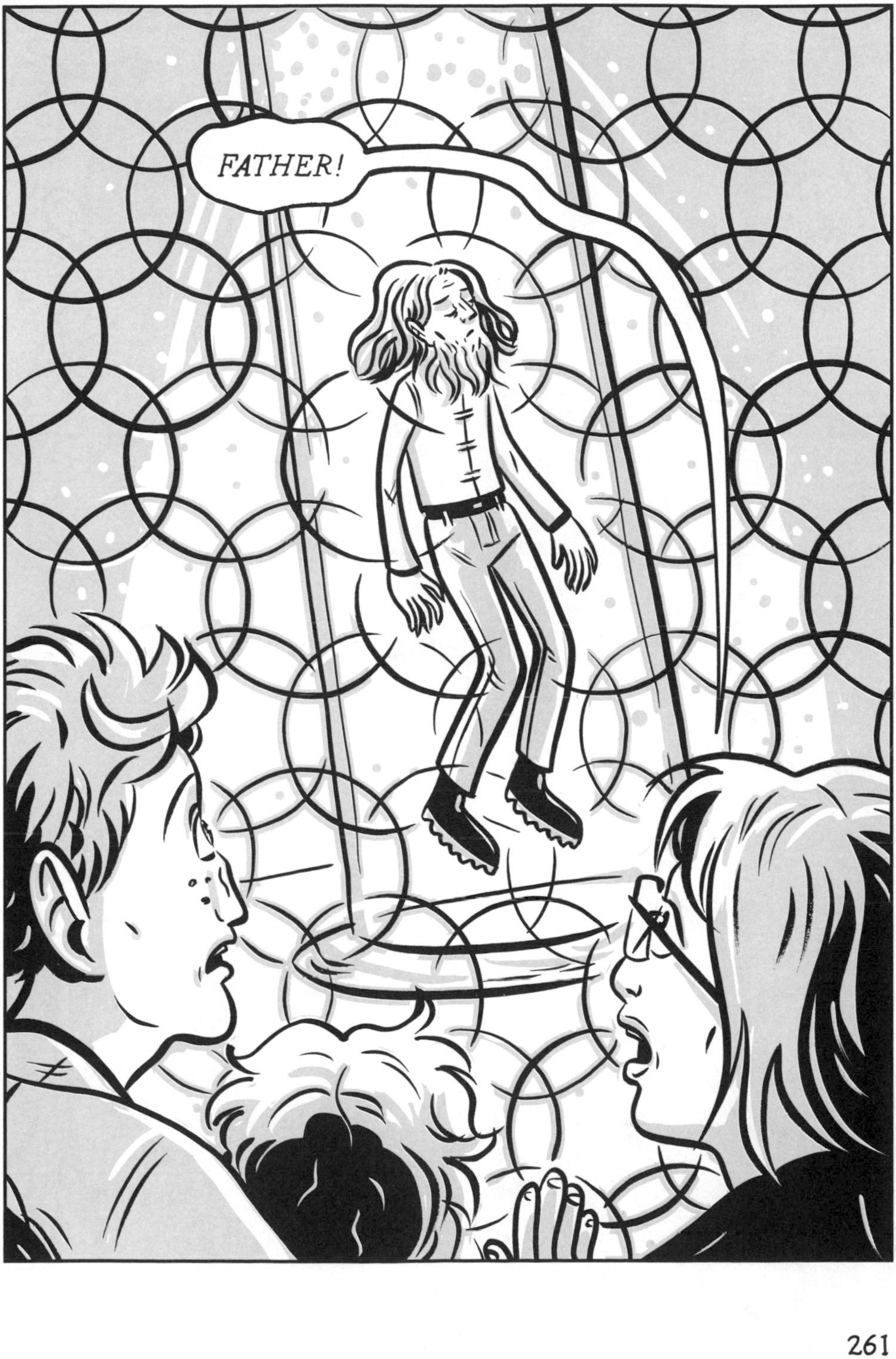
FATHER!

9

IT

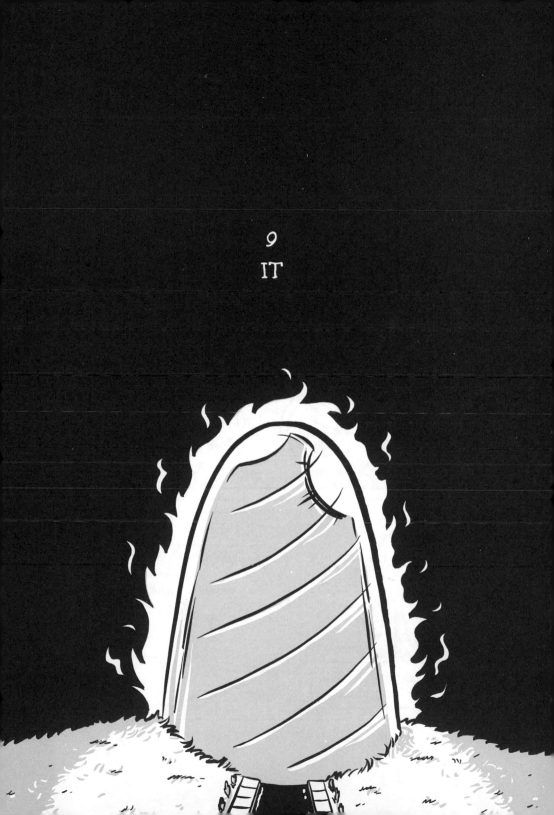

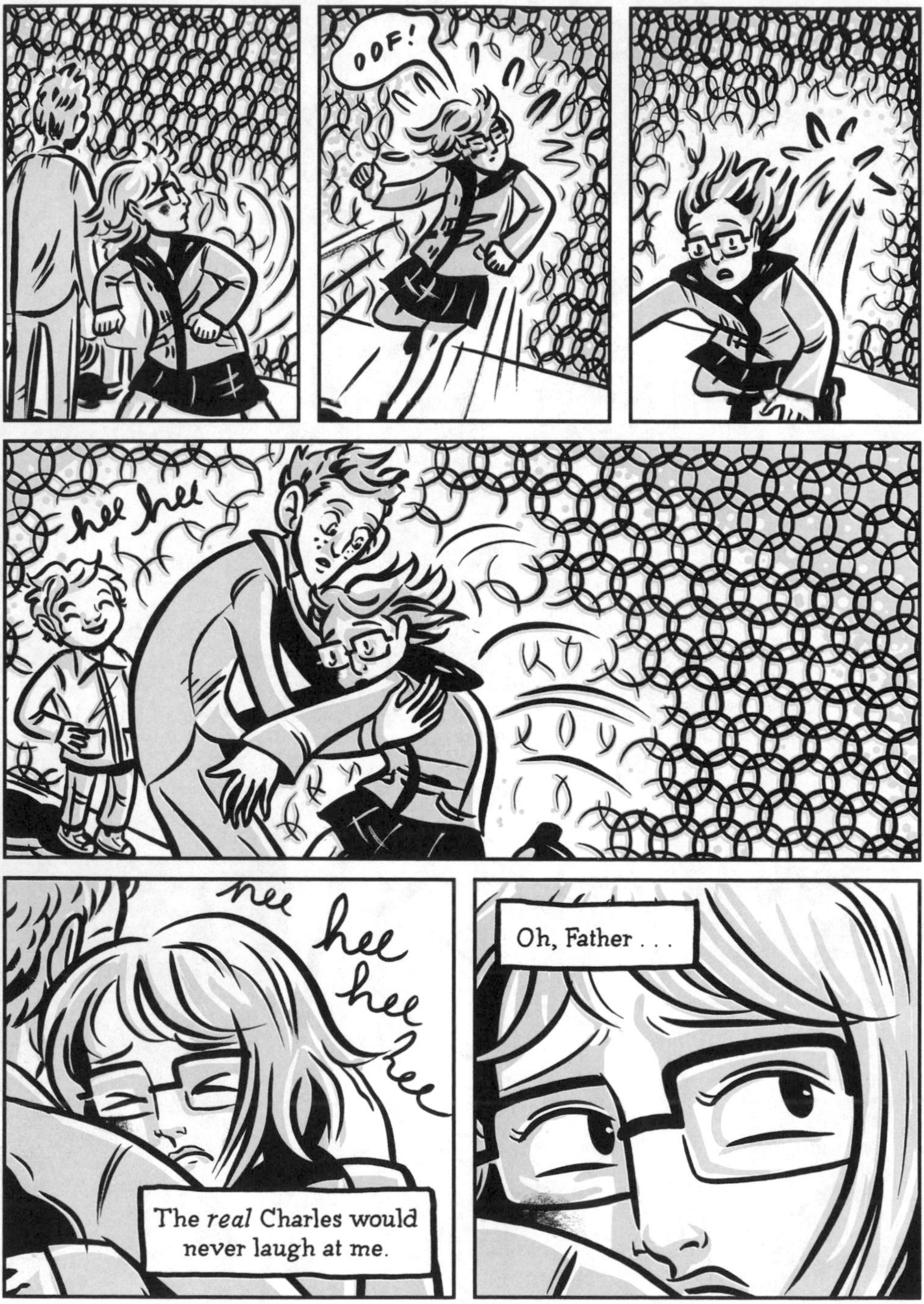
OOF!
hee hee
hee
hee
hee
hee
Oh, Father . . .
The *real* Charles would never laugh at me.

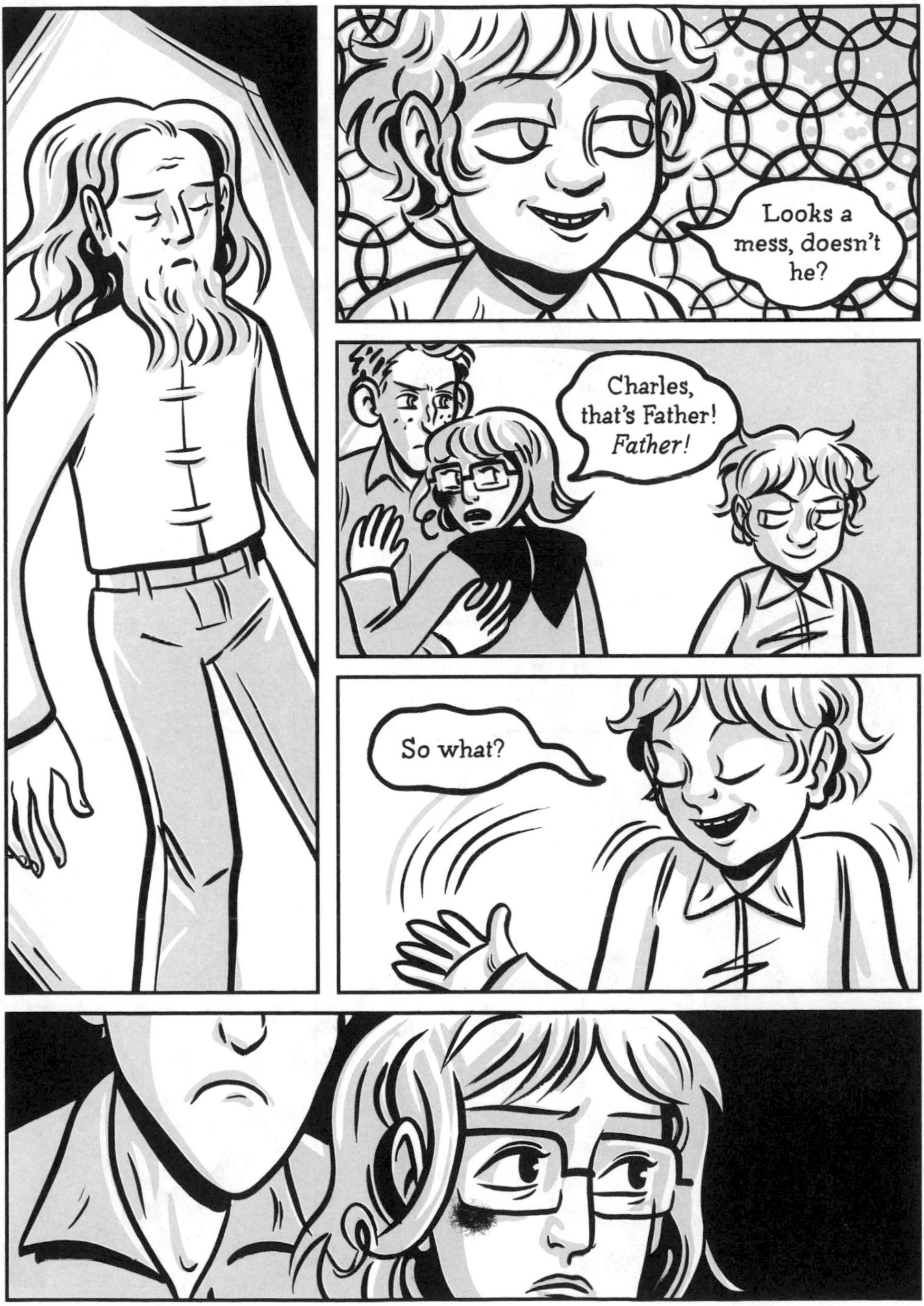
Looks a mess, doesn't he?
Charles, that's Father! *Father!*
So what?

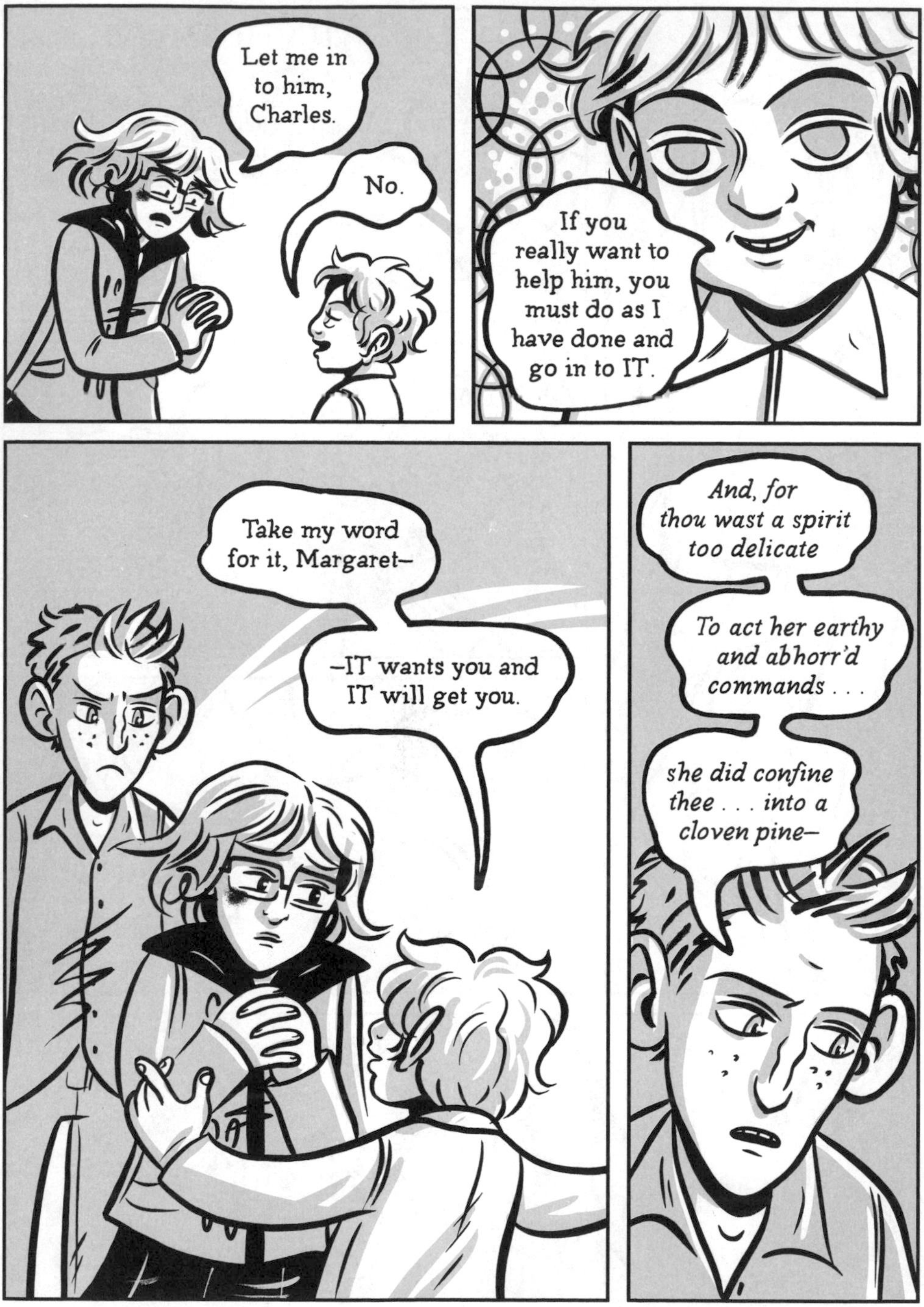
Let me in to him, Charles.
No.
If you really want to help him, you must do as I have done and go in to IT.
Take my word for it, Margaret–
–IT wants you and IT will get you.
And, for thou wast a spirit too delicate
To act her earthy and abhorr'd commands . . .
she did confine thee . . . into a cloven pine–

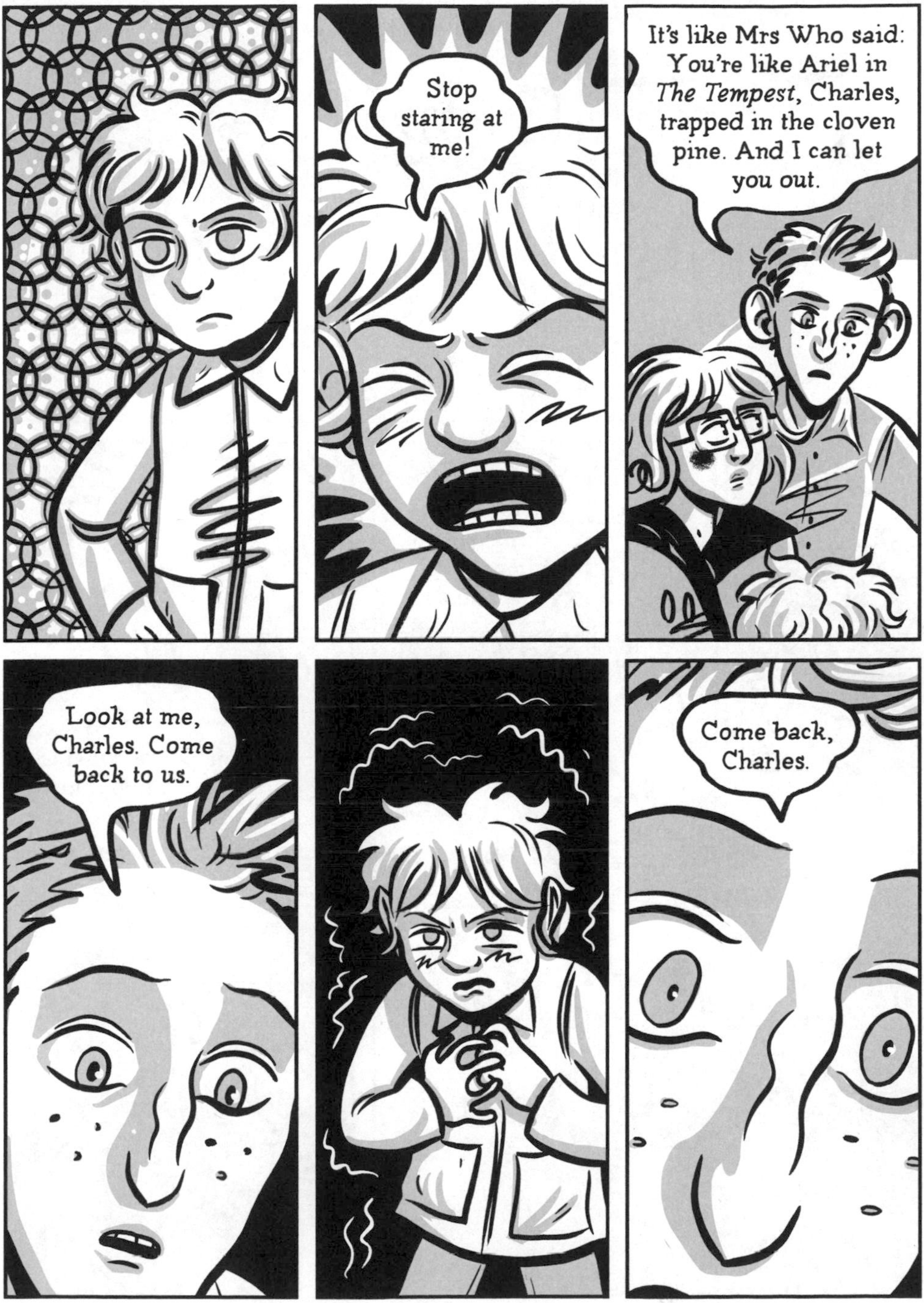
Stop staring at me!
It's like Mrs Who said: You're like Ariel in *The Tempest*, Charles, trapped in the cloven pine. And I can let you out.
Look at me, Charles. Come back to us.
Come back, Charles.

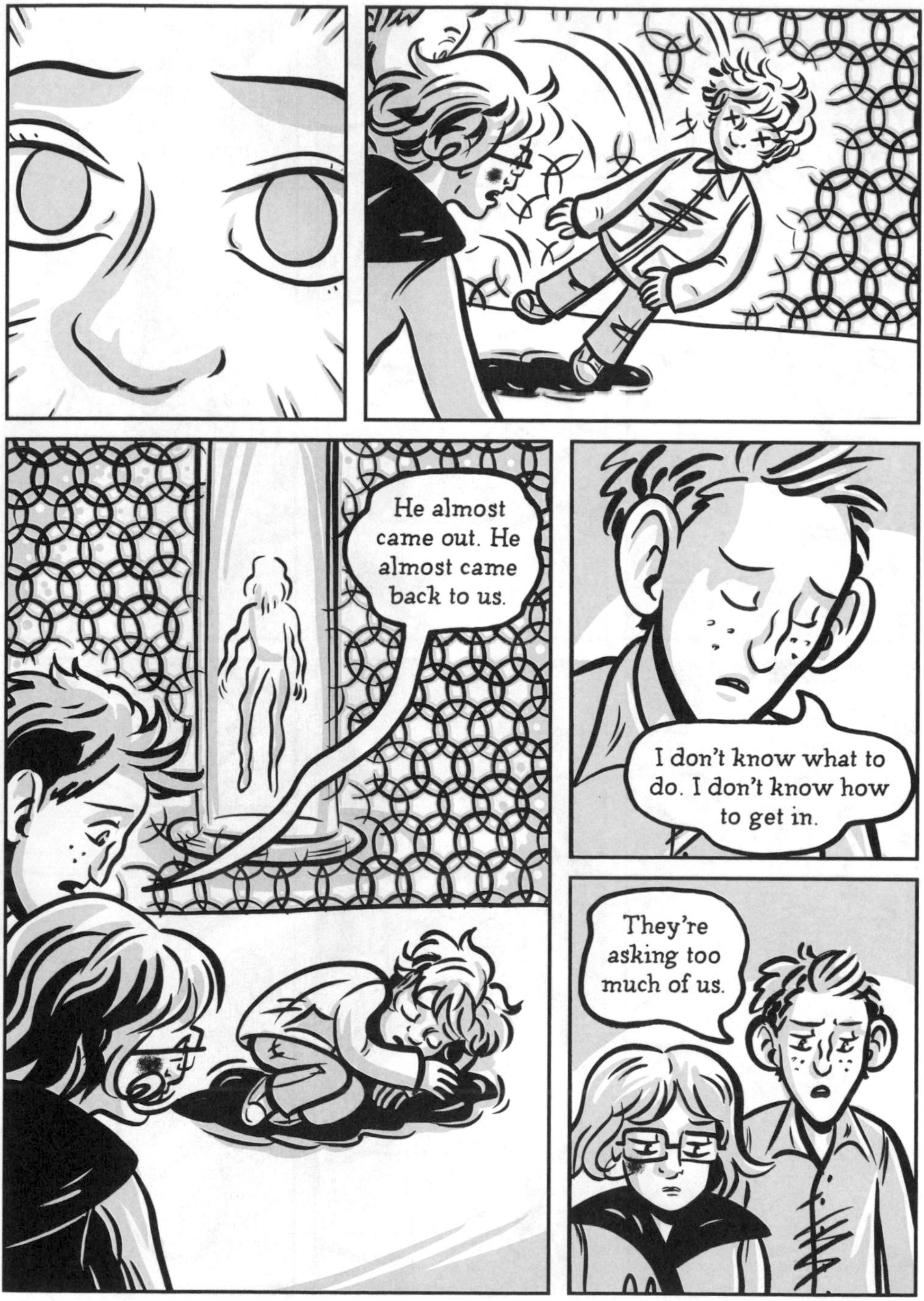
He almost came out. He almost came back to us.
I don't know what to do. I don't know how to get in.
They're asking too much of us.

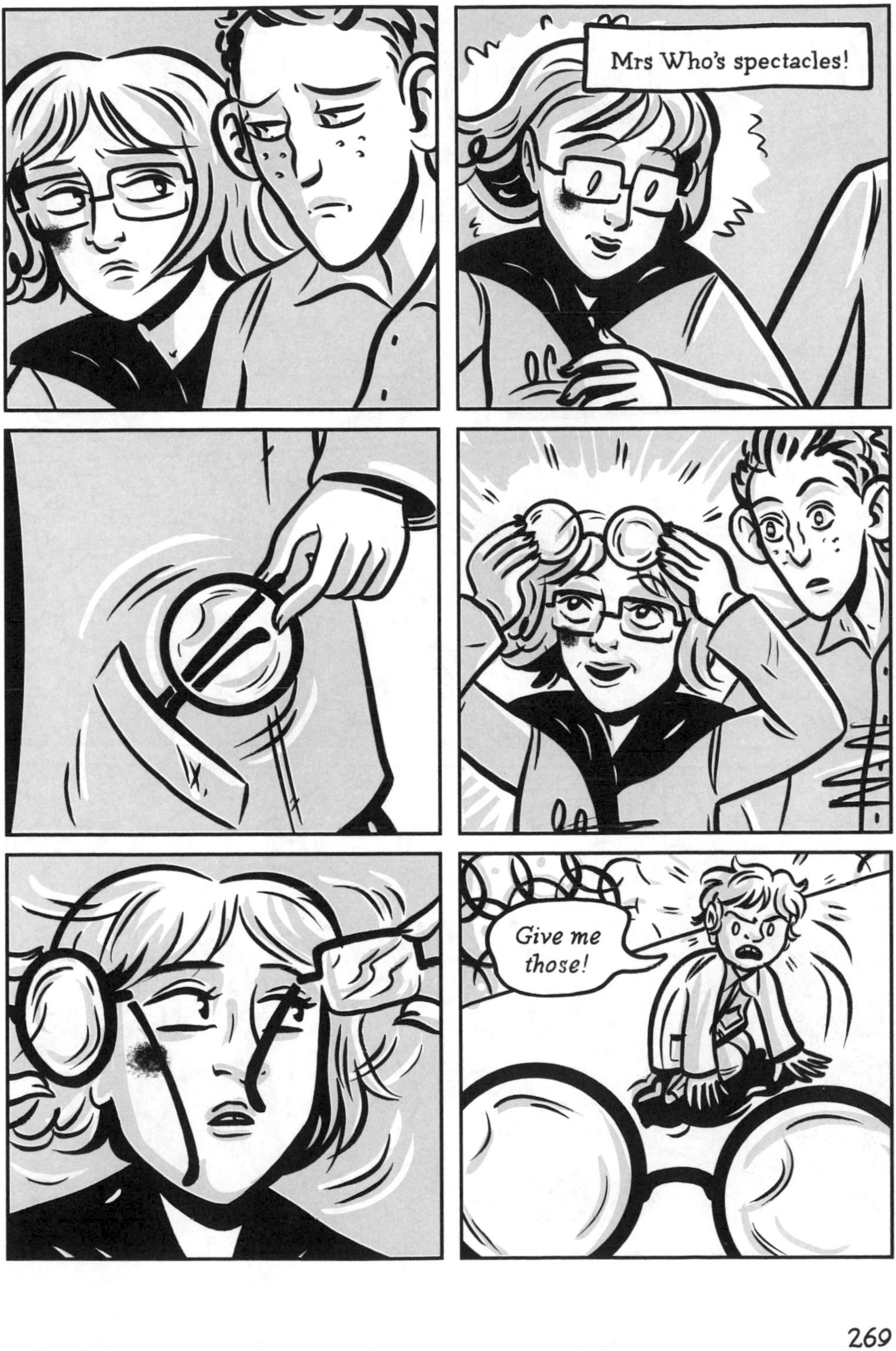
Mrs Who's spectacles!
Give me those!

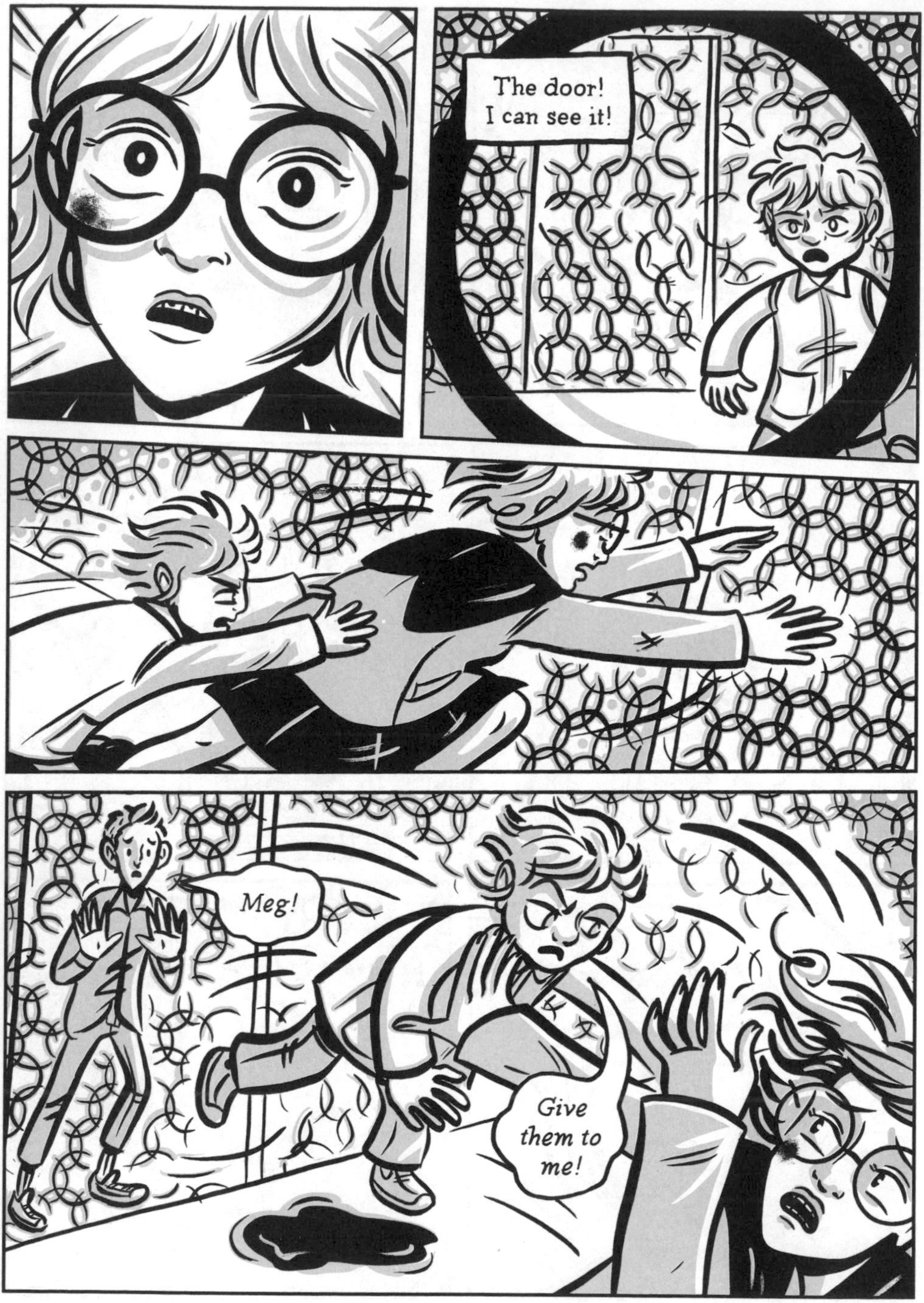
The door! I can see it!
Meg!
Give them to me!

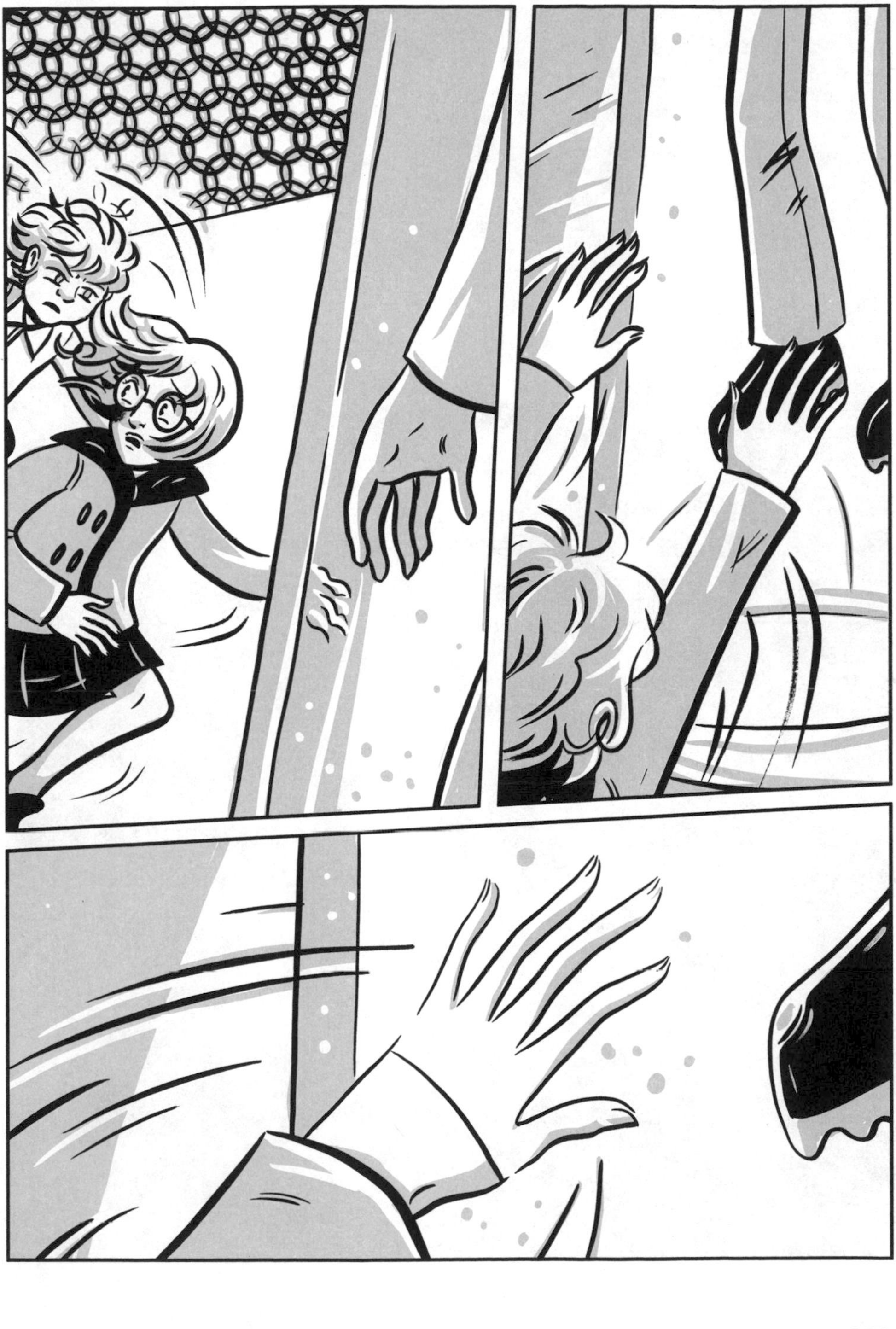

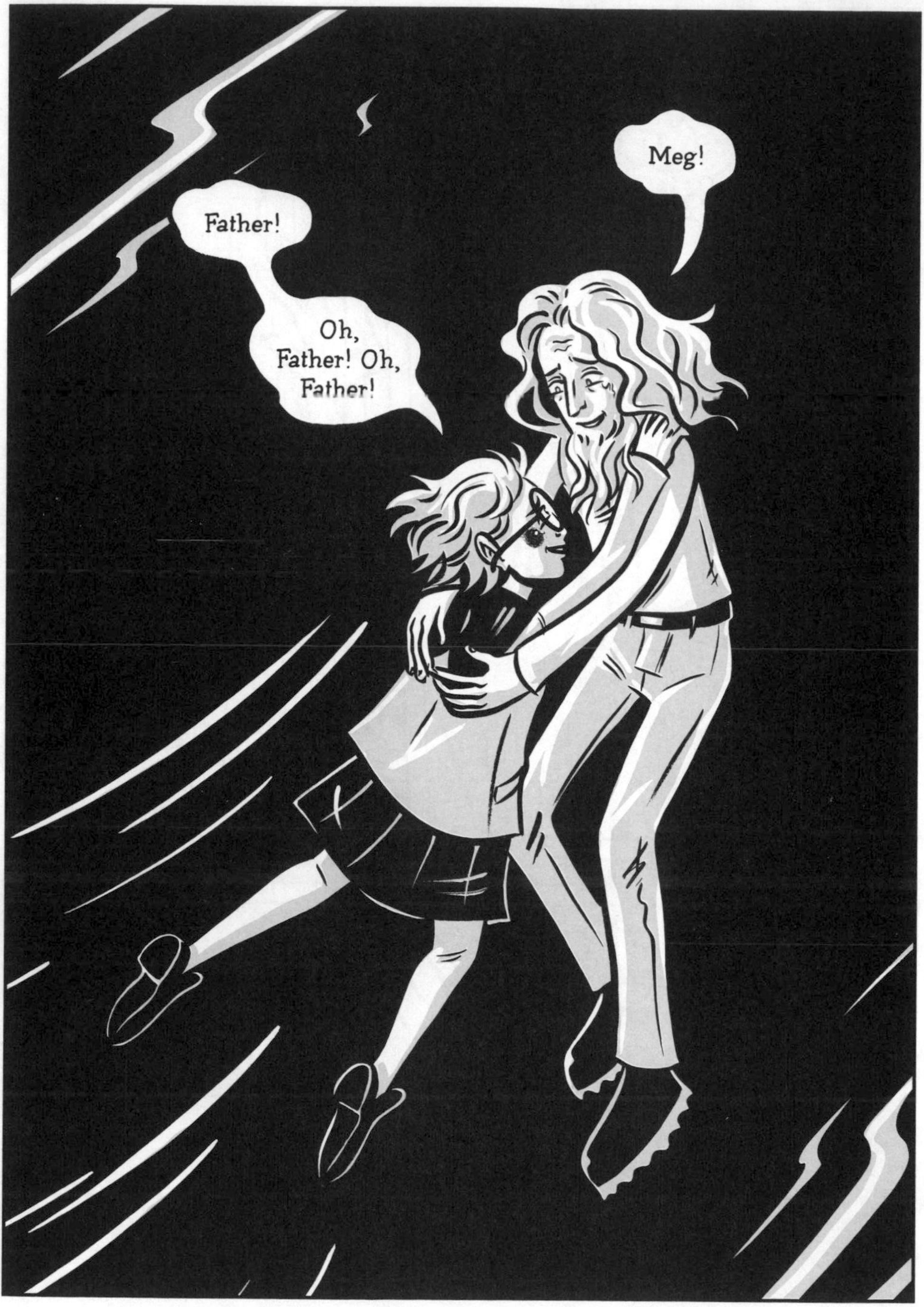
Father!
Oh, Father! Oh, Father!
Meg!

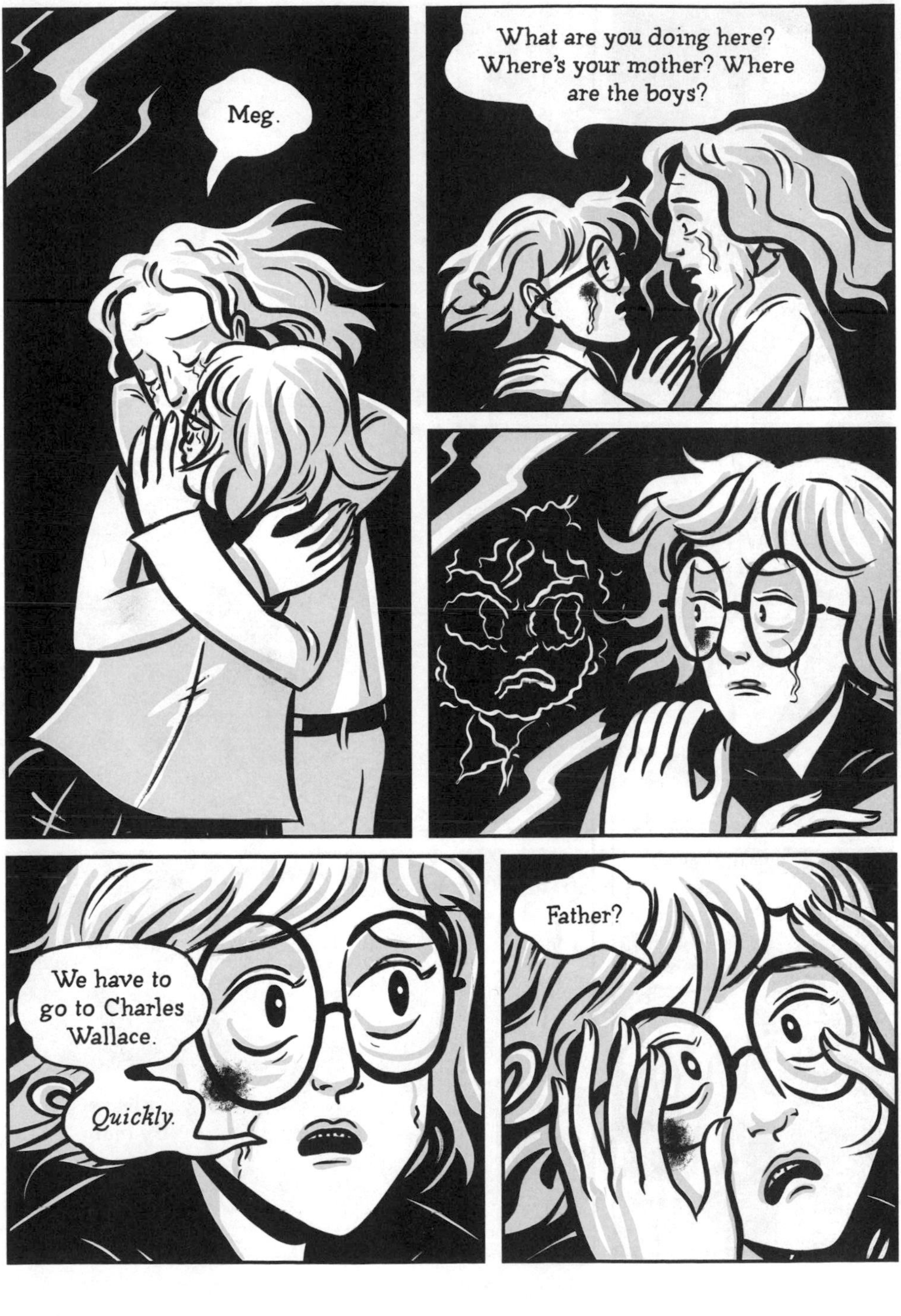
Meg.
What are you doing here? Where's your mother? Where are the boys?
We have to go to Charles Wallace.
Quickly.
Father?

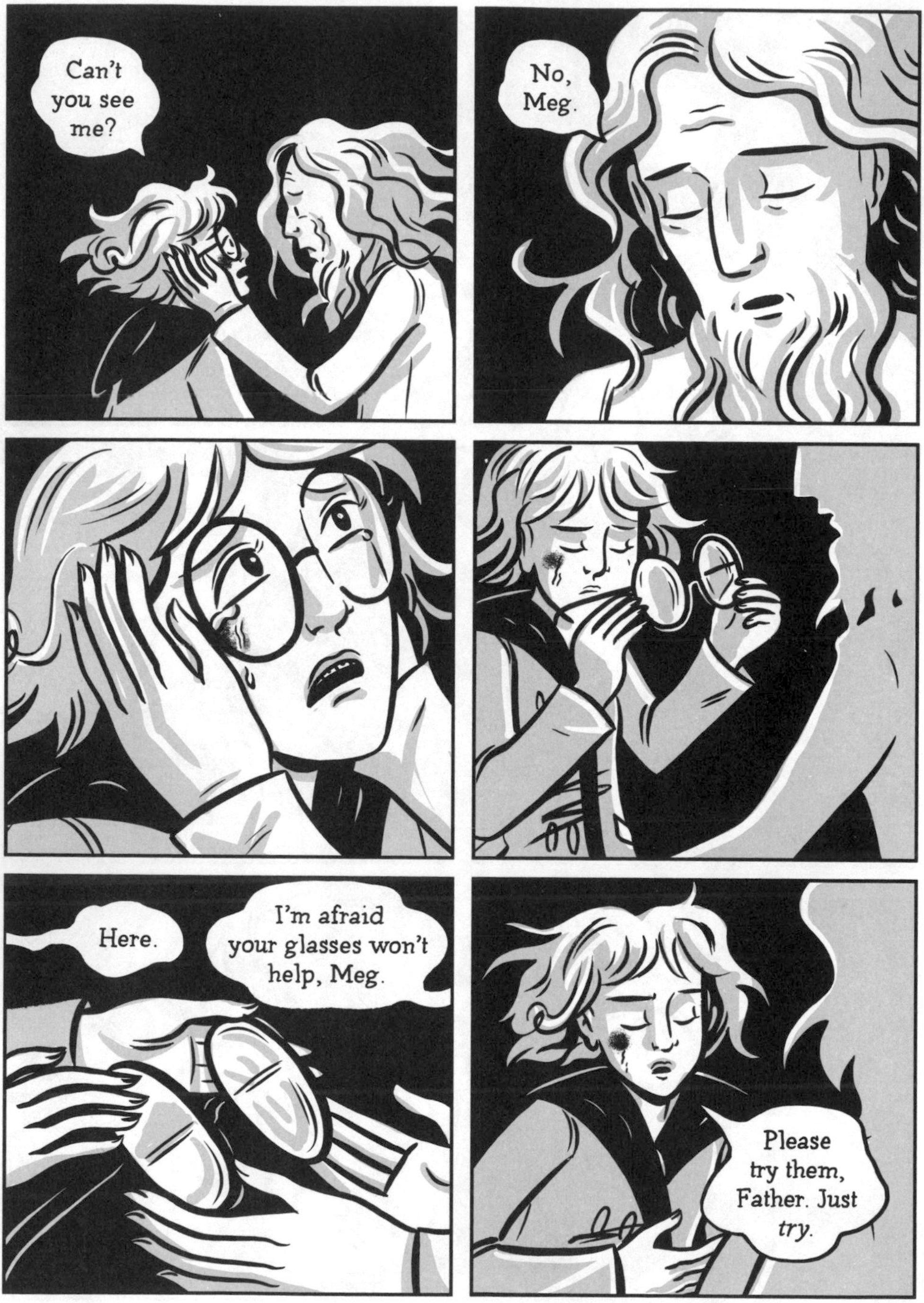
Can't you see me?
No, Meg.
Here.
I'm afraid your glasses won't help, Meg.
Please try them, Father. Just *try*.

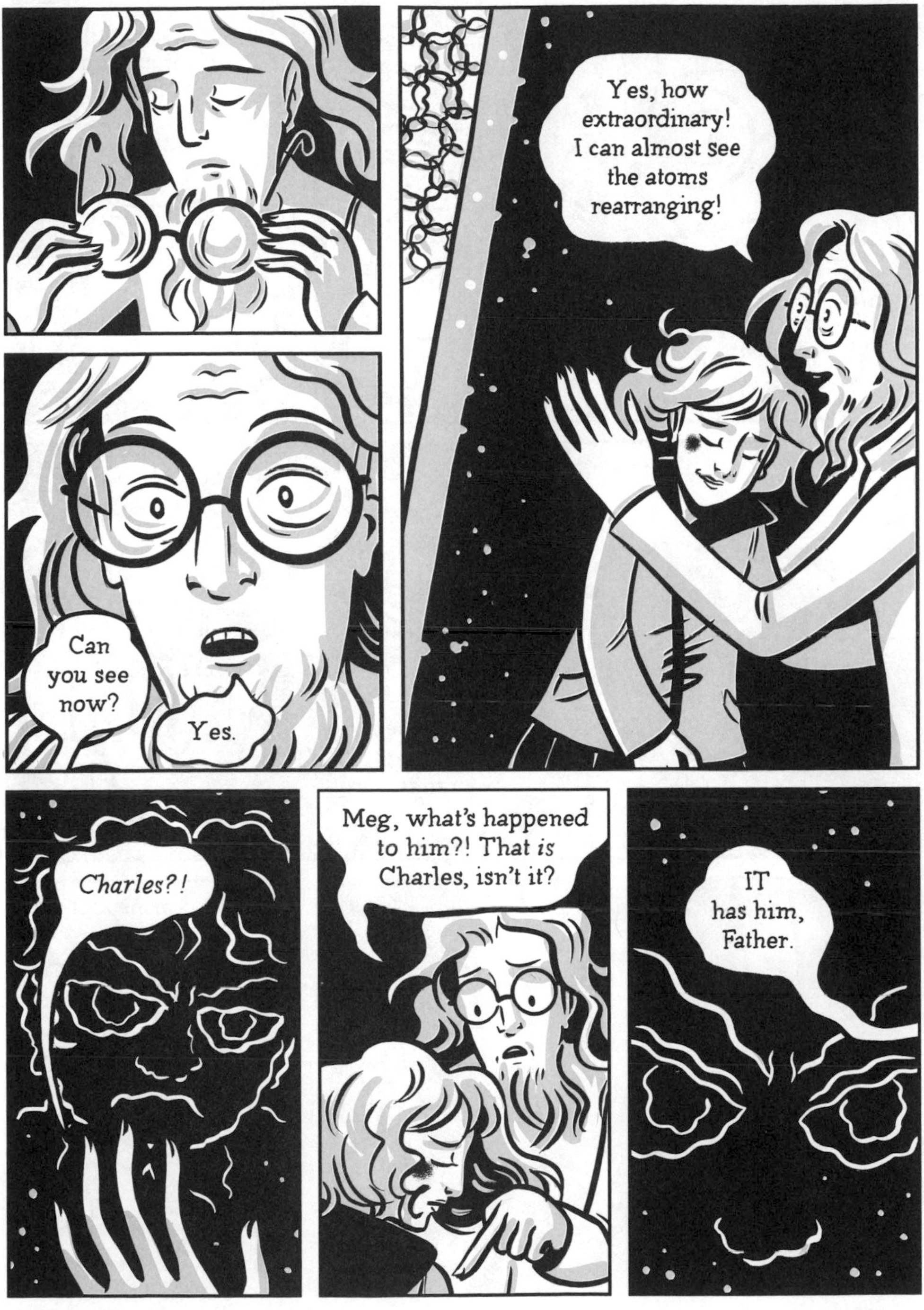
Yes, how extraordinary! I can almost see the atoms rearranging!
Can you see now?
Yes.
Charles?!
Meg, what's happened to him?! That *is* Charles, isn't it?
IT has him, Father.

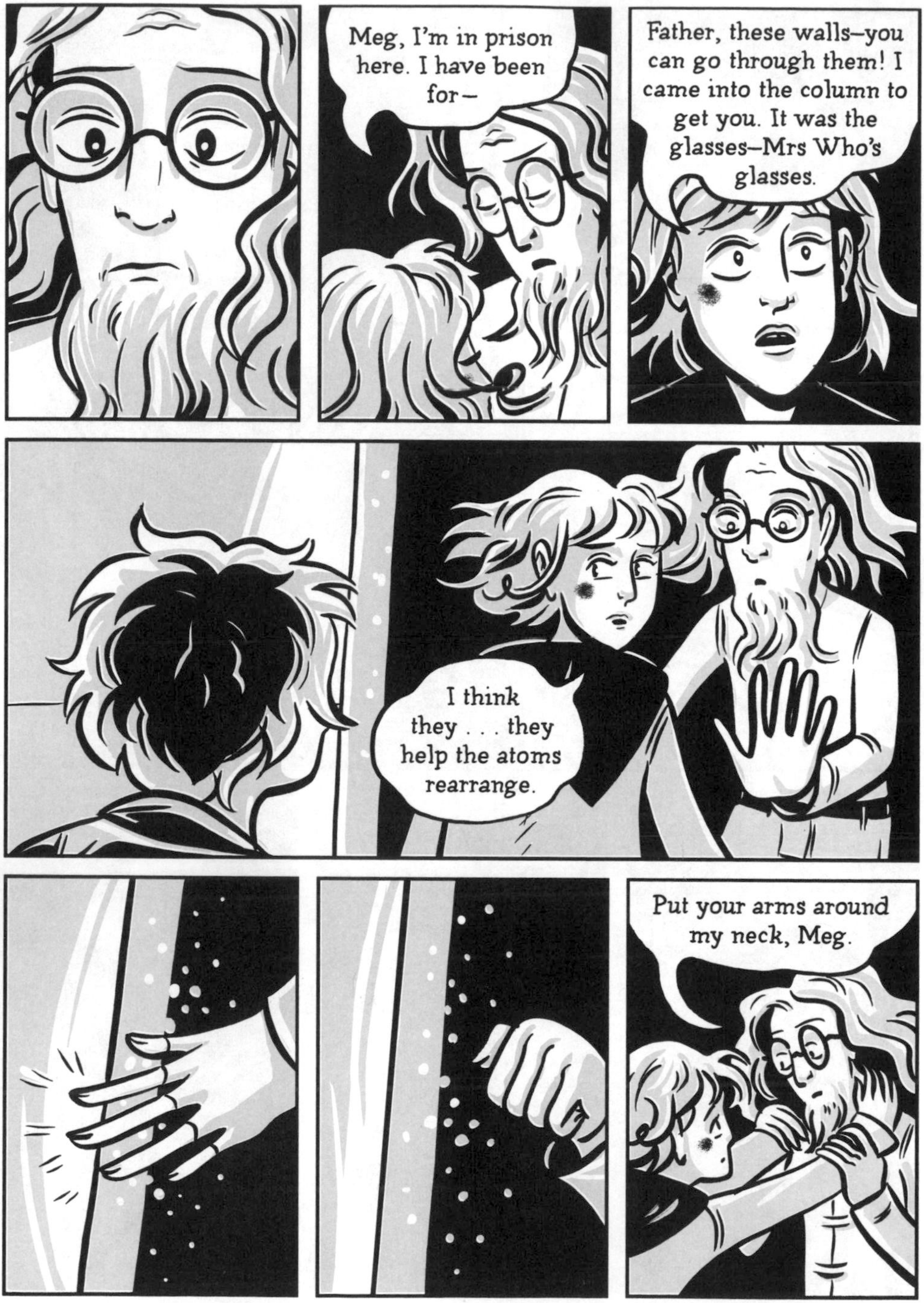
Meg, I'm in prison here. I have been for—
Father, these walls—you can go through them! I came into the column to get you. It was the glasses—Mrs Who's glasses.
I think they . . . they help the atoms rearrange.
Put your arms around my neck, Meg.

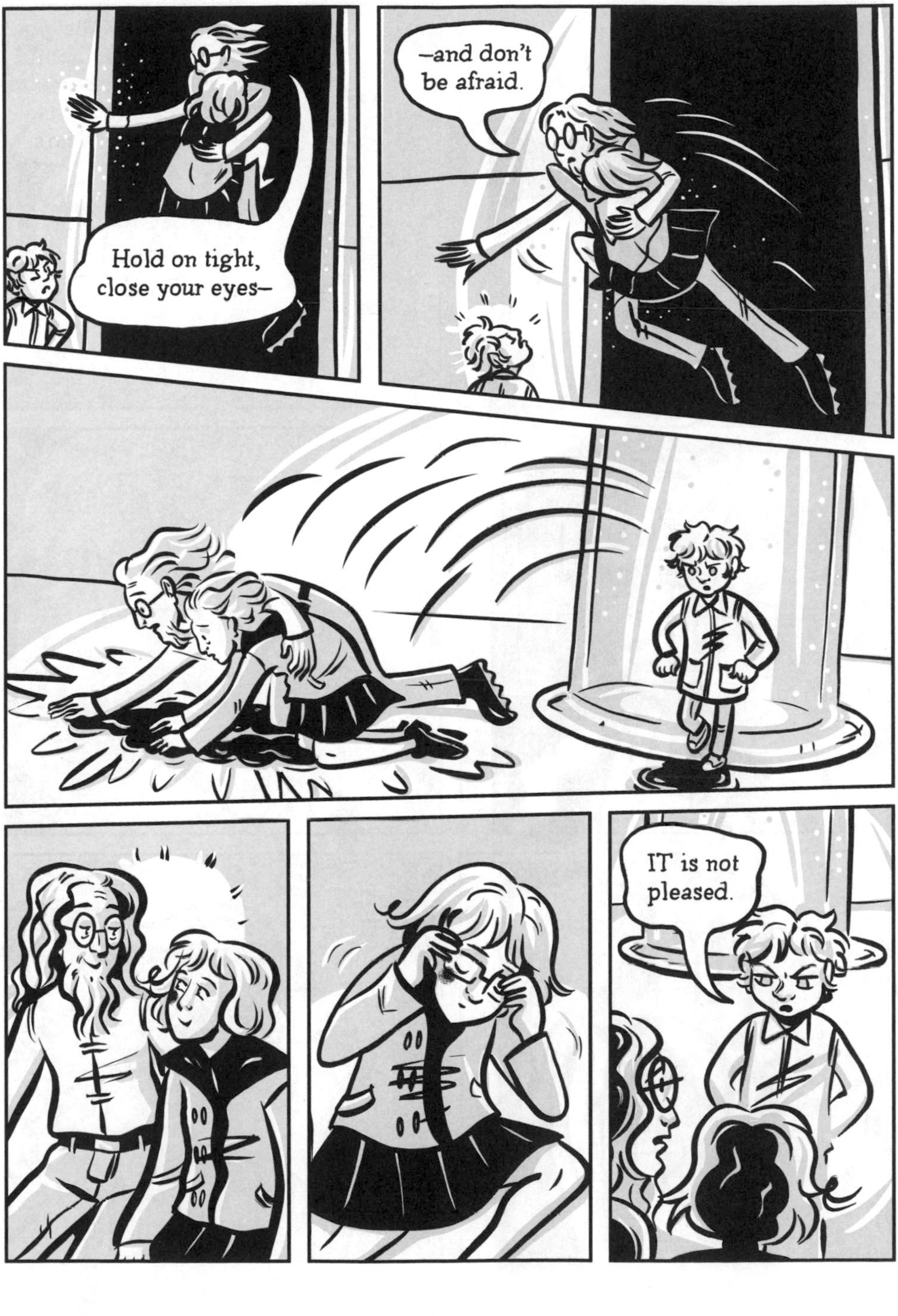
Hold on tight, close your eyes—
—and don't be afraid.
IT is not pleased.

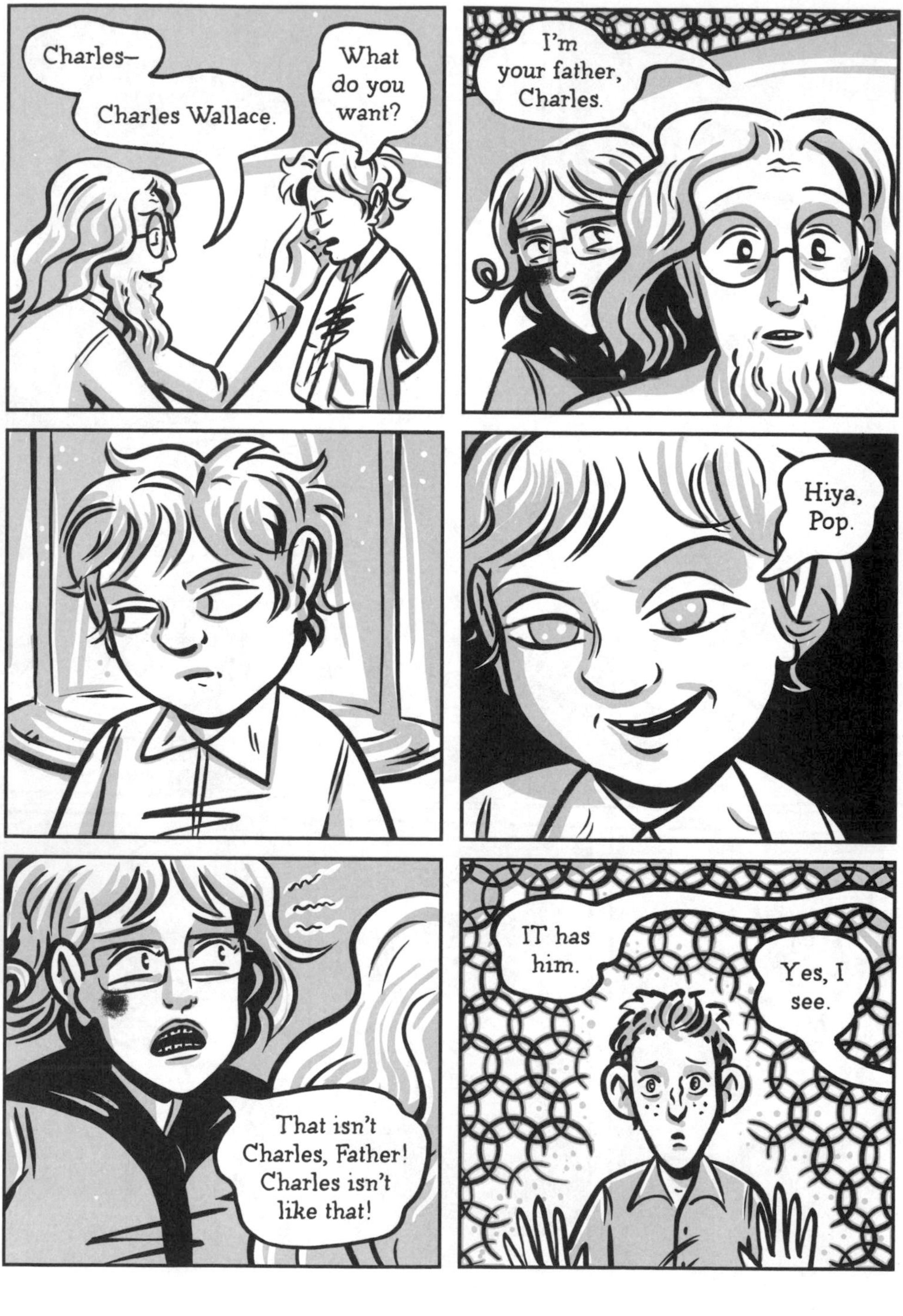
Charles—
Charles Wallace.
What do you want?
I'm your father, Charles.
Hiya, Pop.
That isn't Charles, Father! Charles isn't like that!
IT has him.
Yes, I see.

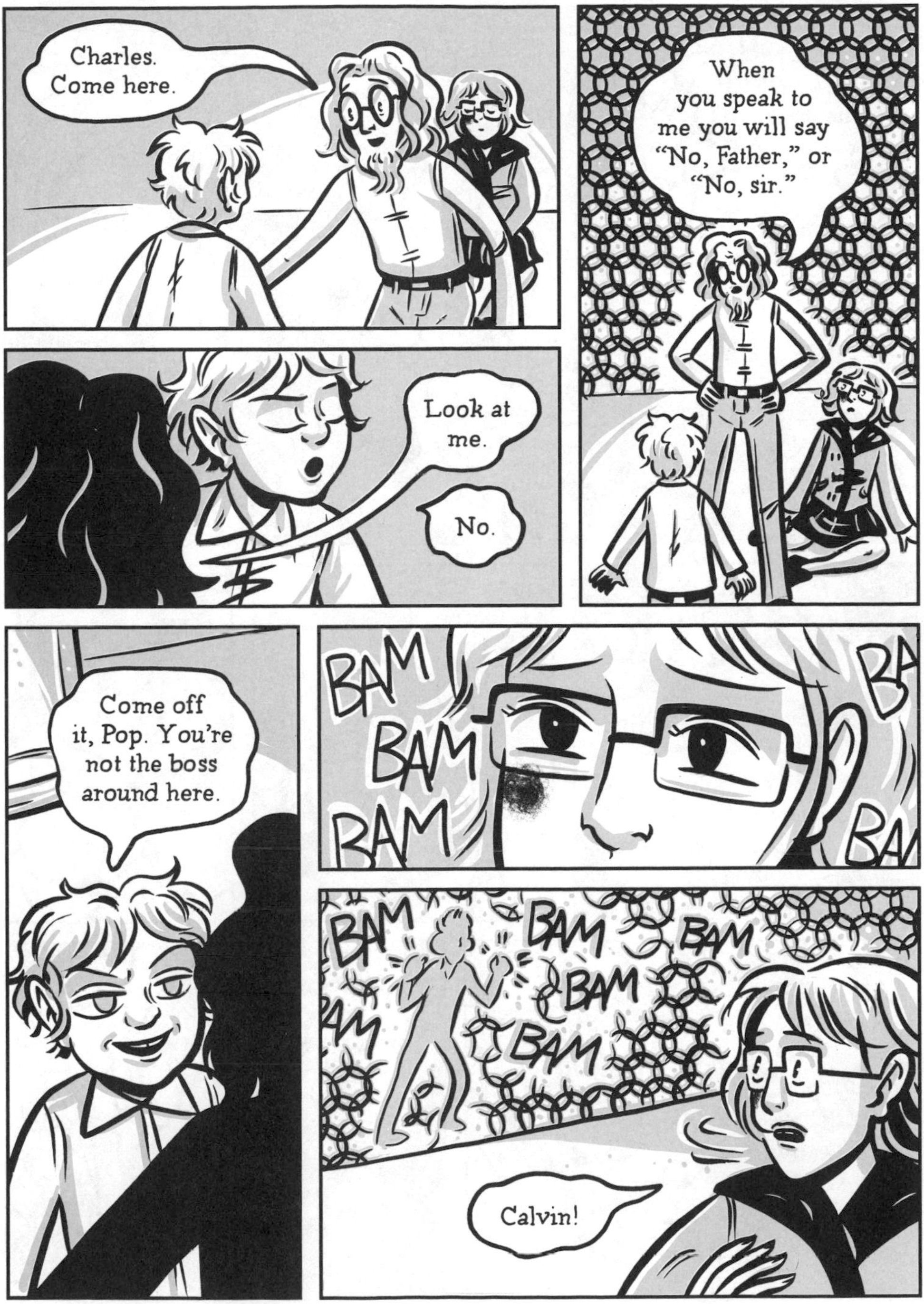
Charles. Come here.
When you speak to me you will say "No, Father," or "No, sir."
Look at me.
No.
Come off it, Pop. You're not the boss around here.
BAM BAM BAM
BAM BAM BAM BAM BAM
Calvin!

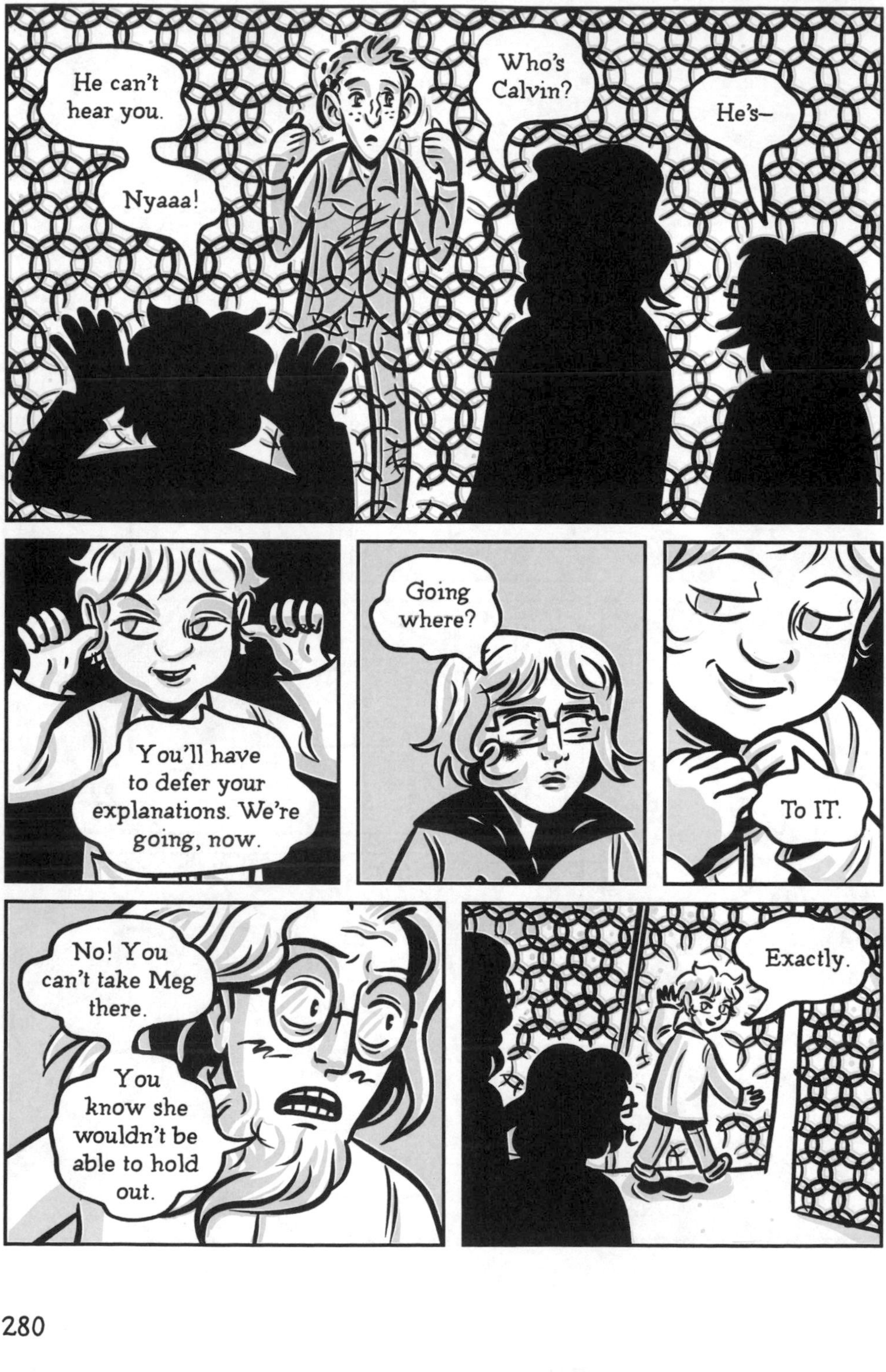
He can't hear you.
Nyaaa!
Who's Calvin?
He's–
You'll have to defer your explanations. We're going, now.
Going where?
To IT.
No! You can't take Meg there.
You know she wouldn't be able to hold out.
Exactly.

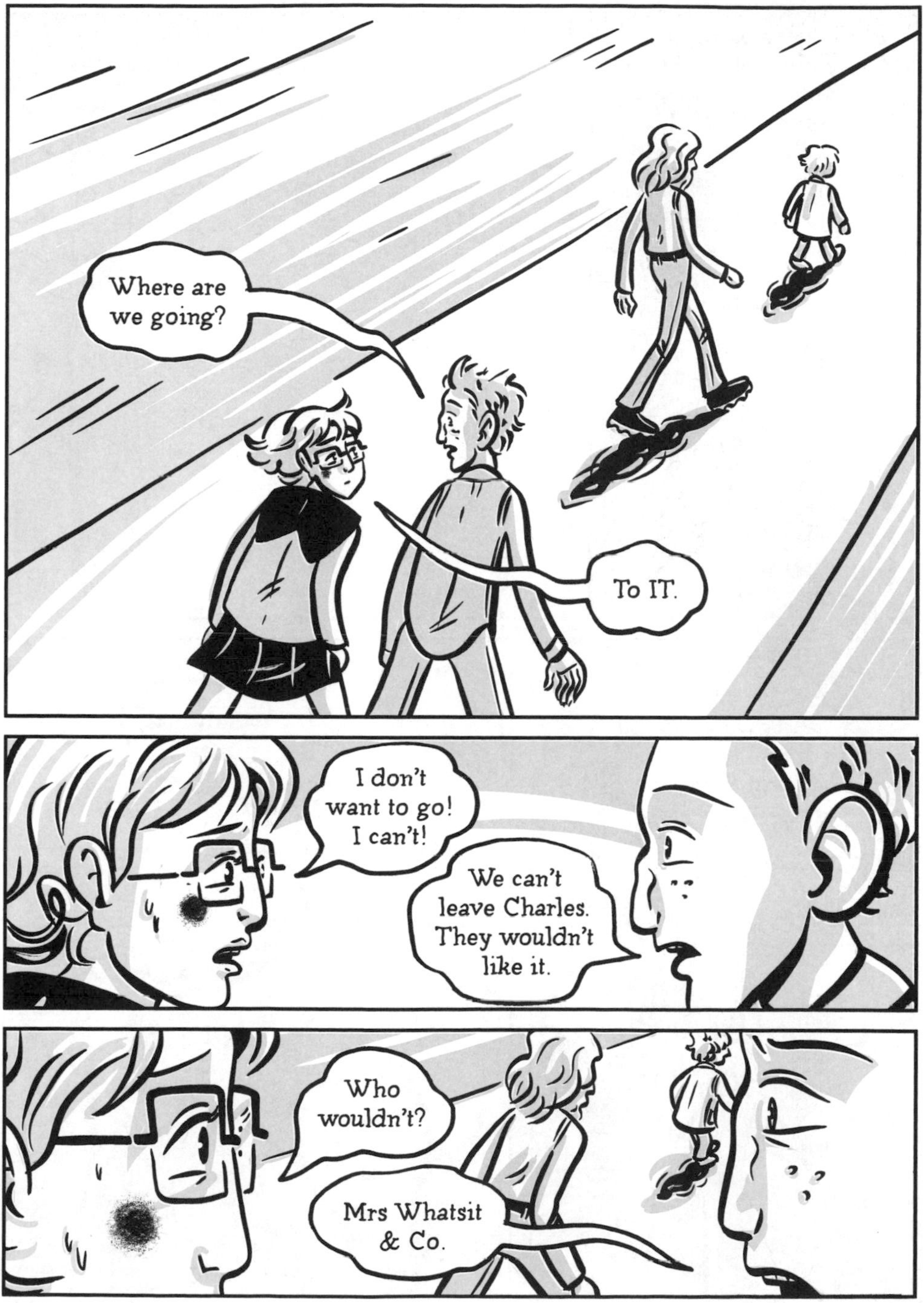
Where are we going?
To IT.
I don't want to go! I can't!
We can't leave Charles. They wouldn't like it.
Who wouldn't?
Mrs Whatsit & Co.

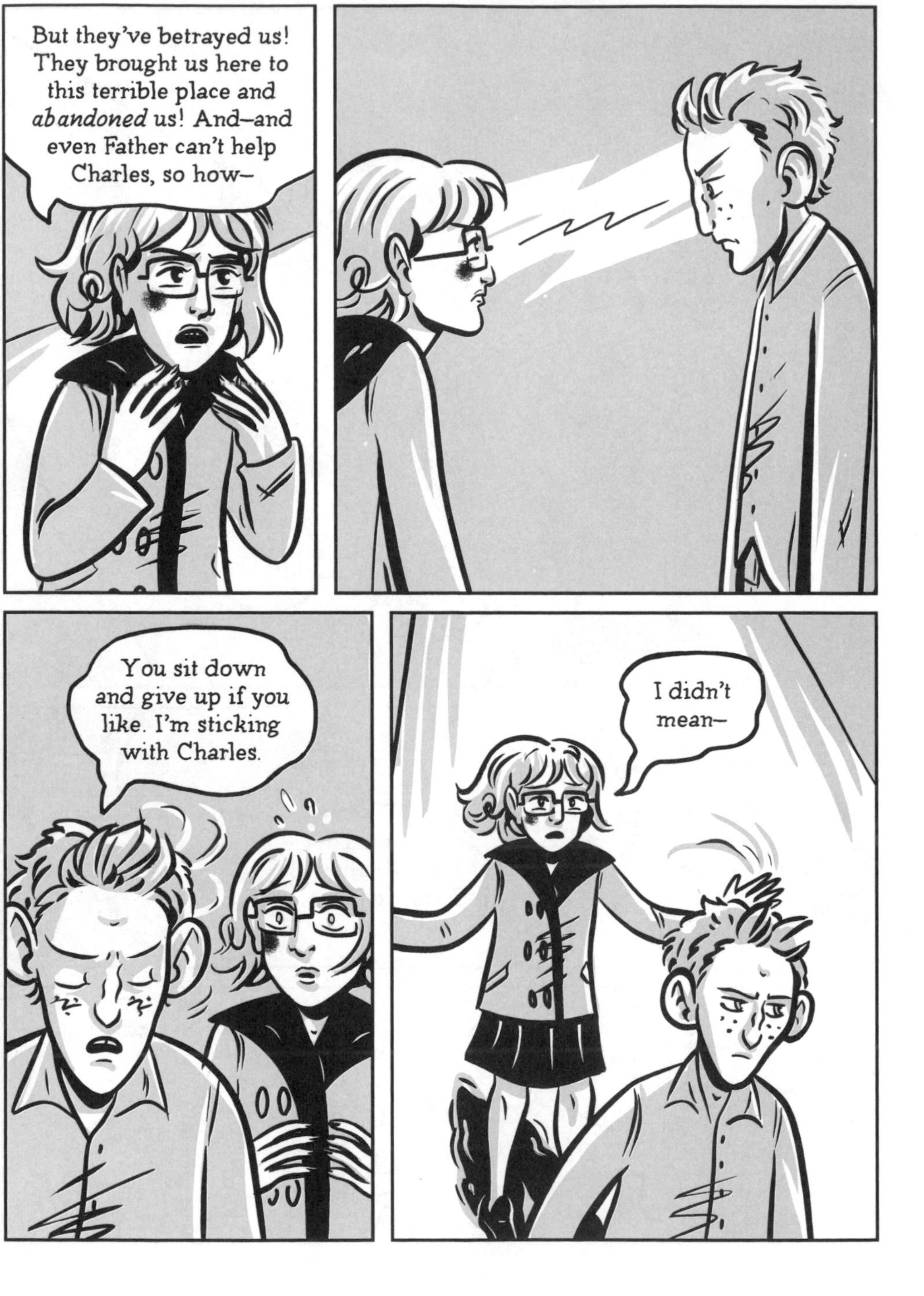
But they've betrayed us! They brought us here to this terrible place and *abandoned* us! And–and even Father can't help Charles, so how–
You sit down and give up if you like. I'm sticking with Charles.
I didn't mean–

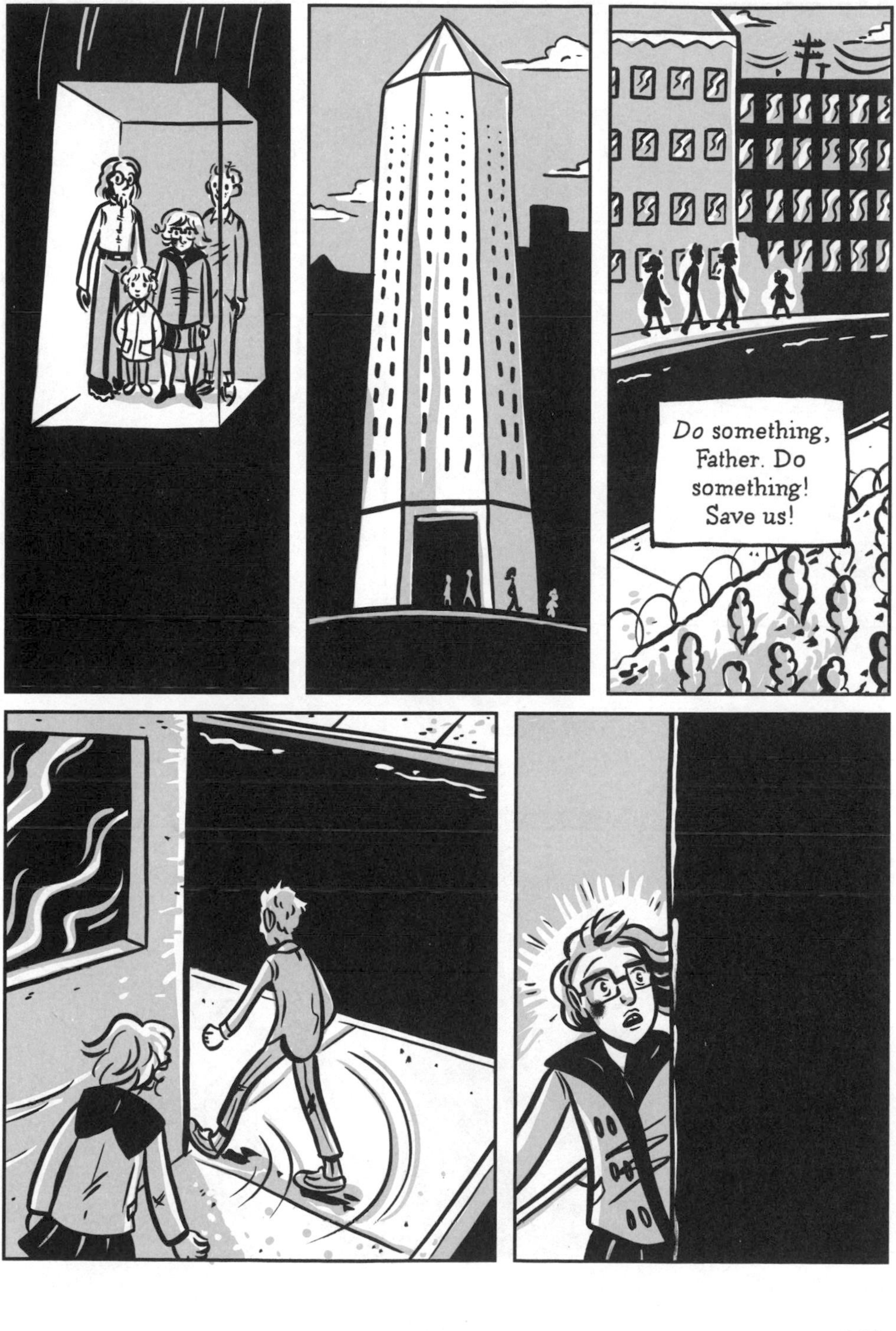
Do something, Father. Do something! Save us!

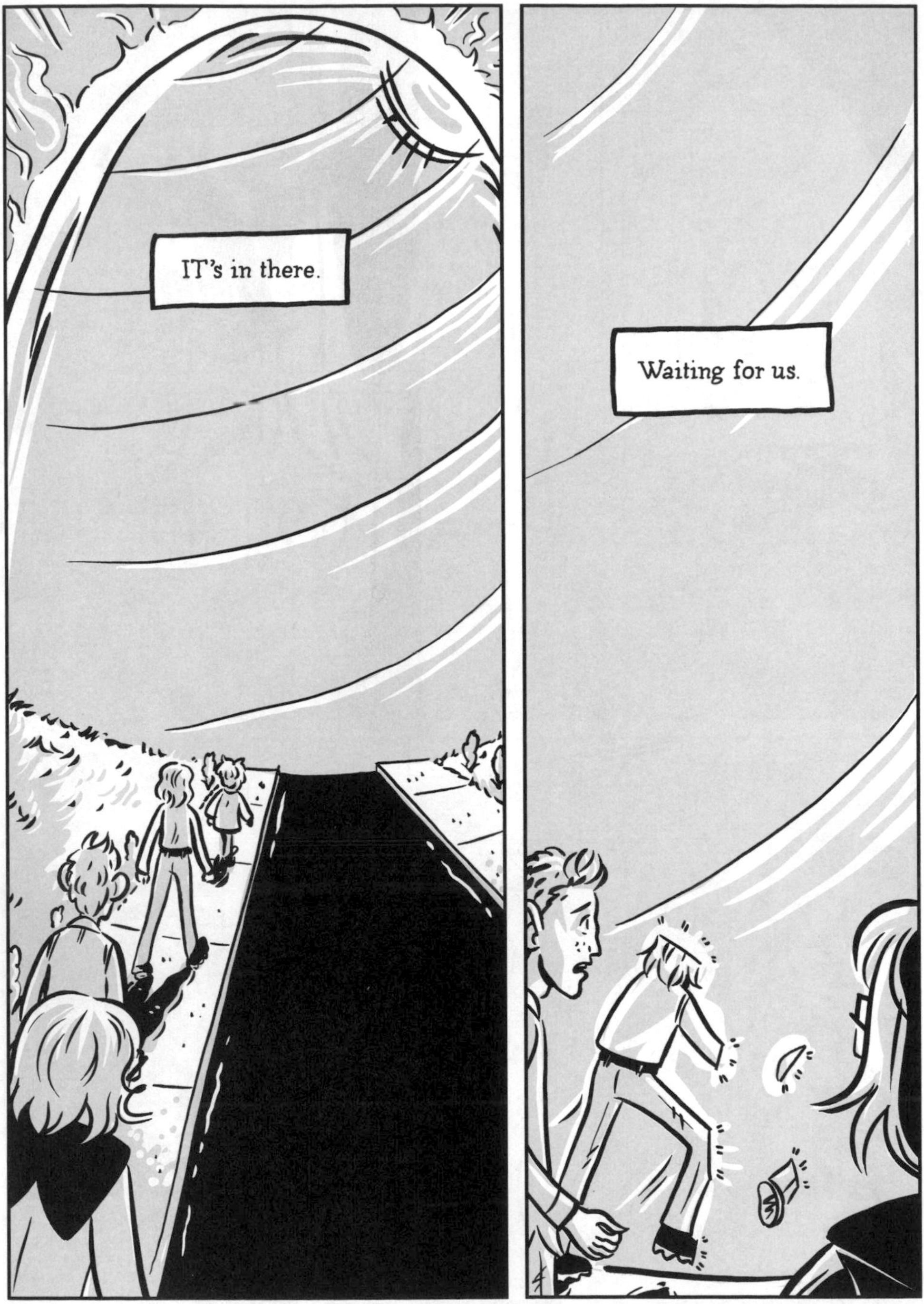
IT's in there.
Waiting for us.

CLICK
CLICK
CLICK
CLICK

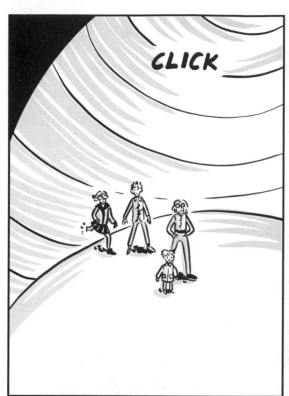

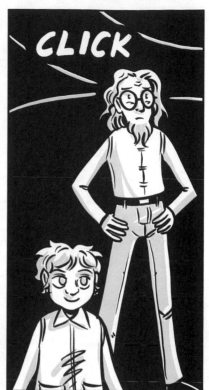

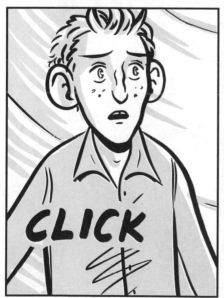

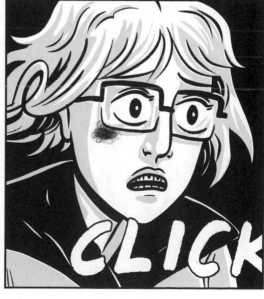

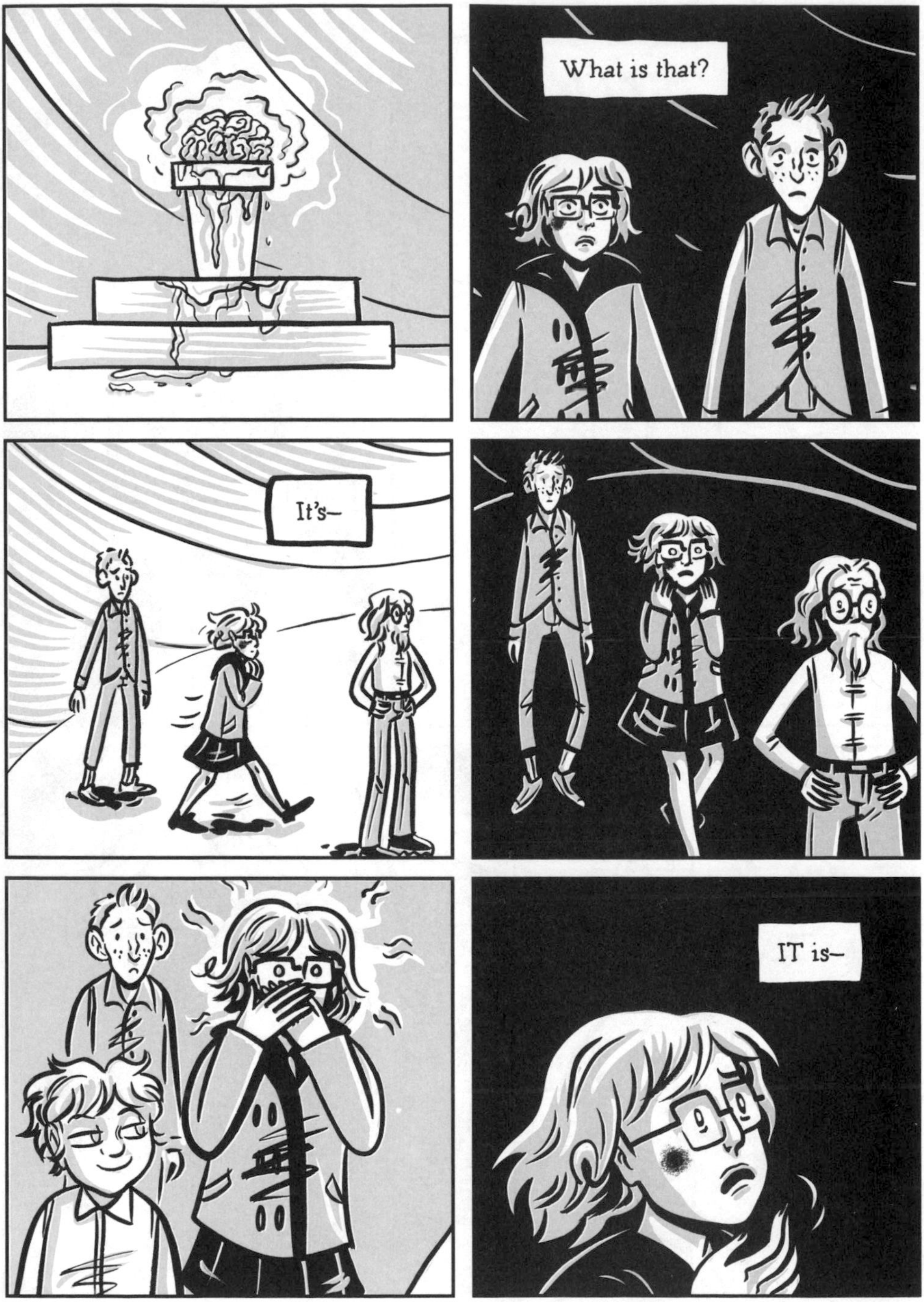
What is that?
It's—
IT is—

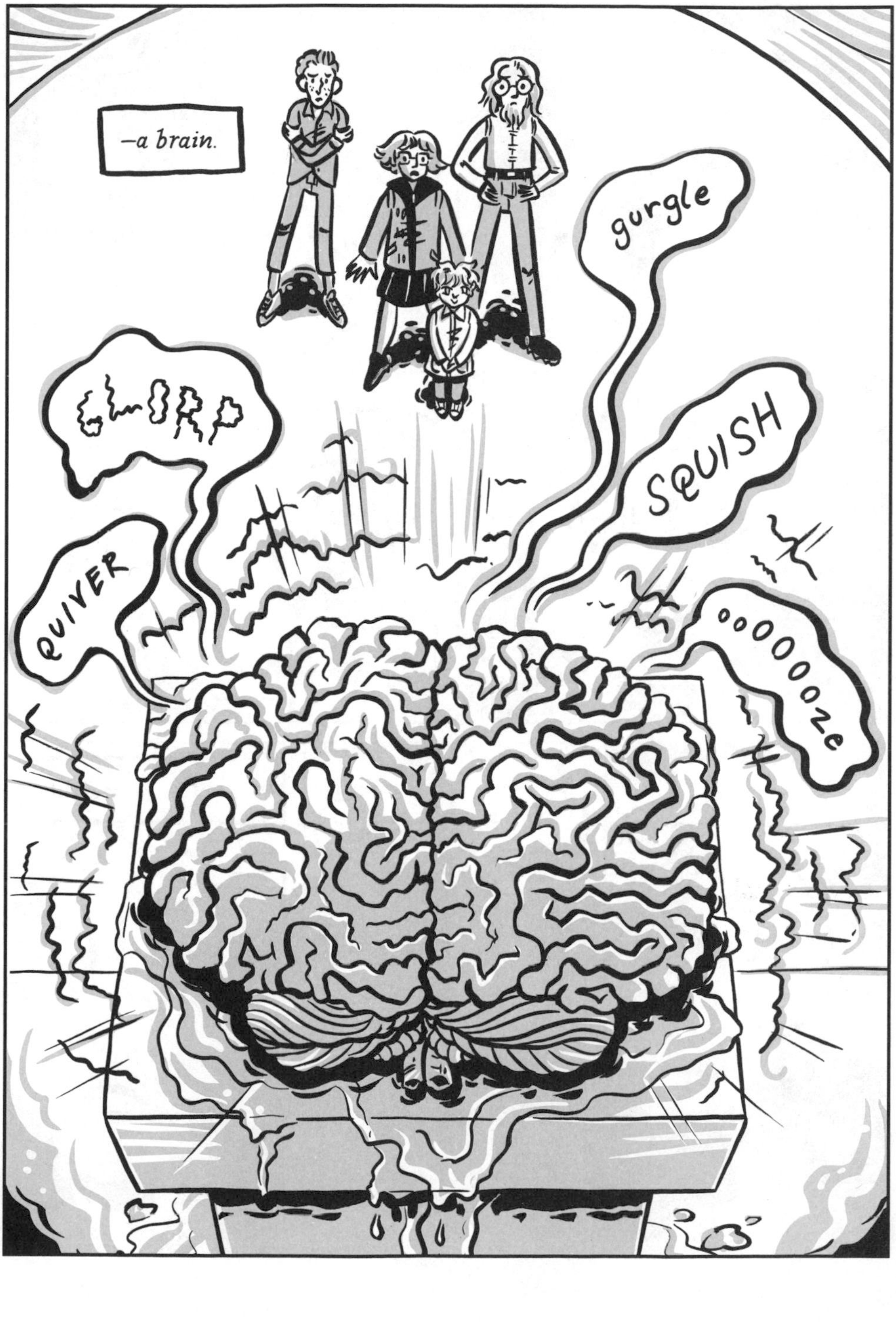
—a brain.
GLORP
gurgle
SQUISH
QUIVER
ooOOOOoze

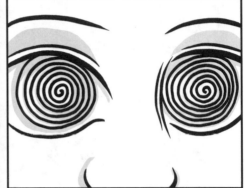

Charles's eyes—

Don't give in!

I won't!

Help, Meg!

That pulsing light—

I can *feel* it.

BA

In my heart.

DUM

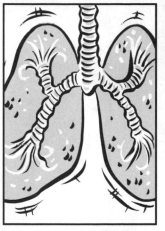

In my lungs.

IT's trying to—

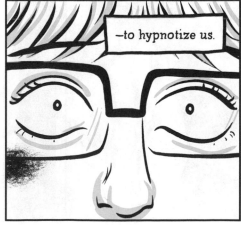

—to hypnotize us.

289

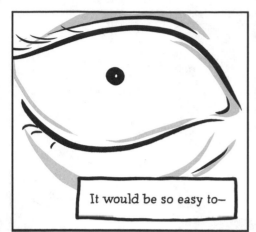

It would be so easy to—

—let go.

Meg.

I give you your faults.

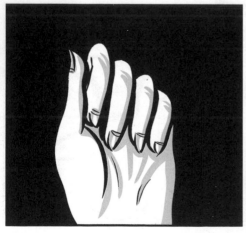

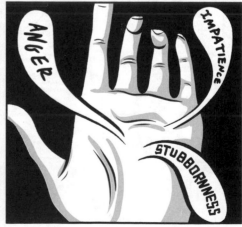

ANGER

IMPATIENCE

STUBBORNNESS

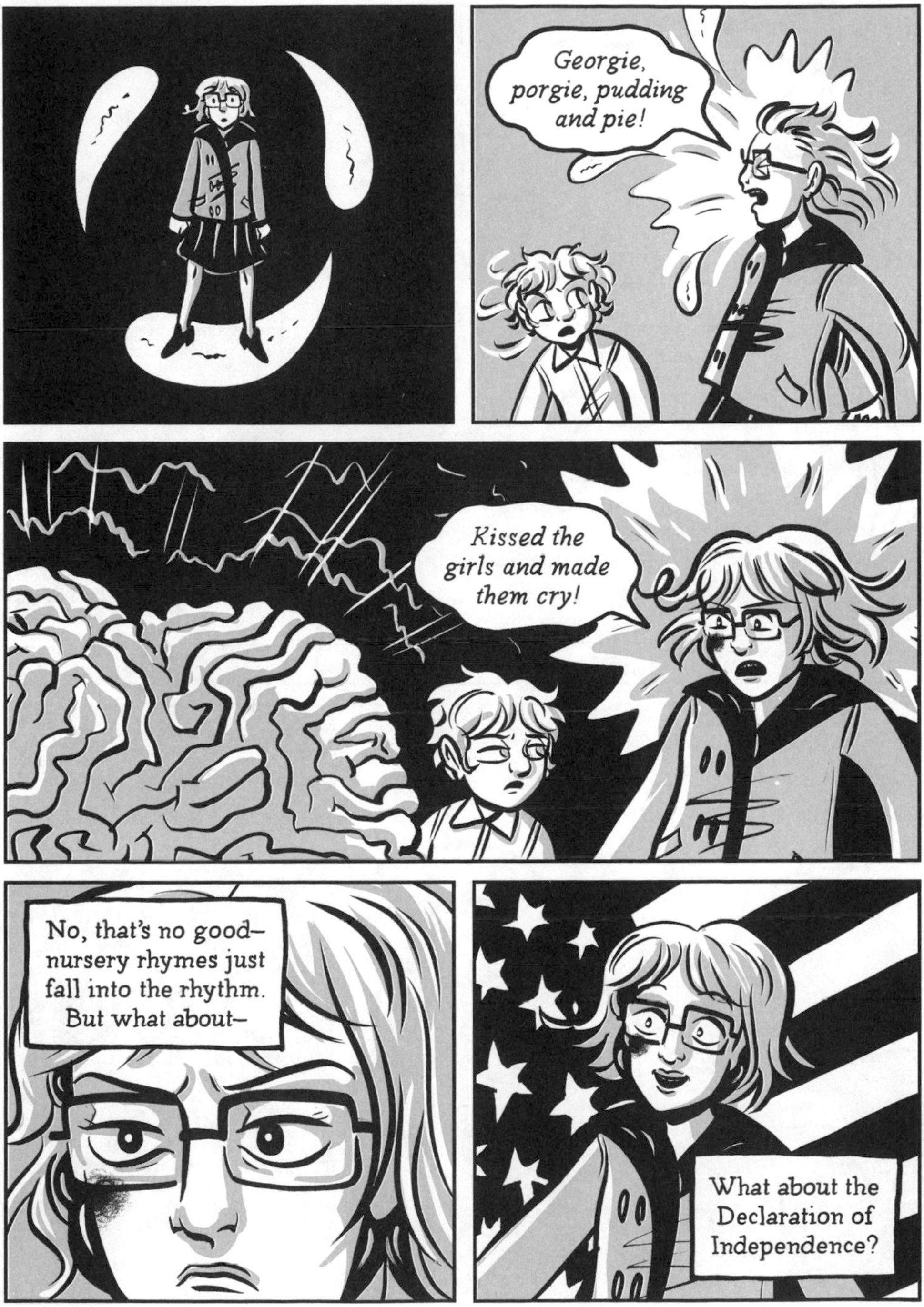
Georgie, porgie, pudding and pie!
Kissed the girls and made them cry!
No, that's no good—nursery rhymes just fall into the rhythm. But what about—
What about the Declaration of Independence?

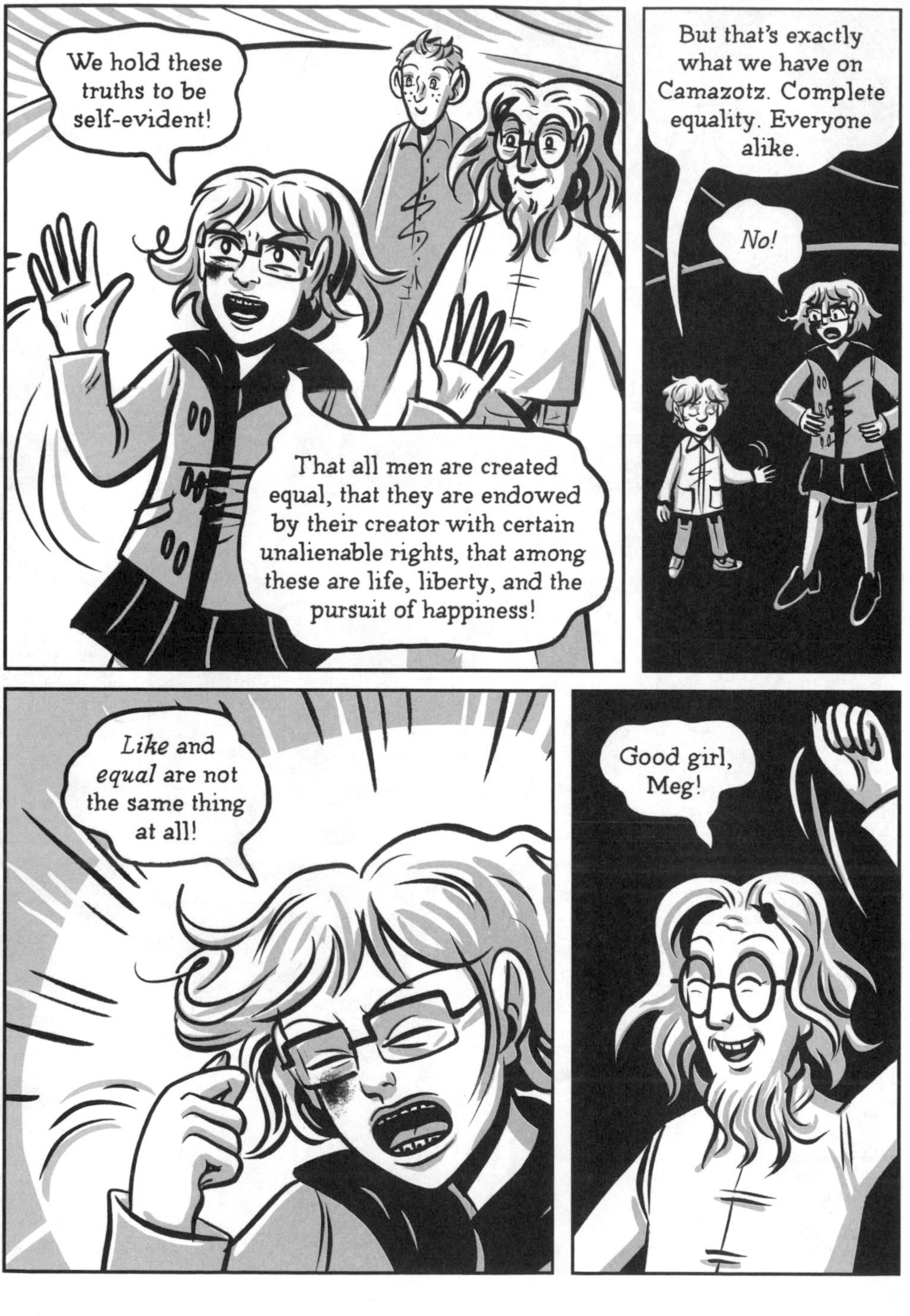
We hold these truths to be self-evident!
That all men are created equal, that they are endowed by their creator with certain unalienable rights, that among these are life, liberty, and the pursuit of happiness!
But that's exactly what we have on Camazotz. Complete equality. Everyone alike.
No!
Like and *equal* are not the same thing at all!
Good girl, Meg!

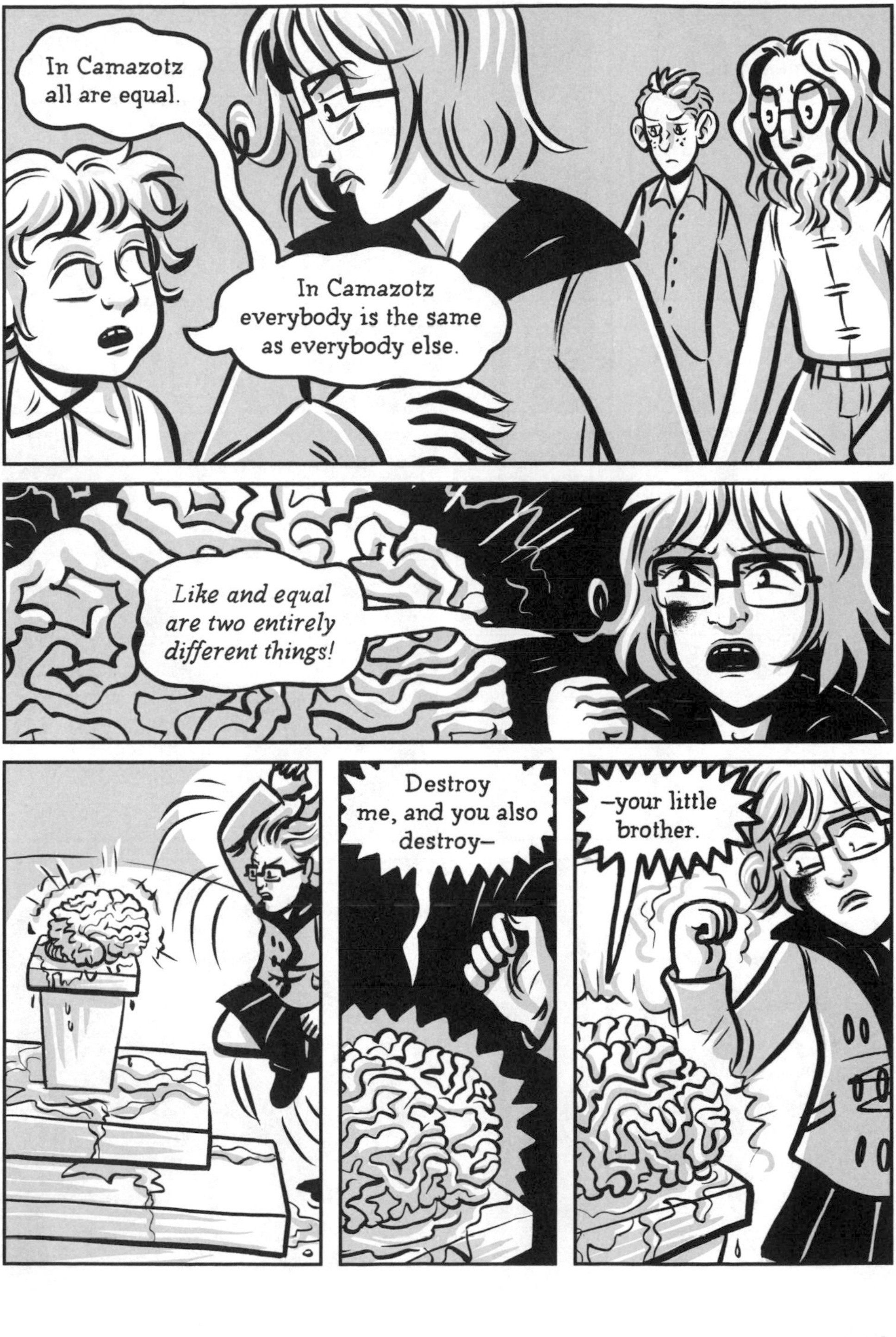
In Camazotz all are equal.
In Camazotz everybody is the same as everybody else.
Like and equal are two entirely different things!
Destroy me, and you also destroy—
—your little brother.

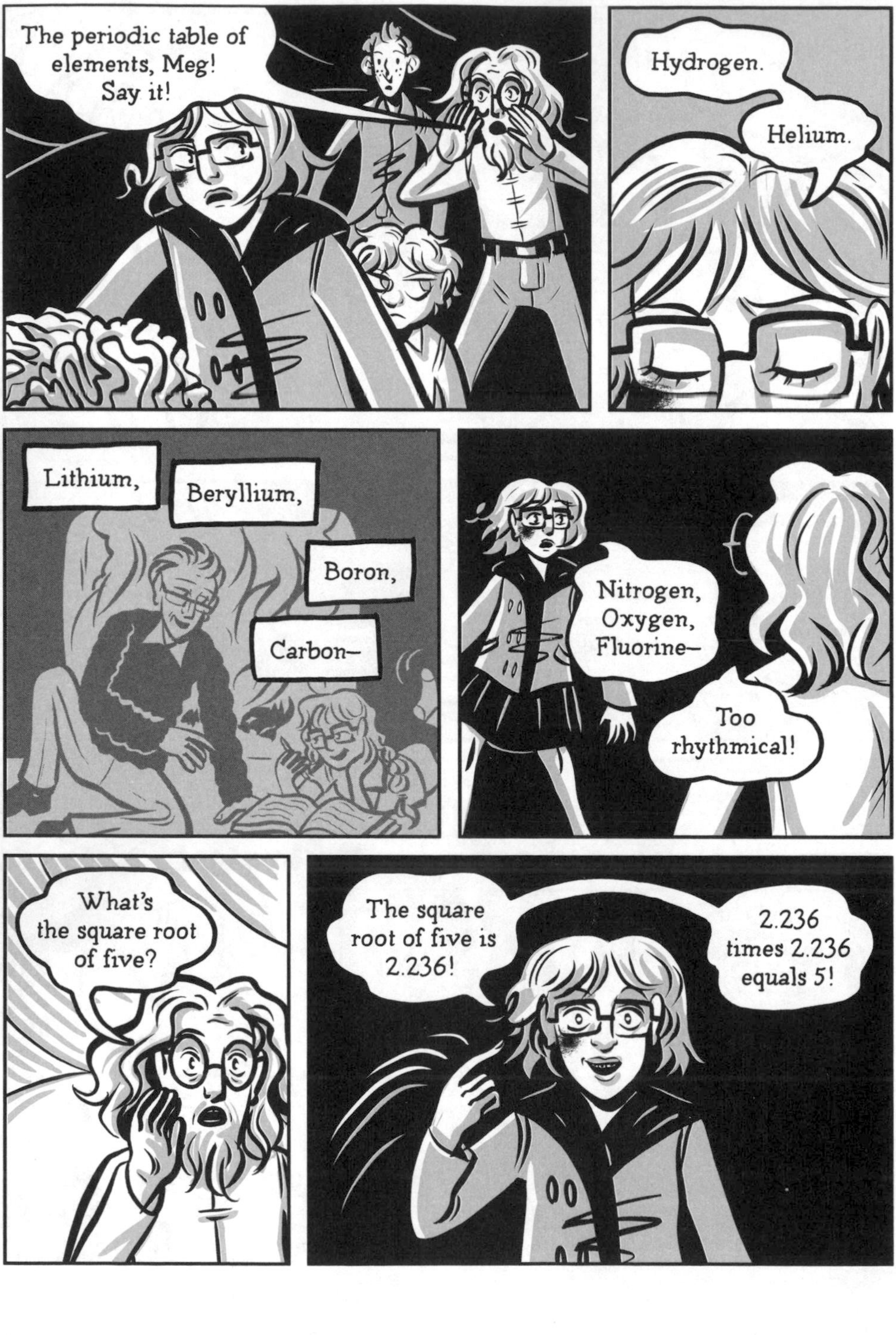
The periodic table of elements, Meg! Say it!
Hydrogen.
Helium.
Lithium,
Beryllium,
Boron,
Carbon—
Nitrogen, Oxygen, Fluorine—
Too rhythmical!
What's the square root of five?
The square root of five is 2.236!
2.236 times 2.236 equals 5!

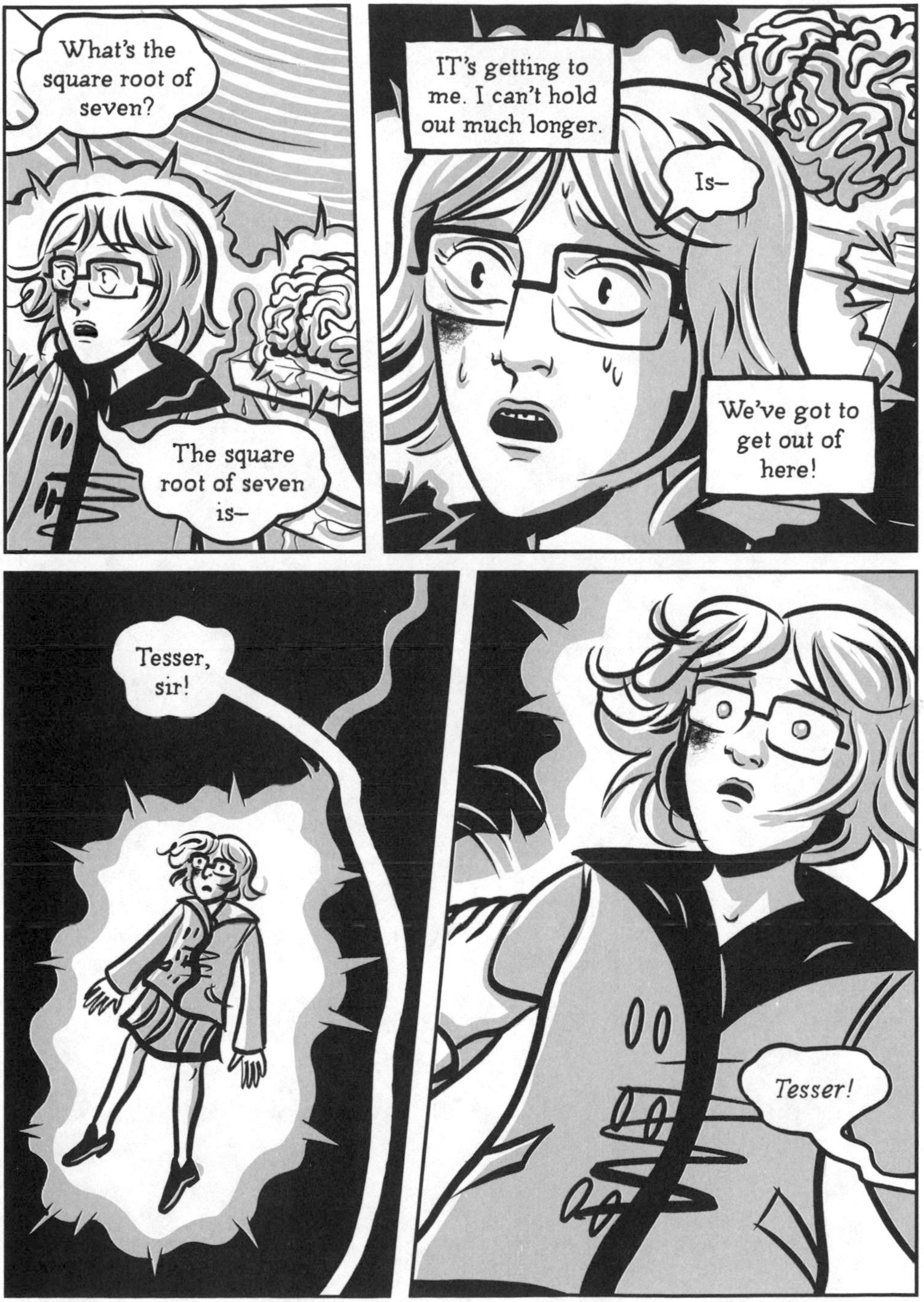
What's the square root of seven?
The square root of seven is—
IT's getting to me. I can't hold out much longer.
Is—
We've got to get out of here!
Tesser, sir!
Tesser!

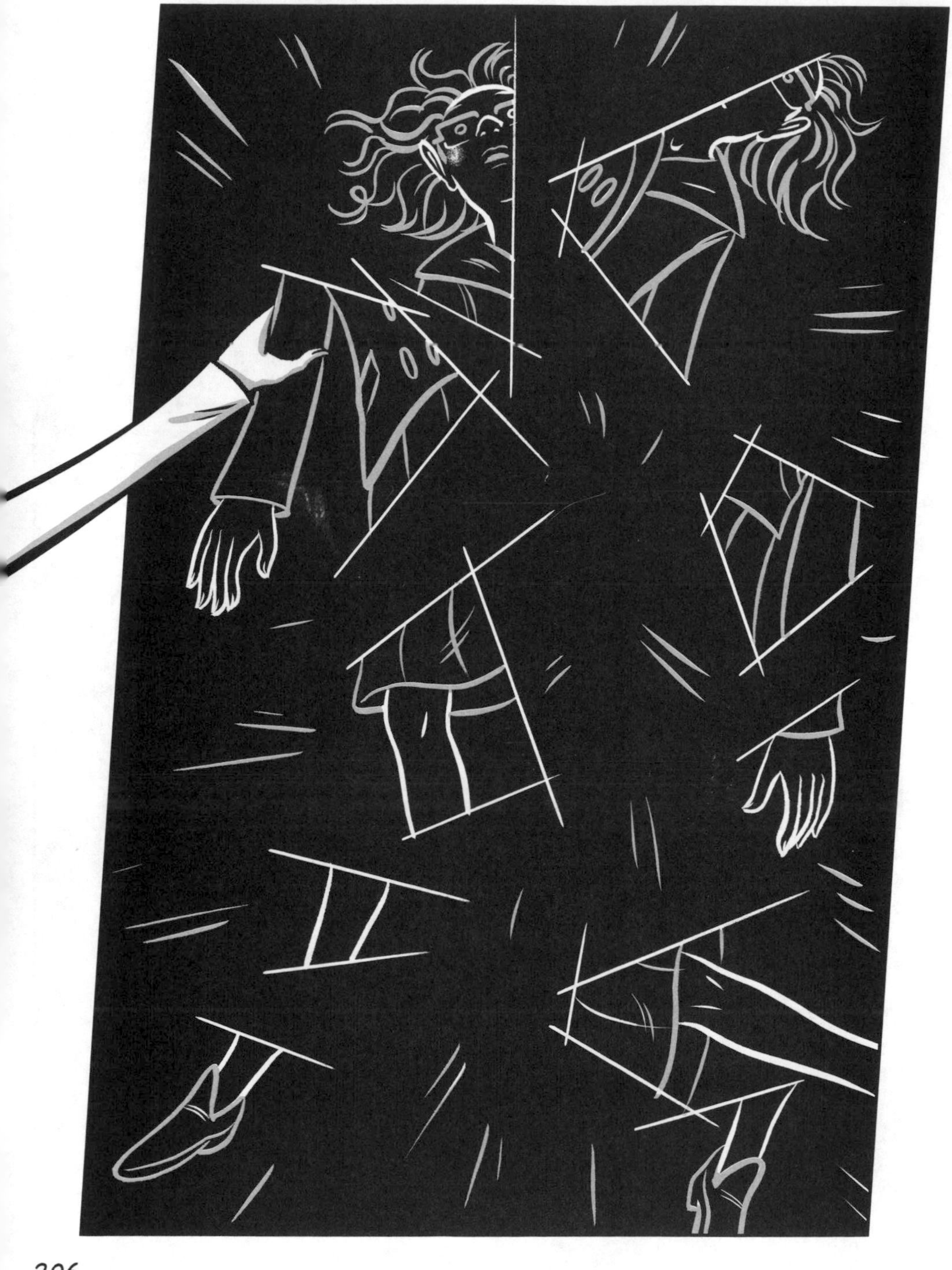

10
Absolute Zero

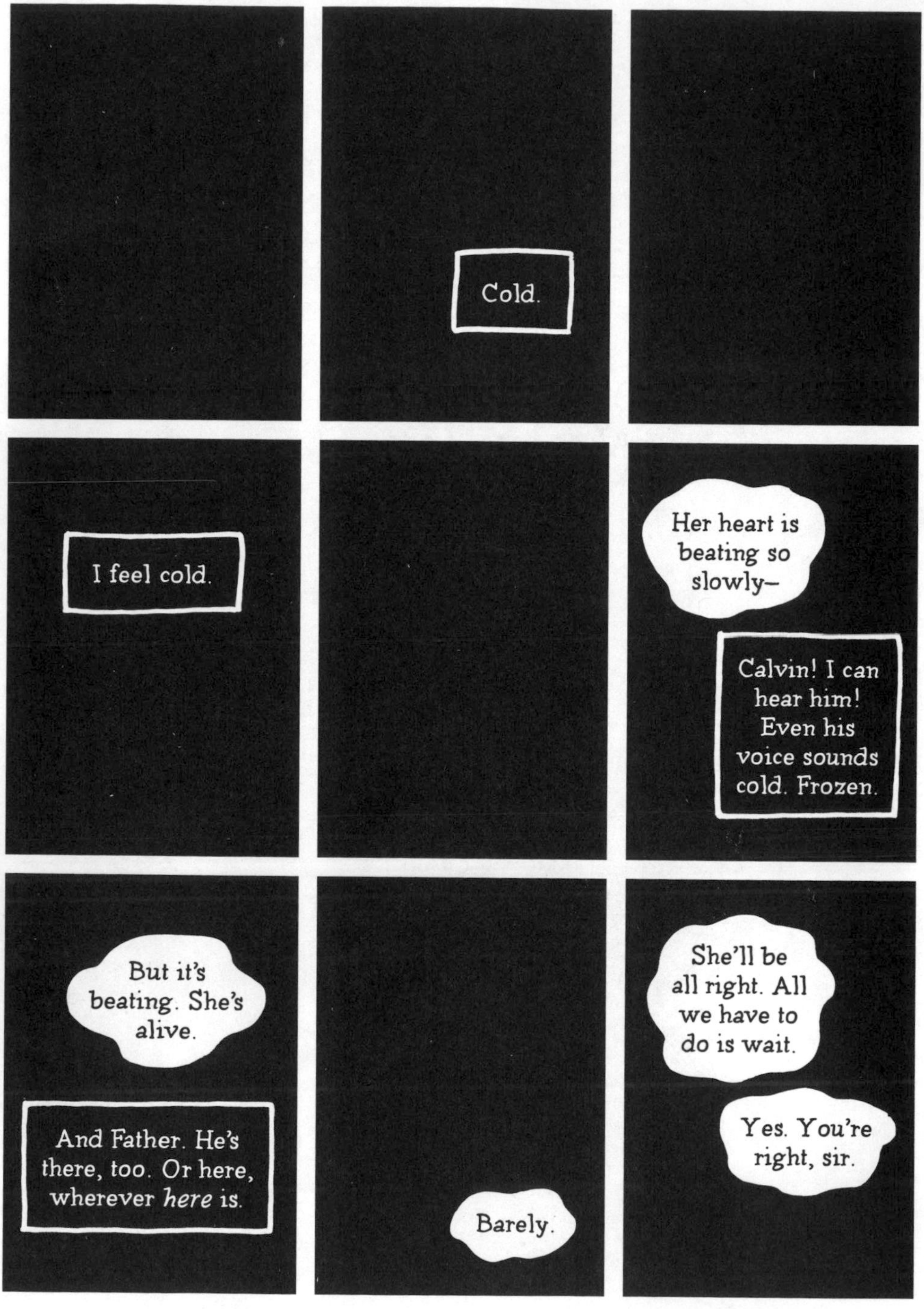
Cold.
I feel cold.
Her heart is beating so slowly—
Calvin! I can hear him! Even his voice sounds cold. Frozen.
But it's beating. She's alive.
And Father. He's there, too. Or here, wherever *here* is.
Barely.
She'll be all right. All we have to do is wait.
Yes. You're right, sir.

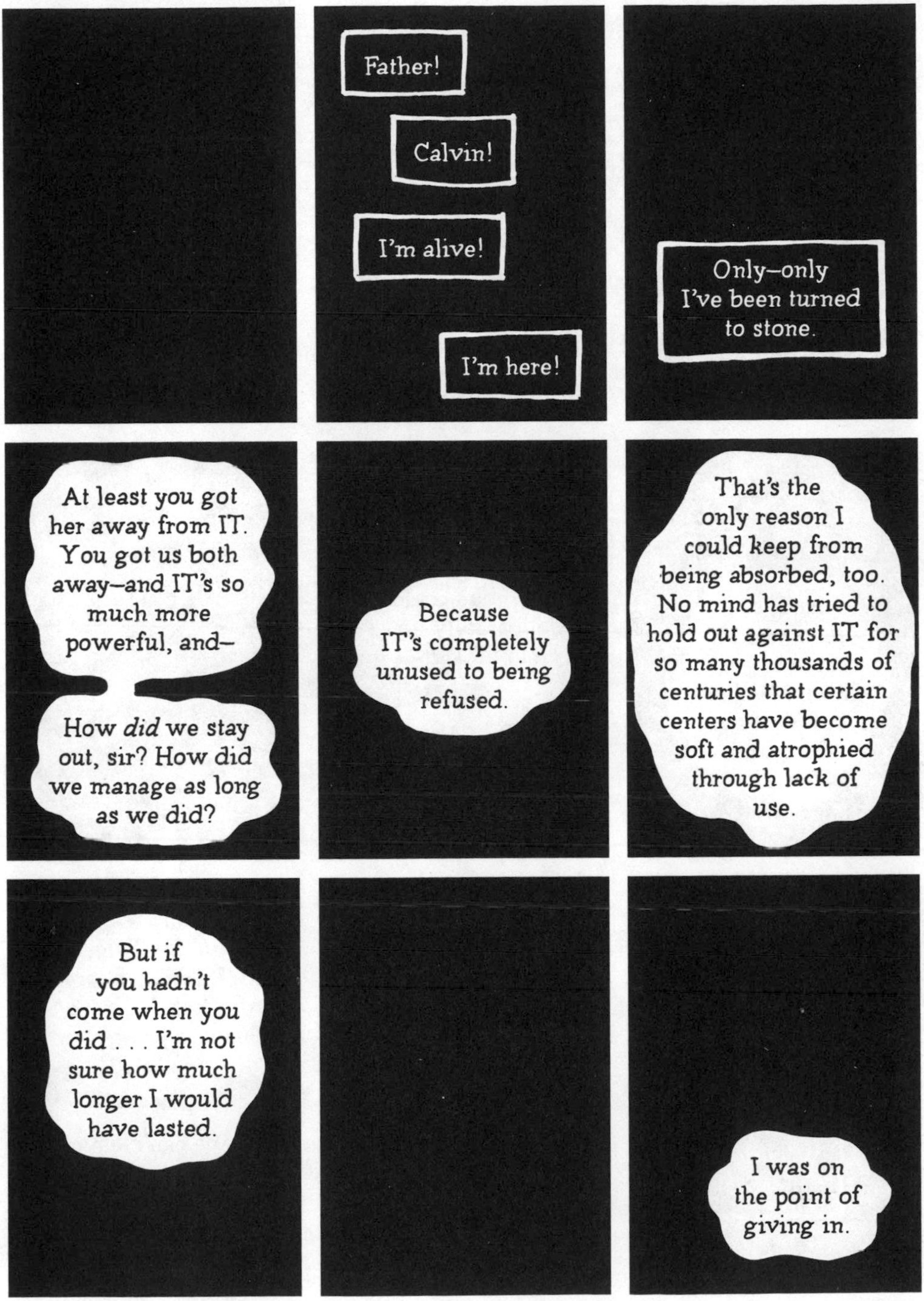
Father!
Calvin!
I'm alive!
I'm here!
Only—only I've been turned to stone.
At least you got her away from IT. You got us both away—and IT's so much more powerful, and—
How *did* we stay out, sir? How did we manage as long as we did?
Because IT's completely unused to being refused.
That's the only reason I could keep from being absorbed, too. No mind has tried to hold out against IT for so many thousands of centuries that certain centers have become soft and atrophied through lack of use.
But if you hadn't come when you did . . . I'm not sure how much longer I would have lasted.
I was on the point of giving in.

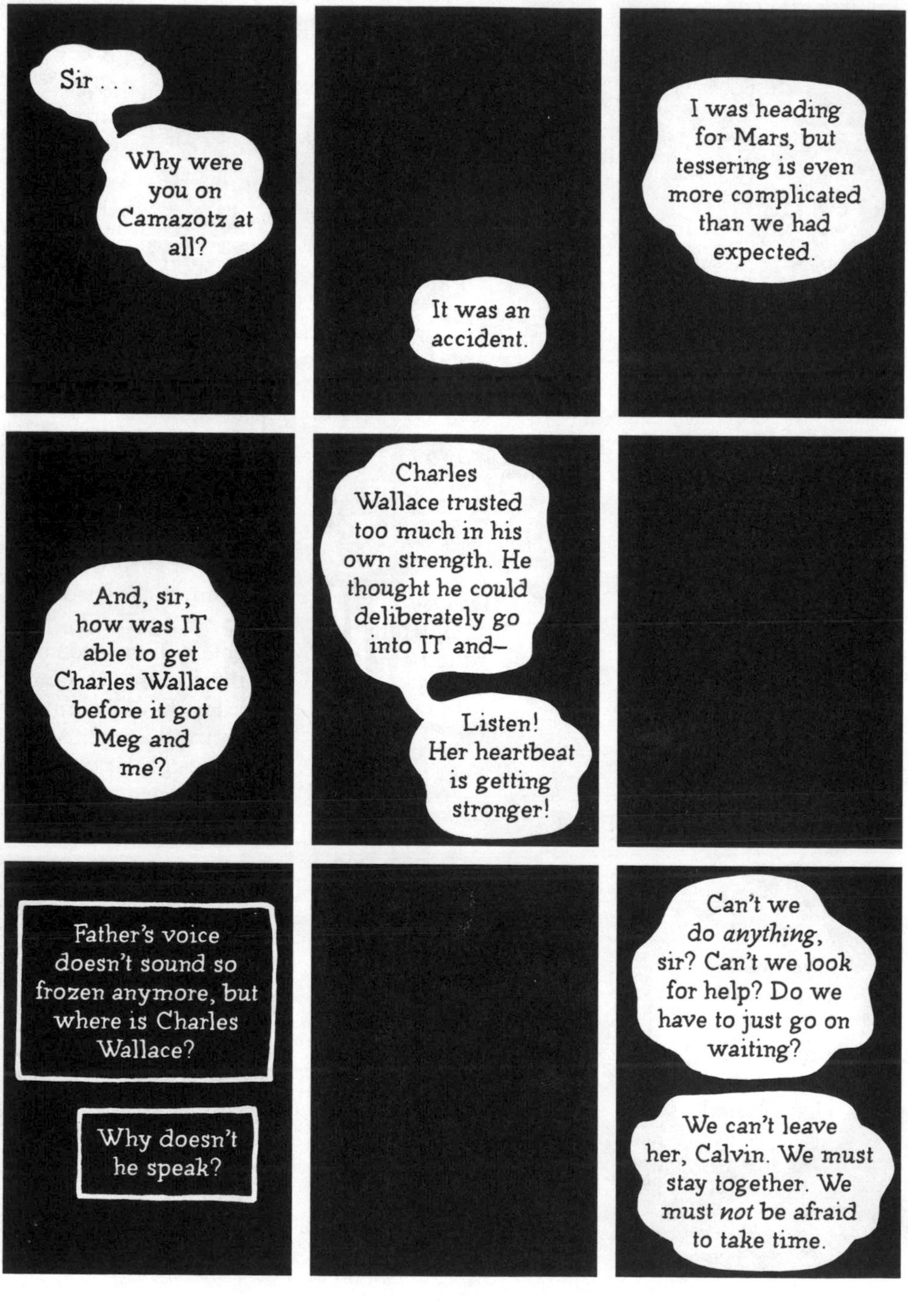
Sir . . .
Why were you on Camazotz at all?
It was an accident.
I was heading for Mars, but tessering is even more complicated than we had expected.
And, sir, how was IT able to get Charles Wallace before it got Meg and me?
Charles Wallace trusted too much in his own strength. He thought he could deliberately go into IT and–
Listen! Her heartbeat is getting stronger!
Father's voice doesn't sound so frozen anymore, but where is Charles Wallace?
Why doesn't he speak?
Can't we do *anything*, sir? Can't we look for help? Do we have to just go on waiting?
We can't leave her, Calvin. We must stay together. We must *not* be afraid to take time.

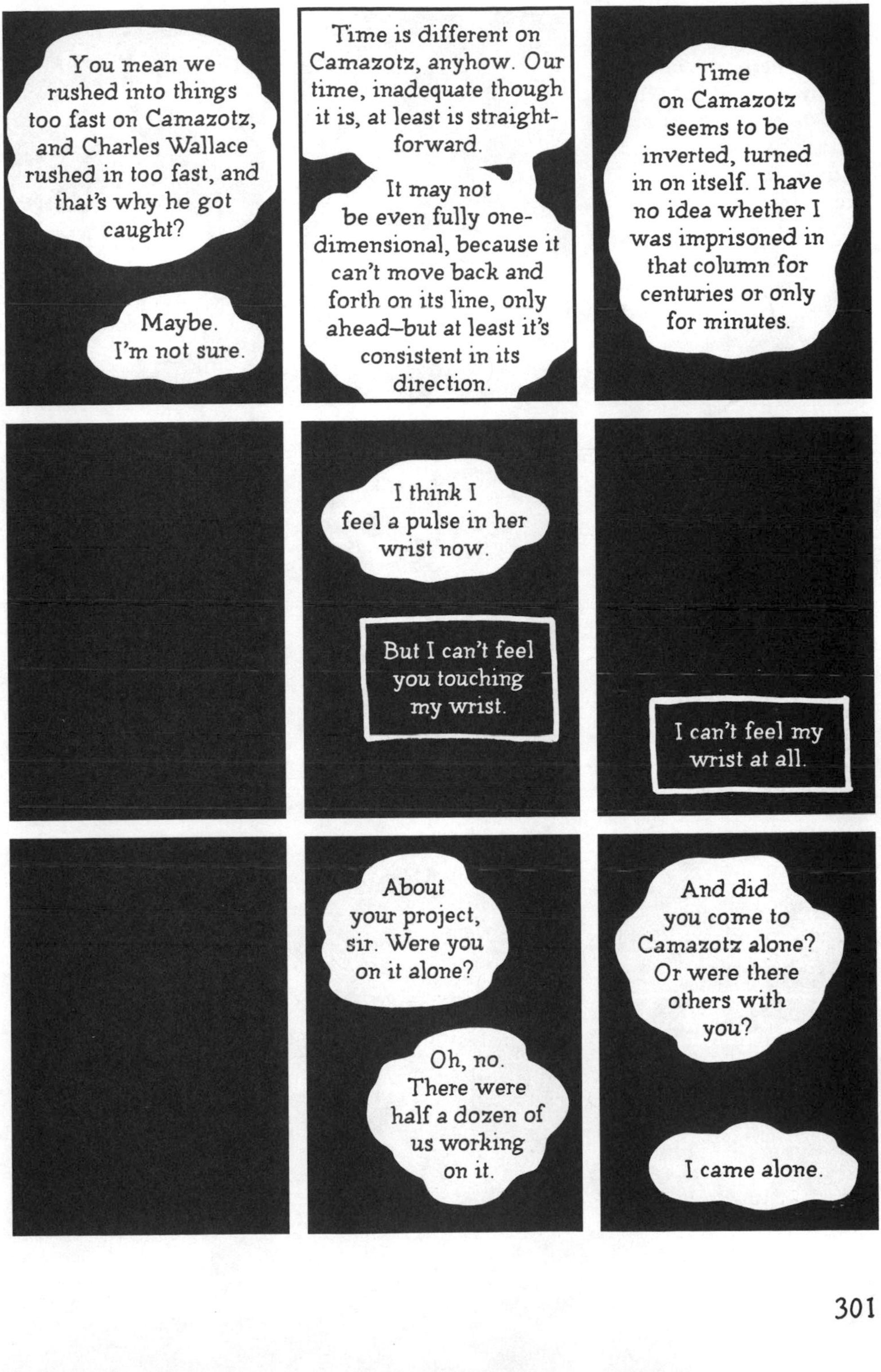
You mean we rushed into things too fast on Camazotz, and Charles Wallace rushed in too fast, and that's why he got caught?
Maybe. I'm not sure.
Time is different on Camazotz, anyhow. Our time, inadequate though it is, at least is straight-forward.
It may not be even fully one-dimensional, because it can't move back and forth on its line, only ahead–but at least it's consistent in its direction.
Time on Camazotz seems to be inverted, turned in on itself. I have no idea whether I was imprisoned in that column for centuries or only for minutes.
I think I feel a pulse in her wrist now.
But I can't feel you touching my wrist.
I can't feel my wrist at all.
About your project, sir. Were you on it alone?
Oh, no. There were half a dozen of us working on it.
And did you come to Camazotz alone? Or were there others with you?
I came alone.

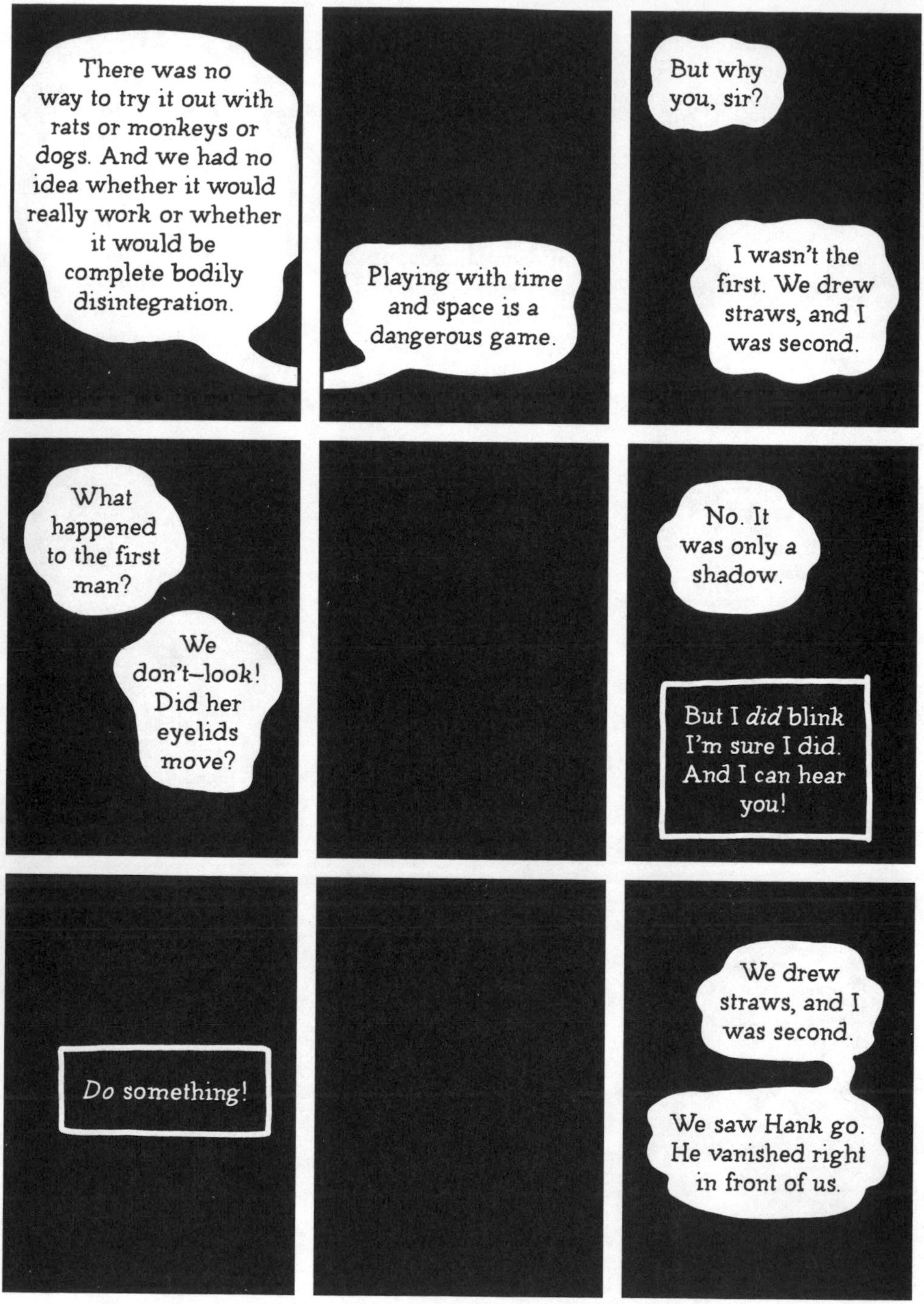
There was no way to try it out with rats or monkeys or dogs. And we had no idea whether it would really work or whether it would be complete bodily disintegration.
Playing with time and space is a dangerous game.
But why you, sir?
I wasn't the first. We drew straws, and I was second.
What happened to the first man?
We don't—look! Did her eyelids move?
No. It was only a shadow.
But I *did* blink I'm sure I did. And I can hear you!
Do something!
We drew straws, and I was second.
We saw Hank go. He vanished right in front of us.

We waited a year for his return, for a message.

But . . . Nothing.

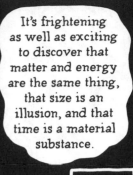

It's frightening as well as exciting to discover that matter and energy are the same thing, that size is an illusion, and that time is a material substance.

Father.

We can know this, but it's far more than we can understand with our puny little brains.

I think you will be able to comprehend far more than I—and Charles Wallace even more than—

Father!

Father!

Gnnnrrgh!

Meg!

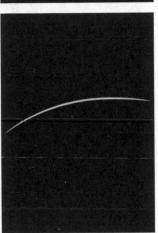

Can you feel my fingers?

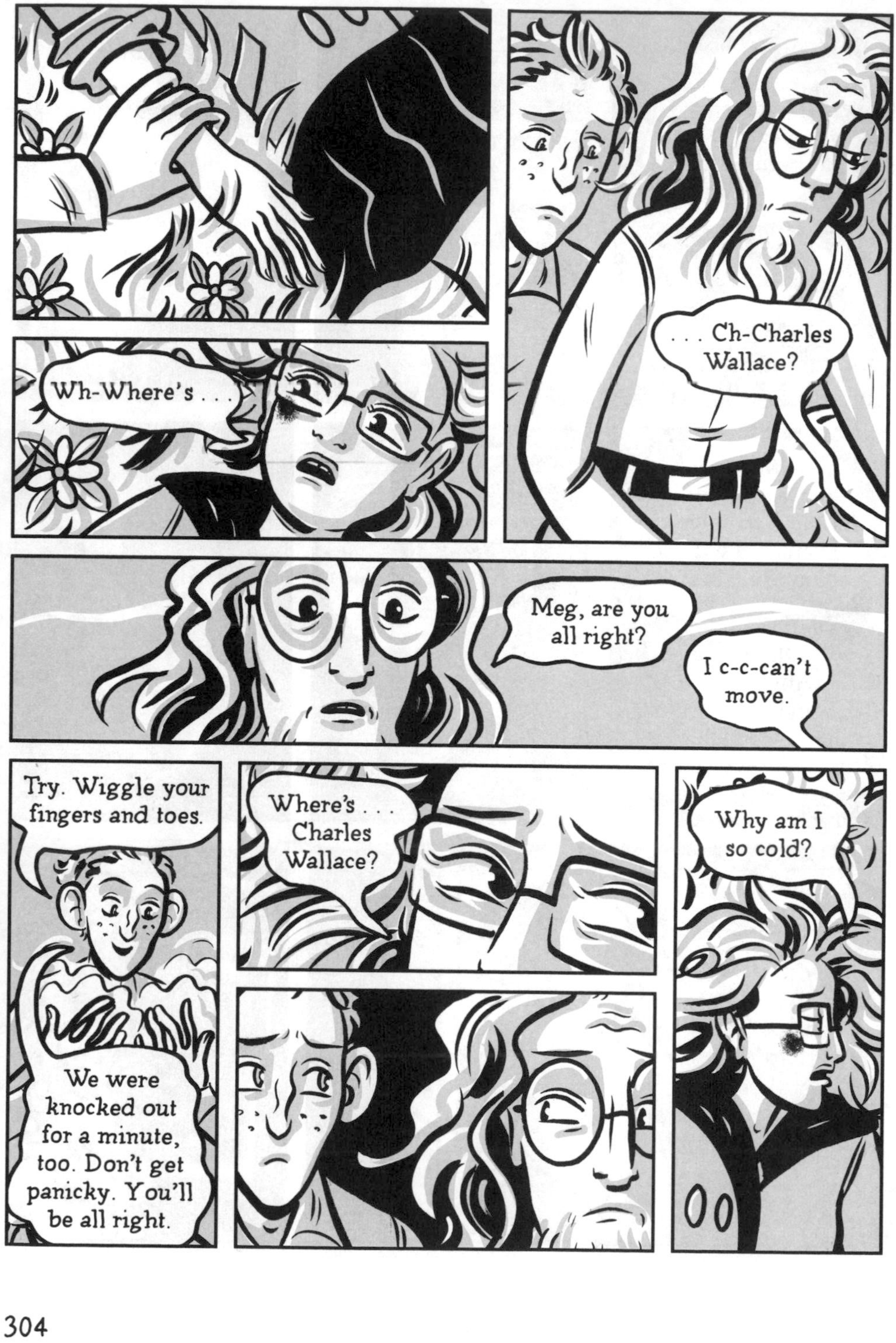
. . . Ch-Charles Wallace?
Wh-Where's . . .
Meg, are you all right?
I c-c-can't move.
Try. Wiggle your fingers and toes.
We were knocked out for a minute, too. Don't get panicky. You'll be all right.
Where's . . . Charles Wallace?
Why am I so cold?

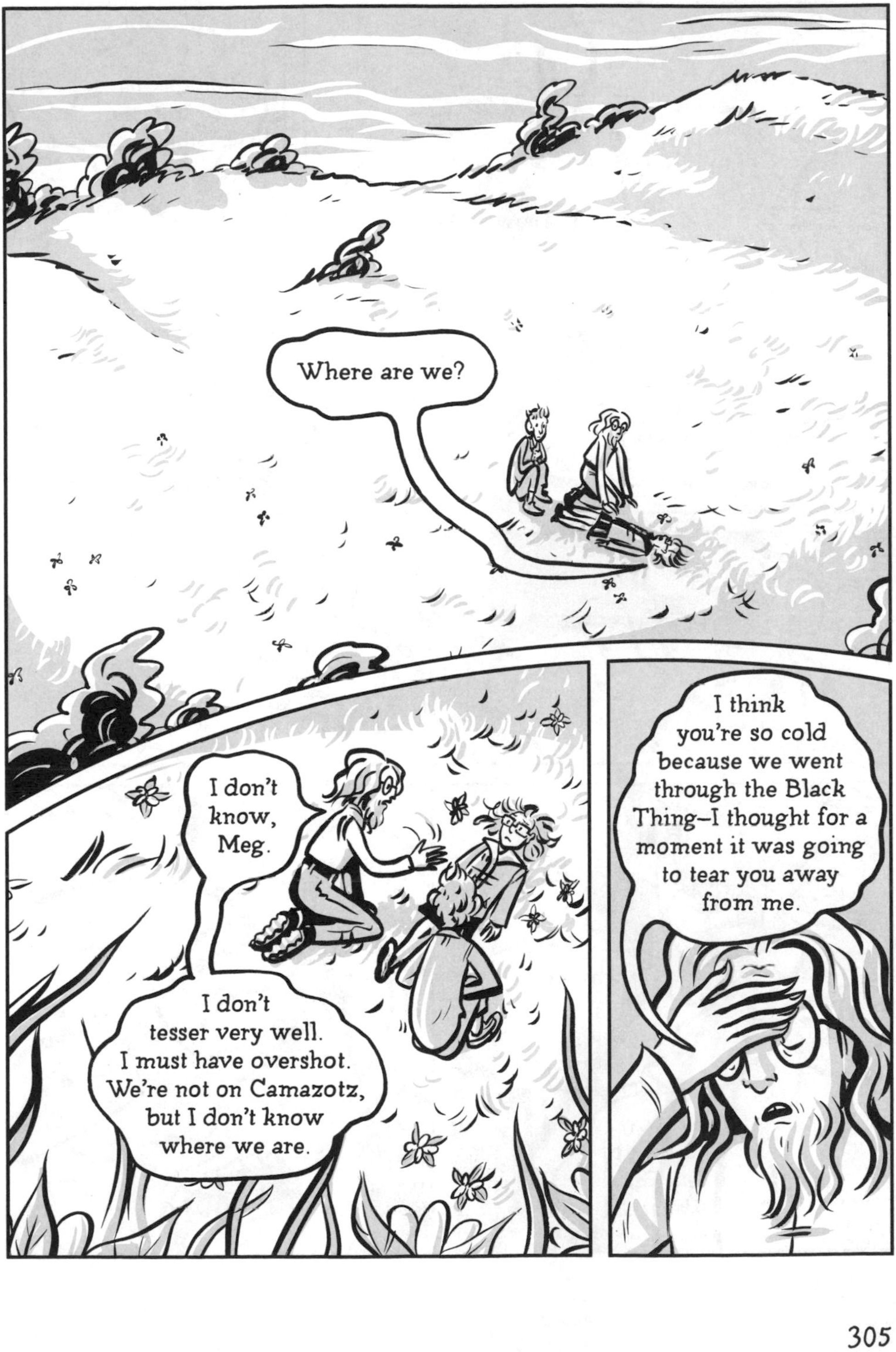
Where are we?
I don't know, Meg.
I don't tesser very well. I must have overshot. We're not on Camazotz, but I don't know where we are.
I think you're so cold because we went through the Black Thing—I thought for a moment it was going to tear you away from me.

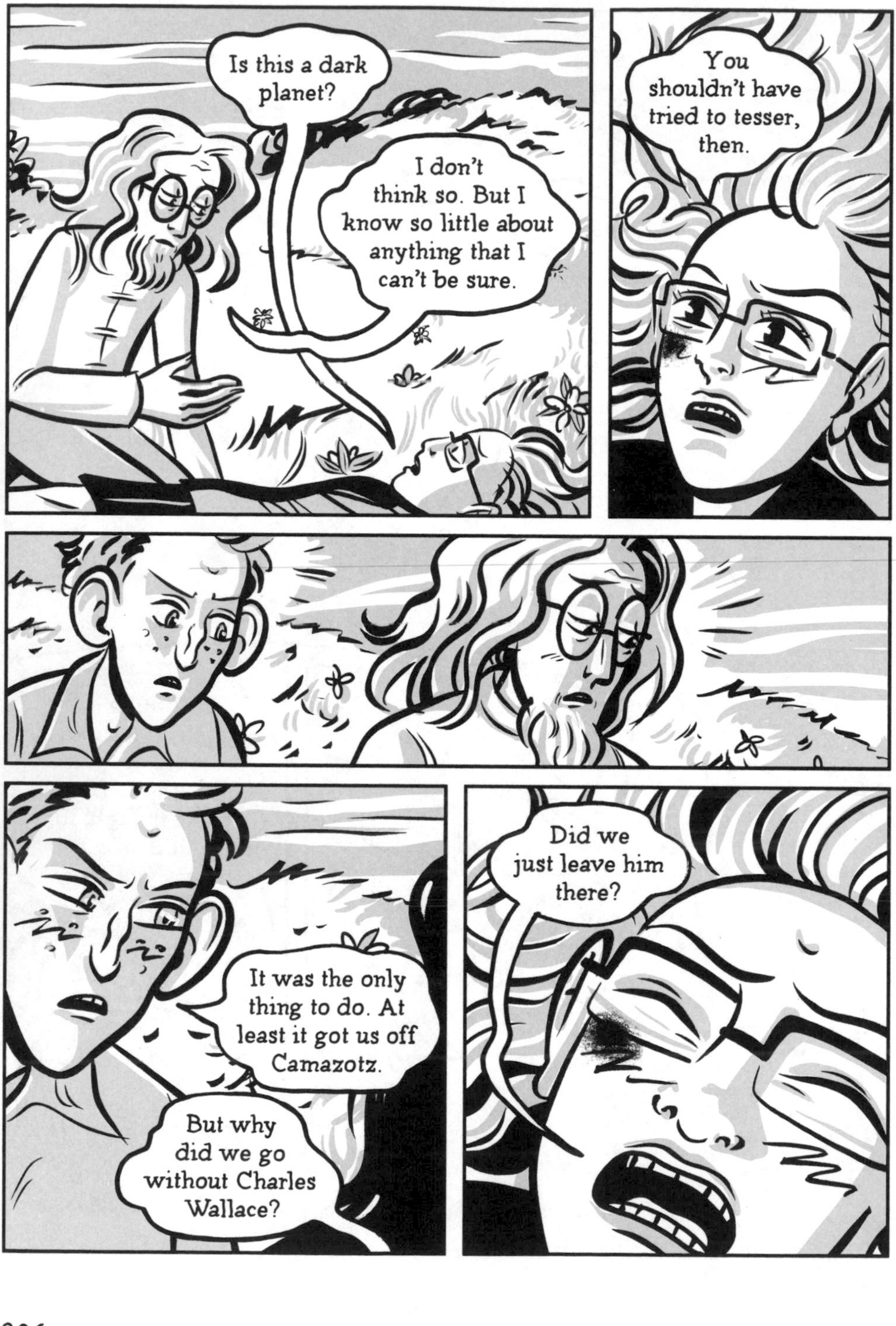
Is this a dark planet?
I don't think so. But I know so little about anything that I can't be sure.
You shouldn't have tried to tesser, then.
It was the only thing to do. At least it got us off Camazotz.
But why did we go without Charles Wallace?
Did we just leave him there?

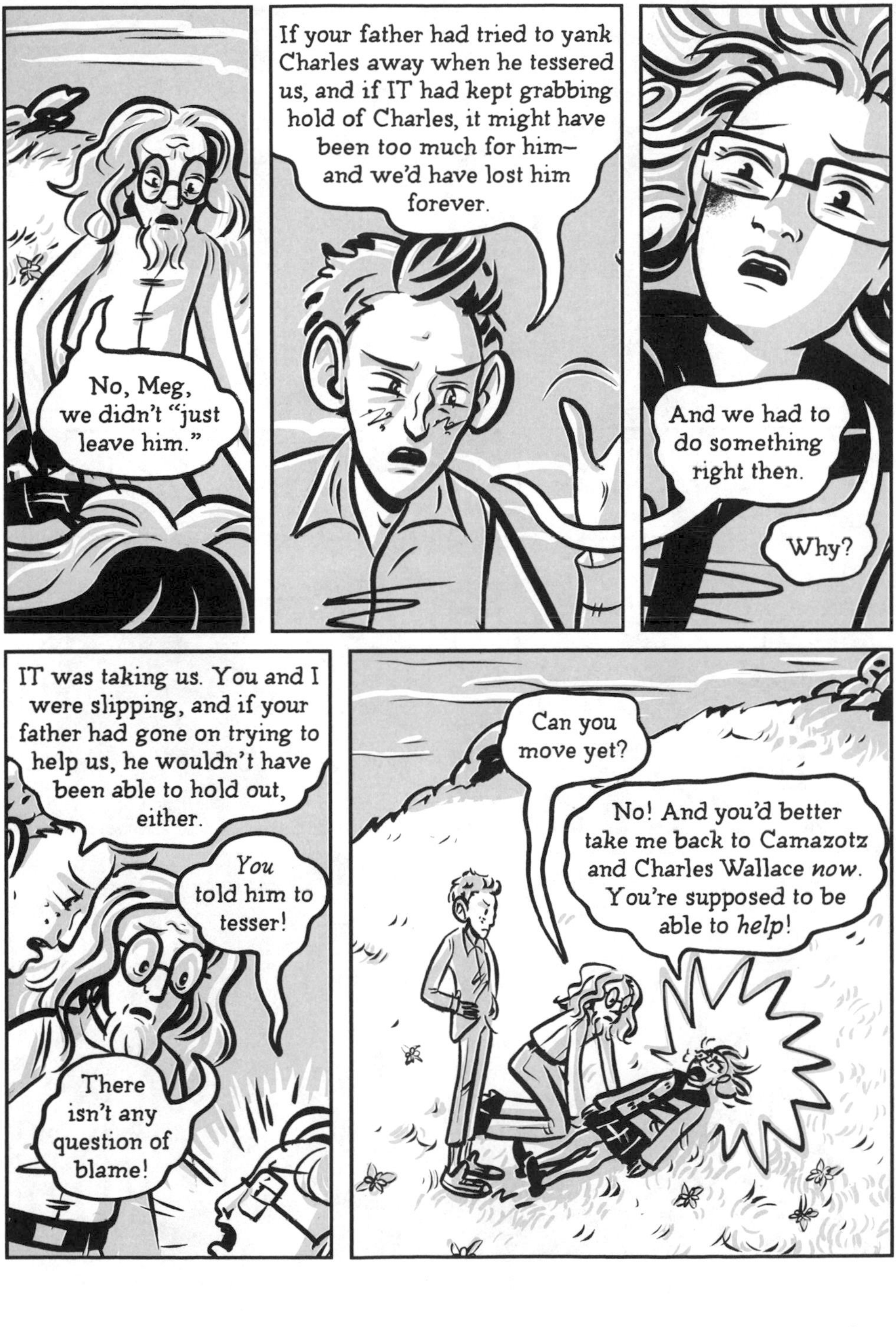

No, Meg, we didn't "just leave him."
If your father had tried to yank Charles away when he tessered us, and if IT had kept grabbing hold of Charles, it might have been too much for him— and we'd have lost him forever.
And we had to do something right then.
Why?
IT was taking us. You and I were slipping, and if your father had gone on trying to help us, he wouldn't have been able to hold out, either.
You told him to tesser!
There isn't any question of blame!
Can you move yet?
No! And you'd better take me back to Camazotz and Charles Wallace *now*. You're supposed to be able to *help*!

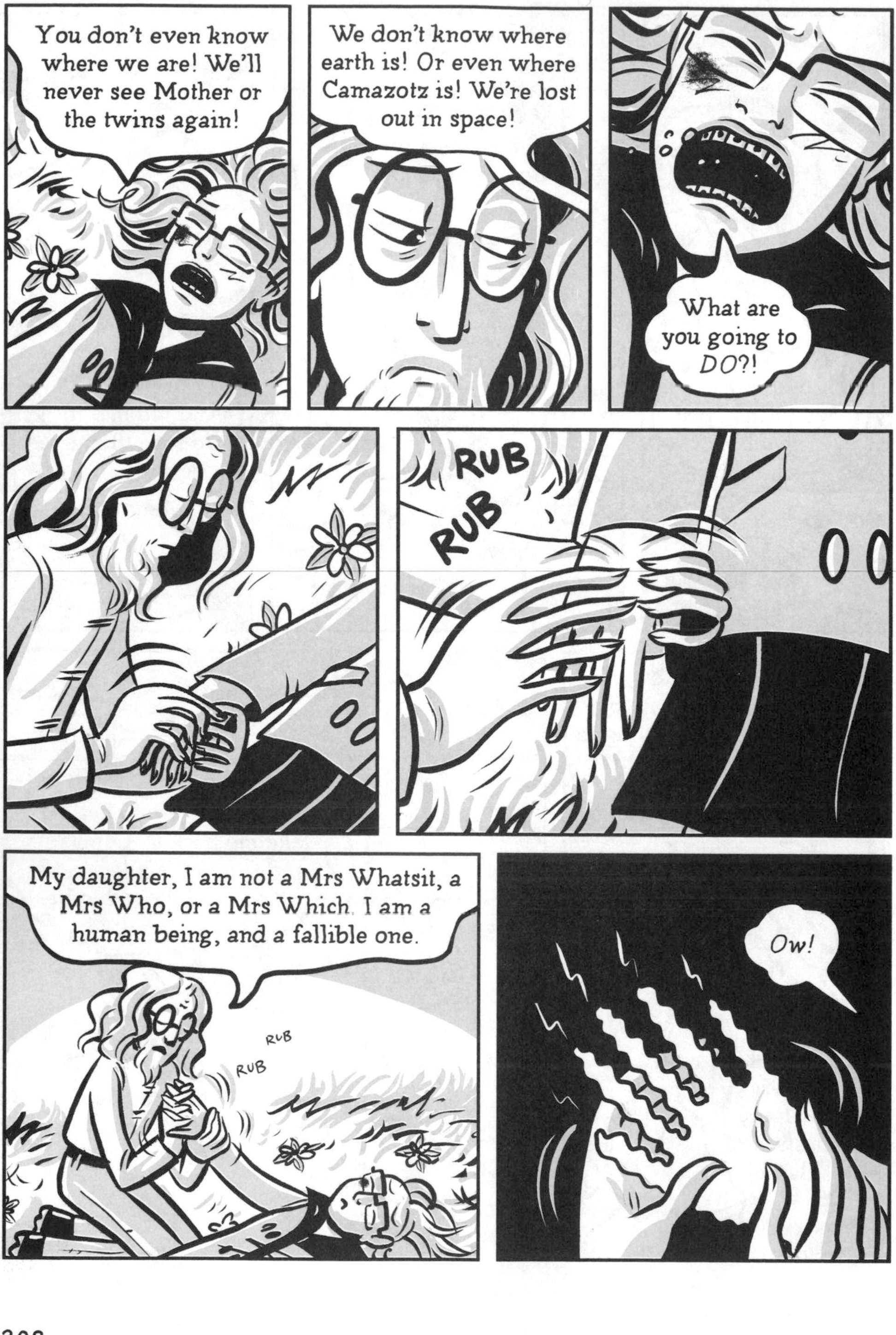
You don't even know where we are! We'll never see Mother or the twins again!
We don't know where earth is! Or even where Camazotz is! We're lost out in space!
What are you going to DO?!
RUB
RUB
My daughter, I am not a Mrs Whatsit, a Mrs Who, or a Mrs Which. I am a human being, and a fallible one.
RUB
RUB
Ow!

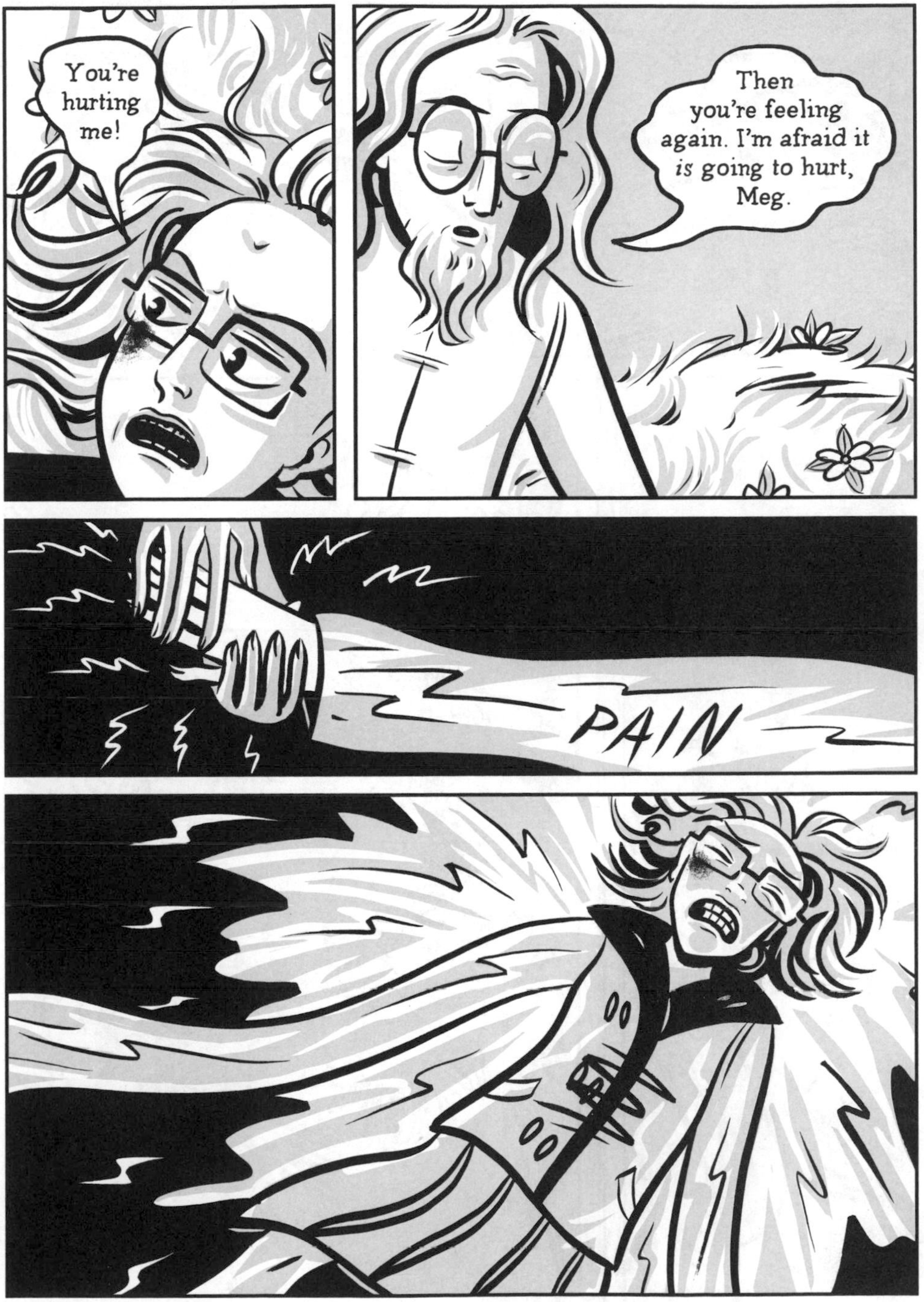
You're hurting me!
Then you're feeling again. I'm afraid it *is* going to hurt, Meg.
PAIN

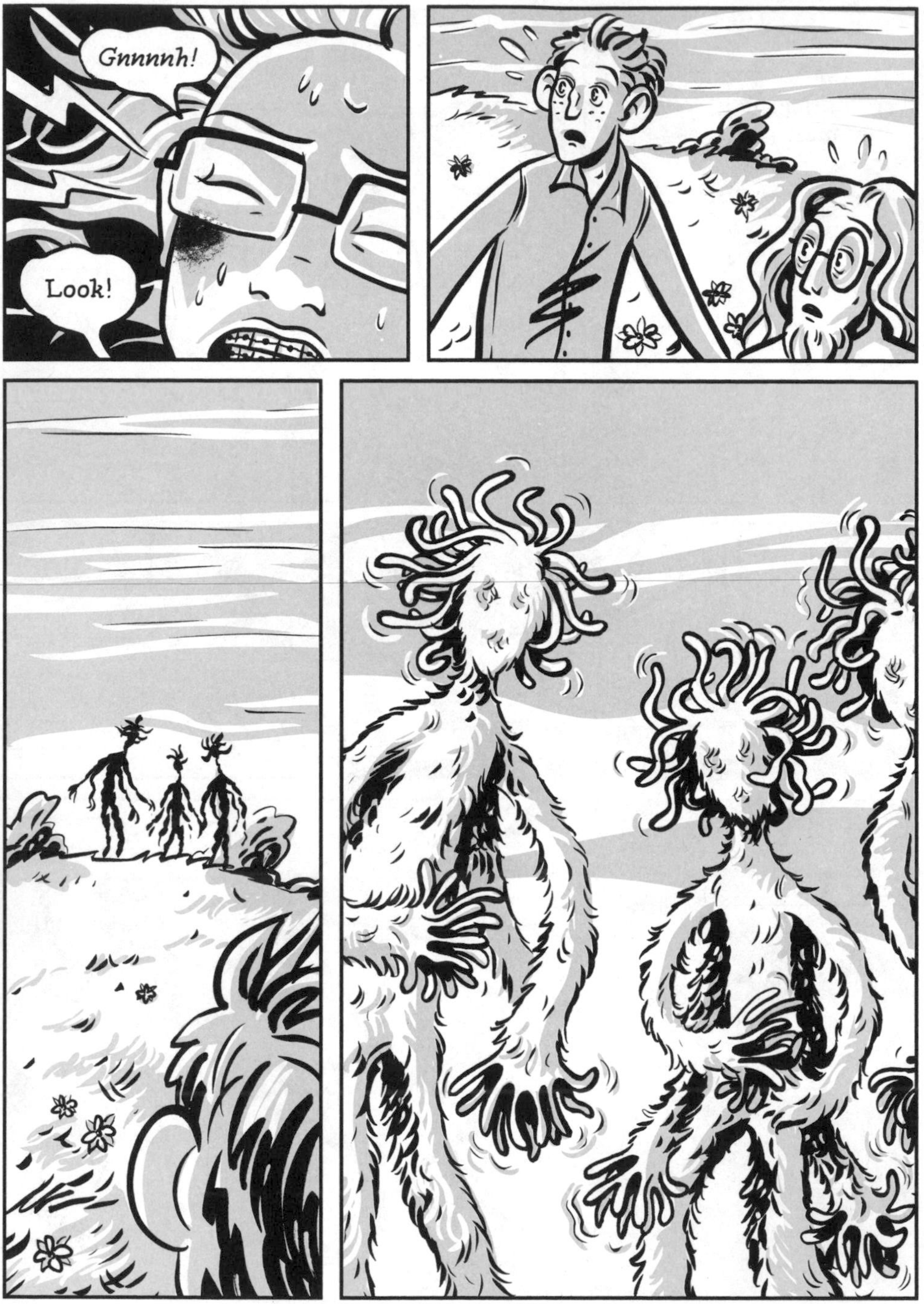
Gnnnnh!
Look!

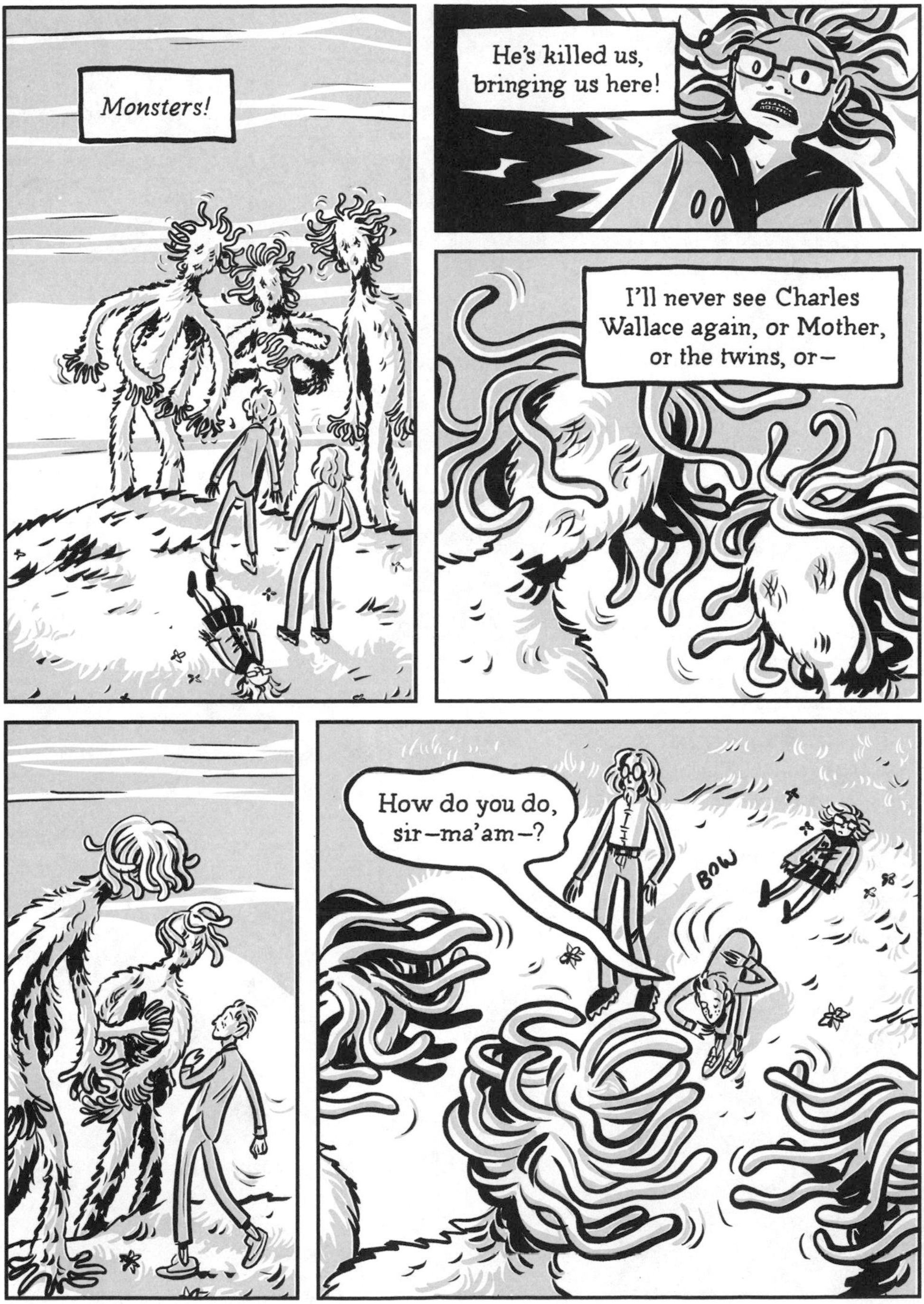
Monsters!
He's killed us, bringing us here!
I'll never see Charles Wallace again, or Mother, or the twins, or–
How do you do, sir–ma'am–?
BOW

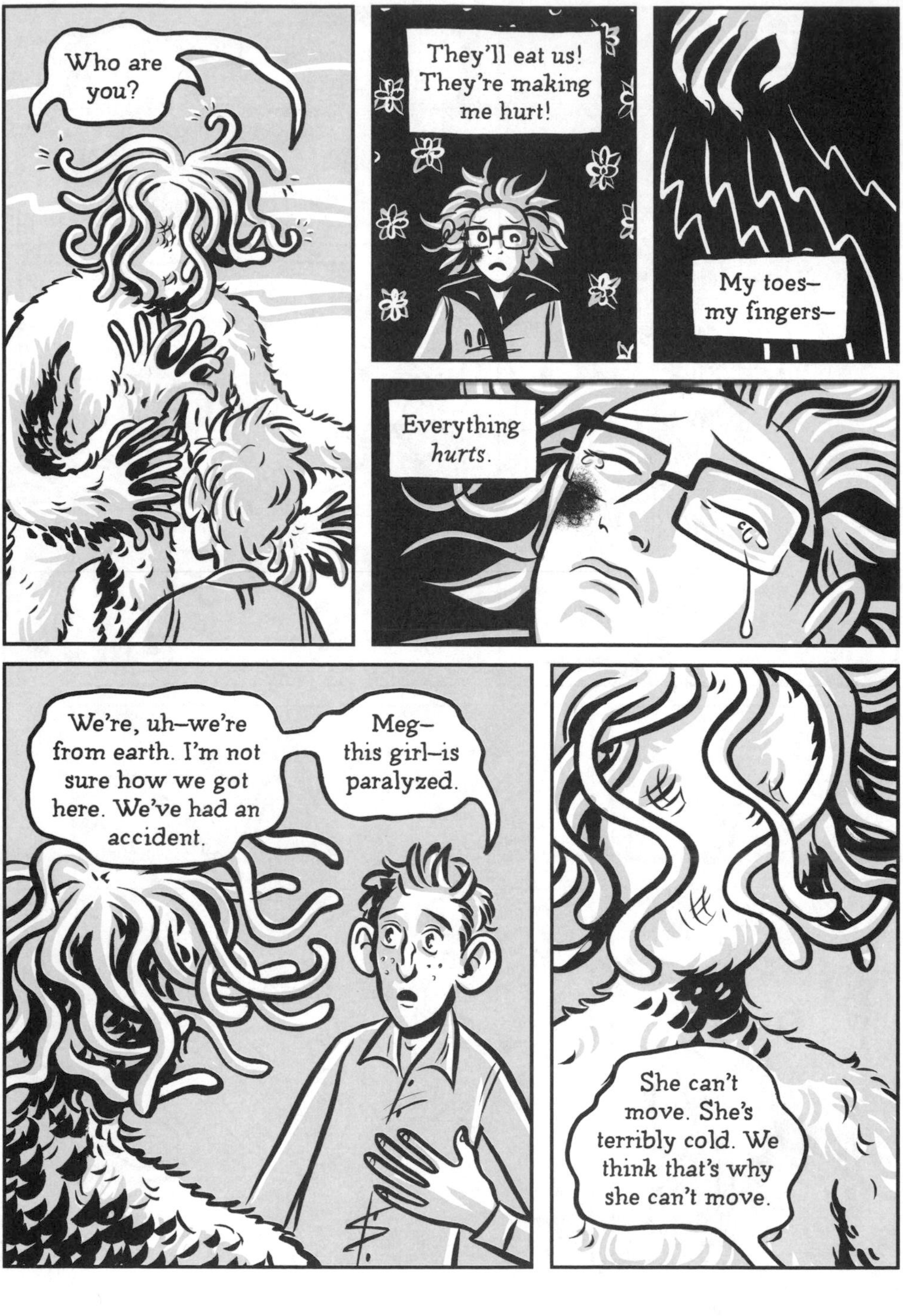
Who are you?
They'll eat us! They're making me hurt!
My toes— my fingers—
Everything *hurts*.
We're, uh—we're from earth. I'm not sure how we got here. We've had an accident.
Meg— this girl—is paralyzed.
She can't move. She's terribly cold. We think that's why she can't move.

Ugh!
No, don't—

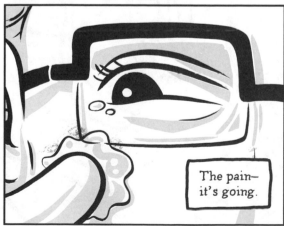

The pain—
it's going.

And what is that
wonderful smell?

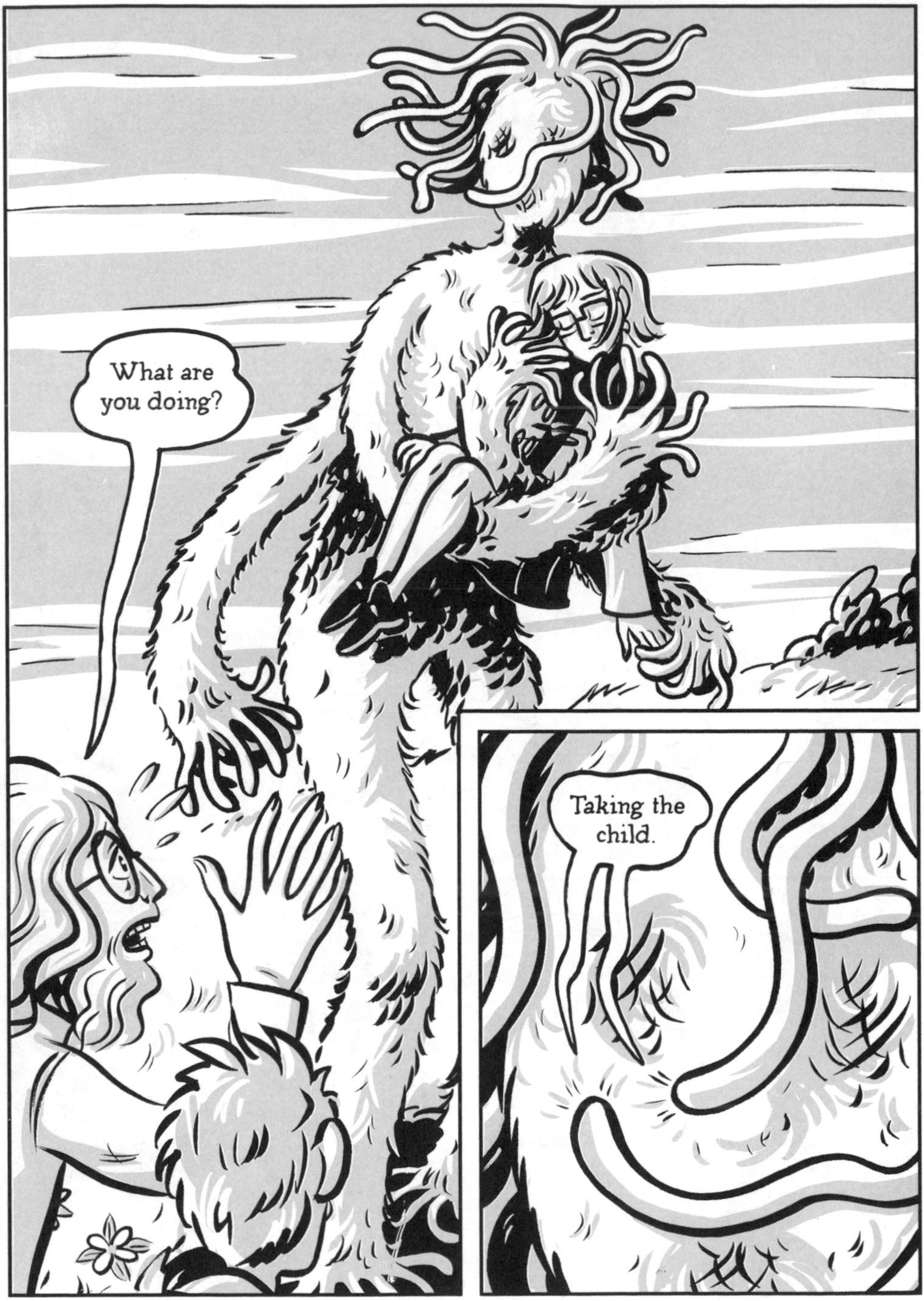
What are you doing?
Taking the child.

11
Aunt Beast

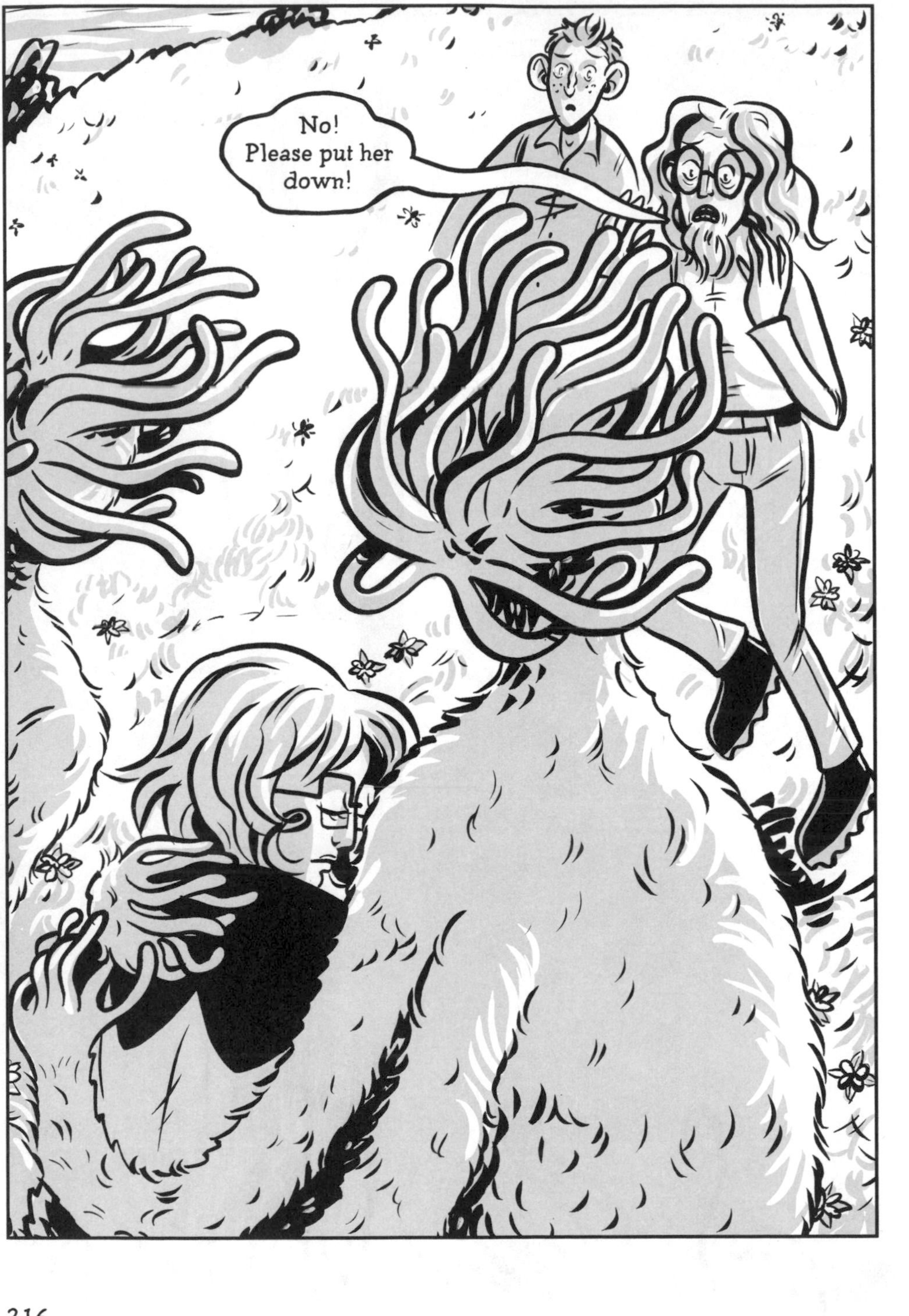
No! Please put her down!

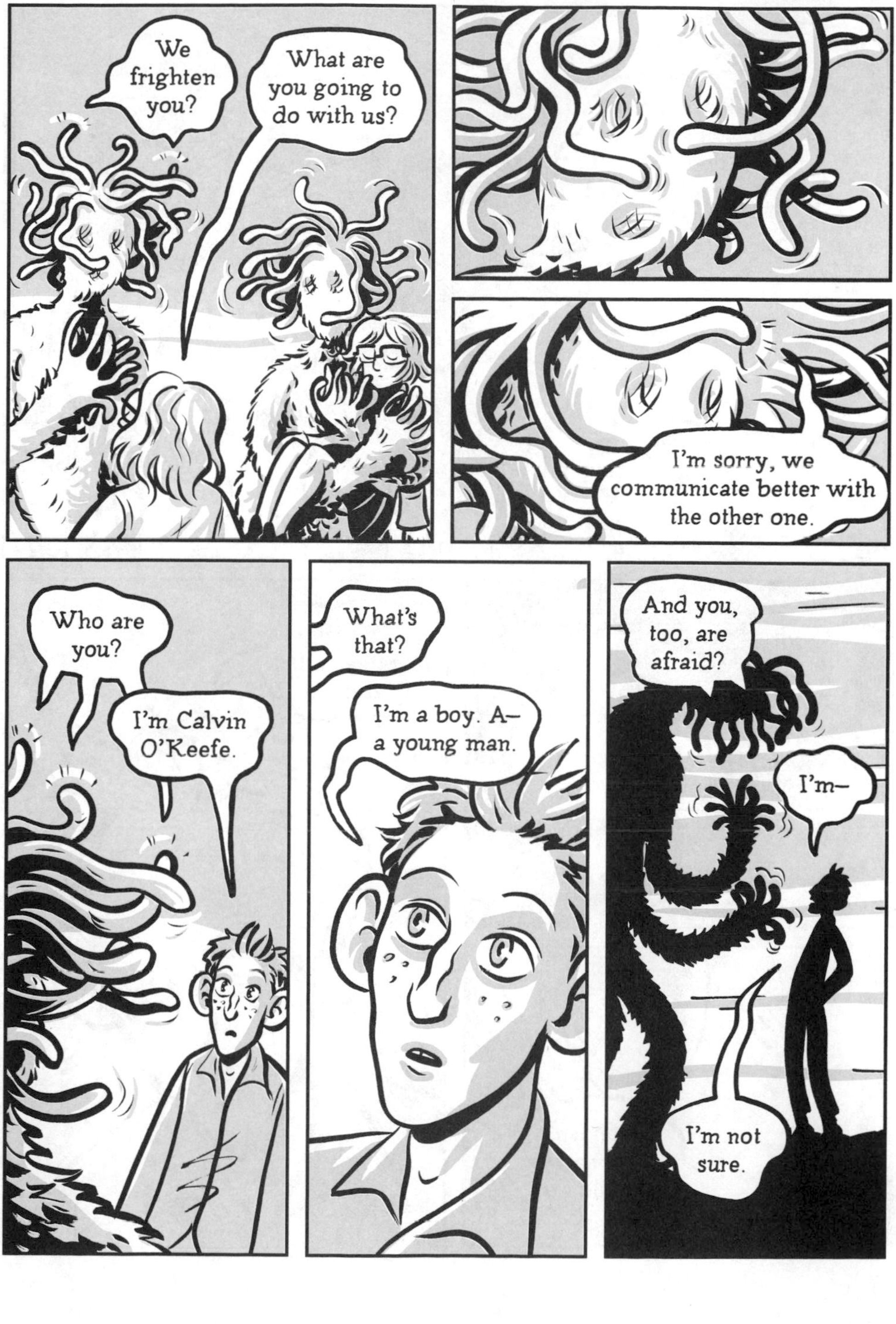
We frighten you?
What are you going to do with us?
I'm sorry, we communicate better with the other one.
Who are you?
I'm Calvin O'Keefe.
What's that?
I'm a boy. A— a young man.
And you, too, are afraid?
I'm—
I'm not sure.

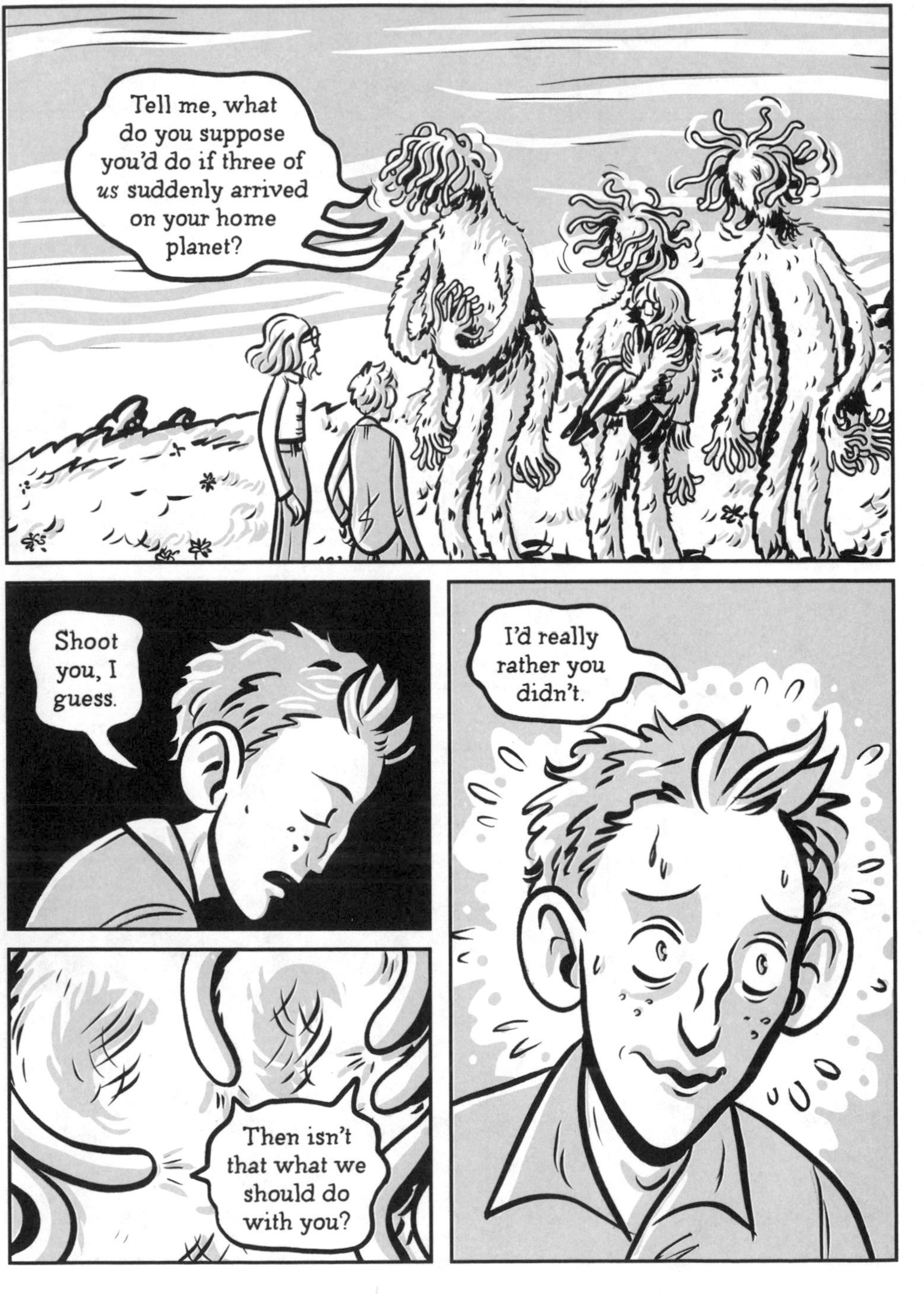
Tell me, what do you suppose you'd do if three of *us* suddenly arrived on your home planet?
Shoot you, I guess.
Then isn't that what we should do with you?
I'd really rather you didn't.

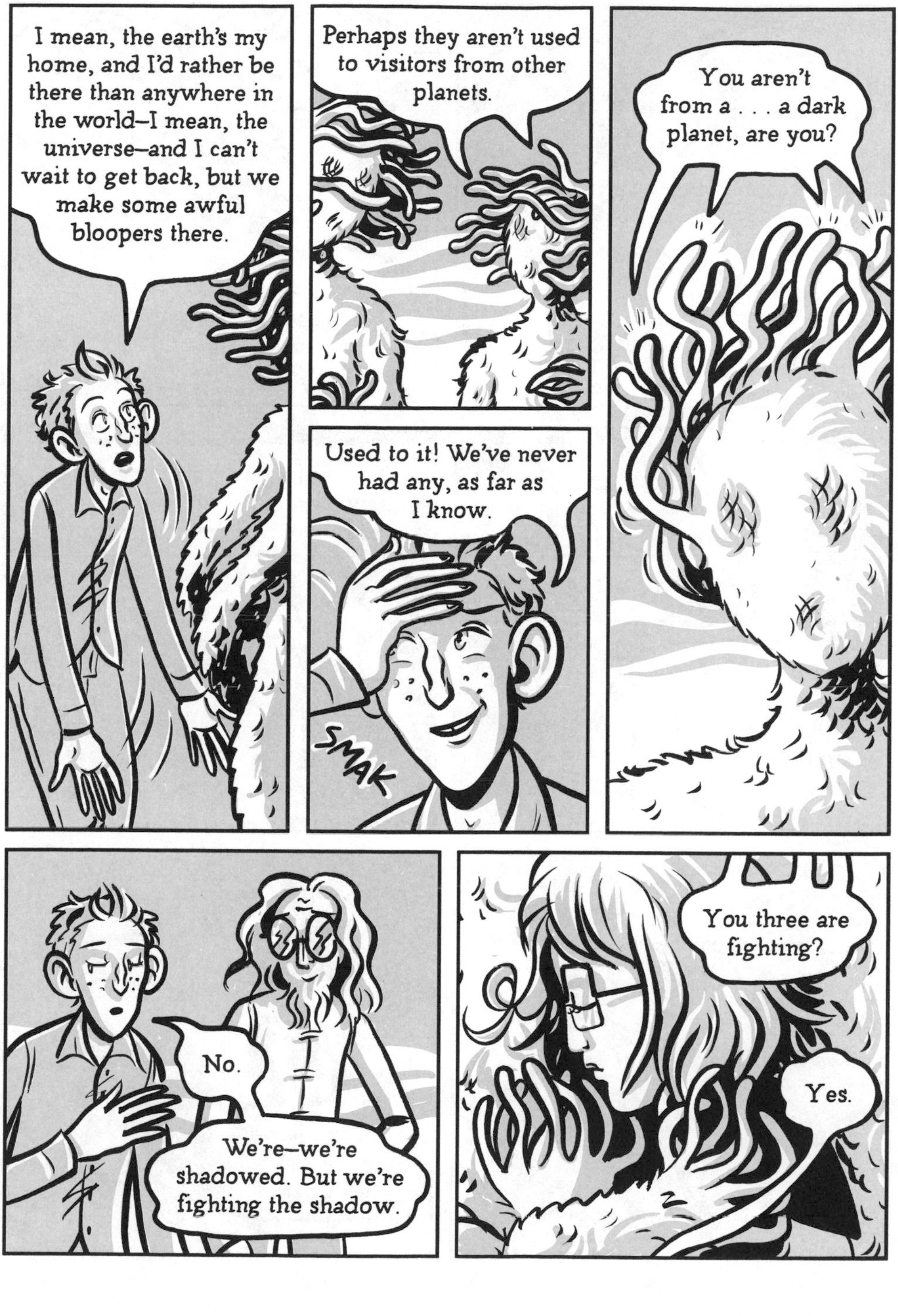
I mean, the earth's my home, and I'd rather be there than anywhere in the world–I mean, the universe–and I can't wait to get back, but we make some awful bloopers there.
Perhaps they aren't used to visitors from other planets.
Used to it! We've never had any, as far as I know.
SMAK
You aren't from a . . . a dark planet, are you?
No.
We're–we're shadowed. But we're fighting the shadow.
You three are fighting?
Yes.

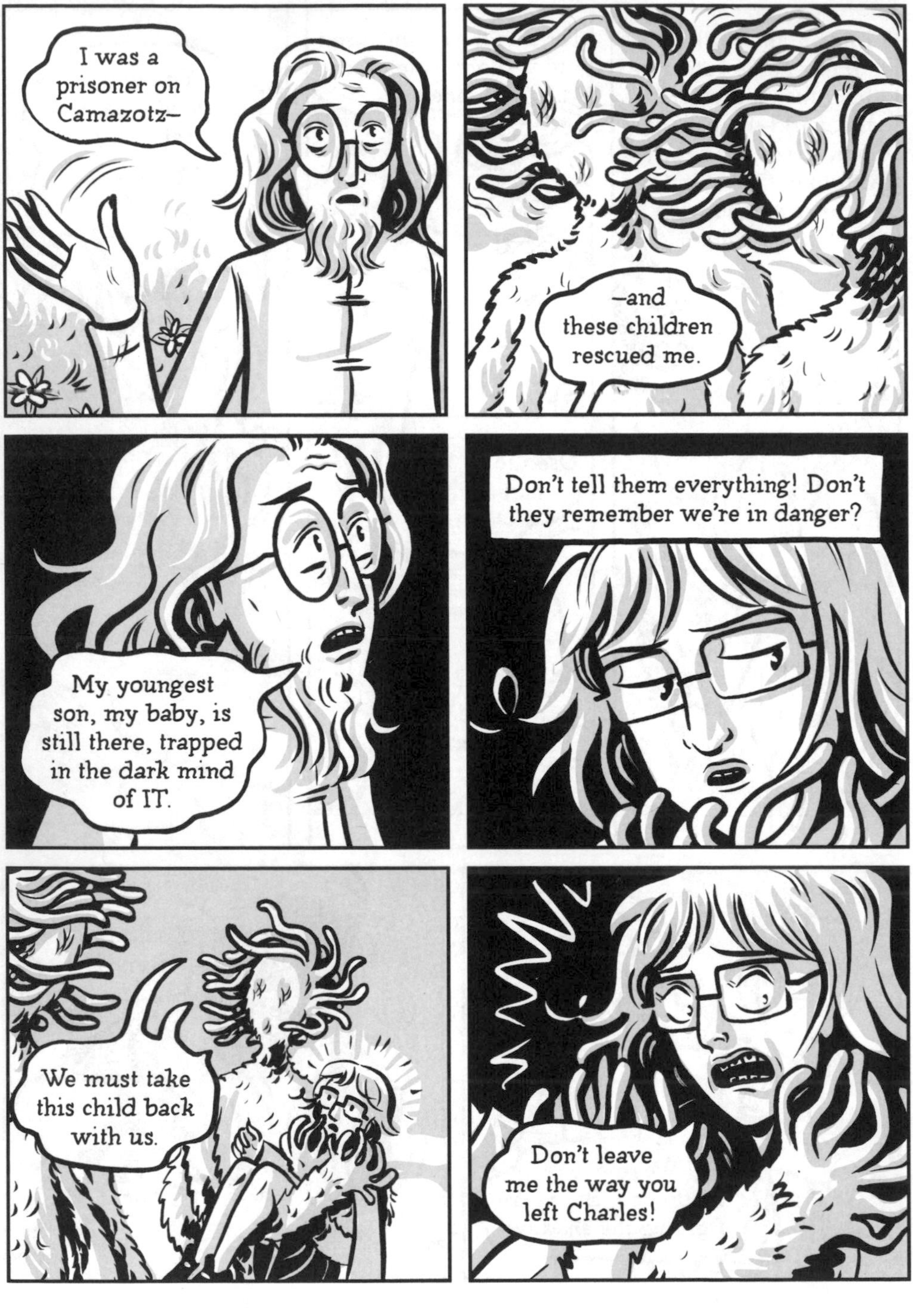
I was a prisoner on Camazotz—
—and these children rescued me.
My youngest son, my baby, is still there, trapped in the dark mind of IT.
Don't tell them everything! Don't they remember we're in danger?
We must take this child back with us.
Don't leave me the way you left Charles!

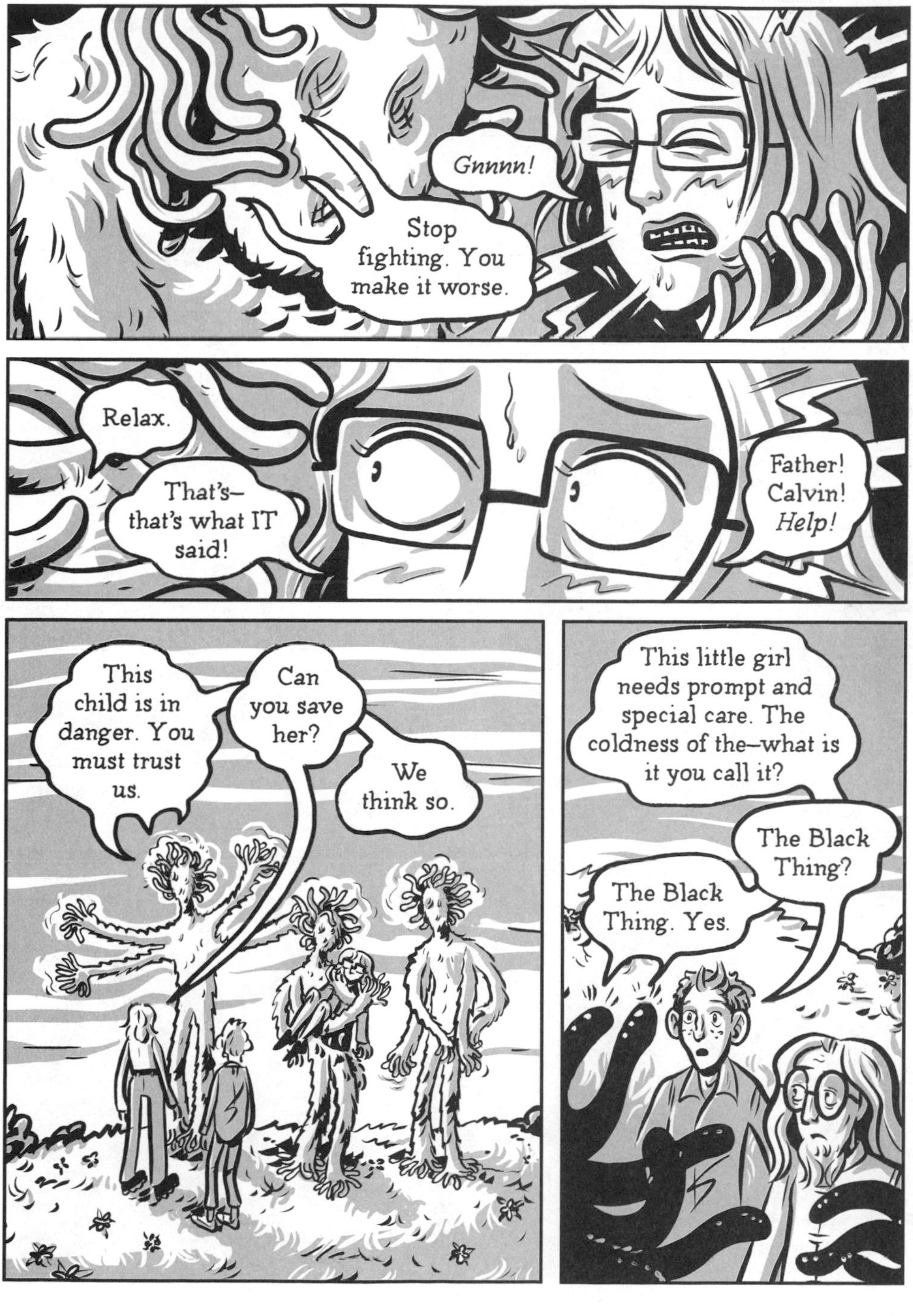
Gnnnn!
Stop fighting. You make it worse.
Relax.
That's—that's what IT said!
Father! Calvin! *Help!*
This child is in danger. You must trust us.
Can you save her?
We think so.
This little girl needs prompt and special care. The coldness of the—what is it you call it?
The Black Thing?
The Black Thing. Yes.

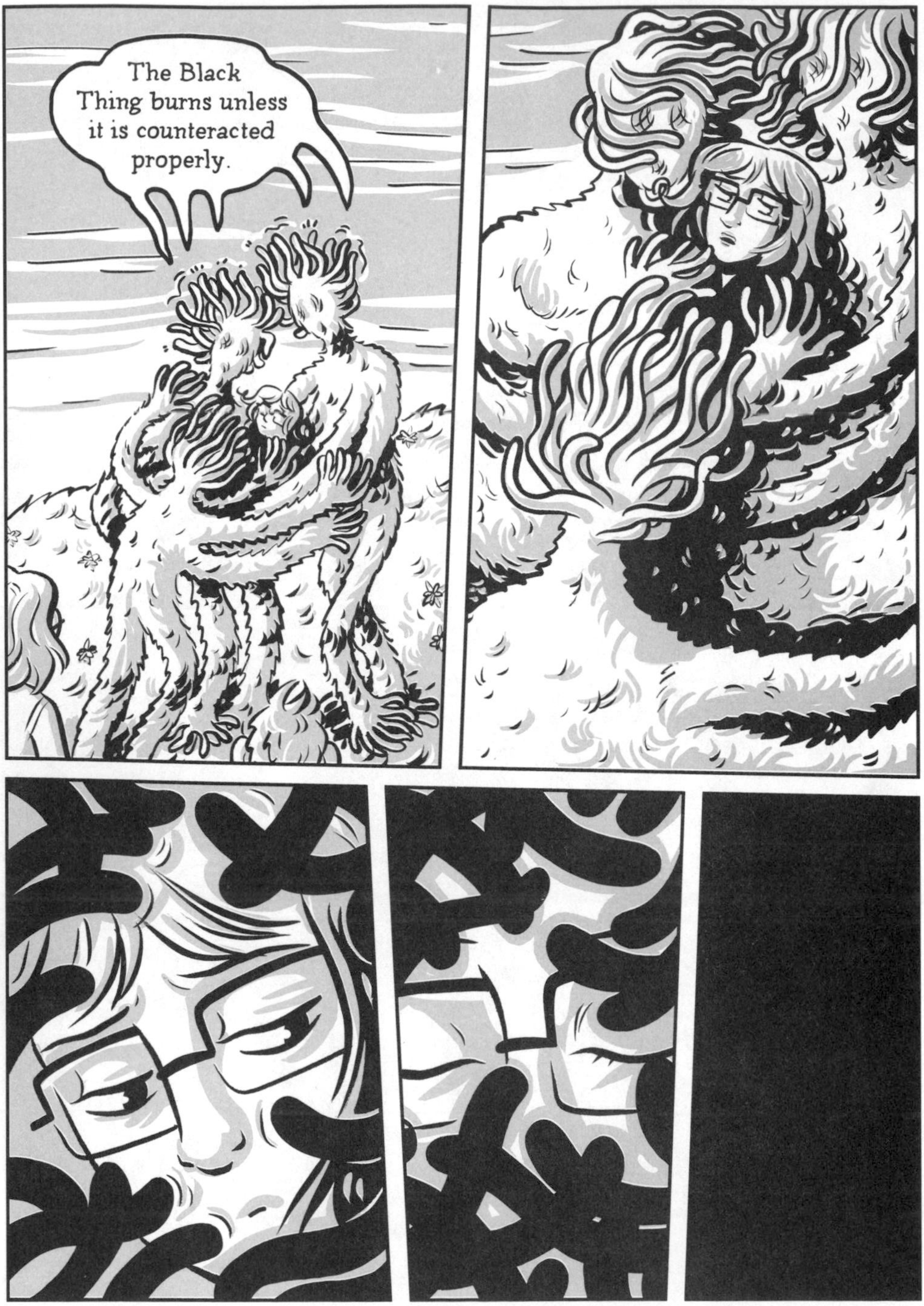
The Black Thing burns unless it is counteracted properly.

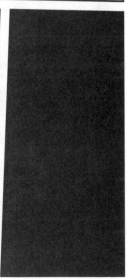

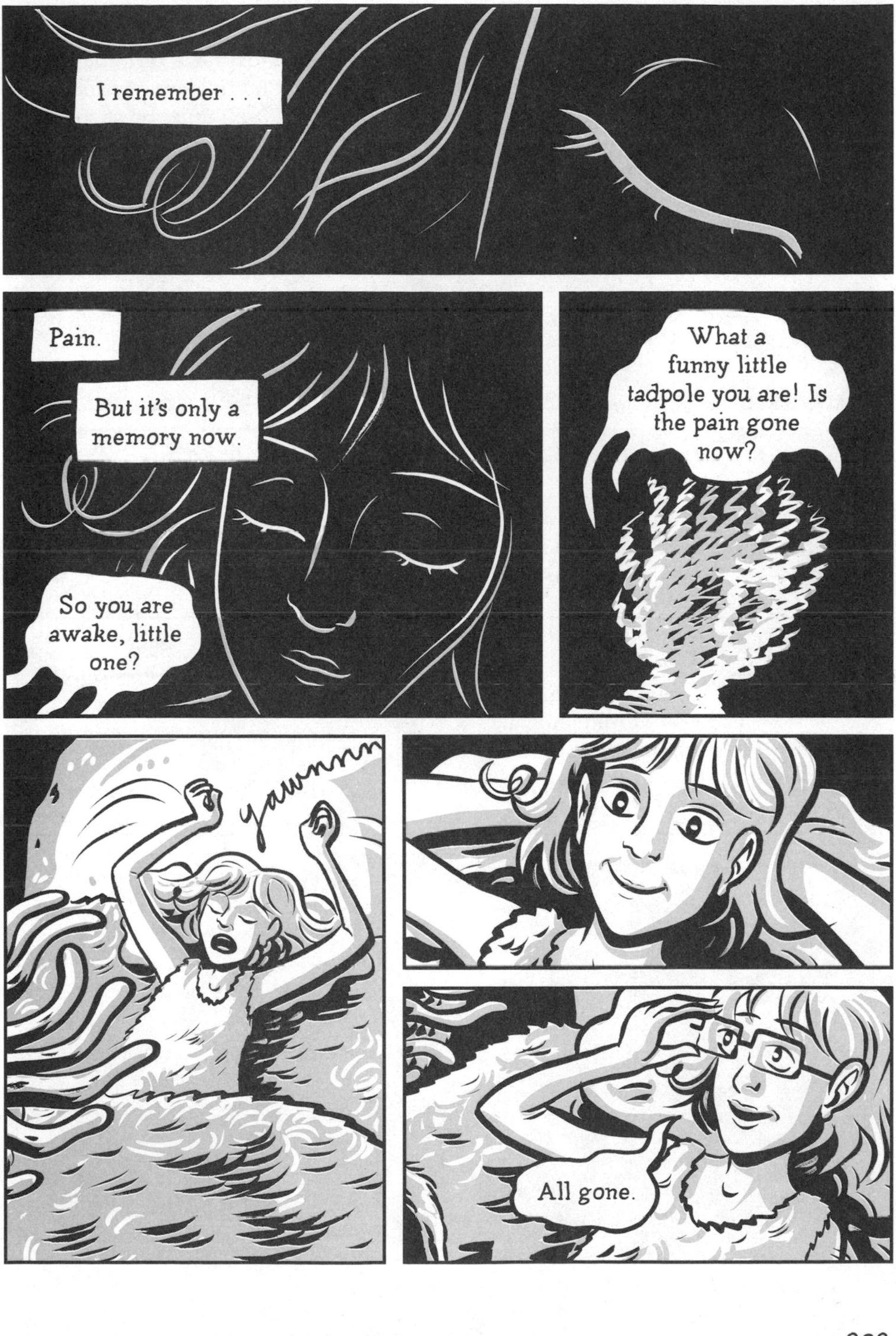
I remember . . .
Pain.
But it's only a memory now.
So you are awake, little one?
What a funny little tadpole you are! Is the pain gone now?
yawnnnn
All gone.

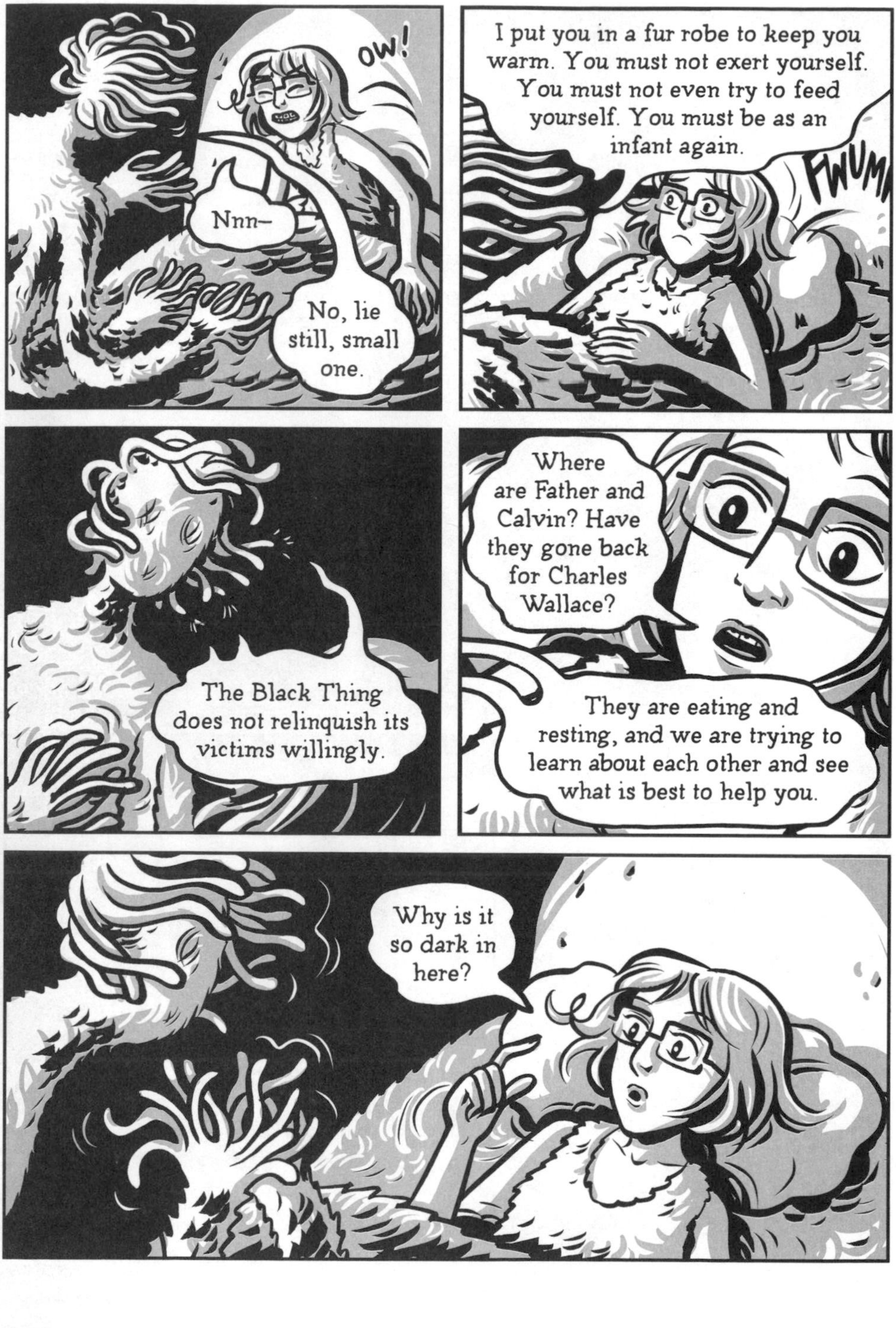
OW!
Nnn–
No, lie still, small one.
I put you in a fur robe to keep you warm. You must not exert yourself. You must not even try to feed yourself. You must be as an infant again.
FWUM
The Black Thing does not relinquish its victims willingly.
Where are Father and Calvin? Have they gone back for Charles Wallace?
They are eating and resting, and we are trying to learn about each other and see what is best to help you.
Why is it so dark in here?

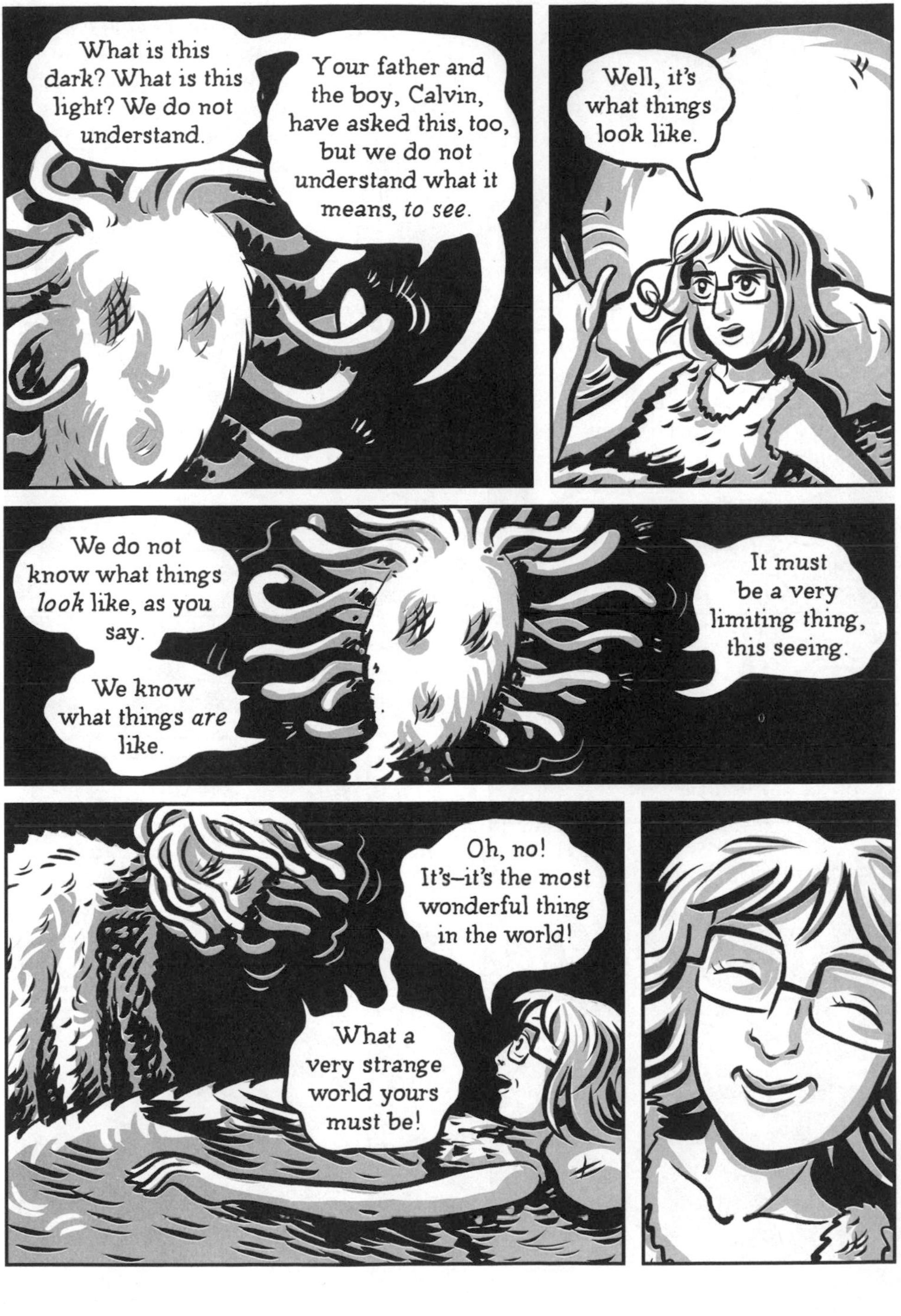
What is this dark? What is this light? We do not understand.
Your father and the boy, Calvin, have asked this, too, but we do not understand what it means, *to see*.
Well, it's what things look like.
We do not know what things *look* like, as you say.
We know what things *are* like.
It must be a very limiting thing, this seeing.
Oh, no! It's–it's the most wonderful thing in the world!
What a very strange world yours must be!

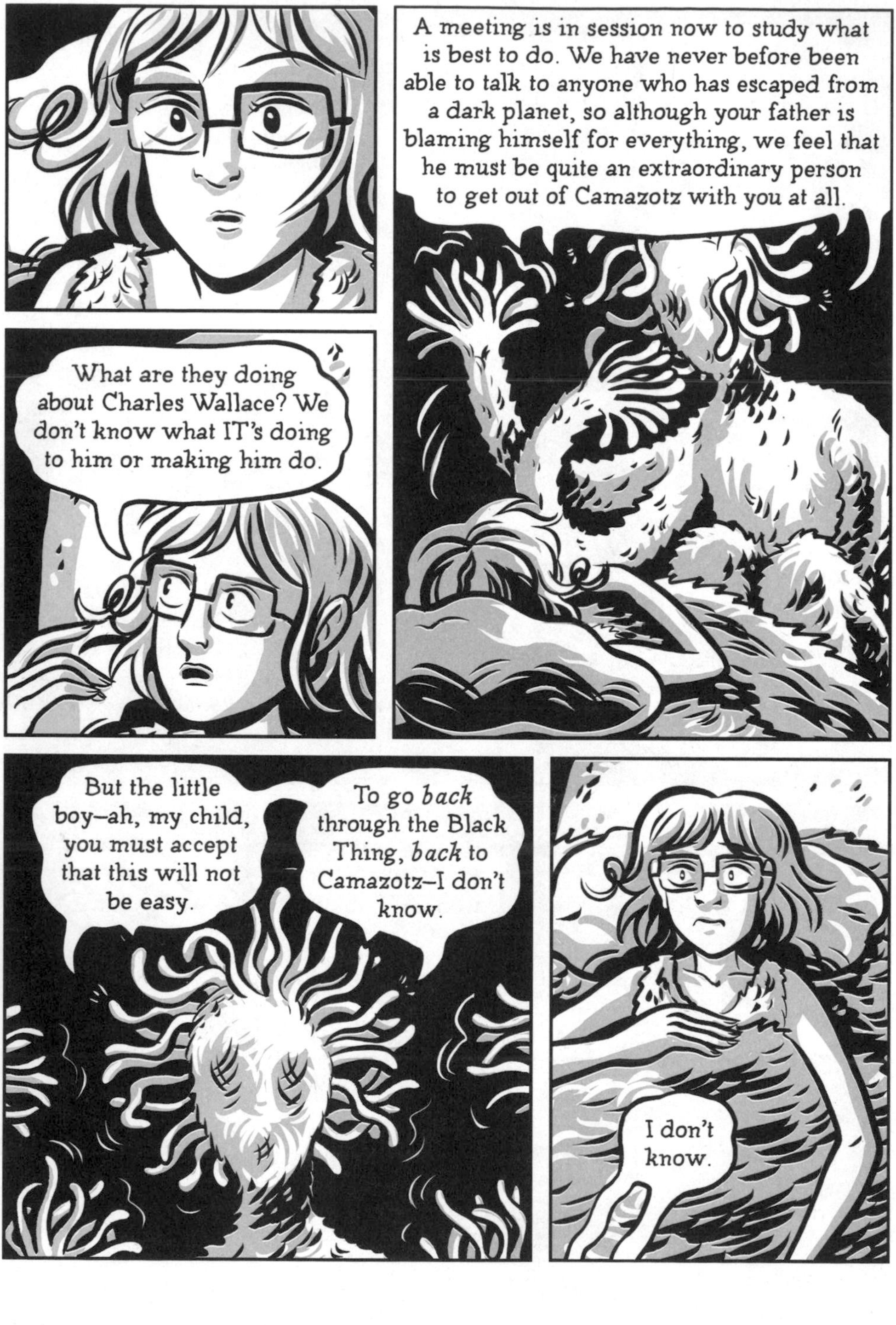
A meeting is in session now to study what is best to do. We have never before been able to talk to anyone who has escaped from a dark planet, so although your father is blaming himself for everything, we feel that he must be quite an extraordinary person to get out of Camazotz with you at all.
What are they doing about Charles Wallace? We don't know what IT's doing to him or making him do.
But the little boy–ah, my child, you must accept that this will not be easy.
To go *back* through the Black Thing, *back* to Camazotz–I don't know.
I don't know.

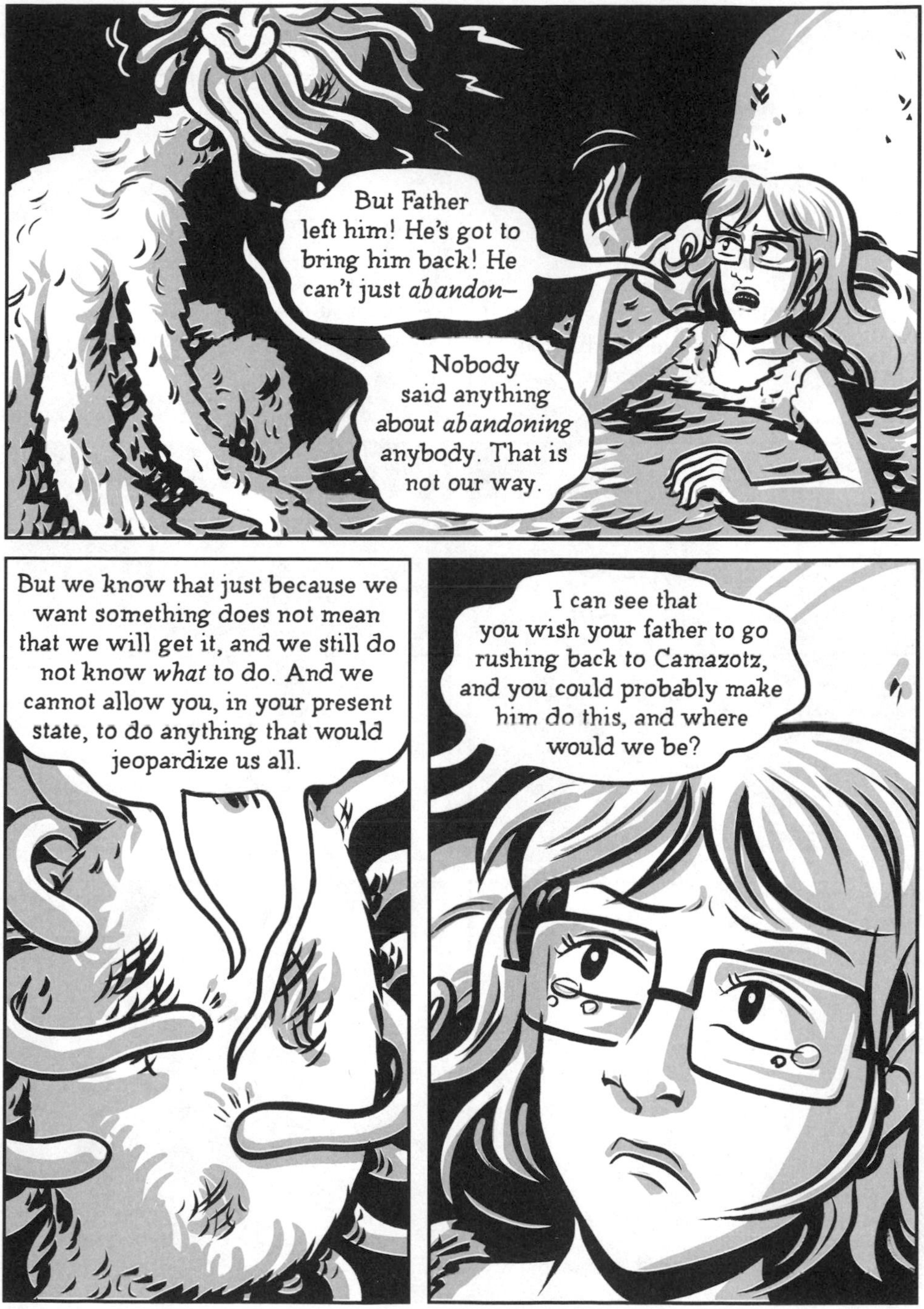
But Father left him! He's got to bring him back! He can't just *abandon*—
Nobody said anything about *abandoning* anybody. That is not our way.
But we know that just because we want something does not mean that we will get it, and we still do not know *what* to do. And we cannot allow you, in your present state, to do anything that would jeopardize us all.
I can see that you wish your father to go rushing back to Camazotz, and you could probably make him do this, and where would we be?

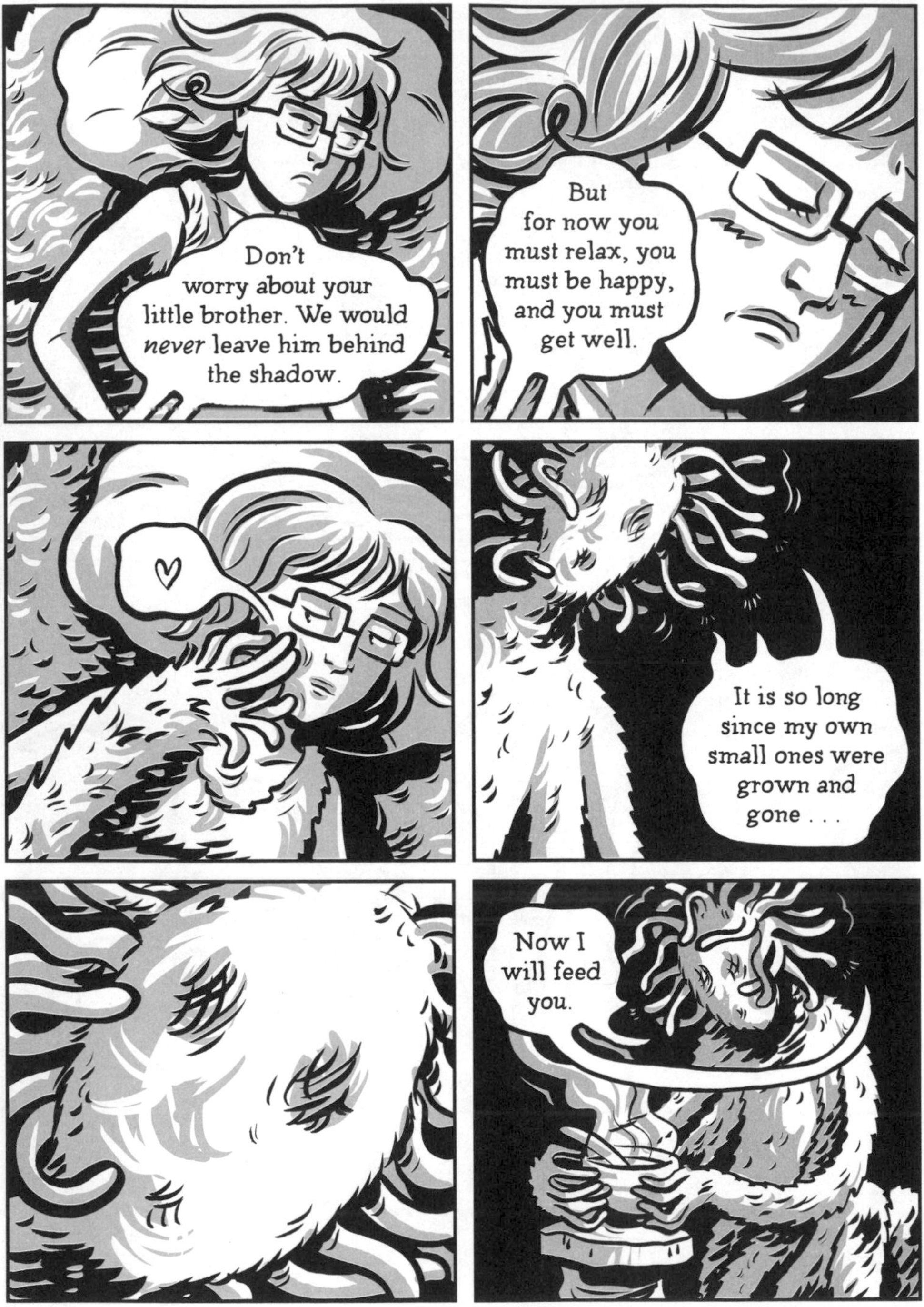
Don't worry about your little brother. We would *never* leave him behind the shadow.
But for now you must relax, you must be happy, and you must get well.
♡
It is so long since my own small ones were grown and gone . . .
Now I will feed you.

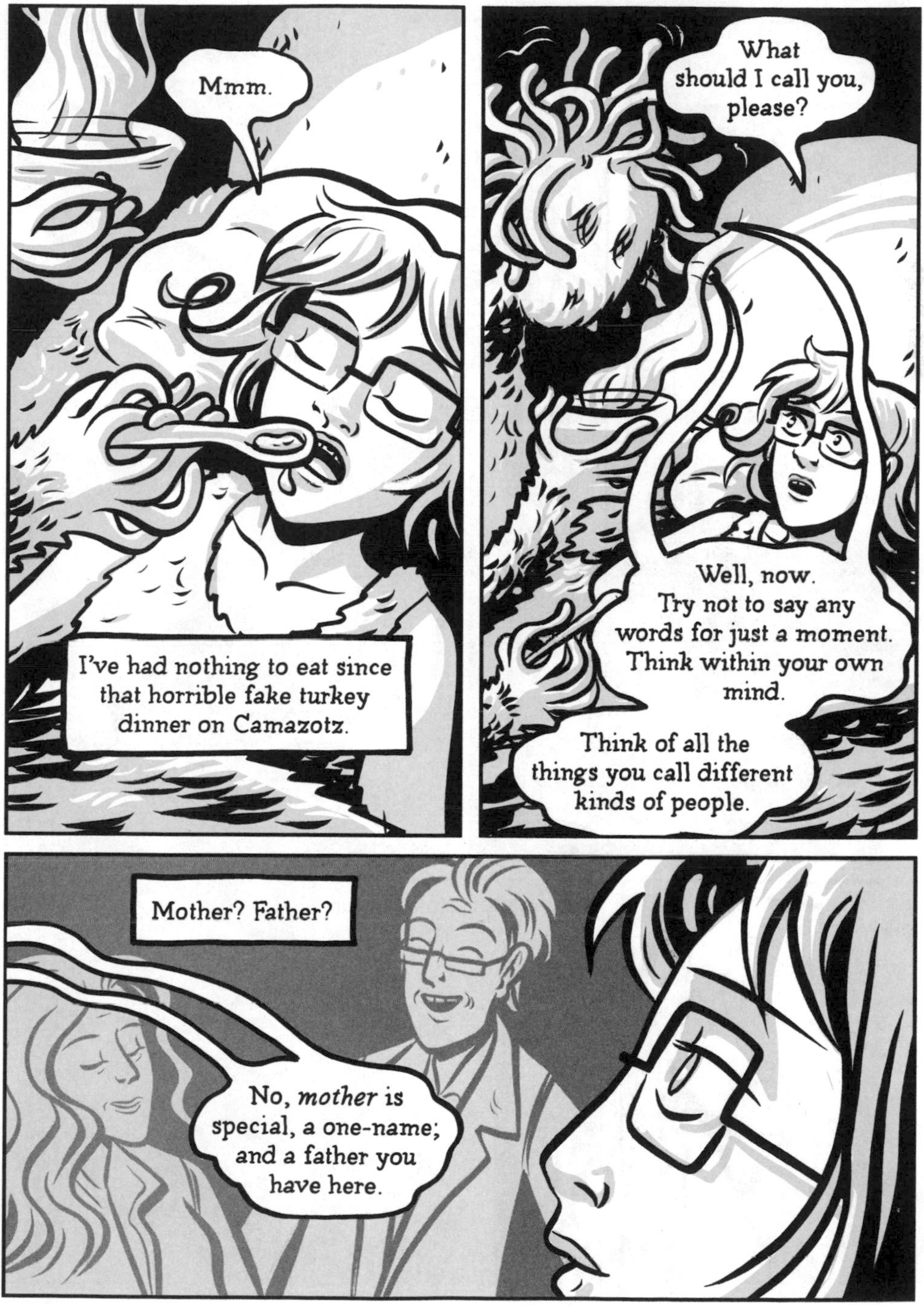

Mmm.
I've had nothing to eat since that horrible fake turkey dinner on Camazotz.
What should I call you, please?
Well, now. Try not to say any words for just a moment. Think within your own mind.
Think of all the things you call different kinds of people.
Mother? Father?
No, *mother* is special, a one-name; and a father you have here.

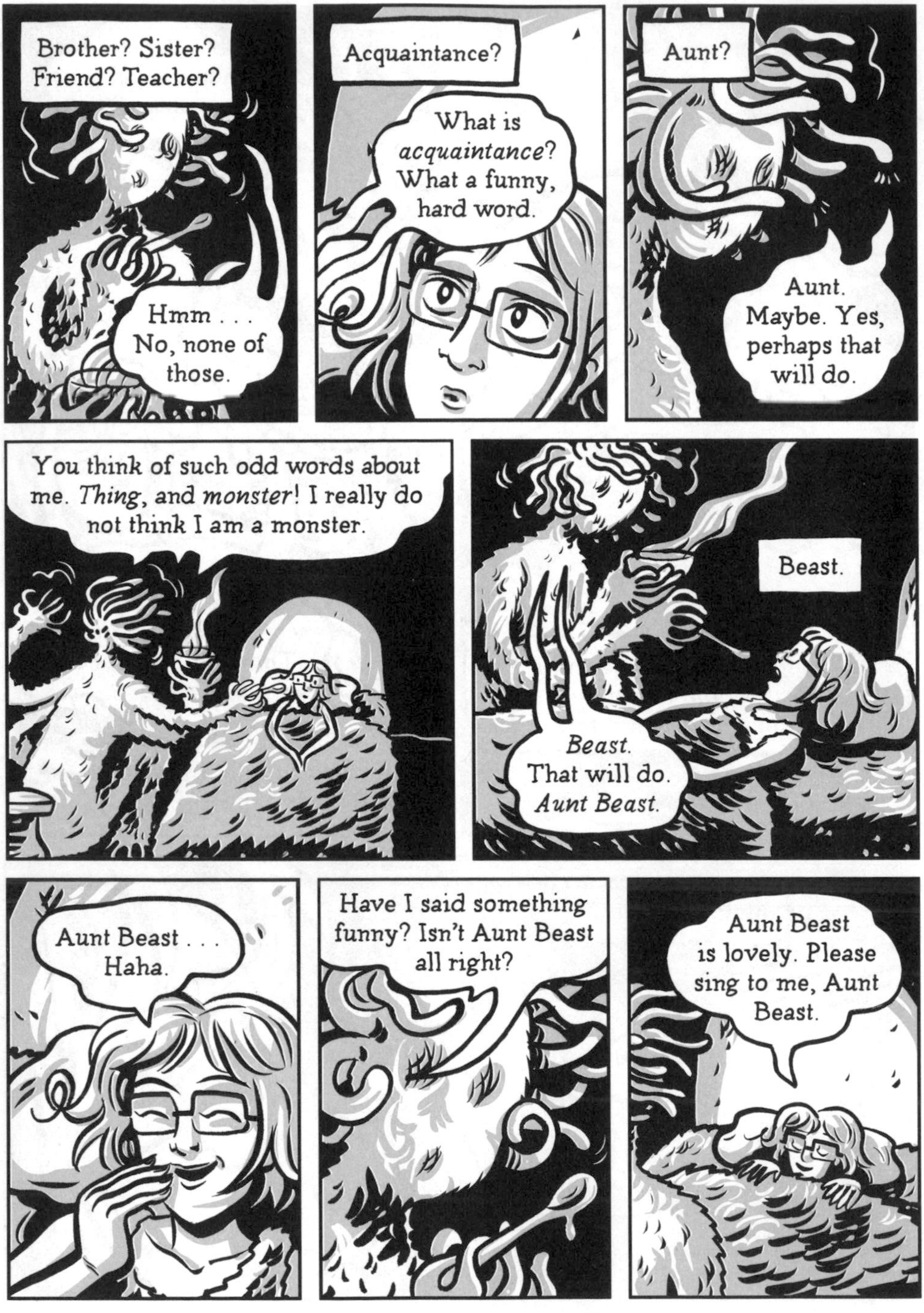
Brother? Sister? Friend? Teacher?
Hmm . . . No, none of those.
Acquaintance?
What is *acquaintance*? What a funny, hard word.
Aunt?
Aunt. Maybe. Yes, perhaps that will do.
You think of such odd words about me. *Thing*, and *monster*! I really do not think I am a monster.
Beast.
Beast. That will do. *Aunt Beast.*
Aunt Beast . . . Haha.
Have I said something funny? Isn't Aunt Beast all right?
Aunt Beast is lovely. Please sing to me, Aunt Beast.

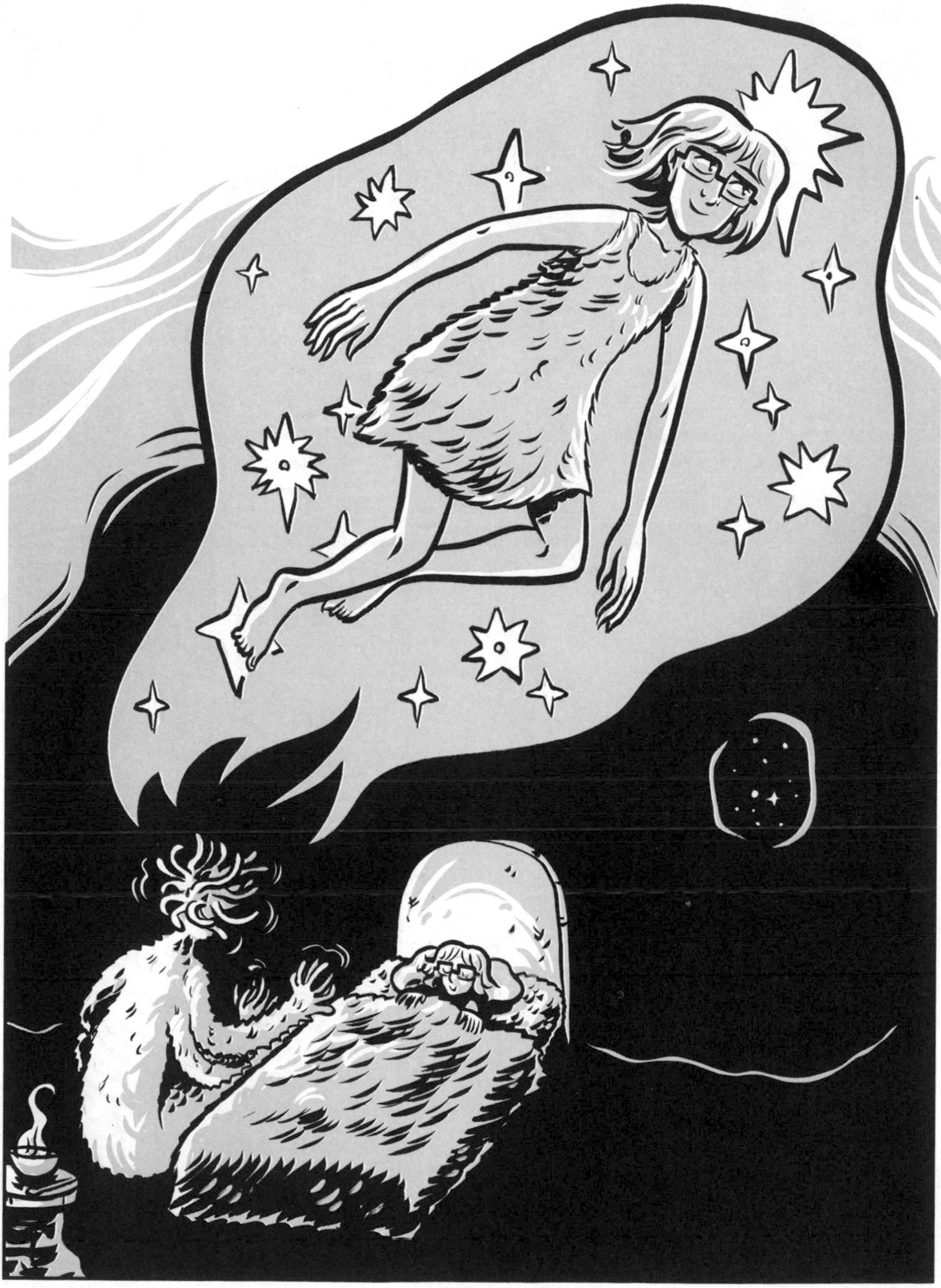

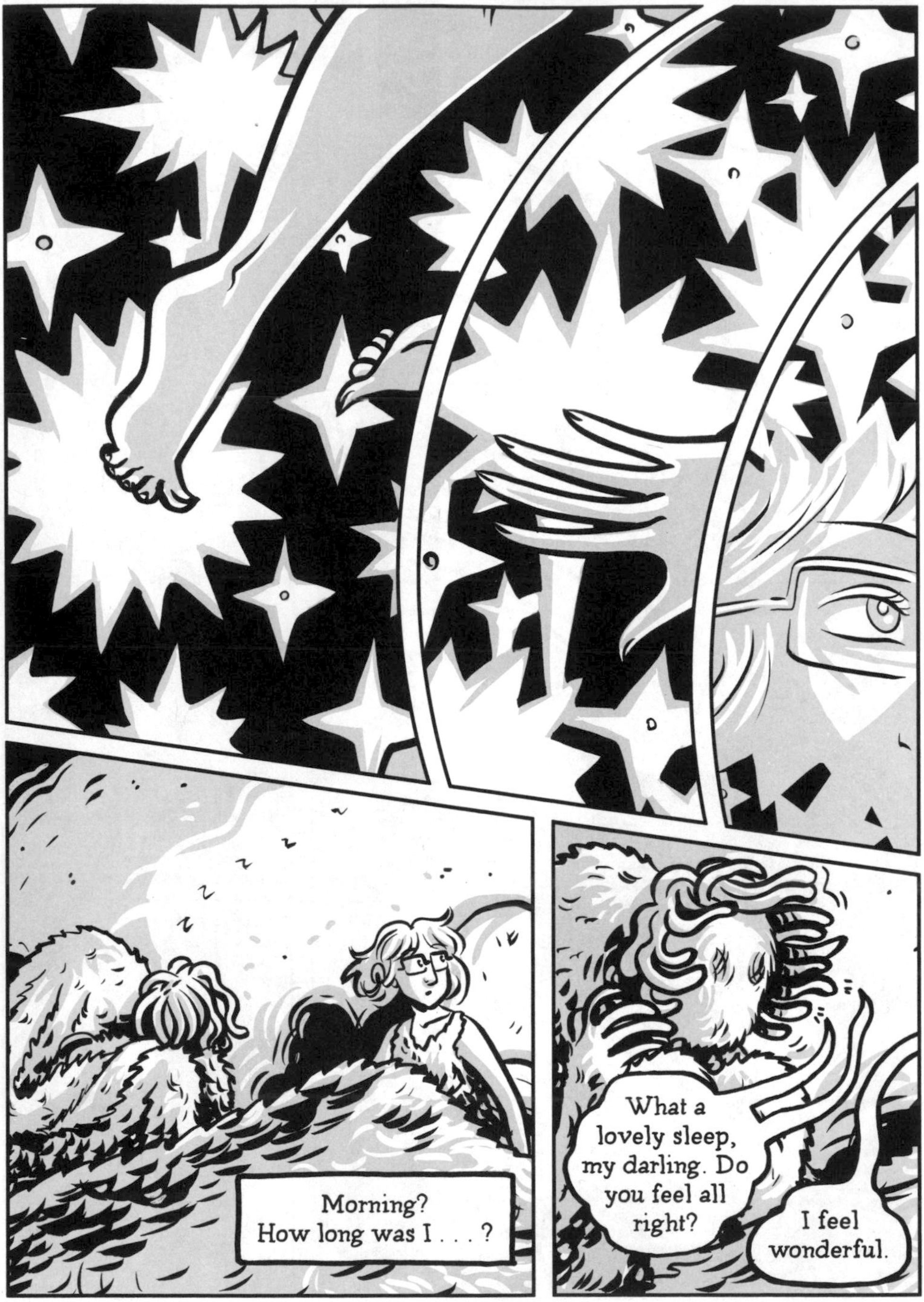
Morning?
How long was I . . . ?
What a lovely sleep, my darling. Do you feel all right?
I feel wonderful.

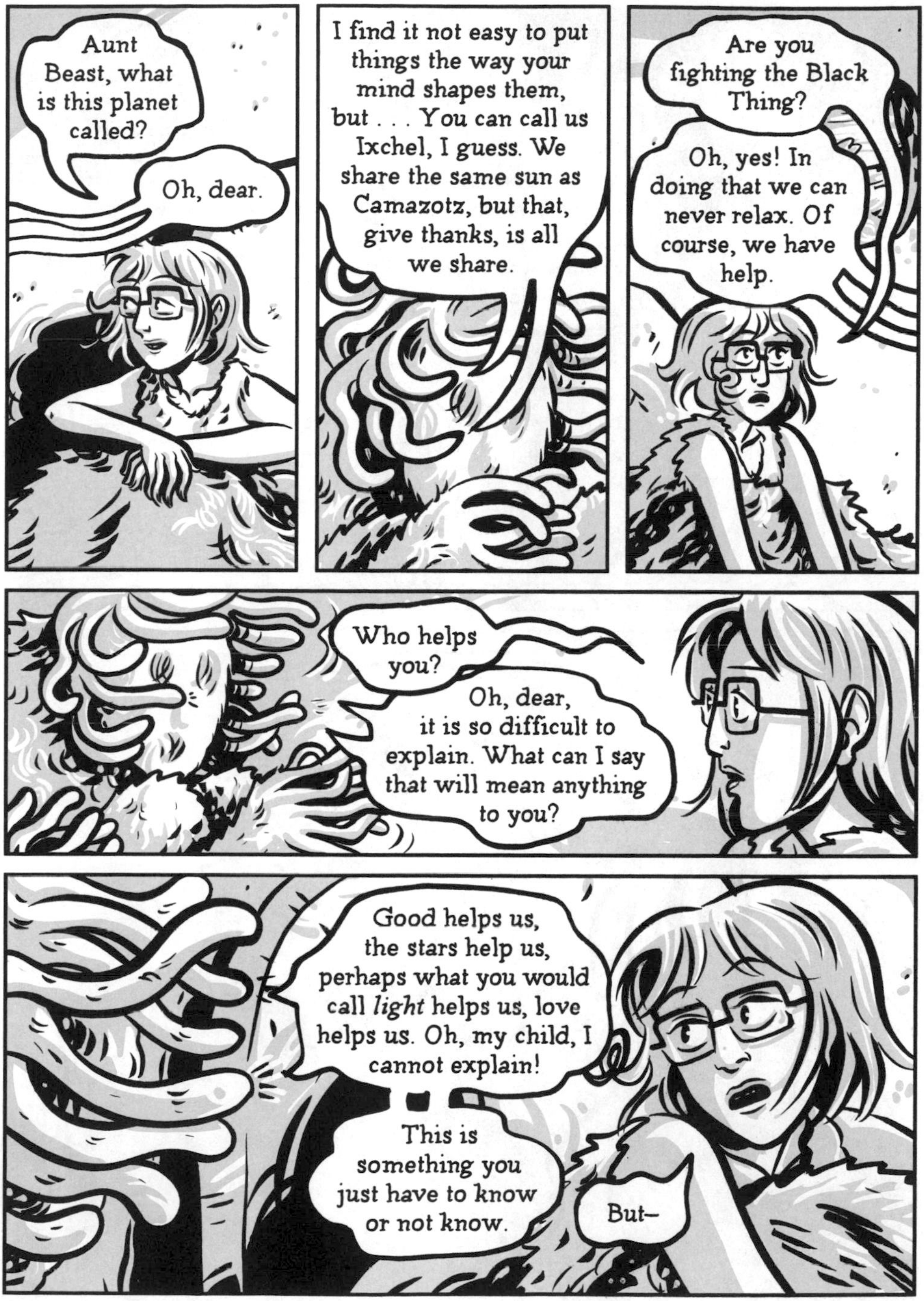
Aunt Beast, what is this planet called?
Oh, dear.
I find it not easy to put things the way your mind shapes them, but . . . You can call us Ixchel, I guess. We share the same sun as Camazotz, but that, give thanks, is all we share.
Are you fighting the Black Thing?
Oh, yes! In doing that we can never relax. Of course, we have help.
Who helps you?
Oh, dear, it is so difficult to explain. What can I say that will mean anything to you?
Good helps us, the stars help us, perhaps what you would call *light* helps us, love helps us. Oh, my child, I cannot explain!
This is something you just have to know or not know.
But—

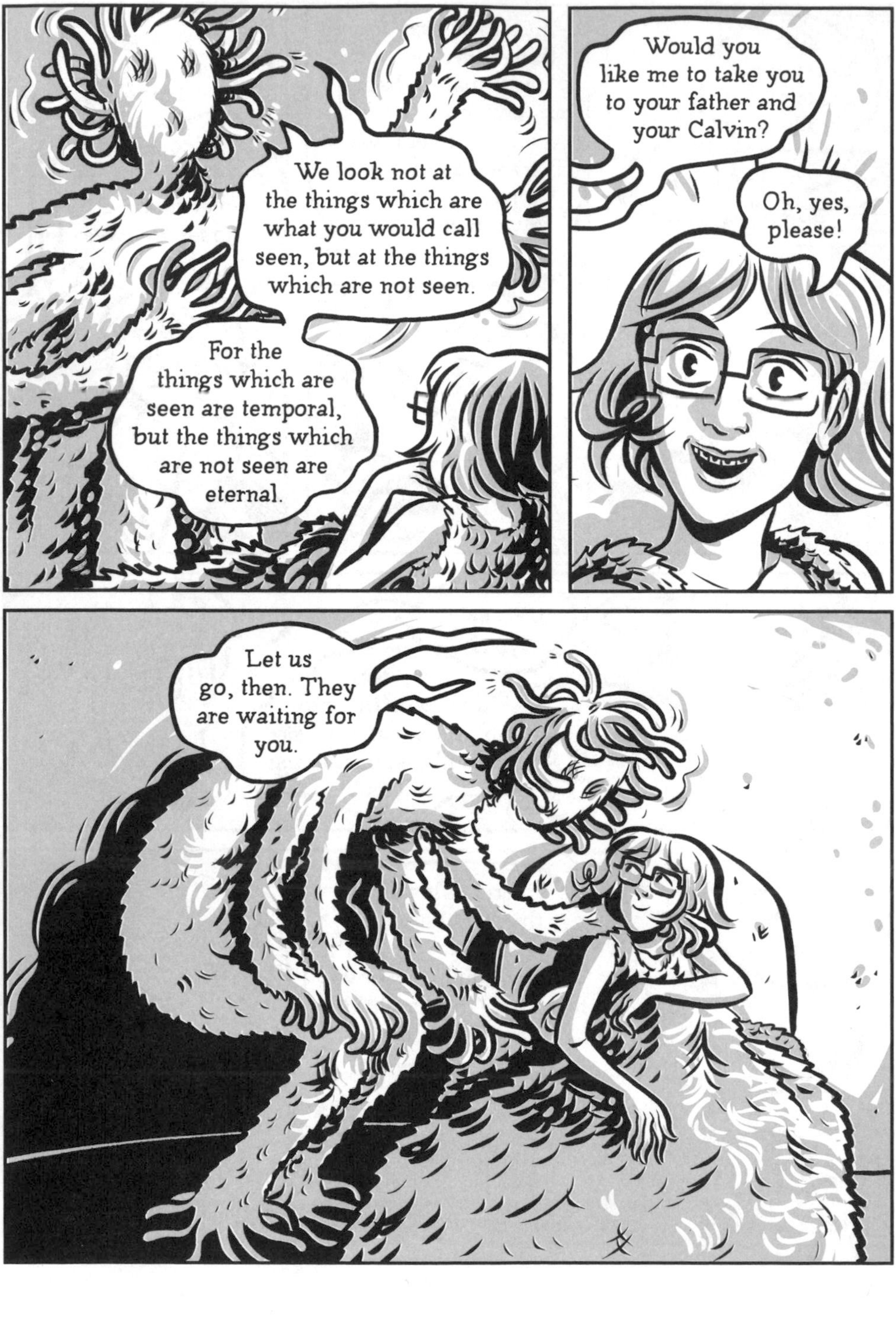
We look not at the things which are what you would call seen, but at the things which are not seen.
For the things which are seen are temporal, but the things which are not seen are eternal.
Would you like me to take you to your father and your Calvin?
Oh, yes, please!
Let us go, then. They are waiting for you.

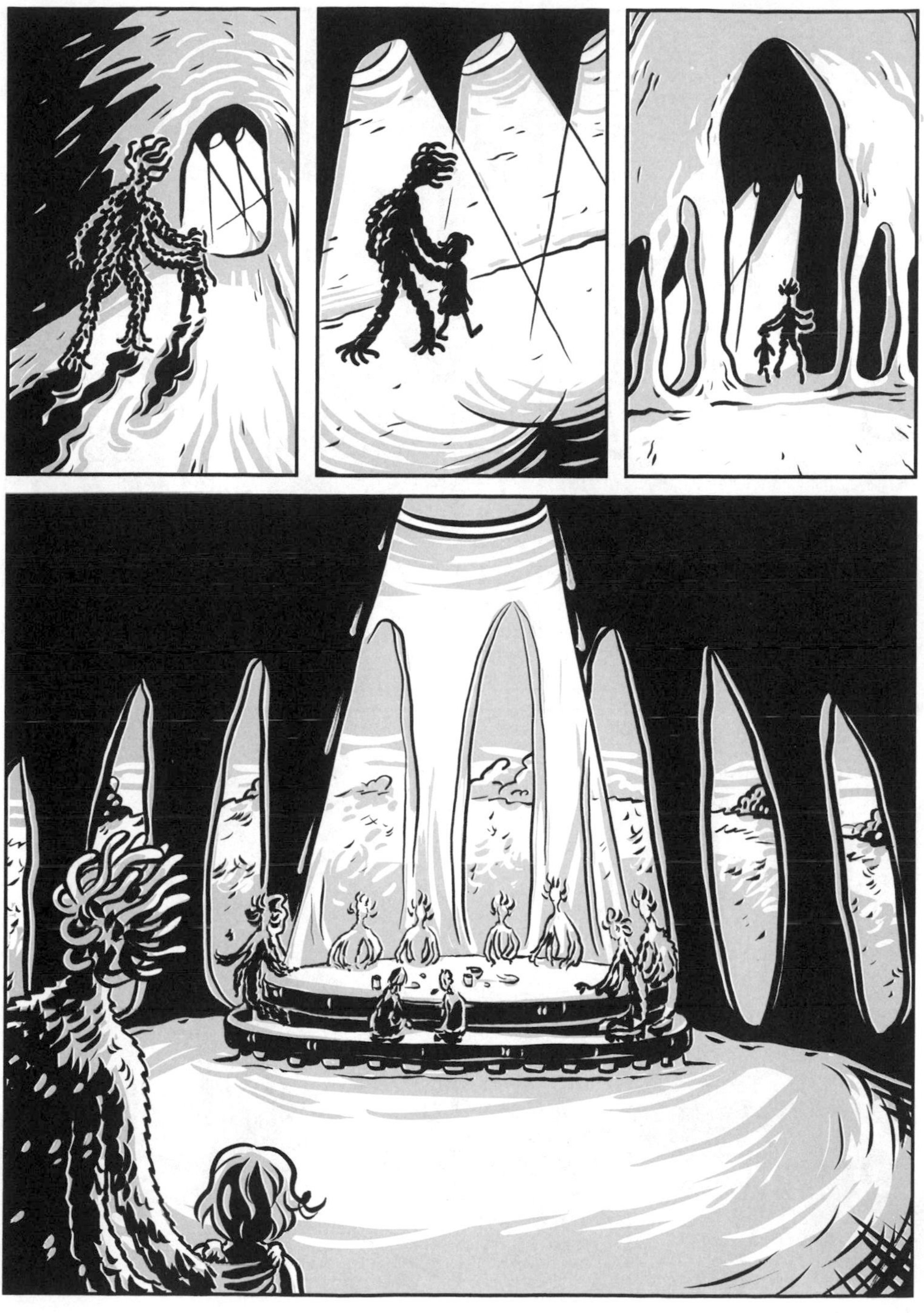

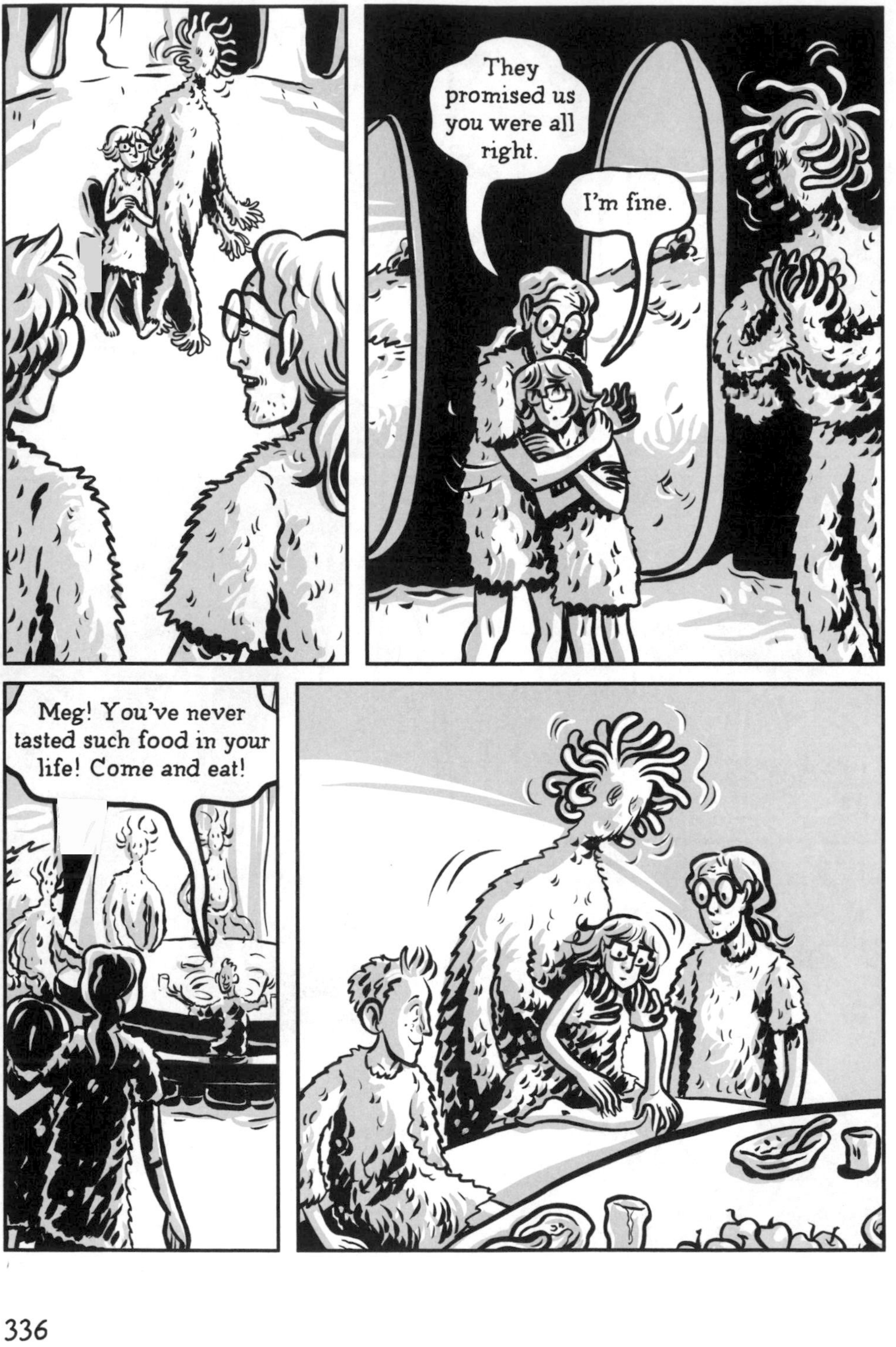
They promised us you were all right.
I'm fine.
Meg! You've never tasted such food in your life! Come and eat!

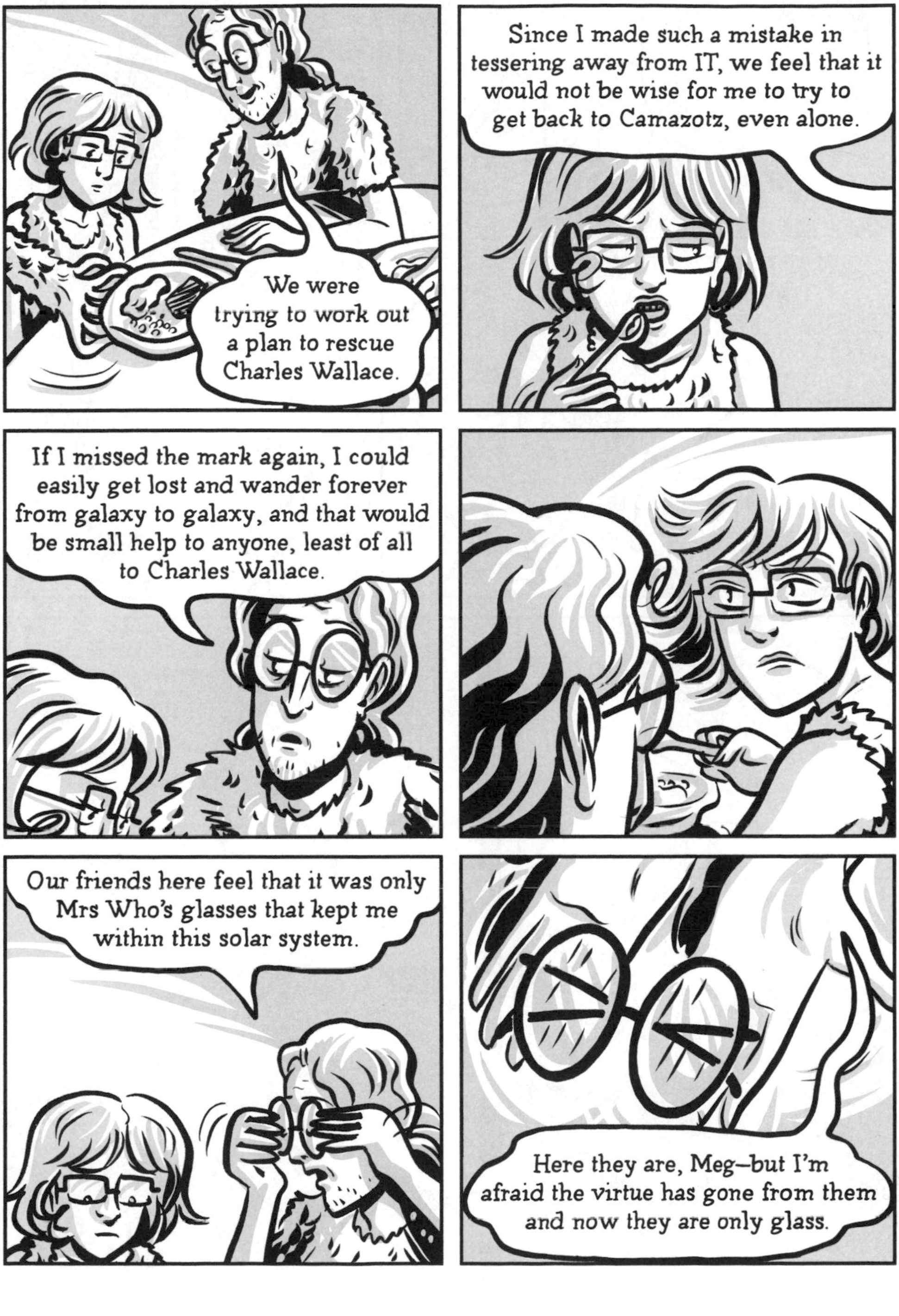
We were trying to work out a plan to rescue Charles Wallace.
Since I made such a mistake in tessering away from IT, we feel that it would not be wise for me to try to get back to Camazotz, even alone.
If I missed the mark again, I could easily get lost and wander forever from galaxy to galaxy, and that would be small help to anyone, least of all to Charles Wallace.
Our friends here feel that it was only Mrs Who's glasses that kept me within this solar system.
Here they are, Meg—but I'm afraid the virtue has gone from them and now they are only glass.

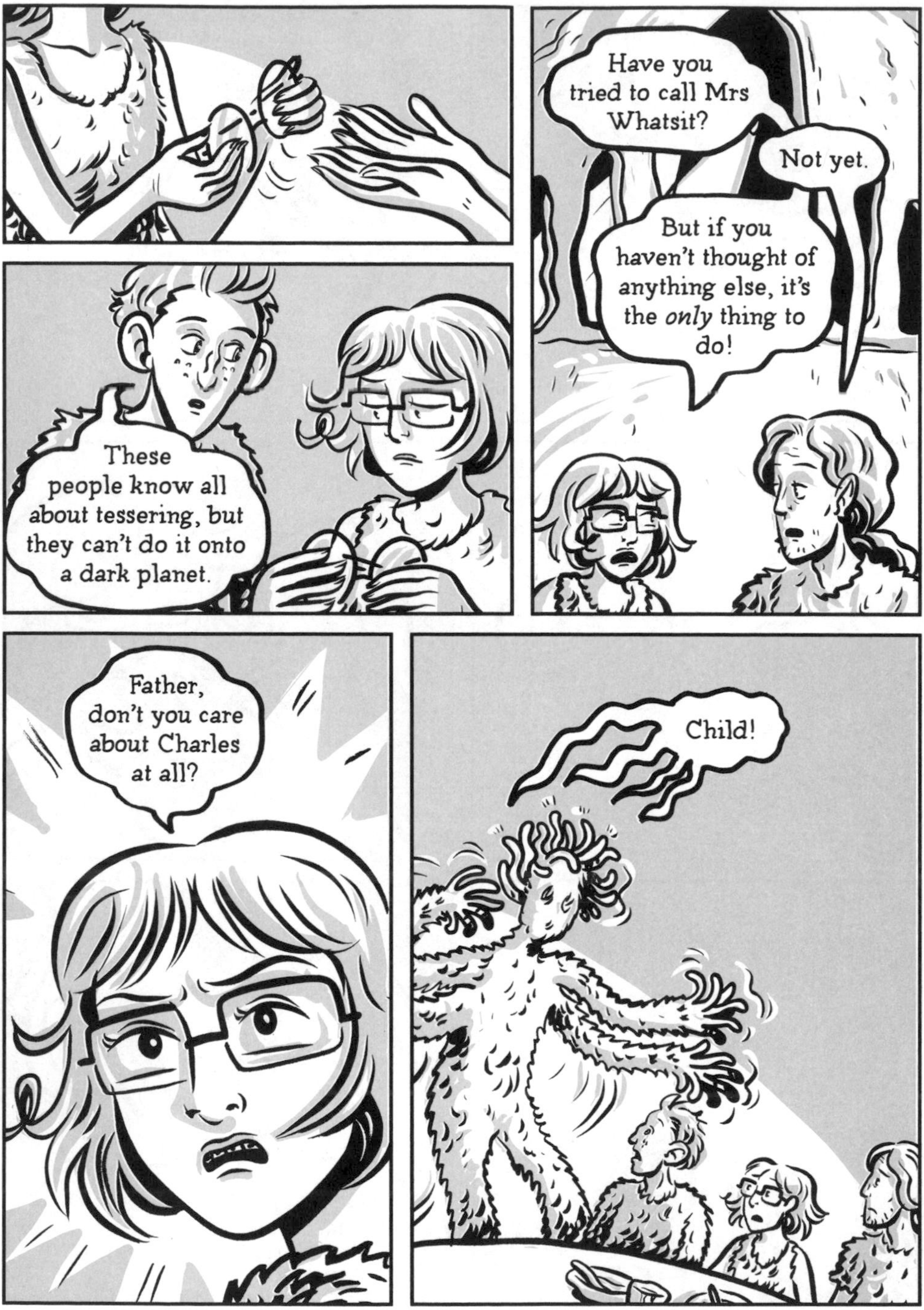

Have you tried to call Mrs Whatsit?
Not yet.
But if you haven't thought of anything else, it's the *only* thing to do!
These people know all about tessering, but they can't do it onto a dark planet.
Father, don't you care about Charles at all?
Child!

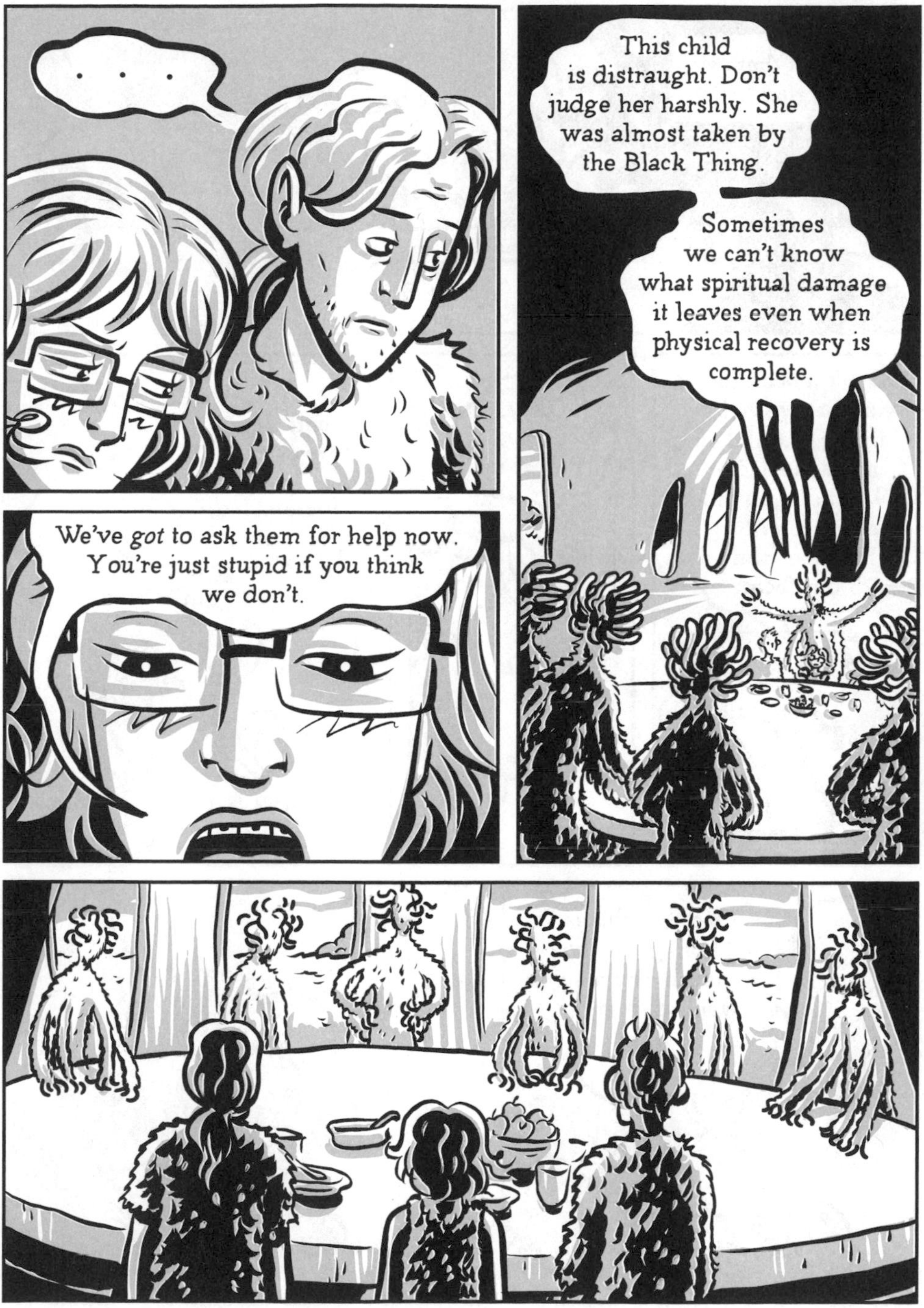
. . .
This child is distraught. Don't judge her harshly. She was almost taken by the Black Thing.
Sometimes we can't know what spiritual damage it leaves even when physical recovery is complete.
We've *got* to ask them for help now. You're just stupid if you think we don't.

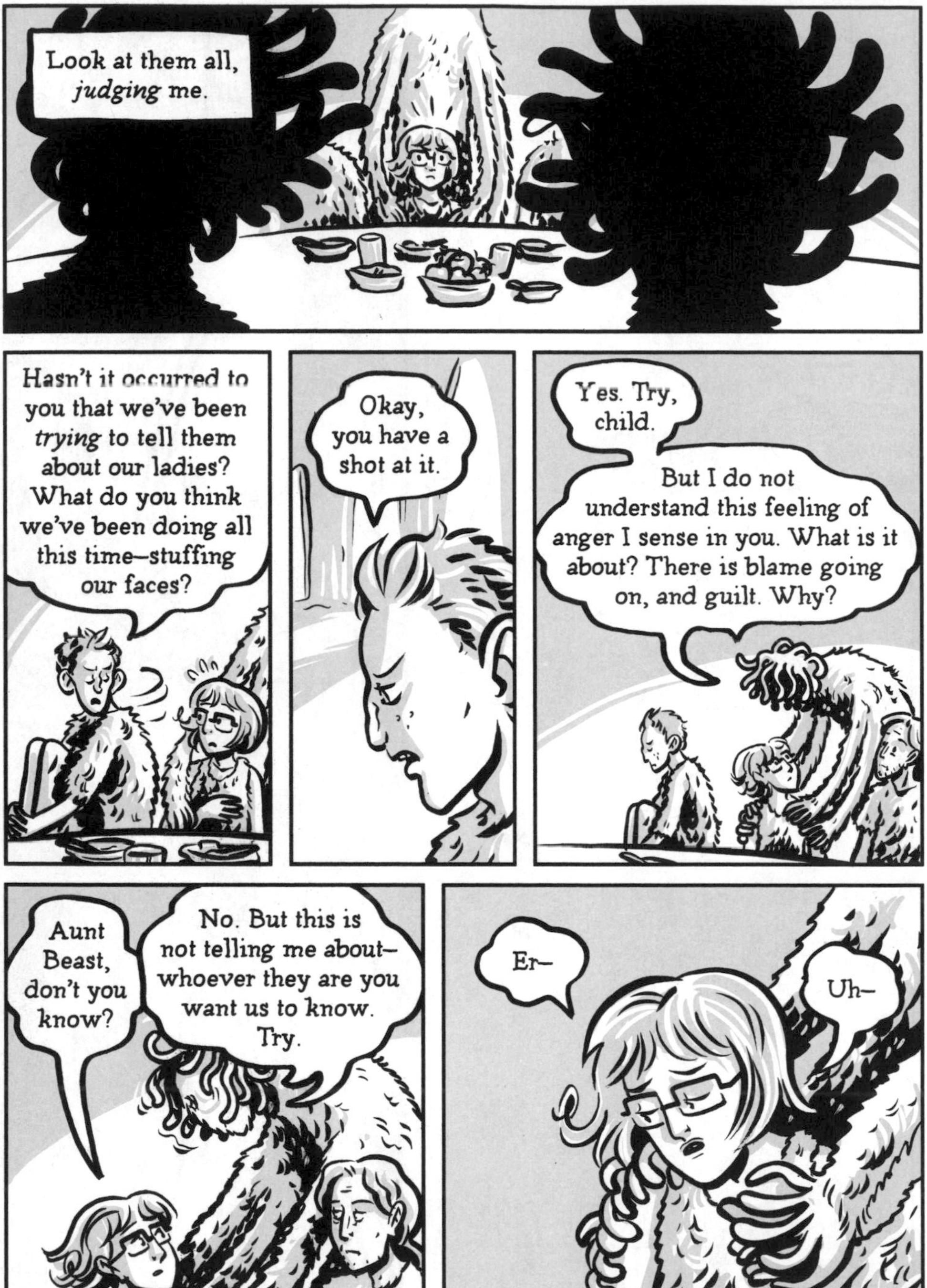
Look at them all, *judging* me.
Hasn't it occurred to you that we've been *trying* to tell them about our ladies? What do you think we've been doing all this time—stuffing our faces?
Okay, you have a shot at it.
Yes. Try, child.
But I do not understand this feeling of anger I sense in you. What is it about? There is blame going on, and guilt. Why?
Aunt Beast, don't you know?
No. But this is not telling me about—whoever they are you want us to know. Try.
Er—
Uh—

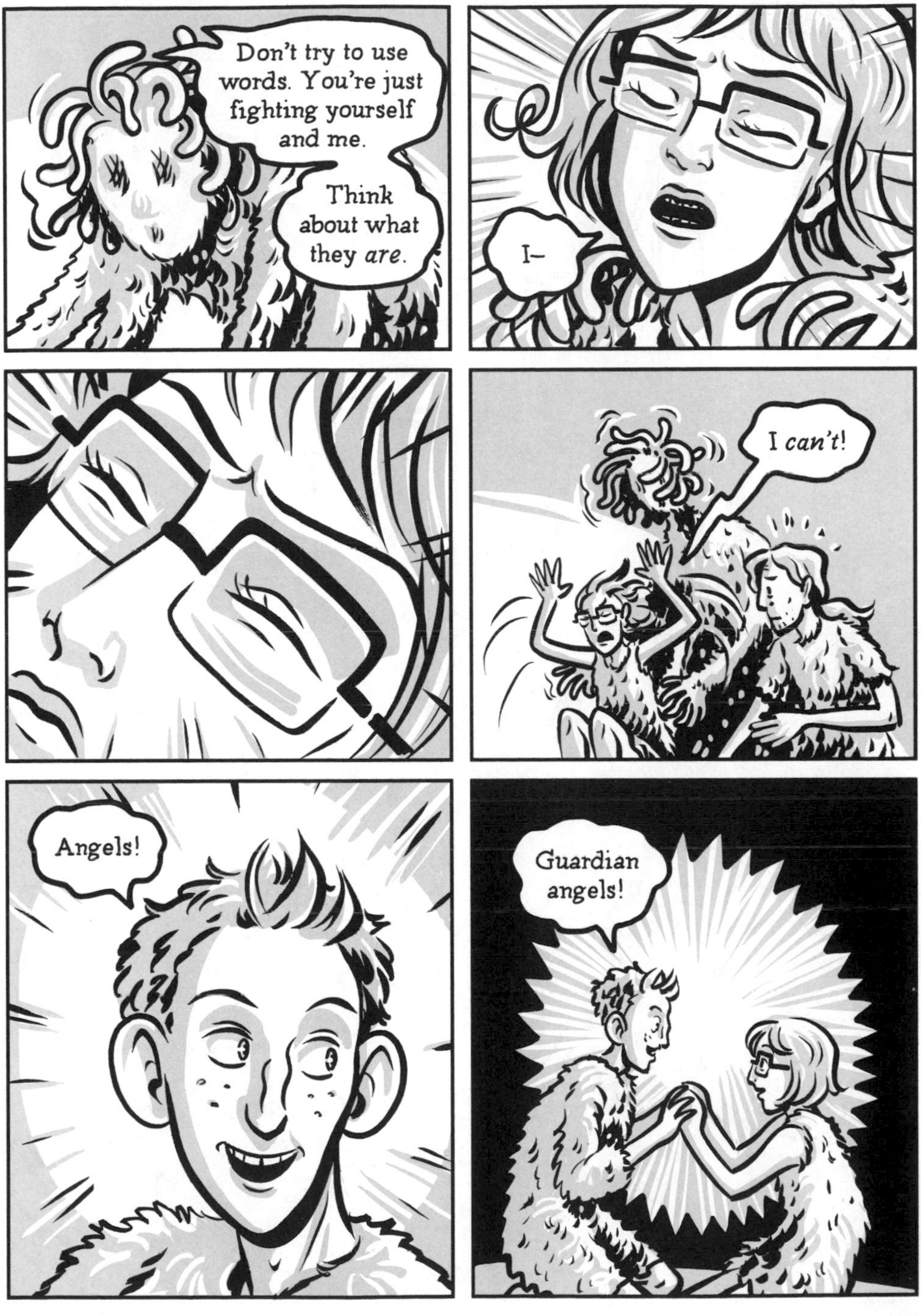
Don't try to use words. You're just fighting yourself and me.
Think about what they *are*.
I–
I *can't*!
Angels!
Guardian angels!

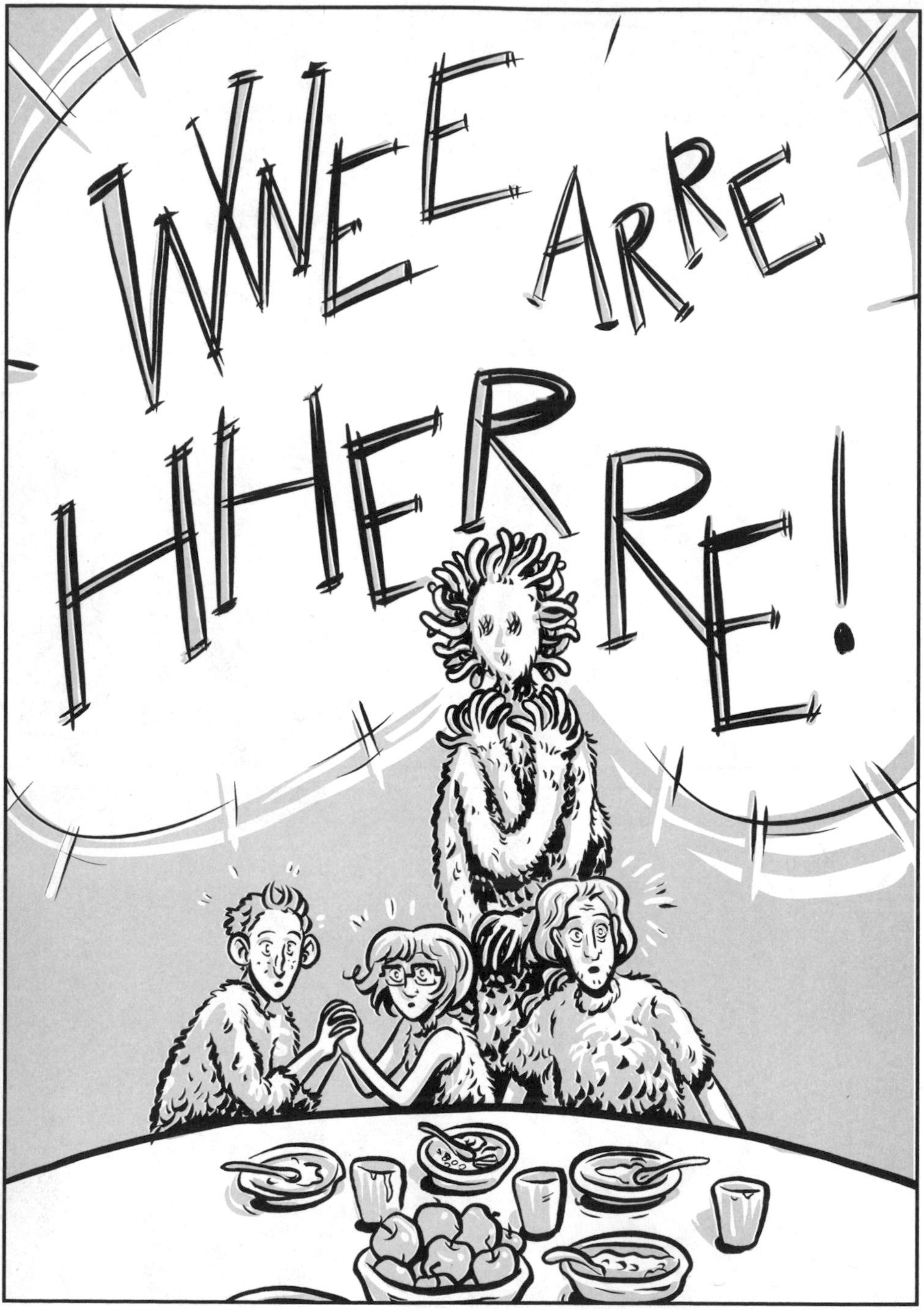
WWEE ARRE HHERRE!

12
The Foolish and the Weak

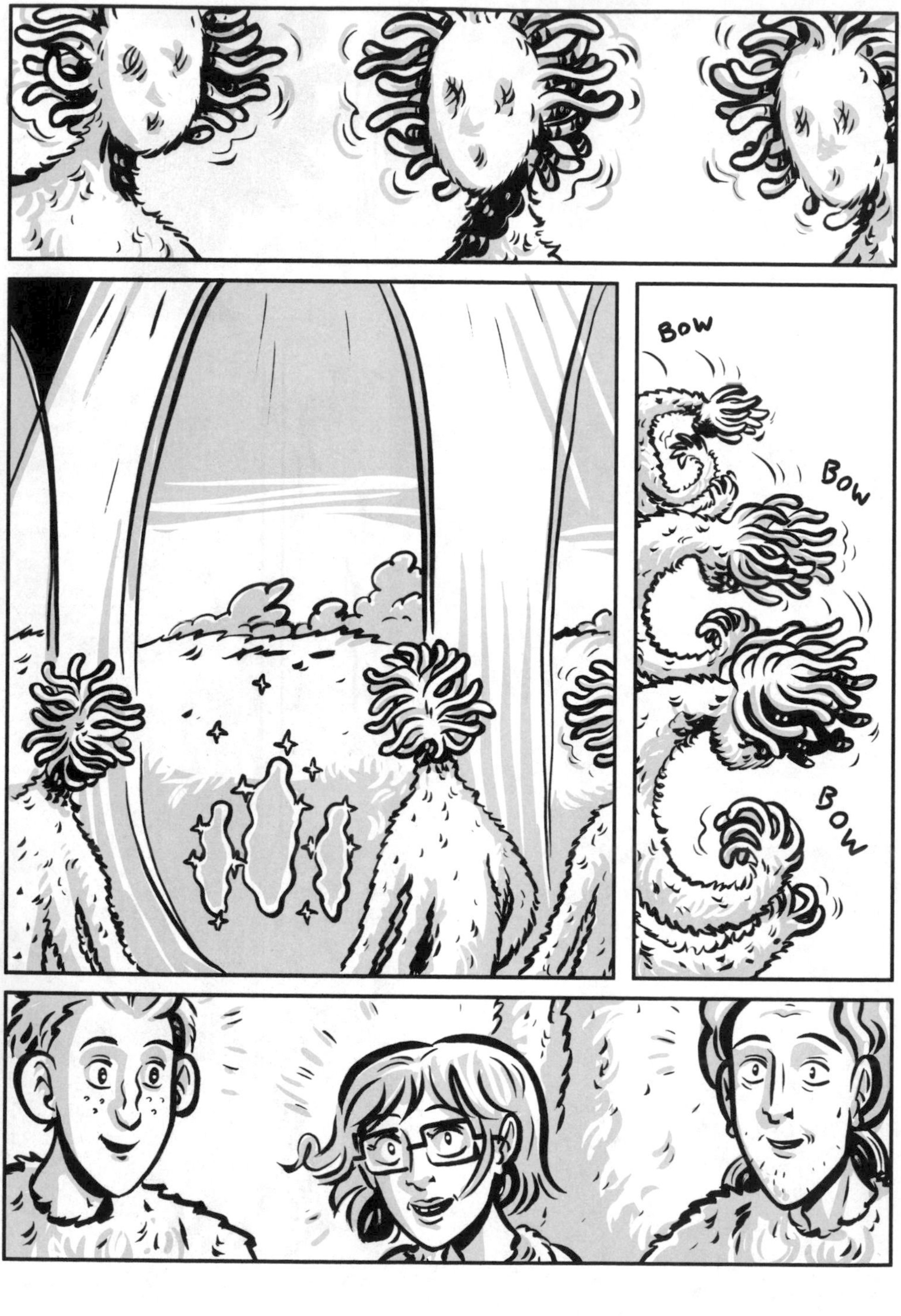
BOW
BOW
BOW

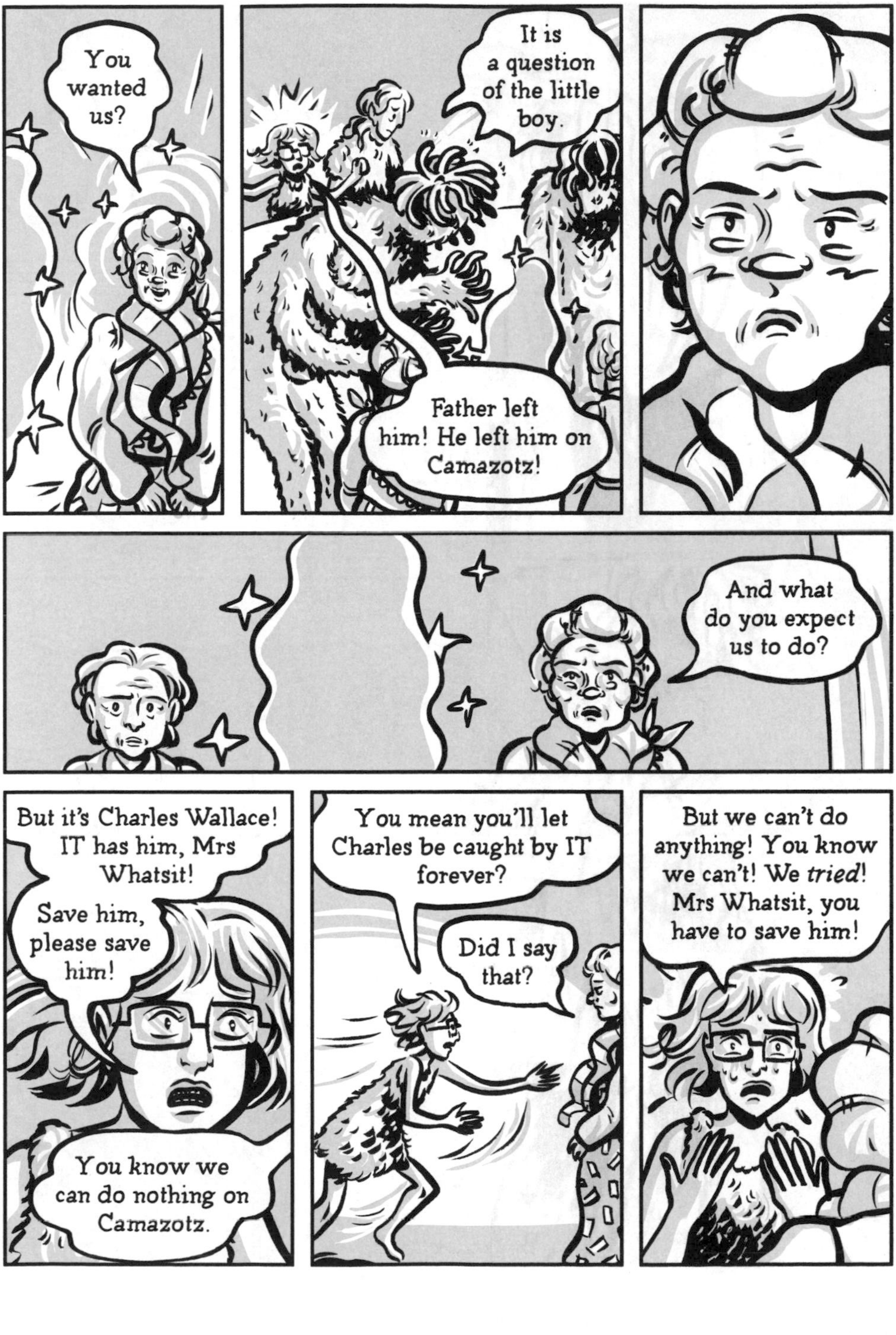
You wanted us?
It is a question of the little boy.
Father left him! He left him on Camazotz!
And what do you expect us to do?
But it's Charles Wallace! IT has him, Mrs Whatsit!
Save him, please save him!
You know we can do nothing on Camazotz.
You mean you'll let Charles be caught by IT forever?
Did I say that?
But we can't do anything! You know we can't! We *tried*! Mrs Whatsit, you have to save him!

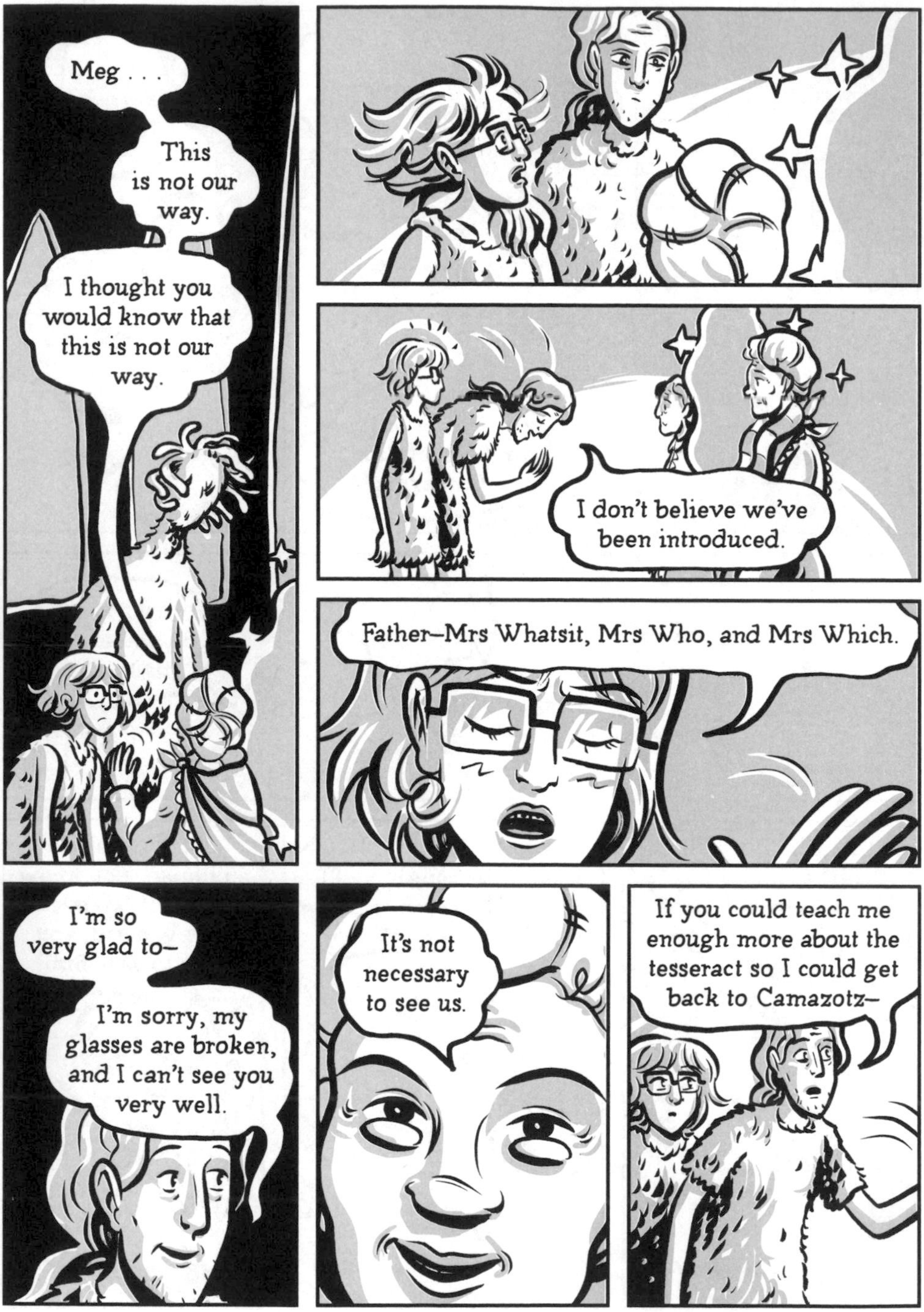

Meg . . .
This is not our way.
I thought you would know that this is not our way.
I don't believe we've been introduced.
Father—Mrs Whatsit, Mrs Who, and Mrs Which.
I'm so very glad to—
I'm sorry, my glasses are broken, and I can't see you very well.
It's not necessary to see us.
If you could teach me enough more about the tesseract so I could get back to Camazotz—

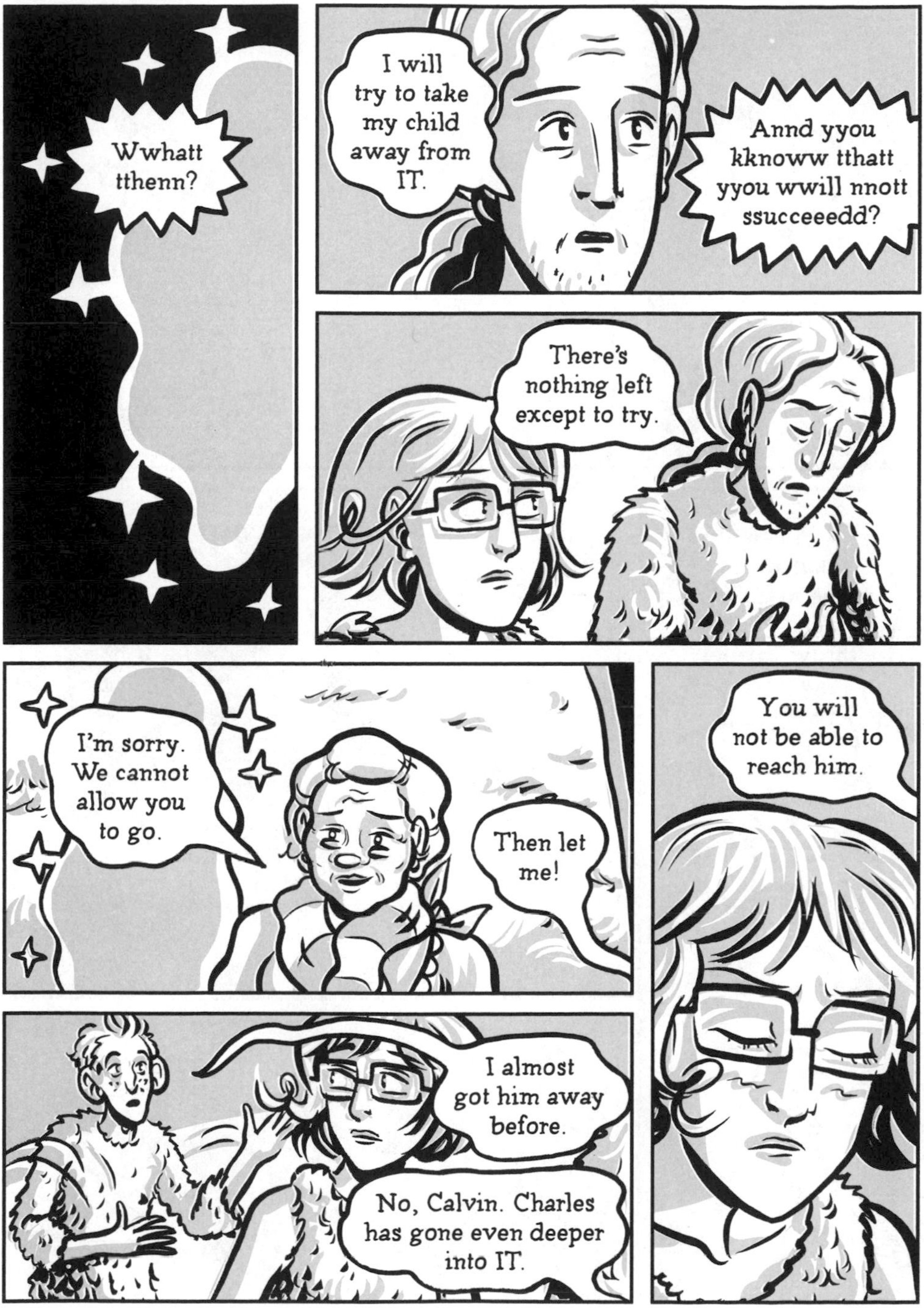
Wwhatt tthenn?
I will try to take my child away from IT.
Annd yyou kknoww tthatt yyou wwill nnott ssucceeedd?
There's nothing left except to try.
I'm sorry. We cannot allow you to go.
Then let me!
You will not be able to reach him.
I almost got him away before.
No, Calvin. Charles has gone even deeper into IT.

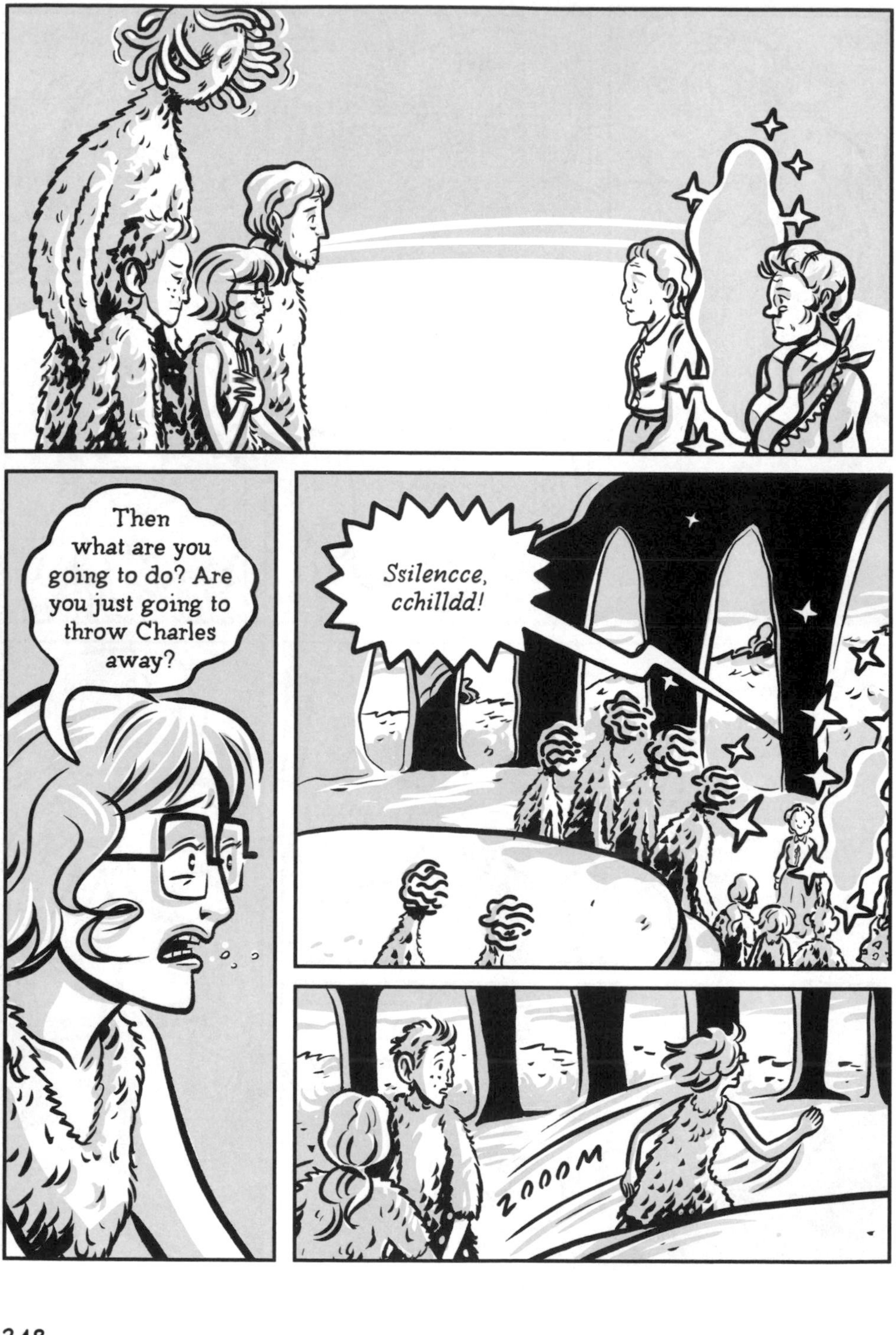
Then what are you going to do? Are you just going to throw Charles away?
Ssilencce, cchilldd!
ZOOOM

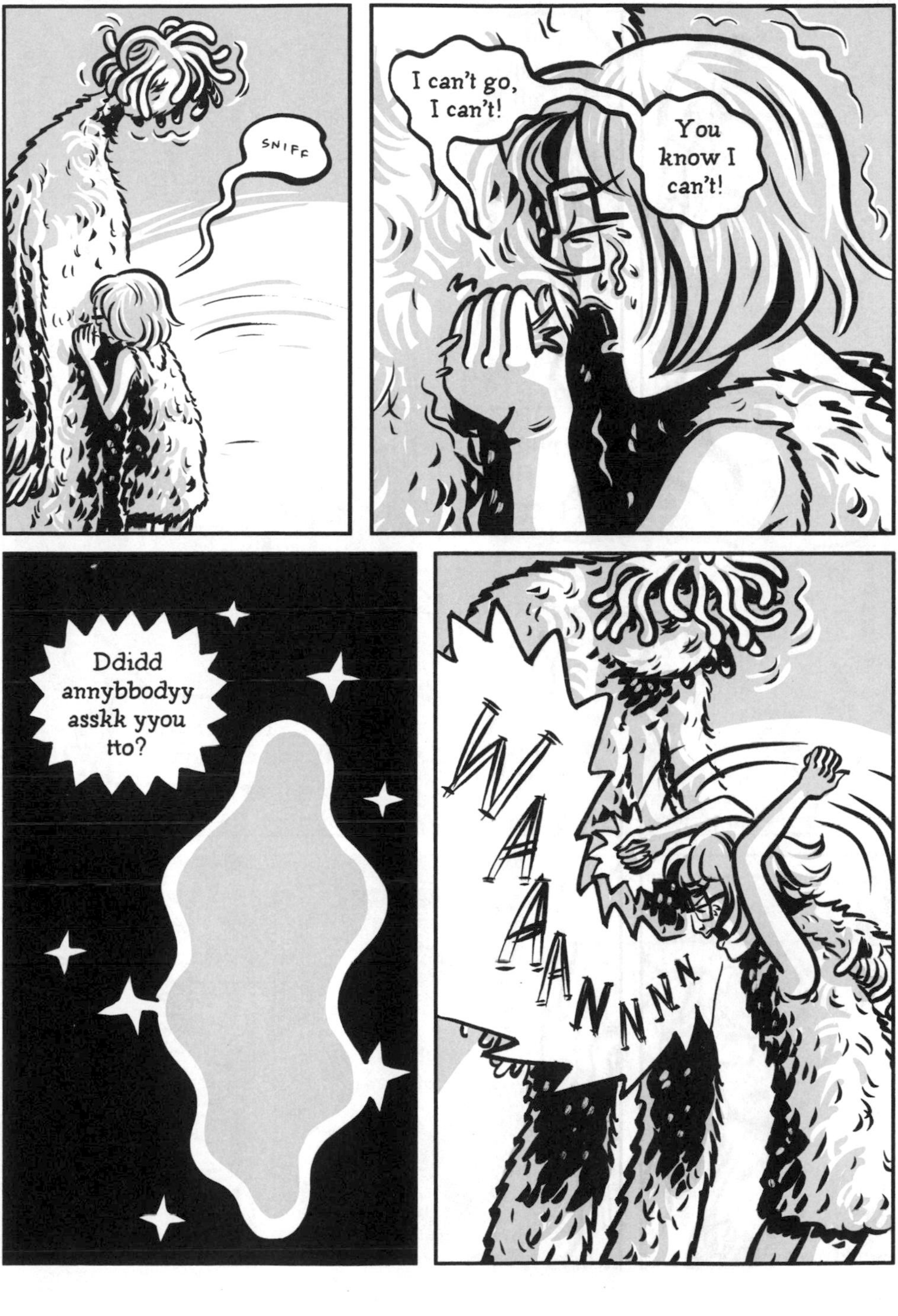
SNIFF
I can't go, I can't!
You know I can't!
Ddidd annybbodyy asskk yyou tto?
WAAAANNNN

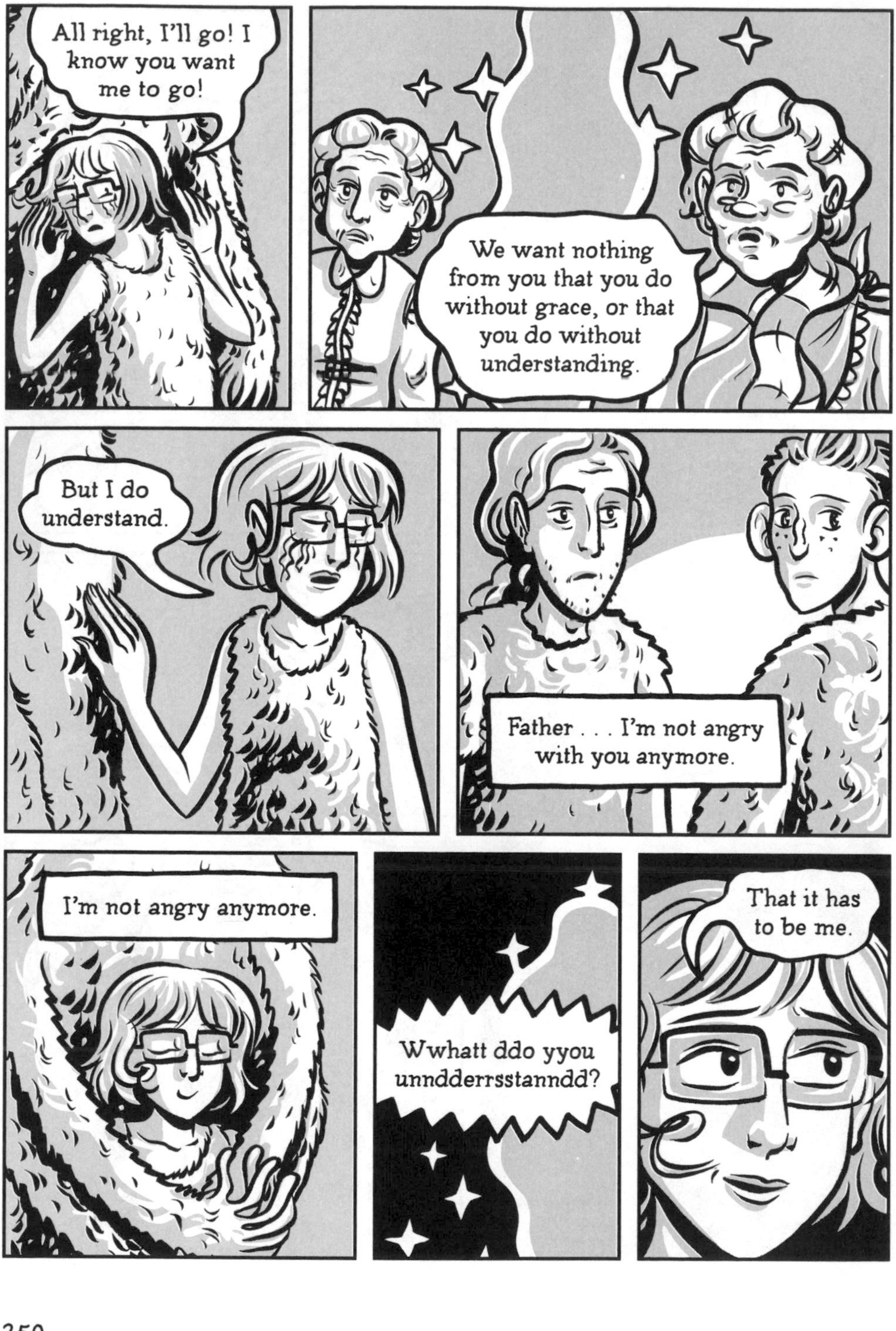
All right, I'll go! I know you want me to go!
We want nothing from you that you do without grace, or that you do without understanding.
But I do understand.
Father . . . I'm not angry with you anymore.
I'm not angry anymore.
Wwhatt ddo yyou unnddderrsstanndd?
That it has to be me.

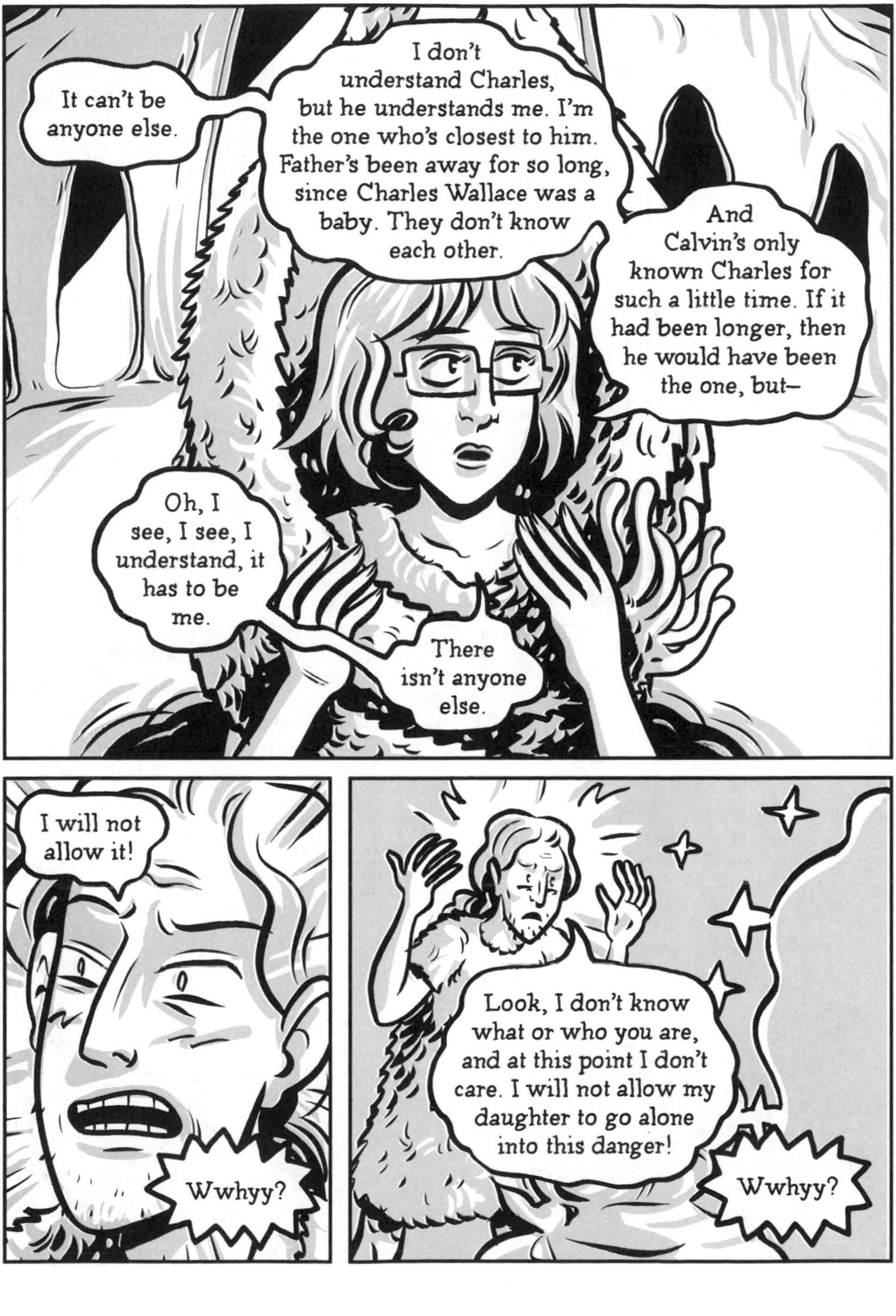
It can't be anyone else.
I don't understand Charles, but he understands me. I'm the one who's closest to him. Father's been away for so long, since Charles Wallace was a baby. They don't know each other.
And Calvin's only known Charles for such a little time. If it had been longer, then he would have been the one, but—
Oh, I see, I see, I understand, it has to be me.
There isn't anyone else.
I will not allow it!
Wwhyy?
Look, I don't know what or who you are, and at this point I don't care. I will not allow my daughter to go alone into this danger!
Wwhyy?

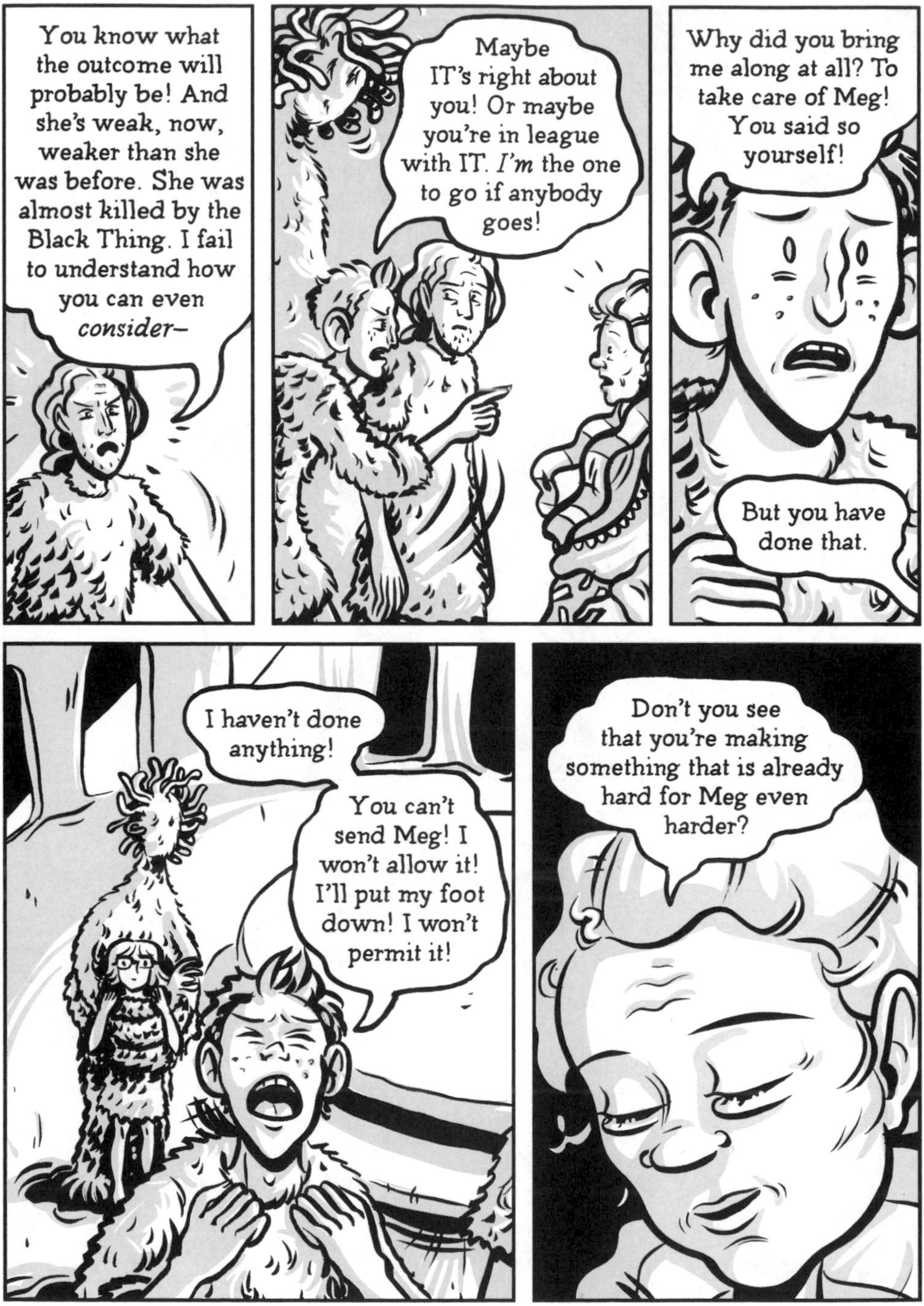
You know what the outcome will probably be! And she's weak, now, weaker than she was before. She was almost killed by the Black Thing. I fail to understand how you can even *consider*–
Maybe IT's right about you! Or maybe you're in league with IT. *I'm* the one to go if anybody goes!
Why did you bring me along at all? To take care of Meg! You said so yourself!
But you have done that.
I haven't done anything!
You can't send Meg! I won't allow it! I'll put my foot down! I won't permit it!
Don't you see that you're making something that is already hard for Meg even harder?

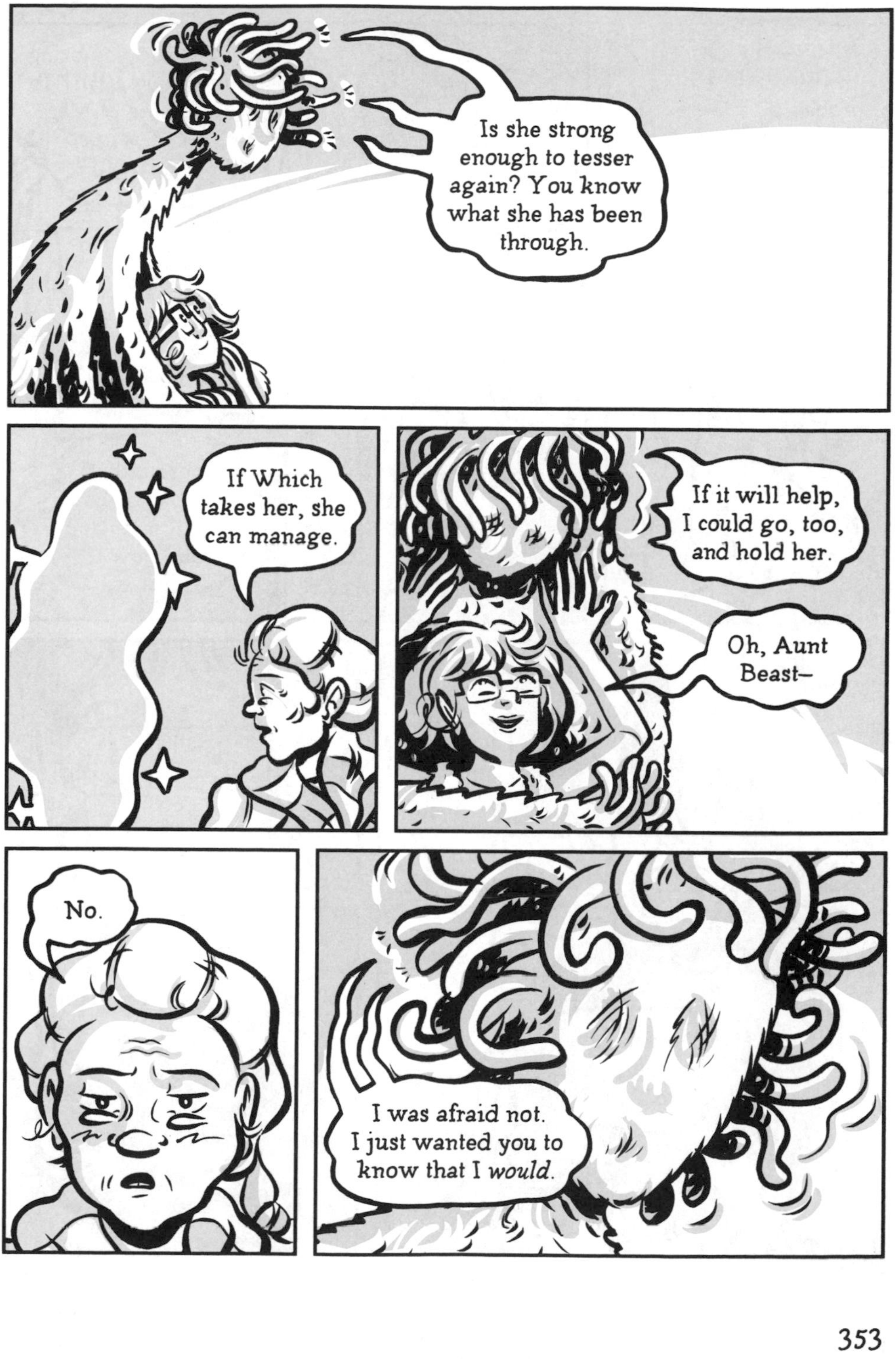
Is she strong enough to tesser again? You know what she has been through.
If Which takes her, she can manage.
If it will help, I could go, too, and hold her.
Oh, Aunt Beast–
No.
I was afraid not. I just wanted you to know that I *would*.

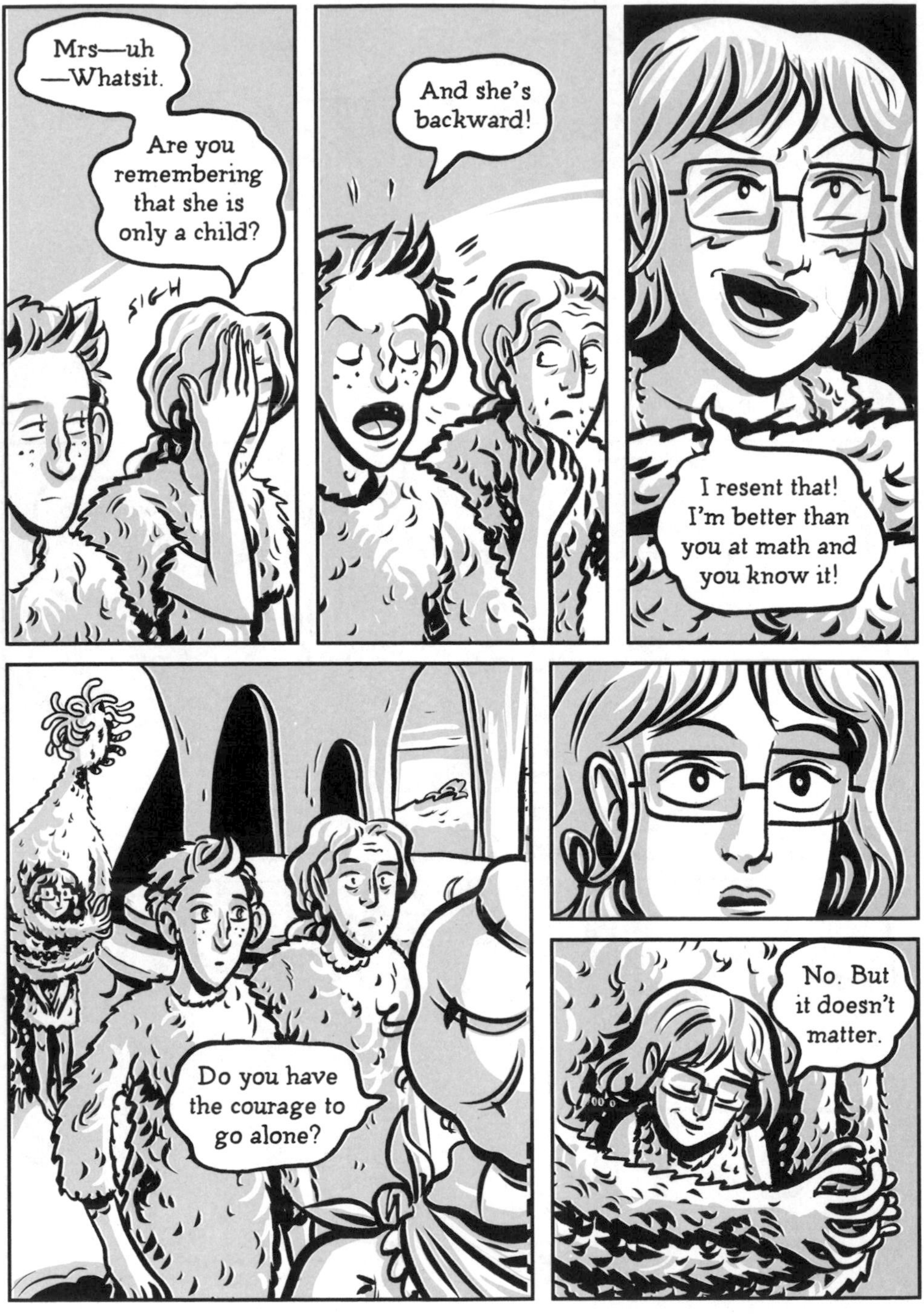
Mrs—uh —Whatsit.
Are you remembering that she is only a child?
SIGH
And she's backward!
I resent that! I'm better than you at math and you know it!
Do you have the courage to go alone?
No. But it doesn't matter.

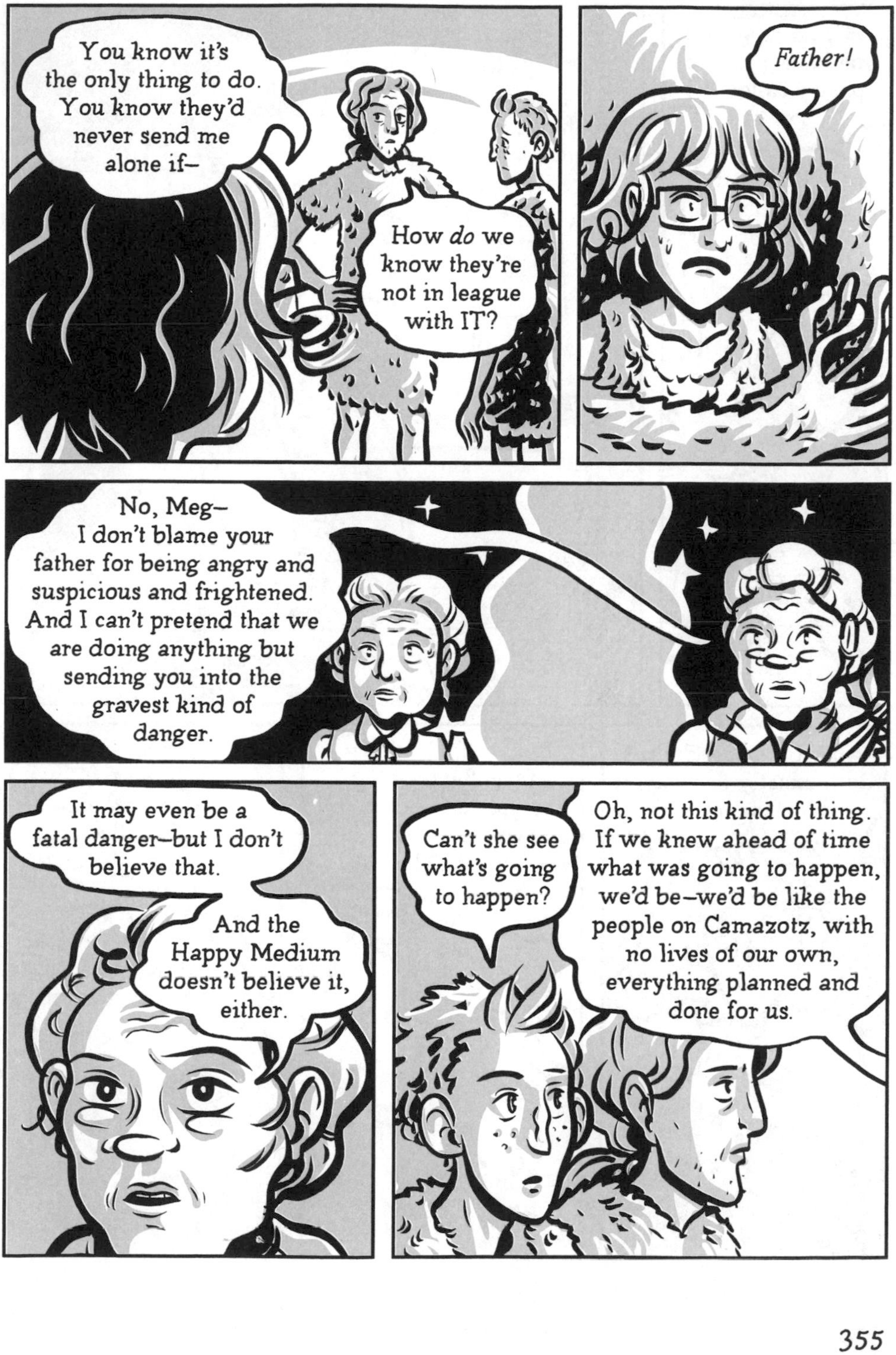
You know it's the only thing to do. You know they'd never send me alone if–
How *do* we know they're not in league with IT?
Father!
No, Meg– I don't blame your father for being angry and suspicious and frightened. And I can't pretend that we are doing anything but sending you into the gravest kind of danger.
It may even be a fatal danger–but I don't believe that.
And the Happy Medium doesn't believe it, either.
Can't she see what's going to happen?
Oh, not this kind of thing. If we knew ahead of time what was going to happen, we'd be–we'd be like the people on Camazotz, with no lives of our own, everything planned and done for us.

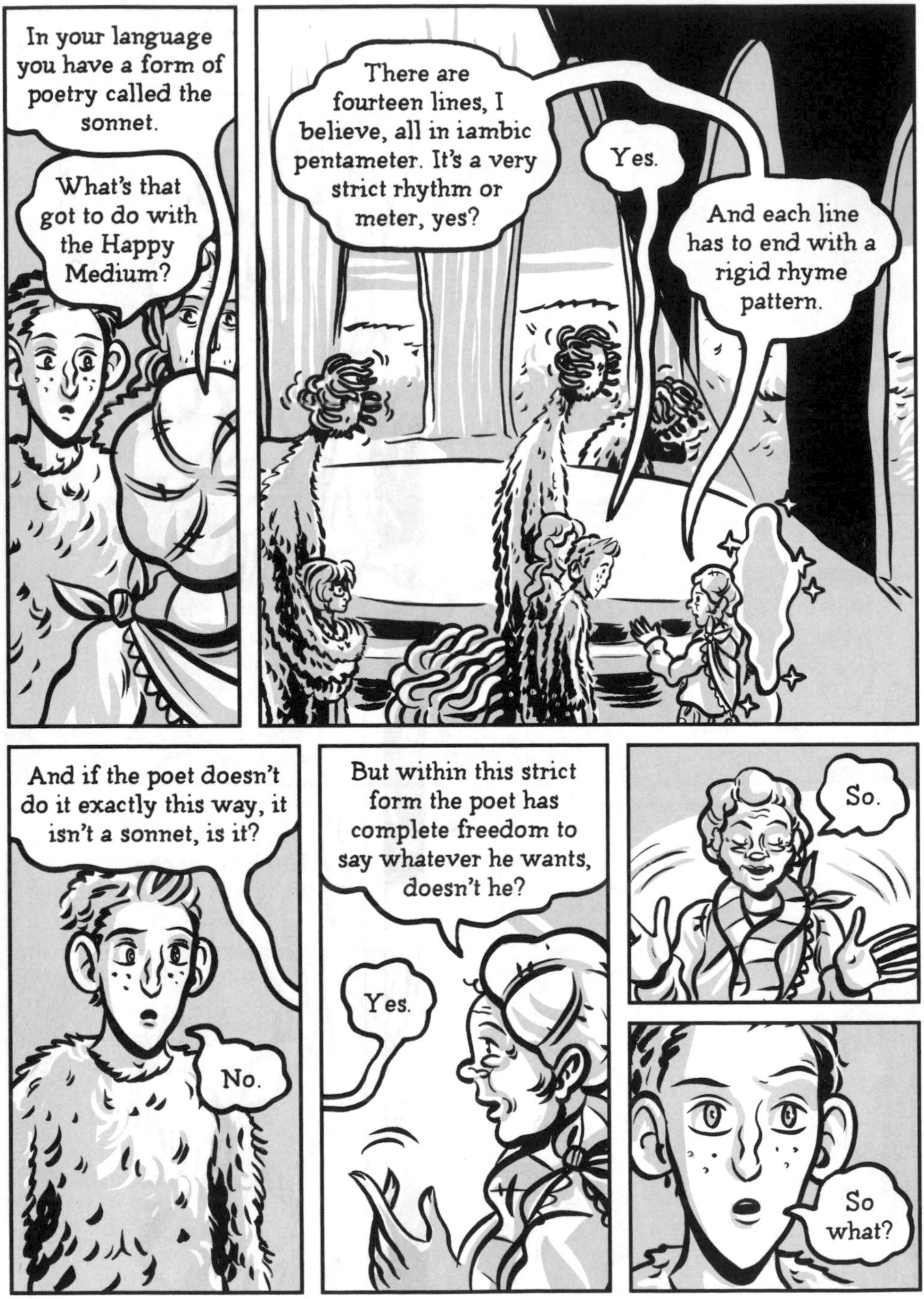
In your language you have a form of poetry called the sonnet.
What's that got to do with the Happy Medium?
There are fourteen lines, I believe, all in iambic pentameter. It's a very strict rhythm or meter, yes?
Yes.
And each line has to end with a rigid rhyme pattern.
And if the poet doesn't do it exactly this way, it isn't a sonnet, is it?
No.
But within this strict form the poet has complete freedom to say whatever he wants, doesn't he?
Yes.
So.
So what?

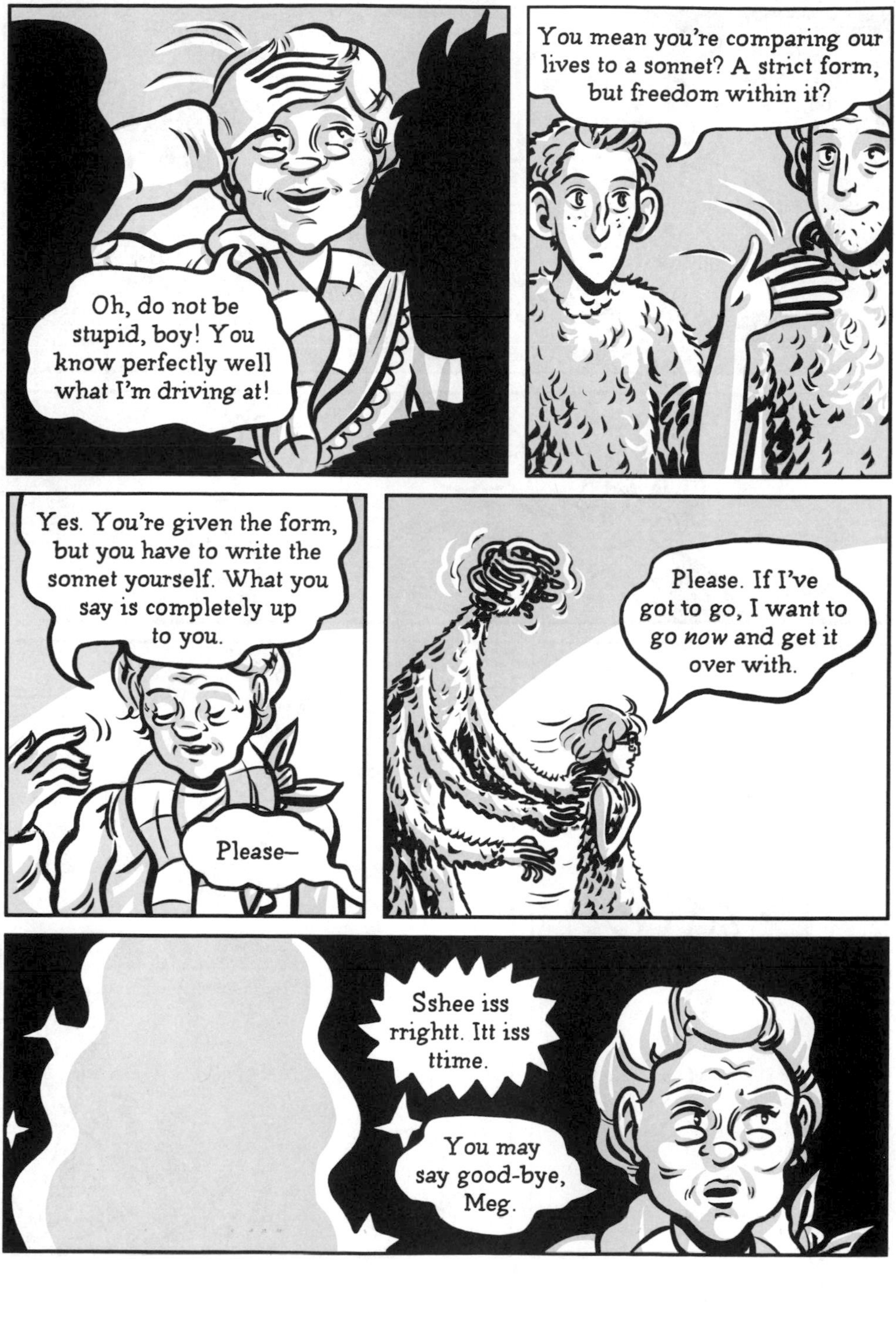
Oh, do not be stupid, boy! You know perfectly well what I'm driving at!
You mean you're comparing our lives to a sonnet? A strict form, but freedom within it?
Yes. You're given the form, but you have to write the sonnet yourself. What you say is completely up to you.
Please–
Please. If I've got to go, I want to go *now* and get it over with.
Sshee iss rrightt. Itt iss ttime.
You may say good-bye, Meg.

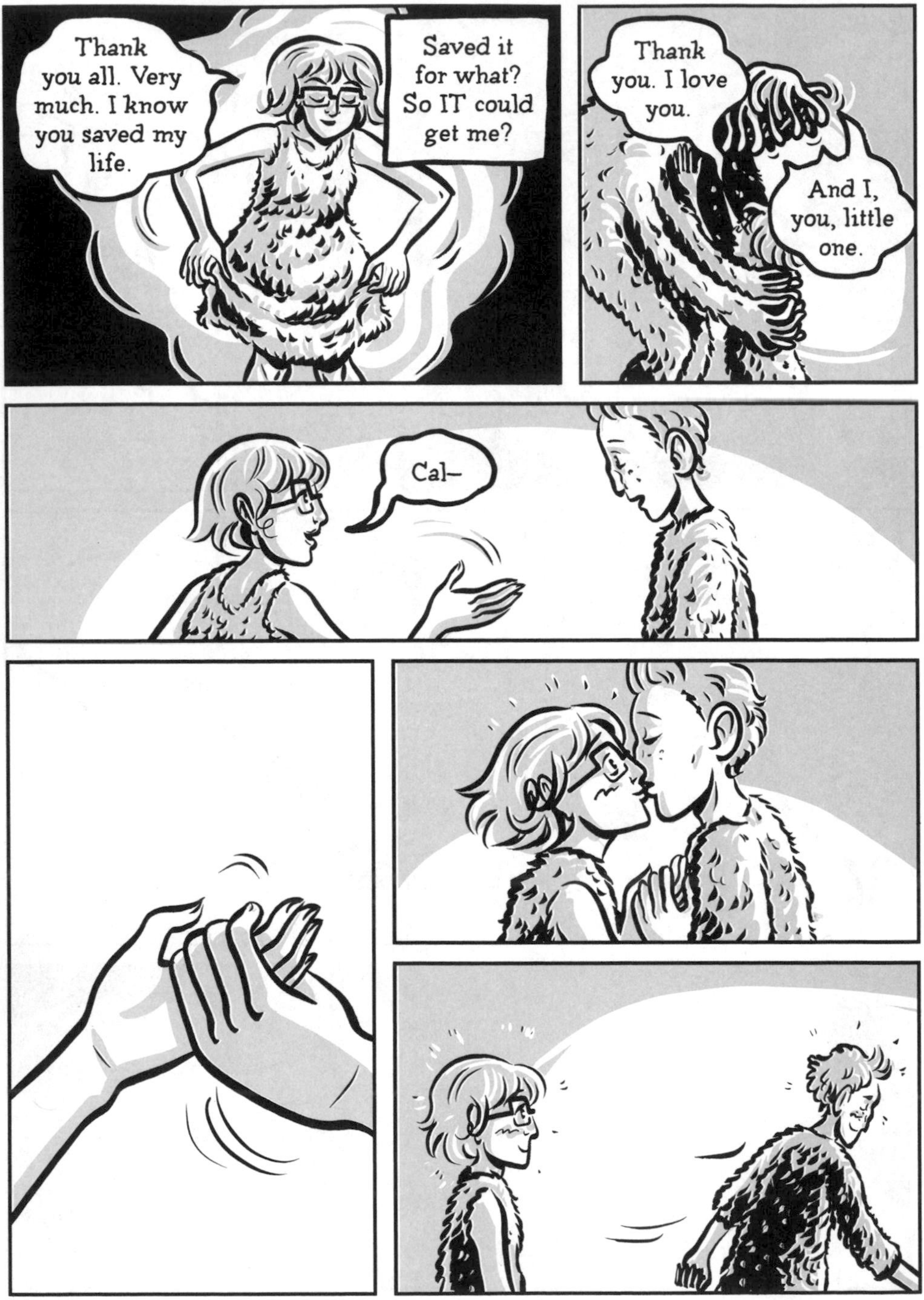
Thank you all. Very much. I know you saved my life.
Saved it for what? So IT could get me?
Thank you. I love you.
And I, you, little one.
Cal–

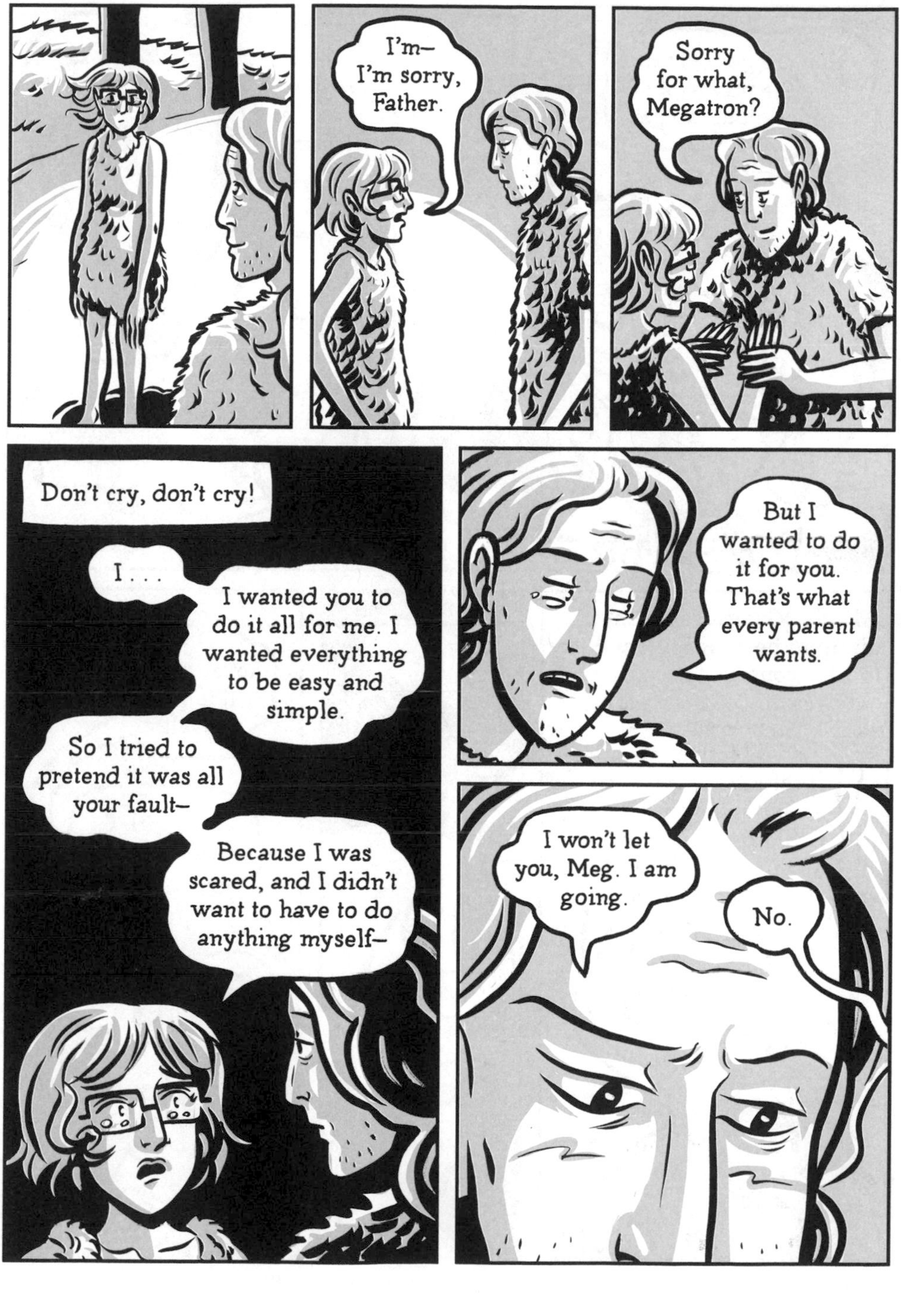
I'm—
I'm sorry, Father.
Sorry for what, Megatron?
Don't cry, don't cry!
I...
I wanted you to do it all for me. I wanted everything to be easy and simple.
So I tried to pretend it was all your fault—
Because I was scared, and I didn't want to have to do anything myself—
But I wanted to do it for you. That's what every parent wants.
I won't let you, Meg. I am going.
No.

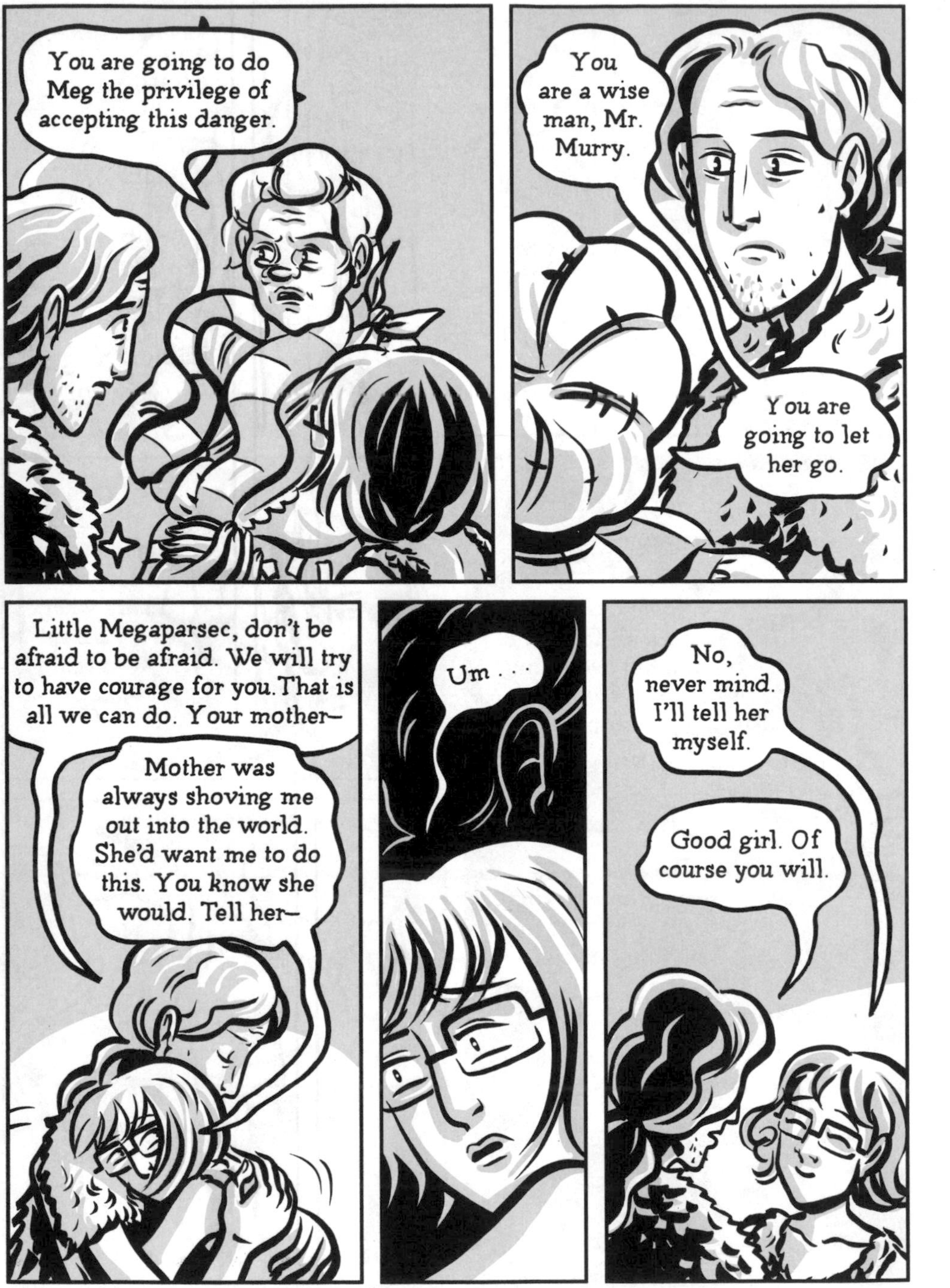
You are going to do Meg the privilege of accepting this danger.
You are a wise man, Mr. Murry.
You are going to let her go.
Little Megaparsec, don't be afraid to be afraid. We will try to have courage for you. That is all we can do. Your mother—
Mother was always shoving me out into the world. She'd want me to do this. You know she would. Tell her—
Um . . .
No, never mind. I'll tell her myself.
Good girl. Of course you will.

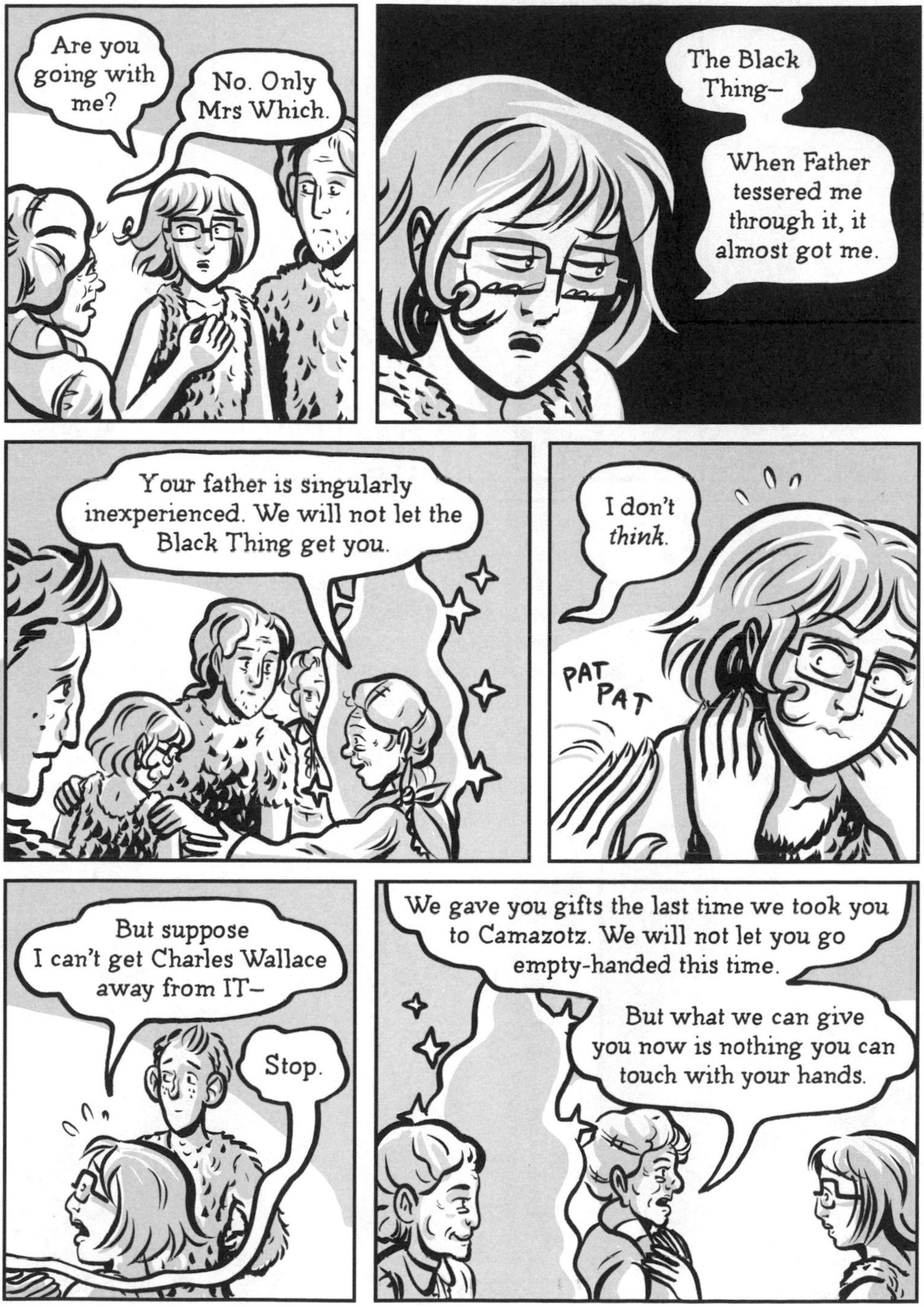
Are you going with me?
No. Only Mrs Which.
The Black Thing—
When Father tessered me through it, it almost got me.
Your father is singularly inexperienced. We will not let the Black Thing get you.
I don't *think*.
PAT PAT
But suppose I can't get Charles Wallace away from IT—
Stop.
We gave you gifts the last time we took you to Camazotz. We will not let you go empty-handed this time.
But what we can give you now is nothing you can touch with your hands.

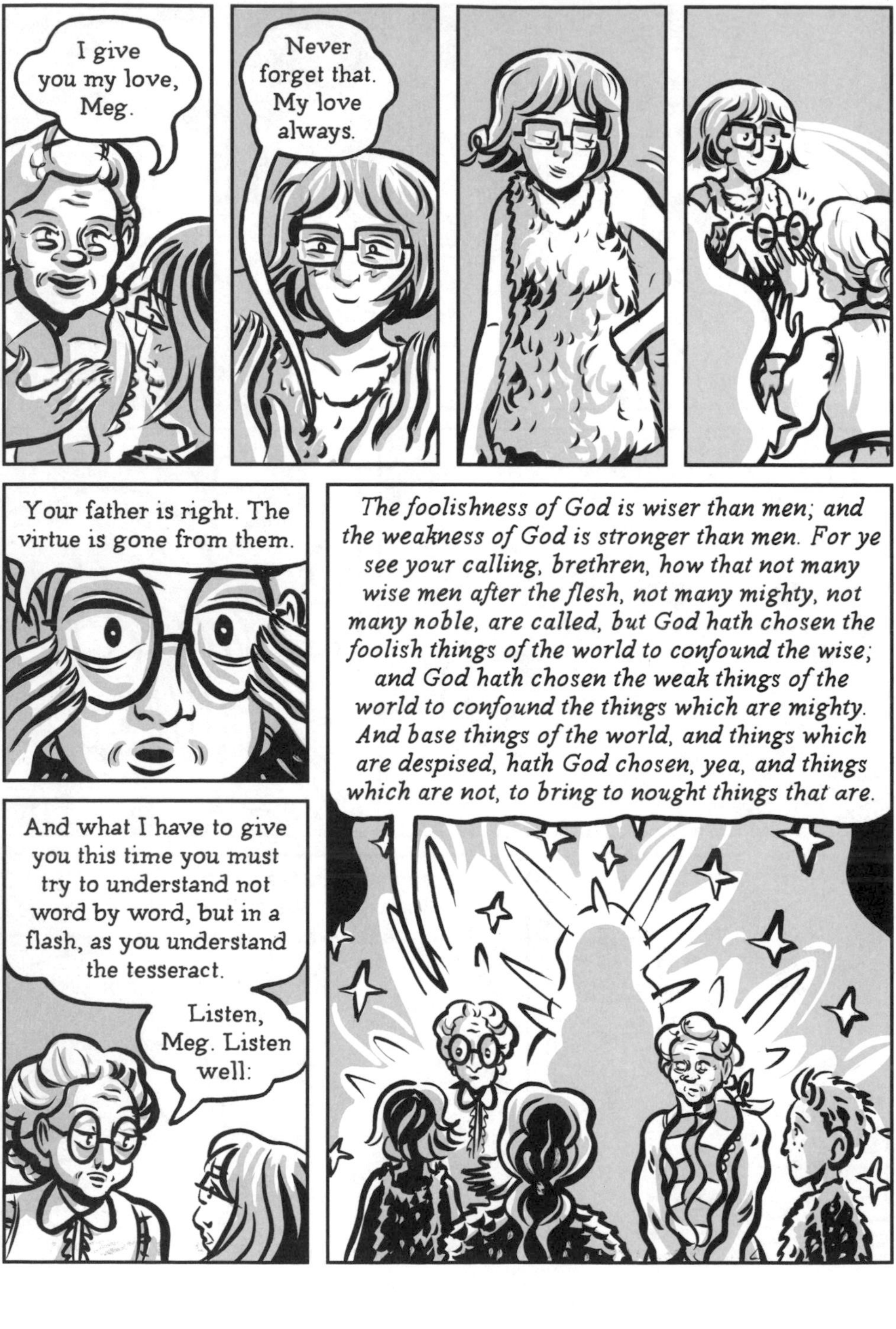
I give you my love, Meg.
Never forget that. My love always.
Your father is right. The virtue is gone from them.
And what I have to give you this time you must try to understand not word by word, but in a flash, as you understand the tesseract.
Listen, Meg. Listen well:
The foolishness of God is wiser than men; and the weakness of God is stronger than men. For ye see your calling, brethren, how that not many wise men after the flesh, not many mighty, not many noble, are called, but God hath chosen the foolish things of the world to confound the wise; and God hath chosen the weak things of the world to confound the things which are mighty. And base things of the world, and things which are despised, hath God chosen, yea, and things which are not, to bring to nought things that are.

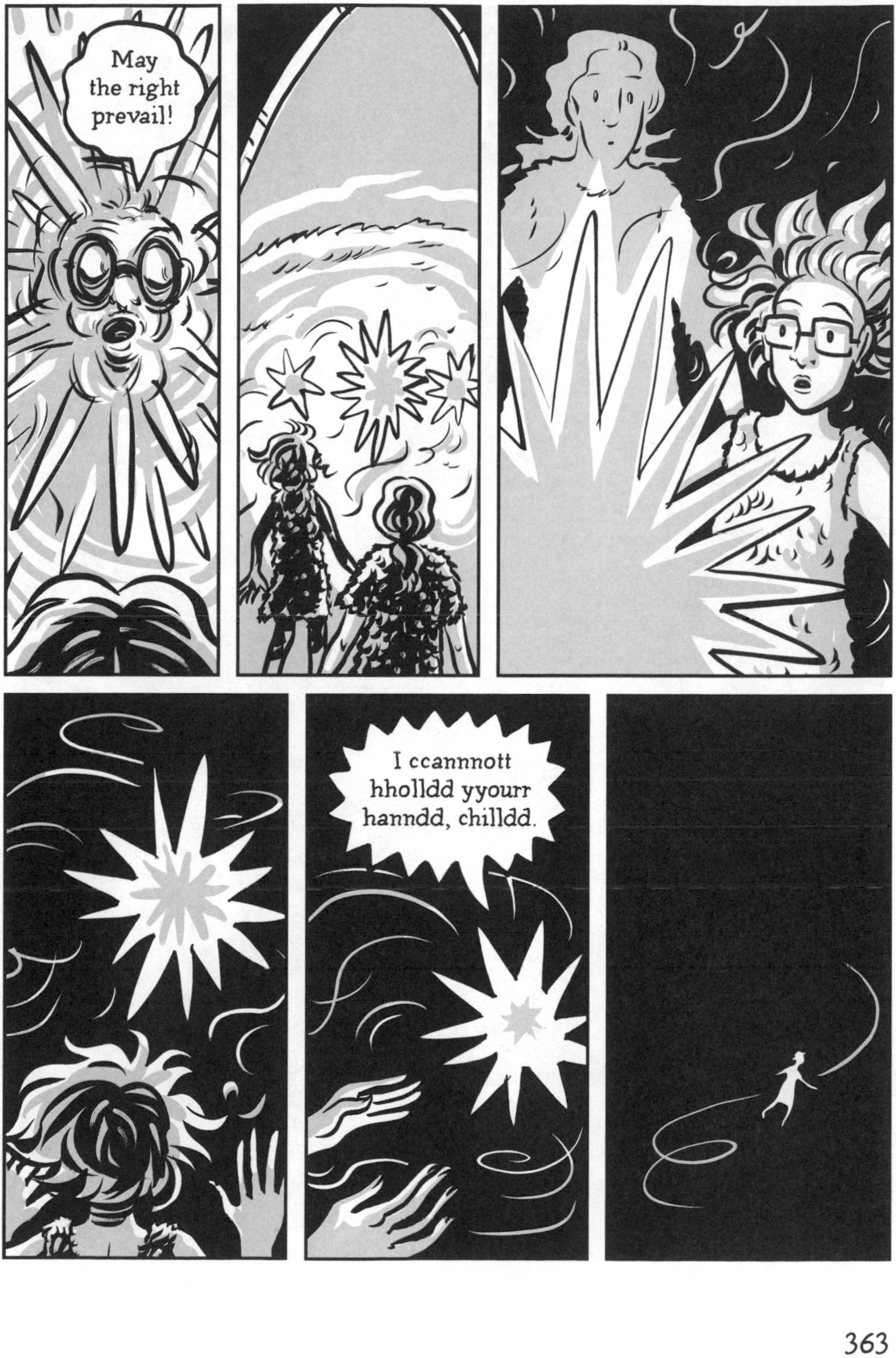
May the right prevail!
I ccannnott hhollldd yyourr hanndd, chillldd.

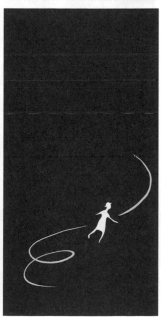

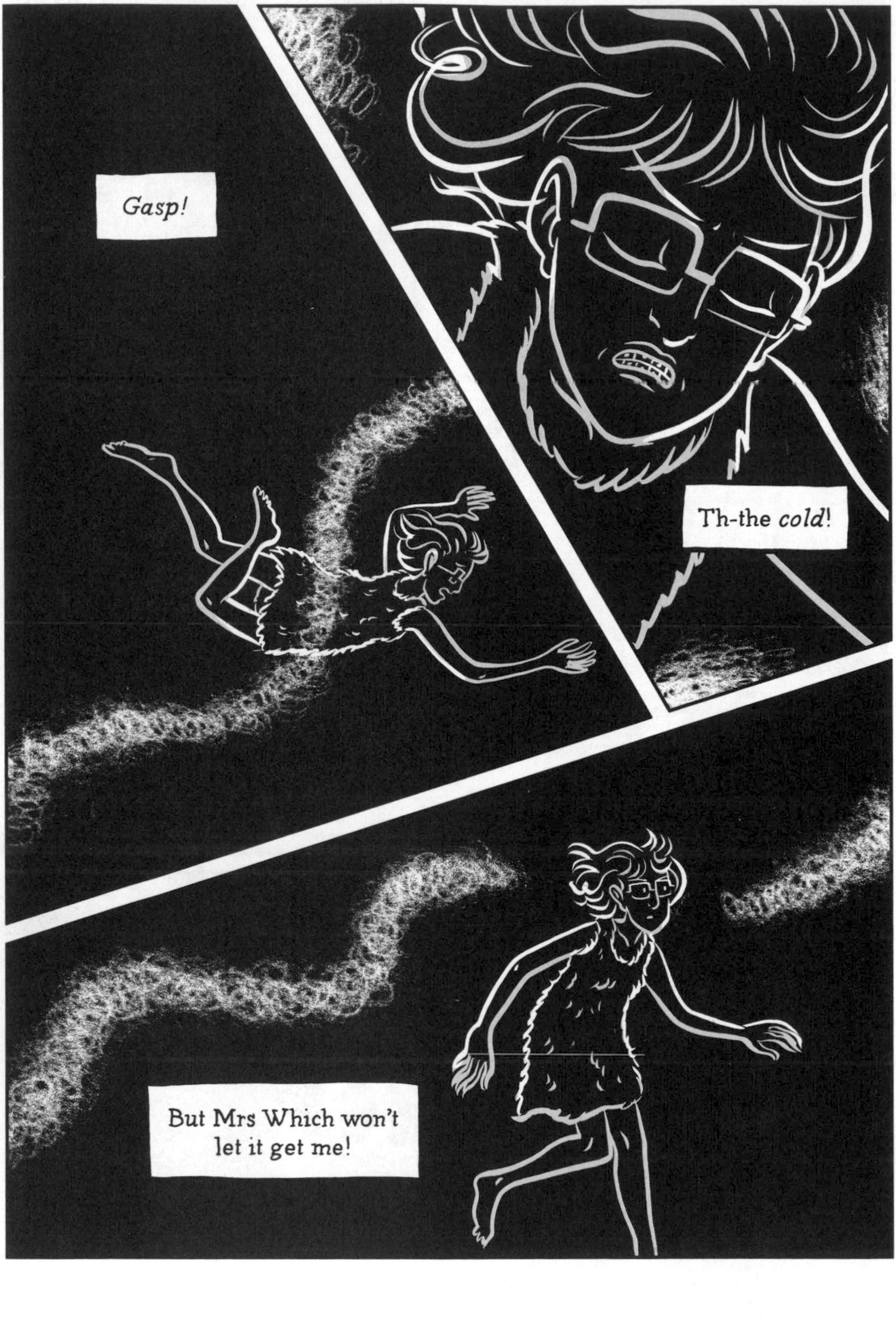

Gasp!
Th-the *cold*!
But Mrs Which won't let it get me!

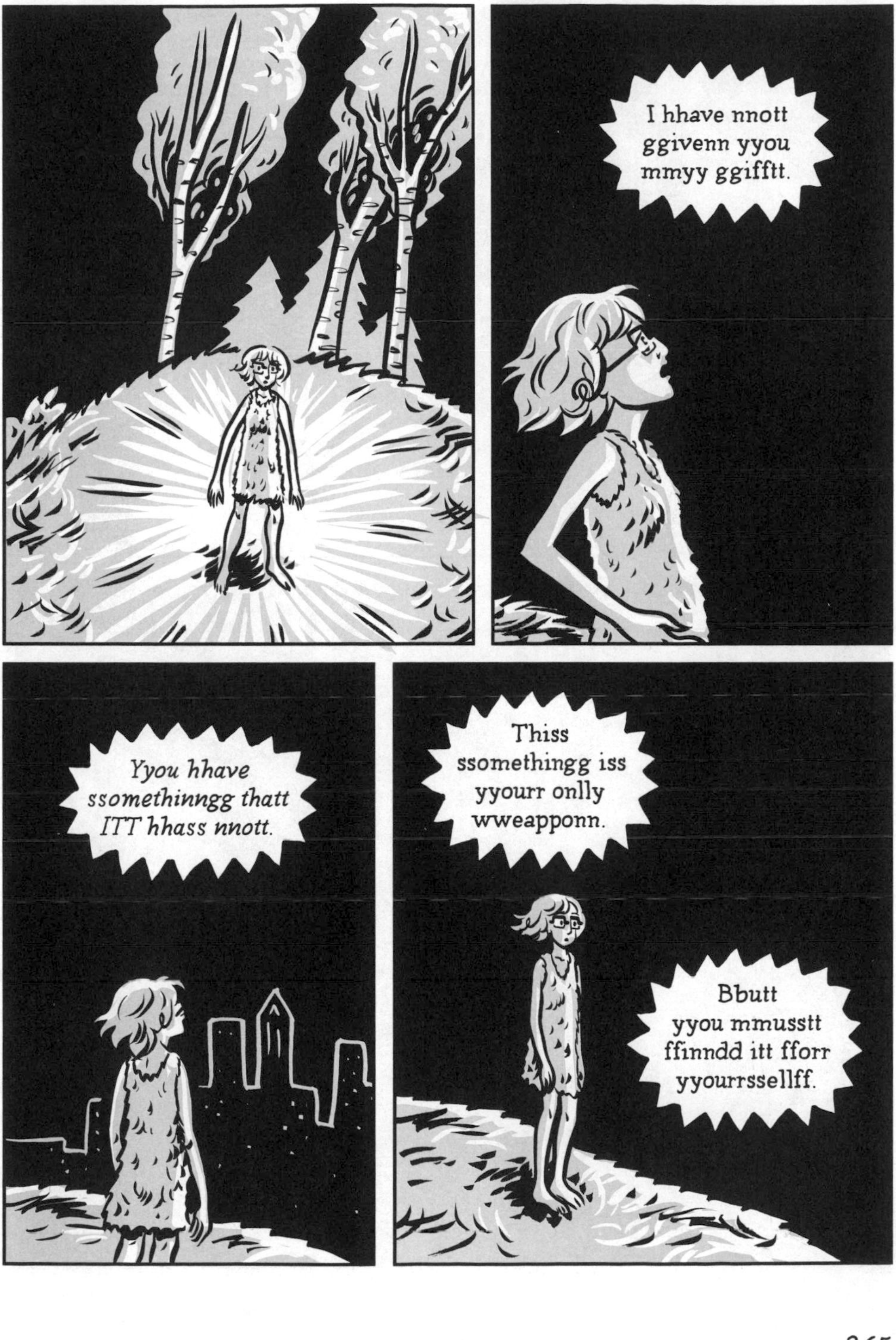
I hhave nnott ggivenn yyou mmyy ggiffttt.
Yyou hhave ssomethinngg thatt ITT hhass nnott.
Thiss ssomethingg iss yyourr onlly wweapponn.
Bbutt yyou mmusstt ffinndd itt fforr yyourrssellff.

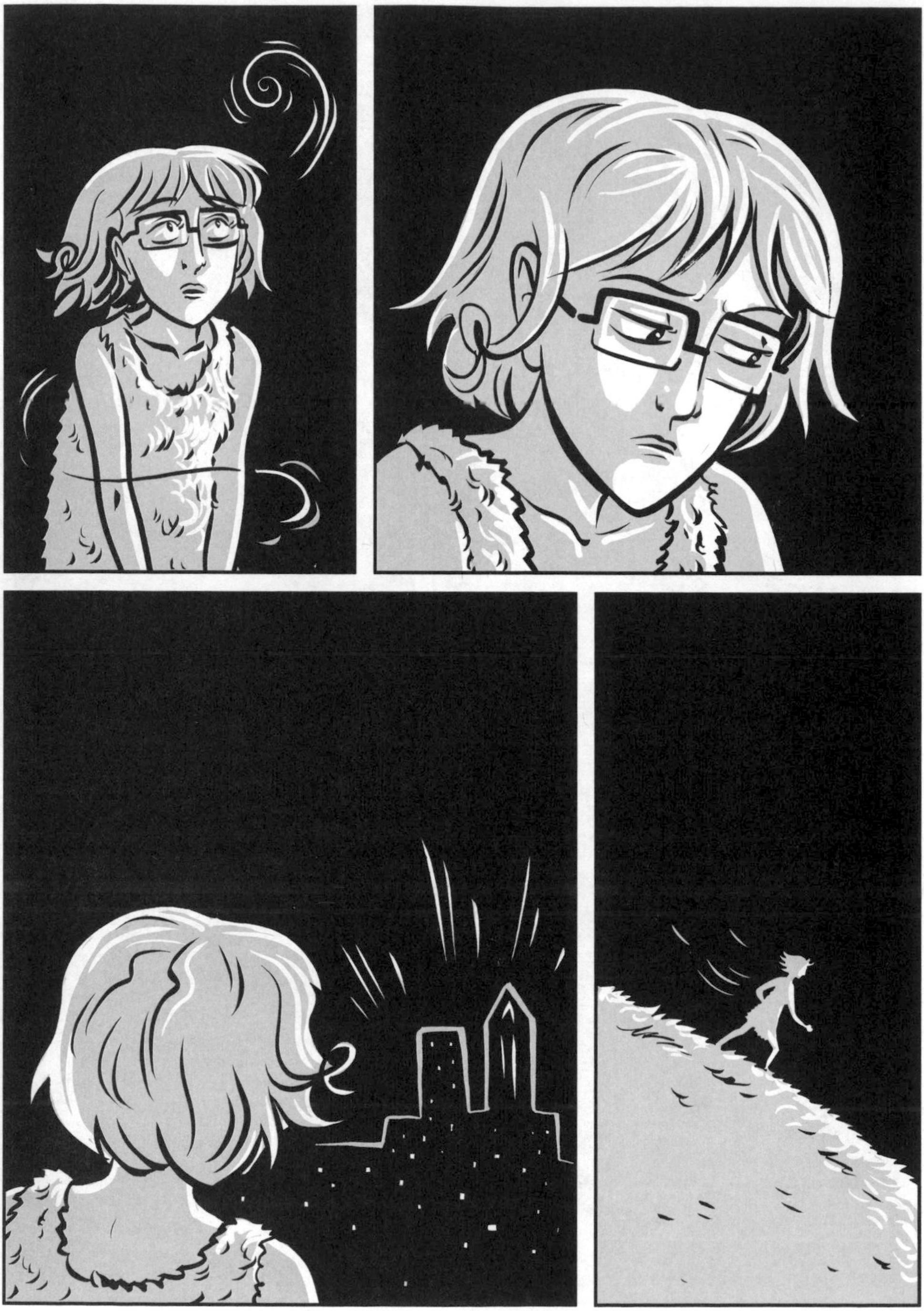

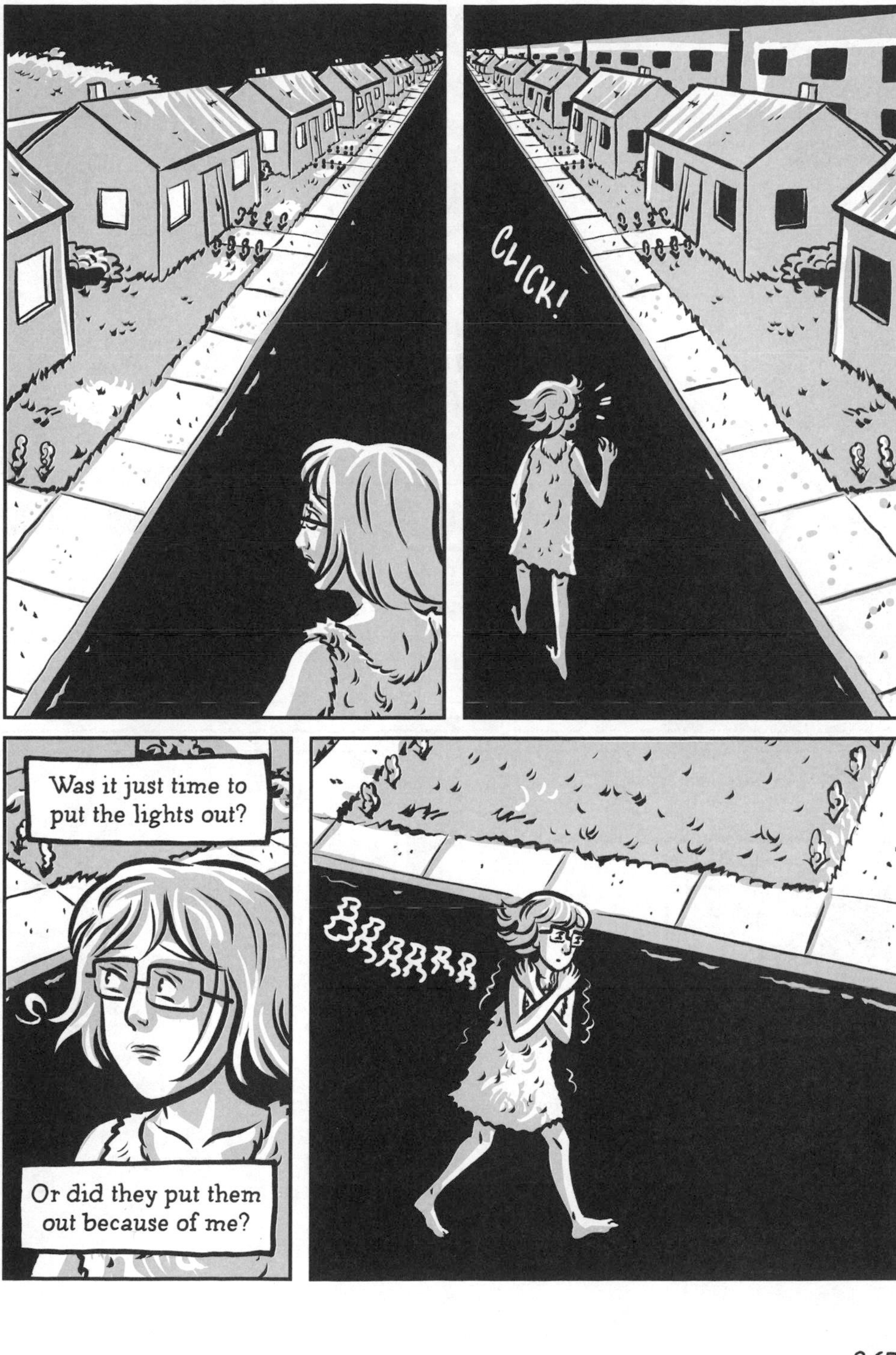
CLICK!
Was it just time to put the lights out?
Or did they put them out because of me?
BRRRRR

What have I got that IT hasn't got?

What?

IT isn't used to being resisted.

Father said that's how he managed, and how Calvin and I managed as long as we did.

Father saved me then, but there's nobody to save me now.

I have to resist IT by myself. Is that what I have that IT hasn't got?

I have to do it myself.

No, I'm sure IT can resist. IT just isn't used to having other people resist.

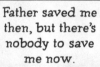

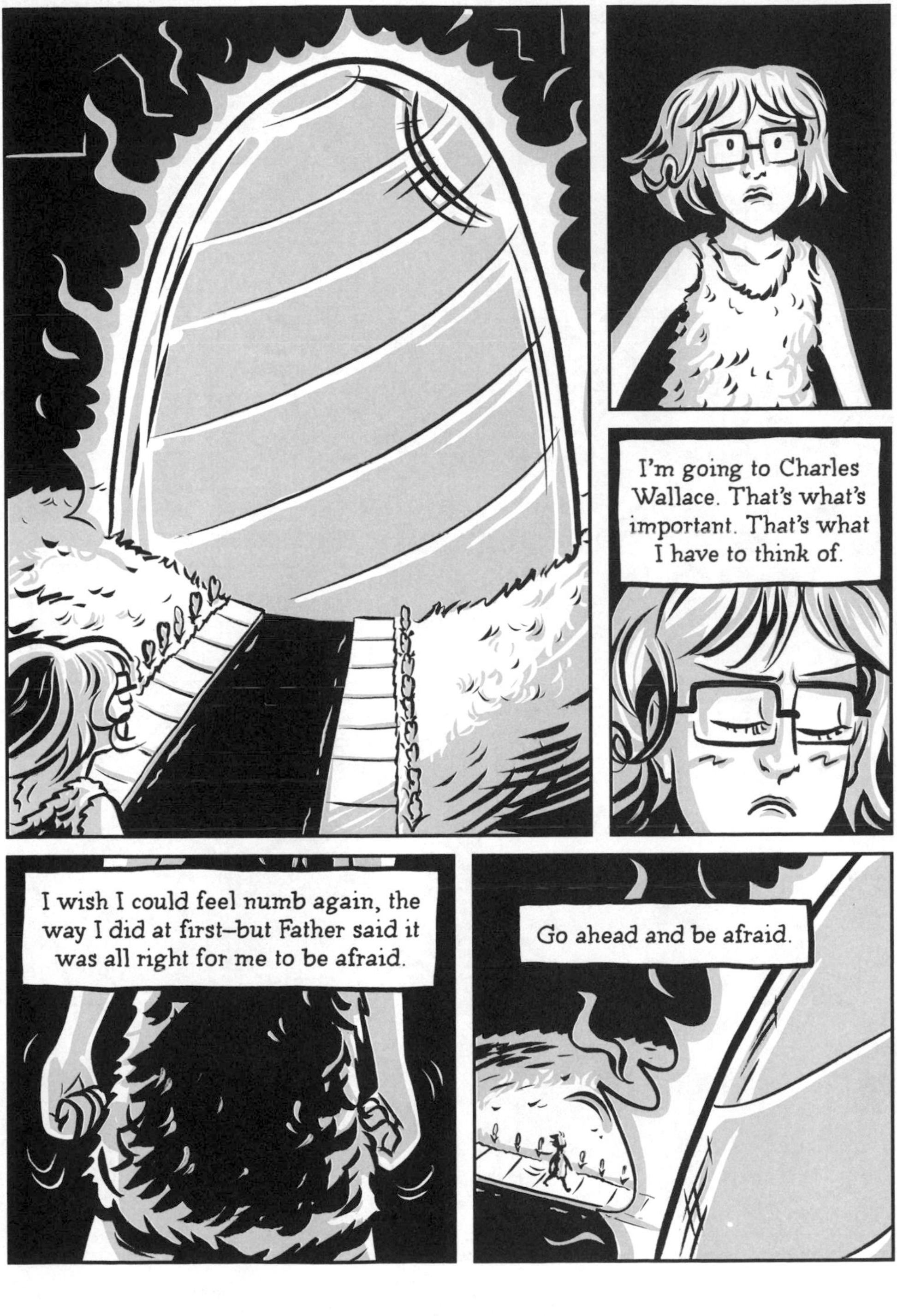
I'm going to Charles Wallace. That's what's important. That's what I have to think of.
I wish I could feel numb again, the way I did at first—but Father said it was all right for me to be afraid.
Go ahead and be afraid.

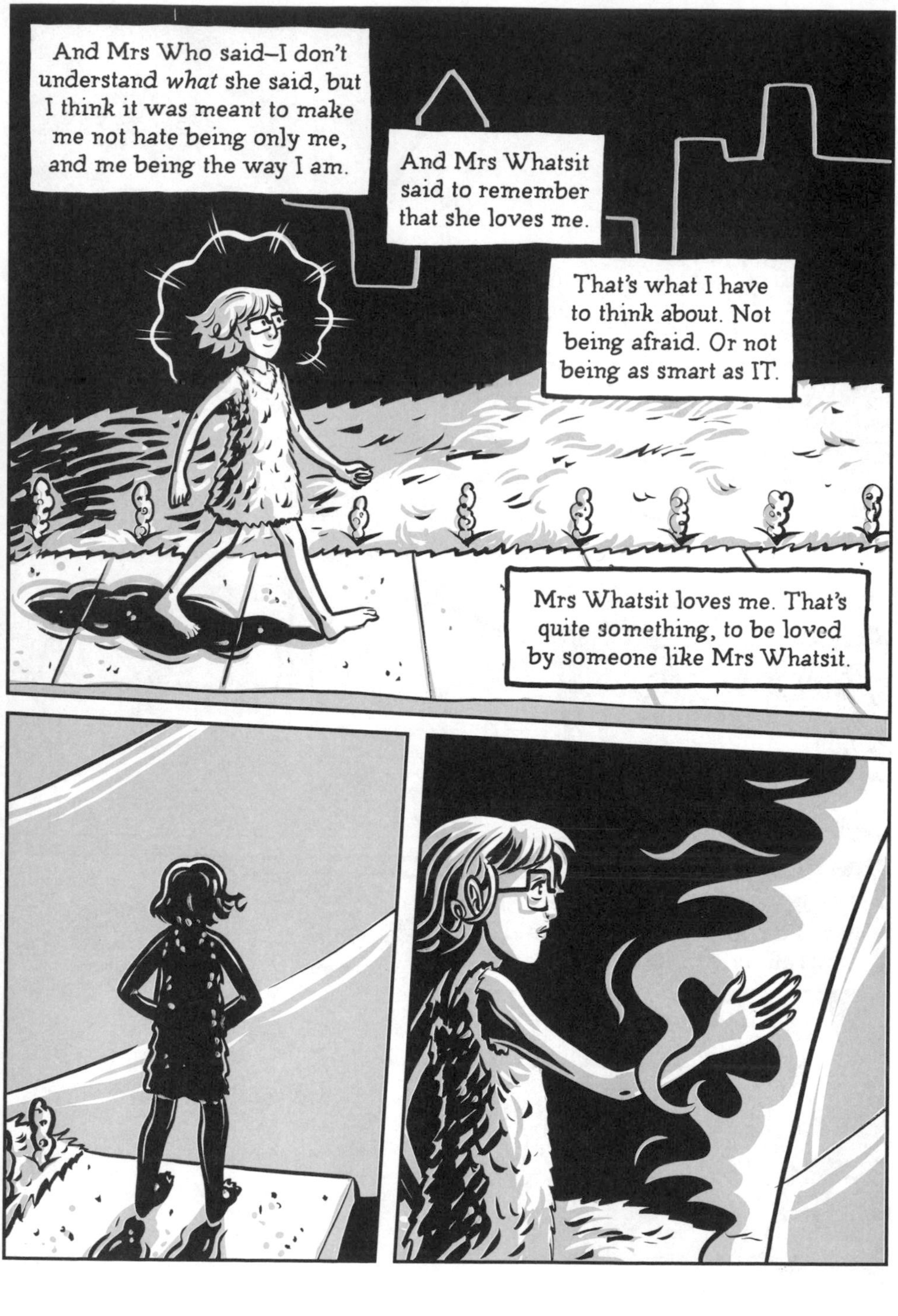
And Mrs Who said–I don't understand *what* she said, but I think it was meant to make me not hate being only me, and me being the way I am.
And Mrs Whatsit said to remember that she loves me.
That's what I have to think about. Not being afraid. Or not being as smart as IT.
Mrs Whatsit loves me. That's quite something, to be loved by someone like Mrs Whatsit.

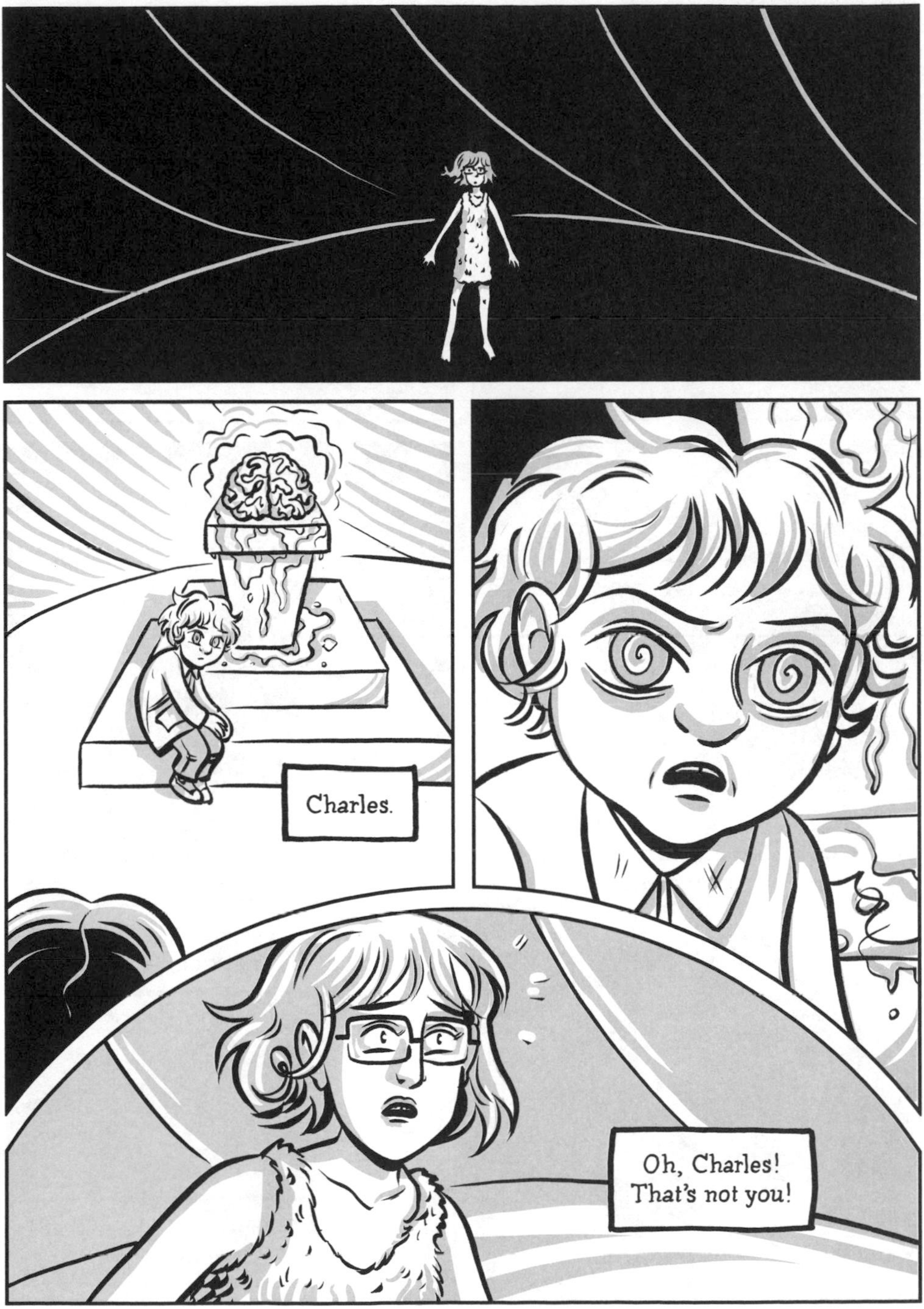
Charles.
Oh, Charles! That's not you!

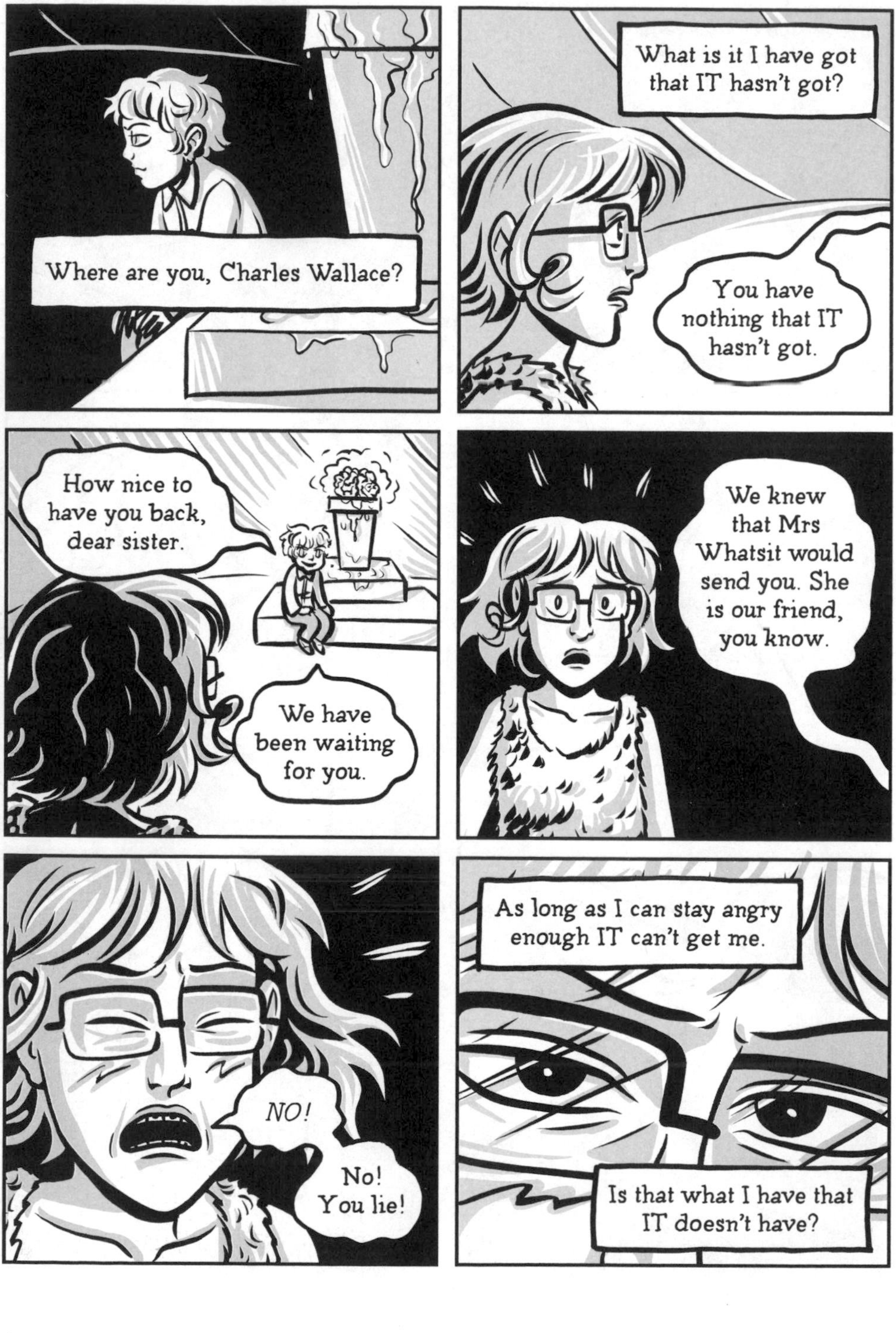
Where are you, Charles Wallace?
What is it I have got that IT hasn't got?
You have nothing that IT hasn't got.
How nice to have you back, dear sister.
We have been waiting for you.
We knew that Mrs Whatsit would send you. She is our friend, you know.
NO!
No! You lie!
As long as I can stay angry enough IT can't get me.
Is that what I have that IT doesn't have?

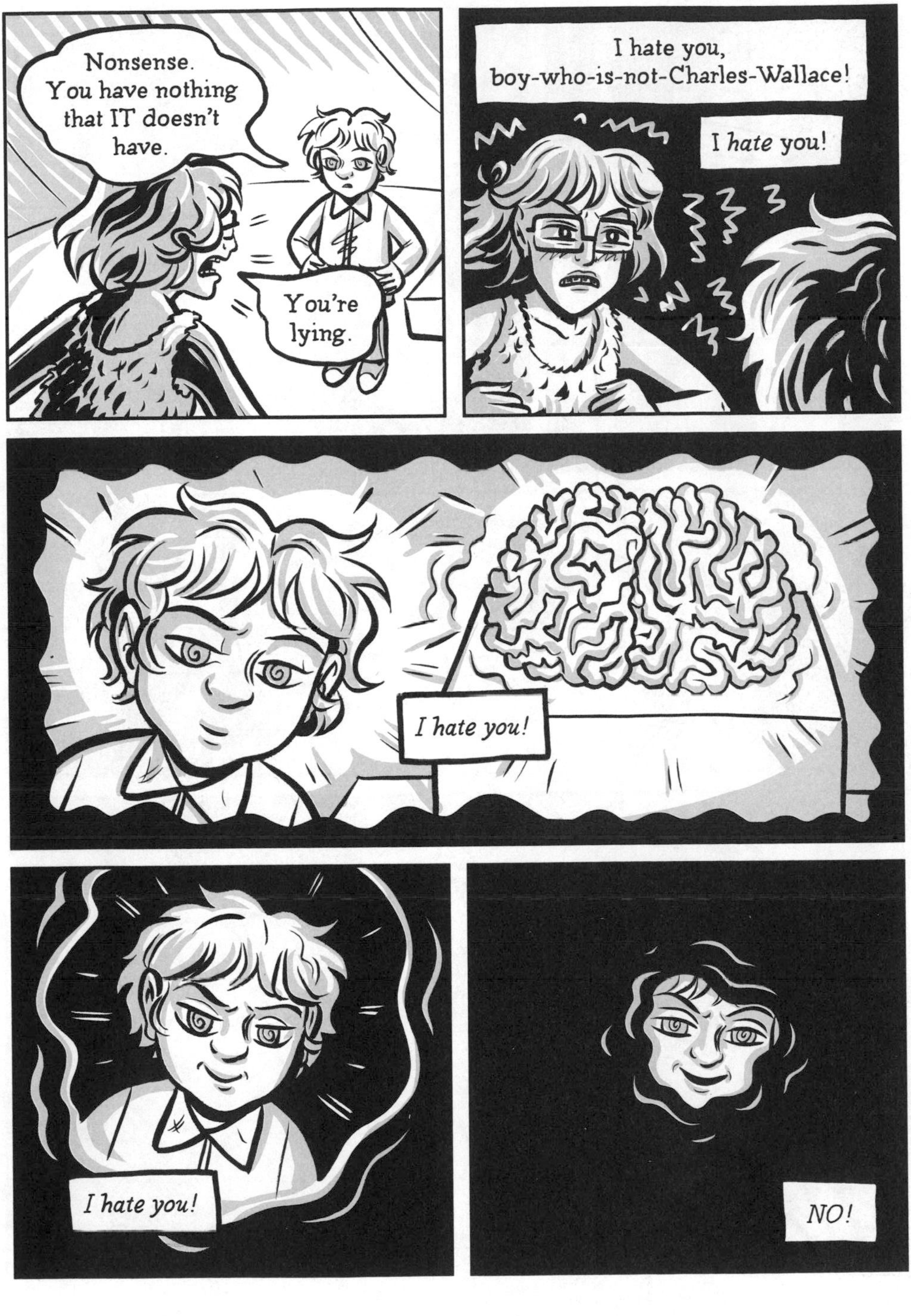
Nonsense. You have nothing that IT doesn't have.
You're lying.
I hate you, boy-who-is-not-Charles-Wallace!
I *hate* you!
I hate you!
I hate you!
NO!

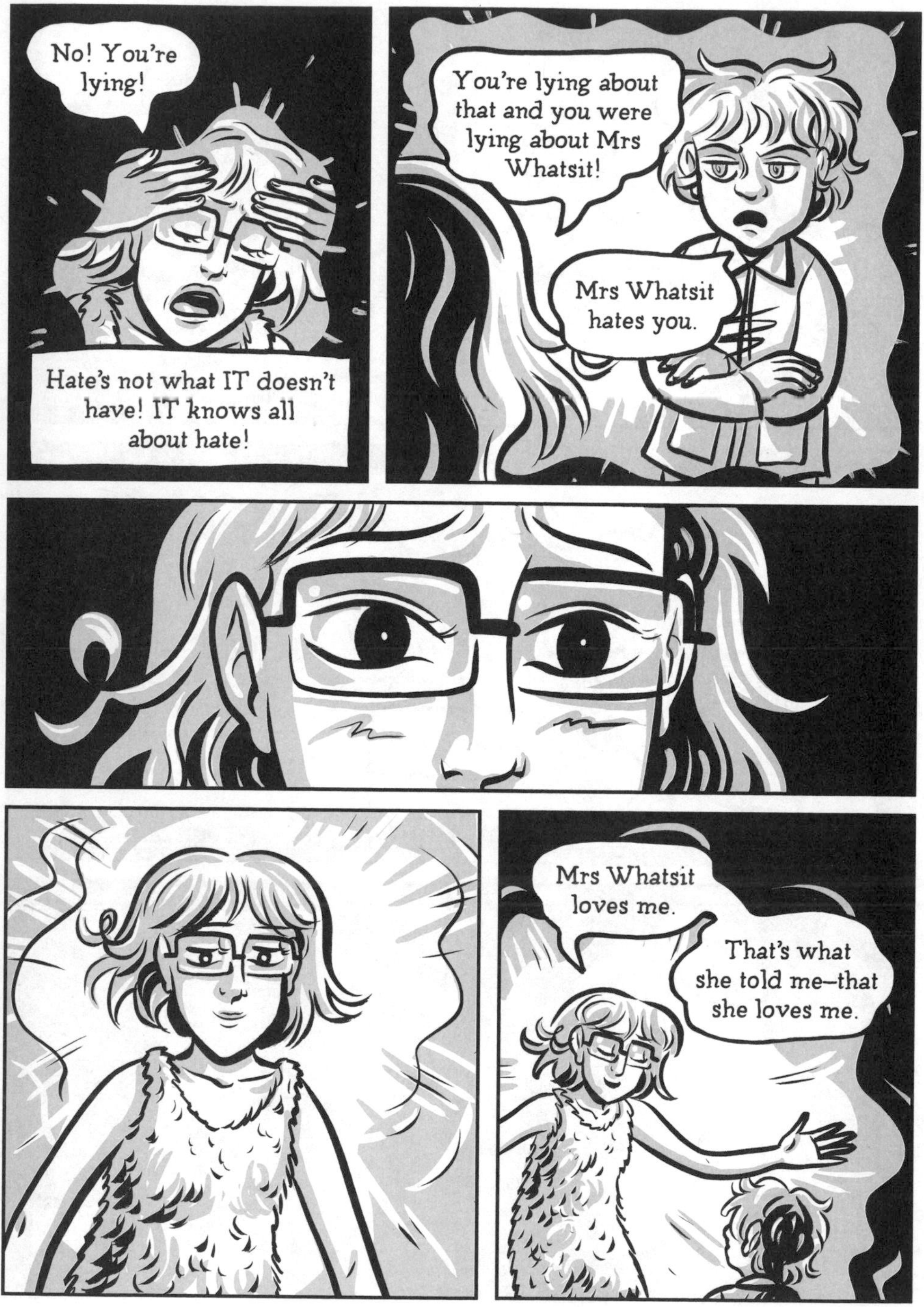
No! You're lying!
Hate's not what IT doesn't have! IT knows all about hate!
You're lying about that and you were lying about Mrs Whatsit!
Mrs Whatsit hates you.
Mrs Whatsit loves me.
That's what she told me—that she loves me.

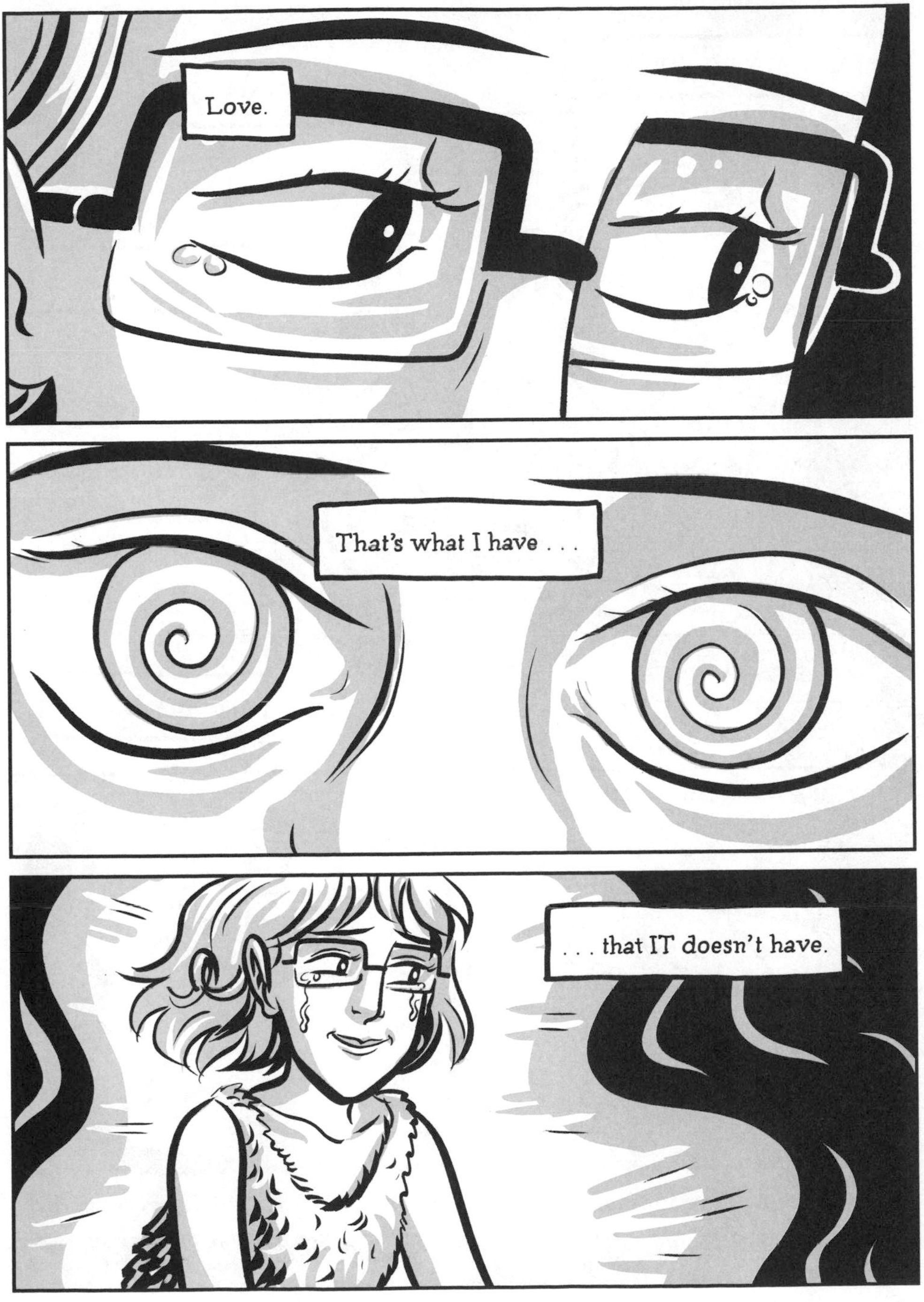
Love.
That's what I have . . .
. . . that IT doesn't have.

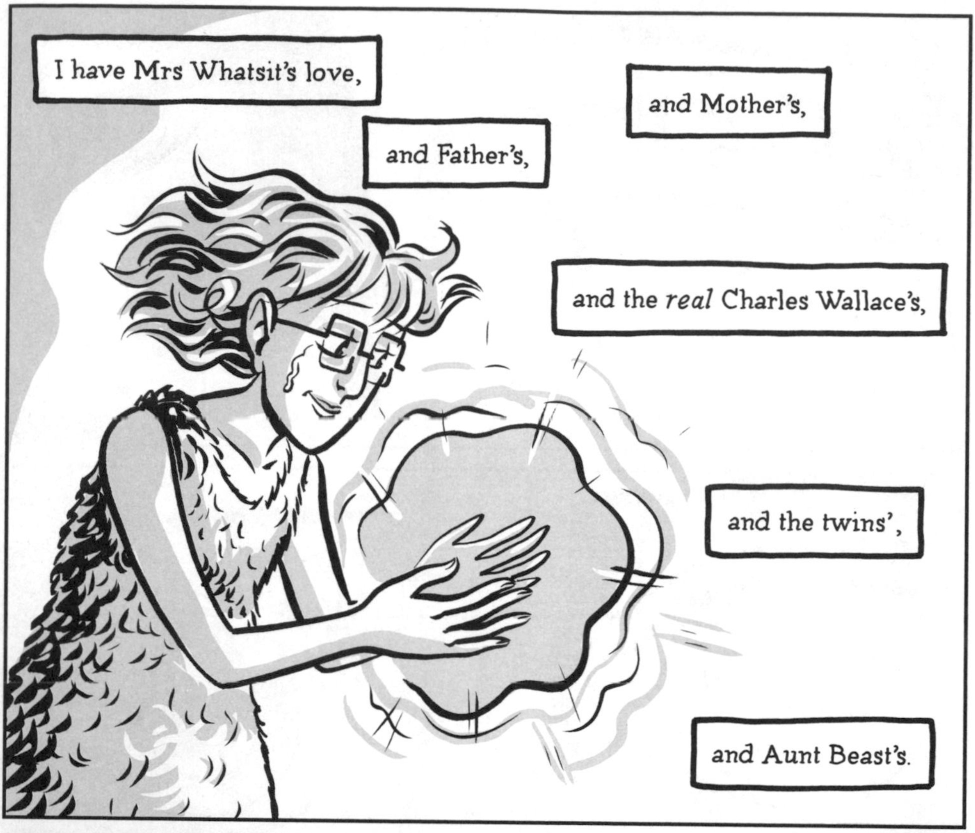
I have Mrs Whatsit's love,
and Father's,
and Mother's,
and the *real* Charles Wallace's,
and the twins',
and Aunt Beast's.

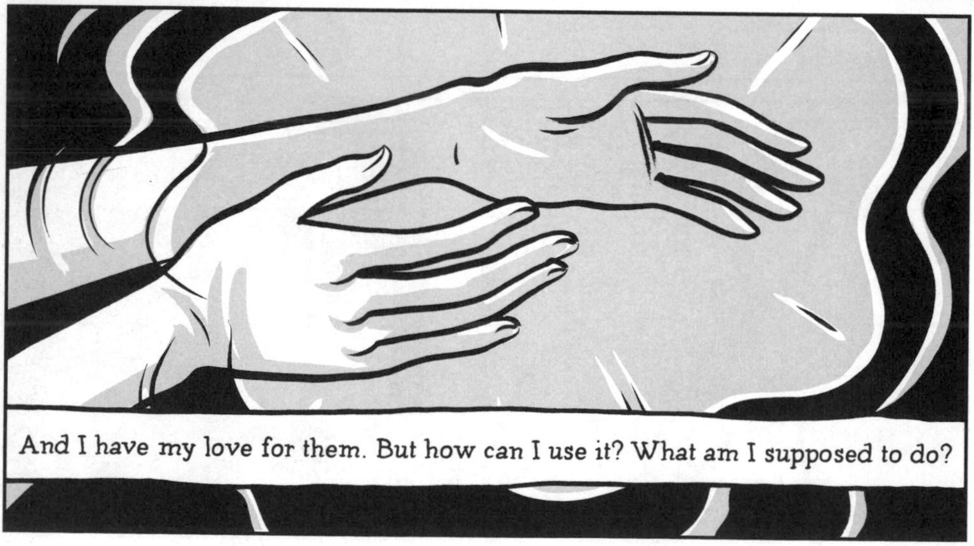
And I have my love for them. But how can I use it? What am I supposed to do?

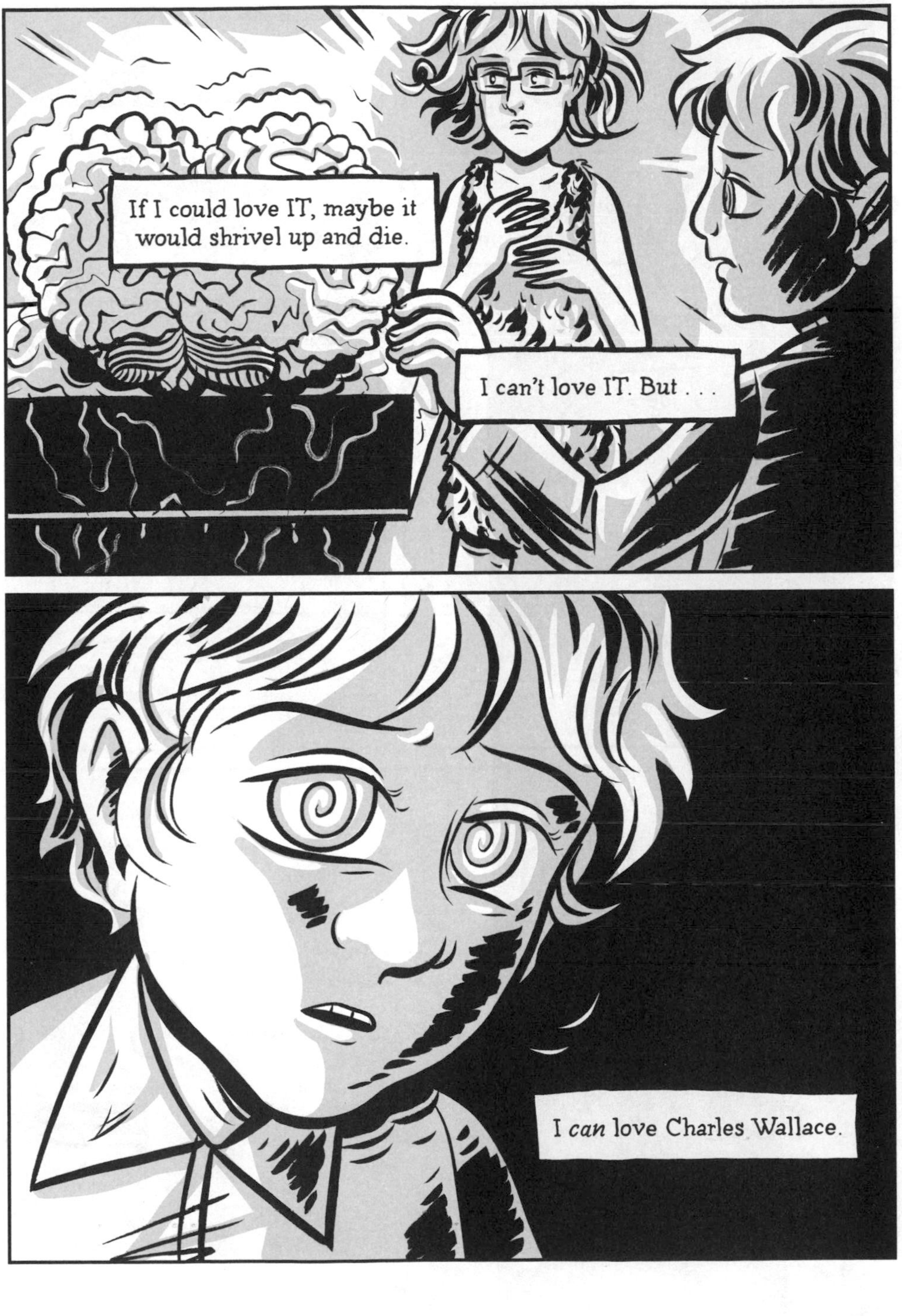
If I could love IT, maybe it would shrivel up and die.
I can't love IT. But . . .
I *can* love Charles Wallace.

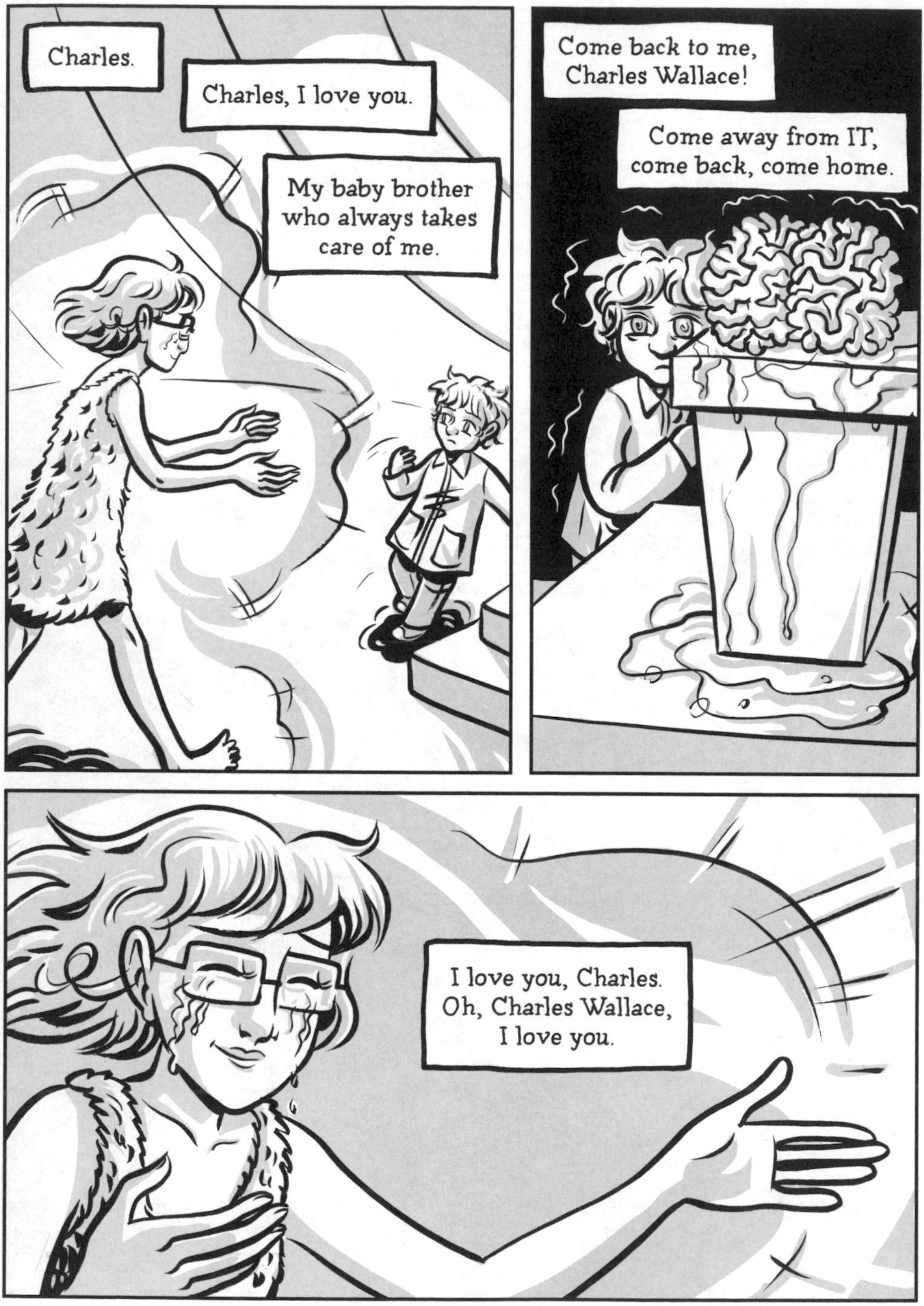
Charles.
Charles, I love you.
My baby brother who always takes care of me.
Come back to me, Charles Wallace!
Come away from IT, come back, come home.
I love you, Charles. Oh, Charles Wallace, I love you.

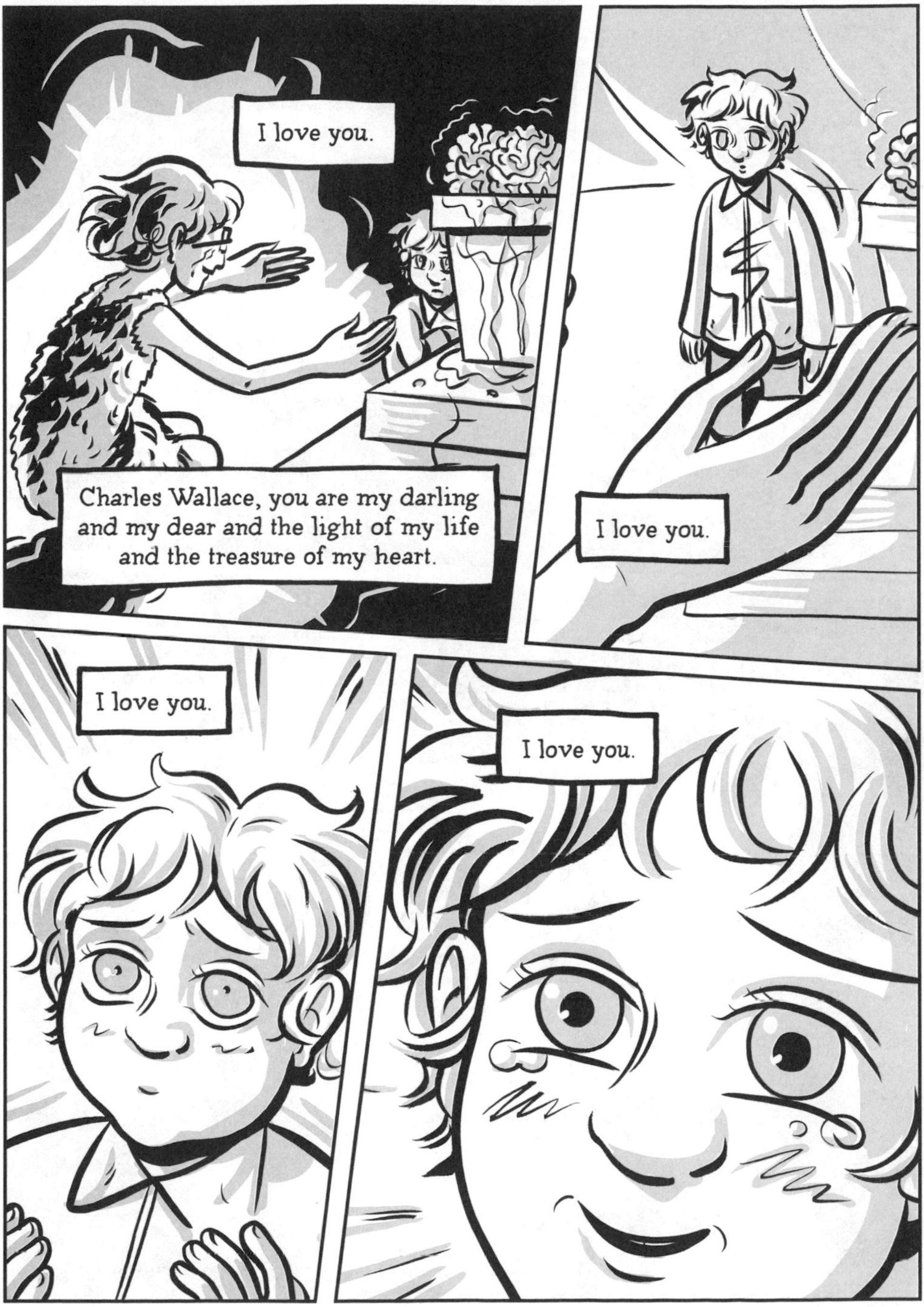
I love you.
Charles Wallace, you are my darling and my dear and the light of my life and the treasure of my heart.
I love you.
I love you.
I love you.

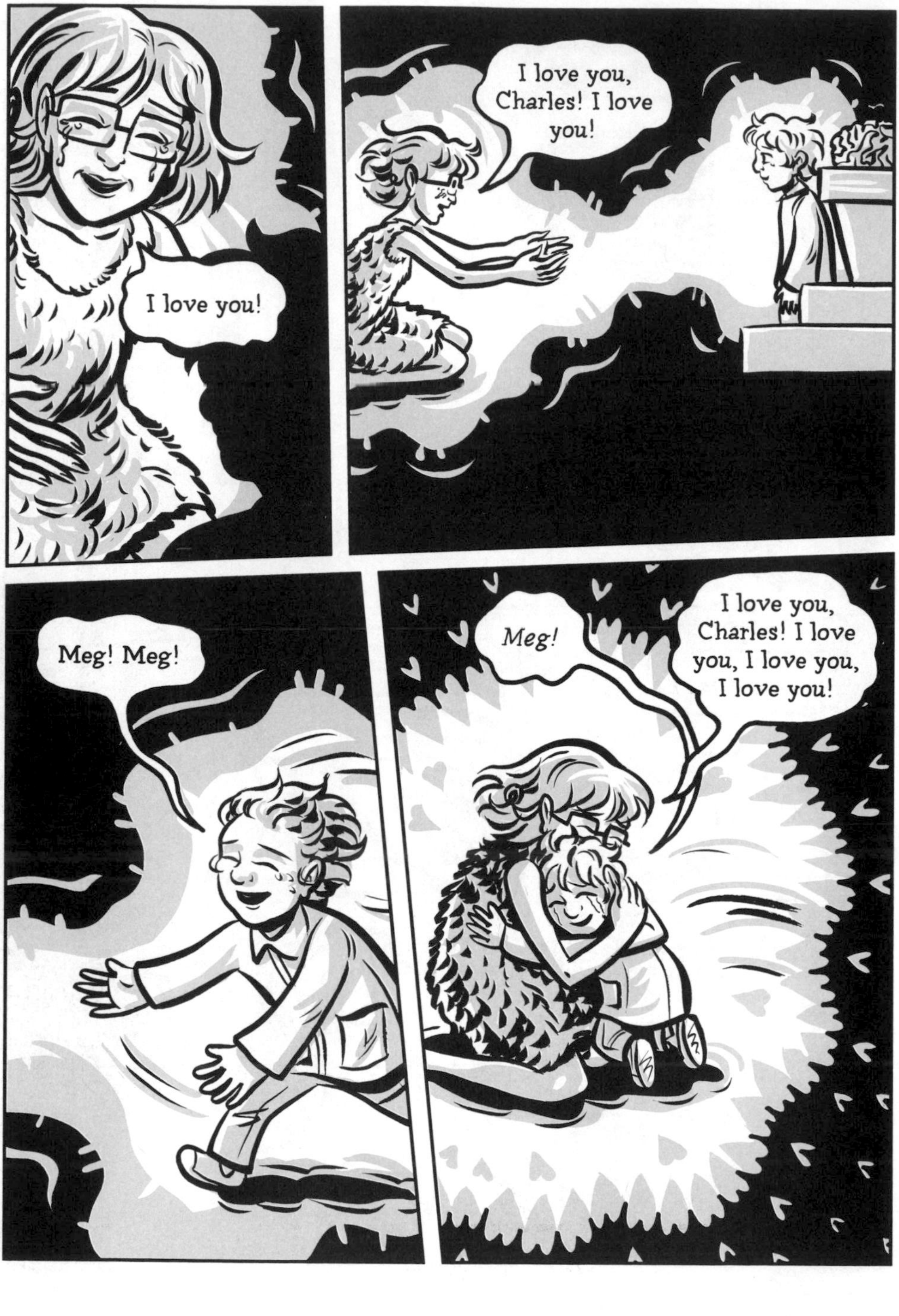
I love you!
I love you, Charles! I love you!
Meg! Meg!
Meg!
I love you, Charles! I love you, I love you, I love you!

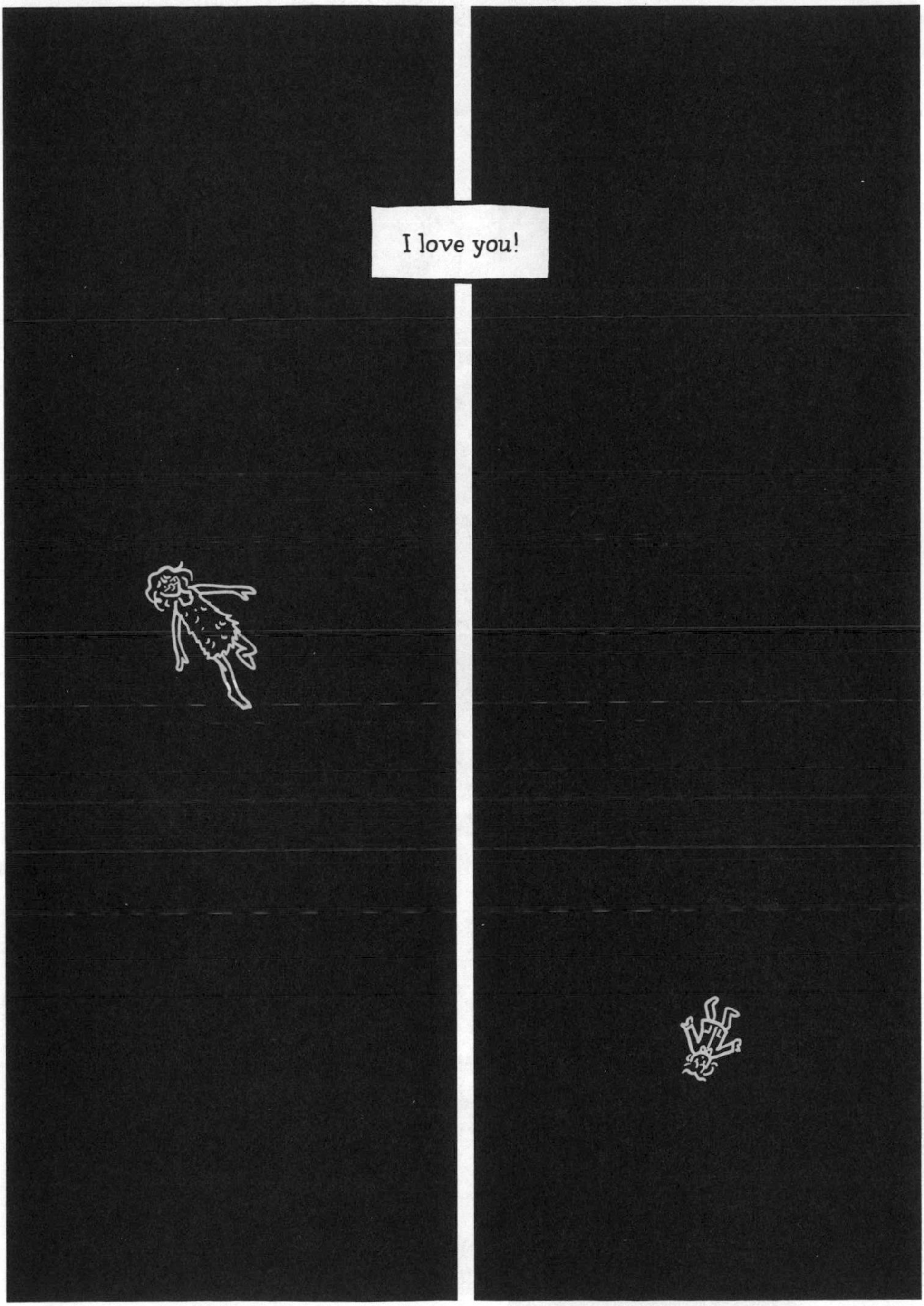
I love you!

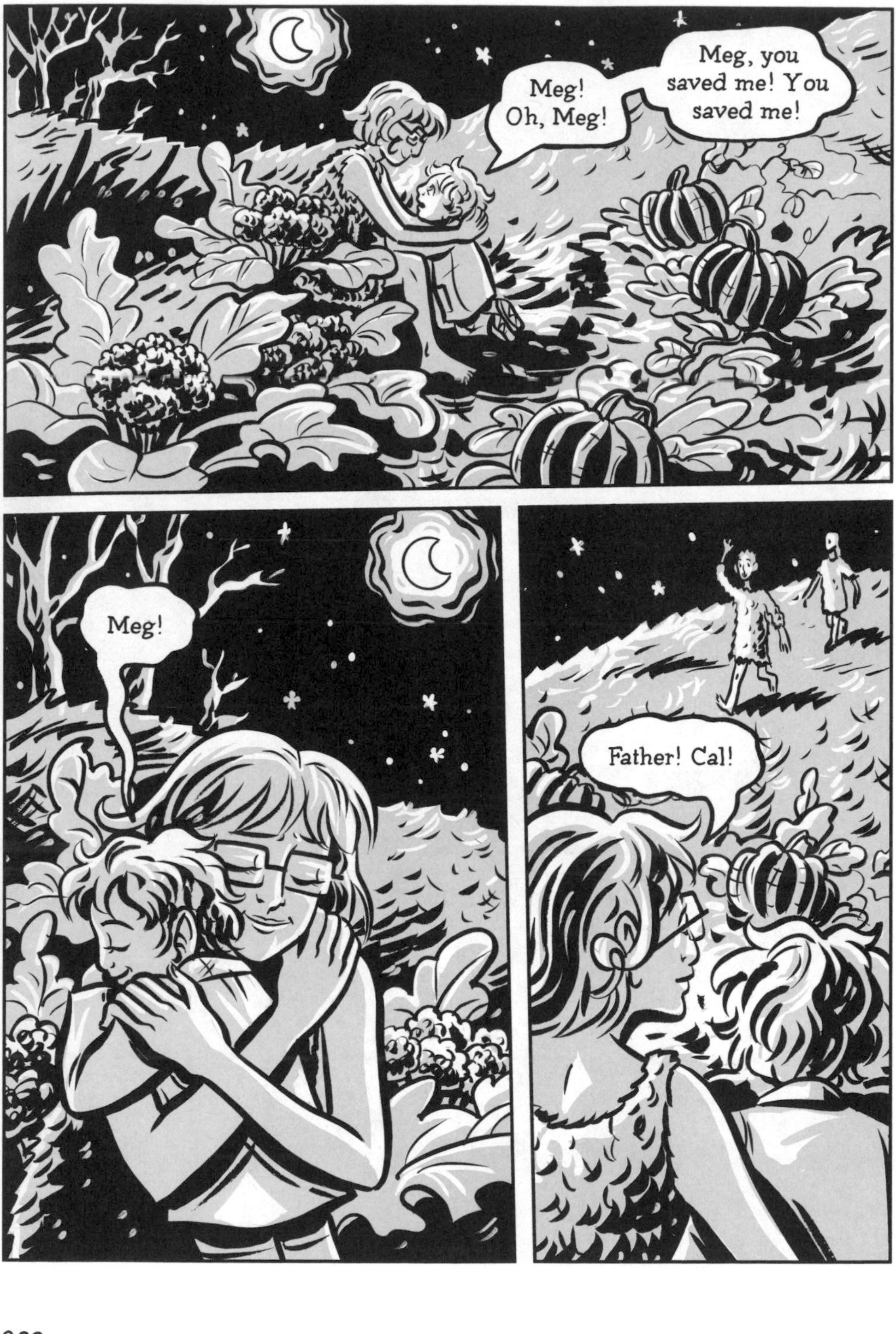
Meg! Oh, Meg!
Meg, you saved me! You saved me!
Meg!
Father! Cal!

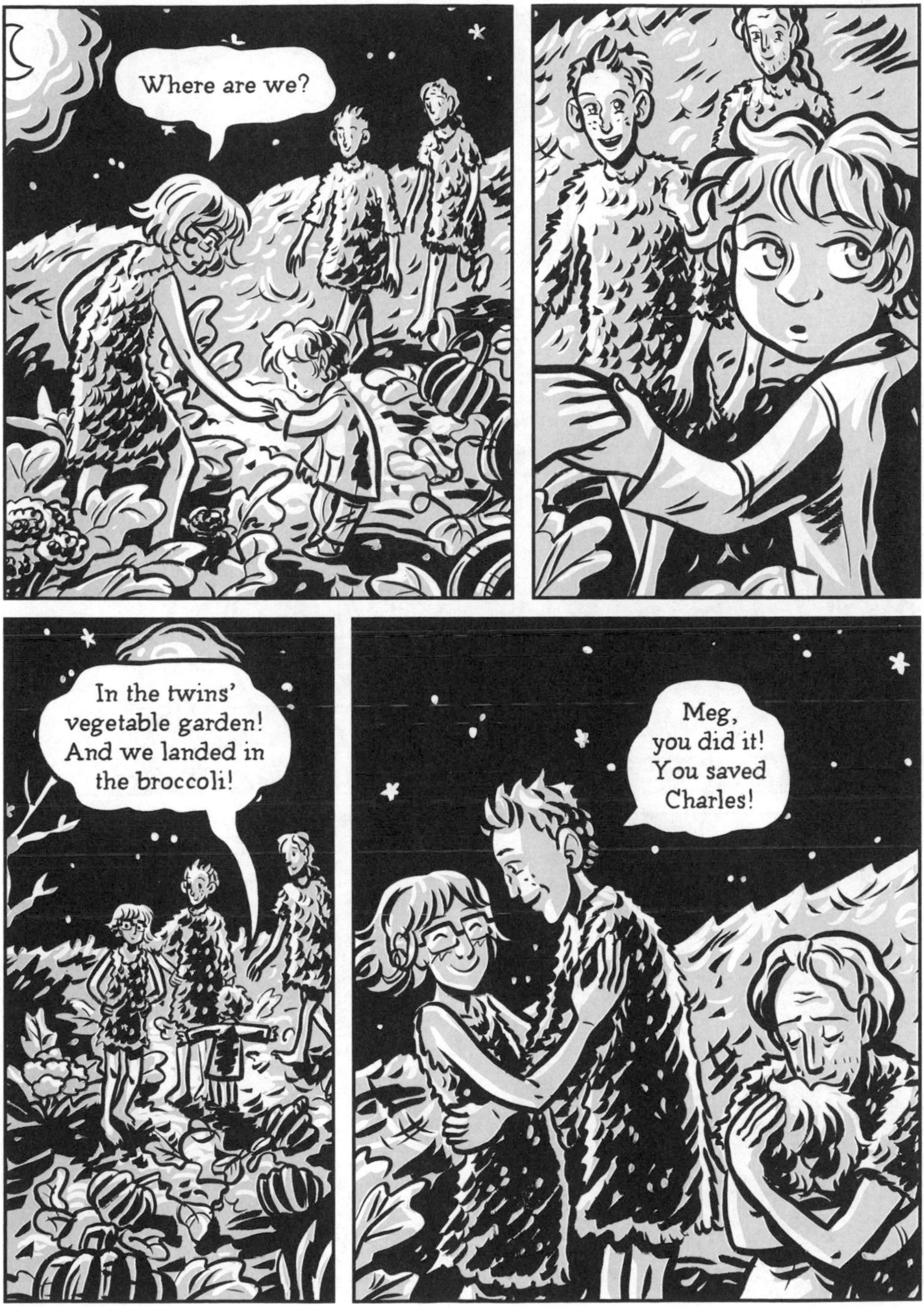
Where are we?
In the twins' vegetable garden! And we landed in the broccoli!
Meg, you did it! You saved Charles!

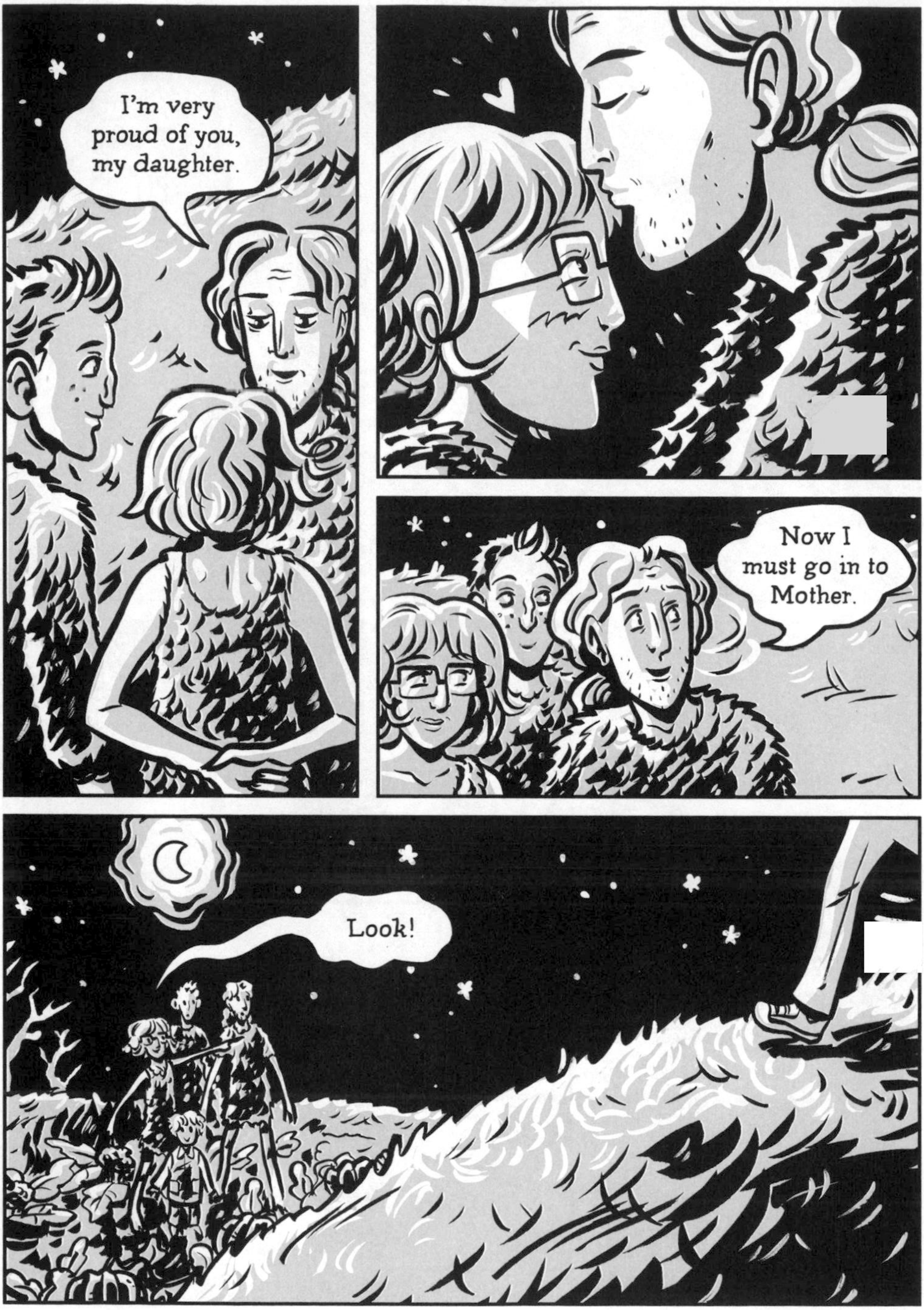
I'm very proud of you, my daughter.
Now I must go in to Mother.
Look!

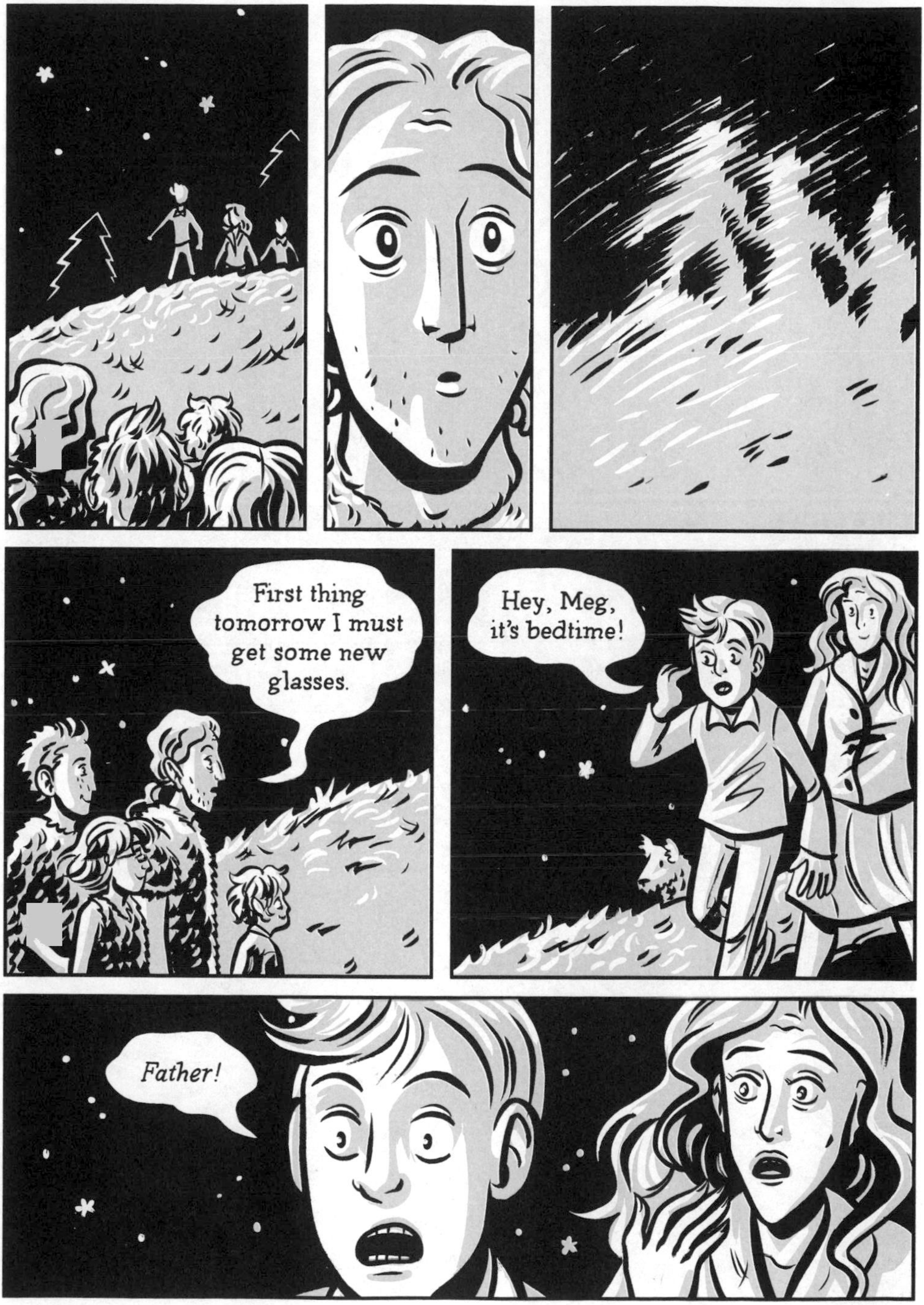

First thing tomorrow I must get some new glasses.
Hey, Meg, it's bedtime!
Father!

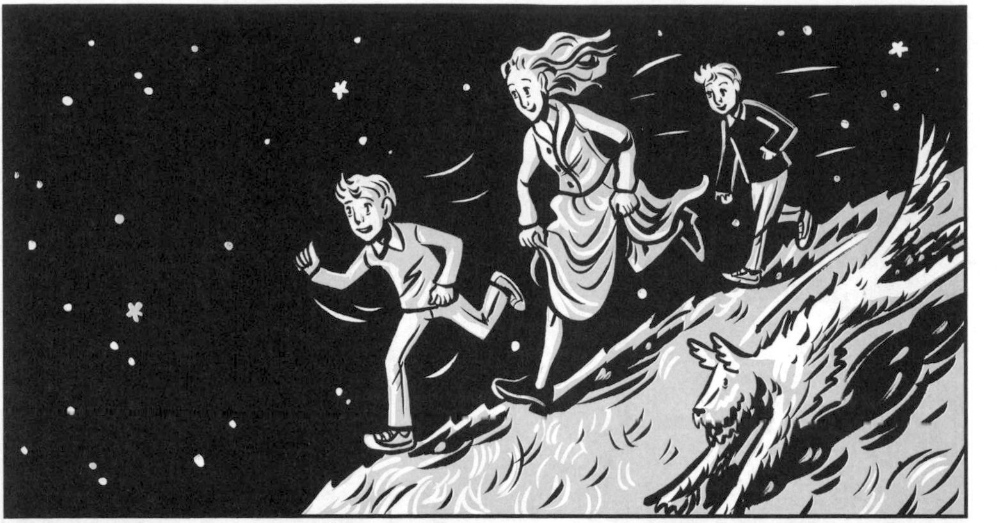

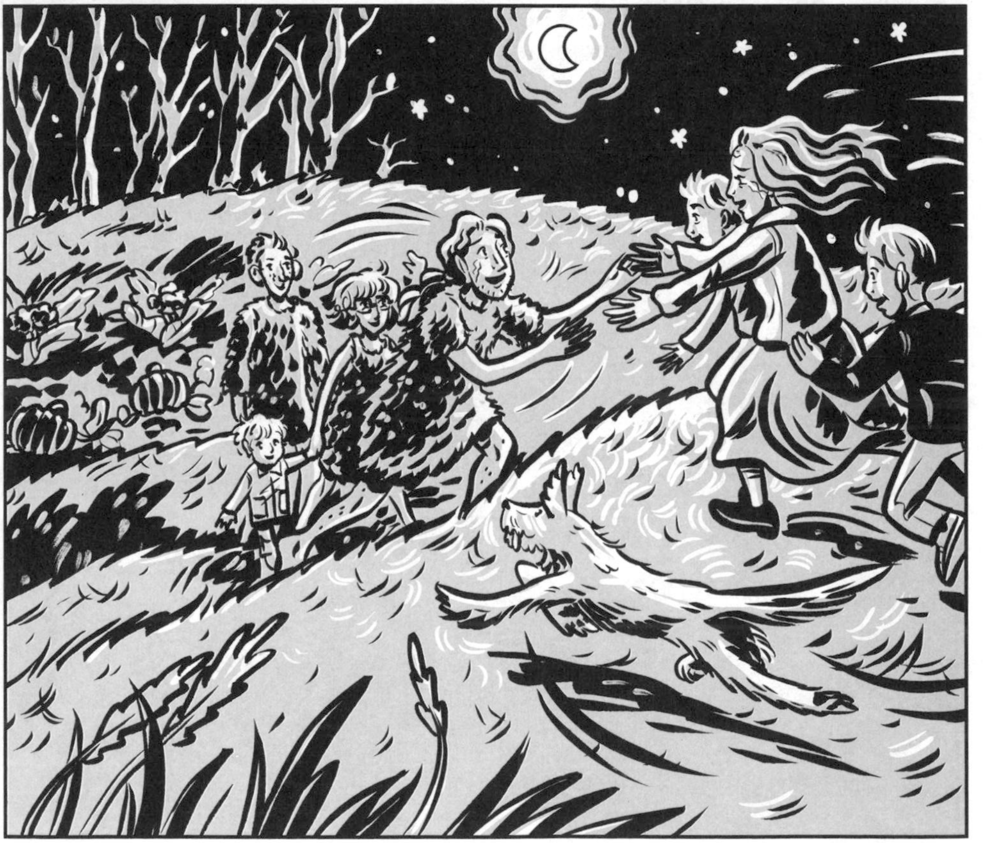

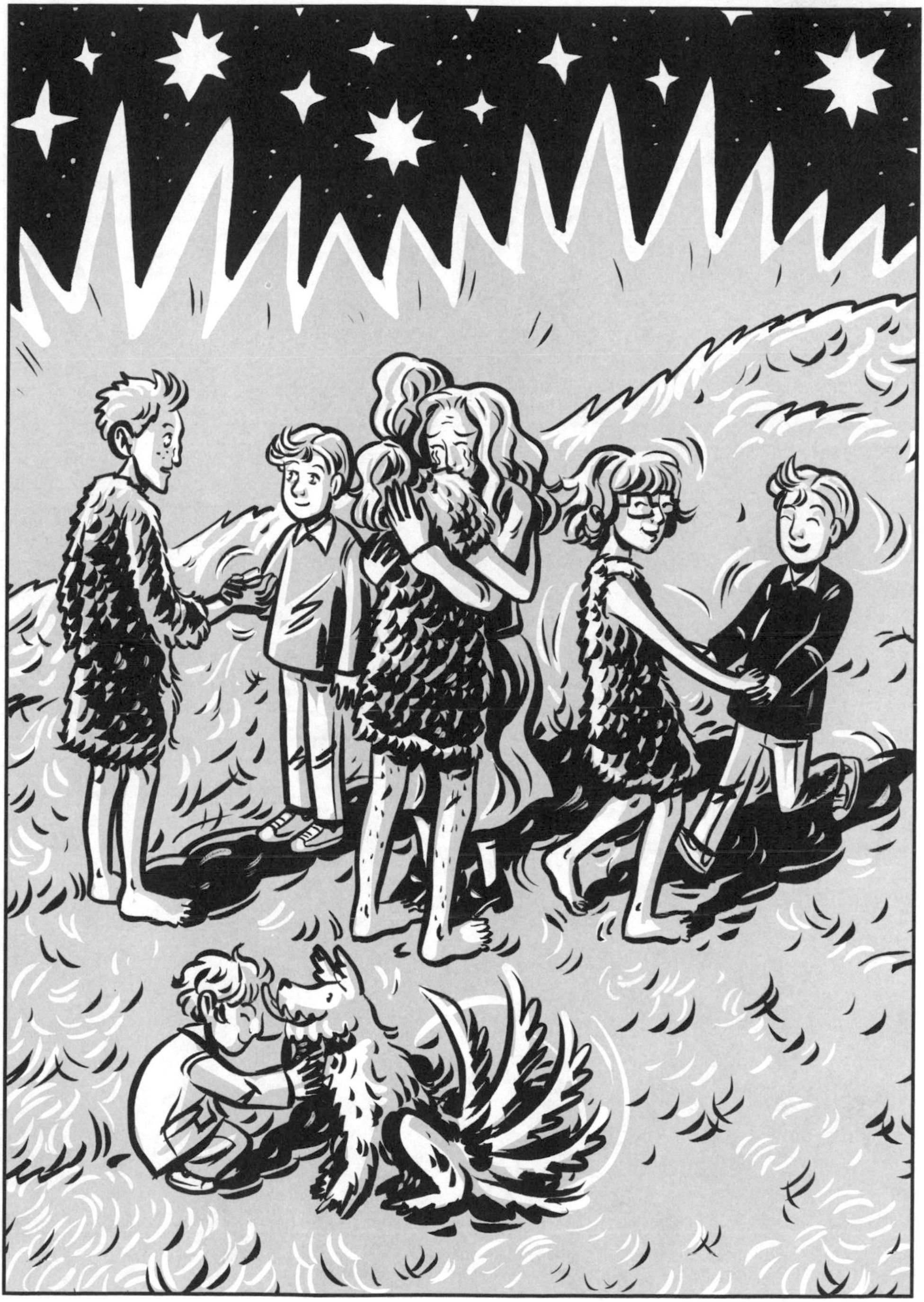

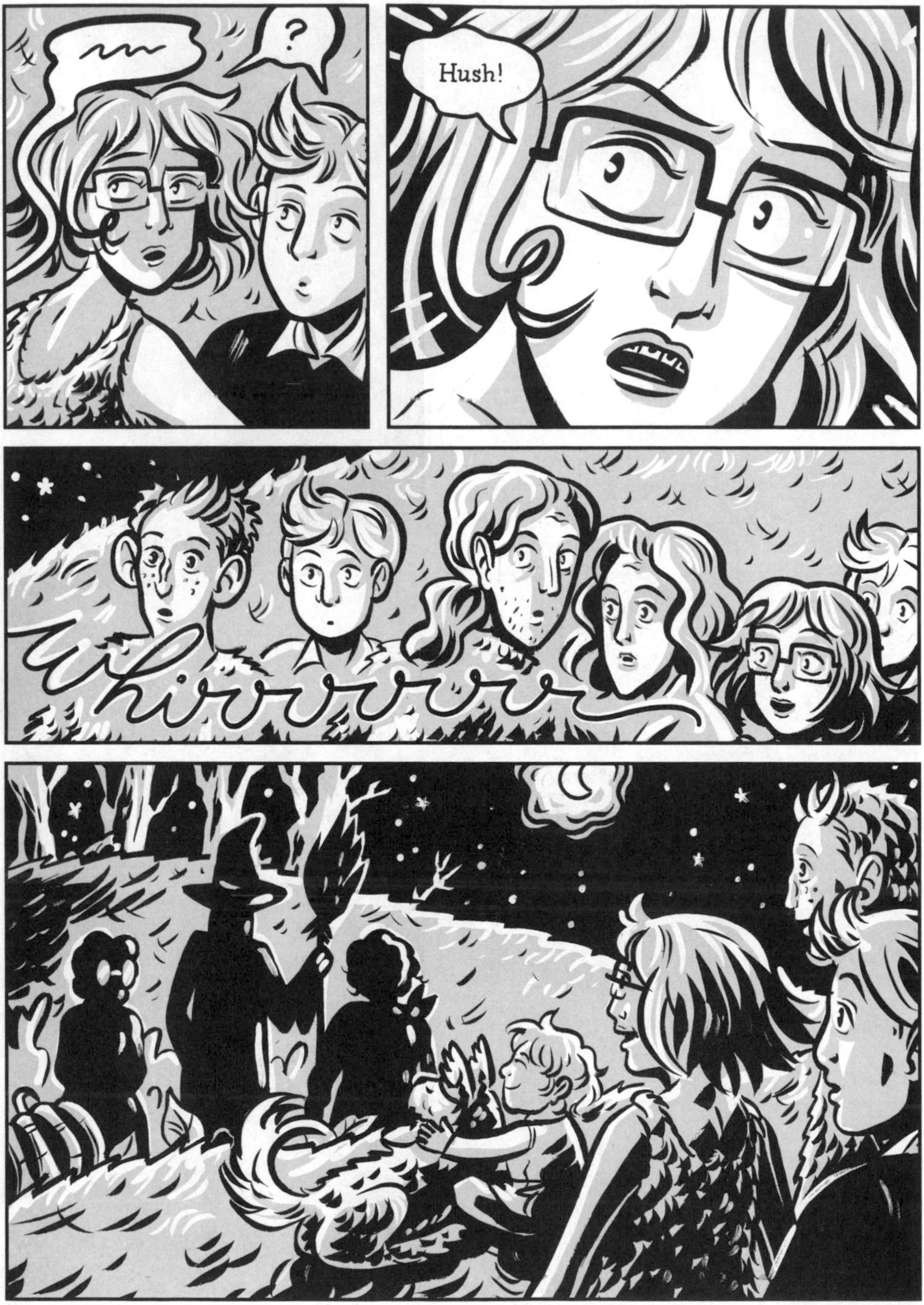
?
Hush!

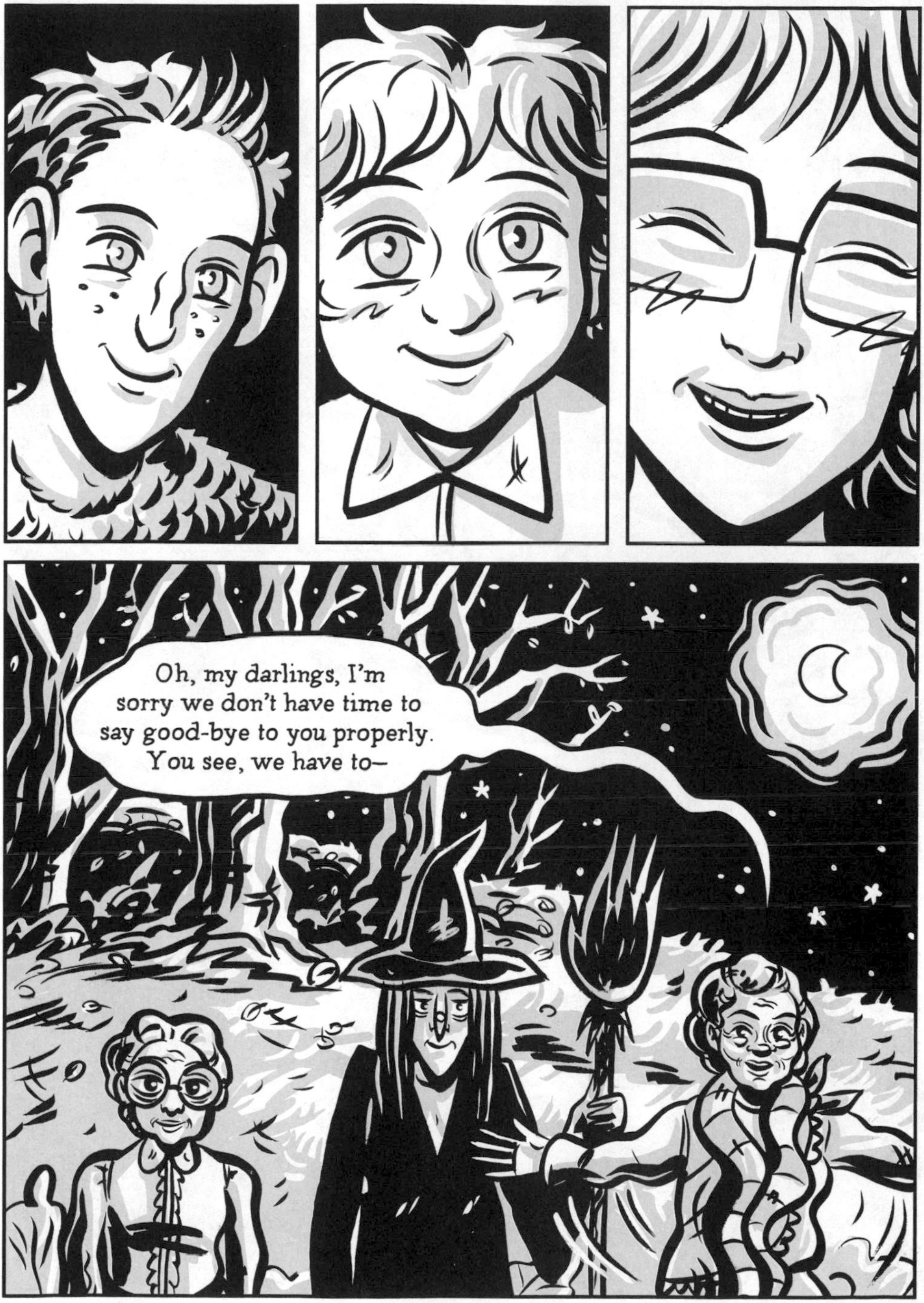
Oh, my darlings, I'm sorry we don't have time to say good-bye to you properly. You see, we have to–

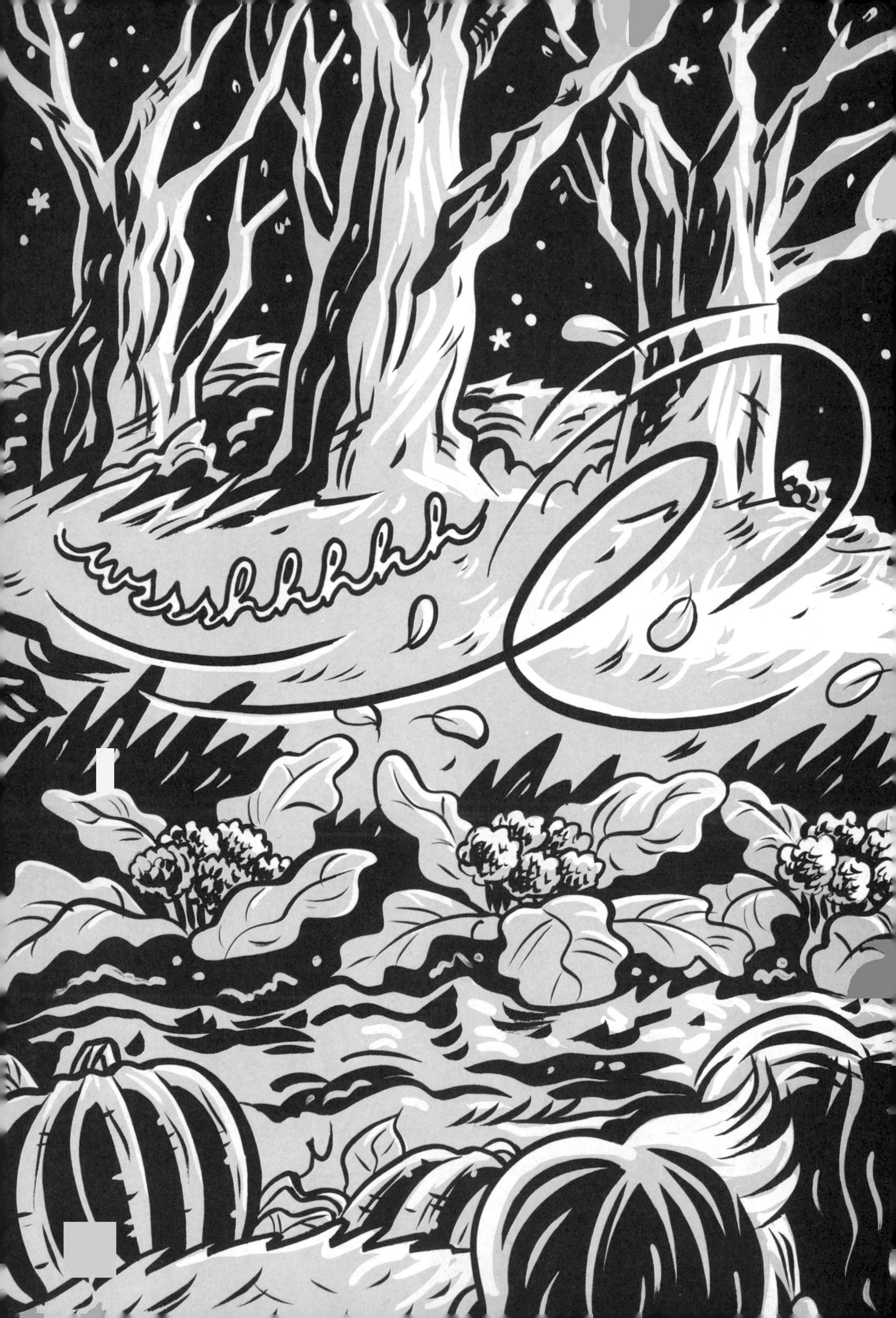
wssshhhhhh

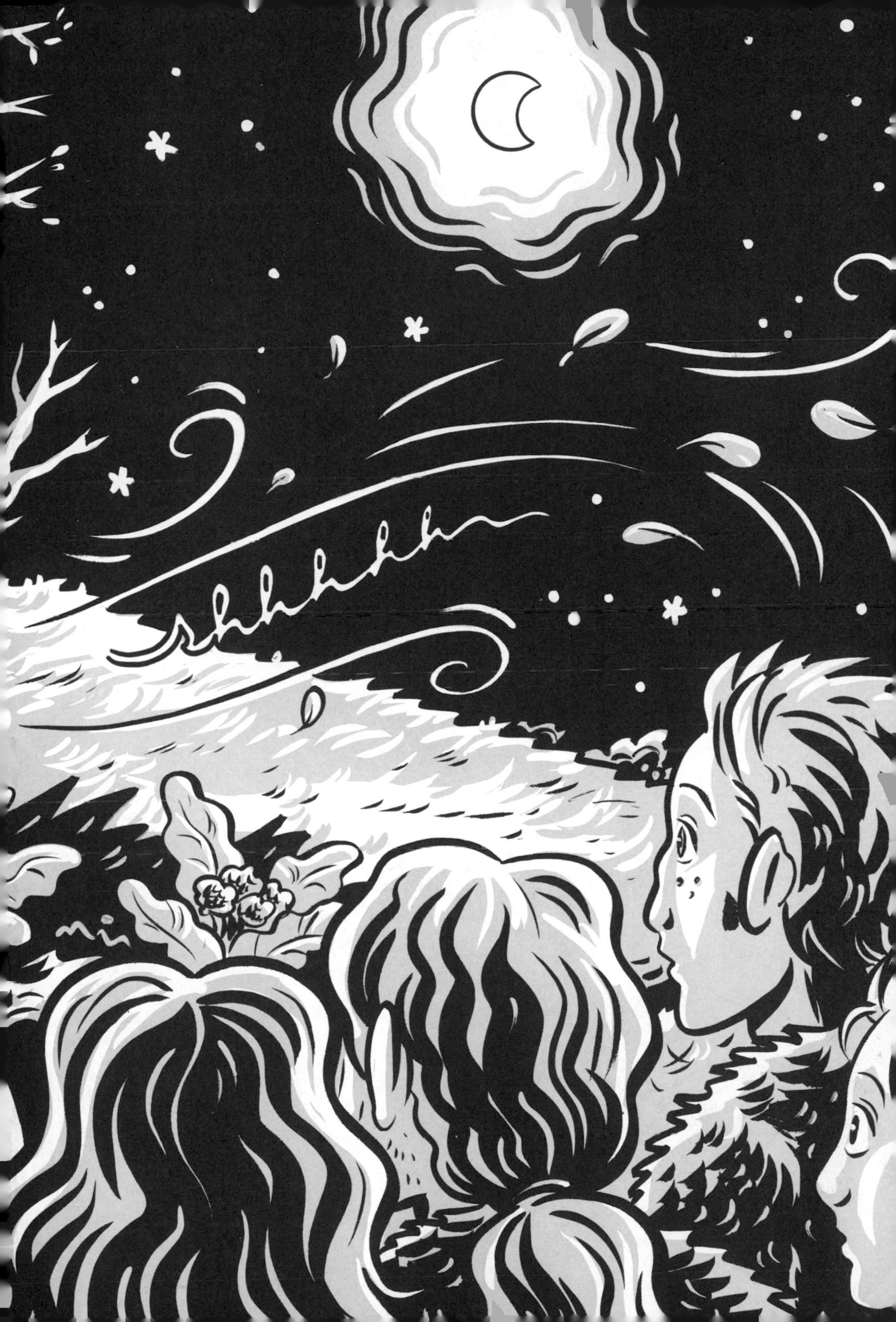
shhhhhh

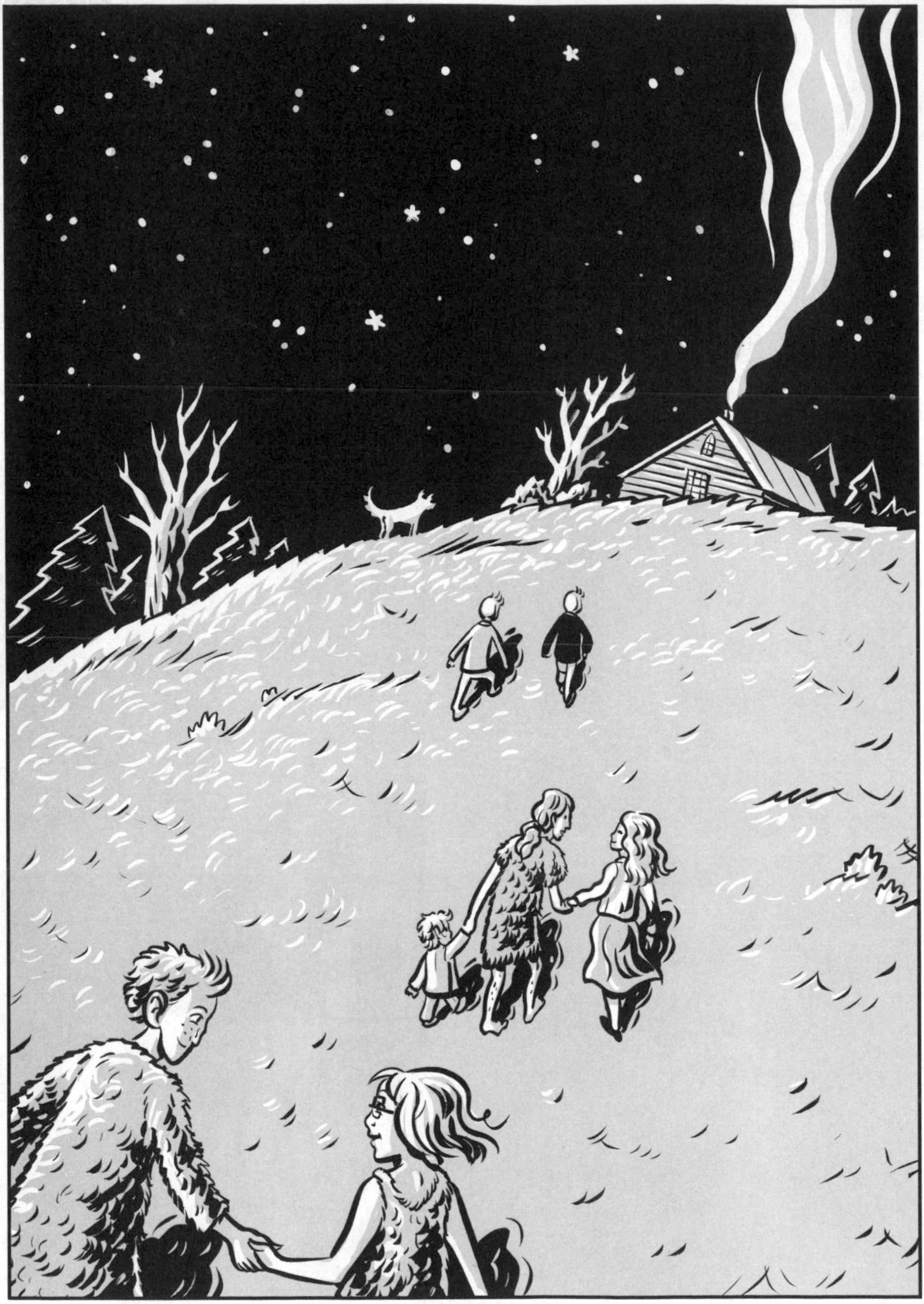